THE LIFE AND ADVENTURES OF
NICHOLAS NICKLEBY

CHARLES DICKENS

THE LIFE AND ADVENTURES OF
NICHOLAS NICKLEBY

Reproduced in facsimile from the
original monthly parts of 1838–9
with an essay by

MICHAEL SLATER

VOLUME TWO

CHAPTERS XXXIV TO LXV

UNIVERSITY OF PENNSYLVANIA PRESS
Philadelphia
1982

First published in monthly parts by Chapman and Hall
2 April 1838 to 1 October 1839
This edition first published in the United States by
the University of Pennsylvania Press, 1982
This edition first published in Great Britain by
Scolar Press, 1982
"The Composition and Monthly Publication of *Nicholas Nickleby*"
copyright © Michael Slater, 1972, 1982

Library of Congress Cataloging in Publication Data

Dickens, Charles, 1812-1870.
The life and adventures of Nicholas Nickleby.

Reprint. Originally published: London: Chapman and
Hall, 1838-1839.
I. Slater, Michael.   II. Title.
PR4565.A1   1982b   823'.8   82-21971
ISBN 0-8122-7873-9
ISBN 0-8122-1135-9 (pbk.)

Printed in the United States of America

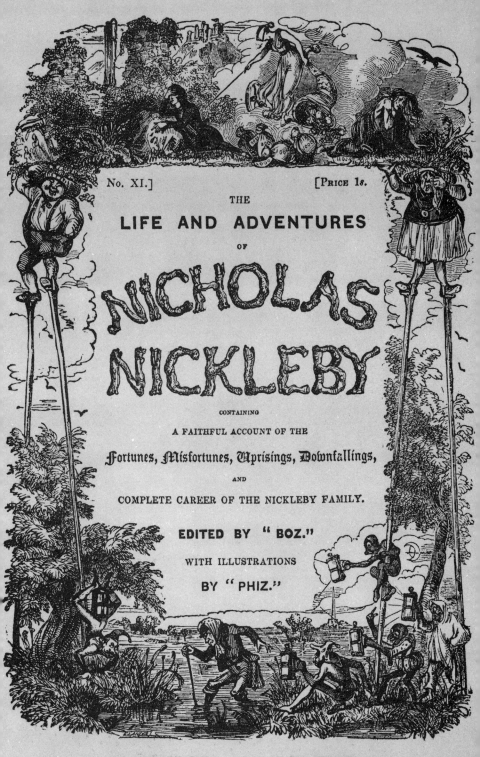

No. XI.]   [PRICE 1s.

THE

LIFE AND ADVENTURES

OF

NICHOLAS NICKLEBY

CONTAINING

A FAITHFUL ACCOUNT OF THE

Fortunes, Misfortunes, Uprisings, Downfallings,

AND

COMPLETE CAREER OF THE NICKLEBY FAMILY.

EDITED BY "BOZ."

WITH ILLUSTRATIONS

BY "PHIZ."

LONDON: CHAPMAN AND HALL, 186, STRAND.

CATALOGUE OF OPERAS,

PUBLISHED BY

J. J. EWER & Co.

BOW CHURCH-YARD, LONDON.

THE WHOLE OF THE MUSIC ARRANGED FOR THE PIANO-FORTE SOLO.

	BY	PRICE		BY	PRICE
Don Juan	Mozart	5s.	Tancredi	Rossini.	5s.
The Marriage of Figaro	Do.	5s.	Othello	Do.	5s.
Cosi fan tutte	Do.	5s.	La Gazza Ladra	Do.	5s.
Die Zauberflœte	Do.	5s.	Semiramide	Do.	6s.
Clemenza de Tito	Do.	5s.	Cenerentola	Do.	6s.
Idomeneo	Do.	5s.	La Donna del Lago	Do.	5s.
The Seraglio	Do.	5s.	I Montechi e Capuletti	Bellini	5s.
Die Gærtnerinn	Do.	6s.	La Straniera	Do.	5s.
Der Freischütz	V. Weber	5s.	Norma	Do.	5s.
Jessonda	Spohr	5s.	Il Pirata	Do.	5s.
Fidelio	Beethoven	5s.	Masaniello	Auber	5s.
The Swiss Family	Weigl	5s.	Zampa	Herold	5s.
Das Opferfest	Winter	5s.	La Dame Blanche	Boieldieu	5s.
The Eagle's Haunt	Glæser	6s.	Anna Bolena	Donnizetti	6s.
The Barber of Seville	Rossini	5s.	L'Elisire d'Amore	Do.	5s.

OPERAS

FOR PIANO-FORTE AND VOICE, WITH GERMAN AND ITALIAN, AND FRENCH AND GERMAN WORDS.

	BY		PRICE		BY		PRICE
Don Juan	Mozart.	G. & I.	10s. 6d.	Othello	Rossini	G. & I.	10s. 6d.
The Marriage of Figaro	Do.	Do.	10s. 6d.	La Gazza Ladra	. Do.	Do.	12s. 0d.
Cosi fan tutte	Do.	Do.	10s. 6d.	Sargin	Paer.	Do.	10s. 6d.
Die Zauberflœte	Do.	Do.	10s. 6d.	La Vestale	Spontini.	G. & F.	10s. 6d.
Idomeneo	Do.	Do.	10s. 6d	La Dame Blanche	Boieldieu.	Do.	10s. 6d.
Clemenza de Tito	Do.	Do.	8s. 0d.	Jean de Paris	. Do.	Do.	10s. 6d.
The Seraglio	Do.	Do.	8s. 0d.	Masaniello	Auber	Do.	12s. 0d.
Fidelio	Beethoven.	G.	10s. 6d.	Joseph in Egypt	Méhul.	Do.	8s. 0d.
Das Opferfest	Winter.	G. & F.	10s. 6d.	Les deux Journées	Cherubini.	Do.	8s. 0d.
The Swiss Family	Weigl.	G.	8s. 0d.	Il Matrimonio segreto	Cimarosa.	G. & I.	10s. 6d.
Barber of Seville	Rossini.	G. & I.	10s. 6d.	Norma	Bellini.	Do.	10s. 6d.
Tancredi	Do.	Do.	10s. 6d.	La Straniera	Do.	Do.	10s. 6d.

OPERAS

ARRANGED FOR THE PIANO-FORTE, FOR TWO PERFORMERS.

	BY	PRICE		BY	PRICE
Norma	Bellini	10s.	The Barber of Seville	Rossini	10s.
Don Juan	Mozart	12s.	Masaniello	Auber	10s.

SOCIETY OF GUARDIANS
FOR THE PROTECTION OF TRADE.
ESTABLISHED MARCH 25, 1776.

CHARLES FAREBROTHER, Esq., Alderman, President.
WILLIAM TAYLOR COPELAND, Esq., Alderman and M.P., Vice-President.
Messrs. WILLIAM PRAED & Co., Bankers, Treasurers.

The objects of this Society, which is an Association of Merchants, Bankers, and Traders,—are, PROTECTION from Fraudulent Practices, and the PUNISHMENT of Offenders guilty of FRAUD or ROBBERY. These are effected

FIRST—BY MUTUAL INFORMATION:—
The Subscribers send to the Secretary the earliest information of such Facts, of a peculiar or suspicious character, as come within their knowledge, for the consideration of the Committee, by whose order the information so given is immediately communicated *to every* MEMBER *of the* SOCIETY.

An annual recapitulation, arranged alphabetically, is sent to each Member.

*** To every NEW MEMBER on his election, a LIST of the Names and Bills noticed for the TWENTY PREVIOUS YEARS is given.

SECONDLY—BY BRINGING THE OFFENDERS TO JUSTICE:—
When a Member is DEFRAUDED, the Offender is prosecuted by and at the expense of the Society.

THIRDLY—Every Member is entitled to the payment of a certain Sum for his Expenses in all Prosecutions for ROBBERY of *any* description.
☞ THE ANNUAL SUBSCRIPTION IS ONE GUINEA.

The Committee have just published the following Report:—

THE Society is now in the SIXTY-THIRD year of its existence; and the Committee conceive that they cannot do better than remind the Subscribers and the public of what were the intentions of its Founders, and what benefits were contemplated in its institution.

It is a lamentable truth, that in every society there are some individuals to whom the course of honest industry is distasteful; who, exulting in the cunning of low minds, exert their depraved intellect in crafty attempts to overreach the unwary, and to take advantage of those unguarded moments to which even the most cautious are liable. Assuming, for their disreputable purposes, the appearance of respectability, they gradually insinuate themselves into confidence; and, gaining a temporary credit, they extend their ramifications, and establish new firms, assisting each other by mutual references and concerted characters,—and thus, by various deceptions, and false ledgers, they for a time succeed; until, all their subterfuges failing, their artificial fabric is suddenly destroyed, and the hopes of those who have trusted them are at once blighted.

Sensible of the inutility of solitary exertions to counteract frauds thus practised, some eminent Merchants, in the year 1776, originated this Society, from the well-founded conviction, that those stratagems which might succeed when practised on individuals, would become powerless when the system was exposed among many; and that by an immediate communication of them to a body of Subscribers, each would be fortified by preparation, and the nefarious efforts of unprincipled ingenuity would be paralyzed in succession.

The Books of the Society form a gratifying record of the success which has accompanied its endeavours. Parties who have lived by deception have been traced from the commencement to the termination of their career; their various modes of dealing have been fully described; their connexions regularly noted; and the perpetual changes of character and name they have assumed have been constantly communicated. Systematic Bill connexions, concocted in fraud, extending not only through the British Isles, but to various places on the Continent, and comprehending almost innumerable firms, have been promptly exposed; the false pretences of persons offering pecuniary accommodation to parties in difficulty have been brought to light; and fac-similes of the handwriting of persons in the country ordering goods under an infinite variety of names have been published. The best proof which the Committee can give of the benefits which have resulted from the operations of this Society is, that while numerous individuals, unconnected with it, have suffered largely by the machinations of the fraudulent, many of its members have been preserved from serious losses, which they would inevitably have incurred had it not been for its cautionary correspondence.

At this period the efforts of the Society are peculiarly necessary. Though fraud may for a time be defeated, experience proves that it cannot be wholly exterminated. One generation succeeds another, and each brings its new systems of deception. It is the duty and the anxiety of the Committee to discover, to expose, and to counteract these as they arise. *But all efforts would be useless without the assistance of the Members themselves;* since it is only by their CONFIDENTIAL COMMUNICATIONS to the Secretary, that the schemes which are daily adopted can be disclosed. Thus, each member contributes to the general good, while at the same time each profits by the experience of his neighbour; and consequently it has been always found, that the larger the number of Subscribers to the Society, the more efficient have been its exertions.

The Committee, in reminding the Members that they have recently received a supply of recommendatory letters, beg to express a hope, *that each Member will introduce at least one new Subscriber,* since it must be apparent to all, that every increase in the numbers must proportionally augment the utility of the Society.

The Committee trust that they have not diminished the respect in which the Society has been hitherto held; a respect which has always given weight to its communications, and which has been established from steadily pursuing the principles on which it was originally founded. Those principles consist in the rejection of every information from a suspicious source; whether by anonymous communications, or by paid informers; the one being never employed, the other never acted upon; but those facts only published, which are detailed or authenticated by the Members themselves. Thus, notwithstanding the thousands of names which have been exposed by the Society, the facts communicated have never been disproved, and its motives have never been questioned.

By Order of the Committee, EDWARD FOSS, Secretary.

36, *Essex Street, January*, 1839.

*** Recommendatory Letters for persons desirous of joining the Soc   may be had at the Secretary's Office.

APSLEY PELLATT'S

ABRIDGED LIST OF

Net Cash Prices for the best Flint Glass Ware.

DECANTERS.

25 Strong quart Nelson shape decanters,
cut all over, bold flutes and cut
brim & stopper, P.M. each 10s6d. to 12 0

26 Do. three-ringed royal shape, cut on
and between rings, turned out stop,
P.M. each 10 0

Do. do. not cut on or between rings,
'nor turned out stopper, P.M. ea. 8s to 9 0

27 Fancy shapes, cut all over, eight flutes,
spire stopper, &c. each, P.M. 16s. to 18 0

Do. six flutes only, each, P.M. 24s. to 27 0

DISHES.

31 Dishes, oblong, pillar moulded, scolloped
edges, cut star.

5-in.   7-in.   9-in.   10-in.
3s. 6d. 6s. 6d. 11s.   13s. each.

32 Oval cup sprig, shell pattern,

5-in.   7-in.   9-in.   11-in.
7s. 6d. 9s. 6d. 16s.   19s. each.

33 Square shape pillar, moulded star,

5-in.   7-in.   9-in.   10-in.
4s.   8s.   12s. 6d. 15s. each.

FINGER CUPS.

37 Fluted finger-cups, strong, about 14
oz. each 2 6

Do. plain flint, punted, per doz..... 18 0

Do. coloured, per doz......18s. to 21 0

38 Ten-fluted round, very strong, each . 5 0

Eight-fluted do., each 8 0

39 Medicean shape, moulded pillar, pearl
upper part, cut flat flutes, each .. 5 0

PICKLES

46 Pickles, half fluted for 3 in. holes, RM ea. 4 6

47 Strong, moulded bottom, 3-in. hole,
cut all over, flat flutes, R.M. each . 5 0

Best cut star do. for 3½-in. hole, PM ea. 7 6

Very strong and best cut, P.M. each 14 6

WATER JUGS

59 Quarts, neatly fluted and cut rings,
each.....................14s. to 18 0

60 Ewer shape, best cut handles, &c... 21 0

61 Silver do. scolloped edges, ex. lar. flutes 25 0

WATER BOTTLES

70 Moulded pillar body, cut neck, each . 3 0

71 Cut neck and star................. 3 0

72 Double fluted cut rings 3 6

73 Very strong pillar, moulded body, cut
neck and rings 5 6

74 Grecian shape, fluted all over 7 0

TUMBLERS

	78	79	80	81	82	83	84	85	86	87	
Tale	5s.										
Flint,	7s.	10s.	12s.	12s.	10s.	12s.	14s.	18s.	18s.		Doz.
	to	to	to	to	to		to	to	to		
	8s.	12s.	14s.	15s.	12s.		18s.	21s.	21s.	30s.	do.

WINES

	88	89	90	91	92	93	94	95	96	97	98	99
	7s.	7s.	7s.	7s.	8s.	14s.	12s.	13s.	15s.	18s.	21s.	20s.
	to	to	to	to								
	8s.	9s.	9s.	9s.	10s.							

*Glass Blowing, Cutting, and Engraving, may
be inspected by Purchasers, at Mr. Pellatt's Extensive Flint Glass and Steam Cutting Works, in
Holland Street, near Blackfriars' Bridge, any
Tuesday, Wednesday, or Thursday.*

Merchants and the Trade supplied on equitable
Terms.

No Abatement from the above specified Ready Money Prices.

No Connexion with any other Establishment.

LEADENHALL STREET, LONDON.
MECHI'S NEW YEAR'S PRESENTS.
MANUFACTORY, No. 4, LEADENHALL STREET, LONDON.

LADIES' COMPANIONS, or Work Cases 15s. to 2l.

LADIES' CARD CASES, in Pearl, Ivory, and Tortoiseshell . . . . . 10s. to 5l. each.

LADIES' WORK BOXES . 25s. to 10 Guineas.

LADIES' DRESSING CASES . 2l. 10s. to 50 Guineas.

LADIES' SCOTCH WORK BOXES at all prices.

LADIES' ROSEWOOD AND MAHOGANY DESKS 12s. 6d. to 10 Guineas.

LADIES' MOROCCO AND RUSSIA LEATHER WRITING CASES . . . . 5s. to 5l.

LADIES' ENVELOPE CASES, various prices.

LADIES' TABLE INKSTANDS, made of British Coal (quite a novelty) . . . 7s. 6d. to 30s.

LADIES' SCOTCH TOOTH-PICK CASES.

LADIES' IVORY AND TORTOISESHELL HAIR BRUSHES . . . at 2l. to 5l. per Pair.

LADIES' SCENT AND TOILET BOTTLES in great variety.

LADIES' SCOTCH TEA CADDIES . 21s. to 40s.

LADIES' PLAYING CARD BOXES . 30s. to 5l.

LACIES' JAPAN DRESSING CASES . 7s. to 15s.

LADIES' TORTOISESHELL DRESSING & SIDE COMBS.

LADIES' HAND GLASSES.

LADIES' PATENT INSTANTANEOUS PEN-MAKERS . . . 10s. 6d. and 12s. 6d.

LADIES' ELEGANT PENKNIVES AND SCISSORS 5s. to 30s.

MISCELLANEOUS.

BAGATELLE TABLES	.	.	£3	10	0 to	£5	0	0
BACKGAMMON TABLES	.	.	1	0	0 to	5	10	0
CHESS BOARDS	.	.	0	4	0 to	3	0	0
POPE JOAN BOARDS	.	.	0	13	0 to	1	0	0
IVORY CHESSMEN	.	.	1	1	0 to	10	10	0
BONE AND WOOD DITTO	.	.		Various Prices.				
WHIST MARKERS, COUNTERS, &c.								

GENT.'S DRESSING CASES, in Wood 2l. to 50l.

GENT.'S LEATHER DRESSING CASES 25s. to 24l.

GENT.'S WRITING DESKS, in Wood 30s. to 16l.

GENT.'S LEATHER WRITING DESKS 24s. 6d. to 5l.

GENT.'S WRITING & DRESSING CASE COMBINED . . . . 5l. to 16l.

GENT.'S POCKET BOOKS WITH INSTRUMENTS 20s. to 40s.

GENT.'S ELEGANT CASES OF RAZORS 12s. to 3l.

GENT.'S SEVEN DAY RAZORS, in Fancy Woods 25s. to 5l.

GENT.'S RAZOR STROPS . . 2s. to 30s.

GENT.'S SPORTING KNIVES . . 12s. to 5l.

GENT.'S FANCY PENKNIVES . 5s. to 15s.

GENT.'S PEARL AND SHELL POCKET COMBS 3s. 6d. to 15s.

GENT.'S SCOTCH CIGAR BOXES 3s. 6d. to 40s.

GENT.'S COAL AND EBONY INKSTANDS 7s. 6d. to 50s.

GENT.'S IVORY AND FANCY WOOD HAIR BRUSHES . . . 20s. to 3l. 10s.

GENT.'S SETS OF BRUSHES, in Russia Cases 25s. to 4l. 10s.

GENT.'S SILVER AND IVORY SHAVING BRUSHES In elegant Patterns.

GENT.'S SILVER AND SHELL TABLETS.

MECHI,  MECHI,

Submits, to public inspection, his Manufactures, as being of the finest quality this kingdom can produce, and at moderate prices.

A large Stock of Table Cutlery, Plated Tea and Coffee Services, Dish Covers, Hash Covers, &c.

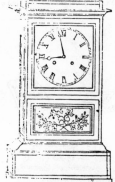

NORWICH UNION LIFE OFFICE.

For the convenience of Insurers, the article in the *Norwich Mercury* of January 19th, in reply to the assertions of Mr. Bignold, has been reprinted in a separate form, and may be had of

W. PICKERING, CHANCERY LANE, LONDON;

SOMERSEALE, W. E.	Leeds.	MILLIKEN and SON	Dublin.
GRAPEL, W.	Liverpool.	ROBERTSON, D.	Glasgow.
G. SIMONS	Manchester.	LAING and FORBES	Edinburgh.
WRIGHTSON and WEBB	Birmingham.	BRYANT, L.	Gloucester.
WHITLEY and BOOTH	Halifax.	LIGHT and RIDLER	Bristol.
CURRIE and BOWMAN	Newcastle-on-Tyne.	SIMONS, S.	Bath.
SANTER, R.	York.	DAVIES, H.	Cheltenham.

The attention of all Persons interested is most earnestly called to the subject.

TO SOUTH AUSTRALIAN EMIGRANTS.

" For the purchase of Ironmongery, it is necessary to be very particular as to the description, sizes, and quality ; what you want, therefore, should be procured of a person who well knows the market ; if the things are not the patterns in use, they will not be even looked at, much less purchased."—*Widdowson on Van Diemen's Land,* page 42.

" The patterns of the above articles may be seen and bought at Messrs. RICHARDS, WOOD, & CO."—*Widdowson on Van Diemen's Land,* page 41.

" I bought my ironmongery of Messrs. RICHARDS, WOOD, & CO., 117 and 118, Bishopsgate-street Within, and upon comparison of invoices with some of my friends in the Colony, I found I had been well used, and the quality of things furnished me was excellent ; they have been for years in the Australian trade, and understand the kind of articles required in these colonies."—*Gouger's South Australia,* page 126.

MOST IMPORTANT INFORMATION.
BY HIS MAJESTY'S ROYAL LETTERS PATENT.
33, GERRARD STREET, SOHO.

G. MINTER begs to inform the Nobility, Gentry, &c., that he has invented an EASY CHAIR, that will recline and elevate, into an innumerable variety of positions, without the least trouble or difficulty to the occupier ; and there being no machinery, rack, catch, or spring, it is only for persons sitting in the chair merely to wish to recline or elevate themselves, and the seat and back take any desired inclination, without requiring the least assistance or exertion whatever, owing to the weight on the seat acting as a counterbalance to the pressure against the back by the application of a self-adjusting leverage ; and for which G. M. has obtained his Majesty's Letters Patent. G. M. particularly recommends this invention to Invalids, or to those who may have lost the use of their hands or legs, as they are by it enabled to vary their position without requiring the use of either to obtain that change of position, from its endless variety, so necessary for the relief and comfort of the afflicted.

The Chair is made by the Inventor only, at his Wholesale Cabinet and Upholstery Manufactory, 33, Gerrard-street, Soho. G. M. is confident an inspection only is required to be convinced of its superiority over all others.

Merlin, Bath, Brighton, and every other description of Garden Wheel Chairs, much improved by G. Minter, with his self-acting reclining backs, so as to enable an invalid to lie at full length. Spinal Carriages, Portable Carriage Chairs, Water Beds, and every article for the comfort of the invalid.

THOMAS FOX

Respectfully announces to Noblemen, Gentlemen, and Families connected with or returning from the East Indian and Colonial Possessions, that he has a large and splendid assortment of every article in the

UPHOLSTERY, DECORATIVE, AND FURNISHING DEPARTMENT,

And has endeavoured to combine in his Stock, Elegance of Style and Fashion and Superiority of Manufacture, adapted for Tropical Climates as well as for Domestic use, and at prices commanding attention. To enable his patrons, the Public, to judge how far he has succeeded in these objects, he solicits an inspection of his Stock at

93, BISHOPSGATE STREET WITHIN,

THE OLDEST PLATE GLASS ESTABLISHMENT IN LONDON.

In the Agency Department will be found a variety of Houses and Properties for Letting or Disposal, connected with the Valuation and Sale of Effects and Estates by public or private channels.

ROWLAND'S MACASSAR OIL.

A VEGETABLE PRODUCTION.

This elegant, fragrant, and pellucid OIL, far surpasses any preparation ever discovered for the Hair, and is in universal high repute for its unequalled Restorative, Preservative, and Beautifying properties.

It is the only article that really produces and restores Hair, even at a late period of life, prevents it from falling off or turning Grey, and possesses the desirable property of preserving it in its natural shade (which renders it invaluable to those whose hair is of a delicate and light colour), frees it from scurf, and renders the most harsh and dry hair as soft as silk, curly and glossy; preserves it in curl and other decorative formation—unimpaired by the damp atmosphere, violent exercise, or the relaxing tendencies of the Ball Room. To CHILDREN it is invaluable, as it lays a foundation for

A BEAUTIFUL HEAD OF HAIR.

TESTIMONIAL.

GENTLEMEN,—I have been prevailed upon by a friend to try your Macassar Oil, and have indeed found it of amazing benefit in my family; four of my children, a few years ago, were ill with the Scarlet Fever, and for many months there was not the least appearance of hair upon their heads. The medical gentlemen who attended them gave no hopes of it ever returning; but, after using your Macassar Oil a short time, I found, to my great delight, their heads covered with short strong hair, which is now daily improving. You are at liberty to make whatever use you please of this letter to your advantage; as I live in the country, I have taken the present opportunity of a friend going to London to convey this letter to you.

I am, Gentlemen, your humble servant,

Ottringham, Yorkshire, June 8th, 1829. JANET SMITH.

CAUTION.—Ask for "Rowland's Macassar Oil," and observe their Name and Address, in Red, on Lace-work, on the wrapper thus—

A. ROWLAND & SON, 20, HATTON GARDEN,
Counter-signed ALEX. ROWLAND.

The lowest price is 3s. 6d.; the next 7s.; or Family Bottles (containing four small) at 10s. 6d.; or double that size, 1l. 1s.

MOSLEY'S METALLIC PENS.

R. MOSLEY & CO. beg to call the attention of Mercantile Men, and the Public in general, to their superior Metallic Pens. They possess the highest degree of elasticity and flexibility, and are found perfectly free from all those inconveniences which have prevented so many persons making use of Metallic Pens.

Every description of writer may be suited, as these pens are manufactured of various qualities, degrees of hardness, &c. They may be had at all respectable Stationers throughout the kingdom.

Observe that every Pen is stamped, R. MOSLEY &-CO., LONDON.

Now publishing, in Monthly Parts, price One Shilling,

BY CHARLES TILT, 86, FLEET STREET;

SOLD BY

SIMPKIN, MARSHALL, AND CO., STATIONERS' COURT; AND ALL BOOKSELLERS.

A SPLENDID LIBRARY EDITION

OF

ILLUSTRATED FABLES;

BY THE MOST EMINENT

BRITISH, FRENCH, GERMAN, AND SPANISH AUTHORS:

ILLUSTRATED WITH NUMEROUS ENGRAVINGS,

BY ORRIN SMITH, BREVIERE, AND OTHER CELEBRATED ENGRAVERS, AFTER ORIGINAL DESIGNS BY M. GRANDVILLE.

The work is printed in the best manner, with new type, on fine paper, and will be completed in Twelve Monthly Parts, forming One Handsome Octavo Volume, uniform with the recent editions of BYRON, SCOTT, CRABBE, &c.

OPINIONS OF THE PUBLIC PRESS.

" A comprehensive collection of the best Fables, with many original translations from the languages of the Continent; the whole richly and profusely illustrated by woodcuts, which, taking the present number as an exemplar, may be described as being exquisitely beautiful. The typography is clear, and equal to the most elaborate attempts at perfection in printing, and the entire work reflects credit on the taste and enterprise employed in its production. To the lovers of Fables—that is to say, to everybody who has imagination and the moral sense—this publication ought to be a welcome and grateful offering. For a holiday present it is worth all the annuals together."—*Atlas.*

" Part I., now before us, containing fifty-nine Fables, with seven illustrations on wood, most of them ranking high in merit, is strong in promise. The work is printed on fine paper, with great accuracy and beauty."—*Aldine Magazine.*

" A compilation of the most esteemed Fables of the most eminent writers ; at the same time, it professes some originality, and promises to become a very amusing series. The present number is profusely embellished with pictorial illustrations, and is a favourable specimen of what is to be expected when the whole is completed."—*Conservative Jour.*

" We can confidently recommend this work to our readers, as one of the cheapest and best of its class. The present number contains seven exquisite woodcuts, and upwards of fifty fables, for one shilling : surely ' the force of cheapness can no further go.' The book, when completed, will form an invaluable source of entertainment and instruction, for many high moral lessons are inculcated in the fictions introduced ; while, from the style in which the first number is got up, it promises to be a work as fitted for the drawing-room of the lady, as it is for the library of the student."—*Court Gazette.*

" The present series, if we may judge of the whole work by the Part before us, will be a valuable addition to the library of all who love wit for its own sake, no less than to those who hold that a humorous incident well related, has a good effect upon the morals of the reader or auditor. The engravings are superb, both as regards their design and execution. The work is beautifully got up, and is sold remarkably cheap—even for this age of cheap printing. We cordially recommend it to our readers."—*Satirist.*

" The mode of teaching wisdom by Fables or parables, has a divine approval and example ; therefore, we need not here insist on it. All we have to observe, being the great merit of the plan adopted here, of culling every good one wheresoever found "—*News.*

" Mr. Tilt has long been celebrated for the neat and tasteful manner in which he produces his publications. The selection has been made with care and attention; it is characterised by a total absence of everything gross."—*Morning Advertiser.*

" Mr. Tilt's splendid Library Edition of Fables has come out this month with increased splendour. Half-a-dozen woodcuts such as these for a shilling ! The publisher should advertise that, with a view to the advancement of morality, he gives away the letter-press for nothing to the purchasers of the plates."—*Era.*

" Neatly printed, and illustrated by humorous woodcuts : the personations of animals are very felicitous."—*Court Jour.*

" A work, the design and execution of which it would be almost impossible to praise too highly. The Fables are well chosen and judiciously commented on, the letter-press is beautifully printed, the engravings are humorous and characteristic, and the price very moderate. It can scarcely fail, we think, to meet with a very extensive circulation."—*Recorder.*

" Printed by Messrs. Willoughby and Co., of Goswell-street, they present a good example of the beauty and perfection to which, even for cheap editions of standard works, typography has been brought ; and consist of a judicious selection of the best Fables of four principal European nations. With all people, and in every stage of life, Fables have had a great and just influence, and it is strange that we have had in England so few readable editions. The defect will be supplied by the present publication. With thirty-two pages of letter-press, and half-a-dozen of these appropriate and superior illustrations for a single shilling, the proprietors seem to us to be fully justified in challenging comparison with any existing efforts."—*Brighton Herald.*

[BRADBURY AND EVANS, PRINTERS, WHITEFRIARS.]

CHAPTER XXXIV.

**WHEREIN MR. RALPH NICKLEBY IS VISITED BY PERSONS WITH WHOM
THE READER HAS BEEN ALREADY MADE ACQUAINTED.**

" WHAT a demnition long time you have kept me ringing at this confounded old cracked tea-kettle of a bell, every tinkle of which is enough
to throw a strong man into blue convulsions, upon my life and soul,
oh demmit,"—said Mr. Mantalini to Newman Noggs, scraping his boots,
as he spoke, on Ralph Nickleby's scraper.

" I didn't hear the bell more than once," replied Newman.

"Then you are most immensely and outr*i*geously deaf," said Mr.
Mantalini, " as deaf as a demnition post."

Mr. Mantalini had got by this time into the passage, and was making
his way to the door of Ralph's office with very little ceremony, when
Newman interposed his body; and hinting that Mr. Nickleby was
unwilling to be disturbed, enquired whether the client's business was of
a pressing nature.

" It is most demnebly particular," said Mr. Mantalini. " It is to
melt some scraps of dirty paper into bright, shining, chinking, tinkling,
demd mint sauce."

Newman uttered a significant grunt, and taking Mr. Mantalini's
proffered card, limped with it into his master's office. As he thrust his
head in at the door, he saw that Ralph had resumed the thoughtful
posture into which he had fallen after perusing his nephew's letter, and
that he seemed to have been reading it again, as he once more held it open
in his hand. The glance was but momentary, for Ralph, being disturbed,
turned to demand the cause of the interruption.

As Newman stated it, the cause himself swaggered into the room, and
grasping Ralph's horny hand with uncommon affection, vowed that he
had never seen him looking so well in all his life.

" There is quite a bloom upon your demd countenance," said Mr.
Mantalini, seating himself unbidden, and arranging his hair and
whiskers. " You look quite juvenile and jolly, demmit ! "

" We are alone," returned Ralph, tartly. " What do you want with
me ? "

" Good ! " cried Mr. Mantalini, displaying his teeth. " What did I
want ! Yes. Ha ha ! Very good. *What* did I want. Ha ha !
Oh dem ! "

" What *do* you want, man ? " demanded Ralph, sternly.

" Demnition discount," returned Mr. Mantalini, with a grin, and
shaking his head waggishly.

" Money is scarce," said Ralph.

" Demd scarce, or I shouldn't want it," interrupted Mr. Mantalini.

" The times are bad, and one scarcely knows whom to trust," continued Ralph. " I don't want to do business just now, in fact I would
rather not; but as you are a friend—how many bills have you there?"

" Two," returned Mr. Mantalini.

" What is the gross amount ? "

" Demd trifling—five-and-seventy."

" And the dates ? "

" Two months, and four."

" I'll do them for you—mind, for *you;* I wouldn't for many people—for five-and-twenty pounds," said Ralph, deliberately.

" Oh demmit ! " cried Mr. Mantalini, whose face lengthened considerably at this handsome proposal.

" Why, that leaves you fifty," retorted Ralph. " What would you have ? Let me see the names."

" You are so demd hard, Nickleby," remonstrated Mr. Mantalini.

" Let me see the names," replied Ralph, impatiently extending his hand for the bills. " Well ! They are not sure, but they are safe enough. Do you consent to the terms, and will you take the money ? I don't want you to do so. I would rather you didn't."

" Demmit, Nickleby, can't you——" began Mr. Mantalini.

" No," replied Ralph, interrupting him. " I can't. Will you take the money—down, mind ; no delay, no going into the city and pretending to negotiate with some other party who has no existence and never had. Is it a bargain or is it not ? "

Ralph pushed some papers from him as he spoke, and carelessly rattled his cash-box, as though by mere accident. The sound was too much for Mr. Mantalini. He closed the bargain directly it reached his ears, and Ralph told the money out upon the table.

He had scarcely done so, and Mr. Mantalini had not yet gathered it all up, when a ring was heard at the bell, and immediately afterwards Newman ushered in no less a person than Madame Mantalini, at sight of whom Mr. Mantalini evinced considerable discomposure, and swept the cash into his pocket with remarkable alacrity.

" Oh, you *are* here," said Madame Mantalini, tossing her head.

" Yes, my life and soul, I am," replied her husband, dropping on his knees, and pouncing with kitten-like playfulness upon a stray sovereign. " I am here, my soul's delight, upon Tom Tidler's ground, picking up the demnition gold and silver."

" I am ashamed of you," said Madame Mantalini, with much indignation.

" Ashamed—of *me,* my joy ? It knows it is talking demd charming sweetness, but naughty fibs," returned Mr. Mantalini. " It knows it is not ashamed of its own popolorum tibby."

Whatever were the circumstances which had led to such a result, it certainly appeared as though the popolorum tibby had rather miscalculated, for the nonce, the extent of his lady's affection. Madame Mantalini only looked scornful in reply ; and, turning to Ralph, begged him to excuse her intrusion.

" Which is entirely attributable," said Madame, " to the gross misconduct and most improper behaviour of Mr. Mantalini."

" Of me, my essential juice of pine-apple ! "

" Of you," returned his wife. " But I will not allow it. I will not

Mr and Mrs Mantalini in Ralph Nickleby's Office.

submit to be ruined by the extravagance and profligacy of any man. I call Mr. Nickleby to witness the course I intend to pursue with you."

"Pray don't call me to witness anything, ma'am," said Ralph. "Settle it between yourselves, settle it between yourselves."

"No, but I must beg you as a favour," said Madame Mantalini, "to hear me give him notice of what it is my fixed intention to do—my fixed intention sir," repeated Madame Mantalini, darting an angry look at her husband.

"Will she call me, 'Sir'!" cried Mantalini. "Me who doat upon her with the demdest ardour! She, who coils her fascinations round me like a pure and angelic rattle-snake! It will be all up with my feelings; she will throw me into a demd state."

"Don't talk of feelings, Sir," rejoined Madame Mantalini, seating herself, and turning her back upon him. "You don't consider mine."

"I do not consider yours, my soul!" exclaimed Mr. Mantalini.

"No," replied his wife.

And notwithstanding various blandishments on the part of Mr. Mantalini, Madame Mantalini still said no, and said it too with such determined and resolute ill temper, that Mr. Mantalini was clearly taken aback.

"His extravagance, Mr. Nickleby," said Madame Mantalini, addressing herself to Ralph, who leant against his easy-chair with his hands behind him, and regarded the amiable couple with a smile of the supremest and most unmitigated contempt,—"His extravagance is beyond all bounds."

"I should scarcely have supposed it," answered Ralph, sarcastically.

"I assure you, Mr. Nickleby, however, that it is," returned Madame Mantalini. "It makes me miserable; I am under constant apprehensions, and in constant difficulty. And even this," said Madame Mantalini, wiping her eyes, "is not the worst. He took some papers of value out of my desk this morning without asking my permission."

Mr. Mantalini groaned slightly, and buttoned his trowsers pocket.

"I am obliged," continued Madame Mantalini, "since our late misfortunes, to pay Miss Knag a great deal of money for having her name in the business, and I really cannot afford to encourage him in all his wastefulness. As I have no doubt that he came straight here, Mr. Nickleby, to convert the papers I have spoken of, into money, and as you have assisted us very often before, and are very much connected with us in these kind of matters, I wish you to know the determination at which his conduct has compelled me to arrive."

Mr. Mantalini groaned once more from behind his wife's bonnet, and fitting a sovereign into one of his eyes, winked with the other at Ralph. Having achieved this performance with great dexterity, he whipped the coin into his pocket, and groaned again with increased penitence.

"I have made up my mind," said Madame Mantalini, as tokens of impatience manifested themselves in Ralph's countenance, "to allowance him."

"To do what, my joy?" inquired Mr. Mantalini, who did not seem to have caught the words.

"To put him," said Madame Mantalini, looking at Ralph, and prudently abstaining from the slightest glance at her husband, lest his many graces should induce her to falter in her resolution, "to put him upon a fixed allowance; and I say that if he has a hundred and twenty pounds a-year for his clothes and pocket-money, he may consider himself a very fortunate man."

Mr. Mantalini waited with much decorum to hear the amount of the proposed stipend, but when it reached his ears, he cast his hat and cane upon the floor, and drawing out his pocket-handkerchief, gave vent to his feelings in a dismal moan.

"Demnition!" cried Mr. Mantalini, suddenly skipping out of his chair, and as suddenly skipping into it again, to the great discomposure of his lady's nerves. "But no. It is a demd horrid dream. It is not reality. No."

Comforting himself with this assurance, Mr. Mantalini closed his eyes and waited patiently till such time as he should wake up.

"A very judicious arrangement," observed Ralph with a sneer, "if your husband will keep within it, ma'am—as no doubt he will."

"Demmit!" exclaimed Mr. Mantalini, opening his eyes at the sound of Ralph's voice, "it is a horrid reality. She is sitting there before me. There is the graceful outline of her form; it cannot be mistaken—there is nothing like it. The two countesses had no outlines at all, and the dowager's was a demd outline. Why is she so excruciatingly beautiful that I cannot be angry with her even now?"

"You have brought it upon yourself, Alfred," returned Madame Mantalini—still reproachfully, but in a softened tone.

"I am a demd villain!" cried Mr. Mantalini, smiting himself on the head. "I will fill my pockets with change for a sovereign in halfpence, and drown myself in the Thames; but I will not be angry with her even then, for I will put a note in the twopenny-post as I go along, to tell her where the body is. She will be a lovely widow. I shall be a body. Some handsome women will cry; she will laugh demnebly."

"Alfred, you cruel, cruel, creature," said Madame Mantalini, sobbing at the dreadful picture.

"She calls me cruel—me—me—who for her sake will become a demd damp, moist, unpleasant body!" exclaimed Mr. Mantalini.

"You know it almost breaks my heart, even to hear you talk of such a thing," replied Madame Mantalini.

"Can I live to be mistrusted?" cried her husband. "Have I cut my heart into a demd extraordinary number of little pieces, and given them all away one after another to the same little engrossing demnition captivater, and can I live to be suspected by her! Demmit, no I can't."

"Ask Mr. Nickleby whether the sum I have mentioned is not a proper one," reasoned Madame Mantalini.

"I don't want any sum," replied her disconsolate husband; "I shall require no demd allowance—I will be a body."

On this repetition of Mr. Mantalini's fatal threat, Madame Mantalini wrung her hands and implored the interference of Ralph Nickleby; and after a great quantity of tears and talking, and several attempts on the part of Mr. Mantalini to reach the door, preparatory to straightway committing violence upon himself, that gentleman was prevailed upon, with difficulty, to promise that he wouldn't be a body. This great point attained, Madame Mantalini argued the question of the allowance, and Mr. Mantalini did the same, taking occasion to show that he could live with uncommon satisfaction upon bread and water and go clad in rags, but that he could not support existence with the additional burden of being mistrusted by the object of his most devoted and disinterested affection. This brought fresh tears into Madame Mantalini's eyes, which having just begun to open to some few of the demerits of Mr. Mantalini, were only open a very little way, and could be easily closed again. The result was, that without quite giving up the allowance question, Madame Mantalini postponed its further consideration; and Ralph saw clearly enough that Mr. Mantalini had gained a fresh lease of his easy life, and that, for some time longer at all events, his degradation and downfall were postponed.

" But it will come soon enough," thought Ralph; " all love—bah! that I should use the cant of boys and girls—is fleeting enough; though that which has its sole root in the admiration of a whiskered face like that of yonder baboon, perhaps lasts the longest, as it originates in the greater blindness and is fed by vanity. Meantime the fools bring grist to my mill, so let them live out their day, and the longer it is, the better."

These agreeable reflections occurred to Ralph Nickleby, as sundry small caresses and endearments, supposed to be unseen, were exchanged between the objects of his thoughts.

" If you have nothing more to say, my dear, to Mr. Nickleby," said Madame Mantalini, " we will take our leaves. I am sure we have detained him much too long already."

Mr. Mantalini answered, in the first instance, by tapping Madame Mantalini several times on the nose, and then, by remarking in words that he had nothing more to say.

" Demmit! I have, though," he added almost immediately, drawing Ralph into a corner. " Here's an affair about your friend Sir Mulberry. Such a demd extraordinary out-of-the-way kind of thing as never was —eh?"

" What do you mean?" asked Ralph.

" Don't you know, demmit?" asked Mr. Mantalini.

" I see by the paper that he was thrown from his cabriolet last night and severely injured, and that his life is in some danger," answered Ralph with great composure; " but I see nothing extraordinary in that—accidents are not miraculous events, when men live hard and drive after dinner."

" Whew!" cried Mr. Mantalini in a long shrill whistle. " Then don't you know how it was?"

" Not unless it was as I have just supposed," replied Ralph, shrugging his shoulders carelessly, as if to give his questioner to understand that he had no curiosity upon the subject.

" Demmit, you amaze me," cried Mantalini.

Ralph shrugged his shoulders again, as if it were no great feat to amaze Mr. Mantalini, and cast a wistful glance at the face of Newman Noggs, which had several times appeared behind a couple of panes of glass in the room door ; it being a part of Newman's duty, when unimportant people called, to make various feints of supposing that the bell had rung for him to show them out, by way of a gentle hint to such visitors that it was time to go.

"Don't you know," said Mr. Mantalini, taking Ralph by the button, "that it wasn't an accident at all, but a demd furious manslaughtering attack made upon him by your nephew ? "

"What !" snarled Ralph, clenching his fists and turning a livid white.

"Demmit, Nickleby, you're as great a tiger as he is," said Mantalini, alarmed at these demonstrations.

"Go on," cried Ralph, savagely. "Tell me what you mean. What is this story ? Who told you ? Speak," growled Ralph. "Do you hear me ?"

" 'Gad, Nickleby," said Mr. Mantalini, retreating towards his wife, "what a demneble fierce old evil genius you are. You're enough to frighten my life and soul out of her little delicious wits—flying all at once into such a blazing, ravaging, raging passion as never was, demmit."

" 'Pshaw," rejoined Ralph, forcing a smile. "It is but manner."

"It is a demd uncomfortable and private-madhouse-sort of manner," said Mr. Mantalini, picking up his cane.

Ralph affected to smile, and once more inquired from whom Mr. Mantalini had derived his information.

"From Pyke ; and a demd, fine, pleasant, gentlemanly dog it is," replied Mantalini. "Demnition pleasant, and a tip-top sawyer."

"And what said he ?" asked Ralph, knitting his brows.

"That it happened this way—that your nephew met him at a coffee-house, fell upon him with the most demneble ferocity, followed him to his cab, swore he would ride home with him if he rode upon the horse's back or hooked himself on to the horse's tail ; smashed his countenance, which is a demd fine countenance in its natural state ; frightened the horse, pitched out Sir Mulberry and himself, and——"

"And was killed ?" interposed Ralph with gleaming eyes. "Was he ? Is he dead ?"

Mantalini shook his head.

"Ugh," said Ralph, turning away, "Then he has done nothing—stay," he added, looking round again. "He broke a leg or an arm, or put his shoulder out, or fractured his collar-bone, or ground a rib or two ? His neck was saved for the halter, but he got some painful and slow-healing injury for his trouble—did he ? You must have heard that, at least."

"No," rejoined Mantalini, shaking his head again. "Unless he was dashed into such little pieces that they blew away, he wasn't hurt, for he went off as quiet and comfortable as—as—as demnition," said Mr. Mantalini, rather at a loss for a simile.

"And what," said Ralph, hesitating a little, "what was the cause of quarrel?"

"You are the demdest, knowing hand," replied Mr. Mantalini, in an admiring tone, "the cunningest, rummest, superlativest old fox—oh dem—to pretend now not to know that it was the little bright-eyed niece—the softest, sweetest, prettiest——"

"Alfred!" interposed Madame Mantalini.

"She is always right," rejoined Mr. Mantalini soothingly, "and when she says it is time to go, it is time, and go she shall; and when she walks along the streets with her own tulip, the women shall say with envy, she has got a demd fine husband, and the men shall say with rapture, he has got a demd fine wife, and they shall both be right and neither wrong, upon my life and soul—oh demmit!"

With which remarks, and many more no less intellectual and to the purpose, Mr. Mantalini kissed the fingers of his gloves to Ralph Nickleby, and drawing his lady's arm through his, led her mincingly away.

"So, so," muttered Ralph, dropping into his chair; "this devil is loose again, and thwarting me, as he was born to do, at every turn. He told me once there should be a day of reckoning between us, sooner or later. I'll make him a true prophet, for it shall surely come."

"Are you at home?" asked Newman, suddenly popping in his head.

"No," replied Ralph, with equal abruptness.

Newman withdrew his head, but thrust it in again.

"You're quite sure you're not at home, are you?" said Newman.

"What does the idiot mean?" cried Ralph, testily.

"He has been waiting nearly ever since they first came in, and may have heard your voice—that's all," said Newman, rubbing his hands.

"Who has?" demanded Ralph, wrought by the intelligence he had just heard, and his clerk's provoking coolness, to an intense pitch of irritation.

The necessity of a reply was superseded by the unlooked-for entrance of a third party—the individual in question—who, bringing his one eye (for he had but one) to bear on Ralph Nickleby, made a great many shambling bows, and sat himself down in an arm-chair, with his hands on his knees, and his short black trousers drawn up so high in the legs by the exertion of seating himself, that they scarcely reached below the tops of his Wellington boots.

"Why, this *is* a surprise," said Ralph, bending his gaze upon the visitor, and half smiling as he scrutinized him attentively; "I should know your face, Mr. Squeers."

"Ah!" replied that worthy, "and you'd have know'd it better, Sir, if it hadn't been for all that I've been a-going through. Just lift that little boy off the tall stool in the back office, and tell him to come in here, will you, my man?" said Squeers, addressing himself to Newman. "Oh, he's lifted his-self off. My son, Sir, little Wackford: What do you think of him, Sir, for a specimen of the Dotheboys Hall feeding? ain't he fit to bust out of his clothes, and start the seams, and make the very buttons fly off with his fatness. Here's flesh!" cried Squeers, turning the boy about, and indenting the plumpest parts of his figure with divers pokes and punches, to the great discomposure of his son and heir. "Here's firmness, here's solidness! why you can hardly get up enough of him between your finger and thumb to pinch him anywheres."

In however good condition Master Squeers might have been, he certainly did not present this remarkable compactness of person, for on his father's closing his finger and thumb in illustration of his remark, he uttered a sharp cry, and rubbed the place in the most natural manner possible.

"Well," remarked Squeers, a little disconcerted, "I had him there; but that's because we breakfasted early this morning, and he hasn't had his lunch yet. Why you couldn't shut a bit of him in a door, when he's had his dinner. Look at them tears, Sir," said Squeers, with a triumphant air, as Master Wackford wiped his eyes with the cuff of his jacket, "there's oiliness!"

"He looks well, indeed," returned Ralph, who for some purposes of his own seemed desirous to conciliate the schoolmaster. "But how is Mrs. Squeers, and how are you?"

"Mrs. Squeers, sir," replied the proprietor of Dotheboys, "is as she always is—a mother to them lads, and a blessing, and a comfort, and a joy to all them as knows her. One of our boys—gorging his-self with vittles, and then turning ill; that's their way—got a abscess on him last week. To see how she operated upon him with a pen-knife! Oh Lor!" said Squeers, heaving a sigh, and nodding his head a great many times, "what a member of society that woman is!"

Mr. Squeers indulged in a retrospective look for some quarter of a minute, as if this allusion to his lady's excellencies had naturally led his mind to the peaceful village of Dotheboys near Greta Bridge in Yorkshire, and then looked at Ralph, as if waiting for him to say something.

"Have you quite recovered that scoundrel's attack?" asked Ralph.

"I've only just done it, if I've done it now," replied Squeers. "I was one blessed bruise, Sir," said Squeers, touching first the roots of his hair, and then the toes of his boots, "from *here* to *there*. Vinegar and brown paper, vinegar and brown paper, from morning to night. I suppose there was a matter of half a ream of brown paper stuck upon me from first to last. As I laid all of a heap in our kitchen, plastered all over, you might have thought I was a large brown paper parcel, chock full of nothing but groans. Did I groan loud, Wackford, or did I groan soft?" asked Mr. Squeers, appealing to his son.

"Loud," replied Wackford.

"Was the boys sorry to see me in such a dreadful condition, Wackford, or was they glad?" asked Mr. Squeers, in a sentimental manner.

"Gl—"

"Eh?" cried Squeers, turning sharp round.

"Sorry," rejoined his son.

"Oh!" said Squeers, catching him a smart box on the ear. "Then take your hands out of your pockets, and don't stammer when you're asked a question. Hold your noise, sir, in a gentleman's office, or I'll run away from my family and never come back any more; and then what would become of all them precious and forlorn lads as would be let loose on the world, without their best friend at their elbers!"

"Were you obliged to have medical attendance?" inquired Ralph.

"Ay, was I," rejoined Squeers, "and a precious bill the medical attendant brought in too : but I paid it though."

Ralph elevated his eyebrows in a manner which might be expressive of either sympathy or astonishment—just as the beholder was pleased to take it.

"Yes, I paid it, every farthing," replied Squeers, who seemed to know the man he had to deal with, too well to suppose that any blinking of the question would induce him to subscribe towards the expenses ; "I wasn't out of pocket by it after all, either."

"No!" said Ralph.

"Not a halfpenny," replied Squeers. "The fact is, that we have only one extra with our boys, and that is for doctors when required—and not then, unless we're sure of our customers. Do you see?"

"I understand," said Ralph.

"Very good," rejoined Squeers. "Then after my bill was run up, we picked out five little boys (sons of small tradesmen, as was sure pay) that had never had the scarlet fever, and we sent one to a cottage where they'd got it, and he took it, and then we put the four others to sleep with him, and *they* took it, and then the doctor came and attended 'em once all round, and we divided my total among 'em, and added it on to their little bills, and the parents paid it. Ha! ha! ha!"

"And a good plan too," said Ralph, eyeing the schoolmaster stealthily.

"I believe you," rejoined Squeers. "We always do it. Why, when Mrs. Squeers was brought to bed with little Wackford here, we ran the hooping-cough through half-a-dozen boys, and charged her expenses among 'em, monthly nurse included. Ha, ha, ha!"

Ralph never laughed, but on this occasion he produced the nearest approach to it that he could, and waiting until Mr. Squeers had enjoyed the professional joke to his heart's content, enquired what had brought him to town.

"Some bothering law business," replied Squeers, scratching his head, "connected with an action, for what they call neglect of a boy. I don't know what they would have. He had as good grazing, that boy had, as there is about us."

Ralph looked as if he did not quite understand the observation.

"Grazing," said Squeers, raising his voice, under the impression that as Ralph failed to comprehend him, he must be deaf. "When a boy gets weak and ill and don't relish his meals, we give him a change of diet—turn him out for an hour or so every day into a neighbour's turnip field, or sometimes, if it's a delicate case, a turnip field and a piece of carrots alternately, and let him eat as many as he likes. There an't better land in the county than this perwerse lad grazed on, and yet he goes and catches cold and indigestion and what not, and then his friends brings a law-suit against *me*. Now, you'd hardly suppose," added Squeers, moving in his chair with the impatience of an ill-used man, " that people's ingratitude would carry them quite as far as that; would you ?"

" A hard case, indeed," observed Ralph.

" You don't say more than the truth when you say that," replied Squeers. " I don't suppose there's a man going, as possesses the fondness for youth that I do. There's youth to the amount of eight hundred pound a-year at Dotheboys Hall at this present time. I'd take sixteen hundred pound worth if I could get 'em, and be as fond of every individual twenty pound among 'em as nothing should equal it !"

" Are you stopping at your old quarters ?" asked Ralph.

" Yes, we are at the Saracen," replied Squeers, " and as it don't want very long to the end of the half-year, we shall continney to stop there till I've collected the money, and some new boys too, I hope. I've brought little Wackford up, on purpose to show to parents and guardians. I shall put him in the advertisement this time. Look at that boy—himself a pupil—why he's a miracle of high feeding, that boy is."

" I should like to have a word with you," said Ralph, who had both spoken and listened mechanically for some time, and seemed to have been thinking.

" As many words as you like, Sir," rejoined Squeers. " Wackford, you go and play in the back office, and don't move about too much or you'll get thin, and that won't do. You haven't got such a thing as twopence, Mr. Nickleby, have you ?" said Squeers, rattling a bunch of keys in his coat pocket, and muttering something about its being all silver.

" I—think I have," said Ralph, very slowly, and producing, after much rummaging in an old drawer, a penny, a halfpenny, and two farthings.

" Thankee," said Squeers, bestowing it upon his son. " Here, you go and buy a tart—Mr. Nickleby's man will show you where—and mind you buy a rich one. Pastry," added Squeers, closing the door on Master Wackford, " makes his flesh shine a good deal, and parents thinks that's a healthy sign."

With which explanation, and a peculiarly knowing look to eke it out, Mr. Squeers moved his chair so as to bring himself opposite to Ralph Nickleby at no great distance off ; and having planted it to his entire satisfaction, sat down.

" Attend to me," said Ralph, bending forward a little.

Squeers nodded.

" I am not to suppose," said Ralph, " that you are dolt enough to forgive or forget very readily the violence that was committed upon you, or the exposure which accompanied it ?"

" Devil a bit," replied Squeers, tartly.

" Or to lose an opportunity of repaying it with interest, if you could get one ?" said Ralph.

" Show me one and try," rejoined Squeers.

" Some such object it was that induced you to call on me ?" said Ralph, raising his eyes to the schoolmaster's face.

" N—n—no, I don't know that," replied Squeers. " I thought that if it was in your power to make me, besides the trifle of money you sent, any compensation——"

" Ah !" cried Ralph, interrupting him. " You needn't go on."

After a long pause, during which Ralph appeared absorbed in contemplation, he again broke silence, by asking—

" Who is this boy that he took with him ?"

Squeers stated his name.

" Was he young or old, healthy or sickly, tractable or rebellious ? Speak out, man," retorted Ralph quickly.

" Why, he wasn't young," answered Squeers ; " that is, not young for a boy you know."

" That is, that he was not a boy at all, I suppose ?" interrupted Ralph.

" Well," returned Squeers briskly, as if he felt relieved by the suggestion, " he might have been nigh twenty. He wouldn't seem so old though to them as didn't know him, for he was a little wanting here," touching his forehead, " nobody at home you know, if you knocked ever so often."

" And you *did* knock pretty often, I dare say ?" muttered Ralph.

" Pretty well," returned Squeers with a grin.

" When you wrote to acknowledge the receipt of this trifle of money as you call it," said Ralph, " you told me his friends had deserted him long ago, and that you had not the faintest clue or trace to tell you who he was. Is that the truth ?"

" It is ; worse luck !" replied Squeers, becoming more and more easy and familiar in his manner, as Ralph pursued his enquiries with the less reserve. " It's fourteen year ago, by the entry in my book, since a strange man brought him to my place one autumn night, and left him there, paying five pound five, for his first quarter in advance. He might have been five or six year old at that time—not more."

" What more do you know about him ?" demanded Ralph.

" Devilish little, I'm sorry to say," replied Squeers. " The money was paid for some six or eight year, and then it stopped. He had given an address in London, had this chap ; but when it came to the point, of course nobody knowed anything about him. So I kept the lad out of—out of—"

" Charity ?" suggested Ralph drily.

" Charity, to be sure," returned Squeers, rubbing his knees, " and when he begins to be useful in a certain sort of a way, this young scoundrel of a Nickleby comes and carries him off. But the most vexatious and aggeravating part of the whole affair is," said Squeers, dropping his voice, and drawing his chair still closer to Ralph, " that some questions have been asked about him at last—not of me, but in a round-about kind of way of people in our village. So, that just when I might have had all arrears paid up, perhaps, and perhaps—who knows ? such things have happened in our business before—a present besides for putting him out to a farmer or sending him to sea, so that he might never turn up to disgrace his parents, supposing him to be a natural boy, as many of our boys are—damme, if that villain of a Nickleby don't collar him in open day, and commit as good as highway robbery upon my pocket."

" We will both cry quits with him before long," said Ralph, laying his hand on the arm of the Yorkshire schoolmaster.

" Quits!" echoed Squeers. " Ah! and I should like to leave a small balance in his favour, to be settled when he can. I only wish Mrs. Squeers could catch hold of him. Bless her heart! She'd murder him, Mr. Nickleby—she would, as soon as eat her dinner."

" We will talk of this again," said Ralph. " I must have time to think of it. To wound him through his own affections or fancies——. If I can strike him through this boy——"

" Strike him how you like, Sir," interrupted Squeers, " only hit him hard enough, that's all—and with that, I'll say good morning. Here! —just chuck that little boy's hat off that corner-peg, and lift him off the stool, will you?"

Bawling these requests to Newman Noggs, Mr. Squeers betook himself to the little back office, and fitted on his child's hat with parental anxiety, while Newman, with his pen behind his ear, sat stiff and immovable on his stool, regarding the father and son by turns with a broad stare.

" He's a fine boy, an't he?" said Squeers, throwing his head a little on one side, and falling back to the desk, the better to estimate the proportions of little Wackford.

" Very," said Newman.

" Pretty well swelled out, an't he?" pursued Squeers. " He has the fatness of twenty boys, he has."

" Ah!" replied Newman, suddenly thrusting his face into that of Squeers, " he has;—the fatness of twenty!—more. He's got it all. God help the others. Ha! ha! Oh Lord!"

Having uttered these fragmentary observations, Newman dropped upon his desk and began to write with most marvellous rapidity.

" Why, what does the man mean?" cried Squeers, colouring. " Is he drunk?"

Newman made no reply.

" Is he mad?" said Squeers.

But still Newman betrayed no consciousness of any presence save his own; so Mr. Squeers comforted himself by saying that he was both drunk *and* mad; and, with this parting observation, he led his hopeful son away.

In exact proportion as Ralph Nickleby became conscious of a struggling and lingering regard for Kate, had his detestation of Nicholas augmented. It might be, that to atone for the weakness of inclining to any one person, he held it necessary to hate some other more intensely than before; but such had been the course of his feelings. And now, to be defied and spurned, to be held up to her in the worst and most repulsive colours, to know that she was taught to hate and despise him; to feel that there was infection in his touch and taint in his companionship—to know all this, and to know that the mover of it all, was that same boyish poor relation who had twitted him in their very first interview, and openly bearded and braved him since, wrought his quiet and stealthy malignity to such a pitch, that there was scarcely anything he would not have hazarded to gratify it, if he could have seen his way to some immediate retaliation.

But fortunately for Nicholas, Ralph Nickleby did not; and although he cast about all that day, and kept a corner of his brain working on the one anxious subject through all the round of schemes and business that came with it, night found him at last still harping on the same theme, and still pursuing the same unprofitable reflections.

"When my brother was such as he," said Ralph, "the first comparisons were drawn between us—always in my disfavour. *He* was open, liberal, gallant, gay; *I* a crafty hunks of cold and stagnant blood, with no passion but love of saving, and no spirit beyond a thirst for gain. I recollected it well when I first saw this whipster; but I remember it better now."

He had been occupied in tearing Nicholas's letter into atoms, and as he spoke he scattered it in a tiny shower about him.

"Recollections like these," pursued Ralph, with a bitter smile, "flock upon me—when I resign myself to them—in crowds, and from countless quarters. As a portion of the world affect to despise the power of money, I must try and show them what it is."

And being by this time in a pleasant frame of mind for slumber, Ralph Nickleby went to bed.

CHAPTER XXXV.

SMIKE BECOMES KNOWN TO MRS. NICKLEBY AND KATE. NICHOLAS ALSO MEETS WITH NEW ACQUAINTANCES, AND BRIGHTER DAYS SEEM TO DAWN UPON THE FAMILY.

HAVING established his mother and sister in the apartments of the kind-hearted miniature painter, and ascertained that Sir Mulberry Hawk was in no danger of losing his life, Nicholas turned his thoughts to poor Smike, who, after breakfasting with Newman Noggs, had remained in a disconsolate state at that worthy creature's lodgings, waiting with much anxiety for further intelligence of his protector.

"As he will be one of our own little household, wherever we live, or whatever fortune is in reserve for us," thought Nicholas, "I must present the poor fellow in due form. They will be kind to him for his own sake, and if not (on that account solely) to the full extent I could wish, they will stretch a point, I am sure, for mine."

Nicholas said "they," but his misgivings were confined to one person. He was sure of Kate, but he knew his mother's peculiarities, and was not quite so certain that Smike would find favour in the eyes of Mrs. Nickleby.

"However," thought Nicholas, as he departed on his benevolent errand; "she cannot fail to become attached to him when she knows what a devoted creature he is, and as she must quickly make the discovery, his probation will be a short one."

"I was afraid," said Smike, overjoyed to see his friend again, "that you had fallen into some fresh trouble; the time seemed so long at last, that I almost feared you were lost."

"Lost!" replied Nicholas gaily. "You will not be rid of me so easily, I promise you. I shall rise to the surface many thousand times yet, and the harder the thrust that pushes me down, the more quickly I shall rebound, Smike. But come; my errand here is to take you home."

"Home!" faltered Smike, drawing timidly back.

"Ay," rejoined Nicholas, taking his arm. "Why not?"

"I had such hopes once," said Smike; "day and night, day and night, for many years. I longed for home till I was weary, and pined away with grief, but now——"

"And what now?" asked Nicholas, looking kindly in his face. "What now, old friend?"

"I could not part from you to go to any home on earth," replied Smike, pressing his hand; "except one, except one. I shall never be an old man; and if your hand placed me in the grave, and I could think before I died that you would come and look upon it sometimes with one of your kind smiles, and in the summer weather, when everything was alive—not dead like me—I could go to that home almost without a tear."

"Why do you talk thus, poor boy, if your life is a happy one with me?" said Nicholas.

"Because *I* should change; not those about me. And if they forgot me, *I* should never know it," replied Smike. "In the churchyard we are all alike, but here there are none like me. I am a poor creature, but I know that well."

"You are a foolish, silly creature," said Nicholas cheerfully. "If that is what you mean, I grant you that. Why, here's a dismal face for ladies' company—my pretty sister too, whom you have so often asked me about. Is this your Yorkshire gallantry? For shame! for shame!"

Smike brightened up, and smiled.

"When I talk of homes," pursued Nicholas, "I talk of mine—which is yours of course. If it were defined by any particular four walls and a roof, God knows I should be sufficiently puzzled to say whereabouts it lay; but that is not what I mean. When I speak of home, I speak of the place where—in default of a better—those I love are gathered together; and if that place were a gipsy's tent or a barn, I should call it by the same good name notwithstanding. And now for what is my present home, which, however alarming your expectations may be, will neither terrify you by its extent nor its magnificence."

So saying, Nicholas took his companion by the arm, and saying a great deal more to the same purpose, and pointing out various things to amuse and interest him as they went along, led the way to Miss La Creevy's house.

" And this, Kate," said Nicholas, entering the room where his sister sat alone, " is the faithful friend and affectionate fellow-traveller whom I prepared you to receive."

Poor Smike was bashful and awkward and frightened enough at first, but Kate advanced towards him so kindly, and said in such a sweet voice, how anxious she had been to see him after all her brother had told her, and how much she had to thank him for having comforted Nicholas so greatly in their very trying reverses, that he began to be very doubtful whether he should shed tears or not, and became still more flurried. However, he managed to say, in a broken voice, that Nicholas was his only friend, and that he would lay down his life to help him ; and Kate, although she was so kind and considerate, seemed to be so wholly unconscious of his distress and embarrassment, that he recovered almost immediately and felt quite at home.

Then Miss La Creevy came in, and to her Smike had to be presented also. And Miss La Creevy was very kind too, and wonderfully talkative :—not to Smike, for that would have made him uneasy at first, but to Nicholas and his sister. Then, after a time, she would speak to Smike himself now and then, asking him whether he was a judge of likenesses, and whether he thought that picture in the corner was like herself, and whether he didn't think it would have looked better if she had made herself ten years younger, and whether he didn't think, as a matter of general observation, that young ladies looked better, not only in pictures but out of them too, than old ones ; with many more small jokes and facetious remarks, which were delivered with such good humour and merriment that Smike thought within himself she was the nicest lady he had ever seen ; even nicer than Mrs. Grudden, of Mr. Vincent Crummles's theatre, and she was a nice lady too, and talked, perhaps more, but certainly louder than Miss La Creevy.

At length the door opened again, and a lady in mourning came in ; and Nicholas kissing the lady in mourning affectionately, and calling her his mother, led her towards the chair from which Smike had risen when she entered the room.

" You are always kind-hearted, and anxious to help the oppressed, my dear mother," said Nicholas, " so you will be favourably disposed towards him, I know."

" I am sure, my dear Nicholas," replied Mrs. Nickleby, looking very hard at her new friend, and bending to him with something more or majesty than the occasion seemed to require,—" I am sure any friend of yours has, as indeed he naturally ought to have, and must have, of course, you know—a great claim upon me, and of course, it is a very great pleasure to me to be introduced to anybody you take an interest in—there can be no doubt about that ; none at all ; not the least in the world," said Mrs. Nickleby. " At the same time I must say, Nicholas, my dear, as I used to say to your poor dear papa, when he *would* bring gentlemen home to dinner, and there was nothing in the house, that if he had come the day before yesterday—no, I don't mean the day before yesterday now; I should have said, perhaps, the year before last—we should have been better able to entertain him."

With which remarks Mrs. Nickleby turned to her daughter, and inquired, in an audible whisper, whether the gentleman was going to stop all night.

"Because if he is, Kate, my dear," said Mrs. Nickleby, "I don't see that it's possible for him to sleep anywhere, and that's the truth."

Kate stepped gracefully forward, and without any show of annoyance or irritation, breathed a few words into her mother's ear.

"La, Kate, my dear," said Mrs. Nickleby, shrinking back, "how you do tickle one. Of course, I understand *that*, my love, without your telling me; and I said the same to Nicholas, and I *am* very much pleased. You didn't tell me, Nicholas, my dear," added Mrs. Nickleby, turning round with an air of less reserve than she had before assumed, " what your friend's name is."

" His name, mother," replied Nicholas, " is Smike."

The effect of this communication was by no means anticipated ; but the name was no sooner pronounced, than Mrs. Nickleby dropped upon a chair, and burst into a fit of crying.

" What is the matter ?" exclaimed Nicholas, running to support her.

" It's so like Pyke," cried Mrs. Nickleby; " so exactly like Pyke, that's all. Oh ! don't speak to me—I shall be better presently."

And after exhibiting every symptom of slow suffocation, in all its stages, and drinking about a tea-spoonful of water from a full tumbler, and spilling the remainder, Mrs. Nickleby *was* better, and remarked, with a feeble smile, that she was very foolish, she knew.

" It's a weakness in our family," said Mrs. Nickleby, " so, of course, I can't be blamed for it. Your grandmama, Kate, was exactly the same—precisely. The least excitement, the slightest surprise, she fainted away directly. I have heard her say, often and often, that when she was a young lady, and before she was married, she was turning a corner into Oxford-street one day, when she ran against her own hair-dresser, who, it seems, was escaping from a bear ;—the mere suddenness of the encounter made her faint away directly. Wait, though," added Mrs. Nickleby, pausing to consider, " Let me be sure I'm right. Was it her hair-dresser who had escaped from a bear, or was it a bear who had escaped from her hair-dresser's ? I declare I can't remember just now, but the hair-dresser was a very handsome man, I know, and quite a gentleman in his manners ; so that it has nothing to do with the point of the story."

Mrs. Nickleby having fallen imperceptibly into one of her retrospective moods, improved in temper from that moment, and glided, by an easy change of the conversation occasionally, into various other anecdotes, no less remarkable for their strict application to the subject in hand.

" Mr. Smike is from Yorkshire, Nicholas, my dear?" said Mrs. Nickleby, after dinner, and when she had been silent for some time.

" Certainly, mother," replied Nicholas. " I see you have not forgotten his melancholy history."

" O dear no," cried Mrs. Nickleby. "Ah! melancholy, indeed. You don't happen, Mr. Smike, ever to have dined with the Grimbles of Grimble Hall, somewhere in the North Riding, do you ?" said the good lady, addressing herself to him. " A very proud man, Sir Thomas Grimble, with six grown-up and most lovely danghters, and the finest park in the county."

" My dear mother," reasoned Nicholas, " Do you suppose that the unfortunate outcast of a Yorkshire school was likely to receive many cards of invitation from the nobility and gentry in the neighbourhood?"

" Really, my dear, I don't know why it should be so very extraordinary," said Mrs. Nickleby. "I know that when *I* was at school, I always went at least twice every half-year to the Hawkinses at Taunton Vale, and they are much richer than the Grimbles, and connected with them in marriage ; so you see it's not so very unlikely, after all."

Having put down Nicholas in this triumphant manner, Mrs. Nickleby was suddenly seized with a forgetfulness of Smike's real name, and an irresistible tendency to call him Mr. Slammons ; which circumstance she attributed to the remarkable similarity of the two names in point of sound, both beginning with an S, and moreover being spelt with an M. But, whatever doubt there might be on this point, there was none as to his being a most excellent listener ; which circumstance had considerable influence in placing them on the very best terms, and in inducing Mrs. Nickleby to express the highest opinion of his general deportment and disposition.

Thus the little circle remained, on the most amicable and agreeable footing, until the Monday morning, when Nicholas withdrew himself from it for a short time, seriously to reflect upon the state of his affairs, and to determine, if he could, upon some course of life, which would enable him to support those who were so entirely dependent upon his exertions.

Mr. Crummles occurred to him more than once ; but although Kate was acquainted with the whole history of his connection with that gentleman, his mother was not ; and he foresaw a thousand fretful objections, on her part, to his seeking a livelihood upon the stage. There were graver reasons, too, against his returning to that mode of life. Independently of those arising out of its spare and precarious earnings, and his own internal conviction that he could never hope to aspire to any great distinction, even as a provincial actor, how could he carry his sister from town to town, and place to place, and debar her from any other associates than those with whom he would be compelled, almost without distinction, to mingle? " It won't do," said Nicholas, shaking his head ; " I must try something else."

It was much easier to make this resolution than to carry it into effect. With no greater experience of the world than he had acquired for himself in his short trials ; with a sufficient share of headlong rashness and precipitation, (qualities not altogether unnatural at his time of life) with a very slender stock of money, and a still more scanty stock of friends, what could he do ? " Egad !" said Nicholas, " I'll try that Register Office again."

He smiled at himself as he walked away with a quick step; for, an instant before, he had been internally blaming his own precipitation. He did not laugh himself out of the intention, however, for on he went; picturing to himself, as he approached the place, all kinds of splendid possibilities, and impossibilities too, for that matter, and thinking himself, perhaps with good reason, very fortunate to be endowed with so buoyant and sanguine a temperament.

The office looked just the same as when he had left it last, and, indeed, with one or two exceptions, there seemed to be the very same placards in the window that he had seen before. There were the same unimpeachable masters and mistresses in want of virtuous servants, and the same virtuous servants in want of unimpeachable masters and mistresses, and the same magnificent estates for the investment of capital, and the same enormous quantities of capital to be invested in estates, and, in short, the same opportunities of all sorts for people who wanted to make their fortunes. And a most extraordinary proof it was of the national prosperity, that people had not been found to avail themselves of such advantages long ago.

As Nicholas stopped to look in at the window, an old gentleman happened to stop too, and Nicholas carrying his eye along the window-panes from left to right in search of some capital-text placard, which should be applicable to his own case, caught sight of this old gentleman's figure, and instinctively withdrew his eyes from the window, to observe the same more closely.

He was a sturdy old fellow in a broad-skirted blue coat, made pretty large, to fit easily, and with no particular waist; his bulky legs clothed in drab breeches and high gaiters, and his head protected by a low-crowned broad-brimmed white hat, such as a wealthy grazier might wear. He wore his coat buttoned; and his dimpled double-chin rested in the folds of a white neckerchief—not one of your stiff starched apoplectic cravats, but a good easy old-fashioned white neckcloth that a man might go to bed in and be none the worse for it. But what principally attracted the attention of Nicholas, was the old gentleman's eye,—never was such a clear, twinkling, honest, merry, happy eye, as that. And there he stood, looking a little upward, with one hand thrust into the breast of his coat, and the other playing with his old-fashioned gold watch-chain: his head thrown a little on one side, and his hat a little more on one side than his head, (but that was evidently accident; not his ordinary way of wearing it,) with such a pleasant smile playing about his mouth, and such a comical expression of mingled slyness, simplicity, kind-heartedness, and good-humour, lighting up his jolly old face, that Nicholas would have been content to have stood there and looked at him until evening, and to have forgotten meanwhile that there was such a thing as a soured mind or a crabbed countenance to be met with in the whole wide world.

But, even a very remote approach to this gratification was not to be made, for although he seemed quite unconscious of having been the subject of observation, he looked casually at Nicholas; and the latter, fearful of giving offence, resumed his scrutiny of the window instantly.

Still, the old gentleman stood there, glancing from placard to placard, and Nicholas could not forbear raising his eyes to his face again. Grafted upon the quaintness and oddity of his appearance, was something so indescribably engaging and bespeaking so much worth, and there were so many little lights hovering about the corners of his mouth and eyes, that it was not a mere amusement, but a positive pleasure and delight to look at him.

This being the case, it is no wonder that the old man caught Nicholas in the fact more than once. At such times, Nicholas coloured and looked embarrassed, for the truth is, that he had begun to wonder whether the stranger could by any possibility be looking for a clerk or secretary; and thinking this, he felt as if the old gentleman must know it.

Long as all this takes to tell, it was not more than a couple of minutes in passing. As the stranger was moving away, Nicholas caught his eye again, and, in the awkwardness of the moment, stammered out an apology.

" No offence—Oh no offence ! " said the old man.

This was said in such a hearty tone, and the voice was so exactly what it should have been from such a speaker, and there was such a cordiality in the manner, that Nicholas was emboldened to speak again.

" A great many opportunities here, sir," he said, half-smiling as he motioned towards the window.

" A great many people willing and anxious to be employed have seriously thought so very often, I dare say," replied the old man. " Poor fellows, poor fellows ! "

He moved away as he said this ; but seeing that Nicholas was about to speak, good-naturedly slackened his pace, as if he were unwilling to cut him short. After a little of that hesitation which may be sometimes observed between two people in the street who have exchanged a nod, and are both uncertain whether they shall turn back and speak, or not, Nicholas found himself at the old man's side.

" You were about to speak, young gentleman ; what were you going to say ? "

" Merely that I almost hoped—I mean to say, thought—you had some object in consulting those advertisements," said Nicholas.

" Ay, ay ? what object now—what object ? " returned the old man, looking slyly at Nicholas. " Did you think I wanted a situation now—Eh ? Did you think I did ? "

Nicholas shook his head.

" Ha ! ha ! " laughed the old gentleman, rubbing his hands and wrists as if he were washing them. " A very natural thought at all events, after seeing me gazing at those bills. I thought the same of you at first, upon my word I did."

" If you had thought so at last, too, sir, you would not have been far from the truth," rejoined Nichol .

" Eh ? " cried the old man, surveying him from head to foot. " What ! Dear me ! No, no. Well-behaved young gentleman reduced to such a necessity ! No no, no no."

Nicholas bowed, and bidding him good morning, turned upon his heel.

" Stay," said the old man, beckoning him into a bye street, where they could converse with less interruption. " What d'ye mean, eh ? What d'ye mean ?"

" Merely that your kind face and manner—both so unlike any I have ever seen—tempted me into an avowal, which, to any other stranger in this wilderness of London, I should not have dreamt of making," returned Nicholas.

" Wilderness ! Yes it is, it is. Good. It *is* a wilderness," said the old man with much animation. " It was a wilderness to me once. I came here barefoot—I have never forgotten it. Thank God !" and he raised his hat from his head, and looked very grave.

" What's the matter—what is it—how did it all come about ?" said the old man, laying his hand on the shoulder of Nicholas, and walking him up the street. " You're—Eh ?" laying his finger on the sleeve of his black coat. " Who's it for—eh ?"

" My father," replied Nicholas.

" Ah !" said the old gentleman quickly. " Bad thing for a young man to lose his father. Widowed mother, perhaps ?"

Nicholas sighed.

" Brothers and sisters too—eh ?"

" One sister," rejoined Nicholas.

" Poor thing, poor thing. You're a scholar too, I dare say ?" said the old man, looking wistfully into the face of the young one.

" I have been tolerably well educated," said Nicholas.

" Fine thing," said the old gentleman, " education a great thing—a very great thing—I never had any. I admire it the more in others. A very fine thing—yes, yes. Tell me more of your history. Let me hear it all. No impertinent curiosity—no, no, no."

There was something so earnest and guileless in the way in which all this was said, and such a complete disregard of all conventional restraints and coldnesses, that Nicholas could not resist it. Among men who have any sound and sterling qualities, there is nothing so contagious as pure openness of heart. Nicholas took the infection instantly, and ran over the main points of his little history without reserve, merely suppressing names, and touching as lightly as possible upon his uncle's treatment of Kate. The old man listened with great attention, and when he had concluded, drew his arm eagerly through his own.

" Don't say another word—not another word," said he. " Come along with me. We must n't lose a minute."

So saying, the old gentleman dragged him back into Oxford Street, and hailing an omnibus on its way to the city, pushed Nicholas in before him, and followed himself.

As he appeared in a most extraordinary condition of restless excitement, and whenever Nicholas offered to speak, immediately interposed with—" Don't say another word, my dear sir, on any account—not another word," the young man thought it better to attempt no further interruption. Into the city they journeyed accordingly, without interchanging any conversation ; and the further they went, the more Nicholas wondered what the end of the adventure could possibly be.

The old gentleman got out with great alacrity when they reached the Bank, and once more taking Nicholas by the arm, hurried him along Threadneedle Street, and through some lanes and passages on the right, until they at length emerged in a quiet shady little square. Into tho oldest and cleanest-looking house of business in the square, he led the way. The only inscription on the door-post was "Cheeryble, Brothers;" but from a hasty glance at the directions of some packages which were lying about, Nicholas supposed that the Brothers Cheeryble were German-merchants.

Passing through a warehouse which presented every indication of a thriving business, Mr. Cheeryble (for such Nicholas supposed him to be, from the respect which had been shown him by the warehousemen and porters whom they passed) led him into a little partitioned-off counting-house like a large glass case, in which counting-house there sat—as free from dust and blemish as if he had been fixed into the glass case before the top was put on, and had never come out since—a fat, elderly, large-faced, clerk, with silver spectacles and a powdered head.

"Is my brother in his room, Tim?" said Mr. Cheeryble, with no less kindness of manner than he had shown to Nicholas.

"Yes he is, sir," replied the fat clerk, turning his spectacle-glasses towards his principal, and his eyes towards Nicholas, "but Mr. Trimmers is with him."

"Ay! And what has he come about, Tim?" said Mr. Cheeryble.

"He is getting up a subscription for the widow and family of a man who was killed in the East India Docks this morning, sir," rejoined Tim. "Smashed, sir, by a cask of sugar."

"He is a good creature," said Mr. Cheeryble, with great earnestness. "He is a kind soul. I am very much obliged to Trimmers. Trimmers is one of the best friends we have. He makes a thousand cases known to us that we should never discover of ourselves. I am *very* much obliged to Trimmers." Saying which, Mr. Cheeryble rubbed his hands with infinite delight, and Mr. Trimmers happening to pass the door that instant on his way out, shot out after him and caught him by the hand.

"I owe you a thousand thanks, Trimmers—ten thousand thanks—I take it very friendly of you—very friendly indeed," said Mr. Cheeryble, dragging him into a corner to get out of hearing. "How many children are there, and what has my brother Ned given, Trimmers?"

"There are six children," replied the gentleman, "and your brother has given us twenty pounds."

"My brother Ned is a good fellow, and you're a good fellow too, Trimmers," said the old man, shaking him by both hands with trembling eagerness. "Put me down for another twenty—or—stop a minute, stop a minute. We must n't look ostentatious; put me down ten pound, and Tim Linkinwater ten pound. A cheque for twenty pound for Mr. Trimmers, Tim. God bless you, Trimmers—and come and dine with us some day this week; you'll always find a knife and fork, and we shall be delighted. Now, my dear Sir—cheque for Mr. Linkin·

water, Tim. Smashed by a cask of sugar, and six poor children—oh dear, dear, dear !"

Talking on in this strain as fast as he could, to prevent any friendly remonstrances from the collector of the subscription on the large amount of his donation, Mr. Cheeryble led Nicholas, equally astonished and affected by what he had seen and heard in this short space, to the half-opened door of another room.

" Brother Ned," said Mr. Cheeryble, tapping with his knuckles, and stooping to listen, " are you busy, my dear brother, or can you spare time for a word or two with me ?"

" Brother Charles, my dear fellow," replied a voice from the inside ; so like in its tones to that which had just spoken that Nicholas started, and almost thought it was the same, " Don't ask me such a question, but come in directly."

They went in without further parley. What was the amazement of Nicholas when his conducter advanced and exchanged a warm greeting with another old gentleman, the very type and model of himself—the same face, the same figure, the same coat, waistcoat, and neckcloth, the same breeches and gaiters—nay, there was the very same white hat hanging against the wall !

As they shook each other by the hand, the face of each lighted up by beaming looks of affection, which would have been most delightful to behold in infants, and which, in men so old, was inexpressibly touching, Nicholas could observe that the last old gentleman was something stouter than his brother ; this, and a slight additional shade of clumsiness in his gait and stature, formed the only perceptible difference between them. Nobody could have doubted their being twin brothers.

" Brother Ned," said Nicholas's friend, closing the room-door, " here is a young friend of mine that we must assist. We must make proper inquiries into his statements, in justice to him as well as to ourselves, and if they are confirmed—as I feel assured they will be—we must assist him ; we must assist him, brother Ned."

" It is enough, my dear brother, that you say we should," returned the other. " When you say that, no further inquiries are needed. He *shall* be assisted. What are his necessities, and what does he require ? Where is Tim Linkinwater? Let us have him here."

Both the brothers, it may be here remarked, had a very emphatic and earnest delivery, both had lost nearly the same teeth, which imparted the same peculiarity to their speech ; and both spoke as if, besides possessing the utmost serenity of mind that the kindliest and most unsuspecting nature could bestow, they had, in collecting the plums from Fortune's choicest pudding, retained a few for present use, and kept them in their mouths.

" Where is Tim Linkinwater ? " said brother Ned.

" Stop, stop, stop," said brother Charles, taking the other aside. " I've a plan, my dear brother, I've a plan. Tim is getting old, and Tim has been a faithful servant, brother Ned ; and I don't think pensioning Tim's mother and sister, and buying a little tomb for the family when his poor brother died, was a sufficient recompense for his faithful services."

"No, no, no," replied the other. "Certainly not. Not half enough, not half."

"If we could lighten Tim's duties," said the old gentleman, "and prevail upon him to go into the country now and then, and sleep in the fresh air, besides, two or three times a-week, (which he could if he began business an hour later in the morning,) old Tim Linkinwater would grow young again in time; and he's three good years our senior now. Old Tim Linkinwater young again! Eh, brother Ned, eh? Why, I recollect old Tim Linkinwater quite a little boy, don't you? Ha, ha, ha! Poor Tim, poor Tim!"

And the fine old fellows laughed pleasantly together: each with a tear of regard for old Tim Linkinwater, standing in his eye.

"But hear this first—hear this first, brother Ned," said the old man hastily, placing two chairs, one on each side of Nicholas. "I'll tell it you myself, brother Ned, because the young gentleman is modest, and is a scholar, Ned, and I shouldn't feel it right that he should tell us his story over and over again as if he was a beggar, or as if we doubted him. No, no, no."

"No, no, no," returned the other, nodding his head gravely. "Very right, my dear brother, very right."

"He will tell me I'm wrong, if I make a mistake," said Nicholas's friend. "But whether I do or not, you'll be very much affected, brother Ned, remembering the time when we were two friendless lads, and earned our first shilling in this great city."

The twins pressed each other's hands in silence, and, in his own homely manner, brother Charles related the particulars he had heard from Nicholas. The conversation which ensued was a long one, and when it was over a secret conference of almost equal duration took place between brother Ned and Tim Linkinwater in another room. It is no disparagement to Nicholas to say, that before he had been closeted with the two brothers ten minutes, he could only wave his hand at every fresh expression of kindness and sympathy, and sob like a little child.

At length brother Ned and Tim Linkinwater came back together, when Tim instantly walked up to Nicholas and whispered in his ear in a very brief sentence, (for Tim was ordinarily a man of few words,) that he had taken down the address in the Strand, and would call upon him that evening at eight. Having done which, Tim wiped his spectacles and put them on, preparatory to hearing what more the brothers Cheeryble had got to say.

"Tim," said brother Charles, "You understand that we have an intention of taking this young gentleman into the counting-house?"

Brother Ned remarked that Tim was aware of that intention, and quite approved of it; and Tim having nodded, and said he did, drew himself up and looked particularly fat and very important. After which there was a profound silence.

"I'm not coming an hour later in the morning you know," said Tim, breaking out all at once, and looking very resolute. " I'm not going to sleep in the fresh air—no, nor I'm not going into the country either. A pretty thing at this time of day, certainly. Pho!"

" Damn your obstinacy, Tim Linkinwater," said brother Charles, looking at him without the faintest spark of anger, and with a countenance radiant with attachment to the old clerk. " Damn your obstinacy, Tim Linkinwater, what do you mean, Sir ?"

" It's forty-four year," said Tim, making a calculation in the air with his pen, and drawing an imaginary line before he cast it up, " forty-four year, next May, since I first kept the books of Cheeryble, Brothers. I've opened the safe every morning all that time (Sundays excepted) as the clock struck nine, and gone over the house every night at half-past ten (except on Foreign Post nights, and then twenty minutes before twelve) to see the doors fastened and the fires out. I've never slept out of the back attic one single night. There's the same mignionette box in the middle of the window, and the same four flower-pots, two on each side, that I brought with me when I first came. There an't—I've said it again and again, and I'll maintain it— there an't such a square as this in the world. I *know* there an't," said Tim, with sudden energy, and looking sternly about him. " Not one. For business or pleasure, in summer time or winter—I don't care which—there's nothing like it. There's not such a spring in England as the pump under the archway. There's not such a view in England as the view out of my window; I've seen it every morning before I shaved, and I ought to know something about it. I have slept in that room," added Tim, sinking his voice a little, " for four-and-forty year ; and if it wasn't inconvenient, and didn't interfere with business, I should request leave to die there."

" Damn you, Tim Linkinwater, how dare you talk about dying ?" roared the twins by one impulse, and blowing their old noses violently.

" That's what I've got to say, Mr. Edwin and Mr. Charles," said Tim, squaring his shoulders again. " This isn't the first time you've talked about superannuating me ; but if you please we'll make it the last, and drop the subject for evermore."

With these words, Tim Linkinwater stalked out and shut himself up in his glass case, with the air of a man who had had his say, and was thoroughly resolved not to be put down.

The brothers interchanged looks, and coughed some half-dozen times without speaking.

" He must be done something with, brother Ned," said the other, warmly ; " we must disregard his old scruples ; they can't be tolerated or borne. He must be made a partner, brother Ned ; and if he won't submit to it peaceably, we must have recourse to violence."

" Quite right," replied brother Ned, nodding his head as a man thoroughly determined ; " quite right, my dear brother. If he won't listen to reason, we must do it against his will, and show him that we are determined to exert our authority. We must quarrel with him, brother Charles."

" We must—we certainly must have a quarrel with Tim Linkinwater," said the other. "But in the mean time, my dear brother, we are keeping our young friend; and the poor lady and her daughter will be anxious for his return. So let us say good-bye for the present, and—there, there—take care of that box, my dear Sir—and—no, no, no, not a word now; but be careful of the crossings and——"

And with any disjointed and unconnected words which would prevent Nicholas from pouring forth his thanks, the brothers hurried him out, shaking hands with him all the way, and affecting very unsuccessfully —they were poor hands at deception!—to be wholly unconscious of the feelings that completely mastered him.

Nicholas's heart was too full to allow of his turning into the street until he had recovered some composure. When he at last glided out of the dark doorway-corner in which he had been compelled to halt, he caught a glimpse of the twins stealthily peeping in at one corner of the glass-case, evidently undecided whether they should follow up their late attack without delay, or for the present postpone laying further siege to the inflexible Tim Linkinwater.

To recount all the delight and wonder which the circumstances just detailed awakened at Miss La Creevy's, and all the things that were done, said, thought, expected, hoped, and prophesied in consequence, is beside the present course and purpose of these adventures. It is sufficient to state, in brief, that Mr. Timothy Linkinwater arrived punctual to his appointment; that, oddity as he was, and jealous as he was bound to be of the proper exercise of his employers' most comprehensive liberality, he reported strongly and warmly in favour of Nicholas; and that next day he was appointed to the vacant stool in the counting-house of Cheeryble, Brothers, with a present salary of one hundred and twenty pounds a year.

"And I think, my dear brother," said Nicholas's first friend, "that if we were to let them that little cottage at Bow which is empty, at something under the usual rent, now—Eh, brother Ned?"

"For nothing at all," said brother Ned. "We are rich, and should be ashamed to touch the rent under such circumstances as these. Where is Tim Linkinwater?—for nothing at all, my dear brother, for nothing at all."

"Perhaps it would be better to say something, brother Ned," suggested the other, mildly; "it would help to preserve habits of frugality, you know, and remove any painful sense of overwhelming obligations. We might say fifteen pound, or twenty pound, and if it was punctually paid, make it up to them in some other way. And I might secretly advance a small loan towards a little furniture, and you might secretly advance another small loan, brother Ned; and if we find them doing well—as we shall; there's no fear, no fear—we can change the loans into gifts—carefully, brother Ned, and by degrees, and without pressing upon them too much; what do you say now, brother?"

Brother Ned gave his hand upon it, and not only said it should be done, but had it done too: and in one short week Nicholas took possession of the stool, and Mrs. Nickleby and Kate took possession of the house; and all was hope, bustle, and light-heartedness.

There surely never was such a week of discoveries and surprises as the first week of that cottage. Every night when Nicholas came home, something new had been found out. One day it was a grapevine, and another day it was a boiler, and another day it was the key of the front parlour closet at the bottom of the water-butt, and so on through a hundred items. Then, this room was embellished with a muslin curtain, and that room was rendered quite elegant by a window-blind, and such improvements were made as no one would have supposed possible. Then, there was Miss La Creevy, who had come out in the omnibus to stop a day or two and help, and who was perpetually losing a very small brown paper parcel of tin tacks and a very large hammer, and running about with her sleeves tucked up at the wrists, and falling off pairs of steps and hurting herself very much —and Mrs. Nickleby, who talked incessantly, and did something now and then, but not often—and Kate, who busied herself noiselessly everywhere, and was pleased with everything—and Smike, who made the garden a perfect wonder to look upon—and Nicholas, who helped and encouraged them every one—all the peace and cheerfulness of home restored, with such new zest imparted to every frugal pleasure, and such delight to every hour of meeting, as misfortune and separation alone could give.

In short, the poor Nicklebys were social and happy; while the rich Nickleby was alone and miserable.

CHAPTER XXXVI.

PRIVATE AND CONFIDENTIAL; RELATING TO FAMILY MATTERS. SHOW-
ING HOW MR. KENWIGS UNDERWENT VIOLENT AGITATION, AND HOW
MRS. KENWIGS WAS AS WELL AS COULD BE EXPECTED.

IT might have been about seven o'clock in the evening, and it was growing dark in the narrow streets near Golden Square, when Mr. Kenwigs sent out for a pair of the cheapest white kid gloves—those at fourteenpence—and selecting the strongest, which happened to be the right-hand one, walked down stairs with an air of some pomp and much excitement, and proceeded to muffle the knob of the street-door knocker therein. Having executed this task with great nicety, Mr. Kenwigs pulled the door to after him, and just stepped across the road to try the effect from the opposite side of the street. Satisfied that nothing could possibly look better in its way, Mr. Kenwigs then stepped back again, and calling through the keyhole to Morleena to open the door, vanished into the house, and was seen no longer.

Now, considered as an abstract circumstance, there was no more obvious cause or reason why Mr. Kenwigs should take the trouble of muffling this particular knocker, than there would have been for his muffling the knocker of any nobleman or gentleman resident ten miles off; because, for the greater convenience of the numerous lodgers, the street-door always stood wide open, and the knocker was never used at all. The first floor, the second floor, and the third floor, had each a bell of its own. As to the attics, no one ever called on them; if any body wanted the parlours, there they were close at hand, and all he had to do was to walk straight into them; while the kitchen had a separate entrance down the area steps. As a question of mere necessity and usefulness, therefore, this muffling of the knocker was thoroughly incomprehensible.

But knockers may be muffled for other purposes than those of mere utilitarianism, as, in the present instance, was clearly shown. There are certain polite forms and ceremonies which must be observed in civilised life, or mankind relapse into their original barbarism. No genteel lady was ever yet confined—indeed, no genteel confinement can possibly take place—without the accompanying symbol of a muffled knocker. Mrs. Kenwigs was a lady of some pretensions to gentility; Mrs. Kenwigs was confined. And, therefore, Mr. Kenwigs tied up the silent knocker on the premises in a white kid glove.

"I'm not quite certain neither," said Mr. Kenwigs, arranging his shirt-collar, and walking slowly up stairs, whether, "as it's a boy, I won't have it in the papers."

Pondering upon the advisability of this step, and the sensation it was likely to create in the neighbourhood, Mr. Kenwigs betook himself to the sitting-room, where various extremely diminutive articles of clothing were airing on a horse before the fire, and Mr. Lumbey, the doctor, was dandling the baby—that is, the old baby—not the new one.

"It's a fine boy, Mr. Kenwigs," said Mr. Lumbey, the doctor.

"You consider him a fine boy, do you, sir?" returned Mr. Kenwigs.

"It's the finest boy I ever saw in all my life," said the doctor. "I never saw such a baby."

It is a pleasant thing to reflect upon, and furnishes a complete answer to those who contend for the gradual degeneration of the human species, that every baby born into the world is a finer one than the last.

"I ne—ver saw such a baby," said Mr. Lumbey, the doctor.

"Morleena was a fine baby," remarked Mr. Kenwigs; as if this were rather an attack, by implication, upon the family.

"They were all fine babies," said Mr. Lumbey. And Mr. Lumbey went on nursing the baby with a thoughtful look. Whether he was considering under what head he could best charge the nursing in the bill, was best known to himself.

During this short conversation, Miss Morleena, as the eldest of the family, and natural representative of her mother during her indisposition, had been hustling and slapping the three younger Miss Kenwigses, without intermission; which considerate and affectionate conduct brought tears into the eyes of Mr. Kenwigs, and caused him to declare that, in understanding and behaviour, that child was a woman.

"She will be a treasure to the man she marries, sir," said Mr.

Kenwigs, half aside; "I think she'll marry above her station, Mr. Lumbey."

"I shouldn't wonder at all," replied the doctor.

"You never see her dance, sir, did you?" asked Mr. Kenwigs. The doctor shook his head.

"Ay!" said Mr. Kenwigs, as though he pitied him from his heart, "then you don't know what she's capable of."

All this time there had been a great whisking in and out of the other room; the door had been opened and shut very softly about twenty times a minute, (for it was necessary to keep Mrs. Kenwigs quiet), and the baby had been exhibited to a score or two of deputations from a select body of female friends, who had assembled in the passage, and about the street-door, to discuss the event in all its bearings. Indeed, the excitement extended itself over the whole street, and groups of ladies might be seen standing at the doors,—some in the interesting condition in which Mrs. Kenwigs had last appeared in public,—relating their experiences of similar occurrences. Some few acquired great credit from having prophesied, the day before yesterday, exactly when it would come to pass; others again related, how that they guessed what it was, directly they saw Mr. Kenwigs turn pale and run up the street as hard as ever he could go. Some said one thing, and some another; but all talked together, and all agreed upon two points: first, that it was very meritorious and highly praiseworthy in Mrs. Kenwigs, to do as she had done; and secondly, that there never was such a skilful and scientific doctor as that Doctor Lumbey.

In the midst of this general hubbub, Doctor Lumbey sat in the first floor front, as before related, nursing the deposed baby, and talking to Mr. Kenwigs. He was a stout bluff-looking gentleman, with no shirt-collar, to speak of, and a beard that had been growing since yesterday morning; for Doctor Lumbey was popular, and the neighbourhood was prolific; and there had been no less than three other knockers muffled, one after the other, within the last forty-eight hours.

"Well, Mr. Kenwigs," said Dr. Lumbey, "this makes six. You'll have a fine family in time, sir."

"I think six is almost enough, sir," returned Mr. Kenwigs.

"Pooh! pooh!" said the doctor. "Nonsense! not half enough."

With this the doctor laughed; but he didn't laugh half as much as a married friend of Mrs. Kenwigs's, who had just come in from the sick-chamber, to report progress and take a small sip of brandy-and-water; and who seemed to consider it one of the best jokes ever launched upon society.

"They're not altogether dependent upon good fortune, neither," said Mr. Kenwigs, taking his second daughter on his knee; "they have expectations."

"Oh, indeed!" said Mr. Lumbey, the doctor.

"And very good ones too, I believe, haven't they?" asked the married lady.

"Why, ma'am," said Mr. Kenwigs, "it's not exactly for me to say what they may be, or what they may not be. It's not for me to boast of any family with which I have the honour to be connected; at the same time, Mrs. Kenwigs's is——I should say," said Mr. Kenwigs, abruptly, and raising his voice as he spoke, "that my children might come into a matter of a hundred pound a-piece, perhaps. Perhaps more, but certainly that."

"And a very pretty little fortune," said the married lady.

"There are some relations of Mrs. Kenwigs's," said Mr. Kenwigs, taking a pinch of snuff from the doctor's box, and then sneezing very hard, for he wasn't used to it, "that might leave their hundred pound a-piece to ten people, and yet not go begging when they had done it."

"Ah! I know who you mean," observed the married lady, nodding her head.

"I made mention of no names, and I wish to make mention of no names," said Mr. Kenwigs, with a portentous look. "Many of my friends have met a relation of Mrs. Kenwigs's in this very room, as would do honour to any company; that's all."

"I've met him," said the married lady, with a glance towards Doctor Lumbey.

"It's naterally very gratifying to my feelings as a father, to see such a man as that, a kissing and taking notice of my children," pursued Mr. Kenwigs. "It's naterally very gratifying to my feelings as a man, to know that man. It will be naterally very gratifying to my feelings as a husband, to make that man acquainted with this ewent."

Having delivered his sentiments in this form of words, Mr. Kenwigs arranged his second daughter's flaxen tail, and bade her be a good girl and mind what her sister, Morleena, said.

"That girl grows more like her mother every day," said Mr. Lumbey, suddenly stricken with an enthusiastic admiration of Morleena.

"There!" rejoined the married lady. "What I always say—what I always did say. She's the very picter of her." And having thus directed the general attention to the young lady in question, the married lady embraced the opportunity of taking another sip of the brandy-and-water—and a pretty long sip too.

"Yes! there is a likeness," said Mr. Kenwigs, after some reflection. "But such a woman as Mrs. Kenwigs was, afore she was married! Good gracious, such a woman!"

Mr. Lumbey shook his head with great solemnity, as though to imply that he supposed she must have been rather a dazzler.

"Talk of fairies!" cried Mr. Kenwigs. "I never see anybody so light to be alive—never. Such manners too; so playful, and yet so sewerely proper! As for her figure! It isn't generally known," said Mr. Kenwigs, dropping his voice; "but her figure was such at that time, that the sign of the Britannia over in the Holloway road, was painted from it!"

"But only see what it is now," urged the married lady. "Does *she* look like the mother of six?"

"Quite ridiculous," cried the doctor.

"She looks a deal more like her own daughter," said the married lady.

" So she does," assented Mr. Lumbey. " A great deal more."

Mr. Kenwigs was about to make some further observations, most probably in confirmation of this opinion, when another married lady, who had looked in to keep up Mrs. Kenwigs' spirits, and help to clear off anything in the eating and drinking way that might be going about, put in her head to announce that she had just been down to answer the bell, and that there was a gentleman at the door who wanted to see Mr. Kenwigs " most particular."

Shadowy visions of his distinguished relation flitted through the brain of Mr. Kenwigs, as this message was delivered ; and under their influence, he despatched Morleena to show the gentleman up straightway.

" Why, I do declare," said Mr. Kenwigs, standing opposite the door so as to get the earliest glimpse of the visitor, as he came up-stairs, " it's Mr. Johnson. How do you find yourself, sir ?"

Nicholas shook hands, kissed his old pupils all round, entrusted a large parcel of toys to the guardianship of Morleena, bowed to the doctor and the married ladies, and inquired after Mrs. Kenwigs in a tone of interest, which went to the very heart and soul of the nurse, who had come in to warm some mysterious compound in a little saucepan over the fire.

" I ought to make a hundred apologies to you for calling at such a season," said Nicholas, " but I was not aware of it until I had rung the bell, and my time is so fully occupied now, that I feared it might be some days before I could possibly come again."

" No time like the present, sir," said Mr. Kenwigs. " The sitiwation of Mrs. Kenwigs, sir, is no obstacle to a little conversation between you and me, I hope ?"

" You are very good," said Nicholas.

At this juncture proclamation was made by another married lady, that the baby had begun to eat like anything ; whereupon the two married ladies, already mentioned, rushed tumultuously into the bedroom to behold him in the act.

" The fact is," resumed Nicholas, " that before I left the country, where I have been for some time past, I undertook to deliver a message to you."

" Ay, ay ?" said Mr. Kenwigs.

" And I have been," added Nicholas, " already in town for some days without having had an opportunity of doing so."

" It's no matter sir," said Mr. Kenwigs. " I dare say it's none the worse for keeping cold. Message from the country !" said Mr. Kenwigs, ruminating ; " that's curious. I don't know any body in the country."

" Miss Petowker," suggested Nicholas.

" Oh ! from her, is it ?" said Mr. Kenwigs. " Oh dear, yes. Ah ! Mrs. Kenwigs will be glad to hear from her. Henrietta Petowker, eh ? How odd things come about, now ! That you should have met her in the country—Well !"

Hearing this mention of their old friend's name, the four Miss Kenwigses gathered round Nicholas, open eyed and mouthed, to hear more. Mr. Kenwigs looked a little curious too, but quite comfortable and unsuspecting.

Emotion of Mr Kenwigs on hearing the family news from Nicholas.

"The message relates to family matters," said Nicholas, hesitating.

"Oh, never mind," said Kenwigs, glancing at Mr. Lumbey, who having rashly taken charge of little Lillyvick, found nobody disposed to relieve him of his precious burden. "All friends here."

Nicholas hemmed once or twice, and seemed to have some difficulty in proceeding.

"At Portsmouth Henrietta Petowker is," observed Mr. Kenwigs.

"Yes," said Nicholas. "Mr. Lillyvick is there."

Mr. Kenwigs turned pale, but he recovered and said, *that* was an odd coincidence also.

"The message is from him," said Nicholas.

Mr. Kenwigs appeared to revive. He knew that his niece was in a delicate state, and had no doubt sent word that they were to forward full particulars:—Yes. That was very kind of him—so like him too!

"He desired me to give his kindest love," said Nicholas.

"Very much obliged to him, I'm sure. Your great-uncle, Lillyvick, my dears," interposed Mr. Kenwigs, condescendingly explaining it to the children.

"His kindest love," resumed Nicholas; "and to say that he had no time to write, but that he was married to Miss Petowker."

Mr. Kenwigs started from his seat with a petrified stare, caught his second daughter by the flaxen tail, and covered his face with his pocket-handkerchief. Morleena fell, all stiff and rigid, into the baby's chair, as she had seen her mother fall when she fainted away, and the two remaining little Kenwigses shrieked in affright.

"My children, my defrauded, swindled infants!" cried Mr. Kenwigs, pulling so hard, in his vehemence, at the flaxen tail of his second daughter, that he lifted her up on tiptoe, and kept her for some seconds in that attitude. "Villain, ass, traitor!"

"Drat the man!" cried the nurse, looking angrily round. "What does he mean by making that noise here?"

"Silence, woman!" said Mr. Kenwigs fiercely.

"I won't be silent," returned the nurse. "Be silent yourself, you wretch. Have you no regard for your baby?"

"No!" returned Mr. Kenwigs.

"More shame for you," retorted the nurse. "Ugh! you unnatural monster."

"Let him die," cried Mr. Kenwigs, in the torrent of his wrath. "Let him die. He has no expectations, no property to come into. We want no babies here," said Mr. Kenwigs recklessly. "Take 'em away, take 'em away to the Fondling!"

With these awful remarks Mr. Kenwigs sat himself down in a chair, and defied the nurse, who made the best of her way into the adjoining room, and returned with a stream of matrons: declaring that Mr. Kenwigs had spoken blasphemy against his family, and must be raving mad.

Appearances were certainly not in Mr. Kenwigs's favour, for the exertion of speaking with so much vehemence, and yet in such a tone as should prevent his lamentations reaching the ears of Mrs. Kenwigs, had made him very black in the face; besides which, the excitement of the occasion, and an unwonted indulgence in various strong cordials to celebrate it, had swollen and dilated his features to a most unusual extent. But Nicholas and the doctor—who had been passive at first, doubting very much whether Mr. Kenwigs could be in earnest—interfering to explain the immediate cause of his condition, the indignation of the matrons was changed to pity, and they implored him with much feeling to go quietly to bed.

"The attention," said Mr. Kenwigs, looking around with a plaintive air, "the attention that I've shown to that man. The hyseters he has eat, and the pints of ale he has drank, in this house—!"

"It's very trying, and very hard to bear, we know," said one of the married ladies; "but think of your dear darling wife."

"Oh yes, and what she's been a undergoing of, only this day," cried a great many voices. "There's a good man, do."

"The presents that have been made to him," said Mr. Kenwigs, reverting to his calamity, "the pipes, the snuff-boxes—a pair of india-rubber goloshes, that cost six and sixpence—"

"Ah! it won't bear thinking of, indeed," cried the matrons generally; "but it 'll all come home to him, never fear."

Mr. Kenwigs looked darkly upon the ladies as if he would prefer its all coming home to *him*, as there was nothing to be got by it; but he said nothing, and resting his head upon his hand, subsided into a kind of doze.

Then the matrons again expatiated on the expediency of taking the good gentleman to bed; observing that he would be better to-morrow, and that they knew what was the wear and tear of some men's minds when their wives were taken as Mrs. Kenwigs had been that day, and that it did him great credit, and there was nothing to be ashamed of in it; far from it: they liked to see it, they did, for it showed a good heart. And one lady observed, as a case bearing upon the present, that her husband was often quite light-headed from anxiety on similar occasions, and that once, when her little Johnny was born, it was nearly a week before he came to himself again, during the whole of which time he did nothing but cry "Is it a boy, is it a boy?" in a manner which went to the hearts of all his hearers.

At length Morleena (who quite forgot she had fainted, when she found she was not noticed) announced that a chamber was ready for her afflicted parent; and Mr. Kenwigs, having partially smothered his four daughters in the closeness of his embrace, accepted the doctor's arm on one side, and the support of Nicholas on the other, and was conducted up-stairs to a bedroom which had been secured for the occasion.

Having seen him sound asleep and heard him snore most satisfactorily, and having further presided over the distribution of the toys, to the perfect contentment of all the little Kenwigses, Nicholas took his leave. The matrons dropped off one by one, with the exception of six or eight particular friends, who had determined to stop all night; the lights in the houses gradually disappeared; the last bulletin was issued that Mrs. Kenwigs was as well as could be expected; and the whole family were left to their repose.

TO ALL PROTESTANTS,

AND BY SPECIAL PERMISSION DEDICATED TO

Her Most Gracious Majesty the Queen,

"THE MARTYRS IN PRISON,"

ENGRAVED IN THE FIRST STYLE OF MEZZOTINT BY

S. W. REYNOLDS,

AFTER THE

GRAND HISTORICAL PAINTING, FROM AUTHENTIC & ORIGINAL SOURCES, BY

J. R. HERBERT, Esq.

THIS PRINT REPRESENTS THE MARTYRS,

VIZ.

LATIMER, CRANMER, RIDLEY, & BRADFORD,

When confined together in one room in the Tower, November, 1553, as men not to be accounted of by reason of their preachi Christ's Gospel.

THE MARTYRS ARE FAITHFULLY DELINEATED FROM AUTHENTICATED PORTRAITS.

SIZE, THIRTY-FOUR INCHES, BY TWENTY-FOUR.

PRINTS, *£2 2s.*—PROOFS, *£3 13s. 6d.*—INDIA PROOFS, *£5 5s.*

N. B.—The Proofs are accompanied with fac-similes of the Autographs of those celebrated Characters, and a brief Memoir of each accompanies the Engraving.

The following distinguished Names honour the Subscription List of this most interesting and truly national production.

HER MOST GRACIOUS MAJESTY THE QUEEN,

HER MAJESTY THE QUEEN DOWAGER,
HIS MAJESTY THE KING OF HANOVER,
HER ROYAL HIGHNESS THE DUCHESS OF KENT,
HER ROYAL HIGHNESS THE PRINCESS AUGUSTA,
HER ROYAL HIGHNESS THE DUCHESS OF GLOUCESTER,
HER GRACE THE DUCHESS OF SUTHERLAND,
HIS GRACE THE ARCHBISHOP OF CANTERBURY,
HIS GRACE THE ARCHBISHOP OF YORK

AND THEIR RIGHT REVERENDS THE LORDS BISHOPS OF LONDON, DURHAM, CHICHESTER, ROCHESTER, RIPPON, SODER AND MAN, LINCOLN, LLANDAFF, ST. ASAPH, EXETER, BATH AND WELLS, ELY, MADRAS, BOMBAY, &c. &c. &c.

LONDON:

PUBLISHED BY ACKERMANN & Co., 96, STRAND,

BY SPECIAL APPOINTMENT,

Printsellers to Her Majesty and Her Royal Highness the Duchess of Kent.

OPINIONS OF THE PRESS.

The appearance of this beautifully-executed engraving is most seasonable, especially at a time when Popery is spreading around us. It should find a place in the home of every Protestant, as a record of the victory which was gained over the Anti-Christian Church of Rome. It is the most magnificent, and decidedly the most interesting engraving, that has appeared this season.—*Church of England Quarterly Review.*

We commend the Queen's taste and interest for this meritorious production, by permitting it to be dedicated to her Majesty—it is truly a national production.—*Conservative Journal and Church of England Gazette.*

Like all Mr. Reynold's works, this is executed in the first style of Mezzotint.—*Literary Gazette.*

This superb engraving represents "the four prime pillars of the Reformed Church of England." when confined together in the Tower. We have seldom seen a print of greater interest.—*Naval and Military Gazette.*

For the mantel-pieces of serious persons, who are not in the habit of framing subjects of a more secular kind, this beautiful and interesting print will form a fitting and appropriate ornament.—*United Service Gazette.*

The attitudes, the countenance, the grouping, the whole expression of the picture, is admirable; and the artists have contributed their united skill to produce an engraving of unrivalled excellence.—To Protestants, its associations are of the most interesting description.—*Oxford Herald.*

This plate of the "Martyrs," may justly be considered a National work, and is well deserving a place in the room of all seriously disposed individuals.—*Cambridge Chronicle.*

Nothing can be better than the grouping of these Protestant Champions; men who sealed their faith with their blood ; and whose lives bore testimony to the excellence of their principles. It is most spirited and beautifully engraved by Mr. Reynolds—*Gloucester Chronicle.*

Among those works of pictorial skill which constantly appeal to the highest impulses of the mind and heart, this plate of the "Martyrs in Prison" must take a prominent place, if not the first.—*Winchester Chronicle.*

The publication of these illustrious Martyrs, of an Anti-Christian Church, at this moment is most seasonable.—*Bristol Mirror.*

This admirable work of art will, we trust, be duly appreciated by all who love their country and their religion.—*Exeter Flying Post.*

The subject of this splendid engraving cannot fail to be sought after by the religious world generally, but more especially by the members of the Reformed Catholic Church established in this realm.—*Liverpool Mail.*

To the labours of these Martyrs we owe whatever of religious liberty we enjoy, and any memorial of them must be valuable to Protestants—this one is inestimable.—*Doncaster Chronicle.*

The Christian Public has now an opportunity of possessing itself of one of the finest gems of art, in perpetuation of that memorial, which impelled these righteous men to seal the purity of their faith with their blood—no Protestant Christian family should be without it.—*Edinburgh Weekly Journal.*

This splendid engraving surpasses all recent productions, not only as respects interest of subject, but in general execution. It is indeed a sublime and noble subject, well conceived, and as admirably carried out by both painter and engraver.—*Glasgow Courier.*

THE following eloquent and soul-stirring verses, the inspiration of the moment upon seeing this *splendid and truly national production*, are from "THE TIMES," and were thence copied into most of the leading Conservative and Protestant Journals throughout the country.

ODE TO
THE MARTYRS IN PRISON,

(*Vide* ACKERMANN's celebrated National Picture.)

WITHIN the old Tower's* iron doors
  No frowning gaoler waits;
The painter's art hath here unbarr'd
  Its everlasting gates;
And thou, O gazer, standest now
  Where, in their prison cell,
As in some chamber of the past,
  The ancient martyrs dwell.

Four men of God,—while that drear place
  Half shrouds the form of light—
Doth not their holy presence there
  Still seem to keep it bright!
And lustre crown each pious brow
  With glory mid the gloom,
And faith undimm'd, that even now
  Shines upward from the tomb!

The thunderbolt of tyranny
  Drops powerless to-day,
And all its fetters seem to burst
  When those old martyrs pray.
The dungeon whence they heavenward look
  To their eternal goal,
Hath suddenly become to them
  A mansion of the soul.

One reverend venerable man
  Kneels by the "Saviour-word;"
And from its page of truth invokes
  The spirit of their Lord,
Whose blest communions on the heart
  Pour Mercy's holiest flood,
And symbolize in sacred forms
  The "body" and the "blood!" †

And lo; while listen all, absorbed,
  Devotion in their eyes,
The mantle of immortal truth
  Falls on them from the skies,
Conviction strengthens in the soul,
  And lingering doubt departs;
And Popish superstitions fade
  For ever from their hearts.

All in a moment—all alike
  The true faith treasure now,
The kneeler's fervid face it fills,
  It shines on Ridley's brow;
Cranmer hath closed the book, as though
  Belief could claim no more,
And Bradford ponders o'er the truth
  His pen had mark'd before!

Enough! as from a broken spell,
  Each soul now heavenward springs;
And Inspiration bears it on
  Upon its soaring wings!
Rapture hath rush'd upon the heart
  And lighted up the eye,
And fill'd the martyrs' dungeon with
  The brightness of the sky!

O, painter, honoured be the hour
  When first thy genius trod
The path that led thee before those
  Who shed their blood for God;
For God, and for a holy faith
  That still the stronger grew,—
The faith our country clings to now,
  The only and the true!

'Tis well that memory bore thee back,
  Amid the past to search,
And found for thee in martyrs cell
  Those "pillars of the Church,"‡—
The Church that ever since defies
  The taint of Popery's breath,
Is proud of their eternal life,
  Was hallow'd by their death.

---

* The Tower of London.

† Latimer is represented kneeling, and is supposed to have just read the passage 1 Cor. x. 16, "The cup of blessing which we bless, is it not the communion of the blood of Christ? The bread which we break, is it not the communion of the body of Christ?" Cranmer has shut his book, and, by the action of his hands, points to the irresistible proof contained in that verse, in which Ridley joins, while Bradford seems to have recorded it with his pen, wrapt in solemn thought.

‡ Styrpe.

PORTRAIT

OF HER MOST GRACIOUS MAJESTY

THE QUEEN,

SEATED IN THE CHAIR OF STATE.

PAINTED BY G. SWANDALE, IN MEZZOTINT BY W. O. GELLER.

SIZE 26½ INCHES BY 20.

PRINTS, £1 1s.—PROOFS, £2 2s.—PROOFS BEFORE LETTERS, £3 3s.

The following Eulogiums on this interesting Portrait of our beloved Queen, which have appeared in some of the leading Journals, will no doubt afford sincere gratification to every person desirous of possessing this most faithful Likeness.

This portrait of our youthful and beloved Sovereign, painted by Mr. SWANDALE, may be considered a surprising resemblance of the illustrious original. The architectural and other accessories are executed with great care and skill.—*Literary Gazette.*

Mr. SWANDALE's portrait of her Majesty, seated on a chair of state, arrayed in a state robe, and with the riband of the order of the garter over her shoulder, is a dignified work, excellently conceived and executed.—*Athenæum.*

This is one of the best portraits we have seen. The posture is easy and natural, and altogether the design reflects the highest credit on Mr. SWANDALE, who has succeeded admirably.—*Metropolitan Conservative Journal.*

This portrait of her Majesty is an admirable likeness: the composition of the whole picture is excellently conceived, and in the best taste. Too much praise can scarcely be given to both artists, for this very splendid, and, at the same time, most pleasing production.—*Naval and Military Gazette.*

This portrait is a splendid production, and worthy to stand among the works of our best masters; we must add the likeness is the best we have seen.—*Literary Journal.*

This very graceful picture presents us with the best likeness we have seen of her Majesty, who is represented seated on a throne, on a noble terrace, overlooking a landscape, in the background of which are seen the antique towers of Windsor Castle. The composition of the whole piece is exceedingly pleasing and appropriate.—*Morning Chronicle.*

This is the first portrait—at least, the first worthy of being called a portrait—of her Majesty, which has been executed. The likeness is admirable.—*Morning Advertiser.*

This is decidedly the best portrait of her Majesty which has hitherto appeared; it is a whole-length, and her Majesty is represented sitting in a chair of state, wearing the blue riband of the Bath across her right shoulder, and a diadem or open crown on her head. It is a faithful likeness.—*Sunday Times.*

This portrait is an admirable resemblance of the illustrious original, and is beautifully conceived, being full of that easy-grand and dignified deportment for which her Majesty is distinguished; it is executed in the first style of mezzotint.—*Bell's Life.*

We can hardly express ourselves in terms adequate to the gratification we have derived from a view of this *chef d'œuvre*. As a national work of art, it rivals any we have ever had the good fortune to notice.—*Weekly Chronicle.*

This is unquestionably the best picture, and the truest representation of her Majesty's face and figure, we have yet seen; the position of the figure is easy and natural, and the *tout ensemble* full of richness and harmony.—*Weekly Dispatch.*

We recommend this admirable portrait, by SWANDALE, as a most interesting likeness of our young Queen.—*Age.*

This is a work of infinite merit, and reflects great credit both on the painter and engraver; the charming expression of our gracious young Queen is successfully pourtrayed.—*Bell's Weekly Messenger.*

This is one of the very best likenesses of her Majesty we have yet seen, presenting her as she really is, free from exaggeration or artistical flattery.—*Sunbeam.*

A very spirited and faithful likeness.—*National Magazine.*

This beautiful portrait is engraved in the very first style of mezzotint; the execution is admirable.—*Church of England Quarterly Review.*

THE BOOK OF ROYALTY,

OR, CHARACTERISTICS OF BRITISH PALACES;

EDITED BY MRS. S. C. HALL.

Containing Thirteen Fac similes, illustrating incidents during various Reigns of the British Court, after Coloured Drawings by W. Perring and J. Brown.

ELEGANTLY BOUND IN SCARLET MOROCCO, RICHLY EMBLAZONED, AND FORMING THE MOST SPLENDID AND THE ONLY COLOURED ANNUAL HITHERTO PRODUCED.

Imperial 4to., price £2 12s. 6d.

The volume is pictorially gay looking, and its literature is pleasant.—*Literary Gazette.*
The binding is so gorgeous, as not merely to call for praise, but claims precedence in our three-fold commendation of this volume. The illustrations are so carefully finished, as closely to approach what they are intended to represent, viz. coloured drawings.—*Athenæum.*
The BOOK OF ROYALTY must, of course, take precedence. The prints are on a new plan, and not, we think, an unhappy one. A dozen or more of these brightly coloured designs adorn the volume, and pretty little stories and ballads, by Mrs. Hall, illustrate the illustrations.—*Times.*
The most novel and beautiful of all the Annuals. The book opens a new field. Mrs. Hall has put her high powers and correct discrimination to work out an ingenious and delicate design, and has completed an Annual that honestly and fairly fulfils its title of BOOK OF ROYALTY. Its illustrations are full of skilful grouping and general artistical expression, founded upon historical data.—*Morning Post.*
The BOOK OF ROYALTY is the most splendid of all the Annuals.—*Conservative Journal.*

THE FORGET ME NOT,

FOR 1839,

A CHRISTMAS, NEW YEARS', AND BIRTHDAY PRESENT·

EDITED BY FREDRICK SHOBERL;

CONTAINING ENGRAVINGS
By C. and H. Rolls, Davenport, Simmons, Ontrim, Stocks, Periam, Allen, and Hincheliff; from

PAINTINGS AND DRAWINGS
By Cooper, R.A., Parris, Barrett, Jones, Middleton, Joy, Nash, Jennings, Mrs. M'Ian, Miss Adams, and Bell;

AND LITERARY COMPOSITIONS
By T. K. Hervey, D. Jerrold, Calder Campbell, P. H. Fleetwood, Esq., M.P., Dr. Mackenzie, H. F. Chorley, Swain, Mitchell, Richard and Mary Howitt, Miss Landon, Miss Lawrance, Mrs. Lee, Mrs. Sigourney, Miss Gould, Mrs. Walker, Miss M.A. Browne, Miss L. H. Sheridan, &c. &c. &c.

Elegantly bound in maroon morocco, price 12s.

SKETCHES & SCENERY

IN THE

BASQUE PROVINCES OF SPAIN;

With a Selection of National Music.

ILLUSTRATED BY NOTES & REMINISCENCES BY

H. WILKENSON, Esq.

Imperial 4to., cloth lettered, price, plain, £2 2s.; or coloured, in imitation of the Original Drawings, £3 3s.

The Author is induced to hope, that the drawings contained in this Work will prove a welcome addition to the libraries of those officers who have served in Spain, whether belonging to the army of the Duke of Wellington, to the present force stationed on the coast of Cantabria under the command of Lord John Hay, or the late expedition intrusted to the guidance of Sir George de Lacy Evans.

TO THE FASHIONABLE WORLD.

BRILLIANT WRITING INKS.

MESSRS. ACKERMANN & Co. have the pleasure to announce, that they are at length able to supply the Fashionable World with INKS and FLUIDS unparalleled for *beauty and diversity of colour;* which, at the same time, are so soft and so free from every corrosive quality as to injure neither pen nor paper, and to form an ornament, instead of a blemish, to every boudoir and writing-table.

These INKS or FLUIDS are in neat portable Inkstands at 6d. each, and are of the following varieties:—

Violette d'Orleans,	or	Violet Writing Fluid
Verde à Napoléon,	or	Green Writing Fluid
Bleue Nationale,	or	Dark Blue Fluid
Bleue Céleste,	or	Bright Blue Fluid
Rouge d'Oeillet,	or	Crimson Writing Fluid
Jaune Algerine,	or	Yellow Writing Fluid

*These Fluids do not turn Black, but remain of brilliant **Permanent Colours**.*

SOLD IN PARIS BY JANET, RUE DE TEMPLE;

AND IN LONDON BY ACKERMANN & CO. 96, STRAND,

BY WHOM THE TRADE IN ENGLAND WILL BE SUPPLIED.

WHITING, LONDON.

BRITISH COLLEGE OF HEALTH
HAMILTON PLACE, NEW ROAD, LONDON.

CONSUMPTION CURED BY MORISON'S MEDICINES,
ATTESTED BY
LADY SOPHIA GREY, OF ASHTON HAYES, NEAR NORTHWICH, CHESHIRE.

To the Editor of the Times.

Sir,—I now beg to forward for publication, at Lady Sophia Grey's own request, her letter, detailing a Cure of Consumption.

I cannot but express my astonishment, that after the repeated cases of cure which, during a period of fourteen years, have been performed under the Hygeian system—which fact must be within the knowledge of many of the medical body—the truth of that system being moreover confirmed by the most distinguished members of the profession, such as the late Dr. James Hamilton, of Edinburgh, as to the practice, and now by Professor Magendie, as to the theory—the medical profession generally should persist in treating diseases on the principles of Organic Pathology, by multifarious and pernicious drugs.

The cure of Consumption here alluded to, is not by many the only one performed under the Hygeian treatment, as Mr. Tothill, Surgeon, of Heavitree, near Exeter, has effected several cures of that disease by my medicines; and I should also cite the case of Sir Richard Sutton's son, who was cured of it, after having been given over by the faculty. In proof of the case now reported being consumption, we have the sound judgment of Lady Sophia Grey, who had been acquainted with the family twenty-nine years, and knew them to be consumptive, two of its members having fallen victims to the disease. The party took my medicine as a last resort. I am, Sir, yours obediently, JAMES MORISON, the Hygeist.
British College of Health, New Road, London, Jan. 2, 1839.

P.S. I am aware that the faculty deem such cases, and many others, incurable. So should I, did I believe in their untenable doctrine of Organic Pathology, which in the language of Magendie " attributes everything to the solids, and refuses the liquids all participation in the production of morbid alterations."—*Lancet*, page 463, 22d December, 1838. But according to the Hygeian treatment the Blood is purified and the progress of disease stopped.

COPY OF LADY SOPHIA GREY'S LETTER.
Ashton Hayes, near Chester, Dec. 31, 1838.

Sir,—Having so greatly benefited by your invaluable medicines, for the last five years, that if my constitution had not been completely ruined by loss of blood and mercury twenty years before I was so fortunate as to hear of your medicines, I am confident I should now be as strong as the strongest of my age (61); but excepting very slight ailments, I now, comparatively speaking, enjoy good health; and it gives me sincere pleasure in having it in my power to send you to be published a CURE OF CONSUMPTION, under my own eye, of a young man, whom I have known from his birth, and all his family for the last twenty-nine years—two of them died of rapid decline, and he was fast going in the same most dreadful and incurable complaint, and was urged by some friends of his to try your medicines. He began by taking three of No. 1 at night and three of No. 2 the next morning, and continued increasing until he got to ten of each, and then felt so well he decreased to one pill, but the night-sweats returned, and he began taking them again in larger doses, and on a different plan—No. 1 Pills one night and No. 2 Pills the next, and so on till he got to twenty-eight at one dose, and this conquered the complaint; he then decreased them to one pill, and is now in good health. He does not wish to have his name published, but if any one wishes for further particulars, they may apply by letter or in person to me, and may hear everything from him by word-of-mouth. He lives in the parish of Tarven.—Your medicines are highly valued in this parish, and the poor are most grateful for them. If I had permission, I could tell you of many that are rich, who have been restored to health by them. Whenever I have any case that I have attended and can vouch for the truth of, you may depend on my informing you of it, for merit and benevolence ought to be encouraged, and it is hard that those who cannot afford advice, or are called incurable, should not benefit, as I have done, by your wonderful medicines. I remain, Sir, your obedient and obliged,
To JAMES MORISON, Esq.   SOPHIA GREY.

CAUTION.

Whereas spurious imitations of my Medicines are now in circulation, I, JAMES MORISON, the Hygeist, hereby give notice, that I am in no wise connected with the following Medicines purporting to be mine, and sold under the various names of " Dr. Morrison's Pills;" " The Hygeian Pills;" " The Improved Vegetable Universal Pills ;" " The Original Morison's Pills, as compounded by the late Mr. Moat ;" " The Original Hygeian Vegetable Pills ;" "The Original Morison's Pills ;" &c. &c.

That my Medicines are prepared only at the British College of Health, Hamilton Place, King's Cross, London ; and sold by the General Agents to the British College of Health, and their Sub-Agents ; and that no Chemist or Druggist is authorised by me to dispose of the same.

None can be genuine, without the words " MORISON'S UNIVERSAL MEDICINES " are engraved on the Government Stamp, in white letters upon a red ground.—In witness whereof I have hereunto set my hand.
British College of Health, King's Cross.   JAMES MORISON, the Hygeist.

Sold in Boxes, at 1s. 1¼d., 2s. 9d., 4s. 6d., and Family Packets, containing three 4s. 6d. Boxes, at 11s. each.

GENERAL DEPOTS IN LONDON FOR THE SALE OF THE MEDICINES.

Medical Dissenter Office, 368, Strand ; Mrs. Twell, 10, Hand-court, Holborn ; Mr. Good, Western Branch, 72, Edgeware-road ; Mr. Field, 65, Quadrant, Regent-street ; Mr. Haslett, 118, Ratcliffe-highway ; Mr. Lofts, 3, Park-place, Mile-end-road ; Messrs. Hannay & Co., 63, Oxford-street ; Mr. Chappell, 84, Lombard-street.

N.B.—Sub-Agents may be found in every Town or Village throughout the Kingdom, duly appointed by the General Agents ; and the Public are hereby further cautioned against purchasing the Medicine, except of the regularly-appointed Agents to the British College of Health, as many spurious imitations are in circulation.

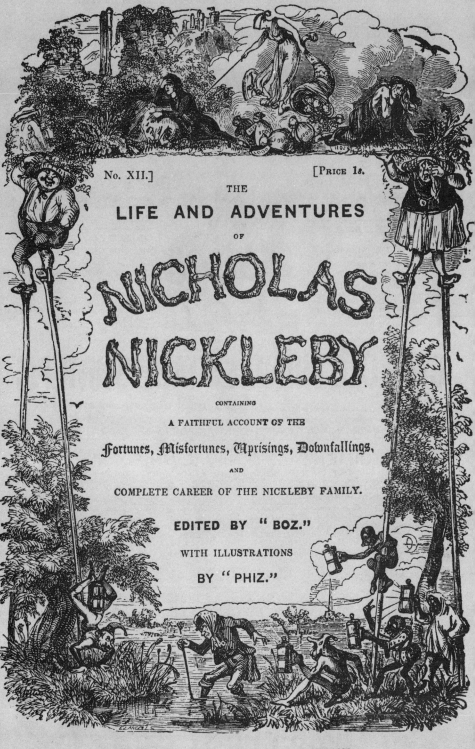

No. XII.] [Price 1s.

THE
LIFE AND ADVENTURES
OF
NICHOLAS NICKLEBY

CONTAINING

A FAITHFUL ACCOUNT OF THE

Fortunes, Misfortunes, Uprisings, Downfallings,

AND

COMPLETE CAREER OF THE NICKLEBY FAMILY.

EDITED BY "BOZ."

WITH ILLUSTRATIONS

BY "PHIZ."

LONDON: CHAPMAN AND HALL, 186 STRAND.

REFORM YOUR TAILORS' BILLS!

LADIES' ELEGANT RIDING HABITS.

Summer Cloth	£3	3	0
Ladies' Cloth	4	4	0
Saxony Cloth	5	5	0

GENTLEMAN'S

Superfine Dress Coat	2	7	6
Extra Saxony, the best that is made	2	15	0
Superfine Frock Coat, silk facings	2	10	0
Buckskin Trousers	1	1	0
Cloth or double-milled Cassimere ditto 17s. 6d. to	1	5	0
New Patterns, Summer Trousers, 10s. 6d. per pr. or 3 pr.	1	10	0
Summer Waistcoats, 7s.; or 3,	1	0	0
Splendid Silk Valencia Dress Waistcoats, 10s. 6d. each, or 3,	1	10	0

FIRST-RATE BOYS' CLOTHING.

Skeleton Dresses	£0	15	0
Tunic and Hussar Suits,	1	10	0
Camlet Cloaks	0	8	6
Cloth Cloaks	0	15	6

GENTLEMAN'S

Morning Coats and Dressing Gowns	0	18	0
Petersham Great Coats and Pilot P Jackets, bound, and Velvet Collar	1	10	0
Camlet Cloak, lined all through	1	1	0
Cloth Opera Cloak	1	10	0
Army Cloth Blue Spanish Cloak, 9½ yards round	2	10	0
Super Cloth ditto	3	3	0
Cloth or Tweed Fishing or Travelling Trousers	0	13	6

THE CELEBRITY THE

CITY CLOTHING ESTABLISHMENT

Has so many years maintained, being the

BEST AS WELL AS THE CHEAPEST HOUSE,

Renders any Assurance as to STYLE and QUALITY unnecessary. The NOBILITY and GENTRY are invited to the SHOW-ROOMS, TO VIEW THE IMMENSE & SPLENDID STOCK.

The numerous Applications for

REGIMENTALS & NAVAL UNIFORMS,

Have induced E. P. D. & SON to make ample Arrangements for an extensive Business in this particular Branch: a perusal of their List of Prices (which can be had gratis) will show the EXORBITANT CHARGES to which OFFICERS OF THE ARMY AND NAVY HAVE SO LONG BEEN SUBJECTED.

CONTRACTS BY THE YEAR,

Originated by E. P. D. & SON, are universally adopted by CLERGYMEN and PROFESSIONAL GENTLEMEN, as being MORE REGULAR and ECONOMICAL. THE PRICES ARE THE LOWEST EVER OFFERED:—

Two Suits per Year, Superfine,	7	7	—Extra Saxony, the best that is made,	8	5	
Three Suits per Year, ditto	10	17	—Extra Saxony, ditto	12	6	
Four Suits per Year, ditto	14	6	—Extra Saxony, ditto	15	18	

(THE OLD SUITS TO BE RETURNED.)

Capital Shooting Jackets, 21s. The new Waterproof Cloak, 21s.

COUNTRY GENTLEMEN,

Preferring their Clothes Fashionably made, at a FIRST-RATE LONDON HOUSE, are respectfully informed, that by a Post-paid Application, they will receive a Prospectus explanatory of the System of Business, Directions for Measurement, and a Statement of Prices. Or if Three or Four Gentlemen unite, one of the Travellers will be dispatched immediately to wait on them.

STATE LIVERIES SPLENDIDLY MADE.

Footman's Suit of Liveries, £3 3. Scarlet Hunting Coat, £3 3

E. P. DOUDNEY AND SON,
49, LOMBARD-STREET. 1784.
Established

THE
NICKLEBY ADVERTISER.

MAXWELL'S LIFE OF WELLINGTON.

MESSRS. A. H. BAILY and CO. have the honour to announce the Publication of a

LIFE OF FIELD-MARSHAL
THE DUKE OF WELLINGTON, K.G.
&c. &c.

BY THE AUTHOR OF THE
" STORIES OF WATERLOO," "THE BIVOUAC," "WILD SPORTS OF THE WEST," AND " VICTORIES OF THE BRITISH ARMIES."

This Work will be completed in Twelve Parts; each Part beautifully embellished by two or more highly-finished Line Engravings on Steel, from pictures by the most eminent living and deceased Artists; and many well-executed Wood Engravings, illustrative of Native and Military Costume. A Part will be published every alternate month, elegantly printed in demy 8vo, price 5s.; and royal 8vo, with proof impressions of the plates on India paper, price 7s. 6d. each Part. This truly National Work, when complete, will form Three handsome Volumes, and contain Twenty-seven splendid Plates, including Three Vignette Titles.

EMBELLISHMENTS TO PART I.

DEATH OF DOONDHIA............... BY A. COOPER, R.A.

THE MARQUIS WELLESLEY...... BY SIR THOMAS LAWRENCE.

VIEW OF STRATHFIELDSAYE... *From an original Drawing taken for this Work.*

AND SEVERAL WOOD ENGRAVINGS.

PROSPECTUS.

AWARE of the difficulties before them, the Publishers undertake the Work, nevertheless, with full assurance of perfect success, having at the outset of their undertaking great advantages already in their possession, and a certain promise of obtaining most valuable assistance during the further progress of their labours.

The name of Mr. Maxwell, the Author and Editor of the Work,—his general literary reputation,—and his particular celebrity as a terse, powerful, and vigorous writer upon military affairs,—are guarantees of a high degree of merit in its composition. Nor will public confidence be lessened by the information that its preparation has been Mr. Maxwell's cherished task for several years; and that he commences the execution of his work, satisfied as to the extent and readiness of his resources, the large accession of documents from best authority, and the active contributive co-operation of his military connexions. A great extent and variety of exclusive information will thus be published for the first time within its pages.

In regard to its Embellishments, they will comprise a beautiful series of highly-finished engravings upon steel, executed in the most exquisite and expensive style, from the easels and burins of the most eminent painters and engravers. The subjects will be principally portraits and battle-pieces,—victories won under Wellington,—and portraits of the Generals who assisted him in gaining them. For the excellence of the more technical department of the publication, the Publishers can make themselves responsible. The work will be remarkable for the beauty of its typography,—and printed in the most handsome and appropriate form. The Parts will appear at two-month intervals, at Five Shillings each, so that a handsome guinea volume will be completed at the end of every eight months; and the whole work at the expiration of two years.

This mode of publication has been adopted, after mature consideration, for several cogent reasons,—not the least important of which, has been a consultation of the convenience of that very large class of readers, who would not willingly let such a work pass,—but who might feel a sensible difference between an immediate payment of Three Guineas, and a periodical instalment of Five Shillings.

₊ *Subscribers' Names received by every respectable Bookseller in the Kingdom.*

LONDON: A. H. BAILY AND CO., 83, CORNHILL.

APSLEY PELLATT'S
ABRIDGED LIST OF
Net Cash Prices for the best Flint Glass Ware.

DECANTERS.

25 Strong quart Nelson shape decanters, cut all over, bold flutes and cut brim & stopper, P.M. each 10s6d: to 12 0

26 Do. three-ringed royal shape, cut on and between rings, turned out stop, P.M. each 10 0
Do. do. not cut on or between rings, nor turned out stopper, P.M. ea. 8s to 9 0

27 Fancy shapes, cut all over, eight flutes, spire stopper, &c. each, P.M. 16s. to 18 0
Do. six flutes only, each, P.M. 24s. to 27 0

DISHES.

31 Dishes, oblong, pillar moulded, scolloped edges, cut star.
| 5-in. | 7-in. | 9-in. | 10-in. |
| 3s. 6d. | 6s. 6d. | 11s. | 13s. each. |

32 Oval cup sprig, shell pattern,
| 5-in. | 7-in. | 9-in. | 11-in. |
| 7s. 6d. | 9s. 6d. | 16s. | 19s. each. |

33 Square shape pillar, moulded star,
| 5-in. | 7-in | 9-in. | 10-in. |
| 4s. | 8s. | 12s. 6d. | 15s. each. |

FINGER CUPS.

37 Fluted finger-cups, strong, about 14 oz. each 2 6
Do. plain flint, punted, per doz..... 18 0
Do. coloured, per doz......18s. to 21 0

38 Ten-fluted round, very strong, each . 5 0
Eight-fluted do., each 8 0

39 Medicean shape, moulded pillar, pearl upper part, cut flat flutes, each .. 5 0

PICKLES

46 Pickles, half fluted for 3 in. holes, RM ea. 4 6

47 Strong, moulded bottom, 3-in. hole, cut all over, flat flutes, R.M. each . 5 0
Best cut star do. for 3½-in. hole, PM ea. 7 6
Very strong and best cut, P.M. each 14 6

WATER JUGS

59 Quarts, neatly fluted and cut rings, each.....................14s. to 18 0

60 Ewer shape, best cut handles, &c... 21 0

61 Silver do. scolloped edges, ex. lar. flutes 25 0

WATER BOTTLES

70 Moulded pillar body, cut neck, each . 3 0

71 Cut neck and star.................. 3 0

72 Double fluted cut rings 3 6

73 Very strong pillar, moulded body, cut neck and rings 5 6

74 Grecian shape, fluted all over 7 0

TUMBLERS

	78	79	80	81	82	83	84	85	86	87	
Tale 5s.											
Flint,	7s.	10s.	12s	12s.	10s.	12s.	14s.	18s.	18s.		Doz.
	to to	to	to	to		to	to	to			
	8s.	12s	14s.	15s.	12s.		15s.	21s.	21s.	30s	do.

WINES

	88	89	90	91	92	93	94	95	96	97	98	99
Tale	7s.	7s.	7s.	8s.	14s.	12s.	13s.	15s.	18s.	21s.	20s.	
	to	to	to	to								
	8s.	9s.	9s.	9s.	10s.							

Glass Blowing, Cutting, and Engraving, may be inspected by Purchasers, at Mr. Pellatt's Extensive Flint Glass and Steam Cutting Works, in Holland Street, near Blackfriars' Bridge, any Tuesday, Wednesday, or Thursday.

Merchants and the Trade supplied on equitable Terms.

No Abatement from the above specified Ready Money Prices.

No Connexion with any other Establishment.

M. & W. Collis, Printers, 104, Bishopsgate Street Within.

LEADENHALL STREET, LONDON.

MECHI'S NOVEL AND SPLENDID
PAPIER MACHIE ARTICLES,

CONSISTING OF

TEA TRAYS, TEA CADDIES, LADIES' WORK, CAKE, AND NOTE BASKETS, CARD CASES, CARD POOLS, FRUIT PLATES, FRUIT BASKETS, NETTING BOXES, HAND SCREENS, CARD RACKS, CHESS BOARDS.

LADIES' COMPANIONS, or Work Cases 15s. to 2l.

LADIES' CARD CASES, in Pearl, Ivory, and Tortoiseshell . . . . . 10s. to 5l. each.

LADIES' WORK BOXES . . 25s. to 10 Guineas.

LADIES' DRESSING CASES 2l. 10s. to 50 Guineas.

LADIES' SCOTCH WORK BOXES at all prices.

LADIES' ROSEWOOD AND MAHOGANY DESKS 12s. 6d. to 10 Guineas.

LADIES' MOROCCO AND RUSSIA LEATHER WRITING CASES . . . . 5s. to 5l.

LADIES' ENVELOPE CASES, various prices.

LADIES' TABLE INKSTANDS, made of British Coal (quite a novelty) . . . 7s. 6d. to 30s.

LADIES' SCOTCH TOOTH-PICK CASES.

LADIES' IVORY AND TORTOISESHELL HAIR BRUSHES . . . at 2l. to 5l. per Pair.

LADIES' SCENT AND TOILET BOTTLES in great variety.

LADIES' SCOTCH TEA CADDIES . 21s. to 40s.

LADIES' PLAYING CARD BOXES . 30s. to 5l.

LADIES' JAPAN DRESSING CASES . 7s. to 15s.

LADIES' TORTOISESHELL DRESSING & SIDE COMBS.

LADIES' HAND GLASSES.

LADIES' PATENT INSTANTANEOUS PEN-MAKERS . . . . 10s. 6d. and 12s. 6d.

LADIES' ELEGANT PENKNIVES AND SCISSORS 5s. to 30s.

MISCELLANEOUS.

BAGATELLE TABLES £3 10 to 5 0

BACKGAMMON TABLES 1 0 to 5 10

CHESS BOARDS . . . 0 4 to 3 0

POPE JOAN BOARDS £0 13 to 1 0

IVORY CHESSMEN . 1 1 to 10 10

BONE & WOOD DITTO Various Prices.

WHIST MARKERS, COUNTERS, &c.

GENT.'S DRESSING CASES, in Wood 2l. to 50l.

GENT.'S LEATHER DRESSING CASES 25s. to 24l.

GENT.'S WRITING DESKS, in Wood 30s. to 16l.

GENT.'S LEATHER WRITING DESKS 24s. 6d. to 5l.

GENT.'S WRITING & DRESSING CASE COMBINED . . . . . 5l. to 16l.

GENT.'S POCKET BOOKS WITH INSTRUMENTS 20s. to 40s.

GENT.'S ELEGANT CASES OF RAZORS 12s. to 3l.

GENT.'S SEVEN DAY RAZORS, in Fancy Woods 25s. to 5l.

GENT.'S RAZOR STROPS . . 2s. to 30s.

GENT.'S SPORTING KNIVES . . 12s. to 5l.

GENT.'S FANCY PENKNIVES . 5s. to 15s.

GENT.'S PEARL AND SHELL POCKET COMBS 3s. 6d. to 15s.

GENT.'S SCOTCH CIGAR BOXES 3s. 6d. to 40s.

GENT.'S COAL AND EBONY INKSTANDS 7s. 6d. to 50s.

GENT.'S IVORY AND FANCY WOOD HAIR BRUSHES . . . . 20s. to 3l. 10s.

GENT.'S SETS OF BRUSHES, in Russia Cases 25s. to 4l. 10s.

GENT.'S SILVER AND IVORY SHAVING BRUSHES In elegant Patterns.

GENT.'S SILVER AND SHELL TABLETS.

MECHI,      MECHI,

Submits, to public inspection, his Manufactures, as being of the finest quality this kingdom can produce, and at moderate prices.

A large Stock of Table Cutlery, Plated Tea and Coffee Services, Dish Covers, Hash Covers, &c.

COMFORT FOR TENDER FEET, &c.

WELLINGTON STREET,

STRAND, LONDON.

HALL & CO.

PATENTEES OF THE PANNUS CORIUM,

OR

Leather Cloth Boots & Shoes,

FOR LADIES AND GENTLEMEN.

These articles have borne the test and received the approbation of all who have worn them. Such as are troubled with Corns, Bunions, Gout, Chilblains, or Tenderness of Feet from any other cause, will find them the softest and most comfortable ever invented—they never draw the feet or get hard, are very durable, adapted for every Climate—they resemble the finest Leather, and are cleaned with common Blacking.

The Patent India-Rubber Goloshes

ARE LIGHT, DURABLE, ELASTIC, AND WATERPROOF;

They thoroughly protect the feet from damp or cold; are excellent preservatives against Gout, Chilblains, &c.; and when worn over a Boot or Shoe, no sensible addition is felt to the weight. *Ladies and Gentlemen may be fitted with either of the above by sending a Boot or Shoe.*

HALL & CO.'S PORTABLE WATER-PROOF DRESSES

FOR LADIES AND GENTLEMEN.

This desirable article claims the attention of all who are exposed to the wet.

Ladies' Cardinal Cloaks, with Hoods........................... **18s.**
Gentlemen's Dresses, comprising Cape, Overalls, & Hood ·· **21s**

The whole can be carried with convenience in the Pocket.
A variety of Water-Proof Garments at proportionable Prices.

Wellington Street Strand, London.

MOSLEY'S METALLIC PENS.

R. MOSLEY & CO. beg to call the attention of Mercantile Men, and the Public in general, to their superior Metallic Pens. They possess the highest degree of elasticity and flexibility, and are found perfectly free from all those inconveniences which have prevented so many persons making use of Metallic Pens.

Every description of writer may be suited, as these pens are manufactured of various qualities, degrees of hardness, &c. They may be had at all respectable Stationers throughout the kingdom.

Observe that every Pen is stamped, R. MOSLEY & CO., LONDON.

LABERN'S BOTANIC CREAM.

By appointment, patronised by her Most Gracious Majesty, celebrated for strengthening and promoting the growth of Hair, and completely freeing it from Scurf.—Sold by the Proprietor, H. Labern, Perfumer to her Majesty, 49, Judd Street, Brunswick Square, in pots, 1s. 6d., 2s. 6d., 3s. 6d., and 5s. each, and by all Perfumers and Medicine Venders. Beware of counterfeits. Ask for "Labern's Botanic Cream."

*** Trade Orders from the Country to come through the London Wholesale Houses.

LITHOGRAPHY. & ZINCOGRAPHY.

The attention of ARTISTS, PUBLISHERS, ARCHITECTS, &c. is respectfully called to STRAKER's Establishment, 3, George Yard, Lombard Street, London,

For the execution, either on ZINC or STONE, of every Description of **Landscapes, Portraits, Botanical, Mechanical, Anatomical,** and other Drawings, Maps and Plans of Estates, Elevations, Fac Similes, Writings, Circular Letters, &c. &c. With the utmost Dispatch, and on the most moderate Terms.

STRAKER'S IMPROVED LITHOGRAPHIC PRESSES, WARRANTED OF THE BEST CONSTRUCTION At the following greatly Reduced Prices for Cash: 8 in. by 14 £5 5s.; 14 in. by 18 £7 10s.; 18 in. by 23 £9 10s; 20 in. by 26 £12 12s. Larger sizes in like proportion.

ZINC PLATES, STONES, and EVERY MATERIAL REQUIRED IN THE ART, forwarded to all Parts of the World. Country and Foreign Orders punctually executed.

Zinc Door and Window Plates of every description.

BEAUFOY'S
INSTANT CURE FOR THE TOOTH-ACHE.

This article has been extensively and successfully used for some time past in a populous Neighbourhood, and has proved to be an INSTANT CURE in most cases.

The Selling Price to the Public has been fixed purposely so low as

to render the

"INSTANT CURE FOR THE TOOTH-ACHE"

accessible to all Classes.

MADE BY BEAUFOY & CO., SOUTH LAMBETH, LONDON,

And Sold by most Respectable Druggists and Patent Medicine Venders
in Town and Country.

The Bottles, with ample Directions for Use, Price 1s. 1½d. each, Stamp included.

[BRADBURY AND EVANS, PRINTERS, WHITEFRIARS.]

CHAPTER XXXVII.

NICHOLAS FINDS FURTHER FAVOUR IN THE EYES OF THE BROTHERS
CHEERYBLE AND MR. TIMOTHY LINKINWATER. THE BROTHERS
GIVE A BANQUET ON A GREAT ANNUAL OCCASION; NICHOLAS, ON
RETURNING HOME FROM IT, RECEIVES A MYSTERIOUS AND IM-
PORTANT DISCLOSURE FROM THE LIPS OF MRS. NICKLEBY.

THE Square in which the counting-house of the brothers Cheeryble
was situated, although it might not wholly realize the very sanguine
expectations which a stranger would be disposed to form on hearing
the fervent encomiums bestowed upon it by Tim Linkinwater, was,
nevertheless, a sufficiently desirable nook in the heart of a busy town
like London, and one which occupied a high place in the affectionate
remembrances of several grave persons domiciled in the neighbourhood,
whose recollections, however, dated from a much more recent period,
and whose attachment to the spot was far less absorbing than were the
recollections and attachment of the enthusiastic Tim.

And let not those whose eyes have been accustomed to the aristo-
cratic gravity of Grosvenor Square and Hanover Square, the dowager
barrenness and frigidity of Fitzroy Square, or the gravel walks and
garden seats of the Squares of Russell and Euston, suppose that the
affections of Tim Linkinwater, or the inferior lovers of this particular
locality, had been awakened and kept alive by any refreshing associations with leaves however dingy, or grass, however bare and thin.
The City square has no inclosure, save the lamp-post in the middle,
and no grass but the weeds which spring up round its base. It is a
quiet, little-frequented, retired spot, favourable to melancholy and contemplation, and appointments of long-waiting; and up and down its
every side the Appointed saunters idly by the hour together, wakening
the echoes with the monotonous sound of his footsteps on the smooth
worn stones, and counting first the windows and then the very bricks
of the tall silent houses that hem him round about. In winter-time the
snow will linger there, long after it has melted from the busy streets
and highways. The summer's sun holds it in some respect, and while
he darts his cheerful rays sparingly into the square, he keeps his fiery
heat and glare for noisier and less-imposing precincts. It is so quiet
that you can almost hear the ticking of your own watch when you
stop to cool in its refreshing atmosphere. There is a distant hum—of
coaches, not of insects—but no other sound disturbs the stillness of the
square. The ticket-porter leans idly against the post at the corner,
comfortably warm, but not hot, although the day is broiling. His
white apron flaps languidly in the air, his head gradually droops upon
his breast, he takes very long winks with both eyes at once; even he
is unable to withstand the soporific influence of the place, and is
gradually falling asleep. But now he starts into full wakefulness,
recoils a step or two, and gazes out before him with eager wildness in

his eye. Is it a job, or a boy at marbles ? Does he see a ghost, or hear an organ ? No ; sight more unwonted still—there is a butterfly in the square—a real, live, butterfly ! astray from flowers and sweets, and fluttering among the iron heads of the dusty area railings !

But if there were not many matters immediately without the doors of Cheeryble Brothers, to engage the attention or distract the thoughts of the young clerk, there were not a few within to interest and amuse him. There was scarcely an object in the place, animate or inanimate, which did not partake in some degree of the scrupulous method and punctuality of Mr. Timothy Linkinwater. Punctual as the counting-house dial, which he maintained to be the best time-keeper in London next after the clock of some old, hidden, unknown church hard by, (for Tim held the fabled goodness of that at the Horse Guards to be a pleasant fiction, invented by jealous West-enders,) the old clerk performed the minutest actions of the day, and arranged the minutest articles in the little room, in a precise and regular order, which could not have been exceeded if it had actually been a real glass case fitted with the choicest curiosities. Paper, pens, ink, ruler, sealing-wax, wafers, pounce-box, string-box, fire-box, Tim's hat, Tim's scrupulously-folded gloves, Tim's other coat—looking precisely like a back view of himself as it hung against the wall—all had their accustomed inches of space. Except the clock, there was not such an accurate and unimpeachable instrument in existence as the little thermometer which hung behind the door. There was not a bird of such methodical and business-like habits in all the world as the blind blackbird, who dreamed and dozed away his days in a large snug cage, and had lost his voice from old age years before Tim first bought him. There was not such an eventful story in the whole range of anecdote as Tim could tell concerning the acquisition of that very bird : how, compassionating his starved and suffering condition, he had purchased him with the view of humanely terminating his wretched life ; how he determined to wait three days and see whether the bird revived ; how, before half the time was out, the bird did revive ; and how he went on reviving and picking up his appetite and good looks until he gradually became what—" what you see him now, Sir"—Tim would say, glancing proudly at the cage. And with that, Tim would utter a melodious chirrup, and cry " Dick ;" and Dick, who, for any sign of life he had previously given, might have been a wooden or stuffed representation of a blackbird indifferently executed, would come to the side of the cage in three small jumps, and, thrusting his bill between the bars, turn his sightless head towards his old master—and at that moment it would be very difficult to determine which of the two was the happier, the bird, or Tim Linkinwater.

Nor was this all. Everything gave back, besides, some reflection of the kindly spirit of the brothers. The warehousemen and porters were such sturdy jolly fellows that it was a treat to see them. Among the shipping-announcements and steam-packet lists which decorated the counting-house wall, were designs for alms-houses, statements of charities, and plans for new hospitals. A blunderbuss and two swords hung above the chimney-piece for the terror of evil-doers, but the blunderbuss was rusty and shattered, and the swords were broken and edgeless. Elsewhere, their open display in such a condition would have raised a smile, but there it seemed as though even violent and offensive weapons partook of the reigning influence, and became emblems of mercy and forbearance.

Such thoughts as these, occurred to Nicholas very strongly on the morning when he first took possession of the vacant stool, and looked about him more freely and at ease than he had before enjoyed an opportunity of doing. Perhaps they encouraged and stimulated him to exertion, for, during the next two weeks, all his spare hours, late at night and early in the morning, were incessantly devoted to acquiring the mysteries of book-keeping and some other forms of mercantile account. To these he applied himself with such steadiness and perseverance that, although he brought no greater amount of previous knowledge to the subject than certain dim recollections of two or three very long sums entered into a cyphering-book at school, and relieved for parental inspection by the effigy of a fat swan tastefully flourished by the writing-master's own hand, he found himself, at the end of a fortnight, in a condition to report his proficiency to Mr. Linkinwater, and to claim his promise that he, Nicholas Nickleby, should now be allowed to assist him in his graver labours.

It was a sight to behold Tim Linkinwater slowly bring out a massive ledger and day-book, and, after turning them over and over and affectionately dusting their backs and sides, open the leaves here and there, and cast his eyes half-mournfully, half-proudly, upon the fair and unblotted entries.

" Four-and-forty year, next May !" said Tim. " Many new ledgers since then. Four-and-forty year !"

Tim closed the book again.

" Come, come," said Nicholas, " I am all impatience to begin."

Tim Linkinwater shook his head with an air of mild reproof. Mr. Nickleby was not sufficiently impressed with the deep and awful nature of his undertaking. Suppose there should be any mistake— any scratching out——

Young men are adventurous. It is extraordinary what they will rush upon sometimes. Without even taking the precaution of sitting himself down upon his stool, but standing leisurely at the desk, and with a smile upon his face—actually a smile ; (there was no mistake about it ; Mr. Linkinwater often mentioned it afterwards ;) Nicholas dipped his pen into the inkstand before him, and plunged into the books of Cheeryble Brothers !

Tim Linkinwater turned pale, and tilting up his stool on the two legs nearest Nicholas, looked over his shoulder in breathless anxiety. Brother Charles and brother Ned entered the counting house together ; but Tim Linkinwater, without looking round, impatiently waved his hand as a caution that profound silence must be observed, and followed the nib of the inexperienced pen with strained and eager eyes.

The brothers looked on with smiling faces, but Tim Linkinwater smiled not, nor moved for some minutes. At length he drew a long slow breath, and still maintaining his position on the tilted stool, glanced at brother Charles, secretly pointed with the feather of his pen towards Nicholas, and nodded his head in a grave and resolute manner, plainly signifying " He'll do."

Brother Charles nodded again, and exchanged a laughing look with brother Ned; but just then Nicholas stopped to refer to some other page, and Tim Linkinwater, unable to contain his satisfaction any longer, descended from his stool and caught him rapturously by the hand.

" He has done it," said Tim, looking round at his employers and shaking his head triumphantly. " His capital B's and D's are exactly like mine; he dots all his small i's and crosses every t as he writes it. There an't such a young man as this in all London," said Tim, clapping Nicholas on the back; " not one. Don't tell me. The City can't produce his equal. I challenge the City to do it !"

With this casting down of his gauntlet, Tim Linkinwater struck the desk such a blow with his clenched fist, that the old blackbird tumbled off his perch with the start it gave him, and actually uttered a feeble croak in the extremity of his astonishment.

" Well said, Tim—well said, Tim Linkinwater !" cried Brother Charles, scarcely less pleased than Tim himself, and clapping his hands gently as he spoke, " I knew our young friend would take great pains, and I was quite certain he would succeed, in no time. Didn't I say so, brother Ned ?"

" You did, my dear brother—certainly, my dear brother, you said so, and you were quite right," replied Ned. " Quite right. Tim Linkinwater is excited, but he is justly excited, properly excited. Tim is a fine fellow. Tim Linkinwater, Sir—you're a fine fellow."

" Here's a pleasant thing to think of," said Tim, wholly regardless of this address to himself, and raising his spectacles from the ledger to the brothers. " Here's a pleasant thing. Do you suppose I haven't often thought what would become of these books when I was gone? Do you suppose I haven't often thought that things might go on irregular and untidy here, after I was taken away ? But now," said Tim, extending his fore-finger towards Nicholas, " now, when I've shown him a little more, I'm satisfied. The business will go on when I'm dead as well as it did when I was alive—just the same; and I shall have the satisfaction of knowing that there never were such books—never were such books ! No, nor never will be such books— as the books of Cheeryble Brothers."

Having thus expressed his sentiments, Mr. Linkinwater gave vent to a short laugh, indicative of defiance to the cities of London and Westminster, and turning again to his desk quietly carried seventy-six from the last column he had added up, and went on with his work.

" Tim Linkinwater, Sir," said brother Charles; " give me your hand, Sir. This is your birth-day. How dare you talk about any-thing else till you have been wished many happy returns of the day, Tim Linkinwater ? God bless you, Tim ! God bless you !"

Linkinwater intimates his approval of Nicholas.

"My dear brother," said the other, seizing Tim's disengaged fist, "Tim Linkinwater looks ten years younger than he did on his last birth-day."

"Brother Ned, my dear boy," returned the other old fellow, "I believe that Tim Linkinwater was born a hundred-and-fifty years old, and is gradually coming down to five-and-twenty ; for he's younger every birth-day than he was the year before."

"So he is, brother Charles, so he is," replied brother Ned. "There's not a doubt about it."

"Remember, Tim," said brother Charles, "that we dine at half-past five to-day instead of two o'clock ; we always depart from our usual custom on this anniversary, as you very well know, Tim Linkinwater. Mr. Nickleby, my dear sir, you will make one. Tim Linkinwater, give me your snuff-box as a remembrance to brother Charles and myself of an attached and faithful rascal, and take that in exchange as a feeble mark of our respect and esteem, and don't open it until you go to bed, and never say another word upon the subject, or I'll kill the blackbird. A dog ! He should have had a golden cage half-a-dozen years ago, if it would have made him or his master a bit the happier. Now, brother Ned, my dear fellow, I'm ready. At half-past five, remember, Mr. Nickleby. Tim Linkinwater, sir, take care of Mr. Nickleby at half-past five. Now, brother Ned."

Chattering away thus, according to custom, to prevent the possibility of any thanks or acknowledgment being expressed on the other side, the twins trotted off arm in arm, having endowed Tim Linkinwater with a costly gold snuff-box, inclosing a bank-note worth more than its value ten times told.

At a quarter past five o'clock, punctual to the minute, arrived, according to annual usage, Tim Linkinwater's sister ; and a great to-do there was between Tim Linkinwater's sister and the old house-keeper respecting Tim Linkinwater's sister's cap, which had been despatched, per boy, from the house of the family where Tim Linkinwater's sister boarded, and had not yet come to hand : notwithstanding that it had been packed up in a bandbox, and the bandbox in a handkerchief, and the handkerchief tied on to the boy's arm ; and notwithstanding, too, that the place of its consignment had been duly set forth at full length on the back of an old letter, and the boy enjoined, under pain of divers horrible penalties, the full extent of which the eye of man could not foresee, to deliver the same with all possible speed and not to loiter by the way. Tim Linkinwater's sister lamented ; the housekeeper condoled, and both kept thrusting their heads out of the second-floor window to see if the boy was " coming,"—which would have been highly satisfactory, and, upon the whole, tantamount to his being come, as the distance to the corner was not quite five yards—when all of a sudden, and when he was least expected, the messenger, carrying the bandbox with elaborate caution, appeared in an exactly opposite direction, puffing and panting for breath, and flushed with recent exercise, as well he might be ; for he had taken the air, in the first instance, be-- hind a hackney-coach that went to Camberwell, and had followed two

Punches afterwards, and had seen the Stilts home to their own door. The cap was all safe, however—that was one comfort—and it was no use scolding him—that was another; so the boy went upon his way rejoicing, and Tim Linkinwater's sister presented herself to the company below stairs just five minutes after the half-hour had struck by Tim Linkinwater's own infallible clock.

The company consisted of the brothers Cheeryble, Tim Linkinwater, a ruddy-faced white-headed friend of Tim's, (who was a superannuated bank clerk,) and Nicholas, who was presented to Tim Linkinwater's sister with much gravity and solemnity. The party being now complete, brother Ned rang for dinner, and, dinner being shortly afterwards announced, led Tim Linkinwater's sister into the next room where it was set forth with great preparation. Then brother Ned took the head of the table and brother Charles the foot; and Tim Linkinwater's sister sat on the left-hand of brother Ned, and Tim Linkinwater himself on his right; and an ancient butler of apoplectic appearance, and with very short legs, took up his position at the back of brother Ned's arm-chair, and, waving his right arm preparatory to taking off the covers with a flourish, stood bolt upright and motionless.

"For these and all other blessings, brother Charles," said Ned.

"Lord, make us truly thankful, brother Ned," said Charles.

Whereupon the apoplectic butler whisked off the top of the soup tureen, and shot all at once into a state of violent activity.

There was abundance of conversation, and little fear of its ever flagging, for the good-humour of the glorious old twins drew everybody out, and Tim Linkinwater's sister went off into a long and circumstantial account of Tim Linkinwater's infancy, immediately after the very first glass of champagne—taking care to premise that she was very much Tim's junior, and had only become acquainted with the facts from their being preserved and handed down in the family. This history concluded, brother Ned related how that, exactly thirty-five years ago, Tim Linkinwater was suspected to have received a love-letter, and how that vague information had been brought to the counting-house of his having been seen walking down Cheapside with an uncommonly handsome spinster; at which there was a roar of laughter, and Tim Linkinwater being charged with blushing, and called upon to explain, denied that the accusation was true; and further, that there would have been any harm in it if it had been; which last position occasioned the superannuated bank clerk to laugh tremendously, and to declare that it was the very best thing he had ever heard in his life, and that Tim Linkinwater might say a great many things before he said anything which would beat *that*.

There was one little ceremony peculiar to the day, both the matter and manner of which made a very strong impression upon Nicholas. The cloth having been removed and the decanters sent round for the first time, a profound silence succeeded, and in the cheerful faces of the brothers there appeared an expression, not of absolute melancholy, but of quiet thoughtfulness very unusual at a festive table. As Nicholas, struck by this sudden alteration, was wondering what it could portend, the brothers rose together, and the one at the top of the table leaning forward towards the other, and speaking in a low voice as if he were addressing him individually, said—

"Brother Charles, my dear fellow, there is another association connected with this day which must never be forgotten, and never can be forgotten, by you and me. This day, which brought into the world a most faithful and excellent and exemplary fellow, took from it the kindest and very best of parents—the very best of parents to us both. I wish that she could have seen us in our prosperity, and shared it, and had the happiness of knowing how dearly we loved her in it, as we did when we were two poor boys—but that was not to be. My dear brother—The Memory of our Mother."

"Good God!" thought Nicholas, "and there are scores of people of their own station, knowing all this, and twenty thousand times more, who wouldn't ask these men to dinner because they eat with their knives and never went to school!"

But there was no time to moralize, for the joviality again became very brisk, and the decanter of port being nearly out, brother Ned pulled the bell, which was instantly answered by the apoplectic butler.

"David," said brother Ned.

"Sir," replied the butler.

"A magnum of the double-diamond, David, to drink the health of Mr. Linkinwater."

Instantly, by a feat of dexterity, which was the admiration of all the company, and had been annually for some years past, the apoplectic butler bringing his left hand from behind the small of his back, produced the bottle with the corkscrew already inserted; uncorked it at a jerk, and placed the magnum and the cork before his master with the dignity of conscious cleverness.

"Ha!" said brother Ned, first examining the cork and afterwards filling his glass, while the old butler looked complacently and amiably on, as if it were all his own property but the company were quite welcome to make free with it, "this looks well, David."

"It ought to, sir," replied David. "You'd be troubled to find such a glass of wine as is our double-diamond, and that Mr. Linkinwater knows very well. That was laid down when Mr. Linkinwater first come, that wine was, gentlemen."

"Nay, David, nay," interposed brother Charles.

"I wrote the entry in the cellar-book myself, sir, if you please," said David, in the tone of a man, quite confident in the strength of his facts. "Mr. Linkinwater had only been here twenty year, sir, when that pipe of double-diamond was laid down."

"David is quite right—quite right, brother Charles," said Ned: "are the people here, David?"

"Outside the door, sir," replied the butler.

"Show 'em in, David, show 'em in."

At this bidding, the old butler placed before his master a small tray of clean glasses, and opening the door admitted the jolly porters and warehousemen whom Nicholas had seen below. There were four in all, and as they came in, bowing, and grinning, and blushing, the house-keeper and cook and housemaid brought up the rear.

" Seven," said brother Ned, filling a corresponding number of glasses with the double-diamond, " and David, eight—There. Now, you're all of you to drink the health of your best friend Mr. Timothy Linkin-water, and wish him health and long life and many happy returns of this day, both for his own sake and that of your old masters, who consider him an inestimable treasure. Tim Linkinwater, sir, your health. Devil take you, Tim Linkinwater, sir, God bless you."

With this singular contradiction of terms, brother Ned gave Tim Linkinwater a slap on the back which made him look for the moment almost as apoplectic as the butler: and tossed off the contents of his glass in a twinkling.

The toast was scarcely drunk with all honour to Tim Linkinwater, when the sturdiest and jolliest subordinate elbowed himself a little in advance of his fellows, and exhibiting a very hot and flushed counte-nance, pulled a single lock of grey hair in the middle of his forehead as a respectful salute to the company, and delivered himself as follows—rubbing the palms of his hands very hard on a blue cotton handkerchief as he did so :

" We 're allowed to take a liberty once a year, gen'lemen, and if you please we'll take it now; there being no time like the present, and no two birds in the hand worth one in the bush, as is well known—least-ways in a contrairy sense, which the meaning is the same. (A pause—the butler unconvinced.) What we mean to say is, that there never was (looking at the butler)—such—(looking at the cook) noble—excel-lent—(looking everywhere and seeing nobody) free, generous, spirited masters as them as has treated us so handsome this day. And here's thanking 'em for all their goodness as is so constancy a diffusing of itself over everywhere, and wishing they may live long and die happy !"

When the foregoing speech was over, and it might have been much more elegant and much less to the purpose, the whole body of subordi-nates under command of the apoplectic butler gave three soft cheers ; which, to that gentleman's great indignation, were not very regular, inasmuch as the women persisted in giving an immense number of little shrill hurrahs among themselves, in utter disregard of the time. This done, they withdrew; shortly afterwards, Tim Linkinwater's sister withdrew; and in reasonable time after that, the sitting was broken up for tea and coffee and a round game of cards.

At half-past ten—late hours for the square—there appeared a little tray of sandwiches and a bowl of bishop, which bishop coming on the top of the double-diamond, and other excitements, had such an effect upon Tim Linkinwater, that he drew Nicholas aside, and gave him to understand confidentially that it was quite true about the uncommonly handsome spinster, and that she was to the full as good-looking as she had been described—more so, indeed—but that she was in too much of a hurry to change her condition, and consequently, while Tim was courting her and thinking of changing his, got married to somebody else. " After all, I dare say it was my fault," said Tim. " I 'll show you a print I have got up stairs, one of these days. It cost me five-and-twenty shillings. I bought it soon after we were cool to each other. Don't mention it, but it's the most extraordinary accidental likeness you ever saw—her very portrait, sir !"

By this time it was past eleven o'clock, and Tim Linkinwater's sister declaring that she ought to have been at home a full hour ago, a coach was procured, into which she was handed with great ceremony by brother Ned, while brother Charles imparted the fullest directions to the coachman, and, besides paying the man a shilling over and above his fare in order that he might take the utmost care of the lady, all but choked him with a glass of spirits of uncommon strength, and then nearly knocked all the breath out of his body in his energetic endeavours to knock it in again.

At length the coach rumbled off, and Tim Linkinwater's sister being now fairly on her way home, Nicholas and Tim Linkinwater's friend took their leaves together, and left old Tim and the worthy brothers to their repose.

As Nicholas had some distance to walk, it was considerably past midnight by the time he reached home, where he found his mother and Smike sitting up to receive him. It was long after their usual hour of retiring, and they had expected him at the very latest two hours ago ; but the time had not hung heavily on their hands, for Mrs. Nickleby had entertained Smike with a genealogical account of her family by the mother's side, comprising biographical sketches of the principal members, and Smike had sat wondering what it was all about, and whether it was learnt from a book, or said out of Mrs. Nickleby's own head ; so that they got on together very pleasantly.

Nicholas could not go to bed without expatiating on the excellences and munificence of the Brothers Cheeryble, and relating the great success which had attended his efforts that day. But before he had said a dozen words, Mrs. Nickleby with many sly winks and nods, observed, that she was sure Mr. Smike must be quite tired out, and that she positively must insist on his not sitting up a minute longer.

"A most biddable creature he is, to be sure," said Mrs. Nickleby, when Smike had wished them good night and left the room. "I know you'll excuse me, Nicholas, my dear, but I don't like to do this before a third person ; indeed, before a young man it would not be quite proper, though really after all, I don't know what harm there is in it, except that to be sure it's not a very becoming thing, though some people say it is very much so, and really I don't know why it should not be, if it's well got up, and the borders are small-plaited ; of course, a good deal depends upon that."

With which preface Mrs. Nickleby took her night-cap from between the leaves of a very large prayer-book where it had been folded up small, and proceeded to tie it on : talking away in her usual discursive manner all the time.

"People may say what they like," observed Mrs. Nickleby, " but there's a great deal of comfort in a night-cap, as I'm sure you would confess, Nicholas my dear, if you would only have strings to yours,

and wear it like a christian, instead of sticking it upon the very top of
your head like a blue-coat boy; you needn't think it an unmanly or
quizzical thing to be particular about your night-cap, for I have often
heard your poor dear papa, and the reverend Mr. what's his name, who
used to read prayers in that old church with the curious little steeple
that the weathercock was blown off the night week before you were
born, I have often heard them say, that the young men at college are
uncommonly particular about their nightcaps, and that the Oxford
nightcaps are quite celebrated for their strength and goodness; so much
so, indeed, that the young men never dream of going to bed without
'em, and I believe it's admitted on all hands that *they* know what's
good, and don't coddle themselves."

Nicholas laughed, and entering no further into the subject of this
lengthened harangue, reverted to the pleasant tone of the little birth-
day party. And as Mrs. Nickleby instantly became very curious
respecting it, and made a great number of inquiries touching what they
had had for dinner, and how it was put on table, and whether it was
overdone or underdone, and who was there, and what "the Mr.
Cherrybles" said, and what Nicholas said, and what the Mr. Cherrybles said when he said that; Nicholas described the festivities at full
length, and also the occurrences of the morning.

"Late as it is," said Nicholas, "I am almost selfish enough to wish
that Kate had been up; to hear all this. I was all impatience, as I
came along, to tell her."

"Why, Kate" said Mrs. Nickleby, putting her feet upon the
fender, and drawing her chair close to it, as if settling herself for a long
talk. "Kate has been in bed—oh! a couple of hours—and I'm very
glad, Nicholas my dear, that I prevailed upon her not to sit up, for I
wished very much to have an opportunity of saying a few words to
you. I am naturally anxious about it, and of course it's a very delightful and consoling thing to have a grown-up son that one can put
confidence in, and advise with—indeed I don't know any use there
would be in having sons at all, unless people could put confidence in
them."

Nicholas stopped in the middle of a sleepy yawn, as his mother
began to speak, and looked at her with fixed attention.

"There was a lady in our neighbourhood," said Mrs. Nickleby,
"speaking of sons puts me in mind of it—a lady in our neighbourhood
when we lived near Dawlish, I think her name was Rogers; indeed I
am sure it was if it wasn't Murphy, which is the only doubt I
have—"

"Is it about her, mother, that you wished to speak to me?" said
Nicholas, quietly.

"About *her*!" cried Mrs. Nickleby. "Good gracious, Nicholas, my
dear, how *can* you be so ridiculous? But that was always the way
with your poor dear papa,—just his way, always wandering, never able
to fix his thoughts on any one subject for two minutes together. I
think I see him now!" said Mrs. Nickleby, wiping her eyes, "looking
at me while I was talking to him about his affairs, just as if his ideas

were in a state of perfect conglomeration! Anybody who had come in upon us suddenly, would have supposed I was confusing and distracting him instead of making things plainer; upon my word they would!"

"I am very sorry, mother, that I should inherit this unfortunate slowness of apprehension," said Nicholas, kindly, "but I'll do my best to understand you if you'll only go straight on, indeed I will."

"Your poor papa!" said Mrs. Nickleby, pondering. "He never knew, 'till it was too late, what I would have had him do!"

This was undoubtedly the case, inasmuch as the deceased Mr. Nickleby had not arrived at the knowledge when he died. Neither had Mrs. Nickleby herself; which is in some sort an explanation of the circumstance.

"However," said Mrs. Nickleby, drying her tears, "this has nothing to do—certainly, nothing whatever to do—with the gentleman in the next house."

"I should suppose that the gentleman in the next house has as little to do with us," returned Nicholas.

"There can be no doubt," said Mrs. Nickleby, "that he *is* a gentleman, and has the manners of a gentleman, and the appearance of a gentleman, although he does wear smalls and grey worsted stockings. That may be eccentricity, or he may be proud of his legs. I don't see why he shouldn't be. The Prince Regent was proud of his legs, and so was Daniel Lambert, who was also a fat man; *he* was proud of his legs. So was Miss Biffin: she was—no," added Mrs. Nickleby, correcting herself, "I think she had only toes, but the principle is the same."

Nicholas looked on, quite amazed at the introduction of this new theme, which seemed just what Mrs. Nickleby had expected him to be.

"You may well be surprised, Nicholas, my dear," she said, "I am sure *I* was. It came upon me like a flash of fire, and almost froze my blood. The bottom of his garden joins the bottom of ours, and of course I had several times seen him sitting among the scarlet-beans in his little arbour, or working at his little hot-beds. I used to think he stared rather, but I didn't take any particular notice of that, as we were new-comers, and he might be curious to see what we were like. But when he began to throw his cucumbers over our wall—"

"To throw his cucumbers over our wall!" repeated Nicholas, in great astonishment.

"Yes, Nicholas, my dear," replied Mrs. Nickleby, in a very serious tone; "his cucumbers over our wall. And vegetable-marrows likewise."

"Confound his impudence!" said Nicholas, firing immediately. "What does he mean by that?"

"I don't think he means it impertinently at all," replied Mrs. Nickleby.

"What!" said Nicholas, "cucumbers and vegetable-marrows flying at the heads of the family as they walk in their own garden, and not meant impertinently! Why, mother—"

Nicholas stopped short, for there was an indescribable expression of placid triumph, mingled with a modest confusion, lingering between the borders of Mrs. Nickleby's nightcap which arrested his attention suddenly.

" He must be a very weak, and foolish, and inconsiderate man," said Mrs. Nickleby ; " blameable indeed—at least I suppose other people would consider him so ; of course I can't be expected to express any opinion on that point, especially after always defending your poor dear papa when other people blamed him for making proposals to me ; and to be sure there can be no doubt that he has taken a very singular way of showing it. Still at the same time, his attentions are—that is, as far as it goes, and to a certain extent of course—a flattering sort of thing ; and although I should never dream of marrying again with a dear girl like Kate still unsettled in life—"

" Surely, mother, such an idea never entered your brain for an instant ? " said Nicholas.

" Bless my heart, Nicholas my dear," returned his mother in a peevish tone, " isn't that precisely what I am saying, if you would only let me speak ? Of course, I never gave it a second thought, and I am surprised and astonished that you should suppose me capable of such a thing. All I say, is, what step is the best to take so as to reject these advances civilly and delicately, and without hurting his feelings too much, and driving him to despair, or anything of that kind ? My goodness me ! " exclaimed Mrs. Nickleby, with a half simper, " suppose he was to go doing anything rash to himself, could I ever be happy again Nicholas ? "

Despite his vexation and concern, Nicholas could scarcely help smiling, as he rejoined, " Now, do you think, mother, that such a result would be likely to ensue from the most cruel repulse ? "

" Upon my word, my dear, I don't know," returned Mrs. Nickleby ; " really, I don't know. I am sure there was a case in the day before yesterday's paper, extracted from one of the French newspapers, about a journeyman shoemaker who was jealous of a young girl in an adjoining village, because she wouldn't shut herself up in an air-tight three-pair-of stairs and charcoal herself to death with him, and who went and hid himself in a Wood with a sharp-pointed knife, and rushed out as she was passing by with a few friends, and killed himself first, and then all the friends, and then her—no, killed all the friends first, and then herself, and then *him*self—which it is quite frightful to think of. Somehow or other," added Mrs. Nickleby, after a momentary pause, " they always *are* journeyman shoemakers who do these things in France, according to the papers. I don't know how it is—something in the leather, I suppose."

" But this man, who is not a shoemaker—what has he done, mother, what has he said ? " inquired Nicholas, fretted almost beyond endurance, but looking nearly as resigned and patient as Mrs. Nickleby herself. " You know, there is no language of vegetables which converts a cucumber into a formal declaration of attachment."

" My dear," replied Mrs. Nickleby, tossing her head and looking at the ashes in the grate, " he has done and said all sorts of things."

"Is there no mistake on your part?" asked Nicholas.

"Mistake!" cried Mrs. Nickleby. "Lord, Nicholas my dear, do you suppose I don't know when a man's in earnest?"

"Well, well!" muttered Nicholas.

"Every time I go to the window," said Mrs. Nickleby, "he kisses one hand, and lays the other upon his heart—of course it's very foolish of him to do so, and I dare say you'll say it's very wrong, but he does it very respectfully—very respectfully indeed—and very tenderly, extremely tenderly. So far he deserves the greatest credit: there can be no doubt about that. Then there are the presents which come pouring over the wall every day, and very fine they certainly are, very fine; we had one of the cucumbers at dinner yesterday, and think of pickling the rest for next winter. And last evening," added Mrs. Nickleby, with increased confusion, "he called gently over the wall, as I was walking in the garden, and proposed marriage and an elopement. His voice is as clear as a bell or a musical glass—very like a musical glass indeed—but of course I didn't listen to it. Then the question is, Nicholas my dear, what am I to do?"

"Does Kate know of this?" asked Nicholas.

"I have not said a word about it yet," answered his mother.

"Then for Heaven's sake," rejoined Nicholas, rising, "do not, for it would make her very unhappy. And with regard to what you should do, my dear mother, do what your better sense and feeling, and respect for my father's memory, would prompt. There are a thousand ways in which you can show your dislike of these preposterous and doting attentions. If you act as decidedly as you ought, and they are still continued, and to your annoyance, I can speedily put a stop to them. But I should not interfere in a matter so ridiculous, and attach importance to it, until you have vindicated yourself. Most women can do that, but especially one of your age and condition in circumstances like these, which are unworthy of a serious thought. I would not shame you by seeming to take them to heart, or treat them earnestly for an instant. Absurd old idiot!"

So saying, Nicholas kissed his mother and bade her good night, and they retired to their respective chambers.

To do Mrs. Nickleby justice, her attachment to her children would have prevented her seriously contemplating a second marriage, even if she could have so far conquered her recollections of her late husband as to have any strong inclinations that way. But, although there was no evil and little real selfishness in Mrs. Nickleby's heart, she had a weak head and a vain one; and there was something so flattering in being sought (and vainly sought) in marriage at this time of day, that she could not dismiss the passion of the unknown gentleman quite so summarily or lightly as Nicholas appeared to deem becoming.

"As to its being preposterous, and doting, and ridiculous," thought Mrs. Nickleby, communing with herself in her own room, "I don't see that at all. It's hopeless on his part, certainly; but why he should be an absurd idiot, I confess I don't see. He is not to be supposed to know it's hopeless. Poor fellow, he is to be pitied, *I* think!"

Having made these reflections, Mrs. Nickleby looked in her little dressing-glass, and walking backward a few steps from it tried to remember who it was who used to say that when Nicholas was one-and-twenty he would have more the appearance of her brother than her son. Not being able to call the authority to mind, she extinguished her candle, and drew up the window-blind to admit the light of morning which had by this time begun to dawn.

"It's a bad light to distinguish objects in," murmured Mrs. Nickleby, peering into the garden, "and my eyes are not very good—I was short-sighted from a child—but, upon my word, I think there's another large vegetable-marrow sticking at this moment on the broken glass bottles at the top of the wall!"

CHAPTER XXXVIII.

COMPRISES CERTAIN PARTICULARS ARISING OUT OF A VISIT OF CON-
DOLENCE, WHICH MAY PROVE IMPORTANT HEREAFTER. SMIKE
UNEXPECTEDLY ENCOUNTERS A VERY OLD FRIEND, WHO INVITES
HIM TO HIS HOUSE, AND WILL TAKE NO DENIAL.

QUITE unconscious of the demonstrations of their amorous neighbour, or their effects upon the susceptible bosom of her mama, Kate Nickleby had, by this time begun to enjoy a settled feeling of tranquillity and happiness, to which, even in occasional and transitory glimpses, she had long been a stranger. Living under the same roof with the beloved brother from whom she had been so suddenly and hardly separated ; with a mind at ease, and free from any persecutions which could call a blush into her cheek, or a pang into her heart, she seemed to have passed into a new state of being. Her former cheerfulness was restored, her step regained its elasticity and lightness, the colour which had forsaken her cheek visited it once again, and Kate Nickleby looked more beautiful than ever.

Such was the result to which Miss La Creevy's ruminations and observations led her, when the cottage had been, as she emphatically said, "thoroughly got to rights, from the chimney-pots to the street-door scraper," and the busy little woman had at length a moment's time to think about its inmates.

"Which I declare I haven't had since I first came down here," said Miss La Creevy, "for I have thought of nothing but hammers, nails, screw-drivers and gimlets, morning, noon, and night."

"You never bestow one thought upon yourself, I believe," returned Kate, smiling.

"Upon my word, my dear, when there are so many pleasanter things to think of, I should be a goose if I did," said Miss La Creevy. "By the bye, I have thought of somebody too. Do you know, that I observe a great change in one of this family—a very extraordinary change ? "

"In whom?" asked Kate, anxiously. "Not in—"

"Not in your brother, my dear," returned Miss La Creevy, anticipating the close of the sentence, "for he is always the same affectionate good-natured clever creature, with a spice of the—I won't say who—in him when there's any occasion, that he was when I first knew you. No. Smike, as he will be called, poor fellow! for he won't hear of a *Mr.* before his name, is greatly altered, even in this short time."

"How?" asked Kate. "Not in health?"

"N-n-o; perhaps not in health exactly," said Miss La Creevy, pausing to consider, "although he is a worn and feeble creature, and has that in his face which it would wring my heart to see in yours. No; not in health."

"How then?"

"I scarcely know," said the miniature-painter. "But I have watched him, and he has brought the tears into my eyes many times. It is not a very difficult matter to do that, certainly, for I am very easily melted; still, I think these came with good cause and reason. I am sure that since he has been here, he has grown, from some strong cause, more conscious of his weak intellect. He feels it more. It gives him greater pain to know that he wanders sometimes, and cannot understand very simple things. I have watched him when you have not been by, my dear, sit brooding by himself with such a look of pain as I could scarcely bear to see, and then get up and leave the room: so sorrowfully, and in such dejection, that I cannot tell you how it has hurt me. Not three weeks ago, he was a light-hearted busy creature, overjoyed to be in a bustle, and as happy as the day was long. Now, he is another being—the same willing, harmless, faithful, loving creature—but the same in nothing else."

"Surely this will all pass off," said Kate. "Poor fellow!"

"I hope," returned her little friend, with a gravity very unusual in her, "it may. I hope, for the sake of that poor lad, it may. However," said Miss La Creevy, relapsing into the cheerful, chattering tone, which was habitual to her, "I have said my say, and a very long say it is, and a very wrong say too, I shouldn't wonder at all. I shall cheer him up to-night at all events, for if he is to be my squire all the way to the Strand, I shall talk on, and on, and on, and never leave off, till I have roused him into a laugh at something. So the sooner he goes the better for him, and the sooner I go, the better for me, I am sure, or else I shall have my maid gallivanting with somebody who may rob the house—though what there is to take away besides tables and chairs, I don't know, except the miniatures, and he is a clever thief who can dispose of them to any great advantage, for *I* can't, I know, and that's the honest truth."

So saying, little Miss La Creevy hid her face in a very flat bonnet, and herself in a very big shawl, and fixing herself tightly into the latter by means of a large pin, declared that the omnibus might come as soon as it pleased, for she was quite ready.

But there was still Mrs. Nickleby to take leave of; and long before that good lady had concluded some reminiscences, bearing upon and appropriate to the occasion, the omnibus arrived. This put Miss La Creevy in a great bustle, in consequence whereof, as she secretly rewarded the servant-girl with eighteen-pence behind the street-door, she pulled out of her reticule ten-pennyworth of halfpence which rolled into all possible corners of the passage, and occupied some considerable time in the picking-up. This ceremony had, of course, to be succeeded by a second kissing of Kate and Mrs. Nickleby, and a gathering together of the little basket and the brown-paper parcel, during which proceedings, "the omnibus," as Miss La Creevy protested, "swore so dreadfully, that it was quite awful to hear it." At length and at last, it made a feint of going away, and then Miss La Creevy darted out and darted in, apologising with great volubility to all the passengers, and declaring that she wouldn't purposely have kept them waiting on any account whatever. While she was looking about for a convenient seat, the conductor pushed Smike in, and cried that it was all right—though it wasn't—and away went the huge vehicle, with the noise of half a dozen brewers' drays at least.

Leaving it to pursue its journey at the pleasure of the conductor afore-mentioned, who lounged gracefully on his little shelf behind, smoking an odoriferous cigar; and leaving it to stop, or go on, or gallop, or crawl, as that gentleman deemed expedient and advisable, this narrative may embrace the opportunity of ascertaining the condition of Sir Mulberry Hawk, and to what extent he had by this time recovered from the injuries consequent upon being flung violently from his cabriolet, under the circumstances already detailed.

With a shattered limb, a body severely bruised, a face disfigured by half-healed scars, and pallid from the exhaustion of recent pain and fever, Sir Mulberry Hawk lay stretched upon his back, on the couch to which he was doomed to be a prisoner for some weeks yet to come. Mr. Pyke and Mr. Pluck sat drinking hard in the next room, now and then varying the monotonous murmurs of their conversation with a half-smothered laugh, while the young lord—the only member of the party who was not thoroughly irredeemable, and who really had a kind heart—sat beside his Mentor, with a cigar in his mouth, and read to him, by the light of a lamp, such scraps of intelligence from a paper of the day as were most likely to yield him interest or amusement.

"Curse those hounds!" said the invalid, turning his head impatiently towards the adjoining room; "will nothing stop their infernal throats?"

Messrs. Pyke and Pluck heard the exclamation, and stopped immediately, winking to each other as they did so, and filling their glasses to the brim, as some recompense for the deprivation of speech.

"Damn!" muttered the sick man between his teeth, and writhing impatiently in his bed. "Isn't this mattrass hard enough, and the room dull enough, and the pain bad enough, but *they* must torture me? What's the time?"

"Half-past eight," replied his friend.

"Here, draw the table nearer, and let us have the cards again," said Sir Mulberry. "More piquet. Come."

It was curious to see how eagerly the sick man, debarred from any change of position save the mere turning of his head from side to side, watched every motion of his friend in the progress of the game; and with what eagerness and interest he played, and yet how warily and coolly. His address and skill were more than twenty times a match for his adversary, who could make little head against them, even when fortune favoured him with good cards, which was not often the case. Sir Mulberry won every game; and when his companion threw down the cards, and refused to play any longer, thrust forth his wasted arm and caught up the stakes with a boastful oath, and the same hoarse laugh, though considerably lowered in tone, that had resounded in Ralph Nickleby's dining-room months before.

While he was thus occupied, his man appeared, to announce that Mr. Ralph Nickleby was below, and wished to know how he was to-night.

"Better," said Sir Mulberry, impatiently.

"Mr. Nickleby wishes to know, sir——"

"I tell you, better," replied Sir Mulberry, striking his hand upon the table.

The man hesitated for a moment or two, and then said that Mr. Nickleby had requested permission to see Sir Mulberry Hawk, if it was not inconvenient.

"It *is* inconvenient. I can't see him. I can't see anybody," said his master, more violently than before. "You know that, you blockhead."

"I am very sorry, sir," returned the man. "But Mr. Nickleby pressed so much, sir——"

The fact was, that Ralph Nickleby had bribed the man, who, being anxious to earn his money with a view to future favours, held the door in his hand, and ventured to linger still.

"Did he say whether he had any business to speak about?" inquired Sir Mulberry, after a little impatient consideration.

"No, sir. He said he wished to see you, sir. Particularly, Mr. Nickleby said, sir."

"Tell him to come up. Here," cried Sir Mulberry, calling the man back, as he passed his hand over his disfigured face, "move that lamp, and put it on the stand behind me. Wheel that table away, and place a chair there—further off. Leave it so."

The man obeyed these directions as if he quite comprehended the motive with which they were dictated, and left the room. Lord Verisopht, remarking that he would look in presently, strolled into the adjoining apartment, and closed the folding-door behind him.

Then was heard a subdued footstep on the stairs; and Ralph Nickleby, hat in hand, crept softly into the room, with his body bent forward as if in profound respect, and his eyes fixed upon the face of his worthy client.

"Well, Nickleby," said Sir Mulberry, motioning him to the chair by the couch side, and waving his hand in assumed carelessness, "I have had a bad accident, you see."

" I see," rejoined Ralph, with the same steady gaze. " Bad, indeed! I should not have known you, Sir Mulberry. Dear, dear. This *is* bad."

Ralph's manner was one of profound humility and respect ; and the low tone of voice was that which the gentlest consideration for a sick man would have taught a visitor to assume. But the expression of his face, Sir Mulberry's being averted, was in extraordinary contrast ; and as he stood, in his usual attitude, calmly looking on the prostrate form before him, all that part of his features which was not cast into shadow by his protruding and contracted brows, bore the impress of a sarcastic smile.

" Sit down," said Sir Mulberry, turning towards him as though by a violent effort. " Am I a sight, that you stand gazing there ? "

As he turned his face, Ralph recoiled a step or two, and making as though he were irresistibly impelled to express astonishment, but was determined not to do so, sat down with well-acted confusion.

" I have inquired at the door, Sir Mulberry, every day," said Ralph, " twice a day, indeed, at first—and to-night, presuming upon old acquaintance, and past transactions by which we have mutually benefited in some degree, I could not resist soliciting admission to your chamber. Have you—have you suffered much ? " said Ralph, bending forward, and allowing the same harsh smile to gather upon his face, as the other closed his eyes.

" More than enough to please me, and less than enough to please some broken-down hacks that you and I know of, and who lay their ruin between us, I dare say," returned Sir Mulberry, tossing his arm restlessly upon the coverlet.

Ralph shrugged his shoulders in deprecation of the intense irritation with which this had been said, for there was an aggravating cold distinctness in his speech and manner which so grated on the sick man that he could scarcely endure it.

" And what is it in these ' past transactions,' that brought you here to-night ? " asked Sir Mulberry.

" Nothing," replied Ralph. " There are some bills of my lord's which need renewal, but let them be till you are well. I—I—came," said Ralph, speaking more slowly, and with harsher emphasis, " I came to say how grieved I am that any relative of mine, although disowned by me, should have inflicted such punishment on you as——"

" Punishment ! " interposed Sir Mulberry.

" I know it has been a severe one," said Ralph, wilfully mistaking the meaning of the interruption, " and that has made me the more anxious to tell you that I disown this vagabond—that I acknowledge him as no kin of mine—and that I leave him to take his deserts from you and every man besides. You may wring his neck if you please. *I* shall not interfere."

" This story that they tell me here, has got abroad then, has it ? " asked Sir Mulberry, clenching his hands and teeth.

" Noised in all directions," replied Ralph. " Every club and gaming-room has rung with it. There has been a good song made about it, as

I am told," said Ralph, looking eagerly at his questioner. "I have not heard it myself, not being in the way of such things, but I have been told it's even printed—for private circulation, but that's all over town, of course."

"It's a lie!" said Sir Mulberry; "I tell you it's all a lie. The mare took fright."

"They *say* he frightened her," observed Ralph, in the same unmoved and quiet manner. "Some say he frightened you, but *that's* a lie, I know. I have said that boldly—oh, a score of times! I am a peaceable man, but I can't hear folks tell that of you—No, no."

When Sir Mulberry found coherent words to utter, Ralph bent forward with his hand to his ear, and a face as calm as if its every line of sternness had been cast in iron.

"When I am off this cursed bed," said the invalid, actually striking at his broken leg in the ecstacy of his passion, "I'll have such revenge as never man had yet. By G— I will! Accident favouring him, he has marked me for a week or two, but I'll put a mark on him that he shall carry to his grave. I'll slit his nose and ears—flog him—maim him for life. I'll do more than that; I'll drag that pattern of chastity, that pink of prudery, the delicate sister, through——"

It might have been that even Ralph's cold blood tingled in his cheeks at that moment. It might have been that Sir Mulberry remembered that, knave and usurer as he was, he must, in some early time of infancy, have twined his arm about her father's neck. He stopped, and, menacing with his hand, confirmed the unuttered threat with a tremendous oath.

"It is a galling thing," said Ralph, after a short term of silence, during which he had eyed the sufferer keenly, "to think that the man about town, the rake, the *roué*, the rook of twenty seasons, should be brought to this pass by a mere boy!"

Sir Mulberry darted a wrathful look at him, but Ralph's eyes were bent upon the ground, and his face wore no other expression than one of thoughtfulness.

"A raw slight stripling," continued Ralph, "against a man whose very weight might crush him; to say nothing of his skill in—I am right, I think," said Ralph, raising his eyes, "you *were* a patron of the ring once, were you not?"

The sick man made an impatient gesture, which Ralph chose to consider as one of acquiescence.

"Ha!" he said, "I thought so. That was before I knew you, but I was pretty sure I couldn't be mistaken. He is light and active, I suppose. But those were slight advantages compared with yours. Luck, luck—these hangdog outcasts have it."

"He'll need the most he has when I am well again," said Sir Mulberry Hawk, "let him fly where he will."

"Oh!" returned Ralph quickly, "he doesn't dream of that. He is here, good Sir, waiting your pleasure—here in London, walking the streets at noonday, carrying it off jauntily; looking for you. I swear," said Ralph, his face darkening, and his own hatred getting the upper hand of him for the first time, as this gay picture of Nicholas presented itself; "if we were only citizens of a country where it could be safely done, I'd give good money to have him stabbed to the heart and rolled into the kennel for the dogs to tear."

As Ralph, somewhat to the surprise of his old client, vented this little piece of sound family feeling and took up his hat preparatory to departing, Lord Frederick Verisopht looked in.

"Why what in the devvle's name, Hawk, have you and Nickleby been talking about?" said the young man. "I neyver heard such an insufferable riot. Croak, croak, croak. Bow, wow, wow. What has it all been about?"

"Sir Mulberry has been angry, my Lord," said Ralph, looking towards the couch.

"Not about money, I hope. Nothing has gone wrong in business, has it, Nickleby?"

"No, my Lord, no," returned Ralph. "On that point we always agree. Sir Mulberry has been calling to mind the cause of——"

There was neither necessity nor opportunity for Ralph to proceed; for Sir Mulberry took up the theme, and vented his threats and oaths against Nicholas almost as ferociously as before.

Ralph, who was no common observer, was surprised to see that as this tirade proceeded, the manner of Lord Verisopht, who at the commencement had been twirling his whiskers with a most dandified and listless air, underwent a complete alteration. He was still more surprised when, Sir Mulberry ceasing to speak, the young lord angrily, and almost unaffectedly, requested never to have the subject renewed in his presence.

"Mind that, Hawk," he added with unusual energy, "I never will be a party to, or permit, if I can help it, a cowardly attack upon this young fellow."

"Cowardly, Lord Verisopht!" interrupted his friend.

"Ye-es," said the other, turning full upon him. "If you had told him who you were; if you had given him your card, and found out afterwards that his station or character prevented your fighting him, it would have been bad enough then; upon my soul it would have been bad enough then. As it is, you did wrong. I did wrong too, not to interfere, and I am sorry for it. What happened to you afterwards was as much the consequence of accident as design, and more your fault than his; and it shall not, with my knowledge, be cruelly visited upon him—it shall not indeed."

With this emphatic repetition of his concluding words, the young lord turned upon his heel, but before he had reached the adjoining room he turned back again, and said, with even greater vehemence than he had displayed before,

"I do believe now, upon my honour I do believe, that the sister is as virtuous and modest a young lady as she is a handsome one; and of the brother, I say this, that he acted as her brother should, and in a manly and spirited manner. And I only wish with all my heart and soul that any one of us came out of this matter half as well as he does."

A sudden recognition, unexpected on both sides.

So saying, Lord Frederick Verisopht walked out of the room, leaving Ralph Nickleby and Sir Mulberry in most unpleasant astonishment.

"Is this your pupil?" asked Ralph, softly, "or has he come fresh from some country parson?"

"Green fools take these fits sometimes," replied Sir Mulberry Hawk, biting his lip, and pointing to the door. "Leave him to me."

Ralph exchanged a familiar look with his old acquaintance, for they had suddenly grown confidential again in this alarming surprise, and took his way home thoughtfully and slowly.

While these things were being said and done, and long before they were concluded, the omnibus had disgorged Miss La Creevy and her escort, and they had arrived at her own door. Now, the good-nature of the little minature-painter would by no means allow of Smike's walking back again, until he had been previously refreshed with just a sip of something comfortable and a mixed biscuit or so ; and Smike entertaining no objection either to the sip of something comfortable or the mixed biscuit, but considering on the contrary that they would be a very pleasant preparation for a walk to Bow, it fell out that he delayed much longer than he originally intended, and that it was some half hour after dusk when he set forth on his journey home.

There was no likelihood of his losing his way, for it lay quite straight before him, and he had walked into town with Nicholas, and back alone, almost every day. So, Miss La Creevy and he shook hands with mutual confidence, and being charged with more kind remembrances to Mrs. and Miss Nickleby, Smike started off.

At the foot of Ludgate Hill, he turned a little out of the road to satisfy his curiosity by having a look at Newgate. After staring up at the sombre walls from the opposite side of the way with great care and dread for some minutes, he turned back again into the old track, and walked briskly through the city; stopping now and then to gaze in at the window of some particularly attractive shop, then running for a little way, then stopping again, and so on, as any other country lad might do.

He had been gazing for a long time through a jeweller's window, wishing he could take some of the beautiful trinkets home as a present, and imagining what delight they would afford if he could, when the clocks struck three-quarters past eight; roused by the sound, he hurried on at a very quick pace, and was crossing the corner of a bye street when he felt himself violently brought to, with a jerk so sudden that he was obliged to cling to a lamp-post to save himself from falling. At the same moment, a small boy clung tight round his leg, and a shrill cry of "Here he is, father,—Hooray!" vibrated in his ears.

Smike knew that voice too well. He cast his despairing eyes downwards towards the form from which it had proceeded, and shuddering from head to foot, looked round. Mr. Squeers had hooked him in the coat-collar with the handle of his umbrella, and was hanging on at the other end with all his might and main. The cry of triumph proceeded from Master Wackford, who, regardless of all his kicks and struggles, clung to him with the tenacity of a bull-dog!

One glance showed him this; and in that one glance the terrified creature became utterly powerless and unable to utter a sound.

"Here's a go!" cried Mr. Squeers, gradually coming hand-over-hand down the umbrella, and only unhooking it when he had got tight hold of the victim's collar. "Here's a delicious go! Wackford, my boy, call up one of them coaches."

"A coach, father!" cried little Wackford.

"Yes, a coach, sir," replied Squeers, feasting his eyes upon the countenance of Smike. "Damn the expense.—Let's have him in a coach."

"What's he been a doing of?" asked a labourer, with a hod of bricks, against whom and a fellow-labourer Mr. Squeers had backed, on the first jerk of the umbrella.

"Everything!" replied Mr. Squeers, looking fixedly at his old pupil in a sort of rapturous trance. "Everything—running away, sir—joining in blood-thirsty attacks upon his master, sir—there's nothing that's bad that he hasn't done. Oh, what a delicious go is this here, good Lord!"

The man looked from Squeers to Smike; but such mental faculties as the poor fellow possessed had utterly deserted him. The coach came up; Master Wackford entered; Squeers pushed in his prize, and following close at his heels, pulled up the glasses. The coachman mounted his box and drove slowly off, leaving the two bricklayers, and an old apple-woman, and a town-made little boy returning from an evening school, who had been the only witnesses of the scene, to meditate upon it at their leisure.

Mr. Squeers sat himself down on the opposite seat to the unfortunate Smike, and planting his hands firmly on his knees looked at him for some five minutes, when, seeming to recover from his trance, he uttered a loud laugh, and slapped his old pupil's face several times—taking the right and left sides alternately.

"It isn't a dream!" said Squeers. "That's real flesh and blood, I know the feel of it;" and being quite assured of his good fortune by these experiments, Mr. Squeers administered a few boxes on the ear, lest the entertainments should seem to partake of sameness, and laughed louder and longer at every one.

"Your mother will be fit to jump out of her skin, my boy, when she hears of this," said Squeers to his son.

"Oh, won't she though, father?" replied Master Wackford.

"To think,"—said Squeers, "that you and me should be turning out of a street, and come upon him at the very nick; and that I should have him tight at only one cast of the umbrella, as if I had hooked him with a grappling-iron!—Ha, ha!"

"Didn't I catch hold of his leg, neither, father?" said little Wackford.

"You did; like a good 'un, my boy," said Mr. Squeers, patting his son's head, "and you shall have the best button-over jacket and waistcoat that the next new boy brings down, as a reward of merit—

mind that. You always keep on in the same path, and do them things that you see your father do, and when you die you'll go right slap to Heaven and be asked no questions."

Improving the occasion in these words, Mr. Squeers patted his son's head again, and then patted Smike's—but harder ; and inquired in a bantering tone how he found himself by this time.

" I must go home," replied Smike, looking wildly round.

" To be sure you must. You're about right there," replied Mr. Squeers. " You'll go home very soon, you will. You'll find yourself at the peaceful village of Dotheboys, in Yorkshire, in something under a week's time, my young friend ; and the next time you get away from there, I give you leave to keep away. Where's the clothes you run off in, you ungrateful robber ?" said Mr. Squeers, in a severe voice.

Smike glanced at the neat attire which the care of Nicholas had provided for him, and wrung his hands.

" Do you know that I could hang you up outside of the Old Bailey, for making away with them articles of property ? " said Squeers. "Do you know that it's a hanging matter—and I an't quite certain whether it an't an anatomy one besides—to walk off with up'ards of the valley of five pound from a dwelling-house ? Eh—do you know that ? What do you suppose was the worth of them clothes you had ? Do you know that that Wellington-boot you wore, cost eight-and-twenty shillings when it was a pair, and the shoe seven-and-six ? But you came to the right shop for mercy when you came to me, and thank your stars that it *is* me as has got to serve you with the article."

Anybody not in Mr. Squeers's confidence would have supposed that he was quite out of the article in question, instead of having a large stock on hand ready for all comers ; nor would the opinion of sceptical persons have undergone much alteration when he followed up the remark by poking Smike in the chest with the ferrule of his umbrella, and dealing a smart shower of blows with the ribs of the same instrument upon his head and shoulders.

" I never threshed a boy in a hackney-coach before," said Mr. Squeers, when he stopped to rest. " There's inconveniency in it, but the novelty gives it a sort of relish too !"

Poor Smike ! He warded off the blows as well as he could, and now shrunk into a corner of the coach, with his head resting on his hands, and his elbows on his knees ; he was stunned and stupefied, and had no more idea that any act of his would enable him to escape from the all-powerful Squeers, now that he had no friend to speak to or advise with, than he had had in all the weary years of his Yorkshire life which preceded the arrival of Nicholas.

The journey seemed endless ; street after street was entered and left behind, and still they went jolting on. At last Mr. Squeers began to thrust his head out at the window every half-minute, and to bawl a variety of directions to the coachman ; and after passing, with some difficulty, through several mean streets which the appearance of the houses and the bad state of the road denoted to have been recently built,

Mr. Squeers suddenly tugged at the check string with all his might, and cried, " Stop !"

" What are you pulling a man's arm off for ?" said the coachman, looking angrily down.

" That's the house," replied Squeers. " The second of them four little houses, one story high, with the green shutters—there's a brass plate on the door with the name of Snawley."

" Couldn't you say that, without wrenching a man's limbs off his body ?" inquired the coachman.

" No !" bawled Mr. Squeers. " Say another word, and I'll summons you for having a broken winder. Stop !"

Obedient to this direction, the coach stopped at Mr. Snawley's door. Mr. Snawley may be remembered as the sleek and sanctified gentleman who confided two sons (*in law*) to the parental care of Mr. Squeers, as narrated in the fourth chapter of this history. Mr. Snawley's house was on the extreme borders of some new settlements adjoining Somers Town, and Mr. Squeers had taken lodgings therein for a short time as his stay was longer than usual, and the Saracen, having experience of Master Wackford's appetite, had declined to receive him on any other terms than as a full-grown customer.

" Here we are !" said Squeers, hurrying Smike into the little parlour, where Mr. Snawley and his wife were taking a lobster supper. " Here's the vagrant—the felon—the rebel—the monster of unthankfulness."

" What ! The boy that run away !" cried Snawley, resting his knife and fork upright on the table, and opening his eyes to their full width.

" The very boy," said Squeers, putting his fist close to Smike's nose, and drawing it away again, and repeating the process several times with a vicious aspect. " If there wasn't a lady present, I'd fetch him such a —— : never mind, I'll owe it him."

And here Mr. Squeers related how, and in what manner, and when and where, he had picked up the runaway.

" It's clear that there has been a Providence in it, sir," said Mr. Snawley, casting down his eyes with an air of humility, and elevating his fork with a bit of lobster on the top of it towards the ceiling.

" Providence is against him, no doubt," replied Mr. Squeers, scratching his nose. " Of course, that was to be expected. Anybody might have known that."

" Hard-heartedness and evil-doing will never prosper, sir," said Mr. Snawley.

" Never was such a thing known," rejoined Squeers, taking a roll of notes from his pocket-book, to see that they were all safe.

" I have been, Mrs. Snawley," said Mr. Squeers, when he had satisfied himself upon this point, " I have been that chap's benefactor, feeder, teacher, and clother. I have been that chap's classical, commercial, mathematical, philosophical, and trigonomical friend. My son —my only son, Wackford—has been his brother; Mrs. Squeers has been his mother, grandmother, aunt,—Ah ! and I may say uncle too, all in one. She never cottoned to anybody except them two engaging and delightful boys of yours, as she cottoned to this chap. What's my return? What's come of my milk of human kindness? It turns into curds and whey when I look at him."

" Well it may, sir," said Mrs. Snawley. " Oh ! Well it may, sir." " Where has he been all this time?" inquired Snawley. " Has he been living with —— ? "

" Ah, sir!" interposed Squeers, confronting him again. " Have you been a living with that there devilish Nickleby, sir ?"

But no threats or cuffs could elicit from Smike one word of reply to this question, for he had internally resolved that he would rather perish in the wretched prison to which he was again about to be consigned, than utter one syllable which could involve his first and true friend. He had already called to mind the strict injunctions of secrecy as to his past life, which Nicholas had laid upon him when they travelled from Yorkshire; and a confused and perplexed idea that his benefactor might have committed some terrible crime in bringing him away, which would render him liable to heavy punishment if detected, had contributed in some degree to reduce him to his present state of apathy and terror.

Such were the thoughts—if to visions so imperfect and undefined as those which wandered through his enfeebled brain, the term can be applied—which were present to the mind of Smike, and rendered him deaf alike to intimidation and persuasion. Finding every effort useless, Mr. Squeers conducted him to a little back room up-stairs where he was to pass the night ; and taking the precaution of removing his shoes, and coat and waistcoat, and also of locking the door on the outside, lest he should master up sufficient energy to make an attempt at escape, that worthy gentleman left him to his meditations.

And what those meditations were, and how the poor creature's heart sunk within him when he thought—when did he, for a moment, cease to think ?—of his late home, and the dear friends and familiar faces with which it was associated, cannot be told. To prepare the mind for such a heavy sleep, its growth must be stopped by rigour and cruelty in childhood ; there must be years of misery and suffering lightened by no ray of hope ; the chords of the heart, which beat a quick response to the voice of gentleness and affection, must have rusted and broken in their secret places, and bear the lingering echo of no old word of love or kindness. Gloomy, indeed, must have been the short day, and dull the long, long twilight, which precedes such a night of intellect as his.

There were voices which would have roused him, even then, but their welcome tones could not penetrate there ; and he crept to bed the same listless, hopeless, blighted creature, that Nicholas had first found him at the Yorkshire school.

CHAPTER XXXIX.

IN WHICH ANOTHER OLD FRIEND ENCOUNTERS SMIKE, VERY OPPOR-
TUNELY AND TO SOME PURPOSE.

THE night fraught with so much bitterness to one poor soul had
given place to a bright and cloudless summer morning, when a north-
country mail-coach traversed with cheerful noise the yet silent streets
of Islington, and, giving brisk note of its approach with the lively
winding of the guard's horn, clattered onward to its halting-place hard
by the Post-office.

The only outside passenger was a burly honest-looking countryman
upon the box, who, with his eyes fixed upon the dome of Saint Paul's
Cathedral, appeared so wrapt in admiring wonder, as to be quite insensible to all the bustle of getting out the bags and parcels, until one of
the coach windows being let sharply down, he looked round and
encountered a pretty female face which was just then thrust out.

" See there, lass ! " bawled the countryman, pointing towards the
object of his admiration. " There be Paul's Church. 'Ecod, he be a
soizable 'un, he be."

" Goodness, John ! I shouldn't have thought it could have been half
the size. What a monster ! "

" Monsther !—Ye're aboot right there, I reckon, Mrs. Browdie," said
the countryman good-humouredly, as he came slowly down in his huge
top-coat, " and wa'at dost thee tak yon place to be noo—thot 'un
ower the wa'. Ye'd never coom near it 'gin ye thried for twelve
moonths. It's na' but a Poast-office. Ho ! ho ! They need to charge
for dooble-latthers. A Poast-office ! Wa'at dost thee think o' thot ?
'Ecod, if thot's on'y a Poast-office, I'd loike to see where the Lord
Mayor o' Lunnun lives."

So saying, John Browdie—for he it was—opened the coach-door,
and tapping Mrs. Browdie, late Miss Price, on the cheek as he looked
in, burst into a boisterous fit of laughter.

" Weel ! " said John—" Dang my bootuns if she bea'nt asleep agean ! "

" She's been asleep all night, and was all yesterday, except for a
minute or two now and then," replied John Browdie's choice, " and I
was very sorry when she woke, for she has been *so* cross ! "

The subject of these remarks was a slumbering figure, so muffled in
shawl and cloak that it would have been matter of impossibility to
guess at its sex but for a brown-beaver bonnet and green veil which
ornamented the head, and which, having been crushed and flattened for
two hundred and fifty miles in that particular angle of the vehicle from
which the lady's snores now proceeded, presented an appearance sufficiently ludicrous to have moved less risible muscles than those of John
Browdie's ruddy face.

" Hollo ! " cried John, twitching one end of the dragged veil. " Coom,
wakken oop, will 'ee."

After several burrowings into the old corner, and many exclamations of impatience and fatigue, the figure struggled into a sitting posture; and there, under a mass of crumpled beaver, and surrounded by a semicircle of blue curl-papers, were the delicate features of Miss Fanny Squeers.

"Oh, 'Tilda!" cried Miss Squeers, "How you have been kicking of me through this blessed night!"

"Well, I do like that," replied her friend, laughing, "when you have had nearly the whole coach to yourself."

"Don't deny it, 'Tilda," said Miss Squeers, impressively, "because you have, and it's no use to go attempting to say you haven't. You mightn't have known it in your sleep, 'Tilda, but I haven't closed my eyes for a single wink, and so I *think* I am to be believed."

With which reply, Miss Squeers adjusted the bonnet and veil, which nothing but supernatural interference and an utter suspension of nature's laws could have reduced to any shape or form; and evidently flattering herself that it looked uncommonly neat, brushed off the sandwich-crumbs and bits of biscuit, which had accumulated in her lap, and availing herself of John Browdie's proffered arm, descended from the coach.

"Noo," said John, when a hackney-coach had been called, and the ladies and the luggage hurried in, "gang to the Sarah's Head, mun."

"To the *vere?*" cried the coachman.

"Lawk, Mr. Browdie!" interrupted Miss Squeers. "The idea! Saracen's Head."

"Sure-ly," said John, "I know'd it was summut aboot Sarah— to the Sarah Son's Head. Dost thou know thot?"

"Oh, ah—I know that," replied the coachman, gruffly, as he banged the door.

"'Tilda, dear—really," remonstrated Miss Squeers, "we shall be taken for I don't know what."

"Let 'em tak us as they foind us;" said John Browdie, "we dean't come to Lunnun to do nought but 'joy oursel, do we?"

"I hope not, Mr. Browdie," replied Miss Squeers, looking singularly dismal.

"Well, then," said John, "it's no matther. I've only been a married mun fower days, 'account of poor old feyther deein' and puttin' it off. Here be a weddin' party—broide and broide'smaid, and the groom—if a mun dean't 'joy himsel noo, when ought he, hey? Draat it all, thot's what I wont to know."

So, in order that he might begin to enjoy himself at once, and lose no time, Mr. Browdie gave his wife a hearty kiss, and succeeded in wresting another from Miss Squeers after a maidenly resistance of scratching and struggling on the part of that young lady, which was not quite over when they reached the Saracen's Head.

Here the party straightway retired to rest, the refreshment of sleep being necessary after so long a journey; and here they met again, about noon, to a substantial breakfast, spread by direction of Mr. John Browdie, in a small private room up-stairs commanding an uninterrupted view of the stables.

To have seen Miss Squeers now, divested of the brown beaver, the green veil, and the blue curl-papers, and arrayed in all the virgin splendour of a white frock and spencer, with a white muslin bonnet, and an imitative damask rose in full bloom on the inside thereof : her luxuriant crop of hair arranged in curls so tight that it was impossible they could come out by any accident, and her bonnet-cap trimmed with little damask roses, which might be supposed to be so many promising scions of the big one—to have seen all this, and to have seen the broad damask belt, matching both the family rose and the little ones, which encircled her slender waist, and by a happy ingenuity took off from the shortness of the spencer behind,—to have beheld all this, and to have taken further into account the coral bracelets (rather short of beads, and with a very visible black string) which clasped her wrists, and the coral necklace which rested on her neck, supporting outside her frock a lonely cornelian heart, typical of her own disengaged affections—to have contemplated all these mute but expressive appeals to the purest feelings of our nature, might have thawed the frost of age, and added new and inextinguishable fuel to the fire of youth.

The waiter was touched. Waiter as he was, he had human passions and feelings, and he looked very hard at Miss Squeers as he handed the muffins.

" Is my pa in, do you know ? " asked Miss Squeers with dignity.

" Beg your pardon, Miss."

" My pa," repeated Miss Squeers ; " is he in ? "

" In where, Miss ? "

" In here—in the house ! " replied Miss Squeers. " My pa—Mr. Wackford Squeers—he's stopping here. Is he at home ? "

" I didn't know there was any gen'lman of that name in the house, Miss," replied the waiter. " There may be, in the coffee-room."

May be. Very pretty this, indeed ! Here was Miss Squeers, who had been depending all the way to London upon showing her friends how much at home she would be, and how much respectful notice her name and connexions would excite, told that her father *might* be there ! " As if he was a feller ! " observed Miss Squeers, with emphatic indignation.

" Ye'd betther inquire, mun," said John Browdie. " An' hond up another pigeon-pie, will 'ee ? Dang the chap," muttered John, looking into the empty dish as the waiter retired ; " Does he ca' this a pie— three yoong pigeons and a troifling matther o' steak, and a crust so loight that you doant know when it's in your mooth and when it's gane ? I wonder hoo many pies goes to a breakfast ! "

After a short interval, which John Browdie employed upon the ham and a cold round of beef, the waiter returned with another pie, and the information that Mr. Squeers was not stopping in the house, but that he came there every day, and that directly he arrived he should be shown up-stairs. With this he retired ; and he had not retired two minutes, when he returned with Mr. Squeers and his hopeful son.

" Why, who'd have thought of this ? " said Mr. Squeers, when he had saluted the party, and received some private family intelligence from his daughter.

"Who, indeed, pa!" replied that young lady, spitefully. "But you see 'Tilda *is* married at last."

"And I stond threat for a soight o' Lunnun, schoolmeasther," said John, vigorously attacking the pie.

"One of them things that young men do when they get married," returned Squeers; "and as runs through with their money like nothing at all. How much better wouldn't it be now, to save it up for the eddication of any little boys, for instance. They come on you," said Mr. Squeers in a moralizing way, "before you're aware of it; mine did upon me."

"Will 'ee pick a bit?" said John.

"I won't myself," returned Squeers; "but if you'll just let little Wackford tuck into something fat, I'll be obliged to you. Give it him in his fingers, else the waiter charges it on, and there's lot of profit on this sort of vittles without that. If you hear the waiter coming, sir, shove it in your pocket and look out of the window, d'ye hear?"

"I'm awake, father," replied the dutiful Wackford.

"Well," said Squeers, turning to his daughter, "It's your turn to be married next. You must make haste."

"Oh, I'm in no hurry," said Miss Squeers, very sharply.

"No, Fanny?" cried her old friend with some archness.

"No, 'Tilda," replied Miss Squeers, shaking her head vehemently. "*I*—can wait."

"So can the young men, it seems, Fanny," observed Mrs. Browdie.

"They an't draw'd into it by *me*, 'Tilda," retorted Miss Squeers.

"No," returned her friend; "that's exceedingly true."

The sarcastic tone of this reply might have provoked a rather acrimonious retort from Miss Squeers, who, besides being of a constitutionally vicious temper—aggravated just now by travel and recent jolting—was somewhat irritated by old recollections and the failure of her own designs upon Mr. Browdie; and the acrimonious retort might have led to a great many other retorts, which might have led to Heaven knows what, if the subject of conversation had not been at that precise moment accidentally changed by Mr. Squeers himself.

"What do you think?" said that gentleman; "who do you suppose we have laid hands on, Wackford and me?"

"Pa! not Mr. ———?" Miss Squeers was unable to finish the sentence, but Mrs. Browdie did it for her, and added, "Nickleby?"

"No," said Squeers. "But next door to him though."

"You can't mean Smike?" cried Miss Squeers, clapping her hands.

"Yes, I can though," rejoined her father. "I've got him hard and fast."

"Wa'at!" exclaimed John Browdie, pushing away his plate. "Got thot poor—dom'd scoondrel,—where?"

"Why, in the top back room, at my lodging," replied Squeers, "with him on one side and the key on the other."

"At thy loodgin'! Thee'st gotten him at thy loodgin'? Ho! ho!

The schoolmeasther agin all England. Give us thee hond, mun;—
I'm darned but I must shak thee by the hond for thot.—Gotten him
at thy loodgin'?"

"Yes," replied Squeers, staggering in his chair under the congratu-
latory blow on the chest which the stout Yorkshireman dealt him—
"thankee. Don't do it again. You mean it kindly, I know, but it
hurts rather—yes, there he is. That's not so bad, is it?"

"Ba'ad!" repeated John Browdie. "It's eneaf to scare a mun to
hear tell on."

"I thought it would surprise you a bit," said Squeers, rubbing his
hands. "It was pretty neatly done, and pretty quick too."

"Hoo wor it?" inquired John, sitting down close to him. "Tell us
all aboot it, mun; coom, quick."

Although he could not keep pace with John Browdie's impatience,
Mr. Squeers related the lucky chance by which Smike had fallen into
his hands, as quickly as he could, and, except when he was interrupted
by the admiring remarks of his auditors, paused not in the recital until
he had brought it to an end.

"For fear he should give me the slip by any chance," observed
Squeers, when he had finished, looking very cunning, "I've taken
three outsides for to-morrow morning, for Wackford and him and me,
and have arranged to leave the accounts and the new boys to the agent,
don't you see? So it's very lucky you come to-day, or you'd have
missed us; and as it is, unless you could come and tea with me to-
night, we shan't see anything more of you before we go away."

"Deant say anoother wurd," returned the Yorkshireman, shaking
him by the hand. "We'd coom if it was twonty mile."

"No, would you though?" returned Mr. Squeers, who had not
expected quite such a ready acceptance of his invitation, or he would
have considered twice before he gave it.

John Browdie's only reply was another squeeze of the hand, and an
assurance that they would not begin to see London till to-morrow, so
that they might be at Mr. Snawley's at six o'clock without fail; and
after some further conversation, Mr. Squeers and his son departed.

During the remainder of the day Mr. Browdie was in a very odd and
excitable state, bursting occasionally into an explosion of laughter, and
then taking up his hat and running into the coach-yard to have it out by
himself. He was very restless too, constantly walking in and out, and
snapping his fingers, and dancing scraps of uncouth country dances,
and, in short, conducting himself in such a very extraordinary manner,
that Miss Squeers opined he was going mad, and, begging her dear
'Tilda not to distress herself, communicated her suspicions in so many
words. Mrs. Browdie, however, without discovering any great alarm,
observed that she had seen him so once before, and that although he was
almost sure to be ill after it, it would not be anything very serious, and
therefore he was better left alone.

The result proved her to be perfectly correct; for while they were all
sitting in Mr. Snawley's parlour that night, and just as it was beginning to get dusk, John Browdie was taken so ill, and seized with such

an alarming dizziness in the head, that the whole company were thrown into the utmost consternation. His good lady, indeed, was the only person present who retained presence of mind enough to observe that if he were allowed to lie down on Mr. Squeers's bed for an hour or so, and left entirely to himself, he would be sure to recover again almost as quickly as he had been taken ill. Nobody could refuse to try the effect of so reasonable a proposal before sending for a surgeon. Accordingly, John was supported up-stairs with great difficulty, being a monstrous weight, and regularly tumbling down two steps every time they hoisted him up three; and being laid on the bed, was left in charge of his wife, who, after a short interval, re-appeared in the parlour with the gratifying intelligence that he had fallen fast asleep.

Now, the fact was, that, at that particular moment, John Browdie was sitting on the bed with the reddest face ever seen, cramming the corner of the pillow into his mouth to prevent his roaring out loud with laughter. He had no sooner succeeded in suppressing this emotion, than he slipped off his shoes, and creeping to the adjoining room where the prisoner was confined, turned the key, which was on the outside, and darting in, covered Smike's mouth with his huge hand before he could utter a sound.

"Ods-bobs, dost thee not know me, mun?" whispered the Yorkshireman to the bewildered lad. " Browdie,—chap as met thee efther schoolmeasther was banged?"

"Yes, yes," cried Smike. "Oh! help me."

"Help thee!" replied John, stopping his mouth again the instant he had said thus much. "Thee didn't need help if thee war'nt as silly yoongster as ever draw'd breath. Wa'at did 'ee come here for, then?"

"He brought me; oh! he brought me," cried Smike.

"Brout thee!" replied John. "Why didn't'ee punch his head, or lay theeself doon and kick, and squeal out for the pollis? I'd ha' licked a doozen such as him when I was yoong as thee. But thee be'est a poor broken-doon chap," said John, sadly, "and God forgi' me for bragging ower yan o' his weakest creeturs."

Smike opened his mouth to speak, but John Browdie stopped him.

"Stan still," said the Yorkshireman, "and doant'ee speak a morsel o' talk till I tell'ee."

With this caution, John Browdie shook his head significantly, and drawing a screw-driver from his pocket, took off the box of the lock in a very deliberate and workmanlike manner, and laid it, together with the implement, on the floor.

"See thot?" said John. "Thot be thy doin'. Noo, coot awa'."

Smike looked vacantly at him, as if unable to comprehend his meaning.

"I say, coot awa'," repeated John, hastily. "Dost thee know where thee livest? Thee dost? Weel. Are yon thy clothes, or schoolmeasther's?"

"Mine," replied Smike, as the Yorkshireman hurried him to the adjoining room, and pointed out a pair of shoes and a coat which were lying on a chair.

" On wi' 'em," said John, forcing the wrong arm into the wrong sleeve, and winding the tails of the coat round the fugitive's neck. " Noo, foller me, and when thee get'st ootside door, turn to the right, and they wean't see thee pass."

" But—but—he'll hear me shut the door," replied Smike, trembling from head to foot.

" Then dean't shut it at all," retorted John Browdie. " Dang it, thee bean't afeard o' schoolmeasther's takkin' cold, I hope?"

" N-no," said Smike, his teeth chattering in his head. " But he brought me back before, and will again. He will, he will indeed."

" He wull, he wull!" replied John impatiently. " He wean't, he wean't. Looke'e. I wont to do this neighbourly loike, and let them think thee's gotten awa' o' theeself, but if he cooms oot o' thot parlour awhiles theer't clearing off, he mun' have mercy on his oun boans, for I wean't. If he foinds it oot soon efther, I'll put 'un on a wrong scent, I warrant'ee. But if thee keeps't a good hart, thee'lt be at whoam afore they know thees't gotten off. Coom."

Smike, who comprehended just enough of this to know it was intended as encouragement, prepared to follow with tottering steps, when John whispered in his ear.

" The'lt just tell yoong Measther, that I'm sploiced to 'Tilly Price, and to be heerd on at the Saracen by latther, and that I bee'nt jealous of 'un—dang it, I'm loike to boost when I think o' that neight ; 'cod, I think I see 'un now, a powderin' awa' at the thin bread an butther!"

It was rather a ticklish recollection for John just then, for he was within an ace of breaking out into a loud guffaw. Restraining himself, however, just in time by a great effort, he glided down stairs, hauling Smike behind him ; and placing himself close to the parlour-door, to confront the first person that might come out, signed to him to make off.

Having got so far, Smike needed no second bidding. Opening the house-door gently, and casting a look of mingled gratitude and terror at his deliverer, he took the direction which had been indicated to him, and sped away like the wind.

The Yorkshireman remained on his post for a few minutes, but, finding that there was no pause in the conversation inside, crept back again unheard, and stood listening over the stair-rail for a full hour. Everything remaining perfectly quiet, he got into Mr. Squeers's bed once more, and drawing the clothes over his head, laughed till he was nearly smothered.

If there could only have been somebody by, to see how the bed-clothes shook, and to see the Yorkshireman's great red face and round head appear above the sheets every now and then, like some jovial monster coming to the surface to breathe, and once more dive down convulsed with the laughter which came bursting forth afresh—that somebody would have been scarcely less amused than John Browdie himself.

NEW AND POPULAR WORKS PUBLISHED BY R. TYAS,

50 CHEAPSIDE, LONDON:

SOLD ALSO BY J. MENZIES, EDINBURGH; AND MACHEN AND CO. DUBLIN.

This Day is Published, No. IV., price Sixpence, and Part I., price Two Shillings, of

THE HISTORY OF
NAPOLEON:

From the French of NORVINS, LAURENT (de l'Ardêche), BOURRIENNE, LAS CASAS, the DUKE DE ROVIGO, LUCIEN BONAPARTE, &c.; with Abstracts from the Works of HAZLITT, CARLYLE, and SIR WALTER SCOTT:

EDITED BY R. H. HORNE, Esq.

Author of "Cosmo de' Medici," "The Death of Marlowe," &c.

RICHLY ILLUSTRATED WITH

MANY HUNDRED ENGRAVINGS ON WOOD,

AFTER DESIGNS BY

RAFFET, HORACE VERNET, JACQUE,

AND OTHER EMINENT ARTISTS.

THIS Work has originated in the belief that the great mass of the English People are imperfectly acquainted with the HISTORY and CHARACTER of NAPOLEON BONAPARTE. Very partial accounts, characterised by extreme eulogy or extreme condemnation, have been diffused in a limited circle, and published at too high a price, and in too voluminous a form, to place them within the means of the General Reader.

The object of the Work now submitted to the Public, is to give an impartial digest of all the best of the numerous publications concerning NAPOLEON; which digest will be condensed into ONE VOLUME.

The present aspect of the social hemisphere in all civilised countries, renders this a peculiarly apt moment for the general diffusion of authentic information respecting NAPOLEON. The most important facts of his eventful period will be displayed in the most concise form, as a vivid series of pictures of those tremendous events of the past, the influence of which has been, and will continue to be, so deep and extensive.

The well known talents of RAFFET (from whose pencil the designs have chiefly emanated), and HORACE VERNET, as depictors of Military Events, will be the best guarantee for the truth and vigour of the illustrations, which delineate in rapid succession those scenes of arduous enterprise abroad, and the no less stirring events at home, that marked the career of NAPOLEON BONAPARTE.

The style of the Engravings and Printing, and the quality of the Paper, will be such as to render the Work one of the choicest specimens of the Typographic Art.

To be completed in about Forty Weekly Numbers, price Sixpence each;
Or, Ten Monthly Parts, price Two Shillings each.

LONDON: ROBERT TYAS, 50 CHEAPSIDE:

J. MENZIES, EDINBURGH; MACHEN AND CO. DUBLIN.

Vizetelly & Co. Printers, 135 Fleet Street.

TO THE READERS OF NICHOLAS NICKLEBY!

This Day is Published, No. I. **PRICE SIXPENCE,** (to be continued Monthly) of

HEADS
FROM
NICHOLAS NICKLEBY

ETCHED

BY

A. DRYPOINT

FROM

DRAWINGS

BY

MISS

LA CREEVY.

These "HEADS" will comprise Portraits of the most interesting individuals that appear in "THE LIFE AND ADVENTURES OF NICHOLAS NICKLEBY," selected at the period when their very actions define their true characters, and exhibit the inward mind by its outward manifestations. Each Portrait will be a literal transcript from the accurate and vividly minute descriptions of this able and most graphic author; and will present to the eye, an equally faithful version of the maiden simplicity of KATE NICKLEBY—the depravity of SIR MULBERRY HAWK—the imbecility of his dupe—the heartless villany of the calculating RALPH—the generosity of the noble-minded NICHOLAS—the broken spirit of poor SMIKE—and the brutality of SQUEERS. These and many others furnish subjects for the display of the artist's genius, and will form an interesting and most desirable addition to the work.

No. I. CONTAINS

KATE NICKLEBY	**SIR MULBERRY HAWK**
RALPH NICKLEBY	**NEWMAN NOGGS.**

LONDON: ROBERT TYAS, 50 CHEAPSIDE:
J. MENZIES, EDINBURGH: MACHEN AND COMPANY, DUBLIN.

Vizetelly & Co. Printers, 135 Fleet Street.

On the Fifteenth of March will be Published, in Imperial Octavo, Price Twopence,

N⁰. I.

(TO BE CONTINUED WEEKLY),

OF

SHAKSPERE

FOR THE PEOPLE:

REVISED FROM THE BEST EDITIONS EXPRESSLY FOR THIS WORK:

WITH ANNOTATIONS, AND INTRODUCTORY REMARKS ON THE PLAYS,

BY MANY DISTINGUISHED WRITERS:

AND A LIFE OF THE AUTHOR, AND AN ESSAY ON HIS WRITINGS,

By DOUGLAS JERROLD:

ILLUSTRATED WITH NEARLY

ONE THOUSAND ENGRAVINGS ON WOOD

FROM DESIGNS

By KENNY MEADOWS.

OBJECT OF THE PROJECTORS.

The purpose of the Projectors of this New Edition of the Works of the WORLD'S POET, is to make the BOOK OF SHAKSPERE literally a household thing; and, whilst its price and mode of publication shall bring it within the means of readers of the humblest fortunes, the novelty of its PICTORIAL ILLUSTRATIONS, with the care bestowed upon its Text, and typographical pretensions, will, it is confidently believed, render it superior to many editions put forth at quadruple its cost: the new resources of mechanical science, and the extraordinary improvement in wood engraving, enabling the Proprietors to diffuse amidst—ay, millions!—those beauties of art, and necessarily those refinements of life, no longer jealously considered as the property of the few, but claimed as the heritage of the many. Time was, when literature and art were to the people—

" Bann'd and barr'd, forbidden fare."

Happily, in our day, the triumphs of the mind have vindicated their first and most sacred purpose—that of being ministrant to the moral improvement, and therefore to the highest happiness, of all men. Books are no longer the exclusive luxuries of the rich—they are become the necessary food of the poor.

It is with this conviction that the Projectors of " SHAKSPERE FOR THE PEOPLE" commence their grateful labours. In the present great moral struggle— in the present conflict of all that ennobles as of all that debases our common nature—good books may be considered as manna, blessing a hungry multitude. This allowed, what human work so irresistibly addresses itself to human sympathies, as the writings of Shakspere? Where shall the people find a nobler teacher—

from whom shall their nature receive such immortal elevation—where shall they behold such vivid, stirring pictures of the world about them—whence learn (and learning, fear, respect, and love) the wondrous mysteries of the human heart—its powers alike for good or evil? Who shall teach them this with a loftier, a sweeter, a simpler, and a more convincing eloquence than Shakspere? Where shall they see and gather this loveliness and wisdom but in the starry page of HIM, whose genius, surpassing the powers of all men in its strength, is tempered with a charity and sweetness, rendering that strength so universal?

It is expected that the forthcoming edition of the Poet will command admission to the libraries of the rich, by the peculiar beauty of its Embellishments; whilst, in the room of the artisan, in the cottage of the labourer, the PEOPLE'S SHAKSPERE (such is the proud hope of the Projectors) shall be as a household oracle; a teacher of the best of human wisdom, the sacredness of human rights; the innocent and ready happiness to be found in this life, even for the lowliest; and the crowning lesson of all life's teaching—the necessity and joyfulness of wise content.

THE ILLUSTRATIONS.

Each Play will be illustrated with numerous Engravings on Wood, executed in a style that shall challenge comparison with the most vigorous and most delicate specimens of the art; the Illustrations to consist of compositions in which there will be an attempt to embody the PORTRAITS OF SHAKSPERE'S CHARACTERS; an attempt, the result of a long, and it may be honestly said, reverential study of the "many-coloured" subjects to be essayed; together with Landscapes illustrative of the Text. Hence, the Work will contain a GALLERY OF SHAKSPERE PORTRAITS AND SHAKSPERE SCENES, executed with that zeal and love for the undertaking, without which there can in no high endeavour be even a promise of success.

THE TEXT AND NOTES.

The Text of Johnson and Steevens will be mainly followed; to which will be appended explanatory Notes, and a Glossary; the Notes from the pens of Writers distinguished by their knowledge and by their reverence of the Author. It is conceived that this most important part of the undertaking may be satisfactorily performed, with a due regard to brevity; nothing being more easy, were such the design, than to load Shakspere with even the whole contents of an Encyclopædia.

THE LIFE OF THE AUTHOR.

A Life of Shakspere, collected from various sources, and containing the results of various late discoveries, will be WRITTEN FOR THE EDITION; with an Essay on the Plays and Poems.

THE PRINTING.

The Work will be confided to the Press of VIZETELLY and Co., a firm already distinguished for the excellence, beauty, and correctness of its works; and from which a new typographical triumph may be confidently predicted, in the edition of SHAKSPERE FOR THE PEOPLE.

EXTENT OF THE WORK.

It is calculated that each Play will occupy from Four to Six Numbers, but in no instance will exceed Six. An Edition will also be published in Monthly Parts.

LONDON: ROBERT TYAS, 50 CHEAPSIDE;

J. MENZIES, EDINBURGH; MACHEN AND CO. DUBLIN.

Vizetelly & Co. Printers, 135 Fleet Street..

THE great number of new Medicines which have within the last few years been offered to the Public would have prevented the Proprietor from submitting to their notice this valuable Extract, had not the fullest and most decided evidence of its superiority convinced him that as far as he could it was strictly right he should make it generally useful. It is purely Vegetable, extracted solely from **CAMOMILE FLOWERS,** *and in all cases where the stomach does not rightly perform its office it is at once the most harmless pleasant, and efficacious assistant possible.*

With the weak, the sickly, and the sedentary, the preventive art of Medicine must be an object worthy of particular attention. The effect of a few doses will fully show its efficacy; for whether the constitution is naturally bad, whether it has been seriously injured by severe attacks of illness or by some inferior dilapidating cause, or whether it has been impaired by time or by neglect, the general effect is similar, and consequently the repairing and propping up of the system are to be accomplished by invigorating and bringing into proper action the digestive organs, so preventing the general breaking up of the constitution. The Proprietor, from experience, is quite confident that by a little attention, and an occasional dose of this Medicine, these important objects may be accomplished; and the period of life may be extended many years beyond the usual number by the use of

NORTON'S
CAMOMILE PILLS,

THE MOST

CERTAIN PRESERVER OF HEALTH,

AND A MILD, YET SPEEDY, SAFE, AND EFFECTUAL CURE OF

INDIGESTION

AND ALL STOMACH COMPLAINTS,

And, as a natural consequence, a purifier of the blood and a sweetener of the whole system.

INDIGESTION is a weakness or want of power of the digestive juices in the stomach to convert what we eat and drink into healthy matter, for the proper nourishment of the whole system. It is caused by every thing which weakens the system in general or the stomach in particular. From it proceeds nearly all the diseases to which we are liable; for it is very certain that if we could always keep the stomach right we should only die by old age or accident. Indigestion produces a great variety of unpleasant sensations: amongst the most prominent of its miserable effects are a want of, or an inordinate, appetite, sometimes attended with a constant craving for drink, a distention or feeling of enlargement of the stomach, belchings or eructations of various kinds, heartburn, pains in the stomach, acidity, unpleasant taste in the mouth, perhaps sickness, rumbling noise in the bowels; in some cases of depraved digestion there is nearly a complete disrelish for food, but still the appetite is not greatly impaired, as at the stated period of meals persons so afflicted can eat heartily, although without much gratification; a long train of nervous symptoms are also frequent attendants, general debility, great languidness, and incapacity for exertion. The minds of persons so afflicted frequently become irritable and desponding, and great anxiety is observable in the countenance; they appear thoughtful, melancholy, and dejected, under great apprehension of some imaginary danger, will start at any unexpected noise or occurrence, and become so agitated that they require some time to calm and collect themselves; yet for all this the mind is exhilarated without much difficulty, pleasing events, society, will for a time dissipate all appearance of disease, but the excitement produced by an agreeable change vanishes soon after the cause has gone by. Other symptoms are violent palpitations, restlessness, the sleep disturbed by frightful dreams and startings and affording little or no refreshment; occasionally there is much moaning, with a sense of weight and oppression upon the chest, night-mare, &c.

It is almost impossible to enumerate all the symptoms of this first invader upon the constitution, as in a hundred cases of *Indigestion* there will probably be something peculiar to each; but, be they what they may, they are all occasioned by the food becoming a burden rather than a support to the stomach; and in all its stages the medicine most wanted is that which will afford speedy and effectual assistance to the digestive organs, and give energy to the nervous and muscular systems: nothing can more speedily or with more certainty effect so desirable an object than *Norton's Extract of Camomile Flowers*. The herb has from time immemorial been highly esteemed in England as a grateful anodyne, imparting an aromatic bitter to the taste and a pleasing degree of warmth and strength to the stomach; and in all cases of indigestion, gout in the stomach, windy colic, and general weakness, it has for ages been strongly recommended by the most eminent practitioners as very useful and beneficial. The great, indeed only objection to their use has been the large quantity of water which it takes to dissolve a small part of the flowers, and which must be taken with it into the Stomach. It requires a quarter of a pint of boiling water to dissolve the soluble portion of one drachm of camomile flowers, and, when one or even two ounces may be taken with advantage, it must at once be seen how impossible it is to take a proper dose of this wholesome herb in the form of tea; and the only reason why it has not long since been placed the very first in rank of all restorative medicines is that in taking it the stomach has always been loaded with water, which tends in a great measure to counteract, and very frequently wholly to destroy, the effect. It must be evident that loading a weak stomach with a large quantity of water, merely for the purpose of conveying into it a small quantity of medicine, must be injurious; and that the medicine must possess powerful renovating properties only to counteract the bad effects likely to be produced by the water. Generally speaking, this has been the case with camomile flowers, a herb possessing the highest restorative qualities, and, when properly taken, decidedly the most speedy restorer and the most certain preserver of health.

These **PILLS** are wholly **CAMOMILE,** prepared by a peculiar process, accidentally discovered, and known only to the Proprietor, and which he firmly believes to be one of the most valuable modern discoveries in medicine, by which all the essential and extractive matter of more than an ounce of the flowers is concentrated in four moderate-sized pills. Experience has afforded the most ample proof that they possess all the fine aromatic and stomachic properties for which the herb has been esteemed; and, as they are taken into the stomach unencumbered by any diluting or indigestible substance, in the same degree has their benefit been more immediate and decided. Mild in their operation and pleasant in their effect, they may be taken at any age and under any circumstance without danger or inconvenience: a person exposed to cold and wet a whole day or night could not possibly receive any injury from taking them, but, on the contrary, they would effectually prevent a cold being taken. After a long acquaintance with and strict observance of the medicinal properties of *Norton's Camomile Pills*, it is only doing them justice to say that they are really the most valuable of all TONIC MEDICINES. By the word tonic is meant a medicine which gives strength to the stomach sufficient to digest in proper quantities all wholesome food, which increases the power of every nerve and muscle of the human body, or, in other words, invigorates the nervous and muscular systems. The solidity or firmness of the whole tissue of the body which so quickly follows the use of *Norton's Camomile Pills*, their certain and speedy effects in repairing the partial dilapidations from time or intemperance, and their lasting salutary influence on the whole frame, is most convincing, that in the smallest compass is contained the largest quantity of the tonic principle, of so peculiar a nature as to pervade the whole system, through which it diffuses health and strength sufficient to resist the formation of disease, and also to fortify the constitution against contagion; as such, their general use is strongly recommended as a preventative during the prevalence of malignant fevers or other infectious diseases, and to persons attending sick rooms they are invaluable, as in no one instance have they ever failed in preventing the taking of illness, even under the most trying circumstances.

As *Norton's Camomile Pills* are particularly recommended for all stomach complaints or indigestion, it will probably be expected that some advice should be given respecting diet, though, after all that has been written upon the subject, after the publication of volume upon volume, after the country has, as it were, been inundated with practical essays on diet as a means of prolonging life, it would be unnecessary to say more did we not feel it our duty to make the humble endeavour of inducing the public to regard them not, but to adopt that course which is dictated by nature, by reason, and by common sense. Those persons who study the wholesomes, and are governed by the opinions of writers on diet, are uniformly both unhealthy in body and weak in mind. There can be no doubt that the palate is designed to inform us what is proper for the stomach, and of course that must best instruct us what food to take and what to avoid: we want no othe adviser. Nothing can be more clear than that those articles which are agreeable to the taste were by nature intended for our food and sustenance, whether liquid or solid, foreign or of native production; if they are pure and unadulterated, no harm need be dreaded by their use; they will only injure by abuse. Consequently, whatever the palate approves, eat and drink, always in moderation, but never in excess; keeping in mind that the first process of digestion is performed in the mouth, the second in the stomach, and that, in order that the stomach may be able to do its work properly, it is requisite the first process should be well performed: this consists in masticating or chewing the solid food so as to break down and separate the fibres and small substances of meat and vegetables, mixing them well, and blending the whole together before they are swallowed; and it is particularly urged upon all to take plenty of time to their meals, and never eat in haste. If you conform to this short and simple but comprehensive advice, and find that there are various things which others eat and drink with pleasure and without inconvenience, and which would be pleasant to yourself only that they disagree, you may at once conclude that the fault is in the stomach, that it does not possess the power which it ought to do, that it wants assistance, and the sooner that assistance is afforded the better. A very short trial of this medicine will best prove how soon it will put the stomach in a condition to perform with ease all the work which nature intended for it. By its use you will soon be able to enjoy, in moderation, whatever is agreeable to the taste, and unable to name one individual article of food which disagrees with or sits unpleasantly on the stomach. Never forget that a small meal well digested affords more nourishment to the system than a large one, even of the same food, when digested imperfectly. Let the dish be ever so delicious, ever so enticing a variety offered, the bottle ever so enchanting, never forget that temperance tends to preserve health, and that health is the soul of enjoyment. But should an impropriety be at any time, or ever so often, committed, by which the stomach becomes overloaded or disordered, render it immediate aid by taking a dose of *Norton's Camomile Pills*, which will so promptly assist in carrying off the burden thus imposed upon it that all will soon be right again.

It is most certainly true that every person in his lifetime consumes a quantity of noxious matter, which if taken at one meal would be fatal: it is these small quantities of noxious matter, which is introduced into our food either by accident or wilful adulteration, which we find so often upset the stomach, and not unfrequently lay the foundation of illness, and perhaps final ruination to health. To preserve the constitution it should be our constant care, if possible, to counteract the effect of these small quantities of unwholesome matter; and whenever, in that way, an enemy to the constitution finds its way into the stomach, a friend should be immediately sent after it, which would prevent its mischievous effects, and expel it altogether: no better friend can be found, nor one which will perform the task with greater certainty, than **NORTON'S CAMOMILE PILLS.** And let it be observed that the longer this medicine is taken the less it will be wanted; it can in no case become habitual, as its entire action is to give energy and force to the stomach, which is the spring of life, the source from which the whole frame draws its succour and support. After an excess of eating or drinking, and upon every occasion of the general health being at all disturbed, these PILLS should be immediately taken, as they will stop and eradicate disease at its commencement. Indeed it is most confidently asserted that by the timely use of this medicine only, and a common degree of caution, any person may enjoy all the comforts within his reach, may pass through life without an illness, and with the certainty of attaining a healthy OLD AGE.

On account of their volatile properties they must be kept in bottles, and if closely corked their qualities are neither impaired by time nor injured by any change of climate whatever. Price 13½d. and 2s. 9d. each, with full directions. The large bottle contains the quantity of three small ones, or PILLS equal to fourteen ounces of CAMOMILE FLOWERS. **TO THE PUBLIC.**

"Having disposed of my whole right and interest in those excellent Medicines known by the name of NORTON'S CAMOMILE PILLS, and NORTON'S EXTRACT OF PEPPERMINT, to the successors of Mr. Benjamin Godfrey Windus, 61, Bishopsgate Street Without, London, both the medicines will in future be prepared by them; and, to protect the Public against Counterfeits, the Government stamp will be engraved, Benjamin Godfrey Windus, 61, Bishopsgate Street.

Beccles 1st. Sept., 1833. "THOS. NORTON."

———

Sold wholesale by Barclay and Sons; T. Butler; E. Edwards; F. Newberry & Sons; W. Sutton & Co., and A. Willoughby & Co. (late B. Godfrey Windus), 61, Bishopsgate Street Without, London, and retail by nearly all respectable Medicine Venders.

Be particular to ask for "NORTON'S PILLS," for in consequence of their great success some unprincipled persons have prepared a spurious imitation.

GODFREY'S
EXTRACT OF ELDER FLOWERS,

For softening the Skin and improving the Complexion.

THIS preparation has by very many years' trial in private practice been found so superlatively efficacious in softening, improving, beautifying, and preserving the skin, and in giving it a blooming and most charming appearance, that the proprietor can with the greatest confidence recommend it as a most fragrant perfume and perfect beautifier. It will speedily and completely remove all Tan, Sunburns, Freckles, Redness, &c., and by its cooling, balsamic, and healing qualities, make the skin soft, pliable, and free from dryness, scurf, &c., clear it from every humour, pimple, and eruption, and, by continuing its use for only a short time, the skin will become and continue delicately clear, soft, and smooth, and the complexion perfectly fair and beautiful.

To children it is singularly beneficial, and perfectly innoxious, even to the youngest infant. It will cleanse the pores of the skin, clear off dandriff much better than combs, will quickly relieve all those inflammatory affections of the face, neck, and ears, occasioned by teething, chafing, &c., and give an appearance of cleanliness and health truly surprising—must be seen to be believed; and will indisputably show that it is alike the *ne plus ultra* of the nursery and of the toilette.

In the process of shaving it is valuable beyond any thing, annihilating every pimple, and all roughness, rendering the skin soft and firm, and its surface even and smooth, and preparing it so completely for the application of the razor that the proprietor earnestly enjoins every gentleman who has any regard for his own comfort to try one bottle, which will so well recommend itself that in all probability he will recommend it to others.

It ought to be observed, that, with whatever indifference some may profess to regard appearances, all are in some degree influenced by them, many much more than they themselves believe or suspect; but, be that as it may, it is certainly to the interest of most, and must be desirable to all, to carry an appearance as pleasing as the nature of things will allow, and, of whatever form the features may be, a clear and wholesome-looking skin must be infinitely preferable to that which is sallow, or covered with numerous eruptive specks and blemishes; therefore it is candidly submitted whether it does not behove every one to make use of the best means which accident or science may have afforded to reduce and obviate as much as possible the ills which flesh is heir to.

As a family lotion, to use on all occasions, Godfrey's Extract of Elder Flowers will be found beyond all praise, and needs only a trial to be approved. Its agreeable perfume, its pleasing and beneficial effects in rendering the complexion delicately fair and beautiful. in softening the skin, cleansing its pores, and freeing it from all pimples and eruptions. in improving its colour and conferring a transcendent transparency and bloom, and rendering it altogether unexceptionable, are so prompt and decided that it must ultimately supersede the use of all other preparations. Indeed it only requires a comparison to show in the strongest light its amazing superiority.

It is prepared only by the Proprietor, and sold wholesale by Messrs. WILLOUGHBY and Co. (successors to Benjamin Godfrey Windus), 61, Bishopsgate Street Without, London; and supplied also by Barclay and Sons; T. Butler; E. Edwards; F. Newberry and Sons; and W. Sutton and Co.; and sold retail in bottles at 2s. 9d. each, by all Booksellers, Druggists, and Patent Medicine Venders in the United Kingdom.

CAUTION TO PURCHASERS.

There are unprincipled persons who are constantly in the habit of imitating every meritorious public medicine, disregarding altogether its qualities. Such a course, though it may yield large profits to the fraudulent, produces to others injury and disappointment; therefore purchasers are particularly requested to observe that the name "Benjamin Godfrey Windus, 61, Bishopsgate Street," is engraved on the Government Stamp, which is pasted over the cork of each bottle; without which none can be genuine.

BRITANNIA LIFE ASSURANCE COMPANY,

No. 1, PRINCES STREET, BANK, LONDON.

CAPITAL, ONE MILLION.

Directors.

WILLIAM BARDGETT, ESQ.
SAMUEL BEVINGTON, ESQ.
WILLIAM FECHNEY BLACK, ESQ.
JOHN BRIGHTMAN, ESQ.
GEORGE COHEN, ESQ.
MILLIS COVENTRY, ESQ.
JOHN DREWETT, ESQ.

ROBERT EGLINTON, ESQ.
ERASMUS ROBERT FOSTER, ESQ.
ALEX. ROBERT IRVINE, ESQ.
PETER MORRISON, ESQ.
WILLIAM SHAND, JUN., ESQ.
HENRY LEWIS SMALE, ESQ.
THOMAS TEED, ESQ.

Medical Officers.

WILLIAM STROUD, M.D., Great Coram Street, Russell Square.
EBENEZER SMITH, ESQ., Surgeon, Billiter Square.

Standing Counsel.

The HON. JOHN ASHLEY, New Square, Lincoln's-Inn.

Solicitor.

WILLIAM BEVAN, ESQ., Old Jewry.

Bankers.

MESSRS. DREWETT & FOWLER, Princes Street.

ADVANTAGES OF THIS INSTITUTION.

A most economical set of Tables—computed expressly for the use of this Establishment, from authentic and complete data ; *and presenting the lowest rates of Assurance that can be offered, without compromising the safety of the Institution.*

Increasing rates of Premium, on a new and remarkable plan, for securing loans on debts, a less immediate payment being required on a Policy for the whole term of life, than in any other office.

Decreasing rates of Premium, also on a novel and remarkable plan ; the Policy-holder having the option of discontinuing the payment of all further premiums after *twenty, fifteen, ten,* and even *five* years ; and the Policy still remaining in force,—in the first case, for the full amount originally assured and in either of the three other cases, for a portion of the same, according to a fixed and equitable scale; endorsed upon the Policy.

Premiums may be paid either Annually, Half-yearly, or Quarterly, in one sum, or in a limited number of payments.

A Board of Directors in attendance daily at Two o'clock.

Age of the assured in every case admitted in the Policy.

All claims payable within one month after proof of death.

Medical attendants remunerated in all cases for their reports.

A liberal commission allowed to solicitors and agents

Age.	Premium per Cent. per Annum payable during				
	First Five Years.	Second Five Years.	Third Five Years.	Fourth Five Years.	Remainder of Life.
	£ s. d.	£ s. d.	£ s. d.	£ s. d.	£ s. d.
20	1 1 0	1 5 10	1 10 11	1 16 9	2 3 6
30	1 6 4	1 12 2	1 19 1	2 7 4	2 17 6
40	1 16 1	2 4 4	2 14 6	3 7 3	4 3 4
50	2 16 7	3 9 4	4 5 5	5 6 3	6 13 0

Officers in the Army and Navy engaged in active service, or residing abroad, and persons afflicted with chronic disorders not attended with immediate danger, assured at the least possible addition to the ordinary rates, regulated in each case by the increased nature of the risk.

PETER MORRISON. *Resident Director.*

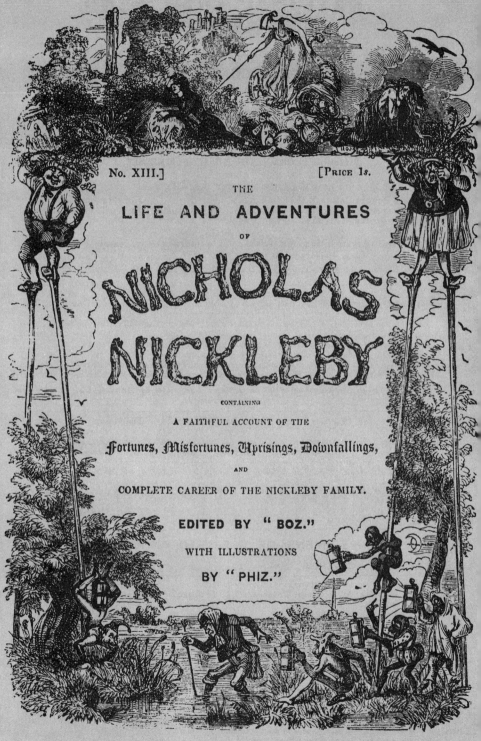

No. XIII.]   [Price 1s.

THE

LIFE AND ADVENTURES

OF

NICHOLAS NICKLEBY

CONTAINING

A FAITHFUL ACCOUNT OF THE

Fortunes, Misfortunes, Uprisings, Downfallings,

AND

COMPLETE CAREER OF THE NICKLEBY FAMILY.

EDITED BY "BOZ."

WITH ILLUSTRATIONS

BY "PHIZ."

LONDON: CHAPMAN AND HALL. 186. STRAND.

NATIONAL LOAN FUND
Life Assurance
AND
DEFERRED ANNUITY SOCIETY,
No. 26, CORNHILL, LONDON;

67, New Buildings, North Bridge, Edinburgh; 36, Westmoreland Street, Dublin; 28, South Castle Street, Liverpool; and 9, Clare Street, Bristol.

CAPITAL, £500,000.
EMPOWERED BY ACT OF PARLIAMENT.

PATRON,—HIS GRACE THE DUKE OF SOMERSET, F.R.S.

DIRECTORS.
T. LAMIE MURRAY, Esq. *Chairman.*

COL. SIR BURGES CAMAC, K.C.S.	H. GORDON, ESQ.	JOHN RAWSON, ESQ.
JOHN ELLIOTSON, M.D., F.R.S.	ROBERT HOLLOND, ESQ., M.P.	JOSEPH THOMPSON, ESQ.
C. FAREBROTHER, ESQ., ALD.	GEORGE LUNGLEY, ESQ.	

AUDITORS.
DR. OLINTHUS GREGORY, F.R.A.S. | PROFESSOR WHEATSTONE, F.R.S.

PHYSICIAN,—J. ELLIOTSON, M.D., F.R.S.   SURGEON,—E. S. SYMES, ESQ.

ACTUARY,—W. S. B. WOOLHOUSE, ESQ., F.R.A.S.

BANKERS,—MESSRS. WRIGHT & CO. and MESSRS. LADBROKES, KINGSCOTE & CO.

STANDING COUNSEL,—W. MILBOURNE JAMES, ESQ.

SOLICITORS,—MESSRS. WEBBER & BLAND.   SECRETARY,—F. FERGUSON CAMROUX, ESQ.

By the new principles of Life Assurance and Deferred Annuities, established by this Society, many essential advantages, besides that of securing a provision for a family, or for old age, are gained by the Assured, and thereby an additional value is given to each Policy effected with the Society.

Every facility is afforded in effecting Assurances.—Premiums payable annually, half-yearly, quarterly, or monthly, or on the increasing or decreasing scales.—Females assured at diminished rates.—Extension of travelling beyond the limits of Europe—and Policies in force seven years not forfeited by suicide.

Premiums for the Assurance of £100 on a Single Life, either by Annual, Half Yearly, or Quarterly Payments.

Age.	For One Year.	For Five Years at an Annual Prem. of	FOR WHOLE LIFE, WITHOUT PROFITS.			FOR WHOLE LIFE, WITH PROFITS.		
			Yearly.	Half Yearly.	Quarterly.	Yearly.	Half Yearly.	Quarterly.
	£ s. d.	£ s. d.	£ s. d.	£ s. d.	£ s. d.	£ s. d.	£ s. d.	£ s. d.
25	0 19 8	1 1 1	1 18 6	0 19 6	0 9 11	2 2 9	1 1 8	0 11 0
35	1 9 2	1 10 9	2 10 11	1 5 10	0 13 2	2 16 6	1 8 8	0 14 7
45	1 14 4	1 15 8	3 9 4	1 15 3	0 17 11	3 17 0	1 19 2	0 19 11
55	2 10 9	2 19 1	5 5 6	2 13 10	1 7 6	5 17 2	2 19 10	1 10 6
65	5 5 0	6 0 4	8 10 5	4 7 6	2 4 11	9 9 4	4 17 3	2 9 11

SPECIMENS OF DEFERRED ANNUITIES.

BENEFITS.				PREMIUMS.			
Options Secured on attaining the age of Sixty-five, by an Annual Premium of £2. 12s.				To secure, on attaining the age of 65, the option of Annuity 10 0 0 Cash... 82 10 0 Policy.. 97 8 6			
Age.	Annuity.	Cash.	Policy.	Age.	Annual.	In one Sum.	Disparity.
	£ s. d.	£ s. d.	£ s. d.		£ s. d.	£ s. d.	£ s. d.
20	47 16 6	394 11 0	466 0 0	20	0 10 11	10 0 10	0 0 0
30	26 15 10	221 0 0	261 0 0	30	0 19 6	16 7 1	7 3 11
40	13 19 9	115 8 0	136 6 0	40	1 17 3	27 3 11	19 4 10

Also Deferred Annuities commencing at the Ages of 50, 55, and 60, and Immediate Annuities for all Ages.

Two-thirds of the Premiums paid, at all times available to the Assured; and the same proportion returnable, in case of premature death.

A Board with a Medical Officer is in daily attendance at Two o'clock.

Prospectuses may be had at the Offices, or any of the Branches in the Principal Towns.

F. FERGUSON CAMROUX, *Sec.*

THE NICKLEBY ADVERTISER.

THE CORONATION.

MR. MOON, Her Majesty's Publisher and Printseller in Ordinary, 20, Threadneedle Street, has the honour to announce that he has received her Majesty's command to publish an Engraving by SAMUEL COUSINS, A.R.A., from the grand Picture by C. R. LESLIE, R.A., painted for and at the express command of her Majesty, of that most solemn and interesting portion of the Coronation ceremony,

HER MAJESTY RECEIVING THE SACRAMENT.

The Portraits of the Royal Family and Noble Personages who were present were taken by the Artist at the special desire of her Majesty.

Also, an Engraving of

THE QUEEN'S FIRST COUNCIL,

THE PROPERTY OF HER MAJESTY, PAINTED AND ENGRAVING BY EXPRESS COMMAND.

This grand historical Picture, by SIR DAVID WILKIE, represents our Sovereign presiding at the Council, upon her Majesty's Accession to the Throne, June 20th, 1837.

And by Authority,

AN ENGRAVING FROM THE SUPERB HISTORICAL PAINTING OF

THE CORONATION.

By E. T. PARRIS, Esq., Historical Painter to the Queen Dowager.

For the treatment of this, the most interesting and important incident of the present day, Mr. PARRIS has secured the most exalted patronage, and commanded the most perfect success. The grand picture—the chef d'œuvre of the talented and popular artist—unites, to an extraordinary extent, the most minute and accurate fidelity, with a grandeur of effect, and a permanent historical interest, infinitely surpassing any similar work of art hitherto attempted.

During the progress of the magnificent ceremonial, Mr. PARRIS was allowed, for the purposes of this Picture, to avail himself of the most eligible situations, and he has in consequence portrayed the scene with a scrupulous fidelity. Subsequently, he has had the advantage of sittings from the greater portion of the illustrious personages present, of whom original portraits are introduced assembled round the throne of our youthful Sovereign. Not only are all the Great Officers of State, the Foreign Visitors, and the Attendant Courtiers, introduced in their respective situations ; but near her Majesty is gathered a rich galaxy of female loveliness, arrayed in all the gorgeous and glittering costumes which the occasion required.

In addition to the original portraits of the attendant members of the Royal Family, of the Duke of Nemours, Marshal Soult, and other illustrious visitors, of the Resident and Extraordinary Ambassadors, and of many members of the Court in immediate attendance on her Majesty,

The following Personages will occupy commanding and prominent stations in the foreground of the Picture:—

Archbishop of Canterbury	Bishop of Durham	Marchioness of Tavistock	Countess of Lichfield
Archbishop of York	Bishop of Bath and Wells	Marchioness of Normanby	Countess of Leicester
Archbishop of Armagh	Sub-Dean of Westminster, &c.	Marchioness of Salisbury	Viscountess Beresford
Lord Chancellor		Marchioness of Londonderry	Lady Willoughby D'Eresby
Duke of Devonshire	Duchess of Sutherland	Marchioness of Aylesbury	Lady Paget
Duke of Sutherland	Duchess of Somerset	Marchioness of Clanricarde	Lady Ada King
Duke of Wellington	Duchess of Richmond	Marchioness of Breadalbane	Lady Barham
Duke of Norfolk	Duchess of Beaufort	Countess of Shrewsbury	Lady Rolle
Duke of Richmond	Duchess of Bedford	Countess of Pembroke	Lady A. Paget
Marquess of Lansdowne	Duchess of Hamilton	Countess of Chesterfield	Lady F. E. Cowper
Marquess of Westminster	Duchess of Buccleuch	Countess of Essex	Lady M. A. F. Grimston
Marquess of Stafford	Duchess of Roxburgh	Countess of Jersey	Lady A. G. Lennox
Marquess of Conyngham	Duchess of Northumberland	Countess Cowper	Lady C. L. W. Stanhope
Viscount Melbourne	Duchess of Leinster	Countess of Wilton	&c. &c. &c.
Bishop of London	Marchioness of Lansdowne		

This great work of Art will, with the grand Portrait of her Majesty by CHALON, the QUEEN'S FIRST COUNCIL, and the Solemnity of HER MAJESTY RECEIVING THE SACRAMENT, form a part of the

REGAL GALLERY OF PICTURES;

Illustrating the incidents of the Reign of QUEEN VICTORIA, which Mr. MOON has arranged to produce as events may transpire.

APSLEY PELLATT'S
ABRIDGED LIST OF
Net Cash Prices for the best Flint Glass Ware.

DECANTERS.

25 Strong quart Nelson shape decanters, cut all over, bold flutes and cut brim & stopper, P.M. each 10s6d. to 12 0

26 Do. three-ringed royal shape, cut on and between rings, turned out stop, P.M. each 10 0

Do. do. not cut on or between rings, nor turned out stopper, P.M. ea. 8s to 9 0

27 Fancy shapes, cut all over, eight flutes, spire stopper, &c. each, P.M. 16s. to 18 0

Do. six flutes only, each, P.M. 24s. to 27 0

DISHES.

31 Dishes, oblong, pillar moulded, scolloped edges, cut star.

5-in.	7-in.	9-in.	10-in.
3s. 6d.	6s. 6d.	11s.	13s. each.

32 Oval cup sprig, shell pattern,

5-in.	7-in.	9-in.	11-in.
7s. 6d.	9s. 6d.	16s.	19s. each.

33 Square shape pillar, moulded star,

5-in.	7-in	9-in.	10-in.
4s.	8s.	12s. 6d.	15s. each.

FINGER CUPS.

37 Fluted finger-cups, strong, about 14 oz. each 2 6

Do. plain flint, punted, per doz..... 18 0

Do. coloured, per doz........18s. to 21 0

38 Ten-fluted round, very strong, each. 5 0

Eight-fluted do., each 8 0

39 Medicean shape, moulded pillar, pearl upper part, cut flat flutes, each .. 5 0

PICKLES

46 Pickles, half fluted for 3 in. holes, RM ea. 4 6

47 Strong, moulded bottom, 3-in. hole, cut all over, flat flutes, R.M. each. 5 0

Best cut star do. for 3½-in. hole, PM ea. 7 6

Very strong and best cut, P.M. each 14 6

WATER JUGS

59 Quarts, neatly fluted and cut rings, each.................14s. to 18 0

60 Ewer shape, best cut handles, &c... 21 0

61 Silver do. scolloped edges, ex. lar. flutes 25 0

WATER BOTTLES

70 Moulded pillar body, cut neck, each. 3 0

71 Cut neck and star.................. 3 0

72 Double fluted cut rings 3 6

73 Very strong pillar, moulded body, cut neck and rings 5 6

74 Grecian shape, fluted all over 7 0

TUMBLERS

	78	79	80	81	82	83	84	85	86	97	
Tale 5s.											
Flint,	7s.	10s.	12s.	12s.	10s.	12s.	14s.	18s.	18s.		Doz.
	to	to	to	to	to	to	to	to	to		
	8s.	12s	14s.	15s.	12s.		18s.	21s.	21s.	30s	do.

WINES

	88	89	90	91	92	93	94	95	96	97	98	99
	7s.	7s.	7s.	7s.	8s.	14s.	12s.	13s.	15s.	18s.	21s.	20s.
	to	to	to	to								
	8s.	9s.	9s.	10s.								

Glass Blowing, Cutting, and Engraving, may be inspected by Purchasers, at Mr. Pellatt's Extensive Flint Glass and Steam Cutting Works, in Holland Street, near Blackfriars' Bridge, any Tuesday, Wednesday, or Thursday.

Merchants and the Trade supplied on equitable Terms.

No Abatement from the above specified Ready Money Prices.

No Connexion with any other Establishment.

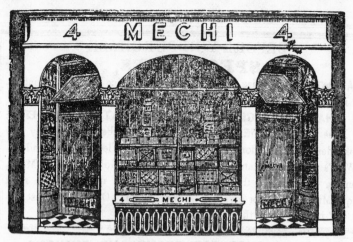

THOMAS FOX

Respectfully announces to Noblemen, Gentlemen, and Families connected with, or returning from, THE EAST INDIAN AND COLONIAL POSSESSIONS, that he has a large and splendid Assortment of every Article in the

UPHOLSTERY, DECORATIVE, AND FURNISHING DEPARTMENT;

and has endeavoured to combine in his Stock elegance of style and superiority of Manufacture, adapted for Tropical Climates, as well as for Domestic Use, and at prices commanding attention. To enable his Patrons, the Public, to judge how far he has succeeded in these objects, he solicits an inspection of his Stock at

93, BISHOPSGATE STREET WITHIN.

In the Agency Department will be found a variety of Houses and Properties for Letting or Disposal, connected with the Valuation and Sale of Effects and Estates by public or private channels.

BISHOPSGATE PLATE GLASS WAREHOUSE.

The late scientific improvements in the manufacture of PLATE GLASS, now enable all parties to embellish with this splendid article of internal and external decoration; and from its greatly improved quality and considerable reduction in cost, will be found for Windows, Conservatories, &c., a most elegant substitute for the Glass in general use, and comparatively more economical.

ENAMELLED, STAINED, & EMBOSSED GLASS,

Embracing Landscapes, Portraits, Maps, and a variety of fancy subjects, with an effect both novel and beautiful, may be adapted as a splendid substitute for every description of fixed blinds for principal windows, at exceedingly low prices.

BRILLIANT PIER AND CHIMNEY GLASSES,

Adapted to the most improved Architectural proportions and embellishments in the richest style of modern taste. Handsome Cottage Chimney-glasses, from £4 upwards; also Cheval and Toilet Glasses in every variety, equally reasonable.

93, BISHOPSGATE STREET WITHIN, LONDON.

LONDON : BRADBURY AND EVANS, PRINTERS, WHITEFRIARS.

CHAPTER XL.

IN WHICH NICHOLAS FALLS IN LOVE. HE EMPLOYS A MEDIATOR,
WHOSE PROCEEDINGS ARE CROWNED WITH UNEXPECTED SUCCESS,
EXCEPTING IN ONE SOLITARY PARTICULAR.

ONCE more out of the clutches of his old persecutor, it needed no
fresh stimulation to call forth the utmost energy and exertion that
Smike was capable of summoning to his aid. Without pausing for a
moment to reflect upon the course he was taking, or the probability of
its leading him homewards or the reverse, he fled away with surprising
swiftness and constancy of purpose, borne upon such wings as only
Fear can wear, and impelled by imaginary shouts in the well-remem-
bered voice of Squeers, who, with a host of pursuers, seemed to the
poor fellow's disordered senses to press hard upon his track; now left at
a greater distance in the rear, and now gaining faster and faster upon
him, as the alternations of hope and terror agitated him by turns.
Long after he had become assured that these sounds were but the
creation of his excited brain, he still held on at a pace, which even
weakness and exhaustion could scarcely retard; and it was not until
the darkness and quiet of a country road recalled him to a sense of
external objects, and the starry sky above warned him of the rapid
flight of time, that, covered with dust and panting for breath, he
stopped to listen and look about him.

All was still and silent. A glare of light in the distance, casting a
warm glow upon the sky, marked where the huge city lay. Solitary
fields, divided by hedges and ditches, through many of which he had
crashed and scrambled in his flight, skirted the road, both by the way
he had come and upon the opposite side. It was late now. They
could scarcely trace him by such paths as he had taken, and if he
could hope to regain his own dwelling, it must surely be at such a
time as that, and under cover of the darkness. This by degrees became
pretty plain even to the mind of Smike. He had at first entertained
some vague and childish idea of travelling into the country for ten or
a dozen miles, and then returning homewards by a wide circuit,
which should keep him clear of London—so great was his apprehension
of traversing the streets alone, lest he should again encounter his
dreaded enemy—but, yielding to the conviction which these thoughts
inspired, he turned back, and taking the open road, though not without
many fears and misgivings, made for London again with scarcely less
speed of foot than that with which he had left the temporary abode of
Mr. Squeers.

By the time he re-entered it at the western extremity, the greater
part of the shops were closed; of the throngs of people who had been
tempted abroad after the heat of the day, but few remained in the
streets, and they were lounging home. But of these he asked his way

from time to time, and by dint of repeated inquiries he at length reached the dwelling of Newman Noggs.

All that evening Newman had been hunting and searching in by-ways and corners for the very person who now knocked at his door, while Nicholas had been pursuing the same inquiry in other directions. He was sitting with a melancholy air at his poor supper, when Smike's timorous and uncertain knock reached his ears. Alive to every sound in his anxious and expectant state, Newman hurried down stairs, and, uttering a cry of joyful surprise, dragged the welcome visitor into the passage and up the stairs, and said not a word until he had him safe in his own garret and the door was shut behind them, when he mixed a great mug-full of gin and water, and holding it to Smike's mouth, as one might hold a bowl of medicine to the lips of a refractory child, commanded him to drain it to the very last drop.

Newman looked uncommonly blank when he found that Smike did little more than put his lips to the precious mixture; he was in the act of raising the mug to his own mouth with a deep sigh of compassion for his poor friend's weakness, when Smike, beginning to relate the adventures which had befallen him, arrested him half-way, and he stood listening with the mug in his hand.

It was odd enough to see the change that came over Newman as Smike proceeded. At first he stood rubbing his lips with the back of his hand, as a preparatory ceremony towards composing himself for a draught; then, at the mention of Squeers, he took the mug under his arm, and opening his eyes very wide, looked on in the utmost astonishment. When Smike came to the assault upon himself in the hackney-coach, he hastily deposited the mug upon the table, and limped up and down the room in a state of the greatest excitement, stopping himself with a jerk every now and then as if to listen more attentively. When John Browdie came to be spoken of, he dropped by slow and gradual degrees into a chair, and rubbing his hands upon his knees—quicker and quicker as the story reached its climax—burst at last into a laugh composed of one loud sonorous "Ha! Ha!" having given vent to which, his countenance immediately fell again as he inquired, with the utmost anxiety, whether it was probable that John Browdie and Squeers had come to blows.

"No! I think not," replied Smike. "I don't think he could have missed me till I had got quite away."

Newman scratched his head with a show of great disappointment, and once more lifting up the mug, applied himself to the contents, smiling meanwhile over the rim with a grim and ghastly smile at Smike.

"You shall stay here," said Newman; "you're tired—fagged. I'll tell them you're come back. They have been half mad about you. Mr. Nicholas—"

"God bless him!" cried Smike.

"Amen!" returned Newman. "He hasn't had a minute's rest or peace; no more has the old lady, nor Miss Nickleby."

"No, no. Has *she* thought about me?" said Smike. "Has she though? oh, has she—has she? Don't tell me so, if she has not."

" She has," cried Newman. " She is as noble-hearted as she is beautiful."

" Yes, yes!" cried Smike. " Well said!"

" So mild and gentle," said Newman.

" Yes, yes!" cried Smike, with increasing eagerness.

" And yet with such a true and gallant spirit," pursued Newman.

He was going on in his enthusiasm, when chancing to look at his companion, he saw that he had covered his face with his hands, and that tears were stealing out between his fingers.

A moment before, the boy's eyes were sparkling with unwonted fire, and every feature had been lighted up with an excitement which made him appear for the moment quite a different being.

" Well, well," muttered Newman, as if he were a little puzzled. " It has touched *me* more than once, to think such a nature should have been exposed to such trials ; this poor fellow—yes, yes,—he feels that too—it softens him—makes him think of his former misery. Hah! That's it! Yes, that's—hum!"

It was by no means clear from the tone of these broken reflections that Newman Noggs considered them as explaining, at all satisfactorily, the emotion which had suggested them. He sat in a musing attitude for some time, regarding Smike occasionally with an anxious and doubtful glance, which sufficiently showed that he was not very remotely connected with his thoughts.

At length he repeated his proposition that Smike should remain where he was for that night, and that he (Noggs) should straightway repair to the cottage to relieve the suspense of the family. But as Smike would not hear of this, pleading his anxiety to see his friends again, they eventually sallied forth together ; and the night being by this time far advanced, and Smike being besides so footsore that he could hardly crawl along, it was within an hour of sunrise when they reached their destination.

At the first sound of their voices outside the house, Nicholas, who had passed a sleepless night, devising schemes for the recovery of his lost charge, started from his bed and joyfully admitted them. There was so much noisy conversation and congratulation and indignation, that the remainder of the family were soon awakened, and Smike received a warm and cordial welcome, not only from Kate, but from Mrs. Nickleby also, who assured him of her future favour and regard ; and was so obliging as to relate, for his entertainment and that of the assembled circle, a most remarkable account extracted from some work the name of which she had never known, of a miraculous escape from some prison, but what one she couldn't remember, effected by an officer whose name she had forgotten, confined for some crime which she didn't clearly recollect.

At first Nicholas was disposed to give his uncle credit for some portion of this bold attempt (which had so nearly proved successful) to carry off Smike, but on more mature consideration he was inclined to think that the full merit of it rested with Mr. Squeers. Determined to ascertain if he could, through John Browdie, how the case really stood, he betook himself to his daily occupation: meditating as he went on a great variety of schemes for the punishment of the Yorkshire schoolmaster, all of which had their foundation in the strictest principles of retributive justice, and had but the one drawback of being wholly impracticable.

"A fine morning, Mr. Linkinwater," said Nicholas, entering the office.

"Ah!" replied Tim, "talk of the country, indeed! What do you think of this now for a day—a London day—eh?"

"It's a little clearer out of town," said Nicholas.

"Clearer!" echoed Tim Linkinwater. "You should see it from my bed-room window."

"You should see it from *mine*," replied Nicholas, with a smile.

"Pooh! pooh!" said Tim Linkinwater, "don't tell me. Country!" (Bow was quite a rustic place to Tim,) "Nonsense. What can you get in the country but new-laid eggs and flowers? I can buy new-laid eggs in Leadenhall market any morning before breakfast; and as to flowers, it's worth a run up-stairs to smell my mignionette, or to see the double-wallflower in the back-attic window, at No. 6, in the court."

"There is a double-wallflower at No. 6, in the court, is there?" said Nicholas.

"Yes, is there," replied Tim, "and planted in a cracked jug, without a spout. There were hyacinths there this last spring, blossoming in——but you'll laugh at that, of course."

"At what?"

"At their blossoming in old blacking-bottles," said Tim.

"Not I, indeed," returned Nicholas.

Tim looked wistfully at him for a moment, as if he were encouraged by the tone of this reply to be more communicative on the subject; and sticking behind his ear a pen that he had been making, and shutting up his knife with a smart click, said,

"They belong to a sickly bed-ridden hump-backed boy, and seem to be the only pleasures, Mr. Nickleby, of his sad existence. How many years is it," said Tim, pondering, "since I first noticed him quite a little child, dragging himself about on a pair of tiny crutches? Well! Well! not many; but though they would appear nothing, if I thought of other things, they seem a long, long time, when I think of him. It is a sad thing," said Tim, breaking off, "to see a little deformed child sitting apart from other children, who are active and merry, watching the games he is denied the power to share in. He made my heart ache very often."

"It is a good heart," said Nicholas, "that disentangles itself from the close avocations of every day, to heed such things. You were saying——"

"That the flowers belonged to this poor boy," said Tim, "that's all. When it is fine weather, and he can crawl out of bed, he draws a chair close to the window, and sits there looking at them, and arranging them all day long. We used to nod at first, and then we came to speak. Formerly, when I called to him of a morning, and asked him how he was, he would smile, and say, ' better ; ' but now he shakes his head, and only bends more closely over his old plants. It must be dull to watch the dark house-tops and the flying clouds for so many months ; but he is very patient."

" Is there nobody in the house to cheer or help him? " asked Nicholas.

" His father lives there I believe," replied Tim," and other people too; but no one seems to care much for the poor sickly cripple. I have asked him very often if I can do nothing for him ; his answer is always the same,—' Nothing.' His voice has grown weak of late, but I can *see* that he makes the old reply. He can't leave his bed now, so they have moved it close beside the window, and there he lies all day : now looking at the sky, and now at his flowers, which he still makes shift to trim and water with his own thin hands. At night, when he sees my candle, he draws back his curtain, and leaves it so till I am in bed. It seems such company to him to know that I am there, that I often sit at my window for an hour and more, that he may see I am still awake ; and sometimes I get up in the night to look at the dull melancholy light in his little room, and wonder whether he is awake or sleeping.

The night will not be long coming," said Tim, "when he will sleep and never wake again on earth. We have never so much as shaken hands in all our lives; and yet I shall miss him like an old friend. Are there any country flowers that could interest me like these, do you think ? Or do you suppose that the withering of a hundred kinds of the choicest flowers that blow, called by the hardest Latin names that were ever invented, would give me one fraction of the pain that I shall feel when these old jugs and bottles are swept away as lumber? Country ! " cried Tim, with a contemptuous emphasis ; " don't you know that I couldn't have such a court under my bed-room window anywhere but in London ? "

With which inquiry, Tim turned his back, and pretending to be absorbed in his accounts, took an opportunity of hastily wiping his eyes when he supposed Nicholas was looking another way.

Whether it was that Tim's accounts were more than usually intricate that morning, or whether it was that his habitual serenity had been a little disturbed by these recollections, it so happened that when Nicholas returned from executing some commission, and inquired whether Mr. Charles Cheeryble was alone in his room, Tim promptly, and without the smallest hesitation, replied in the affirmative, although somebody had passed into the room not ten minutes before, and Tim took especial and particular pride in preventing any intrusion on either of the brothers when they were engaged with any visitor whatever.

" I'll take this letter to him at once," said Nicholas, " if that's the case." And with that he walked to the room and knocked at the door. No answer.

Another knock and still no answer.

" He can't be here," thought Nicholas. " I'll lay it on his table." ﹁

So Nicholas opened the door and walked in ; and very quickly he turned to walk out again, when he saw to his great astonishment and discomfiture a young lady upon her knees at Mr. Cheeryble's feet, and Mr. Cheeryble beseeching her to rise, and entreating a third person, who had the appearance of the young lady's female attendant, to add her persuasions to his to induce her to do so.

Nicholas stammered out an awkward apology, and was precipitately retiring, when the young lady, turning her head a little, presented to his view the features of the lovely girl whom he had seen at the register-office on his first visit long before. Glancing from her to the attendant, he recognised the same clumsy servant who had accompanied her then; and between his admiration of the young lady's beauty, and the confusion and surprise of this unexpected recognition, he stood stock-still, in such a bewildered state of surprise and embarrassment that for the moment he was quite bereft of the power either to speak or move.

" My dear ma'am—my dear young lady," cried brother Charles in violent agitation, " pray don't—not another word, I beseech and entreat you. I implore you—I beg of you—to rise. We—we—are not alone."

As he spoke he raised the young lady, who staggered to a chair and swooned away.

" She has fainted, sir," said Nicholas, darting eagerly forward.

" Poor dear, poor dear!" cried brother Charles. " Where is my brother Ned? Ned, my dear brother, come here pray."

" Brother Charles, my dear fellow," replied his brother, hurrying into the room, " what is the——ah! what——"

" Hush! hush!—not a word for your life, brother Ned," returned the other. " Ring for the housekeeper, my dear brother—call Tim Linkinwater. Here, Tim Linkinwater, sir—Mr. Nickleby, my dear sir, leave the room, I beg and beseech of you."

" I think she is better now," said Nicholas, who had been watching the patient so eagerly that he had not heard the request.

" Poor bird!" cried brother Charles, gently taking her hand in his, and laying her head upon his arm. " Brother Ned, my dear fellow, you will be surprised, I know, to witness this in business hours; but—" here he was again reminded of the presence of Nicholas, and shaking him by the hand, earnestly requested him to leave the room, and to send Tim Linkinwater without an instant's delay.

Nicholas immediately withdrew, and on his way to the counting-house met both the old housekeeper and Tim Linkinwater, jostling each other in the passage, and hurrying to the scene of action with extraordinary speed. Without waiting to hear his message, Tim Linkinwater darted into the room, and presently afterwards Nicholas heard the door shut and locked on the inside.

He had abundance of time to ruminate on this discovery, for Tim Linkinwater was absent during the greater part of an hour, during the whole of which time Nicholas thought of nothing but the young lady and her exceeding beauty, and what could possibly have brought her there, and why they made such a mystery of it. The more he thought of all this, the more it perplexed him, and the more anxious he became to know who and what she was. " I should have known her among ten thousand," thought Nicholas. And with that he walked up and

Nicholas recognizes the Young Lady unknown.

down the room, and recalling her face and figure (of which he had a peculiarly vivid remembrance), discarded all other subjects of reflection and dwelt upon that alone.

At length Tim Linkinwater came back—provokingly cool, and with papers in his hand, and a pen in his mouth, as if nothing had happened.

" Is she quite recovered ?" said Nicholas, impetuously.

" Who ?" returned Tim Linkinwater.

" Who !" repeated Nicholas. " The young lady."

" What do you make, Mr. Nickleby," said Tim, taking his pen out of his mouth, " what do you make of four hundred and twenty-seven times three thousand two hundred and thirty-eight ?"

" Nay," returned Nicholas, " what do you make of my question first ? I asked you——"

" About the young lady," said Tim Linkinwater, putting on his spectacles. " To be sure. Yes. Oh ! she's very well."

" Very well, is she ?" returned Nicholas.

" *Very* well," replied Mr. Linkinwater, gravely.

" Will she be able to go home to-day ?" asked Nicholas.

" She's gone," said Tim.

" Gone !"

" Yes."

" I hope she has not far to go ?" said Nicholas, looking earnestly at the other.

"Ay," replied the immoveable Tim, " I hope she hasn't."

Nicholas hazarded one or two further remarks, but it was evident that Tim Linkinwater had his own reasons for evading the subject, and that he was determined to afford no further information respecting the fair unknown, who had awakened so much curiosity in the breast of his young friend. Nothing daunted by this repulse, Nicholas returned to the charge next day, emboldened by the circumstance of Mr. Linkinwater being in a very talkative and communicative mood ; but directly he resumed the theme, Tim relapsed into a state of most provoking taciturnity, and from answering in monosyllables, came to returning no answers at all, save such as were to be inferred from several grave nods, and shrugs which only served to whet that appetite for intelligence in Nicholas, which had already attained a most unreasonable height.

Foiled in these attempts, he was fain to content himself with watching for the young lady's next visit, but here again he was disappointed. Day after day passed, and she did not return. He looked eagerly at the superscription of all the notes and letters, but there was not one among them which he could fancy to be in her hand-writing. On two or three occasions he was employed on business which took him to a distance, and had formerly been transacted by Tim Linkinwater. Nicholas could not help suspecting that for some reason or other he was sent out of the way on purpose, and that the young lady was there in his absence. Nothing transpired, however, to confirm this suspicion, and Tim could not be entrapped into any confession or admission tending to support it in the smallest degree.

Mystery and disappointment are not absolutely indispensable to the growth of love, but they are very often its powerful auxiliaries. "Out of sight, out of mind," is well enough as a proverb applicable to cases of friendship, though absence is not always necessary to hollowness of heart even between friends, and truth and honesty, like precious stones, are perhaps most easily imitated at a distance, when the counterfeits often pass for real. Love, however, is very materially assisted by a warm and active imagination, which has a long memory, and will thrive for a considerable time on very slight and sparing food. Thus it is that it often attains its most luxuriant growth in separation and under circumstances of the utmost difficulty ; and thus it was that Nicholas, thinking of nothing but the unknown young lady from day to day and from hour to hour, began at last to think that he was very desperately in love with her, and that never was such an ill-used and persecuted lover as he.

Still, though he loved and languished after the most orthodox models, and was only deterred from making a confidante of Kate by the slight considerations of having never, in all his life, spoken to the object of his passion, and having never set eyes upon her except on two occasions, on both of which she had come and gone like a flash of lightning—or, as Nicholas himself said, in the numerous conversations he held with himself, like a vision of youth and beauty much too bright to last—his ardour and devotion remained without its reward. The young lady appeared no more ; so that there was a great deal of love wasted (enough indeed to have set up half-a-dozen young gentlemen, as times go, with the utmost decency) and nobody was a bit the wiser for it ; not even Nicholas himself, who, on the contrary, became more dull, sentimental, and lackadaisical every day.

While matters were in this state, the failure of a correspondent of the Brothers Cheeryble, in Germany, imposed upon Tim Linkinwater and Nicholas the necessity of going through some very long and complicated accounts extending over a considerable space of time. To get through them with the greater despatch, Tim Linkinwater proposed that they should remain at the counting-house for a week or so, until ten o'clock at night ; to this, as nothing damped the zeal of Nicholas in the service of his kind patrons—not even romance, which has seldom business habits—he cheerfully assented. On the very first night of these later hours, at nine exactly, there came : not the young lady herself, but her servant, who being closeted with brother Charles for some time, went away, and returned next night at the same hour, and on the next, and on the next again.

These repeated visits inflamed the curiosity of Nicholas to the very highest pitch. Tantalized and excited beyond all bearing, and unable to fathom the mystery without neglecting his duty, he confided the whole secret to Newman Noggs, imploring him to be on the watch next night, to follow the girl home, to set on foot such inquiries relative to the name, condition, and history of her mistress, as he could without exciting suspicion ; and to report the result to him with the least possible delay.

Beyond all measure proud of this commission, Newman Noggs took up his post in the square on the following evening, a full hour before the needful time, and planting himself behind the pump and pulling his hat over his eyes, began his watch with an elaborate appearance of mystery admirably calculated to excite the suspicion of all beholders. Indeed, divers servant-girls who came to draw water, and sundry little boys who stopped to drink at the ladle, were almost scared out of their senses by the apparition of Newman Noggs looking stealthily round the pump, with nothing of him visible but his face, and that wearing the expression of a meditative Ogre.

Punctual to her time, the messenger came again, and after an interview of rather longer duration than usual, departed. Newman had made two appointments with Nicholas, one for the next evening conditional on his success, and one the next night following which was to be kept under all circumstances. The first night he was not at the place of meeting (a certain tavern about half-way between the City and Golden Square), but on the second night he was there before Nicholas, and received him with open arms.

" It's all right," whispered Newman. " Sit down—sit down, there's a dear young man, and let me tell you all about it."

Nicholas needed no second invitation, and eagerly inquired what was the news.

" There's a great deal of news," said Newman, in a flutter of exultation. " It's all right. Don't be anxious. I don't know where to begin. Never mind that. Keep up your spirits. It's all right."

" Well ?" said Nicholas eagerly. " Yes ?"

" Yes," replied Newman. " That's it."

" What's it ?" said Nicholas. " The name—the name, my dear fellow."

" The name's Bobster," replied Newman.

" Bobster !" repeated Nicholas, indignantly.

" That's the name," said Newman. " I remembered it by lobster."

" Bobster !" repeated Nicholas, more emphatically than before. " That must be the servant's name."

" No, it an't," said Newman, shaking his head with great positiveness. " Miss Cecilia Bobster."

" Cecilia, eh ?" returned Nicholas, muttering the two names together over and over again in every variety of tone, to try the effect. " Well, Cecilia is a pretty name."

" Very. And a pretty creature too," said Newman.

" Who ?" said Nicholas.

" Miss Bobster."

" Why, where have you seen her ?" demanded Nicholas.

" Never mind, my dear boy," retorted Noggs, clapping him on the shoulder. " I *have* seen her. You shall see her. I have managed it all."

" My dear Newman," cried Nicholas, grasping his hand, " are you serious ?"

" I am," replied Newman. " I mean it all. Every word. You shall see her to-morrow night. She consents to hear you speak for yourself. I persuaded her. She is all affability, goodness, sweetness, and beauty."

" I know she is ; I know she must be, Newman," said Nicholas, wringing his hand.

" You are right," returned Newman.

" Where does she live ?" cried Nicholas. " What have you learnt of her history ? Has she a father—mother—any brothers—sisters ? What did she say? How came you to see her? Was she not very much surprised? Did you say how passionately I have longed to speak to her? Did you tell her where I had seen her? Did you tell her how, and when, and where, and how long and how often I have thought of that sweet face which came upon me in my bitterest distress like a glimpse of some better world—did you, Newman—did you ?"

Poor Noggs literally gasped for breath as this flood of questions rushed upon him, and moved spasmodically in his chair at every fresh inquiry, staring at Nicholas meanwhile with a most ludicrous expression of perplexity.

" No," said Newman, " I didn't tell her that."

" Didn't tell her which ?" asked Nicholas.

" About the glimpse of the better world," said Newman. " I didn't tell her who you were, either, or where you'd seen her. I said you loved her to distraction."

" That's true, Newman," replied Nicholas, with his characteristic vehemence. " Heaven knows I do ! "

" I said too, that you had admired her for a long time in secret," said Newman.

" Yes, yes. What did she say to that ?" asked Nicholas.

" Blushed," said Newman.

" To be sure. Of course she would," said Nicholas, approvingly.

Newman then went on to say that the young lady was an only child, that her mother was dead, and that she resided with her father ; and that she had been induced to allow her lover a secret interview at the intercession of her servant, who had great influence with her. He further related how it had required much moving and great eloquence to bring the young lady to this pass ; how it was expressly understood that she merely afforded Nicholas an opportunity of declaring his passion, and how she by no means pledged herself to be favourably impressed with his attentions. The mystery of her visits to the Brothers Cheeryble remained wholly unexplained, for Newman had not alluded to them, either in his preliminary conversations with the servant or his subsequent interview with the mistress, merely remarking that he had been instructed to watch the girl home and plead his young friend's cause, and not saying how far he had followed her, or from what point. But Newman hinted that from what had fallen from the confidante, he had been led to suspect that the young lady led a very miserable and unhappy life, under the strict control of her only parent, who was of a violent and brutal temper—a circumstance which he thought might in some degree account, both for her having sought the protection and friendship of the brothers, and her suffering herself to be prevailed upon to grant the promised interview. The last he held to be a very logical deduction from the premises, inasmuch as it was but natural to suppose that a young lady, whose present condition was so unenviable, would be more than commonly desirous to change it.

It appeared on further questioning—for it was only by a very long and arduous process that all this could be got out of Newman Noggs— that Newman, in explanation of his shabby appearance, had represented himself as being, for certain wise and indispensable purposes connected with that intrigue, in disguise; and being questioned how he had come to exceed his commission so far as to procure an interview, he responded, that the lady appearing willing to grant it, he considered himself bound, both in duty and gallantry, to avail himself of such a golden means of enabling Nicholas to prosecute his addresses. After these and all possible questions had been asked and answered twenty times over, they parted, undertaking to meet on the following night at half-past ten, for the purpose of fulfilling the appointment, which was for eleven o'clock.

" Things come about very strangely," thought Nicholas, as he walked home. " I never contemplated anything of this kind; never dreamt of the possibility of it. To know something of the life of one in whom I felt such interest; to see her in the street, to pass the house in which she lived, to meet her sometimes in her walks, to hope 'that a day might come when I might be in a condition to tell her of my love; this was the utmost extent of my thoughts. Now, however—but I should be a fool, indeed, to repine at my own good fortune."

Still Nicholas was dissatisfied; and there was more in the dissatisfaction than mere revulsion of feeling. He was angry with the young lady for being so easily won, " because," reasoned Nicholas, " it is not as if she knew it was I, but it might have been anybody,"—which was certainly not pleasant. The next moment he was angry with himself for entertaining such thoughts, arguing that nothing but goodness could dwell in such a temple, and that the behaviour of the brothers sufficiently showed the estimation in which they held her. " The fact is, she's a mystery altogether," said Nicholas. This was not more satisfactory than his previous course of reflection, and only drove him out upon a new sea of speculation and conjecture, where he tossed and tumbled in great discomfort of mind until the clock struck ten, and the hour of meeting drew nigh.

Nicholas had dressed himself with great care, and even Newman Noggs had trimmed himself up a little: his coat presenting the phenomenon of two consecutive buttons, and the supplementary pins being inserted at tolerably regular intervals. He wore his hat, too, in the newest taste, with a pocket handkerchief in the crown, and a twisted end of it straggling out behind, after the fashion of a pigtail, though he could scarcely lay claim to the ingenuity of inventing this latter decoration, inasmuch as he was utterly unconscious of it: being in a nervous and excited condition which rendered him quite insensible to everything but the great object of the expedition.

They traversed the streets in profound silence; and after walking at a round pace for some distance, arrived in one of a gloomy appearance and very little frequented, near the Edgeware-road.

" Number twelve," said Newman.

" Oh ! " replied Nicholas, looking about him.

" Good street ? " said Newman.

" Yes," returned Nicholas, " rather dull."

Newman made no answer to this remark, but halting abruptly, planted Nicholas with his back to some area railings, and gave him to understand that he was to wait there, without moving hand or foot, until it was satisfactorily ascertained that the coast was clear. This done, Noggs limped away with great alacrity, looking over his shoulder every instant, to make quite certain that Nicholas was obeying his directions ; and ascending the steps of a house some half-dozen doors off, was lost to view.

After a short delay, he re-appeared, and limping back again, halted midway, and beckoned Nicholas to follow him.

" Well ! " said Nicholas, advancing towards him on tiptoe.

" All right," replied Newman, in high glee. " All ready ; nobody at home. Couldn't be better. Ha ! ha ! "

With this fortifying assurance, he stole past a street-door, on which Nicholas caught a glimpse of a brass plate, with " BOBSTER," in very large letters ; and stopping at the area-gate, which was open, signed to his young friend to descend.

" What the devil ! " cried Nicholas, drawing back. " Are we to sneak into the kitchen as if we came after the forks ? "

" Hush ! " replied Newman. " Old Bobster—ferocious Turk. He'd kill 'em all—box the young lady's ears—he does—often."

" What ! " cried Nicholas, in high wrath, " do you mean to tell me that any man would dare to box the ears of such a—— "

He had no time to sing the praises of his mistress just then, for Newman gave him a gentle push which had nearly precipitated him to the bottom of the area steps. Thinking it best to take the hint in good part, Nicholas descended without further remonstrance ; but with a countenance bespeaking anything rather than the hope and rapture of a passionate lover. Newman followed—he would have followed head first, but for the timely assistance of Nicholas—and taking his hand, led him through a stone passage, profoundly dark, into a back kitchen or cellar of the blackest and most pitchy obscurity, where they stopped.

" Well ! " said Nicholas, in a discontented whisper, " this is not all, I suppose, is it ? "

" No, no," rejoined Noggs ; " they'll be here directly. It's all right."

" I am glad to hear it," said Nicholas. " I shouldn't have thought it, I confess."

They exchanged no further words, and there Nicholas stood, listening to the loud breathing of Newman Noggs, and imagining that his nose seemed to glow like a red-hot coal, even in the midst of the darkness which enshrouded them. Suddenly the sound of cautious footsteps attracted his ear, and directly afterwards a female voice inquired if the gentleman were there.

" Yes," replied Nicholas, turning towards the corner from which the voice proceeded. " Who is that ? "

" Only me, sir," replied the voice. " Now if you please, ma'am."

A gleam of light shone into the place, and presently the servant-girl appeared, bearing a light, and followed by her young mistress, who seemed to be overwhelmed by modesty and confusion.

At sight of the young lady, Nicholas started and changed colour; his heart beat violently, and he stood rooted to the spot. At that instant, and almost simultaneously with her arrival and that of the candle, there was heard a loud and furious knocking at the street-door, which caused Newman Noggs to jump up with great agility from a beer-barrel, on which he had been seated astride, and to exclaim abruptly, and with a face of ashy paleness, " Bobster, by the Lord ! "

The young lady shrieked, the attendant wrung her hands, Nicholas gazed from one to the other in apparent stupefaction, and Newman hurried to and fro, thrusting his hands into all his pockets successively, and drawing out the linings of every one in the excess of his irresolution. It was but a moment, but the confusion crowded into that one moment no imagination can exaggerate.

" Leave the house, for Heaven's sake! We have done wrong—we deserve it all," cried the young lady. " Leave the house, or I am ruined and undone for ever."

" Will you hear me say but one word?" cried Nicholas. " Only one. I will not detain you. Will you hear me say one word in explanation of this mischance ?"

But Nicholas might as well have spoken to the wind, for the young lady with distracted looks hurried up the stairs. He would have followed her, but Newman twisting his hand in his coat collar, dragged him towards the passage by which they had entered.

" Let me go, Newman, in the Devil's name," cried Nicholas. " I must speak to her—I will; I will not leave this house without."

" Reputation—character—violence—consider," said Newman, clinging round him with both arms, and hurrying him away. " Let them open the door. We'll go as we came directly it's shut. Come. This way. Here."

Overpowered by the remonstrances of Newman and the tears and prayers of the girl, and the tremendous knocking above, which had never ceased, Nicholas allowed himself to be hurried off; and precisely as Mr. Bobster made his entrance by the street-door, he and Noggs made their exit by the area-gate.

They hurried away through several streets without stopping or speaking. At last they halted and confronted each other with blank and rueful faces.

" Never mind," said Newman, gasping for breath. " Don't be cast down. It's all right. More fortunate next time. It couldn't be helped. I did *my* part."

" Excellently," replied Nicholas, taking his hand. " Excellently, and like the true and zealous friend you are. Only—mind, I am not disappointed, Newman, and feel just as much indebted to you—only *it was the wrong lady*."

" Eh ?" cried Newman Noggs. " Taken in by the servant ?"

" Newman, Newman," said Nicholas, laying his hand upon his shoulder ; " it was the wrong servant too."

Newman's under-jaw dropped, and he gazed at Nicholas with his sound eye fixed fast and motionless in his head.

" Don't take it to heart," said Nicholas ; " it's of no consequence ; you see I don't care about it ; you followed the wrong person, that's all."

That *was* all. Whether Newman Noggs had looked round the pump in a slanting direction so long, that his sight became impaired, or whether, finding that there was time to spare, he had recruited himself with a few drops of something stronger than the pump could yield— by whatsoever means it had come to pass, this was his mistake. And Nicholas went home to brood upon it, and to meditate upon the charms of the unknown young lady, now as far beyond his reach as ever.

CHAPTER XLI.

CONTAINING SOME ROMANTIC PASSAGES BETWEEN MRS. NICKLEBY AND
THE GENTLEMAN IN THE SMALL-CLOTHES NEXT DOOR.

EVER since her last momentous conversation with her son, Mrs. Nickleby had by little and little begun to display unusual care in the adornment of her person, gradually superadding to those staid and matronly habiliments, which had up to that time formed her ordinary attire, a variety of embellishments and decorations, slight perhaps in themselves, but, taken together, and considered with reference to the subject of her disclosure, of no mean importance. Even her black dress assumed something of a deadly-lively air from the jaunty style in which it was worn ; and, eked out as its lingering attractions were, by a prudent disposal here and there of certain juvenile ornaments of little or no value, which had for that reason alone escaped the general wreck and been permitted to slumber peacefully in odd corners of old drawers and boxes where daylight seldom shone, her mourning garments assumed quite a new character, and from being the outward tokens of respect and sorrow for the dead, were converted into signals of very slaughterous and killing designs upon the living.

Mrs. Nickleby might have been stimulated to this proceeding by a lofty sense of duty, and impulses of unquestionable excellence. She might by this time have become impressed with the sinfulness of long indulgence in unavailing woe, or the necessity of setting a proper example of neatness and decorum to her blooming daughter. Considerations of duty and responsibility apart, the change might have taken its rise in feelings of the purest and most disinterested charity. The gentleman next door had been vilified by Nicholas; rudely stigmatised as a dotard and an idiot ; and for these attacks upon his understanding, Mrs. Nickleby was in some sort accountable. She might have felt that it was the act of a good Christian to show, by all means in her power, that the abused gentleman was neither the one nor the other. And what better means could she adopt towards so virtuous and laudable an end, than proving to all men, in her own person, that his passion was the most rational and reasonable in the world, and just the very result of all others which discreet and thinking persons might have foreseen, from her incautiously displaying her matured charms, without reserve, under the very eye, as it were, of an ardent and too-susceptible man?

"Ah!" said Mrs. Nickleby, gravely shaking her head; "if Nicholas knew what his poor dear papa suffered before we were engaged, when I used to hate him, he would have a little more feeling. Shall I ever forget the morning I looked scornfully at him when he offered to carry my parasol? Or that night when I frowned at him? It was a mercy he didn't emigrate. It very nearly drove him to it."

Whether the deceased might not have been better off if he had emigrated in his bachelor days, was a question which his relict did not stop to consider, for Kate entered the room with her work-box in this stage of her reflections; and a much slighter interruption, or no interruption at all, would have diverted Mrs. Nickleby's thoughts into a new channel at any time.

"Kate, my dear," said Mrs. Nickleby; "I don't know how it is, but a fine warm summer day like this, with the birds singing in every direction, always puts me in mind of roast pig, with sage and onion sauce and made gravy."

"That's a curious association of ideas, is it not, mama?"

"Upon my word, my dear, I don't know," replied Mrs. Nickleby. "Roast pig—let me see. On the day five weeks after you were christened, we had a roast—no that couldn't have been a pig, either, because I recollect there were a pair of them to carve, and your poor papa and I could never have thought of sitting down to two pigs—they must have been partridges. Roast pig! I hardly think we ever could have had one, now I come to remember, for your papa could never bear the sight of them in the shops, and used to say that they always put him in mind of very little babies, only the pigs had much fairer complexions; and he had a horror of little babies, too, because he couldn't very well afford any increase to his family, and had a natural dislike to the subject. It's very odd now, what can put that in my head. I recollect dining once at Mrs. Bevan's, in that broad street, round the corner by the coachmaker's, where the tipsy man fell through the cellar-flap of an empty house nearly a week before quarter-day, and wasn't found till the new tenant went in—and we had roast pig there. It must be that, I think, that reminds me of it, especially as there was a little bird in the room that would keep on singing all the time of dinner—at least, not a little bird, for it was a parrot, and he didn't sing exactly, for he talked and swore dreadfully; but I think it must be that. Indeed I am sure it must. Shouldn't you say so, my dear?"

"I should say there was not a doubt about it, mama," returned Kate, with a cheerful smile.

"No; but do you think so, Kate," said Mrs. Nickleby, with as much gravity as if it were a question of the most imminent and thrilling interest.

" If you don't, say so at once, you know; because it's just as well to be correct, particularly on a point of this kind, which is very curious and worth settling while one thinks about it."

Kate laughingly replied that she was quite convinced; and as her mama still appeared undetermined whether it was not absolutely essential that the subject should be renewed, proposed that they should take their work into the summer-house and enjoy the beauty of the afternoon. Mrs. Nickleby readily assented, and to the summer-house they repaired without further discussion.

" Well, I will say," observed Mrs. Nickleby, as she took her seat, " that there never was such a good creature as Smike. Upon my word, the pains he has taken in putting this little arbour to rights and training the sweetest flowers about it, are beyond anything I could have——I wish he wouldn't put *all* the gravel on your side, Kate, my dear, though, and leave nothing but mould for me."

" Dear mama," returned Kate, hastily, " take this seat—do—to oblige me, mama."

" No, indeed, my dear. I shall keep my own side," said Mrs. Nickleby. " Well! I declare!"

Kate looked up inquiringly.

" If he hasn't been," said Mrs. Nickleby, " and got, from somewhere or other, a couple of roots of those flowers that I said I was so fond of the other night, and asked you if you were not—no, that *you* said *you* were so fond of, the other night, and asked me if I wasn't—it's the same thing—now, upon my word, I take that as very kind and attentive indeed! I don't see," added Mrs. Nickleby, looking narrowly about her, " any of them on my side, but I suppose they grow best near the gravel. You may depend upon it they do, Kate, and that's the reason they are all near you, and he has put the gravel there because it's the sunny side. Upon my word, that's very clever now. I shouldn't have had half as much thought myself!"

" Mama," said Kate hurriedly, bending over her work so that her face was almost hidden, " before you were married——"

" Dear me, Kate," interrupted Mrs. Nickleby, " what in the name of goodness graciousness makes you fly off to the time before I was married, when I'm talking to you about his thoughtfulness and attention to me? You don't seem to take the smallest interest in the garden."

" Oh! mama," said Kate, raising her face again, " you know I do."

" Well then, my dear, why don't you praise the neatness and prettiness with which it's kept," said Mrs. Nickleby. " How very odd you are, Kate!"

" I do praise it, mama," answered Kate, gently. " Poor fellow!"

" I scarcely ever hear you, my dear," retorted Mrs. Nickleby; " that's all I've got to say." By this time the good lady had been a long while upon one topic, so she fell at once into her daughter's little trap for changing it—if trap it were—and inquired what she had been going to say.

" About what, mama?" said Kate, who had apparently quite forgotten her diversion.

" Lor, Kate, my dear," returned her mother, " why, you're asleep or stupid. About the time before I was married."

" Oh yes!" said Kate, " I remember. I was going to ask, mama, before you were married, had you many suitors?"

" Suitors, my dear!" cried Mrs. Nickleby, with a smile of wonderful complacency. " First and last, Kate, I must have had a dozen at least."

" Mama!" returned Kate, in a tone of remonstrance.

" I had indeed, my dear," said Mrs. Nickleby; " not including your poor papa, or a young gentleman who used to go at that time to the same dancing-school, and who *would* send gold watches and bracelets to our house in gilt-edged paper, (which were always returned), and who afterwards unfortunately went out to Botany Bay in a cadet ship—a convict ship I mean—and escaped into a bush and killed sheep, (I don't know how they got there) and was going to be hung, only he accidentally choked himself, and the government pardoned him. Then there was young Lukin," said Mrs. Nickleby, beginning with her left thumb and checking off the names on her fingers—" Mogley—Tipslark —Cabbery—Smifser——"

Having now reached her little finger, Mrs. Nickleby was carrying the account over to the other hand, when a loud " Hem!" which appeared to come from the very foundation of the garden wall, gave both herself and her daughter a violent start.

" Mama! what was that?" said Kate, in a low tone of voice.

" Upon my word, my dear," returned Mrs. Nickleby, considerably startled, " unless it was the gentleman belonging to the next house, I don't know what it could possibly—"

" A—hem!" cried the same voice; and that not in the tone of an ordinary clearing of the throat, but in a kind of bellow, which woke up all the echoes in the neighbourhood, and was prolonged to an extent which must have made the unseen bellower quite black in the face.

" I understand it now, my dear," said Mrs. Nickleby, laying her hand on Kate's; "don't be alarmed, my love, it's not directed to you, and is not intended to frighten anybody. Let us give everybody their due Kate; I am bound to say that."

So saying, Mrs. Nickleby nodded her head, and patted the back of her daughter's hand a great many times, and looked as if she could tell something vastly important if she chose, but had self-denial, thank God! and wouldn't do it.

" What do you mean, mama?" demanded Kate, in evident surprise.

" Don't be flurried, my dear," replied Mrs. Nickleby, looking towards the garden-wall, " for you see I'm not, and if it would be excusable in anybody to be flurried, it certainly would—under all the circumstances— be excusable in me, but I am not, Kate—not at all."

" It seems designed to attract our attention, mama," said Kate.

" It *is* designed to attract our attention, my dear—at least," rejoined Mrs. Nickleby, drawing herself up, and patting her daughter's hand more blandly than before, " to attract the attention of one of us. Hem! you needn't be at all uneasy, my dear."

Kate looked very much perplexed, and was apparently about to ask for further explanation, when a shouting and scuffling noise, as of an elderly gentleman whooping, and kicking up his legs on loose gravel with great violence, was heard to proceed from the same direction as the former sounds; and, before they had subsided, a large cucumber was seen to shoot up in the air with the velocity of a sky-rocket, whence it descended, tumbling over and over, until it fell at Mrs. Nickleby's feet.

This remarkable appearance was succeeded by another of a precisely similar description; then a fine vegetable marrow, of unusually large dimensions, was seen to whirl aloft, and come toppling down; then several cucumbers shot up together; and, finally, the air was darkened by a shower of onions, turnip-radishes, and other small vegetables, which fell rolling and scattering and bumping about in all directions.

As Kate rose from her seat in some alarm, and caught her mother's hand to run with her into the house, she felt herself rather retarded than assisted in her intention; and, following the direction of Mrs. Nickleby's eyes, was quite terrified by the apparition of an old black velvet cap, which, by slow degrees, as if its wearer were ascending a ladder or pair of steps, rose above the wall dividing their garden from that of the next cottage, (which, like their own, was a detached building,) and was gradually followed by a very large head, and an old face, in which were a pair of most extraordinary grey eyes, very wild, very wide open, and rolling in their sockets with a dull, languishing, and leering look, most ugly to behold.

" Mama !" cried Kate, really terrified for the moment, " why do you stop, why do you lose an instant ?—Mama, pray come in !"

" Kate, my dear," returned her mother, still holding back, " how can you be so foolish ? I'm ashamed of you. How do you suppose you are ever to get through life, if you're such a coward as this ! What do you want, sir ?" said Mrs. Nickleby, addressing the intruder with a sort of simpering displeasure. " How dare you look into this garden ?"

" Queen of my soul," replied the stranger, folding his hands together, " this goblet sip."

" Nonsense, sir," said Mrs. Nickleby. " Kate, my love, pray be quiet."

" Won't you sip the goblet ?" urged the stranger, with his head imploringly on one side, and his right hand on his breast. " Oh, do sip the goblet !"

" I shall not consent to do any thing of the kind, sir," said Mrs. Nickleby, with a haughty air. " Pray, begone."

" Why is it," said the old gentleman, coming up a step higher, and leaning his elbows on the wall, with as much complacency as if he were looking out of window, " why is it that beauty is always obdurate, even when admiration is as honourable and respectful as mine ?" Here he smiled, kissed his hand, and made several low bows. " Is it owing to the bees, who, when the honey season is over, and they are supposed to have been killed with brimstone, in reality fly to Barbary and lull the captive Moors to sleep with their drowsy songs? Or is it," he added, dropping his voice almost to a whisper, " in consequence of the statue at Charing Cross having been lately seen on the Stock Exchange

The Gentleman next door declares his passion for M.rs Nickleby.

at midnight, walking arm-in-arm with the Pump from Aldgate, in a riding-habit?"

"Mama," murmured Kate, "do you hear him?"

"Hush, my dear!" replied Mrs. Nickleby, in the same tone of voice, "he is very polite, and I think that was a quotation from the poets. Pray, don't worry me so—you'll pinch my arm black and blue. Go away, sir."

"Quite away?" said the gentleman, with a languishing look, "Oh! quite away?"

"Yes," returned Mrs. Nickleby, "certainly. You have no business here. This is private property, sir; you ought to know that."

"I do know," said the old gentleman, laying his finger on his nose with an air of familiarity most reprehensible, "that this is a sacred and enchanted spot, where the most divine charms"—here he kissed his hand and bowed again—"waft mellifluousness over the neighbours' gardens, and force the fruit and vegetables into premature existence. That fact I am acquainted with. But will you permit me, fairest creature, to ask you one question, in the absence of the planet Venus, who has gone on business to the Horse Guards, and would otherwise— jealous of your superior charms—interpose between us?"

"Kate," observed Mrs. Nickleby, turning to her daughter, "it's very awkward, positively. I really don't know what to say to this gentleman. One ought to be civil, you know."

"Dear mama," rejoined Kate, "don't say a word to him, but let us run away as fast as we can, and shut ourselves up till Nicholas comes home."

Mrs. Nickleby looked very grand, not to say contemptuous, at this humiliating proposal; and turning to the old gentleman, who had watched them during these whispers with absorbing eagerness, said—

"If you will conduct yourself, sir, like the gentleman which I should imagine you to be from your language and—and—appearance, (quite the counterpart of your grand-papa, Kate, my dear, in his best days,) and will put your question to me in plain words, I will answer it."

If Mrs. Nickleby's excellent papa had borne, in his best days, a resemblance to the neighbour now looking over the wall, he must have been, to say the least, a very queer-looking old gentleman in his prime. Perhaps Kate thought so, for she ventured to glance at his living portrait with some attention, as he took off his black velvet cap, and, exhibiting a perfectly bald head made a long series of bows, each accompanied with a fresh kiss of the hand. After exhausting himself, to all appearance, with this fatiguing performance, he covered his head once more, pulled the cap very carefully over the tips of his ears, and resuming his former attitude, said,

"The question is——"

Here he broke off to look round in every direction, and satisfy himself beyond all doubt that there were no listeners near. Assured that there were not, he tapped his nose several times, accompanying the action with a cunning look, as though congratulating himself on his caution; and stretching out his neck, said in a loud whisper,

" Are you a princess ?"

" You are mocking me, sir," replied Mrs. Nickleby, making a feint of retreating towards the house.

" No, but are you ?" said the old gentleman.

" You know I am not, sir," replied Mrs. Nickleby.

" Then are you any relation to the Archbishop of Canterbury ?" inquired the old gentleman with great anxiety, " or to the Pope of Rome? or the Speaker of the House of Commons ? Forgive me, if I am wrong, but I was told you were niece to the Commissioners of Paving, and daughter-in-law to the Lord Mayor and Court of Common Council, which would account for your relationship to all three."

" Whoever has spread such reports, sir," returned Mrs. Nickleby, with some warmth, " has taken great liberties with my name, and one which I am sure my son Nicholas, if he was aware of it, would not allow for an instant. The idea !" said Mrs. Nickleby, drawing herself up, " niece to the Commissioners of Paving !"

" Pray, mama, come away !" whispered Kate.

" ' Pray, mama !' Nonsense, Kate," said Mrs. Nickleby, angrily, " but that's just the way. If they had said I was niece to a piping bullfinch, what would you care ! But I have no sympathy"—whimpered Mrs. Nickleby, " I don't expect it, that's one thing."

" Tears !" cried the old gentleman, with such an energetic jump, that he fell down two or three steps, and grated his chin against the wall. " Catch the crystal globules—catch 'em—bottle 'em up—cork 'em tight—put sealing-wax on the top—seal 'em with a cupid—label 'em ' Best quality'—and stow 'em away in the fourteen binn, with a bar of iron on the top to keep the thunder off !"

Issuing these commands, as if there were a dozen attendants all actively engaged in their execution, he turned his velvet cap inside out, put it on with great dignity so as to obscure his right eye and three-fourths of his nose, and sticking his arms a-kimbo, looked very fiercely at a sparrow hard by, till the bird flew away, when he put his cap in his pocket with an air of great satisfaction, and addressed himself with a respectful demeanour to Mrs. Nickleby.

" Beautiful madam," such were his words—" if I have made any mistake with regard to your family or connexions, I humbly beseech you to pardon me. If I supposed you to be related to Foreign Powers or Native Boards, it is because you have a manner, a carriage, a dignity, which you will excuse my saying that none but yourself (with the single exception perhaps of the tragic muse, when playing extemporaneously on the barrel organ before the East India Company) can parallel. I am not a youth, ma'am, as you see ; and although beings like you can never grow old, I venture to presume that we are fitted for each other."

" Really, Kate, my love !" said Mrs. Nickleby faintly, and looking another way.

" I have estates, ma'am," said the old gentleman, flourishing his right hand negligently, as if he made very light of such matters, and speaking very fast; "jewels, light-houses, frsh-ponds, a whalery of my own in the

North Sea, and several oyster-beds of great profit in the Pacific Ocean. If you will have the kindness to step down to the Royal Exchange and to take the cocked hat off the stoutest beadle's head, you will find my card in the lining of the crown, wrapped up in a piece of blue paper. My walking-stick is also to be seen on application to the chaplain of the House of Commons, who is strictly forbidden to take any money for showing it. I have enemies about me, ma'am," he looked towards his house and spoke very low, " who attack me on all occasions, and wish to secure my property. If you bless me with your hand and heart, you can apply to the Lord Chancellor or call out the military if necessary—sending my toothpick to the commander-in-chief will be sufficient—and so clear the house of them before the ceremony is performed. After that, love bliss and rapture; rapture love and bliss. Be mine, be mine!"

Repeating these last words with great rapture and enthusiasm, the old gentleman put on his black velvet cap again, and looking up into the sky in a hasty manner, said something that was not quite intelligible concerning a balloon he expected, and which was rather after its time.

" Be mine, be mine!" repeated the old gentleman.

" Kate, my dear," said Mrs. Nickleby, " I have hardly the power to speak; but it is necessary for the happiness of all parties that this matter should be set at rest for ever."

" Surely there is no necessity for you to say one word, mama?" reasoned Kate.

" You will allow me, my dear, if you please, to judge for myself," said Mrs. Nickleby.

" Be mine, be mine!" cried the old gentleman.

" It can scarcely be expected, sir," said Mrs. Nickleby, fixing her eyes modestly on the ground, " that I should tell a stranger whether I feel flattered and obliged by such proposals, or not. They certainly are made under very singular circumstances; still at the same time, as far as it goes, and to a certain extent of course," (Mrs. Nickleby's customary qualification,) " they must be gratifying and agreeable to one's feelings."

" Be mine, be mine," cried the old gentleman. " Gog and Magog, Gog and Magog. Be mine, be mine!"

" It will be sufficient for me to say, sir," resumed Mrs. Nickleby, with perfect seriousness—" and I am sure you'll see the propriety of taking an answer and going away—that I have made up my mind to remain a widow, and to devote myself to my children. You may not suppose I am the mother of two children—indeed many people have doubted it, and said that nothing on earth could ever make 'em believe it possible—but it is the case, and they are both grown up. We shall be very glad to have you for a neighbour—very glad; delighted, I'm sure—but in any other character it's quite impossible, quite. As to my being young enough to marry again, that perhaps may be so, or it may not be; but I couldn't think of it for an instant, not on any account whatever. I said I never would, and I never will. It's a very painful thing to have to reject proposals, and I would much rather that none were made; at the same time this is the answer that I determined long ago to make, and this is the answer I shall always give."

These observations were partly addressed to the old gentleman, partly to Kate, and partly delivered in soliloquy. Towards their conclusion, the suitor evinced a very irreverent degree of inattention, and Mrs. Nickleby had scarcely finished speaking, when, to the great terror both of that lady and her daughter, he suddenly flung off his coat, and springing on the top of the wall, threw himself into an attitude which displayed his small-clothes and grey worsteds to the fullest advantage, and concluded by standing on one leg, and repeating his favourite bellow with increased vehemence.

While he was still dwelling on the last note, and embellishing it with a prolonged flourish, a dirty hand was observed to glide stealthily and swiftly along the top of the wall, as if in pursuit of a fly, and then to clasp with the utmost dexterity one of the old gentleman's ancles. This done, the companion hand appeared, and clasped the other ancle.

Thus encumbered the old gentleman lifted his legs awkwardly once or twice, as if they were very clumsy and imperfect pieces of machinery, and then looking down on his own side of the wall, burst into a loud laugh.

" It's you, is it ? " said the old gentleman.

" Yes, it's me," replied a gruff voice.

" How's the Emperor of Tartary ? " said the old gentleman.

" Oh ! he's much the same as usual," was the reply. " No better and no worse."

" The young Prince of China," said the old gentleman, with much interest. " Is he reconciled to his father-in-law, the great potato salesman ? "

" No," answered the gruff voice ; " and he says he never will be, that's more."

" If that's the case," observed the old gentleman, " perhaps I'd better come down."

" Well," said the man on the other side, " I think you had, perhaps."

One of the hands being then cautiously unclasped, the old gentleman dropped into a sitting posture, and was looking round to smile and bow to Mrs. Nickleby, when he disappeared with some precipitation, as if his legs had been pulled from below.

Very much relieved by his disappearance, Kate was turning to speak to her mama, when the dirty hands again became visible, and were immediately followed by the figure of a coarse squat man, who ascended by the steps which had been recently occupied by their singular neighbour.

" Beg your pardon, ladies," said this new comer, grinning and touching his hat. " Has he been making love to either of you ? "

" Yes," said Kate.

" Ah ! " rejoined the man, taking his handkerchief out of his hat and wiping his face, " he always will, you know. Nothing will prevent his making love."

" I need not ask you if he is out of his mind, poor creature," said Kate.

"Why no," replied the man, looking into his hat, throwing his handkerchief in at one dab, and putting it on again. "That's pretty plain, that is."

"Has he been long so?" asked Kate.

"A long while."

"And is there no hope for him?" said Kate, compassionately.

"Not a bit, and don't deserve to be," replied the keeper. "He's a deal pleasanter without his senses than with 'em. He was the cruelest, wickedest, out-and-outerest old flint that ever drawed breath."

"Indeed!" said Kate.

"By George!" replied the keeper, shaking his head so emphatically that he was obliged to frown to keep his hat on, "I never come across such a vagabond, and my mate says the same. Broke his poor wife's heart, turned his daughters out of doors, drove his sons into the streets—it was a blessing he went mad at last, through evil tempers, and covetousness, and selfishness, and guzzling, and drinking, or he'd have drove many others so. Hope for *him*, an old rip! There isn't too much hope going, but I'll bet a crown that what there is, is saved for more deserving chaps than him, anyhow."

With which confession of his faith, the keeper shook his head again, as much as to say that nothing short of this would do, if things were to go on at all; and touching his hat sulkily—not that he was in an ill humour, but that his subject ruffled him—descended the ladder, and took it away.

During this conversation, Mrs. Nickleby had regarded the man with a severe and stedfast look. She now heaved a profound sigh, and pursing up her lips, shook her head in a slow and doubtful manner.

"Poor creature!" said Kate.

"Ah! poor indeed!" rejoined Mrs. Nickleby. "It's shameful that such things should be allowed.—Shameful!"

"How can they be helped, mama?" said Kate, mournfully. "The infirmities of nature—"

"Nature!" said Mrs. Nickleby. "What! Do *you* suppose this poor gentleman is out of his mind?"

"Can anybody who sees him entertain any other opinion, mama?"

"Why then, I just tell you this, Kate," returned Mrs. Nickleby, "that he is nothing of the kind, and I am surprised you can be so imposed upon. It's some plot of these people to possess themselves of his property—didn't he say so himself? He may be a little odd and flighty, perhaps, many of us are that; but downright mad! and express himself as he does, respectfully, and in quite poetical language, and making offers with so much thought, and care, and prudence—not as if he ran into the streets, and went down upon his knees to the first chit of a girl he met, as a madman would! No, no, Kate, there's a great deal too much method in *his* madness; depend upon that, my dear."

CHAPTER XLII.

ILLUSTRATIVE OF THE CONVIVIAL SENTIMENT, THAT THE BEST OF
FRIENDS MUST SOMETIMES PART.

THE pavement of Snow Hill had been baking and frying all day in
the heat, and the twain Saracens' heads guarding the entrance to the
hostelry of whose name and sign they are the duplicate presentments,
looked—or seemed in the eyes of jaded and foot-sore passers by, to
look—more vicious than usual, after blistering and scorching in the sun,
when, in one of the inn's smallest sitting-rooms, through whose open
window there rose, in a palpable steam, wholesome exhalations from
reeking coach-horses, the usual furniture of a tea-table was displayed
in neat and inviting order, flanked by large joints of roast and boiled, a
tongue, a pigeon-pie, a cold fowl, a tankard of ale, and other little
matters of the like kind, which, in degenerate towns and cities are
generally understood to belong more particularly to solid lunches, stage-
coach dinners, or unusually substantial breakfasts.

Mr. John Browdie, with his hands in his pockets, hovered restlessly
about these delicacies, stepping occasionally to whisk the flies out of the
sugar-basin with his wife's pocket-handkerchief, or to dip a tea-spoon
in the milkpot and carry it to his mouth, or to cut off a little knob of
crust, and a little corner of meat, and swallow them at two gulps like a
couple of pills. After every one of these flirtations with the eatables,
he pulled out his watch, and declared with an earnestness quite pathetic
that he couldn't undertake to hold out two minutes longer.

" 'Tilly!" said John to his lady, who was reclining half awake and
half asleep upon a sofa.

" Well, John!"

" Weel, John!" retorted her husband, impatiently. " Dost thou feel
hoongry, lass?"

" Not very," said Mrs. Browdie.

" Not vary!" repeated John, raising his eyes to the ceiling. " Hear
her say not vary, and us dining at three, and loonching off pasthry thot
aggravates a mon 'stead of pacifying him ! Not vary!"

" Here's a gen'lman for you, sir," said the waiter, looking in.

" A wa'at, for me?" cried John, as though he thought it must be a
letter, or a parcel.

" A gen'lman, sir."

"Stars and garthers, chap!" said John, " wa'at dost thou coom and
say thot for. In wi' 'un."

" Are you at home, sir?"

" At whoam!" cried John, "I wish I wur; I'd ha tea'd two hour
ago. Why, I told t'oother chap to look sharp ootside door, and tell 'un
d'rectly he coom, thot we war faint wi' hoonger. In wi' 'un. Aha!
Thee hond, Misther Nickleby. This is nigh to be the proodest day o'
my life, sir. Hoo be all wi' ye? Ding! But, I'm glod o' this!"

Quite forgetting even his hunger in the heartiness of his salutation,

John Browdie shook Nicholas by the hand again and again, slapping his palm with great violence between each shake, to add warmth to the reception.

"Ah! there she be," said John, observing the look which Nicholas directed towards his wife. "There she be—we shan't quarrel about her noo—Eh? Ecod, when I think o' thot—but thou want'st soom'at to eat. Fall to, mun, fall to, and for wa'at we're aboot to receive——"

No doubt the grace was properly finished, but nothing more was heard, for John had already begun to play such a knife and fork, that his speech was, for the time, gone.

"I shall take the usual licence, Mr. Browdie," said Nicholas, as he placed a chair for the bride.

"Tak' whatever thou like'st," said John, "and when a's gane, ca' for more."

Without stopping to explain, Nicholas kissed the blushing Mrs. Browdie, and handed her to her seat.

"I say," said John, rather astounded for the moment, "mak' theeself quite at whoam, will 'ee?"

"You may depend upon that," replied Nicholas; "on one condition."

"And wa'at may thot be?" asked John.

"That you make me a godfather the very first time you have occasion for one."

"Eh! d'ye hear thot!" cried John, laying down his knife and fork. "A godfeyther! Ha! ha! ha! Tilly—hear till 'un—a godfeyther! Divn't say a word more, ye'll never beat thot. Occasion for 'un—a godfeyther! Ha! ha! ha!"

Never was man so tickled with a respectable old joke, as John Browdie was with this. He chuckled, roared, half suffocated himself by laughing large pieces of beef into his windpipe, roared again, persisted in eating at the same time, got red in the face and black in the forehead, coughed, cried, got better, went off again laughing inwardly, got worse, choked, had his back thumped, stamped about, frightened his wife, and at last recovered in a state of the last exhaustion and with the water streaming from his eyes, but still faintly ejaculating "A godfeyther—a godfeyther, Tilly!" in a tone bespeaking an exquisite relish of the sally, which no suffering could diminish.

"You remember the night of our first tea-drinking?" said Nicholas.

"Shall I e'er forget it, mun?" replied John Browdie.

"He was a desperate fellow that night though, was he not, Mrs. Browdie?" said Nicholas. "Quite a monster?"

"If you had only heard him as we were going home, Mr. Nickleby, you'd have said so indeed," returned the bride. "I never was so frightened in all my life."

"Coom, coom," said John, with a broad grin; "thou know'st betther than thot, Tilly."

"So I was," replied Mrs. Browdie. "I almost made up my mind never to speak to you again."

"A'most!" said John, with a broader grin than the last. "A'most made up her mind! And she wur coaxin', and coaxin', and wheedlin', and wheedlin', a' the blessed wa'. 'Wa'at did'st thou let yon chap mak' oop tiv'ee for?' says I. 'I deedn't, John,' says she, a squeedgin my arm. ' You deedn't?' says I. ' Noa,' says she, a squeedgin of me agean."

"Lor, John!" interposed his pretty wife, colouring very much. "How can you talk such nonsense? As if I should have dreamt of such a thing!"

" I dinnot know whether thou'd ever dreamt of it, though I think that's loike eneaf, mind," retorted John; "but thou didst it. ' Ye're a feeckle, changeable weathercock, lass,' says I. ' Not feeckle, John,' says she. ' Yes,' says I, ' feeckle, dom'd feeckle. Dinnot tell me thou bean't, efther yon chap at schoolmeasther's,' says I. ' Him!' says she, quite screeching. ' Ah! him!' says I. ' Why, John,' says she—and she coom a deal closer and squeedged a deal harder than she'd deane afore—' dost thou think it's nat'ral noo, that having such a proper mun as thou to keep company wi', I'd ever tak' oop wi' such a leetle scanty whipper-snapper as you?' she says. Ha! ha! ha! She said whipper-snapper! ' Ecod!' I says, ' efther thot, neame the day, and let's have it ower!' Ha! ha! ha!"

Nicholas laughed very heartily at this story, both on account of its telling against himself, and his being desirous to spare the blushes of Mrs. Browdie, whose protestations were drowned in peals of laughter from her husband. His good-nature soon put her at her ease; and although she still denied the charge, she laughed so heartily at it, that Nicholas had the satisfaction of feeling assured that in all essential respects it was strictly true.

" This is the second time," said Nicholas, " that we have ever taken a meal together, and only the third I have ever seen you; and yet it really seems to me as if I were among old friends."

" Weel!" observed the Yorkshireman, " so I say."

" And I am sure I do," added his young wife.

" I have the best reason to be impressed with the feeling, mind," said Nicholas; " for if it had not been for your kindness of heart, my good friend, when I had no right or reason to expect it, I know not what might have become of me or what plight I should have been in by this time."

" Talk aboot soom'at else," replied John, gruffly, "and dinnot bother."

" It must be a new song to the same tune then," said Nicholas, smiling. " I told you in my letter that I deeply felt and admired your sympathy with that poor lad, whom you released at the risk of involving yourself in trouble and difficulty; but I can never tell you how grateful he and I, and others whom you don't know, are to you for taking pity on him."

" Ecod!" rejoined John Browdie, drawing up his chair; " and I can never tell you hoo gratful soom folks that we do know would be loikewise, if they know'd I had takken pity on him."

" Ah!" exclaimed Mrs. Browdie, " what a state I was in, that night!"

" Were they at all disposed to give you credit for assisting in the escape?" inquired Nicholas of John Browdie.

" Not a bit," replied the Yorkshireman, extending his mouth from ear to ear. " There I lay, snoog in schoolmeasther's bed long efther it was dark, and nobody coom nigh the pleace. ' Weel !' thinks I, 'he's got a pretty good start, and if he bean't whoam by noo, he never will be ; so you may coom as quick as you loike, and foind us reddy '—that is, you know, schoolmeasther might coom."

" I understand," said Nicholas.

" Presently," resumed John, " he *did* coom. I heerd door shut doonstairs, and him a warking oop in the daark. ' Slow and steddy,' I says to myself, ' tak' your time, sir—no hurry.' He cooms to the door, turns the key—turns the key when there warn't nothing to hoold the lock—and ca's oot ' Hallo there !'—' Yes,' thinks I, ' you may do thot agean, and not wakken anybody, sir.' ' Hallo, there,' he says, and then he stops. 'Thou'd betthernot aggravate me,' says schoolmeasther, efther a little time. ' I'll brak' every boan in your boddy, Smike,' he says, efther another little time. Then all of a soodden, he sings oot for a loight, and when it cooms—ecod, such a hoorly-boorly ! ' Wa'ats the matter ?' says I. ' He's gane,' says he,—stark mad wi' vengeance. ' Have you heerd nought ?' ' Ees,' says I, ' I heerd street door shut, no time at a' ago. I heerd a person run doon there' (pointing t'other wa'—eh ?) ' Help !' he cries. ' I'll help you,' says I ; and off we set—the wrong wa' ! Ho ! ho ! ho !"

" Did you go far ?" asked Nicholas.

" Far !" replied John ; " I run him clean off his legs in quarther of an hoor. To see old schoolmeasther wi'out his hat, skimming along oop to his knees in mud and wather, tumbling over fences, and rowling into ditches, and bawling oot like mad, wi' his one eye looking sharp out for the lad, and his coat-tails flying out behind, and him spattered wi' mud all ower, face and all ;—I thot I should ha' dropped doon, and killed myself wi' laughing."

John laughed so heartily at the mere recollection, that he communicated the contagion to both his hearers, and all three burst into peals of laughter, which were renewed again and again, until they could laugh no longer.

" He's a bad 'un," said John, wiping his eyes ; " a vary bad 'un, is schoolmeasther."

" I can't bear the sight of him, John," said his wife.

" Coom," retorted John, " thot's tidy in you, thot is. If it wa'nt along o' you, we shouldn't know nought aboot 'un. Thou know'd 'un first, Tilly, didn't thou ?"

" I couldn't help knowing Fanny Squeers, John," returned his wife ; " she was an old playmate of mine, you know."

" Weel," replied John, " dean't I say so, lass ? It's best to be neighbourly, and keep up old acquaintance loike ; and what I say is, dean't quarrel if 'ee can help it. Dinnot think so, Mr. Nickleby ?"

" Certainly," returned Nicholas ; " and you acted upon that principle when I met you on horseback on the road, after our memorable evening."

" Sure-ly," said John. " Wa'at I say, I stick by."

" And that's a fine thing to do, and manly too," said Nicholas, " though it's not exactly what we understand by ' coming Yorkshire over us' in London. Miss Squeers is stopping with you, you said in your note."

" Yes," replied John, " Tilly's bridesmaid ; and a queer bridesmaid she be, too. She wean't be a bride in a hurry, I reckon."

" For shame, John," said Mrs. Browdie ; with an acute perception of the joke though, being a bride herself.

" The groom will be a blessed mun," said John, his eyes twinkling at the idea. " He'll be in luck, he will."

" You see, Mr. Nicklebly," said his wife, " that it was in consequence of her being here, that John wrote to you and fixed to-night, because we thought that it wouldn't be pleasant for you to meet, after what has passed—"

" Unquestionably. You were quite right in that," said Nicholas, interrupting.

" Especially," observed Mrs. Browdie, looking very sly, " after what we know about past and gone love matters."

" We know, indeed ! " said Nicholas, shaking his head. " You behaved rather wickedly there, I suspect."

" O' course she did," said John Browdie, passing his huge fore-finger through one of his wife's pretty ringlets, and looking very proud of her. " She wur always as skittish and full o' tricks as a——"

" Well, as a what ? " said his wife.

" As a woman," returned John. " Ding ! But I dinnot know ought else that cooms near it."

" You were speaking about Miss Squeers," said Nicholas, with the view of stopping some slight connubialities which had begun to pass between Mr. and Mrs. Browdie, and which rendered the position of a third party in some degree embarrassing, as occasioning him to feel rather in the way than otherwise.

" Oh yes," rejoined Mrs. Browdie. " John, ha' done —— John fixed to-night, because she had settled that she would go and drink tea with her father. And to make quite sure of there being nothing amiss, and of your being quite alone with us, he settled to go out there and fetch her home. "

" That was a very good arrangement," said Nicholas ; " though I am sorry to be the occasion of so much trouble."

" Not the least in the world," returned Mrs. Browdie ; " for we have looked forward to seeing you—John and I have—with the greatest possible pleasure. Do you know, Mr. Nickleby," said Mrs. Browdie, with her archest smile, " that I really think Fanny Squeers was very fond of you ?"

" I am very much obliged to her," said Nicholas ; " but, upon my word, I never aspired to making any impression upon her virgin heart."

" How you talk ! " tittered Mrs. Browdie. " No, but do you know that really—seriously now and without any joking—I was given to understand by Fanny herself, that you had made an offer to her, and that you two were going to be engaged quite solemn and regular."

" Was you, ma'am—was you ?" cried a shrill female voice, " was you given to understand that I—I—was going to be engaged to an assassinating thief that shed the gore of my pa ? Do you—do you think, ma'am—that I was very fond of such dirt beneath my feet, as I couldn't condescend to touch with kitchen tongs, without blacking and crocking myself by the contract ? Do you, ma'am—do you ? Oh! base and degrading 'Tilda !"

With these reproaches Miss Squeers flung the door wide open, and disclosed to the eyes of the astonished Browdies and Nicholas, not only her own symmetrical form, arrayed in the chaste white garments before described, (a little dirtier) but the form of her brother and father, the pair of Wackfords.

" This is the hend, is it ?" continued Miss Squeers, who, being excited, aspirated her h's strongly; " this is the hend, is it, of all my forbearance and friendship for that double-faced thing—that viper, that—that— mermaid ?" (Miss Squeers hesitated a long time for this last epithet, and brought it out triumphantly at last, as if it quite clinched the business.) " This is the hend, is it, of all my bearing with her deceitfulness, her lowness, her falseness, her laying herself out to catch the admiration of vulgar minds, in a way which made me blush for my— for my——"

" Gender," suggested Mr. Squeers, regarding the spectators with a malevolent eye—literally a malevolent eye.

" Yes," said Miss Squeers ; " but I thank my stars that my ma' is of the same——"

" Hear, hear !" remarked Mr. Squeers ; " and I wish she was here to have a scratch at this company."

" This is the hend, is it," said Miss Squeers, tossing her head, and looking contemptuously at the floor, " of my taking notice of that rubbishing creature, and demeaning myself to patronise her ?"

" Oh, come," rejoined Mrs. Browdie, disregarding all the endeavours of her spouse to restrain her, and forcing herself into a front row, " don't talk such nonsense as that."

" Have I not patronised you, ma'am ?" demanded Miss Squeers.

" No," returned Mrs. Browdie.

" I will not look for blushes in such a quarter," said Miss Squeers, haughtily, " for that countenance is a stranger to everything but hignominiousness and red-faced boldness."

" I say," interposed John Browdie, nettled by these accumulated attacks on his wife, " dra' it mild, dra' it mild."

" You, Mr. Browdie," said Miss Squeers, taking him up very quickly, " I pity. I have no feeling for you, sir, but one of unliquidated pity."

" Oh !" said John.

" No," said Miss Squeers, looking sideways at her parent, " although I *am* a queer bridesmaid, and *shan't* be a bride in a hurry, and although my husband *will* be in luck, I entertain no sentiments towards you, sir, but sentiments of pity."

Here Miss Squeers looked sideways at her father again, who looked sideways at her, as much as to say, ' There you had him.'

" *I* know what you've got to go through," said Miss Squeers, shaking her curls violently. " *I* know what life is before you, and if you was my bitterest and deadliest enemy, I could wish you nothing worse."

" Couldn't you wish to be married to him yourself, if that was the case ?" inquired Mrs. Browdie, with great suavity of manner.

" Oh, ma'am, how witty you are !" retorted Miss Squeers, with a low curtsey, " almost as witty, ma'am, as you are clever. How very clever it was in you, ma'am, to choose a time when I had gone to tea with my pa', and was sure not to come back without being fetched ! What a pity you never thought that other people might be as clever as yourself, and spoil your plans !"

" You won't vex me, child, with such airs as these," said the late Miss Price, assuming the matron.

" Don't *Missis* me, ma'am, if you please," returned Miss Squeers, sharply. " I'll not bear it. Is *this* the hend——"

" Dang it a'," cried John Browdie, impatiently. " Say thee say out, Fanny, and mak' sure it's the end, and dinnot ask nobody whether it is or not."

" Thanking you for your advice which was not required, Mr. Browdie," returned Miss Squeers, with laborious politeness, " have the goodness not to presume to meddle with my christian name. Even my pity shall never make me forget what's due to myself, Mr. Browdie. 'Tilda," said Miss Squeers, with such a sudden accession of violence that John started in his boots, " I throw you off for ever, Miss. I abandon you, I renounce you. I wouldn't," cried Miss Squeers in a solemn voice, " have a child named 'Tilda—not to save it from its grave."

" As for the matther o' that," observed John, " it'll be time eneaf to think aboot neaming of it when it cooms."

" John !" interposed his wife, " don't tease her."

" Oh! Tease, indeed!" cried Miss Squeers, bridling up. " Tease, indeed! He! he! Tease, too! No, don't tease her. Consider her feelings, pray."

" If it's fated that listeners are never to hear any good of themselves," said Mrs. Browdie, " I can't help it, and I am very sorry for it. But I will say, Fanny, that times out of number I have spoken so kindly of you behind your back, that even you could have found no fault with what I said."

" Oh, I dare say not, ma'am !" cried Miss Squeers, with another curtsey. " Best thanks to you for your goodness, and begging and praying you not to be hard upon me another time !"

" I don't know," resumed Mrs. Browdie, " that I have said anything very bad' of you, even now—at all events, what I did say was quite true ; but if I have, I am very sorry for it, and I beg your pardon. You have said much worse of me, scores of times, Fanny ; but I have never borne any malice to you, and I hope you'll not bear any to me."

Miss Squeers made no more direct reply than surveying her former friend from top to toe, and elevating her nose in the air with ineffable disdain. But some indistinct allusions to a ' puss,' and a ' minx,' and a ' contemptible creature,' escaped her ; and this, together with a severe biting of the lips, great difficulty in swallowing, and very frequent comings and goings of breath, seemed to imply that feelings were swelling in Miss Squeers's bosom too great for utterance.

While the foregoing conversation was proceeding, Master Wackford, finding himself unnoticed, and feeling his preponderating inclinations strong upon him, had by little and little sidled up to the table and attacked the food with such slight skirmishing as drawing his fingers round and round the inside of the plates, and afterwards sucking them with infinite relish—picking the bread, and dragging the pieces over the surface of the butter—pocketing lumps of sugar, pretending all the time to be absorbed in thought—and so forth. Finding that no interference was attempted with these small liberties, he gradually mounted to greater, and, after helping himself to a moderately good cold collation, was, by this time, deep in the pie.

Nothing of this had been unobserved by Mr. Squeers, who, so long as the attention of the company was fixed upon other objects, hugged himself to think that his son and heir should be fattening at the enemy's expense. But there being now an appearance of a temporary calm, in which the proceedings of little Wackford could scarcely fail to be observed, he feigned to be aware of the circumstance for the first time, and inflicted upon the face of that young gentleman a slap that made the very tea-cups ring.

" Eating ! " cried Mr. Squeers, " of what his father's enemies has left ! It's fit to go and poison you, you unnat'ral boy."

" It wean't hurt him," said John, apparently very much relieved by the prospect of having a man in the quarrel ; " let 'un eat. I wish the whole school was here. I'd give 'em soom'ut to stay their unfort'nate stomachs wi', if I spent the last penny I had ! "

Squeers scowled at him with the worst and most malicious expression of which his face was capable—it was a face of remarkable capability, too, in that way—and shook his fist stealthily.

" Coom, coom, schoolmeasther," said John, " dinnot make a fool o' thyself ; for if I was to sheake mine—only once—thou'd fa' doon wi' the wind o' it."

" It was you, was it," returned Squeers, " that helped off my runaway boy ? It was you, was it ? "

" Me ! " returned John, in a loud tone. " Yes, it wa' me, coom ; wa'at o' that ! It wa' me. Noo then ! "

" You hear him say he did it, my child ! " said Squeers, appealing to his daughter. " You hear him say he did it ! "

" Did it ! " cried John. " I'll tell'ee more ; hear this, too. If thou'd get another runaway boy, I'd do it agean. If thou'd got twenty roonaway boys, I'd do it twenty times ower, and twenty more to thot ; and I tell thee more," said John, " noo my blood is oop, that thou'rt an old ra'ascal ; and that it's weel for thou, thou be'st an old 'un, or I'd ha poonded thee to flour, when thou told an honest mun hoo' thou'd licked that poor chap in t' coorch."

" An honest man ! " cried Squeers, with a sneer.

" Ah ! an honest man," replied John ; " honest in ought but ever putting legs under seame table wi' such as thou."

" Scandal! " said Squeers, exultingly. " Two witnesses to it ; Wackford knows the nature of an oath, he does—we shall have you there, Sir. Rascal, eh ? " Mr. Squeers took out his pocket-book and made a note of it.—" Very good. I should say that was worth full twenty pound at the next assizes, without the honesty, sir."

" 'Soizes," cried John, " thou'd betther not talk to me o' 'Soizes. York-shire schools have been shown up at 'Soizes afore noo, mun, and it's a ticklish soobjact to revive, I can tell ye."

Mr. Squeers shook his head in a threatening manner, looking very white with passion ; and taking his daughter's arm, and dragging little Wackford by the hand, retreated towards the door.

" As for you," said Squeers, turning round and addressing Nicholas, who, as he had caused him to smart pretty soundly on a former occa-sion, purposely abstained from taking any part in the discussion, " see if I ain't down upon you before long. " You'll go a kidnapping of boys, will you ? Take care their fathers don't turn up—mark that— take care their fathers don't turn up, and send 'em back to me to do as I like with, in spite of you."

" I am not afraid of that," replied Nicholas, shrugging his shoulders contemptuously, and turning away.

" Ain't you !" retorted Squeers, with a diabolical look. " Now then, come along."

" I leave such society, with my pa', for *h*ever," said Miss Squeers, looking contemptuously and loftily round. " I am defiled by breathing the air with such creatures. Poor Mr. Browdie ! He! he! he ! I do pity him, that I do ; he's so deluded ! He! he! he!——Artful and designing 'Tilda !"

With this sudden relapse into the sternest and most majestic wrath, Miss Squeers swept from the room ; and having sustained her dignity until the last possible moment, was heard to sob and scream and struggle in the passage.

John Browdie remained standing behind the table, looking from his wife to Nicholas, and back again, with his mouth wide open, until his hand accidentally fell upon the tankard of ale, when he took it up, and having obscured his features therewith for some time, drew a long breath, handed it over to Nicholas, and rang the bell.

" Here, waither," said John, briskly. " Look alive here. Tak' these things awa', and let's have soomat broiled for sooper—vary comfortable and plenty o' it—at ten o'clock. Bring soom brandy and soom wather, and a pair o' slippers—the largest pair in the house—and be quick aboot it. Dash ma' wig!" said John, rubbing his hands, " there's no ganging oot to neeght, noo, to fetch anybody whoam, and ecod, we'll begin to spend the evening in airnest."

IMPORTANT, VALUABLE, AND CHEAP

MAPS,

AND

MISCELLANEOUS WORKS,

PUBLISHED BY

GRATTAN AND GILBERT,

51, PATERNOSTER ROW,

LONDON.

CONTENTS:

WHOLESALE AND EXPORTATION ORDERS

EXECUTED ON LIBERAL TERMS.

SIZE, THREE FEET FIVE INCHES BY TWO FEET FOUR.

In sheet, coloured, only 12s.; *case* 18s.; *black roller, varnished,* 1l. 4s.; *or* MOUNTED ON FRENCH POLISHED MAHOGANY ROLLER, BEAUTIFULLY COLOURED AND VARNISHED, *price* 1l. 8s.

GILBERT'S
NEW MAP OF ENGLAND AND WALES,

ON ONE SHEET,

WITH A

PICTORIAL COMPARATIVE VIEW OF THE MOUNTAINS AND CHART OF THE RIVERS,

AND THE PUBLIC RAILWAYS.

In presenting this much admired Map to the Public, the Publishers beg to direct particular notice to some of the important features, most of which are entirely new. The first, which adds greatly to its perspicuity, is that every name is arranged to read in that county to which its town or village belongs; when it happens that a place is situated in two counties, the name will be found to read partly in each. Great attention has been paid to the boroughs, which may be readily distinguished by the stars attached, which denote the number of Members returned; the contributory boroughs being marked with an arrow head. The market towns, with their distance from London, have had the strictest care bestowed on them relative to the number of miles. In short, no trouble has been spared to produce a striking and decided difference, so as at one glance to ascertain whether any name is that of a City, County Town, Borough, Market Town, or Village. The Railroads are carefully laid down from the most authentic documents. It will also be found that the Mail Coach Roads may be greatly depended upon for accuracy. No Maps hitherto laid before the public have, as *Guides to Travellers,* inserted the Islands of Guernsey, Jersey, &c., in their proper position; these are not only given, but also the coast extending from Calais to Havre de Regneville, the Steam-boat tracks, and the distance from each port.

With every copy of the above Map, sold previous to the 30*th of June,* will be given a Ticket, securing to the Purchaser *gratuitously,* on the 30th of June, a 12mo volume (now preparing), entitled

A POPULAR DESCRIPTION OF ENGLAND AND WALES;

By R. MUDIE, Esq.

The price of this Book, *separately from the Map,* will be 5s.

Price, stitched with the Map coloured, only 2s.; *in case,* 4s. 6d.; *or with the Map mounted on mahogany roller and varnished,* 6s.

GILBERT'S
GEOLOGY OF ENGLAND AND WALES,

WITH A MAP.

It is with great pleasure we introduce to our readers this map, it is a very praiseworthy performance."—*Athenæum.*

All that is necessary to a general survey is compressed with accuracy into its pages.—*Atlas.*

Of great service to those who wish to acquire, in brief, an acquaintance with the geological features of the kingdom. It is plainly written, and contains a vast deal of information. A well-executed map accompanies the treatise, and will give a more correct notion than volumes of dry dissertation.—*Railway Times.*

A large mass of valuable information in a small compass. The map is very excellently executed.—*Court Journal.*

SIZE, FOUR FEET BY FOUR FEET ONE INCH.

Price only 18s. in sheets coloured; 1l. 10s. case; black roller, varnished, 1l. 16s.; or,
MOUNTED ON FRENCH POLISHED MAHOGANY ROLLER, BEAUTIFULLY COLOURED AND
VARNISHED, PRICE 2l. 2s., *the third edition of*

GILBERT'S
NEW MAP OF EUROPE,
With all the Public Railways.

The approval of the two first editions of this cheap and valuable Map has encouraged the Proprietors to add numerous improvements to the new edition. The Map, which is engraved in a bold and distinct character, is laid down from the best authorities, showing in the clearest manner ever yet attempted, its physical features, political divisions, post and railroads, steam communication, population, &c. A Diagram of Hills, in profile, is introduced, and the water is clearly distinguishable from the land, by the former being engine ruled.

This is an useful, valuable, elegant, and carefully executed undertaking, embracing all the most recent improvements. It is got up on a liberal scale that does great credit to the publisher. We heartily recommend it to the traveller, and consider it an acquisition to the public seminary equally as the private library of the gentleman.—*Metropolitan Conservative Journal.*

Price, stitched, with the Map coloured, only 2s. 6d.; in case, 4s. 6d.; or with the Map mounted on mahogany roller and varnished, 6s 6d.

GILBERT'S
RAILWAYS OF ENGLAND AND WALES,
WITH A MAP.

This is a very useful compilation, on an important and interesting subject, containing an account of the origin, progress, and present state of railways in this country, accompanied by a map, with all the lines carefully laid down, both of those already constructed, and those which are projected or in course of execution. The statistics collected in this work are extremely curious, and deserving of attention. We recommend this little *brochure* before us to all who feel an interest in the subject.—*Times, Dec.* 19.

The descriptions are full and clear, and, by the aid of the Map, the reader is enabled to trace with accuracy the course of all these flying paths through the land.—*Atlas.*

This conveys to us a succinct account of the origin and progress of Railroads illustrating an excellent Map, showing their position throughout England and Wales.—*Sunday Times.*

A spirited and entertaining, but at the same time accurate, account of the origin, progress, and present state of our Railways, with a Map, on which not only existing but projected Railways are laid down.—*Weekly True Sun.*

This little work contains an excellent Map of all the Railways commenced and proposed throughout England and Wales. It is accompanied by a good history of Railways—a statement of the different scientific principles upon which they are constructed, with various details respecting the carriages, the steam engine, the weight and structure of the trains, and, in short, numerous particulars, embracing, it appears to us, all points connected with the subject.—*Dispatch.*

SIZE, THIRTY-EIGHT INCHES BY NINETEEN.

In sheet, coloured, only 4s.; case 6s. 6d.; black roller, varnished 9s.; or MOUNTED ON FRENCH
POLISHED MAHOGANY ROLLER, BEAUTIFULLY COLOURED AND VARNISHED, *price* 14s.

GILBERT'S
NEW MAP OF THE WORLD,
FOR 1839.

The Proprietors with confidence beg to submit these Hemispheres to the particular notice of
Scholastic Teachers, those interested in Geographical Science, and the Public generally, as a
spirited attempt to delineate the present state of the known world.

They flatter themselves the work will be universally acknowledged to contain a large mass
of valuable information, and the price of the work is so low as to come within the means of all
classes of society.

It is clearly executed, and can thus be readily consulted. The other general information,
supplied on a single sheet, is also extremely useful. *The height of the principal mountains, the
length of the great rivers, the summary of the chief products of various quarters, and tabular
calculations of population, language, &c. &c.*, are all matters which should be familiar to
intelligent persons.—*Literary Gazette.*

We have hearty commendations to bestow upon Gilbert's Map of the World, which has just
been issued at a cheap rate, in a convenient form, and in a style of execution that leaves
nothing to be desired. It contains a variety of necessary information, extensive tabular
computations, *and the dates of Geographical discoveries.—Court Journal.*

ON THE IMPORTANCE OF A MAP OF THE WORLD.

Of all the furnishings requisite for a family, one of the most valuable is a Map of the World,
on a scale sufficiently large for displaying the great distinguishing points of every country, at
the same time that it presents a general view of the whole.   The great value of such a map
consists in the facility with which it can be made an artificial memory to every kind of knowledge, and a bond of union, uniting the whole together, so that it is as easy to pass from any
one department to any other of a different, or even an opposite character, as it is to pass from
one part to another of the same department.

The earth is sometimes represented by the globe, or model, and sometimes by the plane
picture, or map; and, for all useful purposes, the map, in hemispheres, is beyond comparison
the more serviceable of the two, not only in the details of geography, but more especially the
studying the earth as a whole, in the relations of its different parts, and the results which we
draw from the comparison, at one view, of these with each other.

Such is the importance of studying intimately and correctly a good Map of the World, that,
independently altogether of the characters of the earth itself, considered as a whole, no one is
properly qualified for acting his part well in the common business of life, and no one is capable
of duly appreciating the value of history, enjoying a book of travels, or, in short, of talking
like a rational being about any of those countless foreign substances, which are now met with
as the materials of articles of use or ornament, or as portions of food in almost every house
within these kingdoms.

If all persons could once be led to this, it is incalculable to conceive how much more
delightful it would make the world we live in; because it would enable us to live mentally,
and in our mental life consists our real enjoyment of all the world at once. Thus, for instance,
we should be enabled to drink our coffee in the groves of Yemen, with turbaned Arabs and
loaded camels around us; and, under that balmy sky, we could look across the Red Sea, where
there is in one place an assemblage of worm-built reefs, extending line upon line, and white
with the foam produced by an angry wind, and in another place reeking with the steam of
volcanic fires, while the bottom is as gay as a garden with the vegetation of the deep, and the
waters are literally encumbered with living creatures.   So might we drink our tea in some
fantastic alcove in the pleasure-grounds of a Chinese mandarin, and enjoy the characters of
that most singular country, which has remained changeless for hundreds of years, amid all the
vicissitudes, reverses, and progressions of our part of the world.   We should never taste the
stimulating flavour of cinnamon, without being borne in thought to Ceylon, with its rich fields
of rice; its beautiful copses, which furnish this wholesome and exhilarating spice; its tangled
and swampy woods, with their herds of gigantic elephants; its more dry and inland forests,
peopled with countless thousands of apes, which make the early morn literally hideous with their
cries, and the females of some of which may be occasionally found descending to the brook, in

order to wash the faces of their little ones. So also we should never taste a clove or a nutmeg, without being wafted to the spicy islands of the oriental archipelago, where all is the vigour of growth and beauty, and the richness of perfume ; where perpetual health is carried on the gentle gales of the widest ocean of the globe; where some of the fruits combine the qualities of the most racy of their own tribe with the substantial nourishment of delicate animal food, and the admixture of a cooling ice and a cheering cordial ; while the trees around us would be thronged with the loveliest of birds; and the birds of Paradise, with their long and filmy feathers, streaming in every direction through the air, like meteors—meteors which shine but do not burn.

But we must stop, for there is no end to the catalogue, and it is an exhibition of wh. .h we must not see too much at a passing glance, lest it should wile us from our proper purpose. And we have mentioned these few particulars merely to let those who are yet in ignorance of the subject know how well the world is worth our studying—how richly the earth which we inhabit has been endowed by its bountiful Maker—how full the feast which it affords to all; and yet how varied, how free from surfeiting, how healthful !

Now, as we have already said, not only might, but *should*, every commodity of every region transport us to that region, and make it render up to our enjoyment all that it posseses ; but a Map of the World, which has been duly studied, brings the whole before us the moment we glance at it; nor is it confined to the external appearance, and the productions and the present population of the several countries ; for in proportion to the extent of our knowledge, will be the extent of the reminiscence which this most powerful talisman will conjure up. Truly, it is magic,—but it is magic of nature's exhibiting ; the effect of infinite wisdom and goodness, without deception, without any thing to mislead or corrupt, and with every thing to inform the head and soften the heart.

As we look upon these two circular spots of paper, the whole of the human race, from Adam downward, rise in succession to our view ; and every event, pictured to itself, stands out as fresh and as forcible in its colours as if it were before our mortal eyes. Now we see the congregating clouds and the flashing lightnings, and hear the dismal sounds of the volleyed thunder and the rending earth, as " the windows of heaven are opened, and the fountains of the great deep broken up," in order to drown the world sunk in iniquity beyond all mercy and forgiveness; but, in the very depth of the tempest terrors, behold the ark of deliverance for the man who was faithful amid an offending race, riding safely on the top of the swelling waters; and no sooner is the purpose accomplished, and execution done upon the guilty, than, lo ! " the bow of hope is seen in the cloud, and the promise of mercy is declared to a renovated world."

Again, we might call—or rather there would arise without our calling—any one scene in the world's history, whether sacred or profane. We might march through the divided waters with the delivered Israelites, and standing safely on the shore, behold the overwhelming of Pharoah and his host. So might we continue the stream of history down to the present hour, adding nation after nation as it arose, and losing it in the sandy desert of oblivion when it perished from the scroll ; and in tracing the sacred story we should be enabled, if we brought sufficient knowledge to the task, to ascertain in a manner beyond all doubt that the history of the old Testament is so faithful to the natural character of the countries in which the scenes of it are laid, and so entirely free from all allusion to other countries,—so different indeed, from all human record, in this respect, that it cannot but be true to the letter.

Let the knowledge be once fairly acquired, whether it be limited or extended, if it be properly applied to the map, the map will render it up more briefly and clearly than it would be rendered up by any other means. The extent and the readiness of this *memorial* or suggestive power on the map, will astonish those who have not been in the habit of using it; and there is a most agreeable way of finding this out. Let, for instance, the conversation be directed to the varieties of the human race, in appearance and character, and let any one lay his finger successively upon lands strongly contrasted in this respect ; and in whatever order he takes them, he will find that the people stand up, as it were, the instant that his finger touches their country, as if that country was touched by the wand of a magician.

It is the same with every art which mankind have practised, and every science which they have studied. If we once are in possession of the knowledge, and have had the map in juxta-position with us in the study of it, the map will not suffer us to forget it, but will faithfully bring to our recollection, at all times, every thing of weal or woe, that has happened to our kind; and not to our kind only, but to all the creatures that now tenant the earth, or have formerly tenanted it, to every one of its varied localities ; and the revolutions which the earth itself has undergone—either violently by those convulsions which are now and then taken place, or more slowly and silently, but with equal certainty in the lapse of ages—may be equally brought to our recollection by this invaluable record. The map will not furnish us with the knowledge at first, but it will keep for us what we have acquired.

On a great scale, there is no artificial memory half so good for this purpose as a Map of the World. It must, however, be borne in mind, that the map is only the casket, and not the jewels of knowledge; but then it is a casket so perfect, and so permanent in its arrangement, that every jewel which we can put into it is found the very instant that we require it. Every family, therefore, should have a Map of the World, as large and good as their circumstances will admit, and, BESIDES THE PLEASURE OF ITS POSSESSION IT WILL INSURE THEM ITS VALUE MANIFOLD IN THE INSTRUCTION OF BOTH OLD AND YOUNG.

In conclusion it may be truly asserted, that arguments of equal import might be advanced for good maps of separate nations, especially of our native land.

SIZE, THREE FEET BY TWO FEET FIVE INCHES

With numerous engravings, price, coloured, mounted on mahogany roller, and highly var-nished, 14s.; or 6s. in sheet, coloured,

KELVEY'S
ROYAL GENEALOGICAL CHART,

SHOWING

THE DESCENT OF THE BRITISH SOVEREIGNS

From the time of the Conqueror;

AND OF

THE KINGS OF FRANCE FOR ABOVE SIX HUNDRED YEARS.

The Chart is so arranged as to show, in a "bird's eye view," the descent of the English Monarchs in *one continuous line*—and of her present illustrious Majesty, VICTORIA, through the male line of the House of Brunswick, for above 600 years. The different branches of the Capetines are also distinctly traced, showing in what manner the first line of Valois, the first House of Orleans, the second line of Valois, the House of Bourbon, and the present line of Orleans, have descended from Louis IX., great-grandson of Henry II., King of England.

The consanguinity of contemporary monarchs may be easily traced—many of the principal characters mentioned in history are given—and the ancestors of some of the most illustrious of our present nobility, who have descended from the collateral branches of the Royal Family, are pointed out.

The design of the Chart is to render that assistance to a reader of History which a Map affords him when reading the geographical description or situation of a country ; even a reference to it will, by association of ideas, recal to memory many transactions which occurred during that period ; and a slight perusal of it will impress on the mind an outline of the various branches which have emanated from the Conqueror.

Just completed in Eight Parts, Price 1s. each, or bound in One Volume, price 9s

SAMUEL WELLER'S

ILLUSTRATIONS
TO THE PICKWICK CLUB.

These delineations are imputed to no less a person than *Sam Weller* himself ; the characters are graphically conceived, and their features well preserved ; the local scenery is sketched on the spot. The drollness and spirit of these illustrations make us anxious to see more of the artist.—*Atlas.*

We hail with satisfaction the Illustrations to this popular work by *Samuel Weller* himself. Judging from his natural shrewdness, and these his earliest pencillings, we feel confident they will prove a very popular addition to the work. We should advise all the readers of this inimitable work to possess themselves of these Illustrations immediately ; they will form a valuable acquisition to the work or the scrap-book.—*Observer.*

Very clever prints, full of humour, and delightfully etched. Combining as he does the genius of the pencil and graver, he promises to be a second HOGARTH —*Age.*

JUST PUBLISHED,

SIZE, FIFTEEN INCHES BY NINETEEN INCHES,

Price only 4s.; or Proofs on India Paper, 6s.

GRATTAN'S MEDALLION PORTRAIT

OF

HER MOST GRACIOUS MAJESTY,

FROM A PAINTING BY H. MELVILLE, ESQ.,

ENGRAVED ON STEEL BY A NEWLY INVENTED MACHINE ON THE PRINCIPLE OF

M. A. COLLAS.

Now publishing, in Monthly Parts, price One Shilling each, to be completed in Eight,

ILLUSTRATIONS TO NICHOLAS NICKLEBY

BY PETER PALETTE.

And capital illustrations they are. Those who are subcribers to Boz's work will lose half the zest of Nickleby's story if they fail to take Peter Palette.—*Weekly True Sun.*

These illustrations are admirably adapted to the Nickleby Papers.—*Blackwood's Lady's Magazine.*

A series of very clever engravings have been commenced by a talented young artist, named Onwhyn, in illustration of the inimitable Boz. The artist has certainly succeeded in catching the humour of the author; the work deserves encouragement, and every admirer of Nickleby should possess these illustrations.—*Chronicle.*

These are very clever, and extremely well adapted to illustrate the fortunes of Nicholas; we doubt not the success of Peter Palette's Nickleby-isms.—*Age.*

ON THE 1st OCTOBER WILL BE PUBLISHED—SIZE, 3 FEET 8 INCHES, BY 2 FEET 6,

GILBERT'S

STEEL-PLATE MAP OF THE WORLD.

The extraordinary sale of nearly 10,000 of the copper-plate edition of GILBERT'S NEW MAP OF THE WORLD (*see page* 4), has encouraged the Author to prepare an enlarged, improved, and more copious Map, TO BE BEAUTIFULLY AND ACCURATELY ENGRAVED ON STEEL. The price, coloured, will be 7s. on sheet; 9s. in case; 14s. black roller, varnished; 18s. mahogany ditto.

PREPARING FOR PUBLICATION, SAME SIZE AS THE MAP OF EUROPE,

GILBERT'S

NEW MAP OF NORTH AMERICA.

NEW WEEKLY JOURNAL,

THE

SOCIAL GAZETTE:

ITS MOTTO,

"SOCIAL IMPROVEMENT UPON CHRISTIAN PRINCIPLES."

THIS new Journal has been established with a view to supply a deficiency which has been long felt and lamented ; it accordingly appeals to the support of all who approve of its principles and execution, upon the following grounds :—

It is the only Weekly Newspaper, attached to the Established Church, which is issued in the middle of the week, whereby Sunday labour and Sunday trading are wholly avoided.

Like other Weekly Newspapers, it contains Leading Articles upon Political and other Topics of the Day; Domestic and Foreign News; a Digest of Parliamentary Intelligence ; and Reviews of Books and the Fine Arts. But it abstains from fierce party politics and personal invective ; from inflammatory and exaggerated statements; and from all those offensive details by which Newspapers are too often rendered unfit for general reading in families.

It is the vehicle of much interesting, useful, and instructive matter, which has not hitherto formed a substantive portion of any weekly Journal. Of this description may be chiefly noticed :—

1. The PAROCHIAL INTELLIGENCER ; being statements from the only authentic sources, of the actual nature and working of the Religious, Benevolent, and Educational Establishments, in various Parishes throughout the kingdom. Under this head have already been given,—St. George's, Bloomsbury, (Rev. Dr. Short) ; Upper Chelsea, (Rev. R. Burgess) ; Paddington, (Rev. A. M. Campbell); All Soul's, Marylebone, (Very Rev. Dean of Chichester); Leeds, (Rev. Dr. Hook); Whippingham, Isle of Wight, (Hon. and Rev. F. P. Bouverie); St. Giles's in the Fields, (Rev. J. E. Tyler) ; and St. George's, Queen Square, (Rev. W. Short); the Series being continued weekly.

2. The FAMILY INTELLIGENCER: containing information and advice upon matters of Domestic Economy; the general management of a Household; the best methods of effecting Insurance, and investing Money; and of educating Children and bringing them forward in the world.

3. PLANS of SOCIAL IMPROVEMENT; and SOCIAL SKETCHES; calculated to guide, facilitate, and record, the operations of Philanthropic Individuals and Societies, in all parts of the Kingdom.

4. ANALYSES of the REPORTS and other DOCUMENTS of numerous Societies and Associations established throughout the Country for Religious, Instructional, and Benevolent purposes; the end and object of these being to show to all what is doing by all, in promoting Education; in the cultivation of Knowledge, and the spread of Intelligence; in the exercise of Charity, and the practical application of Christian virtues to the every-day duties of life.

5. CORRESPONDENCE, (the extension and continuation of which is earnestly solicited,) whereby an interchange of practical information is obtained, and useful facts promulgated, instead of crude opinions and untried theories.

6. The PHILOSOPHY of PUBLIC EXHIBITIONS; in which accounts of places of public resort, and descriptions of the productions of Nature and works of Art which they contain, are made vehicles of communicating information in various branches of popular knowledge, scientific investigation, and intellectual inquiry.

For the full and effectual carrying out of the important objects to which the Social Gazette is devoted, the co-operation and communications of all who take an interest in the great and sacred cause of Social Improvement upon Christian principles, are most earnestly requested. The Conductors have to offer their grateful acknowledgments for the kind assistance, and promises of further support, already received from Dignitaries of the Church and active parochial Ministers; from Magistrates, Commissioners, and Guardians of the Poor; and from numerous other individuals of station and influence.

The SOCIAL GAZETTE is published every WEDNESDAY afternoon at three o'clock, price Sixpence, stamped for conveyance, postage free. Orders for it will be executed by any Newsman in town or country, and Communications for the Editor (post paid), Books and Works of Art for Review, and Advertisements, will be received by the Publisher, JOHN W. PARKER, West Strand, London.

A SELECT LIST OF BOOKS,

PUBLISHED BY

JOHN W. PARKER, WEST-STRAND, LONDON.

THE WORKS OF DOCTOR DONNE; with a Memoir of
his Life. By HENRY ALFORD, M.A., Vicar of Wymeswold, and late
Fellow of Trinity College, Cambridge. In Six Volumes Octavo, with a
Fine Portrait after an Original Picture by VANDYKE.   3*l.* 12*s.*

IT has often been a subject of regret, that the works of this eminent Divine and Poet have
not been collected in a modern uniform edition, and in a recent Number of the *Quarterly
Review* there occurs a recommendation that such an edition should be undertaken. Many
months, however, before the appearance of that article, the present Editor had commenced
preparing for the Press the Life and Works of Donne now announced, and it is hoped that the
edition will be welcomed by the Public, and found worthy of becoming a standard book in
English Libraries.

THE RISE AND PROGRESS OF THE ENGLISH CON-
STITUTION: with an HISTORICAL and LEGAL INTRODUCTION, and NOTES.
By ARCHIBALD JOHN STEPHENS, M.A., F.R.S., &c., Barrister
at Law. Two Vols. Octavo.   30*s.*

THE Introduction is embodied in the first volume, and extends from the earliest period of
authentic history up to the termination of the reign of William III.; and the Saxon institutions, tenure of lands, domesday, the royal prerogative, origin and progress of the legislative assemblies, privileges of Lords and Commons, pecuniary exactions, administration
of justice, gradual improvements in the laws, judicial powers of the Peers, borough institutions, infamy of the Long Parliament, national dissensions, and the principles under which
the executive power was entrusted to the Prince of Orange, have experienced every illustration.

The doctrinal changes in the Anglican Church which were effected under the Tudors,
are justified by a reference to the records and practice of the primitive church, and the
doctrinal schismatic points of Roman Catholic faith relating to the canons of Scripture,
seven sacraments, sacrifice of the mass, private and solitary mass, communion in one kind,
transubstantiation, image worship, purgatory, indulgences, confession and penance, abso-
lution, &c., &c., are clearly established as being in direct opposition to the opinions of the
early fathers, and the fundamental doctrines of Christianity.

The text of De Lolme is incorporated in the second volume, and the notes affixed extend
to a great length, and embody very valuable and diversified information relative to the rights,
qualifications, and disqualifications of members of Parliament and their constituents; the
unions of Scotland and Ireland with England; the origin, rise, and progress of the civil law
under nine periods of the Roman history; civil process in the English courts of law; history
of the courts of equity, and the principles under which they act; trial by jury, and an
analysis of criminal offences, and the statutes under which they are punishable, with an
analysis of crimes that were committed in 1837, and of the sentences passed. There are
likewise tables of the public income and expenditure in the year ended January 5, 1837; of
the church revenues, in which will be found information relative to the number of benefices
in each diocese; total amount of incomes, gross and net, of the incumbents in each diocese,
also the averages of each respectively; number of curates in each diocese, total amount of
their stipends and average thereof; also four scales of the incomes of the beneficed clergy;
and genealogical tables from the Saxon and Danish kings, to Queen Victoria.

MEMOIRS of the LIFE, CHARACTER, and WRITINGS,
of BISHOP BUTLER, Author of *The Analogy.* By THOMAS BART-
LETT, M.A., One of the Six Preachers of Canterbury Cathedral, and
Rector of Kingstone, Kent. *Dedicated by permission to His Grace the
Archbishop of Canterbury.*   Octavo, with an original Portrait, 12*s.*

ELIZABETHAN RELIGIOUS HISTORY. By HENRY
SOAMES, M.A., Author of *The History of the Reformation; The Anglo-Saxon Church, &c.*   Octavo, 16s.

THIS Work is intended to fill a long-acknowledged chasm in English literature, and especially in that which peculiarly concerns the Church of England. Both Romanists and Protestant Dissenters have been attentive to the important reign of Elizabeth, and by saying very little of each other, have given an invidious colouring to both the Church and the Government. The present work is meant to give every leading fact in sufficient detail, but to avoid unnecessary particulars. It reaches from the establishment of the Thirty-nine Articles, in 1563, to the Hampton-Court Conference, in 1604.

THE ANGLO-SAXON CHURCH; its HISTORY, REVE-
NUES, and General Character. By the Rev. HENRY SOAMES, M.A., Author of the *Elizabethan Religious History*. A NEW EDITION. 10s. 6d.

THE EVIDENCE of PROFANE HISTORY to the TRUTH
of REVELATION. With Numerous Graphic Illustrations. *Dedicated by Permission to Her Majesty the Queen.*   10s. 6d.

IT is the object of this Work to exhibit, from traces afforded in the records and monuments, both sacred and profane, of the ancient world, an unity of purpose maintained by the all-controlling providence of God.

GERMANY, BOHEMIA, and HUNGARY, visited in 1837.
By the Rev. G. R. GLEIG, M.A., Chaplain to the Royal Hospital, Chelsea. Three Volumes, Post Octavo.   1l. 11s. 6d.

THE principal design of this work is to give some account of the state of society as it now exists in Bohemia and Hungary. In order to reach these countries, the Author was, of course, obliged to pass through a large portion of Germany, where the social condition of the people, as well as the civil, ecclesiastical, and military establishments, attracted his attention. Upon these he touches, more especially in reference to Prussia, towards which the eyes of the rest of Europe are at present anxiously turned. But his great design was to obtain and communicate information, respecting countries into which few Englishmen are accustomed to penetrate. Hence a large portion of his tour, both in Bohemia and Hungary, was performed on foot; and the acquaintance which he was thereby enabled to form with all ranks and conditions of the people, was at once more intimate and more familiar than could have taken place had he travelled by a more usual mode of conveyance. He looked into the cottage as well as the palace, and he has given some account of both.

GERMANY, PAST AND PRESENT; or, the SPIRIT of
its HISTORY, LITERATURE, SOCIETY, and NATIONAL ECO-NOMY; combined with Details of Courts, Customs, Laws, and Education; and with the Physical, Moral, and Political Statistics of its various States. By BISSET HAWKINS, M.D., F.R.S., &c.   10s. 6d.

RESEARCHES IN BABYLONIA, ASSYRIA, and CHAL-
DEA; forming part of the Labours of the Euphrates Expedition, and *published with the sanction of the Right Hon. the President of the Board of Control.* By W. AINSWORTH, F.G.S. With Maps, &c.   12s. 6d.

A NEW SYSTEM OF LOGIC, and Developement of the
Principles of Truth and Reasoning; in which a System of Logic, applicable
to Moral and Practical Subjects, is for the first time proposed. By
SAMUEL RICH. BOSANQUET, A.M., of the Inner Temple. 10s. 6d.

BELLINGHAM; or, NARRATIVE of a CHRISTIAN in
SEARCH of the CHURCH. By the Rev. WILLIAM PALIN, B.A.,
Rector of Stifford, Essex; Author of *Village Lectures on the Litany.* 3s. 6d.

THE CATHOLIC CHARACTER OF CHRISTIANITY.
In a SERIES of LETTERS to a FRIEND. By the Rev. FREDERICK
NOLAN, LL.D., F.R.S., Vicar of Prittlewell, and Author of *The Evan-
gelical Character of Christianity,* &c.

The Profits arising from the First Edition of this Work, will be given to the Fund for
erecting a Memorial to the Martyred Bishops at Oxford.

THE SCRIPTURAL CHARACTER of the ENGLISH
CHURCH CONSIDERED, in a SERIES of SERMONS, with Notes
and Illustrations. By the Rev. DERWENT COLERIDGE, Master of
Helleston Grammar School, in Cornwall. *In the Press.*

THE series of Sermons, bearing the above title, were written exclusively for perusal, and are
arranged as a connected whole. The author has adopted this form to avail himself of the
devotional frame of mind, presupposed, on the part of the reader, in this species of composition;
but he has not deemed it as necessary to preserve with strictness the conventional style of the
pulpit, for which these discourses were never intended: they may, consequently, be taken either
as a series of Essays, or as the successive chapters of a general work.

THE NEW CRATYLUS; or, CONTRIBUTIONS towards
a more ACCURATE KNOWLEDGE of the GREEK LANGUAGE.
By JOHN WILLIAM DONALDSON, M.A., Fellow of Trinity College,
Cambridge. 17s.

A DICTIONARY of the MATERIA MEDICA and PRAC-
TICAL PHARMACY; including a Translation of the Formulæ of the
London Pharmacopœia. By WILLIAM THOMAS BRANDE, of Her
Majesty's Mint, Author of the *Manual of Chemistry.* 15s.

A MANUAL OF CHEMISTRY, by W. T. BRANDE, F.R.S.
30s.

AN INTRODUCTION TO THE STUDY OF CHEMIS-
TRY, being a preparatory View of the Forces which concur to the Production of Chemical Phenomena. By J. FREDERIC DANIELL, F.R.S.,
Professor of Chemistry in King's College, London; and Lecturer on Chemistry and Geology in the Hon. East India Company's Military Seminary
at Addiscombe; Author of *Meteorological Essays.* *Nearly Ready.*

LECTURES on ASTRONOMY, delivered at King's College, London. By the Rev. HENRY MOSELEY, M.A., F.R.S., Professor of Astronomy and Natural Philosophy at the College. Numerous Illustrations.   6s. 6d.

MECHANICS APPLIED to the ARTS. By PROFESSOR MOSELEY, of King's College, London. A New Edition, corrected and improved. With numerous Engravings.   6s. 6d.

THE STUDENT'S MANUAL OF NATURAL PHILOSO- PHY; comprising Descriptions, Popular and Practical of the most important Philosophical Instruments, their History, Nature, and Uses; with complete elucidations of the Sciences to which they respectively appertain. Dedicated, by permission, to the Lord Bishop of Salisbury. By CHARLES TOMLINSON.   10s. 6d.

STUDENT'S MANUAL OF ANCIENT HISTORY; Accounts of all the principal Nations of Antiquity. By W. C. TAYLOR, LL.D., of Trin. Coll., Dublin.   10s. 6d.

STUDENT'S MANUAL of MODERN HISTORY; the Rise and Progress of the principal EUROPEAN NATIONS, their Political History, and the changes in their Social Condition; with a History of the COLONIES founded by Europeans; and the general progress of Civilization. By the same Author.   10s. 6d.

LIVES OF EMINENT CHRISTIANS. By R. B. HONE, M.A., Vicar of Hales Owen.   Three Vols., at 4s. 6d. each.

VOL. I.	VOL. II.	VOL. III.
ARCHBISHOP USHER,	BERNARD GILPIN,	BISHOP RIDLEY,
DOCTOR HAMMOND,	PHILIP DE MORNAY,	BISHOP HALL,
JOHN EVELYN,	BISHOP BEDELL,	AND THE
BISHOP WILSON.	DOCTOR HORNECK.	HON. ROBERT BOYLE.

LIVES OF BRITISH SACRED POETS. By R. A. WIL- MOTT, Esq., Trinity College, Cambridge. Now complete, in Two Vols., at 4s. 6d. each.

The FIRST SERIES contains an Historical Sketch of Sacred Poetry, and the Lives of the English Sacred Poets preceding MILTON.

The SECOND SERIES commences with MILTON, and brings down the Lives to that of BISHOP HEBER inclusive.

LETTERS OF EMINENT PERSONS; Selected and Illustrated by ROBERT ARIS WILLMOTT, Esq., of Trinity College, Cambridge : Author of *Lives of the English Sacred Poets.*

THE PHILOSOPHY of LIVING. By HERBERT MAYO, F.R.S., Senior Surgeon of the Middlesex Hospital. 8s. 6d.

CONTENTS.

OF DIVERSITIES OF CONSTITUTION; Temperament; Habit; Diathesis.—Of DIET.—Of DIGESTION; Adaptation of Diet to different Constitutions and Ages; Social Relations of Food.—Of EXERCISE; Exercise proper for Boys; Physical Education of Girls; Spinal Curvature; Exercise proper for Adults; for the Aged.—Of SLEEP.—Of BATHING.—Of CLOTHING.—Of AIR and CLIMATE.—HEALTH of MIND; Self-control; Mental Culture.

MANAGEMENT OF THE ORGANS OF DIGESTION, in HEALTH and in DISEASE. By the Author of the preceding Work. 6s. 6d.

CONTENTS.

Rules of Diet for different Constitutions.—Treatment of the various kinds of Indigestion;—of Looseness; of Costiveness.—Local Diseases of the Lower Bowel, and their Treatment.

THE FAMILY HAND-BOOK, or PRACTICAL INFOR-MATION in DOMESTIC ECONOMY; including Cookery, Household Management, and all other subjects connected with the Health, Comfort, and Expenditure of a Family. With Choice Receipts and Valuable Hints. 5s.

THE YOUNG LADY'S FRIEND; a Manual of Practical Advice and Instruction to Young Females, on their entering upon the Duties of Life, after quitting School. By a LADY. 3s. 6d.

SACRED MINSTRELSY; a COLLECTION OF THE FINEST SACRED MUSIC, by the best Masters, arranged as Solos, Duets, Trios, &c., and Chorusses; and with Accompaniments for the Piano-Forte or Organ. Two Handsome Folio Volumes, price 2l. 2s. Half-bound, or in Nos., I. to XXIV., at 1s. 6d.

NEW WEEKLY JOURNAL,
EXCLUSIVELY DEVOTED TO THE AFFAIRS OF
THE COLONIES:

THE

COLONIAL GAZETTE,

ESTABLISHED FOR THE PURPOSE OF COLLECTING AND DIFFUSING
EVERY SPECIES OF INFORMATION OF USE OR INTEREST TO
THOSE RESIDENT IN, OR CONNECTED WITH
THE COLONIES.

The principles upon which this Journal is conducted are, entire freedom from political or party influences, and exclusive devotion to the welfare of the Colonies in their connexion with the Mother Country.

Its Contents embrace—

NEWS from all the Colonies throughout the world, derived as well from the Journals of the respective Colonies as from Private Correspondents, and the Corresponding Members of the Colonial Society of London.

Papers on the great questions of Colonization, and Intelligence arising in this Country and communicated from Abroad, relating thereto.

Summary of Home News, selected and adapted for readers resident in the Colonies; it being evident that a Journal possessing the special character of a COLONIAL Gazette cannot in any case become a substitute for a London Newspaper.

Leading Articles on the Topics of the Day, so far as they appertain to Colonial Affairs.

Reviews of Books, and Analyses of Parliamentary Papers, and other Documents, relating to the Colonies.

Communications on the Political and Social Condition, the Natural History, Productions, and Commerce, and every other subject of interest, in the various Colonies, will at all times meet with due attention, and whenever possessing sufficient general importance will be published in the Gazette.

The COLONIAL GAZETTE is published every SATURDAY, by JOHN W. PARKER, West Strand, London, price Sixpence, stamped for conveyance, postage free, and is supplied to order by any Newsman.

QUEEN  VICTORIA

AND THE UNIFORM PENNY POSTAGE;

A SCENE AT WINDSOR CASTLE.

Council Chamber in Windsor Castle—Her Majesty is sitting at a large table, on which are lying the Reports on Postage; Copies of the Post Circular; Annual Reports of the French and American Post-Offices—Her Majesty is in deep study over "Post-Office Reform," by Rowland Hill—Lord Melbourne, at the Queen's right hand, is watching her Majesty's countenance.

The Queen (*exclaiming aloud*)—Mothers pawning their clothes to pay the postage of a child's letter! Every subject studying how to evade postage, without caring for the law! Even Messrs Baring sending letters illegally every week, to save postage: such things must not last.—(*To Lord Melbourne.*) I trust, my Lord, you have commanded the attendance of the Postmaster-General and of Mr Rowland Hill, as I directed, in order that I may hear the reasons of both about this Universal Penny Postage Plan, which appears to me likely to remove all these great evils. Moreover, I have made up my mind that the three hundred and twenty petitions presented to the House of Commons during the last session of Parliament, which pray for a fair trial of the plan, shall be at least attended to. (*A pause.*) Are you, my Lord, yourself, able to say anything about this postage plan, which all the country seems talking about?

Lord Melbourne.—May it please your Majesty, I have heard something about it, but—

The Queen.—Heard! So I suppose has every one, from the Land's End to John O'Groat's house? I wish to learn what your Lordship thinks of it?

Lord Melbourne (*aside; I really think nothing, because I know nothing.*)—May it please your Majesty, the Postmaster-General tells me the plan will not do, and that, to confess the truth, is all I know about the matter.

Enter Groom of the Chamber.

Groom.—The Postmaster-General and Mr Rowland Hill await your Majesty's pleasure.

The Queen.—Give them entrance.

Enter Lord Lichfield and Mr Rowland Hill, bowing.

The Queen.—I am happy to see my noble Postmaster-General, and the ingenious author of the Universal Penny Post Plan. Gentlemen, be seated. My Lord Melbourne has told you why I wished for your presence on this occasion. I have been reading carefully, and with great interest, the late discussions and evidence on the postage question, and I now wish to hear what is my Postmaster-General's opinion on the plan, which I therefore beg you, Mr Hill, to describe in a few words.

Rowland Hill.—With your Majesty's leave I will say nothing of the dearness and hardship of the present Post-Office rates, or of Post-Office management itself, but confine myself, according to your Majesty's commands, to the plan you have honoured me by noticing. My plan is, that all letters not weighing more than half an ounce should be charged one penny; and heavier letters one penny for each additional half ounce, whatever may be the distance they are carried. This postage to be paid when the letter is sent, and not when received, as at present.

Lord Lichfield.—Of all the wild and visionary schemes which I have ever heard or read of, it is the most extravagant.[*]

The Queen.—You seem, my Lord, to adhere both

to your opinions and your very words; for the very same expressions were used a year and a half ago. Pray abstain from calling names, and use argument.

Lord Lichfield.—Since I made those observations I have given the subject considerable attention, and I remain, even still more firmly, of the same opinion.[*]

The Queen.—I must again beg of you, my Lord, to state reasons.

Lord Lichfield.—I have no objection to some reduction of postage, and I believe all previous Postmasters-General agree that some reduction is necessary.

The Queen.—Why, then, have the reductions been delayed so long? Proceed, Mr Hill, to say why you fix so low a sum as one penny.

R. Hill.—Your Majesty will see that the cheaper the postage the easier it will be for the poor, who are nearly debarred from the use of the post at present, and all classes, to use the post. Though a penny seems very low, I beg to say that the Post-Office would get at least a halfpenny profit on each letter after paying all expenses. It does not cost the Post-Office a quarter of a farthing to carry a letter from London to Edinburgh, which is 400 miles.

The Queen.—I see, Mr Hill, the Post-Office admit you are correct in that estimate.

Lord Lichfield.—It would be unjust to charge a letter going 100 miles a penny, and a letter going 400 miles only a penny. And, may it please your Majesty to remember that, though according to Mr Hill's mode of reckoning it does not cost us a farthing to carry letters to Edinburgh, 400 miles, it does cost us nearly a halfpenny to carry a letter from London to Louth, which is only 140 miles.

The Queen.—Indeed!—How much, then, is the postage to Edinburgh and to Louth?

Lord Lichfield.—To Edinburgh, 1s. 2d. To Louth, 11d.

The Queen.—It appears, therefore, you think it just to charge my people the highest price for the cheapest business. If an Edinburgh letter cost you a farthing to carry, and a Louth letter a halfpenny, I think in justice the Louth letter should be the dearest and not the cheapest, because all the other expenses on both letters are the same. My agreeable Prime Minister will have this looked to.

Lord Melbourne (*aside.*)—My dear Lichfield, I am afraid the Queen has found you in a scrape.

The Queen.—It is quite clear, from these instances alone, that postage cannot be justly charged according to distance; and I must say, that as the cost of carriage is so trifling in both cases, and the difference so small, whether a letter goes one mile or 500 miles, I think it would be fairer not to consider it at all, and then the rate on all letters would be uniform. Every letter, as you know, my Lord Lichfield, must be put into a Post-Office—must be stamped—must be sorted—must be carried where directed to—and must be delivered. Postage is made up of the expenses of doing all this, and a tax beside. All the labour, except that of carriage, is the same. The carriage being so cheap now-a-days, is hardly worth regarding. Any one can send 1,000 letters, packed in a parcel or bag, as they are in the Post-Office, from London to Edinburgh for 2s. 6d. by steam-boat, which travels as fast as the mail. The tax should be equal on all letters, and not, as at present, the heaviest on letters going the greatest distance. The people who live at York, or at Exeter, or London, pay all other taxes equally, and so they should the postage tax. Mr Hill, I agree with you that there should be a uniform rate; but before I assent to a penny charge, I am bound not to neglect the public revenue. I am afraid that at a penny a great loss will follow. It is true the Post-Office revenue is very bad at present, because it has not increased for these twenty years, though I am sure the numbers of my people, their knowledge, and their commerce, have.

Rowland Hill.—I trust your Majesty will read the evidence taken by the House of Commons respecting the revenue. Every witness says he should rejoice to engage to pay as much postage at a penny rate as he does at the present charges. I reckon that a sixfold increase of letters would yield the present amount of revenue. Many witnesses say the increase would be fifteen-fold; some twentyfold; and some even a hundred-fold. The present high rates cause at least three times as many letters to be sent illegally as are sent by the post. No one thinks it sinful to defraud the Post-Office. There are numerous smugglers in almost every town, who carry letters, and charge only a penny for each letter; and if a private person can carry letters for a penny, with a profit, I think a public body could do so. Moreover, there are above 1,900 penny posts all over the kingdom, which carry letters sometimes as much as 38 miles, and deliver them for a penny; and these penny posts altogether yield nearly 50 per cent., or a halfpenny profit on each letter.

The Queen.—That certainly proves, Mr Hill, that all letters, taking one with another, could be carried for a penny, with large gain. I wish to learn, however, if this great increase of letters takes place, what would be its effect on the expenses of the Post-Office management.

Lord Lichfield.—Effect, indeed! as your Majesty observes; the mails will have to carry twelve times as much in weight, and therefore the charge for transmission, instead of 100,000l. as now, must be twelve times that amount. The walls of the Post-Office would burst, the whole area in which the building stands would not be large enough to receive the clerks and the letters.*

The Queen.—Then it would appear, my Lord, that the mails already are full every night?

Lord Lichfield.—Not quite, your Majesty.

The Queen.—How much weight will the mails carry, according to their contract?

Lord Lichfield.—From eight to fifteen hundred weight.

Rowland Hill.—His Lordship has given some account of the weights carried on several nights.

* 'Mirror of Parliament,' December 18, 1837.

The Queen.—I find, in the Appendix to the Report of the Select Committee, that the Leeds mail on the 20th April weighed only 158 pounds, of which the letters weighed only 38 pounds, the rest being newspapers and letter bags; so that this mail might then have carried twenty-four times the weight of the letters, without overloading the mail. On the 5th April the letters of the Stroud mail weighed less than 10 pounds; so that they might be increased fifty-fold. I find that the average weight of the letters and newspapers of all the mails leaving London nightly is not three hundred weight, and that the average weight of all the letters is only 74 pounds; so that it is proved letters might be increased twelve-fold without increasing the expenses, instead of requiring twelve times the present number of mails, as you thought.

Lord Lichfield.—Please your Majesty, I feel very uneasy.

The Queen.—Support his Lordship, my Lord Melbourne.

Lord Lichfield.—With your Majesty's leave I will retire.

Exit Lord Lichfield.

The Queen (to Lord Melbourne).—It is clear to me that his Lordship had better retire from the Post-Office.

Lord Melbourne.—Certainly, your Majesty; we all thought him the best man to be Postmaster-General, but he has not realized the fond hopes we cherished of him.

The Queen.—It appears to me, my Lord, that the loss of Colonel Maberly to the Post-Office would be another great gain to the public. What I have read, and this interview, have convinced me that a uniform penny post is most advisable. I am sure it would confer a great boon to the poorer classes of my subjects, and would be the greatest benefit to religion, to morals, to general knowledge, and to trade—that uniformity and payment in advance would greatly simplify the Post-Office, and get rid of their troublesome accounts—that it would effectually put down the smuggling postman, and lead my people to obey and not disobey the law.— *(The Queen rises, and in a most emphatic tone)—* My Lord Melbourne, you will please to bear in mind that the Queen agrees with her faithful Commons in recommending an uniform penny post. If your Lordship has any difficulty in finding a minister among your party able to carry the measure into effect, I shall apply to my Lord Ashburton or my Lord Lowther, as circumstances may require. Mr Hill, the nation will owe you a large debt of gratitude, which I am sure it will not be unwilling to repay. I wish you good morning, gentlemen.

Exit the Queen—Lord Melbourne and Rowland Hill bowing.

PLEASE PASS THIS TO YOUR NEIGHBOUR.

Mothers and Fathers that wish to hear from their absent children!—Friends who are parted, that wish to write to each other!—Farmers that wish to hear of the best markets!—Tradesmen that wish to receive orders and money quickly and cheaply!—Mechanics and Labourers that wish to learn where good work and high wages are to be had!—SUPPORT YOUR QUEEN and the Report of the House of Commons with your Petitions for a UNIFORM PENNY POST. Let every one in the kingdom sign a Petition with his name or his mark. This IS NO PARTY QUESTION. The Conservatives may send their Petitions to the Lords to Lord Ashburton, and to the Commons to Lord Lowther;—the Whigs theirs to Earl Fitzwilliam and Lord Seymour;—the Radicals theirs to Lord Brougham and Mr Wallace, M.P., addressed to London. It is only necessary to get two petitions, like the following, written out on paper—one to the Lords, and one to the Commons; and, when signed,

to put them into the Post-Office, addressed as above stated:—

To the Honourable the Lords Spiritual and Temporal [or the Commons, *as the case may be*] in Parliament assembled:—

The humble Petition of the Undersigned SHEWETH,

That your Petitioners earnestly desire a Uniform Penny Post, payable in advance, as proposed by Rowland Hill.

That your Petitioners entreat your Honourable House to give instant effect to the recommendations of the Select Committee of the House of Commons.

And your Petitioners will ever pray.

REMEMBER the 4,000 petitions last year emancipated the slaves. Let there be the same number this year to emancipate the POSTAGE.

Price ¼d. each, or four for 1d., or 40 for 6d., or 100 for 1s., or 500 for 4s., and 1,000 for 7s.

Printed by C. REYNELL, 16 Little Pulteney street, Golden square, London who will supply any quantity at the above price (orders must be post paid).

REFORM YOUR TAILORS' BILLS!

LADIES' ELEGANT
RIDING HABITS.

Summer Cloth	£3 3 0
Ladies' Cloth	4 4 0
Saxony Cloth	5 5 0

GENTLEMAN'S

Superfine Dress Coat	2 7 6
Extra Saxony, the best that is made	2 15 0
Superfine Frock Coat, silk facings	2 10 0
Buckskin Trousers	1 1 0
Cloth or double-milled Cassimere ditto 17s. 6d. to	1 5 0
New Patterns, Summer Trousers, 10s. 6d. per pr. or 3 pr.	1 10 0
Summer Waistcoats, 7s.; or 3,	1 0 0
Splendid Silk Valencia Dress Waistcoats, 10s.6d. each, or 3,	1 10 0

FIRST-RATE
BOYS' CLOTHING.

Skeleton Dresses	£0 15 0
Tunic and Hussar Suits,	1 10 0
Camlet Cloaks	0 8 6
Cloth Cloaks	0 15 6

GENTLEMAN'S

Morning Coats and Dressing Gowns	0 18 0
Petersham Great Coats and Pilot P Jackets, bound, and Velvet Collar	1 10 0
Camlet Cloak, lined all through	1 1 0
Cloth Opera Cloak	1 10 0
Army Cloth Blue Spanish Cloak, 9½ yards round	2 10 0
Super Cloth ditto	3 3 0
Cloth or Tweed Fishing or Travelling Trousers	0 13 6

THE CELEBRITY THE

CITY CLOTHING ESTABLISHMENT

Has so many years maintained, being the

BEST AS WELL AS THE CHEAPEST HOUSE,

Renders any Assurance as to STYLE and QUALITY unnecessary. The NOBILITY and GENTRY are invited to the

SHOW-ROOMS, TO VIEW THE IMMENSE & SPLENDID STOCK.

The numerous Applications for

REGIMENTALS & NAVAL UNIFORMS,

Have induced E. P. D. & SON to make ample Arrangements for an extensive Business in this particular Branch; a perusal of their List of Prices (which can be had gratis) will show the EXORBITANT CHARGES to which OFFICERS OF THE ARMY AND NAVY HAVE SO LONG BEEN SUBJECTED.

CONTRACTS BY THE YEAR,

Originated by E. P. D. & SON, are universally adopted by CLERGYMEN and PROFESSIONAL GENTLEMEN, as being MORE REGULAR and ECONOMICAL. THE PRICES ARE THE LOWEST EVER OFFERED:—

Two Suits per Year, Superfine,	7 7	Extra Saxony, the best that is made,	8 5
Three Suits per Year, ditto	10 17	Extra Saxony, ditto	12 6
Four Suits per Year, ditto	14 6	Extra Saxony, ditto	15 18

(THE OLD SUITS TO BE RETURNED.)

Capital Shooting Jackets, 21s. The new Waterproof Cloak, 21s

COUNTRY GENTLEMEN,

Preferring their Clothes Fashionably made, at a FIRST-RATE LONDON HOUSE, are respectfully informed, that by a Post-paid Application, they will receive a Prospectus explanatory of the System of Business, Directions for Measurement, and a Statement of Prices. Or if Three or Four Gentlemen unite, one of the Travellers will be dispatched immediately to wait on them.

STATE LIVERIES SPLENDIDLY MADE.

Footman's Suit of Liveries, £3 3. Scarlet Hunting Coat, £3 3

E. P. DOUDNEY AND SON,
49, LOMBARD-STREET. 1784.
Established

BRITANNIA LIFE ASSURANCE COMPANY,

No. 1, PRINCES STREET, BANK, LONDON.

CAPITAL, ONE MILLION.

Directors.

WILLIAM BARDGETT, ESQ.
SAMUEL BEVINGTON, ESQ.
WILLIAM FECHNEY BLACK, ESQ.
JOHN BRIGHTMAN, ESQ.
GEORGE COHEN, ESQ.
MILLIS COVENTRY, ESQ.
JOHN DREWETT, ESQ.

ROBERT EGLINTON, ESQ.
ERASMUS ROBERT FOSTER, ESQ.
ALEX. ROBERT IRVINE, ESQ.
PETER MORRISON, ESQ.
WILLIAM SHAND, JUN., ESQ.
HENRY LEWIS SMALE, ESQ.
THOMAS TEED, ESQ.

Medical Officers.

WILLIAM STROUD, M.D., Great Coram Street, Russell Square.
EBENEZER SMITH, ESQ., Surgeon, Billiter Square.

Standing Counsel.

The HON. JOHN ASHLEY. New Square, Lincoln's-Inn.

Solicitor.

WILLIAM BEVAN, ESQ., Old Jewry.

Bankers.

MESSRS. DREWETT & FOWLER, Princes Street.

ADVANTAGES OF THIS INSTITUTION.

A most economical set of Tables—computed expressly for the use of this Establishment, from authentic and complete data ; *and presenting the lowest rates of Assurance that can be offered, without compromising the safety of the Institution.*

Increasing rates of Premium, on a new and remarkable plan, for securing loans on debts, a less immediate payment being required on a Policy for the whole term of life, than in any other office.

Decreasing rates of Premium, also on a novel and remarkable plan; the Policy-holder having the option of discontinuing the payment of all further premiums after *twenty, fifteen, ten,* and even *five* years ; and the Policy still remaining in force,—in the first case, for the full amount originally assured and in either of the three other cases, for a portion of the same, according to a fixed and equitable scale; endorsed upon the Policy.

Premiums may be paid either Annually, Half-yearly, or Quarterly, in one sum, or in a limited number of payments.

A Board of Directors in attendance daily at Two o'clock.

Age of the assured in every case admitted in the Policy.

All claims payable within one month after proof of death.

Medical attendants remunerated in all cases for their reports.

A liberal commission allowed to solicitors and agents.

Age.	Premium per Cent. per Annum payable during				
	First Five Years.	Second Five Years.	Third Five Years.	Fourth Five Years.	Remainder of Life.
	£ s. d.	£ s. d.	£ s. d.	£ s. d.	£ s. d.
20	1 1 0	1 5 10	1 10 11	1 16 9	2 3 8
30	1 6 4	1 12 2	1 19 1	2 7 4	2 17 6
40	1 16 1	2 4 4	2 14 6	3 7 3	4 3 4
50	2 16 7	3 9 4	4 5 5	5 6 3	6 13 0

Officers in the Army and Navy engaged in active service, or residing abroad, and persons aff   with chronic disorders not attended with immediate danger, assured at the least possible addition   rdinary rates, regulated in each case by the increased nature of the risk.

PETER MORRISON, *Resident Director.*

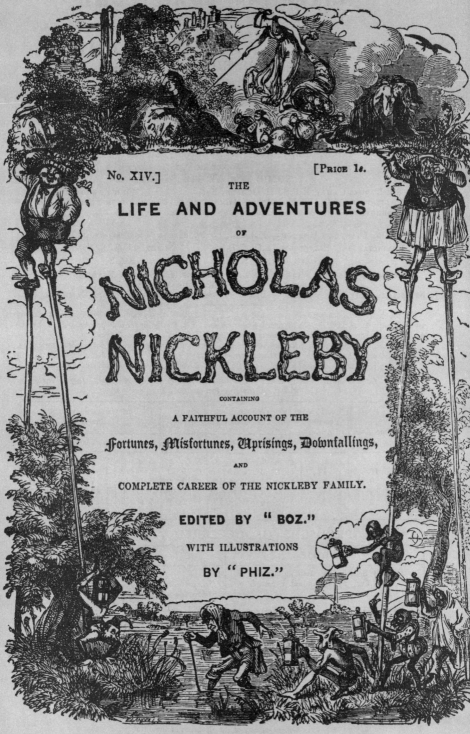

No. XIV.]

[PRICE 1s.

THE
LIFE AND ADVENTURES
OF
NICHOLAS NICKLEBY

CONTAINING

A FAITHFUL ACCOUNT OF THE

Fortunes, Misfortunes, Uprisings, Downfallings,

AND

COMPLETE CAREER OF THE NICKLEBY FAMILY.

EDITED BY "BOZ."

WITH ILLUSTRATIONS

BY "PHIZ."

LONDON: CHAPMAN AND HALL, 186, STRAND.

NATIONAL LOAN FUND
𝕷𝖎𝖋𝖊 𝕬𝖘𝖘𝖚𝖗𝖆𝖓𝖈𝖊
AND
DEFERRED ANNUITY SOCIETY,
No. 26, CORNHILL, LONDON;

67, New Buildings, North Bridge, Edinburgh; 36, Westmoreland Street, Dublin; 28, South Castle Street, Liverpool; and 9, Clare Street, Bristol.

CAPITAL, £500,000.
EMPOWERED BY ACT OF PARLIAMENT.

PATRON,—HIS GRACE THE DUKE OF SOMERSET, F.R.S.

DIRECTORS.

T. LAMIE MURRAY, Esq. *Chairman.*

COL. SIR BURGES CAMAC, K.C.S.	H. GORDON, ESQ.	JOHN RAWSON, ESQ.
JOHN ELLIOTSON, M.D., F.R.S.	ROBERT HOLLOND, ESQ., M.P.	JOSEPH THOMPSON, ESQ.
C. FAREBROTHER, ESQ., ALD.	GEORGE LUNGLEY, ESQ.	

AUDITORS.
DR. OLINTHUS GREGORY, F.R.A.S. | PROFESSOR WHEATSTONE, F.R.S.

PHYSICIAN,—J. ELLIOTSON, M.D., F.R.S.   SURGEON,—E. S. SYMES, ESQ.

ACTUARY,—W. S. B. WOOLHOUSE, ESQ., F.R.A.S.

BANKERS,—MESSRS. WRIGHT & CO., and MESSRS. LADBROKES, KINGSCOTE & CO.

STANDING COUNSEL,—W. MILBOURNE JAMES, ESQ.

SOLICITORS,—MESSRS. WEBBER & BLAND.   SECRETARY,—F. FERGUSON CAMROUX, ESQ.

By the new principles of Life Assurance and Deferred Annuities, established by this Society, many essential advantages, besides that of securing a provision for a family, or for old age, are gained by the Assured, and thereby an additional value is given to each Policy effected with the Society.

Every facility is afforded in effecting Assurances—Premiums payable annually, half-yearly, quarterly, or monthly, or on the increasing or decreasing scales.—Females assured at diminished rates.—Extension of travelling beyond the limits of Europe—and Policies in force seven years not forfeited by suicide.

Premiums for the Assurance of £100 on a Single Life, either by Annual, Half Yearly, or Quarterly Payments.

Age.	For One Year.	For Five Years at an Annual Prem. of	FOR WHOLE LIFE, WITHOUT PROFITS.			FOR WHOLE LIFE, WITH PROFITS.		
			Yearly.	Half Yearly.	Quarterly.	Yearly.	Half Yearly.	Quarterly.
	£ s. d.	£ s. d.	£ s. d.	£ s. d.	£ s. d.	£ s. d.	£ s. d.	£ s. d.
25	0 19 8	1 1 1	1 18 6	0 19 6	0 9 11	2 2 9	1 1 8	0 11 0
35	1 9 2	1 10 9	2 10 11	1 5 10	0 13 2	2 16 6	1 8 8	0 14 7
45	1 14 4	1 15 8	3 9 4	1 15 3	0 17 11	3 17 0	1 19 2	0 19 11
55	2 10 9	2 19 1	5 5 6	2 13 10	1 7 6	5 17 2	2 19 10	1 10 6
65	5 5 0	6 0 4	8 10 5	4 7 6	2 4 11	9 9 4	4 17 3	2 9 11

SPECIMENS OF DEFERRED ANNUITIES.

BENEFITS.	PREMIUMS.
Options Secured on attaining the age of Sixty-five, by an Annual Premium of £2. 12s.	To secure, on attaining the age of 65, the option of Annuity 10 0 0 / Cash... 82 10 0 / Policy.. 97 8 6

Age.	Annuity.	Cash.	Policy.	Age.	Annual.	In one Sum.	Disparity.
	£ s. d.	£ s. d.	£ s. d.		£ s. d.	£ s. d.	£ s. d.
20	47 16 6	394 11 0	466 0 0	20	0 10 11	10 0 10	0 0 0
30	26 15 10	221 0 0	261 0 0	30	0 19 6	16 7 1	7 3 11
40	13 19 9	115 8 0	136 6 0	40	1 17 3	27 3 11	19 4 10

Also Deferred Annuities commencing at the Ages of 50, 55, and 60, and Immediate Annuities for all Ages.

Two-thirds of the Premiums paid, at all times available to the Assured; and the same proportion returnable, in case of premature death.

A Board with a Medical Officer is in daily attendance at Two o'clock.

Prospectuses may be had at the Offices, or any of the Branches in the Principal Towns.

F. FERGUSON CAMROUX, *Sec.*

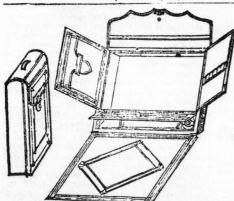

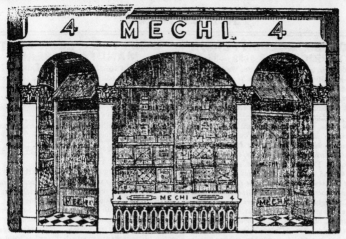

T. COX SAVORY,

GOLDSMITH, SILVERSMITH, WATCHMAKER, &c.,

47, CORNHILL, LONDON, (SEVEN DOORS FROM GRACECHURCH-STREET.)

NEW SILVER SPOONS AND FORKS, 7s. 2d. PER OZ.

ESTIMATE FOR A VERY COMPLETE SMALL SERVICE OF PLATE.

The prices are subject to the Discount taken off at foot. The quantity of any of the articles mentioned below may be increased or decreased as may be preferred, or a single article may be had if required.

	oz	s d	£ s d
12 Fiddle pattern Silver Table Spoons	30 at 7 2		10 15 0
12 Silver Dessert ditto	20	7 2	7 3 4
12 Silver Table Forks	30	7 2	10 15 0
12 Silver Dessert ditto	20	7 2	7 3 4
2 Silver Gravy Spoons	10	7 2	3 11 8
1 Silver Soup Ladle	10	7 2	3 11 8
4 Silver Sauce ditto	10	7 8	3 16 8
4 Silver Salt Spoons (gilt strong)			1 0 0
1 Silver Fish Slice			2 10 0
12 Silver Tea Spoons	10	7 8	3 16 8
1 Pair Silver Sugar Tongs			0 15 0
1 Silver moist Sugar Spoon			0 10 0
1 Silver Sugar Sifter			0 17 0
1 Pair of Silver Pickle Forks, ivory handles			0 12 0
1 Silver Butter Knife, ivory handle			0 12 0
12 Pair of Plated Dessert Fruit Knives and Forks, plated on steel blades			3 3 0
24 Best Steel Table Knives with 12 ditto Forks, balanced handles			3 19 0
24 Best Steel Dessert Pie Knives with 12 Forks, balanced handles			2 19 0
1 Pair Poultry Carvers			0 9 0
1 Pair full size Carvers			0 9 0
2 Pair of Plated Candlesticks, 10½ in. high, at 27s. per pair			2 14 0
1 Pair of Plated Candlesticks, 12 in. high			1 18 0
2 Pair of Plated Branches to fit the above, forming together a Candelabra of five lights when required	55		0
1 Snuffer Tray, Plated, with Silver Shield			0 15 0
1 Pair Plated Snuffers to match			0 10 0
2 Pair of Plated Decanter Stands, at 20s.			2 0 0
1 Liquor Frame, Plated, with three best cut glass Decanters			3 13 6
1 Cruet Frame, Plated, with seven Cruets of best cut glass, silver mounts to the Mustard Pot and Castors			3 17 0
1 Silver Cottage pattern Coffee Pot,			15 0 0
1 Ditto Tea Pot, Silver			12 0 0
1 Ditto Sugar Basin, Silver, gilt inside			6 16 0
1 Ditto Cream Ewer, Silver, gilt inside			4 10 0
1 Pair of Waiters, Plated, 8 inches diameter			2 2 0
1 Waiter, Plated, Silver Shield, 12 in. diameter			2 5 0

Carried forward £131 13 10

	£ s d
Brought forward	131 13 10
1 Waiter, Plated, 20 inches diameter	9 9 0
1 Pickle Frame, Plated, with three best cut Glasses	2 15 0
1 Egg Frame, Plated, with six Cups, gilt inside	3 5 0
2 Plated Chamber Candlesticks, at 14s.	1 8 0
Plated Epergne, with centre glass and four branches supporting four Dishes; the Dishes take off, and nozzles are replaced for candles, forming a splendid centre piece for the table	8 18 6
Set of four Plated Hash Dishes and Covers, the handles to take off the Covers, so as to form eight Dishes when required	9 9 0
Set of four Plated Dish Covers, one 12 inches, one 14, one 18, and one 20	16 0 0
Plated Soup Tureen to match	6 6 0
4 Plated Sauce Tureens to match	8 8 0
A Plated Hot-Water or Venison Dish for the head of the table	8 8 0
4 Plated Salt Cellars	2 0 0
1 Plated Butter Cooler	2 2 0
1 Plated Bread or Cake Basket	2 10 0
1 Pair of Plated Wine Coolers	7 7 0
1 Plated Toast Rack	0 14 0
1 Bronze Tea Urn	2 6 0
4 Plated Knife Rests	0 10 0
1 Plated Asparagus Tongs	0 17 0
1 Plated Grape Scissors	0 10 0
4 Plated Nutcrackers, at 5s each	1 0 0
4 Plated Bottle Labels, at 2s. 6d. each	0 10 0
Pair of Plated Muffineers	0 10 0
Plated Mustard Pot	0 14 0
Plated Wine Funnel	0 11 0
2 Iron bound Plate Cases to contain the above articles, green baize linings and divisions, patent lock, &c	14 0 0
	242 6 4
Discount off Cutlery 25 per cent, and Plated Goods 10 per cent	13 16 0
Total £228 10 4

If for exportation there would be a further deduction of £15, being the drawback allowed by Government on silver exported.

The Service enumerated above is selected so as to furnish strong serviceable articles of elegant plain patterns: but a Pamphlet of thirty-two pages is published by T. Cox Savory, containing a detailed List, illustrated with Drawings of other Patterns of Plate, Plated Goods, &c. The Pamphlet may be had free of charge, by application; or will be sent in reply to a post-paid letter.

HORIZONTAL FLAT WATCHES.

WATCHES ON THIS HIGHLY APPROVED CONSTRUCTION, WITH WELL-FINISHED JEWELLED MOVEMENTS, WARRANTED, ARE OFFERED IN SILVER CASES, PRICE FIVE GUINEAS EACH; IN GOLD CASES WITH SILVER DIALS, NINE GUINEAS EACH; OR IN GOLD CASES WITH GOLD DIALS, TEN GUINEAS EACH.

Watches on the Vertical Construction are offered far cheaper, but unless much thicker, the performance is not so accurate.

N.B.—Second-hand Watches purchased in exchange.

REFORM YOUR TAILORS' BILLS!

LADIES' ELEGANT
RIDING HABITS.

Summer Cloth	£3	3	0
Ladies' Cloth	4	4	0
Saxony Cloth	5	5	0

GENTLEMAN'S

Superfine Dress Coat	2	7	6
Extra Saxony, the best that is made	2	15	0
Superfine Frock Coat, silk facings	2	10	0
Buckskin Trousers	1	1	0
Cloth or double-milled Cassimere ditto 17s. 6d. to	1	5	0
New Patterns, Summer Trousers, 10s. 6d. per pr. or 3 pr.	1	10	0
Summer Waistcoats, 7s.; or 3,	1	0	0
Splendid Silk Valencia Dress Waistcoats, 10s. 6d. each, or 3,	1	10	0

FIRST-RATE
BOYS' CLOTHING.

Skeleton Dresses	£0	15	0
Tunic and Hussar Suits,	1	10	0
Camlet Cloaks	0	8	6
Cloth Cloaks	0	15	6

GENTLEMAN'S

Morning Coats and Dressing Gowns	0	18	0
Petersham Great Coats and Pilot P Jackets, bound, and Velvet Collar	1	10	0
Camlet Cloak, lined all through	1	1	0
Cloth Opera Cloak	1	10	0
Army Cloth Blue Spanish Cloak, 9½ yards round	2	10	0
Super Cloth ditto	3	3	0
Cloth or Tweed Fishing or Travelling Trousers	0	13	6

THE CELEBRITY THE

CITY CLOTHING ESTABLISHMENT

Has so many years maintained, being the

BEST AS WELL AS THE CHEAPEST HOUSE,

Renders any Assurance as to STYLE and QUALITY unnecessary. The NOBILITY and GENTRY are invited to the SHOW-ROOMS, TO VIEW THE IMMENSE & SPLENDID STOCK.

The numerous Applications for

REGIMENTALS & NAVAL UNIFORMS,

Have induced E. P. D. & SON to make ample Arrangements for an extensive Business in this particular Branch: a perusal of their List of Prices (which can be had gratis) will show the EXORBITANT CHARGES to which OFFICERS OF THE ARMY AND NAVY HAVE SO LONG BEEN SUBJECTED.

CONTRACTS BY THE YEAR,

Originated by E. P. D. & SON, are universally adopted by CLERGYMEN and PROFESSIONAL GENTLEMEN, as being MORE REGULAR and ECONOMICAL. THE PRICES ARE THE LOWEST EVER OFFERED:—

Two Suits per Year, Superfine,	7 7—Extra Saxony, the best that is made,	8 5
Three Suits per Year, ditto	10 17—Extra Saxony, ditto	12 6
Four Suits per Year, ditto	14 6—Extra Saxony, ditto	15 18

(THE OLD SUITS TO BE RETURNED.)

Capital Shooting Jackets, 21s. The new Waterproof Cloak, 21s.

COUNTRY GENTLEMEN,

Preferring their Clothes Fashionably made, at a FIRST-RATE LONDON HOUSE, are respectfully informed, that by a Post-paid Application, they will receive a Prospectus explanatory of the System of Business, Directions for Measurement, and a Statement of Prices. Or if Three or Four Gentlemen unite, one of the Travellers will be dispatched immediately to wait on them.

STATE LIVERIES SPLENDIDLY MADE.

Footman's Suit of Liveries, £3 3s. Scarlet Hunting Coat, £3 3

E. P. DOUDNEY AND SON,
49, LOMBARD-STREET. 1784.
Established

NOTICE.

THE Publishers regret to state, that in consequence of the sudden indisposition of the Artist,
the Plates which should have accompanied this
Number are unavoidably postponed till next
Month, when Four will be given.

186, STRAND.
April 30, 1839.

The Publication of the First Part of

PHIZ'S FANCIES,

AND

A PAPER—OF TOBACCO,

Is Postponed for a short time.

CHAPTER XLIII.

OFFICIATES AS A KIND OF GENTLEMAN USHER, IN BRINGING VARIOUS
PEOPLE TOGETHER.

THE storm had long given place to a calm the most profound, and
the evening was pretty far advanced—indeed supper was over, and the
process of digestion proceeding as favourably as, under the influence of
complete tranquillity, cheerful conversation, and a moderate allowance of
brandy and water, most wise men conversant with the anatomy and
functions of the human frame will consider that it ought to have proceeded, when the three friends, or as one might say, both in a civil and
religious sense, and with proper deference and regard to the holy state
of matrimony, the two friends, (Mr. and Mrs. Browdie counting as no
more than one,) were startled by the noise of loud and angry threatenings
below-stairs, which presently attained so high a pitch, and were conveyed besides in language so towering sanguinary and ferocious, that
it could hardly have been surpassed, if there had actually been a
Saracen's head then present in the establishment, supported on the
shoulders and surmounting the trunk of a real, live, furious, and most
unappeasable Saracen.

This turmoil, instead of quickly subsiding after the first outburst,
(as turmoils not unfrequently do, whether in taverns, legislative assemblies, or elsewhere,) into a mere grumbling and growling squabble,
increased every moment; and although the whole din appeared to be
raised by but one pair of lungs, yet that one pair was of so powerful
a quality, and repeated such words as " scoundrel," " rascal," "insolent
puppy," and a variety of expletives no less flattering to the party addressed, with such great relish and strength of tone, that a dozen voices
raised in concert under any ordinary circumstances would have made
far less uproar and created much smaller consternation.

" Why, what's the matter?" said Nicholas, moving hastily towards
the door.

John Browdie was striding in the same direction when Mrs. Browdie
turned pale, and, leaning back in her chair, requested him with a faint
voice to take notice, that if he ran into any danger it was her intention
to fall into hysterics immediately, and that the consequences might be
more serious than he thought for. John looked rather disconcerted by
this intelligence, though there was a lurking grin on his face at the
same time; but, being quite unable to keep out of the fray, he compromised the matter by tucking his wife's arm under his own, and, thus
accompanied, following Nicholas down stairs with all speed.

The passage outside the coffee-room door was the scene of disturbance, and here were congregated the coffee-room customers and waiters,
together with two or three coachmen and helpers from the yard. These

had hastily assembled round a young man who from his appearance might have been a year or two older than Nicholas, and who, besides having given utterance to the defiances just now described, seemed to have proceeded to even greater lengths in his indignation, inasmuch as his feet had no other covering than a pair of stockings, while a couple of slippers lay at no great distance from the head of a prostrate figure in an opposite corner, who bore the appearance of having been shot into his present retreat by means of a kick, and complimented by having the slippers flung about his ears afterwards.

The coffee-room customers, and the waiters, and the coachmen, and the helpers—not to mention a bar-maid who was looking on from behind an open sash window—seemed at that moment, if a spectator might judge from their winks, nods, and muttered exclamations, strongly disposed to take part against the young gentleman in the stockings. Observing this, and that the young gentleman was nearly of his own age and had in nothing the appearance of an habitual brawler, Nicholas, impelled by such feelings as will influence young men sometimes, felt a very strong disposition to side with the weaker party, and so thrust himself at once into the centre of the group, and in a more emphatic tone perhaps than circumstances might seem to warrant, demanded what all that noise was about.

" Hallo ! " said one of the men from the yard, " this is somebody in disguise, this is."

" Room for the eldest son of the Emperor of Roosher, gen'lmen ! " cried another fellow.

Disregarding these sallies, which were uncommonly well received, as sallies at the expense of the best-dressed persons in a crowd usually are, Nicholas glanced carelessly round, and addressing the young gentleman, who had by this time picked up his slippers and thrust his feet into them, repeated his inquiries with a courteous air.

" A mere nothing ! " he replied.

At this a murmur was raised by the lookers-on, and some of the boldest cried, " Oh, indeed !—Wasn't it though ?—Nothing, eh ?—He called that nothing, did he ?   Lucky for him if he found it nothing." These and many other expressions of ironical disapprobation having been exhausted, two or three of the out-of-door fellows began to hustle Nicholas and the young gentleman who had made the noise: stumbling against them by accident, and treading on their toes, and so forth. But this being a round game, and one not necessarily limited to three or four players, was open to John Browdie too, who, bursting into the little crowd—to the great terror of his wife—and falling about in all directions, now to the right, now to the left, now forwards, now backwards, and accidentally driving his elbow through the hat of the tallest helper, who had been particularly active, speedily caused the odds to wear a very different appearance ; while more than one stout fellow limped away to a respectful distance, anathematising with tears in his eyes the heavy tread and ponderous feet of the burly Yorkshireman.

" Let me see him do it again," said he who had been kicked into the corner, rising as he spoke, apparently more from the fear of John Browdie's inadvertently treading upon him, than from any desire to place himself on equal terms with his late adversary. " Let me see him do it again. That's all."

" Let me hear you make those remarks again," said the young man, " and I'll knock that head of yours in among the wine-glasses behind you there."

Here a waiter who had been rubbing his hands in excessive enjoyment of the scene, so long as only the breaking of heads was in question, adjured the spectators with great earnestness to fetch the police, declaring that otherwise murder would be surely done, and that he was responsible for all the glass and china on the premises.

" No one need trouble himself to stir," said the young gentleman, " I am going to remain in the house all night, and shall be found here in the morning if there is any assault to answer for."

" What did you strike him for ? " asked one of the bystanders.

" Ah ! what did you strike him for ?" demanded the others.

The unpopular gentleman looked coolly round, and addressing himself to Nicholas, said :—

" You inquired just now what was the matter here. The matter is simply this. Yonder person, who was drinking with a friend in the coffee-room when I took my seat there for half an hour before going to bed, (for I have just come off a journey, and preferred stopping here to-night, to going home at this hour, where I was not expected until to-morrow,) chose to express himself in very disrespectful, and insolently familiar terms, of a young lady, whom I recognised from his description and other circumstances, and whom I have the honour to know. As he spoke loud enough to be overheard by the other guests who were present, I informed him most civilly that he was mistaken in his conjectures, which were of an offensive nature, and requested him to forbear. He did so for a little time, but as he chose to renew his conversation when leaving the room, in a more offensive strain than before, I could not refrain from making after him, and facilitating his departure by a kick, which reduced him to the posture in which you saw him just now. I am the best judge of my own affairs, I take it," said the young man, who had certainly not quite recovered from his recent heat, " if anybody here thinks proper to make this quarrel his own, I have not the smallest earthly objection, I do assure him."

Of all possible courses of proceeding under the circumstances detailed, there was certainly not one which, in his then state of mind, could have appeared more laudable to Nicholas than this. There were not many subjects of dispute which at that moment could have come home to his own breast more powerfully, for having the unknown uppermost in his thoughts, it naturally occurred to him that he would have done just the same if any audacious gossiper durst have presumed in his hearing to speak lightly of her. Influenced by these considerations, he espoused the young gentleman's quarrel with great warmth, protesting that he had done quite right, and that he respected him for it ; which John

Browdie (albeit not quite clear as to the merits) immediately protested too, with not inferior vehemence.

" Let him take care, that's all," said the defeated party, who was being rubbed down by a waiter, after his recent fall on the dusty boards. " He don't knock me about for nothing, I can tell him that. A pretty state of things, if a man isn't to admire a handsome girl without being beat to pieces for it !"

This reflection appeared to have great weight with the young lady in the bar, who (adjusting her cap as she spoke, and glancing at a mirror) declared that it would be a very pretty state of things indeed ; and that if people were to be punished for actions so innocent and natural as that, there would be more people to be knocked down than there would be people to knock them down, and that she wondered what the gentleman meant by it, that she did.

" My dear girl,'' said the young gentleman in a low voice, advancing towards the sash window.

" Nonsense, sir!" replied the young lady sharply, smiling though as she turned aside, and biting her lip, (whereat Mrs. Browdie, who was still standing on the stairs, glanced at her with disdain, and called to her husband to come away).

" No, but listen to me," said the young man. " If admiration of a pretty face were criminal, I should be the most hopeless person alive, for I cannot resist one. It has the most extraordinary effect upon me, checks and controls me in the most furious and obstinate mood. You see what an effect yours has had upon me already."

" Oh, that's very pretty," replied the young lady, tossing her head, " but—"

" Yes, I know it's very pretty," said the young man, looking with an air of admiration in the bar- maid's face, " I said so, you know, just this moment. But beauty should be spoken of respectfully—respectfully, and in proper terms, and with a becoming sense of its worth and excellence, whereas this fellow has no more notion——"

The young lady interrupted the conversation at this point, by thrusting her head out of the bar-window, and inquiring of the waiter in a shrill voice whether that young man who had been knocked down was going to stand in the passage all night, or whether the entrance was to be left clear for other people. The waiters taking the hint, and communicating it to the hostlers, were not slow to change their tone too, and the result was, that the unfortunate victim was bundled out in a twinkling.

" I am sure I have seen that fellow before," said Nicholas.

" Indeed !" replied his new acquaintance.

" I am certain of it," said Nicholas, pausing to reflect. " Where can I have—stop !—yes, to be sure—he belongs to a register-office up at the west end of the town. I knew I recollected the face."

It was, indeed, Tom—the ugly clerk.

" That's odd enough !" said Nicholas, ruminating upon the strange manner in which that register-office seemed to start up and stare him in the face every now and then, and when he least expected it.

" I am much obliged to you for your kind advocacy of my cause when it most needed an advocate," said the young man, laughing, and drawing a card from his pocket. " Perhaps you'll do me the favour to let me know where I can thank you."

Nicholas took the card, and glancing at it involuntarily as he returned the compliment, evinced very great surprise.

" ' Mr. Frank Cheeryble !' " said Nicholas. " Surely not the nephew of Cheeryble Brothers, who is expected to-morrow !"

" I don't usually call myself the nephew of the firm," returned Mr. Frank, good-humouredly, " but of the two excellent individuals who compose it, I am proud to say I *am* the nephew. And you, I see, are Mr. Nickleby, of whom I have heard so much ! This is a most unexpected meeting, but not the less welcome I assure you."

Nicholas responded to these compliments with others of the same kind, and they shook hands warmly. Then he introduced John Browdie, who had remained in a state of great admiration ever since the young lady in the bar had been so skilfully won over to the right side. Then Mrs. John Browdie was introduced, and finally they all went up-stairs together and spent the next half hour with great satisfaction and mutual entertainment ; Mrs. John Browdie beginning the conversation by declaring that of all the made-up things she ever saw, that young woman below-stairs was the vainest and the plainest.

This Mr. Frank Cheeryble, although, to judge from what had recently taken place, a hot-headed young man, (which is not an absolute miracle and phenomenon in nature) was a sprightly, good-humoured, pleasant fellow, with much both in his countenance and disposition that reminded Nicholas very strongly of the kind-hearted brothers. His manner was as unaffected as theirs, and his demeanour full of that heartiness which, to most people who have anything generous in their composition, is peculiarly prepossessing. Add to this, that he was good-looking and intelligent, had a plentiful share of vivacity, was extremely cheerful, and accommodated himself in five minutes' time to all John Browdie's oddities with as much ease as if he had known him from a boy ; and it will be a source of no great wonder that, when they parted for the night, he had produced a most favourable impression, not only upon the worthy Yorkshireman and his wife, but upon Nicholas also, who, revolving all these things in his mind as he made the best of his way home, arrived at the conclusion that he had laid the foundation of a most agreeable and desirable acquaintance.

" But it's a most extraordinary thing about that register-office fellow !" thought Nicholas. " Is it likely that this nephew can know anything about that beautiful girl ? When Tim Linkinwater gave me to understand the other day that he was coming to take a share in the business here, he said he had been superintending it in Germany for four years, and that during the last six months he had been engaged in establishing an agency in the north of England. That's four years and a half—four years and a half. She can't be more than seventeen—say eighteen at the outside. She was quite a child when he went away, then. I should say he knew nothing about her and had never seen her, so *he* can give me no information. At all events," thought Nicholas, coming to the real point in his mind, " there can be no danger of any prior occupation of her affections in that quarter; that's quite clear."

Is selfishness a necessary ingredient in the composition of that passion called love, or does it deserve all the fine things which poets, in the exercise of their undoubted vocation, have said of it? There are, no doubt, authenticated instances of gentlemen having given up ladies and ladies having given up gentlemen to meritorious rivals, under circumstances of great high-mindedness; but is it quite established that the majority of such ladies and gentlemen have not made a virtue of necessity, and nobly resigned what was beyond their reach; as a private soldier might register a vow never to accept the order of the Garter, or a poor curate of great piety and learning, but of no family—save a very large family of children—might renounce a bishopric?

Here was Nicholas Nickleby, who would have scorned the thought of counting how the chances stood of his rising in favour or fortune with the Brothers Cheeryble, now that their nephew had returned, already deep in calculations whether that same nephew was likely to rival him in the affections of the fair unknown—discussing the matter with himself too, as gravely as if, with that one exception, it were all settled; and recurring to the subject again and again, and feeling quite indignant and ill-used at the notion of anybody else making love to one with whom he had never exchanged a word in all his life. To be sure, he exaggerated rather than depreciated the merits of his new acquaintance; but still he took it as a kind of personal offence that he should have any merits at all—in the eyes of this particular young lady, that is; for elsewhere he was quite welcome to have as many as he pleased. There was undoubted selfishness in all this, and yet Nicholas was of a most free and generous nature, with as few mean or sordid thoughts, perhaps, as ever fell to the lot of any man; and there is no reason to suppose that, being in love, he felt and thought differently from other people in the like sublime condition.

He did not stop to set on foot an inquiry into his train of thought or state of feeling, however, but went thinking on all the way home, and continued to dream on in the same strain all night. For, having satisfied himself that Frank Cheeryble could have no knowledge of, or acquaintance with the mysterious young lady, it began to occur to him that even he himself might never see her again; upon which hypothesis he built up a very ingenious succession of tormenting ideas which answered his purpose even better than the vision of Mr. Frank Cheeryble, and tantalized and worried him, waking and sleeping.

Notwithstanding all that has been said and sung to the contrary, there is no well-established case of morning having either deferred or hastened its approach by the term of an hour or so for the mere gratification of a splenetic feeling against some unoffending lover: the sun having, in the discharge of his public duty, as the books of precedent report, invariably risen according to the almanacks, and without suffering himself to be swayed by any private considerations. So, morning came as usual and with it business-hours, and with them Mr. Frank

Cheeryble, and with him a long train of smiles and welcomes from the worthy brothers, and a more grave and clerk-like, but scarcely less hearty reception, from Mr. Timothy Linkinwater.

"That Mr. Frank and Mr. Nickleby should have met last night," said Tim Linkinwater, getting slowly off his stool, and looking round the counting-house with his back planted against the desk, as was his custom when he had anything very particular to say—"that those two young men should have met last night in that manner is, I say, a coincidence—a remarkable coincidence. Why, I don't believe now," added Tim, taking off his spectacles, and smiling as with gentle pride, "that there's such a place in all the world for coincidences as London is!"

"I don't know about that," said Mr. Frank; "but——"

"Don't know about it, Mr. Francis!" interrupted Tim, with an obstinate air. "Well, but let us know. If there is any better place for such things, where is it? Is it in Europe? No, that it isn't. Is it in Asia? Why, of course it's not. Is it in Africa? Not a bit of it. Is it in America? *You* know better than that, at all events. Well, then," said Tim, folding his arms resolutely, "where is it?"

"I was not about to dispute the point, Tim," said young Cheeryble, laughing. "I am not such a heretic as that. All I was going to say was, that I hold myself under an obligation to the coincidence, that's all."

"Oh! if you don't dispute it," said Tim, quite satisfied, "that's another thing. I'll tell you what though—I wish you had. I wish you or anybody would. I would so put that man down," said Tim, tapping the forefinger of his left hand emphatically with his spectacles, "so put that man down by argument——"

It was quite impossible to find language to express the degree of mental prostration to which such an adventurous wight would be reduced in the keen encounter with Tim Linkinwater, so Tim gave up the rest of his declaration in pure lack of words, and mounted his stool again.

"We may consider ourselves, brother Ned," said Charles, after he had patted Tim Linkinwater approvingly on the back, "very fortunate in having two such young men about us as our nephew Frank and Mr. Nickleby. It should be a source of great satisfaction and pleasure to us."

"Certainly, Charles, certainly," returned the other.

"Of Tim," added brother Ned, "I say nothing whatever, because Tim is a mere child—an infant—a nobody—that we never think of or take into account at all. Tim, you villain, what do you say to that, sir?"

"I am jealous of both of 'em," said Tim, "and mean to look out for another situation; so provide yourselves, gentlemen, if you please."

Tim thought this such an exquisite, unparalleled, and most extraordinary joke, that he laid his pen upon the inkstand, and rather tumbling off his stool than getting down with his usual deliberation, laughed till he was quite faint, shaking his head all the time so that little particles of powder flew palpably about the office. Nor were the brothers at all behind-hand, for they laughed almost as heartily at the ludicrous idea

of any voluntary separation between themselves and old Tim.   Nicholas
and Mr. Frank laughed quite boisterously, perhaps to conceal some
other emotion awakened by this little incident, (and, so indeed, did the
three old fellows after the first burst,) so perhaps there was as much
keen enjoyment and relish in that laugh altogether, as the politest
assembly ever derived from the most poignant witticism uttered at any
one person's expense.

" Mr. Nickleby," said brother Charles, calling him aside, and taking
him kindly by the hand, " I—I—am anxious, my dear sir, to see that
you are properly and comfortably settled in the cottage.   We cannot
allow those who serve us well to labour under any privation or discomfort that it is in our power to remove.   I wish, too, to see your mother
and sister—to know them, Mr. Nickleby, and have an opportunity of
relieving their minds by assuring them that any trifling service we have
been able to do them is a great deal more than repaid by the zeal and
ardour you display.—Not a word, my dear sir, I beg.   To-morrow is
Sunday.   I shall make bold to come out at tea-time, and take the
chance of finding you at home ; if you are not, you know, or the
ladies should feel a delicacy in being intruded on, and would rather not
be known to me just now, why I can come again another time, any
other time would do for me.   Let it remain upon that understanding.
Brother Ned, my dear fellow, let me have a word with you this way."

The twins went out of the office arm in arm, and Nicholas, who
saw in this act of kindness, and many others of which he had been the
subject that morning, only so many delicate renewals on the arrival of
their nephew of the kind assurances which the brothers had given him
in his absence, could scarcely feel sufficient admiration and gratitude for
such extraordinary consideration.

The intelligence that they were to have a visitor— and such a visitor
—next day, awakened in the breast of Mrs. Nickleby mingled feelings
of exultation and regret ; for whereas on the one hand she hailed it as
an omen of her speedy restoration to good society and the almost-for-
gotten pleasures of morning calls and evening tea-drinkings, she could
not, on the other, but reflect with bitterness of spirit on the absence of
a silver teapot with an ivory knob on the lid, and a milk-jug to match,
which had been the pride of her heart in days of yore, and had been
kept from year's end to year's end wrapped up in wash-leather on a
certain top shelf which now presented itself in lively colours to her
sorrowing imagination.

" I wonder who's got that spice-box," said Mrs. Nickleby, shaking
her head.   " It used to stand in the left-hand corner, next but two
to the pickled onions.   You remember that spice-box, Kate ? "

" Perfectly well, mama."

" I shouldn't think you did, Kate," returned Mrs. Nickleby, in a
severe manner, " talking about it in that cold and unfeeling way !   If
there is any one thing that vexes me in these losses more than the losses
themselves, I do protest and declare," said Mrs. Nickleby, rubbing her
nose with an impassioned air, " that it is to have people about me who
take things with such provoking calmness."

" My dear mama," said Kate, stealing her arm round her mother's neck, " why do you say what I know you cannot seriously mean or think, or why be angry with me for being happy and content? You and Nicholas are left to me, we are together once again, and what regard can I have for a few trifling things of which we never feel the want? When I have seen all the misery and desolation that death can bring, and known the lonesome feeling of being solitary and alone in crowds, and all the agony of separation in grief and poverty when we most needed comfort and support from each other, can you wonder that I look upon this as a place of such delicious quiet and rest, that with you beside me I have nothing to wish for or regret? There was a time, and not long since, when all the comforts of our old home did come back upon me, I own, very often—oftener than you would think perhaps—but I affected to care nothing for them, in the hope that you would so be brought to regret them less. I was not insensible, indeed. I might have felt happier if I had been. Dear mama," said Kate, in great agitation, " I know no difference between this home and that in which we were all so happy for so many years, except that the kindest and gentlest heart that ever ached on earth has passed in peace to heaven."

"Kate my dear, Kate," cried Mrs. Nickleby, folding her in her arms.

" I have so often thought," sobbed Kate, " of all his kind words—of the last time he looked into my little room, as he passed up-stairs to bed, and said, ' God bless you, darling.' There was a paleness in his face, mama—the broken heart—I know it was—I little thought so—then—"

A gush of tears came to her relief, and Kate laid her head upon her mother's breast, and wept like a little child.

It is an exquisite and beautiful thing in our nature, that when the heart is touched and softened by some tranquil happiness or affectionate feeling, the memory of the dead comes over it most powerfully and irresistibly. It would almost seem as though our better thoughts and sympathies were charms, in virtue of which the soul is enabled to hold some vague and mysterious intercourse with the spirits of those whom we dearly loved in life. Alas! how often and how long may those patient angels hover above us, watching for the spell which is so seldom uttered, and so soon forgotten!

Poor Mrs. Nickleby, accustomed to give ready utterance to whatever came uppermost in her mind, had never conceived the possibility of her daughter's dwelling upon these thoughts in secret, the more especially as no hard trial or querulous reproach had ever drawn them from her. But now, when the happiness of all that Nicholas had just told them, and of their new and peaceful life, brought these recollections so strongly upon Kate that she could not suppress them, Mrs. Nickleby began to have a glimmering that she had been rather thoughtless now and then, and was conscious of something like self-reproach as she embraced her daughter, and yielded to the emotions which such a conversation naturally awakened.

There was a mighty bustle that night, and a vast quantity of preparation for the expected visitor, and a very large nosegay was brought from a gardener's hard by and cut up into a number of very small ones with which Mrs. Nickleby would have garnished the little sitting-room, in a style that certainly could not have failed to attract anybody's attention, if Kate had not offered to spare her the trouble, and arranged them in the prettiest and neatest manner possible. If the cottage ever looked pretty, it must have been on such a bright and sunshiny day as the next day was. But Smike's pride in the garden, or Mrs. Nickleby's in the condition of the furniture, or Kate's in everything, was nothing to the pride with which Nicholas looked at Kate herself; and surely the costliest mansion in all England might have found in her beautiful face and graceful form its most exquisite and peerless ornament.

About six o'clock in the afternoon Mrs. Nickleby was thrown into a great flutter of spirits by the long-expected knock at the door, nor was this flutter at all composed by the audible tread of two pair of boots in the passage, which Mrs. Nickleby augured, in a breathless state, must be " the two Mr. Cheerybles ;" as it certainly was, though not the two Mrs. Nickleby expected, because it was Mr. Charles Cheeryble, and his nephew, Mr. Frank, who made a thousand apologies for his intrusion, which Mrs. Nickleby (having tea-spoons enough and to spare for all) most graciously received. Nor did the appearance of this unexpected visitor occasion the least embarrassment, (save in Kate, and that only to the extent of a blush or two at first,) for the old gentleman was so kind and cordial, and the young gentleman imitated him in this respect so well, that the usual stiffness and formality of a first meeting showed no signs of appearing, and Kate really more than once detected herself in the very act of wondering when it was going to begin.

At the tea-table there was plenty of conversation on a great variety of subjects, nor were there wanting jocose matters of discussion, such as they were ; for young Mr. Cheeryble's recent stay in Germany happening to be alluded to, old Mr. Cheeryble informed the company that the aforesaid young Mr. Cheeryble was suspected to have fallen deeply in love with the daughter of a certain German burgomaster. This accusation young Mr. Cheeryble most indignantly repelled, upon which Mrs. Nickleby slily remarked, that she suspected, from the very warmth of the denial, there must be something in it. Young Mr. Cheeryble then earnestly entreated old Mr. Cheeryble to confess that it was all a jest, which old Mr. Cheeryble at last did, young Mr. Cheeryble being so much in earnest about it, that—as Mrs. Nickleby said many thousand times afterwards in recalling the scene—he "quite coloured," which she rightly considered a memorable circumstance, and one worthy of remark, young men not being as a class remarkable for modesty or self-denial, especially when there is a lady in the case, when, if they colour at all, it is rather their practice to colour the story, and not themselves.

After tea there was a walk in the garden, and the evening being very fine they strolled out at the garden gate into some lanes and bye-roads, and sauntered up and down until it grew quite dark. The time seemed to pass very quickly with all the party. Kate went first, leaning upon her brother's arm, and talking with him and Mr. Frank Cheeryble; and Mrs. Nickleby and the elder gentleman followed at a short distance, the kindness of the good merchant, his interest in the welfare of Nicholas, and his admiration of Kate, so operating upon the good lady's feelings, that the usual current of her speech was confined within very narrow and circumscribed limits. Smike (who, if he had ever been an object of interest in his life, had been one that day) accompanied them, joining sometimes one group and sometimes the other, as brother Charles, laying his hand upon his shoulder, bade him walk with him, or Nicholas, looking smilingly round, beckoned him to come and talk with the old friend who understood him best, and who could win a smile into his care-worn face when none else could.

Pride is one of the seven deadly sins; but it cannot be the pride of a mother in her children, for that is a compound of two cardinal virtues —faith and hope. This was the pride which swelled Mrs. Nickleby's heart that night, and this it was which left upon her face, glistening in the light when they returned home, traces of the most grateful tears she had ever shed.

There was a quiet mirth about the little supper, which harmonized exactly with this tone of feeling, and at length the two gentlemen took their leave. There was one circumstance in the leave-taking which occasioned a vast deal of smiling and pleasantry, and that was, that Mr. Frank Cheeryble offered his hand to Kate twice over, quite forgetting that he had bade her adieu already. This was held by the elder Mr. Cheeryble to be a convincing proof that he was thinking of his German flame, and the jest occasioned immense laughter. So easy is it to move light hearts.

In short, it was a day of serene and tranquil happiness; and as we all have some bright day—many of us, let us hope, among a crowd of others—to which we revert with particular delight, so this one was often looked back to afterwards, as holding a conspicuous place in the calendar of those who shared it.

Was there one exception, and that one he who needed to have been most happy?

Who was that who, in the silence of his own chamber, sunk upon his knees to pray as his first friend had taught him, and folding his hands and stretching them wildly in the air, fell upon his face in a passion of bitter grief?

CHAPTER XLIV.

MR. RALPH NICKLEBY CUTS AN OLD ACQUAINTANCE. IT WOULD ALSO APPEAR FROM THE CONTENTS HEREOF, THAT A JOKE, EVEN BETWEEN HUSBAND AND WIFE, MAY BE SOMETIMES CARRIED TOO FAR.

THERE are some men, who, living with the one object of enriching themselves, no matter by what means, and being perfectly conscious of the baseness and rascality of the means which they will use every day towards this end, affect nevertheless—even to themselves—a high tone of moral rectitude, and shake their heads and sigh over the depravity of the world. Some of the craftiest scoundrels that ever walked this earth, or rather—for walking implies, at least, an erect position and the bearing of a man—that ever crawled and crept through life by its dirtiest and narrowest ways, will gravely jot down in diaries the events of every day, and keep a regular debtor and creditor account with heaven, which shall always show a floating balance in their own favour. Whether this is a gratuitous (the only gratuitous) part of the false-hood and trickery of such men's lives, or whether they really hope to cheat heaven itself, and lay up treasure in the next world by the same process which has enabled them to lay up treasure in this—not to question how it is, so it is. And, doubtless, such book-keeping (like certain autobiographies which have enlightened the world) cannot fail to prove serviceable, in the one respect of sparing the recording Angel some time and labour.

Ralph Nickleby was not a man of this stamp. Stern, unyielding, dogged, and impenetrable, Ralph cared for nothing in life, or beyond it, save the gratification of two passions, avarice, the first and predominant appetite of his nature, and hatred, the second. Affecting to consider himself but a type of all humanity, he was at little pains to conceal his true character from the world in general, and in his own heart he exulted over and cherished every bad design as it had birth. The only scriptural admonition that Ralph Nickleby heeded, in the letter, was "know thyself." He knew himself well, and choosing to imagine that all mankind were cast in the same mould, hated them; for, though no man hates himself, the coldest among us having too much self-love for that, yet, most men unconsciously judge the world from themselves, and it will be very generally found that those who sneer habitually at human nature, and affect to despise it, are among its worst and least pleasant samples.

But the present business of these adventures is with Ralph himself, who stood regarding Newman Noggs with a heavy frown, while that worthy took off his fingerless gloves, and spreading them carefully on the palm of his left hand, and flattening them with his right to take the creases out, proceeded to roll them up with an absent air as if he were utterly regardless of all things else, in the deep interest of the ceremonial.

"Gone out of town!" said Ralph, slowly. "A mistake of yours. Go back again."

"No mistake," returned Newman. "Not even going;—gone."

"Has he turned girl or baby?" muttered Ralph, with a fretful gesture.

"I don't know," said Newman, "but he's gone."

The repetition of the word, "gone," seemed to afford Newman Noggs inexpressible delight, in proportion as it annoyed Ralph Nickleby. He uttered the word with a full round emphasis, dwelling upon it as long as he decently could, and when he could hold out no longer without attracting observation, stood gasping it to himself, as if even that were a satisfaction.

" And *where* has he gone?" said Ralph.

" France," replied Newman. "Danger of another attack of erysipelas —a worse attack—in the head. So the doctors ordered him off. And he's gone."

" And Lord Frederick——?" began Ralph.

" He's gone too," replied Newman.

" And he carries his drubbing with him, does he !" said Ralph, turning away—" pockets his bruises, and sneaks off without the retaliation of a word, or seeking the smallest reparation !"

" He's too ill," said Newman.

" Too ill !" repeated Ralph. " Why *I* would have it if I were dying; in that case I should only be the more determined to have it, and that without delay—I mean if I were he. But he's too ill ! Poor Sir Mulberry ! Too ill !"

Uttering these words with supreme contempt and great irritation of manner, Ralph signed hastily to Newman to leave the room; and throwing himself into his chair, beat his foot impatiently upon the ground.

" There is some spell about that boy," said Ralph, grinding his teeth. " Circumstances conspire to help him. Talk of fortune's favours ! What is even money to such Devil's luck as this !"

He thrust his hands impatiently into his pockets, but notwithstanding his previous reflection there was some consolation there, for his face relaxed a little; and although there was still a deep frown upon the contracted brow, it was one of calculation, and not of disappointment.

" This Hawk will come back, however," muttered Ralph ; " and if I know the man—and I should by this time—his wrath will have lost nothing of its violence in the meanwhile. Obliged to live in retirement —the monotony of a sick room to a man of his habits—no life—no drink—no play—nothing that he likes and lives by. He is not likely to forget his obligations to the cause of all this. Few men would; but he of all others—no, no !"

He smiled and shook his head, and resting his chin upon his hand fell a musing, and smiled again. After a time he rose and rang the bell.

" That Mr. Squeers ; has he been here?" said Ralph.

" He was here last night. I left him here when I went home," returned Newman.

" I know that, fool, do I not ?" said Ralph, irascibly. " Has he been here since ? Was he here this morning ?"

" No," bawled Newman, in a very loud key.

" If he comes while I am out—he is pretty sure to be here by nine to-night, let him wait. And if there's another man with him, as there will be—perhaps," said Ralph, checking himself, " let him wait too."

" Let 'em both wait ?" said Newman.

" Ay," replied Ralph, turning upon him with an angry look. " Help me on with this spencer, and don't repeat after me, like a croaking parrot."

" I wish I was a parrot," said Newman, sulkily.

" I wish you were," rejoined Ralph, drawing his spencer on; " I'd have wrung your neck long ago."

Newman returned no answer to this compliment, but looked over Ralph's shoulder for an instant, (he was adjusting the collar of the spencer behind, just then,) as if he were strongly disposed to tweak him by the nose. Meeting Ralph's eye, however, he suddenly recalled his wandering fingers, and rubbed his own red nose with a vehemence quite astonishing.

Bestowing no further notice upon his eccentric follower than a threatening look, and an admonition to be careful and make no mistake, Ralph took his hat and gloves, and walked out.

He appeared to have a very extraordinary and miscellaneous connexion, and very odd calls he made—some at great rich houses, and some at small poor ones—but all upon one subject : money. His face was a talisman to the porters and servants of his more dashing clients, and procured him ready admission, though he trudged on foot, and others, who were denied, rattled to the door in carriages. Here he was all softness and cringing civility ; his step so light, that it scarcely produced a sound upon the thick carpets; his voice so soft, that it was not audible beyond the person to whom it was addressed. But in the poorer habitations Ralph was another man ; his boots creaked upon the passage floor as he walked boldly in, his voice was harsh and loud as he demanded the money that was overdue ; his threats were coarse and angry. With another class of customers, Ralph was again another man. These were attorneys of more than doubtful reputation, who helped him to new business, or raised fresh profits upon old. With them Ralph was familiar and jocose—humorous upon the topics of the day, and especially pleasant upon bankruptcies and pecuniary difficulties that made good for trade. In short, it would have been difficult to have recognised the same man under these various aspects, but for the bulky leather case full of bills and notes which he drew from his pocket at every house, and the constant repetition of the same complaint, (varied only in tone and style of delivery,) that the world thought him rich, and that perhaps he might be if he had his own ; but there was no getting money in when it was once out, either principal or interest, and it was a hard matter to live—even to live from day to day.

It was evening before a long round of such visits (interrupted only by a scanty dinner at an eating-house) terminated at Pimlico, and Ralph walked along Saint James's Park, on his way home.

There were some deep schemes in his head, as the puckered brow and firmly-set mouth would have abundantly testified, even if they had been unaccompanied by a complete indifference to, or unconsciousness of, the objects about him. So complete was his abstraction, however, that Ralph, usually as quick-sighted as any man, did not observe that he was followed by a shambling figure, which at one time stole behind him with noiseless footsteps, at another crept a few paces before him, and at another glided along by his side ; at all times regarding him with an eye so keen, and a look so eager and attentive, that it was more like the expression of an intrusive face in some powerful picture or strongly-marked dream, than the scrutiny even of a most interested and anxious observer.

The sky had been lowering and dark for some time, and the commencement of a violent storm of rain drove Ralph for shelter to a tree. He was leaning against it with folded arms, still buried in thought, when, happening to raise his eyes, he suddenly met those of a man who, creeping round the trunk, peered into his face with a searching look. There was something in the usurer's expression at the moment, which the man appeared to remember well, for it decided him; and stepping close up to Ralph, he pronounced his name.

Astonished for the moment, Ralph fell back a couple of paces, and surveyed him from head to foot. A spare, dark, withered man, of about his own age, with a stooping body, and a very sinister face rendered more ill-favoured by hollow and hungry cheeks, deeply sunburnt, and thick black eye-brows, blacker in contrast with the perfect whiteness of his hair; roughly clothed in shabby garments, of a strange and uncouth make; and having about him an indefinable manner of depression and degradation ;—this, for a moment, was all he saw. But he looked again, and the face and person seemed gradually to grow less strange ; to change as he looked, to subside and soften into lineaments that were familiar, until at last they resolved themselves, as if by some strange optical illusion, into those of one whom he had known for many years, and forgotten and lost sight of for nearly as many more.

The man saw that the recognition was mutual, and beckoning to Ralph to take his former place under the tree, and not to stand in the falling rain, of which, in his first surprise, he had been quite regardless, addressed him in a hoarse, faint tone.

" You would hardly have known me from my voice, I suppose, Mr. Nickleby ? " he said.

" No," returned Ralph, bending a severe look upon him. " Though there is something in that, that I remember now."

" There is little in me that you can call to mind as having been there eight years ago, I dare say ? " observed the other.

" Quite enough," said Ralph, carelessly, and averting his face. " More than enough."

" If I had remained in doubt about *you*, Mr. Nickleby," said the other, " this reception, and *your* manner, would have decided me very soon."

" Did you expect any other ? " asked Ralph, sharply.

" No ! " said the man.

" You were right," retorted Ralph ; " and as you feel no surprise, need express none."

" Mr. Nickleby," said the man, bluntly, after a brief pause, during which he had seemed to struggle with an inclination to answer him by some reproach, " will you hear a few words that I have to say ? "

" I am obliged to wait here till the rain holds a little," said Ralph, looking abroad. " If you talk, sir, I shall not put my fingers in my ears, though your talking may have as much effect as if I did."

" I was once in your confidence—," thus his companion began. Ralph looked round, and smiled involuntarily.

" Well," said the other, " as much in your confidence as you ever chose to let anybody be."

" Ah ! " rejoined Ralph, folding his arms ; " that's another thing—quite another thing."

" Don't let us play upon words, Mr. Nickleby, in the name of humanity."

" Of what ? " said Ralph.

" Of humanity," replied the other, sternly. " I am hungry and in want. If the change that you must see in me after so long an absence —must see, for I, upon whom it has come by slow and hard degrees, see it and know it well—will not move you to pity, let the knowledge that bread ; not the daily bread of the Lord's Prayer, which, as it is offered up in cities like this, is understood to include half the luxuries of the world for the rich and just as much coarse food as will support life for the poor—not that, but bread, a crust of dry hard bread, is beyond my reach to-day—let that have some weight with you, if nothing else has."

" If this is the usual form in which you beg, sir," said Ralph, " you have studied your part well ; but if you will take advice from one who knows something of the world and its ways, I should recommend a lower tone—a little lower tone, or you stand a fair chance of being starved in good earnest."

As he said this, Ralph clenched his left wrist tightly with his right hand, and inclining his head a little on one side and dropping his chin upon his breast, looked at him whom he addressed with a frowning, sullen face : the very picture of a man whom nothing could move or soften.

" Yesterday was my first day in London," said the old man, glancing at his travel-stained dress and worn shoes.

" It would have been better for you, I think, if it had been your last also," replied Ralph.

" I have been seeking you these two days, where I thought you were most likely to be found," resumed the other more humbly, " and I met you here at last, when I had almost given up the hope of encountering you, Mr. Nickleby."

He seemed to wait for some reply, but Ralph giving him none, he continued—

" I am a most miserable and wretched outcast, nearly sixty years old, and as destitute and helpless as a child of six."

" I am sixty years old, too," replied Ralph, "and am neither destitute nor helpless. Work. Don't make fine play-acting speeches about bread, but earn it."

" How ?" cried the other. " Where ? Show me the means. Will you give them to me—will you ?"

" I did once," replied Ralph, composedly, " you scarcely need ask me whether I will again."

" It's twenty years ago, or more," said the man, in a suppressed voice, " since you and I fell out. You remember that ? I claimed a share in the profits of some business I brought to you, and, as I persisted, you arrested me for an old advance of ten pounds, odd shillings—including interest at fifty per cent., or so."

" I remember something of it," replied Ralph, carelessly. " What then ?"

" That didn't part us," said the man. " I made submission, being on
the wrong side of the bolts and bars ; and as you were not the made man
then that you are now, you were glad enough to take back a clerk
who wasn't over nice, and who knew something of the trade you drove."

" You begged and prayed, and I consented," returned Ralph. " That
was kind of me. Perhaps I did want you—I forget. I should think
I did, or you would have begged in vain. You were useful—not too
honest, not too delicate, not too nice of hand or heart—but useful."

" Useful, indeed !" said the man. " Come. You had pinched and
ground me down for some years before that, but I had served you
faithfully up to that time, in spite of all your dog's usage—had I ?"

Ralph made no reply.

" Had I ?" said the man again.

" You had had your wages," rejoined Ralph, " and had done your
work. We stood on equal ground so far, and could both cry quits."

" Then, but not afterwards," said the other.

" Not afterwards, certainly, nor even then, for (as you have just
said) you owed me money, and do still," replied Ralph.

" That's not all," said the man, eagerly. " That's not all. Mark
that. I didn't forget that old sore, trust me. Partly in remembrance
of that, and partly in the hope of making money some day by the
scheme, I took advantage of my position about you, and possessed
myself of a hold upon you, which you would give half of all you have,
to know, and never can know but through me. I left you—long after
that time, remember—and, for some poor trickery that came within
the law, but was nothing to what you money-makers daily practise
just outside its bounds, was sent away a convict for seven years. I
have returned what you see me. Now, Mr. Nickleby," said the man,
with a strange mixture of humility and sense of power, " what help
and assistance will you give me—what bribe, to speak out plainly ?
My expectations are not monstrous, but I must live, and to live I must
eat, and drink. Money is on your side, and hunger and thirst on
mine. You may drive an easy bargain."

" Is that all ?" said Ralph, still eyeing his companion with the same
steady look, and moving nothing but his lips.

" It depends on you, Mr. Nickleby, whether that's all or not," was
the rejoinder.

" Why then, harkye, Mr. ——, I don't know by what name I am
to call you," said Ralph.

" By my old one, if you like."

" Why, then, harkye, Mr. Brooker," said Ralph, in his harshest
accents, " and don't expect to draw another speech from me—harkye,
sir. I know you of old for a ready scoundrel, but you never had a stout
heart ; and hard work, with (maybe) chains upon those legs of yours,
and shorter food than when I ' pinched' and ' ground' you, has blunted
your wits, or you would not come with such a tale as this to me. You
a hold upon me ! Keep it, or publish it to the world, if you like."

" I can't do that," interposed Brooker. " That wouldn't serve me."

" Wouldn't it ?" said Ralph. " It will serve you as much as bringing it to me, I promise you.   To be plain with you, I am a careful man, and know my affairs thoroughly.   I know the world, and the world knows me.   Whatever you gleaned, or heard, or saw, when you served me, the world knows and magnifies already.   You could tell it nothing that would surprise it—unless, indeed, it redounded to my credit or honour, and then it would scout you for a liar.   And yet I don't find business slack, or clients scrupulous.   Quite the contrary.   I am reviled or threatened every day by one man or another," said Ralph ; " but things roll on just the same, and I don't grow poorer either."

" I neither revile nor threaten," rejoined the man.   " I can tell you of what you have lost by my act, what I only can restore, and what, if I die without restoring, dies with me, and never can be regained."

" I tell my money pretty accurately, and generally keep it in my own custody," said Ralph.   " I look sharply after most men that I deal with, and most of all I looked sharply after you.   You are welcome to all you have kept from me."

" Are those of your own name dear to you ? " said the man emphatically.   " If they are——"

" They are not," returned Ralph, exasperated at this perseverance, and the thought of Nicholas, which the last question awakened.   " They are not.   If you had come as a common beggar, I might have thrown a sixpence to you in remembrance of the clever knave you used to be ; but since you try to palm these stale tricks upon one you might have known better, I'll not part with a halfpenny—nor would I to save you from rotting.   And remember this, 'scape-gallows," said Ralph, menacing him with his hand, " that if we meet again, and you so much as notice me by one begging gesture, you shall see the inside of a jail once more, and tighten this hold upon me in intervals of the hard labour that vagabonds are put to.   There's my answer to your trash.   Take it."

With a disdainful scowl at the object of his anger, who met his eye but uttered not a word, Ralph walked away at his usual pace, without manifesting the slightest curiosity to see what became of his late companion, or indeed once looking behind him.   The man remained on the same spot with his eyes fixed upon his retreating figure until it was lost to view, and then drawing his arms about his chest, as if the damp and lack of food struck coldly to him, lingered with slouching steps by the wayside, and begged of those who passed along.

Ralph, in no-wise moved by what had lately passed, further than as he had already expressed himself, walked deliberately on, and turning out of the Park and leaving Golden Square on his right, took his way through some streets at the west end of the town until he arrived in that particular one in which stood the residence of Madame Mantalini. The name of that lady no longer appeared on the flaming door-plate, that of Miss Knag being substituted in its stead ; but the bonnets and dresses were still dimly visible in the first-floor windows by the decaying light of a summer's evening, and, excepting this ostensible alteration in the proprietorship, the establishment wore its old appearance.

" Humph ! " muttered Ralph, drawing his hand across his mouth with a connoisseur-like air, and surveying the house from top to bottom ;

Mr Mantalini poisons himself for the seventh time.

" these people look pretty well. They can't last long; but if I know of their going, in good time, I am safe, and a fair profit too. I must keep them closely in view—that's all."

So, nodding his head very complacently, Ralph was leaving the spot, when his quick ear caught the sound of a confused noise and hubbub of voices, mingled with a great running up and down stairs, in the very house which had been the subject of his scrutiny; and while he was hesitating whether to knock at the door or listen at the key-hole a little longer, a female servant of Madame Mantalini's (whom he had often seen) opened it abruptly and bounced out, with her blue cap-ribands streaming in the air.

" Hallo here. Stop!" cried Ralph. " What's the matter. Here am I. Didn't you hear me knock?"

" Oh! Mr. Nickleby, sir," said the girl. " Go up, for the love of Gracious. Master's been and done it again."

" Done what?" said Ralph, tartly. " What d'ye mean?"

" I knew he would if he was drove to it," cried the girl. " I said so all along."

" Come here, you silly wench," said Ralph, catching her by the wrist; " and don't carry family matters to the neighbours, destroying the credit of the establishment. Come here; do you hear me, girl?"

Without any further expostulation, he led or rather pulled the frightened hand-maid into the house, and shut the door; then bidding her walk up-stairs before him, followed without more ceremony.

Guided by the noise of a great many voices all talking together, and passing the girl in his impatience, before they had ascended many steps, Ralph quickly reached the private sitting-room, when he was rather amazed by the confused and inexplicable scene in which he suddenly found himself.

There were all the young-lady workers, some with bonnets and some without, in various attitudes expressive of alarm and consternation; some gathered round Madame Mantalini, who was in tears upon one chair; and others round Miss Knag, who was in opposition tears upon another; and others round Mr. Mantalini, who was perhaps the most striking figure in the whole group, for Mr. Mantalini's legs were extended at full length upon the floor, and his head and shoulders were supported by a very tall footman, who didn't seem to know what to do with them, and Mr. Mantalini's eyes were closed, and his face was pale, and his hair was comparatively straight, and his whiskers and moustache were limp, and his teeth were clenched, and he had a little bottle in his right hand, and a little tea-spoon in his left; and his hands, arms, legs, and shoulders, were all stiff and powerless. And yet Madame Mantalini was not weeping upon the body, but was scolding violently upon her chair; and all this amidst a clamour of tongues, perfectly deafening, and which really appeared to have driven the unfortunate footman to the uttermost verge of distraction.

" What is the matter here?" said Ralph, pressing forward.

At this inquiry, the clamour was increased twenty-fold, and an astounding string of such shrill contradictions as " He's poisoned him-

self"—" He hasn't "—" Send for a doctor "—" Don't "—" He's dying "
—" He isn't, he's only pretending "—with various other cries, poured
forth with bewildering volubility, until Madame Mantalini was seen to
address herself to Ralph, when female curiosity to know what she
would say, prevailed, and, as if by general consent, a dead silence, unbroken by a single whisper, instantaneously succeeded.

" Mr. Nickleby," said Madame Mantalini; " by what chance you
came here, I don't know."

Here a gurgling voice was heard to ejaculate—as part of the wanderings of a sick man—the words " Demnition sweetness ! " but nobody
heeded them except the footman, who, being startled to hear such awful
tones proceeding, as it were, from between his very fingers, dropped his
master's head upon the floor with a pretty loud crash, and then, without an effort to lift it up, gazed upon the bystanders, as if he had done
something rather clever than otherwise.

" I will, however," continued Madame Mantalini, drying her eyes,
and speaking with great indignation, " say before you, and before everybody here, for the first time, and once for all, that I never will supply
that man's extravagances and viciousness again. I have been a dupe
and a fool to him long enough. In future, he shall support himself if he
can, and then he may spend what money he pleases, upon whom and
how he pleases ; but it shall not be mine, and therefore you had better
pause before you trust him further."

Thereupon Madame Mantalini, quite unmoved by some most pathetic
lamentations on the part of her husband, that the apothecary had not
mixed the prussic acid strong enough, and that he must take another
bottle or two to finish the work he had in hand, entered into a catalogue of that amiable gentleman's gallantries, deceptions, extravagances,
and infidelities (especially the last), winding up with a protest against
being supposed to entertain the smallest remnant of regard for him ;
and adducing, in proof of the altered state of her affections, the circumstance of his having poisoned himself in private no less than six times
within the last fortnight, and her not having once interfered by word or
deed to save his life.

" And I insist on being separated and left to myself," said Madame
Mantalini, sobbing. " If he dares to refuse me a separation, I'll have
one in law—I can—and I hope this will be a warning to all girls who
have seen this disgraceful exhibition."

Miss Knag, who was unquestionably the oldest girl in company, said
with great solemnity, that it would be a warning to *her*, and so did the
young ladies generally, with the exception of one or two who appeared
to entertain some doubts whether such whiskers could do wrong.

" Why do you say all this before so many listeners ? " said Ralph, in
a low voice. " You know you are not in earnest."

" I *am* in earnest," replied Madame Mantalini, aloud, and retreating
towards Miss Knag.

" Well, but consider," reasoned Ralph, who had a great interest in
the matter. " It would be well to reflect. A married woman has no
property."

" Not a solitary single individual dem, my soul," said Mr. Mantalini, raising himself upon his elbow.

" I am quite aware of that," retorted Madame Mantalini, tossing her head ; " and *I* have none. The business, the stock, this house, and everything in it, all belong to Miss Knag."

" That's quite true, Madame Mantalini," said Miss Knag, with whom her late employer had secretly come to an amicable understanding on this point. " Very true, indeed, Madame Mantalini—hem—very true. And I never was more glad in all my life, that I had strength of mind to resist matrimonial offers, no matter how advantageous, than I am when I think of my present position as compared with your most unfortunate and most undeserved one, Madame Mantalini."

" Demmit·!" cried Mr. Mantalini, turning his head towards his wife. " Will it not slap and pinch the envious dowager, that dares to reflect upon its own delicious?"

But the day of Mr. Mantalini's blandishments had departed. " Miss Knag, sir," said his wife, " is my particular friend;" and although Mr. Mantalini leered till his eyes seemed in danger of never coming back to their right places again, Madame Mantalini showed no signs of softening.

To do the excellent Miss Knag justice, she had been mainly instrumental in bringing about this altered state of things, for, finding by daily experience, that there was no chance of the business thriving, or even continuing to exist, while Mr. Mantalini had any hand in the expenditure, and having now a considerable interest in its well-doing, she had sedulously applied herself to the investigation of some little matters connected with that gentleman's private character, which she had so well elucidated, and artfully imparted to Madame Mantalini, as to open her eyes more effectually than the closest and most philosophical reasoning could have done in a series of years. To which end, the accidental discovery by Miss Knag of some tender correspondence, in which Madame Mantalini was described as " old" and " ordinary," had most providentially contributed.

However, notwithstanding her firmness, Madame Mantalini wept very piteously; and as she leant upon Miss Knag, and signed towards the door, that young lady and all the other young ladies with sympathising faces, proceeded to bear her out.

" Nickleby," said Mr. Mantalini, in tears, " you have been made a witness to this demnition cruelty, on the part of the demdest enslaver and captivater that never was, oh dem ! I forgive that woman."

" Forgive !" repeated Madame Mantalini, angrily.

" I do forgive her, Nickleby," said Mr. Mantalini. " You will blame me, the world will blame me, the women will blame me; everybody will laugh, and scoff, and smile, and grin most demnebly. They will say, ' She had a blessing. She did not know it. He was too weak ; he was too good ; he was a dem'd fine fellow, but he loved too strong ; he could not bear her to be cross, and call him wicked names. It was a dem'd case, there never was a demder.—But I forgive her."

With this affecting speech Mr. Mantalini fell down again very flat, and lay to all appearance without sense or motion, until all the females had left the room, when he came cautiously into a sitting posture, and confronted Ralph with a very blank face, and the little bottle still in one hand and the tea-spoon in the other.

" You may put away those fooleries now, and live by your wits again," said Ralph, coolly putting on his hat.

" Demmit, Nickleby, you're not serious ?"

" I seldom joke," said Ralph. " Good night."

" No, but Nickleby—" said Mantalini.

" I am wrong, perhaps," rejoined Ralph. " I hope so. You should know best. Good night."

Affecting not to hear his entreaties that he would stay and advise with him, Ralph left the crest-fallen Mr. Mantalini to his meditations, and left the house quietly.

" Oho !" he said, " sets the wind that way so soon ?   Half knave and half fool, and detected in both characters—hum—I think your day is over, sir."

As he said this, he made some memorandum in his pocket-book in which Mr. Mantalini's name figured conspicuously, and finding by his watch that it was between nine and ten o'clock, made all speed home.

" Are they here ?" was the first question he asked of Newman.

Newman nodded. " Been here half-an-hour."

" Two of them ? one a fat sleek man ?"

" Ay," said Newman. " In your room now."

" Good," rejoined Ralph. " Get me a coach."

" A coach ! What you—going to—Eh ?" stammered Newman.

Ralph angrily repeated his orders, and Noggs, who might well have been excused for wondering at such an unusual and extraordinary circumstance—for he had never seen Ralph in a coach in his life—departed on his errand, and presently returned with the conveyance.

Into it went Mr. Squeers, and Ralph, and the third man, whom Newman Noggs had never seen. Newman stood upon the door step to see them off, not troubling himself to wonder where or upon what business they were going, until he chanced by mere accident to hear Ralph name the address whither the coachman was to drive.

Quick as lightning and in a state of the most extreme wonder, Newman darted into his little office for his hat, and limped after the coach as if with the intention of getting up behind ; but in this design he was balked, for it had too much the start of him and was soon hopelessly ahead, leaving him gaping in the empty street.

" I don't know though," said Noggs, stopping for breath, " any good that I could have done by going too. He would have seen me if I had. Drive *there* ! What can come of this ! If I had only known it yesterday I could have told—drive there ! There's mischief in it. There must be."

His reflections were interrupted by a grey-haired man of a very remarkable, though far from prepossessing appearance, who, coming stealthily towards him, solicited relief.

Newman, still cogitating deeply, turned away ; but the man followed him, and pressed him with such a tale of misery that Newman (who might have been considered a hopeless person to beg from, and who had little enough to give) looked into his hat for some halfpence which he usually kept screwed up, when he had any, in a corner of his pocket handkerchief.

While he was busily untwisting the knot with his teeth, the man said something which attracted his attention; whatever that something was, it led to something else, and in the end he and Newman walked away side by side—the strange man talking earnestly, and Newman listening.

CHAPTER XLV.

CONTAINING MATTER OF A SURPRISING KIND.

" As we gang awa' fra' Lunnun tomorrow neeght, and as I dinnot know that I was e'er so happy in a' my days, Misther Nickleby, Ding! but I *will* tak' anoother glass to our next merry meeting ! "

So said John Browdie, rubbing his hands with great joyousness, and looking round him with a ruddy shining face, quite in keeping with the declaration.

The time at which John found himself in this enviable condition, was the same evening to which the last chapter bore reference ; the place was the cottage; and the assembled company were Nicholas, Mrs. Nickleby, Mrs. Browdie, Kate Nickleby, and Smike.

A very merry party they had been. Mrs. Nickleby, knowing of her son's obligations to the honest Yorkshireman, had, after some demur, yielded her consent to Mr. and Mrs. Browdie being invited out to tea ; in the way of which arrangement, there were at first sundry difficulties and obstacles, arising out of her not having had an opportunity of " calling" upon Mrs. Browdie first ; for although Mrs. Nickleby very often observed with much complacency (as most punctilious people do), that she had not an atom of pride or formality about her, still she was a great stickler for dignity and ceremonies ; and as it was manifest that, until a call had been made, she could not be (politely speaking, and according to the laws of society) even cognizant of the fact of Mrs. Browdie's existence, she felt her situation to be one of peculiar delicacy and difficulty.

" The call *must* originate with me, my dear," said Mrs. Nickleby, " that's indispensable. The fact is, my dear, that it's necessary there should be a sort of condescension on my part, and that I should show this young person that I am willing to take notice of her. There's a very respectable-looking young man," added Mrs. Nickleby, after a short consideration, " who is conductor to one of the omnibuses that go by here, and who wears a glazed hat—your sister and I have noticed him very often—he has a wart upon his nose, Kate, you know, exactly like a gentleman's servant."

" Have all gentlemen's servants warts upon their noses, mother ?" asked Nicholas.

" Nicholas, my dear, how very absurd you are," returned his mother ; " of course I mean that his glazed hat looks like a gentleman's
servant, and not the wart upon his nose—though even that is not so
ridiculous as it may seem to you, for we had a footboy once, who had
not only a wart, but a wen also, and a very large wen too, and he
demanded to have his wages raised in consequence, because he found it
came very expensive. Let me see, what was I—oh yes, I know. The
best way that I can think of, would be to send a card, and my compliments, (I've no doubt he'd take 'em for a pot of porter,) by this young
man, to the Saracen with Two Necks—if the waiter took him for a gentleman's servant, so much the better. Then all Mrs. Browdie would
have to do, would be to send her card back by the carrier (he could
easily come with a double knock), and there's an end of it."

" My dear mother," said Nicholas, " I don't suppose such unsophis-
ticated people as these ever had a card of their own, or ever will have."

" Oh that, indeed, Nicholas, my dear," returned Mrs. Nickleby,
" that's another thing. If you put it upon that ground, why, of course,
I have no more to say, than that I have no doubt they are very good
sort of persons, and that I have no kind of objection to their coming
here to tea if they like, and shall make a point of being very civil to
them if they do."

The point being thus effectually set at rest, and Mrs. Nickleby duly
placed in the patronising and mildly-condescending position which
became her rank and matrimonial years, Mr. and Mrs. Browdie were
invited and came ; and as they were very deferential to Mrs. Nickleby,
and seemed to have a becoming appreciation of her greatness, and were
very much pleased with everything, the good lady had more than once
given Kate to understand, in a whisper, that she thought they were the
very best-meaning people she had ever seen, and perfectly well behaved.

And thus it came to pass, that John Browdie declared, in the parlour
after supper, to wit, at twenty minutes before eleven o'clock, P.M., that
he had never been so happy in all his days.

Nor was Mrs. Browdie much behind her husband in this respect, for
that young matron—whose rustic beauty contrasted very prettily with
the more delicate loveliness of Kate, and without suffering by the contrast either, for each served as it were to set off and decorate the other
—could not sufficiently admire the gentle and winning manners of the
young lady, or the engaging affability of the elder one.   Then Kate had
the art of turning the conversation to subjects upon which the country
girl, bashful at first in strange company, could feel herself at home ;
and if Mrs. Nickleby was not quite so felicitous at times in the selection
of topics of discourse, or if she did seem, as Mrs. Browdie expressed it,
" rather high in her notions," still nothing could be kinder, and that she
took considerable interest in the young couple was manifest from the
very long lectures on housewifery with which she was so obliging as to
entertain Mrs. Browdie's private ear, which were illustrated by various
references to the domestic economy of the cottage, in which (those
duties falling exclusively upon Kate) the good lady had about as much
share, either in theory or practice, as any one of the statues of

the Twelve Apostles which embellish the exterior of Saint Paul's cathedral.

" Mr. Browdie," said Kate, addressing his young wife, " is the best humoured, the kindest and heartiest creature I ever saw. If I were oppressed with I don't know how many cares, it would make me happy only to look at him."

" He does seem indeed, upon my word, a most excellent creature, Kate," said Mrs. Nickleby; " most excellent. And I am sure that at all times it will give me pleasure—really pleasure now—to have you, Mrs. Browdie, to see me in this plain and homely manner. We make no display," said Mrs. Nickleby, with an air which seemed to insinuate that they could make a vast deal if they were so disposed—" no fuss, no preparation; I wouldn't allow it. I said ' Kate, my dear, you will only make Mrs. Browdie feel uncomfortable, and how very foolish and inconsiderate that would be ! ' "

" I am very much obliged to you, I am sure, ma'am," returned Mrs. Browdie, gratefully. " It's nearly eleven o'clock, John. I am afraid we are keeping you up very late, ma'am."

" Late !" cried Mrs. Nickleby, with a sharp thin laugh, and one little cough at the end, like a note of admiration expressed. " This is quite early for us. We used to keep such hours ! Twelve, one, two, three o'clock was nothing to us. Balls, dinners, card-parties—never were such rakes as the people about where we used to live. I often think now, I am sure, that how we ever could go through with it is quite astonishing—and that is just the evil of having a large connexion and being a great deal sought after, which I would recommend all young married people steadily to resist; though of course, and it's perfectly clear, and a very happy thing too, *I* think, that very few young married people can be exposed to such temptations. There was one family in particular, that used to live about a mile from us—not straight down the road, but turning sharp off to the left by the turnpike where the Plymouth mail ran over the donkey—that were quite extraordinary people for giving the most extravagant parties, with artificial flowers and champagne, and variegated lamps, and, in short, every delicacy of eating and drinking that the most singular epicure could possibly require—I don't think there ever were such people as those Peltiroguses. You remember the Peltiroguses, Kate ? "

Kate saw that for the ease and comfort of the visitors it was high time to stay this flood of recollection, so answered that she entertained of the Peltiroguses a most vivid and distinct remembrance; and then said that Mr. Browdie had half promised, early in the evening, that he would sing a Yorkshire song, and that she was most impatient that he should redeem his promise, because she was sure it would afford her mama more amusement and pleasure than it was possible to express.

Mrs. Nickleby confirming her daughter with the best possible grace —for there was patronage in that too, and a kind of implication that she had a discerning taste in such matters, and was something of a critic —John Browdie proceeded to consider the words of some north-country ditty, and to take his wife's recollection respecting the same. This done, he made divers ungainly movements in his chair, and singling out one particular fly on the ceiling from the other flies there asleep, fixed his eyes upon him, and began to roar a meek sentiment (supposed to be uttered by a gentle swain fast pining away with love and despair) in a voice of thunder.

At the end of the first verse, as though some person without had waited until then to make himself audible, was heard a loud and violent knocking at the street-door—so loud and so violent, indeed, that the ladies started as by one accord, and John Browdie stopped.

" It must be some mistake," said Nicholas, carelessly. " We know nobody who would come here at this hour."

Mrs. Nickleby surmised, however, that perhaps the counting-house was burnt down, or perhaps ' the Mr. Cheerybles' had sent to take Nicholas into partnership (which certainly appeared highly probable at that time of night) or perhaps Mr. Linkinwater had run away with the property, or perhaps Miss La Creevy was taken ill, or perhaps——

But a hasty exclamation from Kate stopped her abruptly in her conjectures, and Ralph Nickleby walked into the room.

" Stay," said Ralph, as Nicholas rose, and Kate, making her way towards him, threw herself upon his arm. " Before that boy says a word, hear me."

Nicholas bit his lip and shook his head in a threatening manner, but appeared for the moment unable to articulate a syllable. Kate clung closer to his arm, Smike retreated behind them, and John Browdie, who had heard of Ralph, and appeared to have no great difficulty in recognising him, stepped between the old man and his young friend, as if with the intention of preventing either of them from advancing a step further.

" Hear me, I say," said Ralph, " and not him."

" Say what thou'st gotten to say then, sir," retorted John ; " and tak' care thou dinnot put up angry bluid which thou'dst betther try to quiet."

" I should know _you_," said Ralph, " by your tongue; and _him_ " (pointing to Smike) " by his looks."

" Don't speak to him," said Nicholas, recovering his voice. " I will not have it. I will not hear him. I do not know that man. I cannot breathe the air that he corrupts. His presence is an insult to my sister. It is shame to see him. I will not bear it, by —— "

" Stand !" cried John, laying his heavy hand upon his chest.

" Then let him instantly retire," said Nicholas, struggling. " I am not going to lay hands upon him, but he shall withdraw. I will not have him here. John—John Browdie—is this my house—am I a child ? If he stands there," cried Nicholas, burning with fury, " looking so calmly upon those who know his black and dastardly heart, he'll drive me mad."

To all these exclamations John Browdie answered not a word, but he retained his hold upon Nicholas ; and when he was silent again, spoke.

" There's more to say and hear than thou think'st for," said John. " I tell'ee I ha' gotten scent o' thot already. Wa'at be that shadow ootside door there ?   Noo schoolmeasther, show thyself, mun ; dinnot be sheame-feaced.   Noo, auld gen'lm'n, let's have schoolmeasther, coom."

Hearing this adjuration, Mr. Squeers, who had been lingering in the passage until such time as it should be expedient for him to enter and he could appear with effect, was fain to present himself in a somewhat undignified and sneaking way ; at which John Browdie laughed with such keen and heartfelt delight, that even Kate, in all the pain anxiety and surprise of the scene, and though the tears were in her eyes, felt a disposition to join him.

" Have you done enjoying yourself, sir ?" said Ralph, at length.

" Pratty nigh for the prasant time, sir," replied John.

" I can wait," said Ralph.   " Take your own time, pray."

Ralph waited until there was a perfect silence, and then turning to Mrs. Nickleby, but directing an eager glance at Kate, as if more anxious to watch his effect upon her, said :—

" Now, ma'am, listen to me.   I don't imagine that you were a party to a very fine tirade of words sent me by that boy of yours, because I don't believe that under his control, you have the slightest will of your own, or that your advice, your opinion, your wants, your wishes —anything which in nature and reason (or of what use is your great experience ?) ought to weigh with him—has the slightest influence or weight whatever, or is taken for a moment into account."

Mrs. Nickleby shook her head and sighed, as if there were a good deal in that, certainly.

" For this reason," resumed Ralph, "I address myself to you ma'am. For this reason, partly, and partly because I do not wish to be disgraced by the acts of a vicious stripling whom *I* was obliged to disown, and who, afterwards, in his boyish majesty, feigns to—ha ! ha !—to disown *me*, I present myself here to-night.   I have another motive in coming—a motive of humanity.   I come here," said Ralph, looking round with a biting and triumphant smile, and gloating and dwelling upon the words as if he were loath to lose the pleasure of saying them, " to restore a parent his child.   Ay, sir," he continued, bending eagerly forward, and addressing Nicholas, as he marked the change of his countenance, " to restore a parent his child—his son, sir—trepanned, waylaid, and guarded at every turn by you, with the base design of robbing him some day of any little wretched pittance of which he might become possessed."

" In that, you know you lie," said Nicholas, proudly.

" In this, I know I speak the truth—I have his father here," retorted Ralph.

" Here !" sneered Squeers, stepping forward.   " Do you hear that ? Here !   Didn't I tell you to be careful that his father didn't turn up, and send him back to me ?   Why, his father's my friend ; he's to come back to me directly, he is.   Now, what do you say—eh !—now—come— what do you say to that—an't you sorry you took so much trouble for nothing ? an't you ? an't you ?"

" You bear upon your body certain marks I gave you," said Nicholas, looking quietly away, " and may talk in acknowledgment of them as much as you please. You'll talk a long time before you rub them out, Mr. Squeers."

The estimable gentleman last-named, cast a hasty look 'at the table, as if he were prompted by this retort to throw a jug or bottle at the head of Nicholas, but he was interrupted in this design (if such design he had) by Ralph, who, touching him on the elbow, bade him tell the father that he might now appear and claim his son.

This being purely a labour of love, Mr. Squeers readily complied, and leaving the room for the purpose, almost immediately returned, supporting a sleek personage with an oily face, who, bursting from him, and giving to view the form and face of Mr. Snawley, made straight up to Smike, and tucking that poor fellow's head under his arm in a most uncouth and awkward embrace, elevated his broad-brimmed hat at arm's length in the air as a token of devout thanksgiving, exclaiming, meanwhile, " How little did I think of this here joyful meeting, when I saw him last ! Oh, how little did I think it !"

" Be composed, sir," said Ralph, with a gruff expression of sympathy, " you have got him now."

" Got him ! Oh, havn't I got him ! Have I got him, though ?" cried Mr. Snawley, scarcely able to believe it. " Yes, here he is, flesh and blood, flesh and blood."

" Vary little flesh," said John Browdie.

Mr. Snawley was too much occupied by his parental feelings to notice this remark ; and, to assure himself more completely of the restoration of his child, tucked his head under his arm again, and kept it there.

" What was it," said Snawley, " that made me take such a strong interest in him, when that worthy instructor of youth brought him to my house ? What was it that made me burn all over with a wish to chastise him severely for cutting away from his best friends—his pastors and masters ? "

" It was parental instinct, sir," observed Squeers.

" That's what it was, sir," rejoined Snawley ; " the elevated feeling —the feeling of the ancient Romans and Grecians, and of the beasts of the field and birds of the air, with the exception of rabbits and tom-cats, which sometimes devour their offspring. My heart yearned towards him. I could have—I don't know what I couldn't have done to him in the anger of a father."

" It only shows what Natur is, sir," said Mr. Squeers. " She's a rum 'un, is Natur."

" She is a holy thing, sir," remarked Snawley.

" I believe you," added Mr. Squeers, with a moral sigh. " I should like to know how we should ever get on without her. Natur," said Mr. Squeers, solemnly, " is more easier conceived than described. Oh what a blessed thing, sir, to be in a state of natur !"

Pending this philosophical discourse, the bystanders had been quite stupified with amazement, while Nicholas had looked keenly from Snawley to Squeers, and from Squeers to Ralph, divided between his feelings of disgust, doubt, and surprise. At this juncture, Smike escaping from

Mr Snawley enlarges on parental instinct.

his father fled to Nicholas, and implored him, in most moving terms, never to give him up, but to let him live and die beside him.

" If you are this boy's father," said Nicholas, " look at the wreck he is, and tell me that you purpose to send him back to that loathsome den from which I brought him."

"Scandal again!" cried Squeers. "Recollect, you an't worth powder and shot, but I'll be even with you one way or another."

" Stop," interposed Ralph, as Snawley was about to speak. " Let us cut this matter short, and not bandy words here with hare-brained profligates. This is your son, as you can prove—and you, Mr. Squeers, you know this boy to be the same that was with you for so many years under the name of Smike—Do you ? "

" Do I!" returned Squeers. " Don't I ? "

" Good," said Ralph ; " a very few words will be sufficient here. You had a son by your first wife, Mr. Snawley ? "

" I had," replied that person, " and there he stands."

" We'll show that presently," said Ralph. " You and your wife were separated, and she had the boy to live with her, when he was a year old. You received a communication from her, when you had lived apart a year or two, that the boy was dead ; and you believed it ?"

" Of course I did!" returned Snawley. " Oh the joy of——"

" Be rational, sir, pray," said Ralph. " This is business, and transports interfere with it. This wife died a year and a half ago, or thereabouts—not more—in some obscure place, where she was housekeeper in a family. Is that the case ?"

" That's the case," replied Snawley.

" Having written on her death-bed a letter or confession to you, about this very boy, which, as it was not directed otherwise than in your name, only reached you, and that by a circuitous course, a few days since ? "

"' Just so," said Snawley. " Correct in every particular, sir."

" And this confession," resumed Ralph, " is to the effect that his death was an invention of hers to wound you—was a part of a system of annoyance, in short, which you seem to have adopted towards each other—that the boy lived, but was of weak and imperfect intellect—that she sent him by a trusty hand to a cheap school in Yorkshire—that she had paid for his education for some years, and then, being poor, and going a long way off, gradually deserted him, for which she prayed forgiveness ? "

Snawley nodded his head, and wiped his eyes ; the first slightly, the last violently.

" The school was Mr. Squeers's," continued Ralph ; " the boy was left there in the name of Smike ; every description was fully given, dates tally exactly with Mr. Squeers's books, Mr. Squeers is lodging with you at this time ; you have two other boys at his school : you communicated the whole discovery to him, he brought you to me as the person who had recommended to him the kidnapper of his child ; and I brought you here. Is that so ?"

" You talk like a good book, sir, that's got nothing in its inside but what's the truth," replied Snawley.

" This is your pocket-book," said Ralph, producing one from his coat ; " the certificates of your first marriage and of the boy's birth, and your wife's two letters, and every other paper that can support these statements directly or by implication, are here, are they ?"

" Every one of 'em, sir."

" And you don't object to their being looked at here, so that these people may be convinced of your power to substantiate your claim at once in law and reason, and you may resume your controul over your own son without more delay.   Do I understand you ?"

" I couldn't have understood myself better, sir."

" There, then," said Ralph, tossing the pocket-book upon the table. " Let them see them if they like; and as those are the original papers, I should recommend you to stand near while they are being examined, or you may chance to lose some."

With these words Ralph sat down unbidden, and compressing his lips, which were for the moment slightly parted by a smile, folded his arms, and looked for the first time at his nephew.

Nicholas, stung by the concluding taunt, darted an indignant glance at him; but commanding himself as well as he could, entered upon a close examination of the documents, at which John Browdie assisted. There was nothing about them which could be called in question.   The certificates were regularly signed as extracts from the parish books, the first letter had a genuine appearance of having been written and preserved for some years, the hand-writing of the second tallied with it exactly, (making proper allowance for its having been written by a person in extremity,) and there were several other corroboratory scraps of entries and memoranda which it was equally difficult to question.

" Dear Nicholas," whispered Kate, who had been looking anxiously over his shoulder, " can this be really the case ?   Is this statement true ?"

" I fear it is," answered Nicholas.   " What say you, John ?"

John scratched his head and shook it, but said nothing at all.

" You will observe, ma'am," said Ralph, addressing himself to Mrs. Nickleby, " that this boy being a minor and not of strong mind, we might have come here to-night, armed with the powers of the law, and backed by a troop of its myrmidons.   I should have done so, ma'am, unquestionably, but for my regard for the feelings of yourself—and your daughter."

" You have shown your regard for *her* feelings well," said Nicholas, drawing his sister towards him.

" Thank you," replied Ralph.   " Your praise, sir, is commendation, indeed."

" Well," said Squeers, " what's to be done ?   Them hackney-coach horses will catch cold if we don't think of moving ; there's one of 'em a-sneezing now, so that he blows the street door right open.   What's the order of the day—eh ?   Is Master Snawley to come along with us ?"

" No, no, no," replied Smike, drawing back, and clinging to Nicholas. " No.   Pray, no.   I will not go from you with him.   No, no."

"This is a cruel thing," said Snawley, looking to his friends for support. "Do parents bring children into the world for this?"

"Do parents bring children into the world for *thot*?" said John Browdie bluntly, pointing, as he spoke, to Squeers.

"Never you mind," retorted that gentleman, tapping his nose, derisively.

"Never I mind!" said John, "no, nor never nobody mind, say'st thou, schoolmeasther. It's nobody's minding that keeps sike men as thou afloat. Noo then, where be'st thou coomin' to? Dang it, dinnot coom treadin' ower me, mun."

Suiting the action to the word, John Browdie just jerked his elbow into the chest of Mr. Squeers who was advancing upon Smike; with so much dexterity that the schoolmaster reeled and staggered back upon Ralph Nickleby, and being unable to recover his balance, knocked that gentleman off his chair, and stumbled heavily upon him.

This accidental circumstance was the signal for some very decisive proceedings. In the midst of a great noise, occasioned by the prayers and entreaties of Smike, the cries and exclamations of the women, and the vehemence of the men, demonstrations were made of carrying off the lost son by violence: and Squeers had actually begun to haul him out, when Nicholas (who, until then, had been evidently undecided how to act) took him by the collar, and shaking him so that such teeth as he had, chattered in his head, politely escorted him to the room door, and thrusting him into the passage, shut it upon him.

"Now" said Nicholas, to the other two, "have the kindness to follow your friend."

"I want my son," said Snawley.

"Your son," replied Nicholas, "chooses for himself. He chooses to remain here, and he shall."

"You won't give him up?" said Snawley.

"I would not give him up against his will, to be the victim of such brutality as that to which you would consign him," replied Nicholas, "if he were a dog or a rat."

"Knock that Nickleby down with a candlestick," cried Mr. Squeers, through the keyhole, "and bring out my hat, somebody, will you, unless he wants to steal it."

"I am very sorry, indeed," said Mrs. Nickleby, who, with Mrs. Browdie, had stood crying and biting her fingers in a corner, while Kate—very pale, but perfectly quiet—had kept as near her brother as she could. "I am very sorry, indeed, for all this. I really don't know what would be best to do, and that's the truth. Nicholas ought to be the best judge, and I hope he is. Of course, it's a hard thing to have to keep other people's children, though young Mr. Snawley is certainly as useful and willing as it's possible for anybody to be; but, if it could be settled in any friendly manner—if old Mr. Snawley, for instance, would settle to pay something certain for his board and lodging, and some fair arrangement was come to, so that we undertook to have fish twice a-week, and a pudding twice, or a dumpling, or something of that sort, I do think that it might be very satisfactory and pleasant for all parties."

This compromise, which was proposed with abundance of tears and sighs, not exactly meeting the point at issue, nobody took any notice of it; and poor Mrs. Nickleby accordingly proceeded to enlighten Mrs. Browdie upon the advantages of such a scheme, and the unhappy results flowing on all occasions, from her not being attended to when she proffered her advice.

" You, sir," said Snawley, addressing the terrified Smike, " are an unnatural, ungrateful, unloveable boy. You won't let me love you when I want to. Won't you come home—won't you ? "

" No, no, no," cried Smike, shrinking back.

" He never loved nobody," bawled Squeers, through the keyhole. " He never loved me ; he never loved Wackford, who is next door but one to a cherubim. How can you expect that he'll love his father ? He'll never love his father, he won't. He don't know what it is to have a father. He don't understand it. It an't in him."

Mr. Snawley looked stedfastly at his son for a full minute, and then covering his eyes with his hand, and once more raising his hat in the air, appeared deeply occupied in deploring his black ingratitude. Then drawing his arm across his eyes, he picked up Mr. Squeers's hat, and taking it under one arm, and his own under the other, walked slowly and sadly out.

" Your romance, sir," said Ralph, lingering for a moment, " is destroyed, I take it. No unknown ; no persecuted descendant of a man of high degree; but the weak, imbecile son of a poor, petty tradesman. We shall see how your sympathy melts before plain matter of fact."

" You shall," said Nicholas, motioning towards the door.

" And trust me, sir," added Ralph, " that I never supposed you would give him up to-night. Pride, obstinacy, reputation for fine feeling, were all against it. These must be brought down, sir, lowered, crushed, as they shall be soon. The protracted and wearing anxiety and expense of the law in its most oppressive form, its torture from hour to hour, its weary days and sleepless nights—with these I'll prove you, and break your haughty spirit, strong as you deem it now. And when you make this house a hell, and visit these trials upon yonder wretched object (as you will; I know you), and those who think you now a young-fledged hero, we'll go into old accounts between us two, and see who stands the debtor, and comes out best at last—even before the world."

Ralph Nickleby withdrew. But Mr. Squeers, who had heard a portion of this closing address, and was by this time wound up to a pitch of impotent malignity almost unprecedented, could not refrain from returning to the parlour-door, and actually cutting some dozen capers with various wry faces and hideous grimaces, expressive of his triumphant confidence in the downfall and defeat of Nicholas.

Having concluded this war-dance, in which his short trousers and large boots had borne a very conspicuous figure, Mr. Squeers followed his friends, and the family were left to meditate upon recent occurrences.

Table Forks per doz. 0 16 6	Soup Ladles each 0 6 6	Table Spoons pr. doz. 0 16 6	Gravy Spoons, each 0 3 6
Dessert do. do. 0 12 6	Sauce do. do. 0 1 6	Dessert do. do. 0 12 6	Salt do. do. 0 0 6
Fish Knives, each 0 5 6	Mustard do. do. 0 0 6	Tea do. do. 0 5 6	Sugar Tongs do. 0 1 0

An inferior article, nearly equal in make, but not so good in quality, can be supplied in any quantity.
Table Spoons and Forks 10s. per dozen. Dessert and Tea Spoons at the same proportion.
Solid wrought King's pattern, highly-finished at very reduced prices.

Silver Plated on British Plate.

This is a very superior Article, and from having *Sheet Silver Plated upon the British Plate*, their appearance is so alike unto Silver, that the difference cannot be detected without an inspection of the stamp; and, after many years' wear, should the Silver be worn through, the article still preserves the same colour.

Full size Table Forks,	Full-size Table Spoons	Tea Spoons pr doz. 0 19 6	Soup Ladles 0 17 0
pr doz. 2 5 0	pr doz. 2 8 0	Sugar Tongs, per pr 0 4 6	Sauce do. do. 0 4 6
do. Dessert do. 1 12 0	do. Dessert do. 1 16 0	Gravy Spoons, each 0 7 0	Fish Knives do. 0 17 6

Plated on Steel.

Dessert Knives and Forks, in Plain and Carved Ivory Handles.—Plated on Steel Spoons and Forks of the best manufacture.—Plated on Steel Snuffers, Toast Racks, Butter and Cheese Knives, Vegetable Forks, Knife Rests, Nut Cracks, &c. &c.

Paper Tea Trays.

A Handsome and extensive stock of superior Paper Tea Trays, in a variety of new and elegant shapes, and of exquisite workmanship. The largest size made, 30 inches, with neat gold border, only 25s. Waiters, &c. proportionably cheap. New and elegant pattern Fruit Plates, Fruit Baskets, Hand Screens, Card Racks, Card Pools, &c. &c.
Also the largest and best selected Stock in London of

Superior Iron Japan Ware.

Of all the Shapes, Patterns, and Colours that are made in Paper.

Tea Trays and Waiters	Candlesticks and Snuffer Trays	Hat and Umbrella Stands
Bread and Cake Baskets	Spice and Sugar Boxes	Cash Boxes with patent locks
Cheese Trays	Toast and Card Racks	Plate and Vegetable Warmers
Knife and Spoon ditto	Dressing Cases on improved principles	Night Lamps, &c. &c.

Superior Britannia Metal Goods.

Warranted to keep their colour in any climate.

Venison and Haunch of Mutton Dishes	Coffee Pots, and Percolators to match	Mounted Jugs, of various sizes
Beef Steak Dishes and Covers	Sugar Basins and Cream Ewers	Pepper Boxes
Tea Pots of all sizes and in entirely new patterns, mounted in ivory pearl, and silver	Table Candlesticks	Egg Cups
	Chamber ditto	Spoons and Soup Ladles
	Snuffer Trays	Children's Mugs
	Mustard Pots and Salt Cellars	Soap Dishes, &c. &c.

Superior Table Cutlery.

	Table Knives and Forks per Dozen of 24 pieces.		Dessert Knives and Forks per Dozen of 24 pieces.		Carving Knives with Guard Forks per pair.	
	s.	d.	s.	d.	s.	d.
Octagon Ivory Handles, Oval Rim	24	0	17	6	6	6
Balance Octagon Ivory Handles	27	0	20	0	6	6
A large stock of Superfine Transparent Ivory, of various patterns, equally cheap.						
WHITE BONE HANDLES.						
Plain White Bone	9	0				
Octagon White Bone	12	6	10	6	3	0
Octagon White Bone, Oval Rim	17	0	14	6	3	9
SUPERIOR HORN HANDLES.						
Strong Octagon Horn	16	6	8	6	2	9
Plain Black, Three Pins	11	0	9	0	6	0
Octagon Black, Oval Rim	19	0	12	6	3	9

The excellent quality of *Alderman's Table Cutlery* being so long established, it is merely necessary to remark, that every article is warranted, and stamped with the Name and Address, and sold at lower prices than at any other Wholesale Warehouse. The List opposite merits the attention of the Public :—

Purchasers not requiring Forks, one-third of the price is allowed; the Octagon Ivory Handles, Oval Rim, would be 16s. per dozen, Knives only; and all other patterns in the same proportion.

Shipping or large Orders promptly executed, an extensive stock being always kept on hand, and a discount allowed.

IMPROVED KNIFE SHARPENERS AND TABLE STEELS.

Warranted Pen and Pocket Knives,

In a great variety of neat and ornamental patterns.

Capital Single-bladed Pen Knives, *warranted*, from 1s. each
Ditto, Two Blades, Pocket ditto ditto from 1s. each
Desk and Pruning Knives, from 1s. each
Sportmen's Knives of various descriptions
Celebrated Wharncliffe Knives, Two Blades, 1s. 6d
Ditto, Three Blades, 1s. 9d.
Excellent Knives, with Four Blades, 2s. 3d.
Emigrants will find a capital and useful stock to select from, well suited for their purposes, and remarkably cheap.
Foreigners wishing to make purchases of *superior and*
N.B.—Old Patent Corkscrews fitted with New Worms, at 1s. 3d. each.

highly-finished *British Cutlery*, will find ample choice, and at very reduced prices.
Scissors of all descriptions, and the best quality, warranted, from 1s. a pair.—Nail Nippers and Files.
Patent plain and pocket Corkscrews, of superior quality
Champagne Nippers, with screw and brush
Knife Wire-Cutters, for Champagne, Soda Water, &c.
Patent Key Rings, 4d. to 1s. each.
Engraving Name and Address on ditto, 1s. 3d.
Portable and other Boot Hooks.—Button Hooks, &c.

Warranted best Steel Razors,

So justly celebrated for more than 40 years, sold upon the principle, if not approved, exchanged, or the money returned.

Plain Black Handles	per pair 3s. 0d.	Seven-day Razors, in Cases	18s. 0d.
.. Fine Ivory ..	do. 5 0	.. Pair of Razors, in Case	4 6
Fine Ivory, silver mounted	do. 8 6	.. Fine Ivory Handle	6 6

An extensive variety of fine Steel Razors, in Tortoise-shell, Pearl, and Ivory Handles, handsomely mounted with Silver, and fitted in Cases, complete, equally cheap.
Improved Razor Strops of every description.

London Made Bronze Tea and Coffee Urns,

Of the best quality and newest patterns, at reduced prices.

Wright's New Patent Tea Urn	Bronze Lustres	Bronze Candlesticks	Bronze Inkstands
Bronze Coffee Percolators	.. Pastile Burners	.. Taper do.	.. Letter Weights
.. Coffee Pots	.. Thermometers	.. Table Bells	.. Card Racks, &c. &c.

SUNDRIES.

A large stock of Rosewood and Mahogany Writing Desks, Tea Chests and Tea Caddies, of a superior quality, at reduced prices
Handsome Work Boxes, in Rosewood and Mahogany, inlaid with Pearl, &c. &c.
Dressing Cases for Ladies and Gentlemen, Brass bound or inlaid with Pearl, fitted with Looking-Glass and all other necessary articles.
Excellent Hair, Tooth, Nail, and Cloth Brushes

Tortoise-shell and Horn Combs of every description
English and French China Ornaments in great variety
Papier Maché Liquor, Cruet, Pickle, and Soy Frames
Patent and plain Dish and Plate Covers
Palmer's Patent Candle Lamps
Patent Telescope and plain Hearth Brushes
Roasting Jacks, Table Mats, and Beer Taps
Brass Candlesticks, Fender Footmen, and Fire Guards
Fenders, Fire Irons, Copper Scuttles and Kettles

Together with a variety of other useful articles far too numerous to be inserted in the present List.
Proprietors of Hotels, Taverns, and Chop Houses, supplied with any quantity of Plate, Cutlery, Japan Ware, &c., on the lowest Wholesale Terms.

SHIPPING ORDERS EXECUTED AT THE MANUFACTURERS' PRICES.

City Press, 1, Long Lane: D. A. Doudney.

ESTABLISHED 1795.

S. ALDERMAN,

JEWELLER, SILVERSMITH, CUTLER,

ETC. ETC.

16, NORTON FOLGATE,

AND AT

41 & 42, BARBICAN,

LONDON.

KIRBY, BEARD & KIRBY'S
LONDON
NE PLUS ULTRA NEEDLES
AND
ROYAL DIAMOND PATENT PINS.

A NEW YEARS DAY GIFT · AT QUEENS COLLEGE OXFORD

"TAKE THIS AND BE THRIFTY."

MANUFACTURERS BY SPECIAL APPOINTMENT
TO HER MOST EXCELLENT MAJESTY
QUEEN VICTORIA
& THE DOWAGER QUEEN ADELAIDE.

THE surpassing excellence of the above **PINS** and **NEEDLES** has justly rendered them worthy of the most exalted Patronage with which they have been honoured, and combined with all the recent improvements, the effect of long experience and great skill in the application of the most ingenious mechanism, are most confidently recommended to the **LADIES** as possessing every requisite Quality so long sought after in these most useful Articles.

For the convenience of Purchasers (as well as in the usual manner) **KIRBY & C°** make up their **NE PLUS ULTRA NEEDLES** in a variety of Novel and Unique embellished **CASES**, each containing One Hundred of assorted useful sizes; also in Morocco Leather, and Splendid Satin and Rich Velvet Pocket Book Cases, with ornamental Locks, and furnished with every kind of Needle **FOR LADIES' FANCY WORK.** Also their **ROYAL DIAMOND PINS,** in Superb Cases, containing Six Papers of the most approved Sizes, forming a choice of elegant and useful little Presents.

KIRBY & C° rely entirely for a preference given to the Articles of their Manufacture from their uniform Perfection, and respectfully solicit **LADIES** who desire to use them (to prevent mistakes) to ask for **KIRBY & C°.'S PINS** and **NEEDLES,** which are sold by all the Haberdashers and Drapers of the United Kingdom, and Wholesale and for Exportation at their Old-Established Royal Diamond Patent Pin and Needle Manufactory, No. 46, Cannon Street, **LONDON,** and at **GLOUCESTER.**

PARRIS'S GRAND AUTHENTIC CORONATION PICTURE.

MR. MOON, Her Majesty's Publisher and Printseller in Ordinary, 20, Threadneedle Street; has the honour to announce that he has received her Majesty's special command to publish an Engraving from the Superb Historical Painting of

THE CORONATION.

By E. T. PARRIS, Esq., Historical Painter to the Queen Dowager.

This grand picture—the chef d'œuvre of the talented and popular artist—unites, to an extraordinary extent, the most minute and accurate fidelity, with a grandeur of effect, and a permanent historical interest, infinitely surpassing any similar work of art hitherto attempted.

During the progress of the magnificent ceremonial, Mr. PARRIS was allowed, for the purposes of this Picture, to avail himself of the most eligible situations, and he has in consequence portrayed the scene with a scrupulous fidelity. Subsequently, he has had the advantage of sittings from the greater portion of the illustrious personages present, of whom original portraits are introduced assembled round the throne of our youthful Sovereign. Not only are all the Great Officers of State, the Foreign Visitors and the Attendant Courtiers, introduced in their respective situations ; but near her Majesty is gathered a rich galaxy of female loveliness, arrayed in all the gorgeous and glittering costumes which the occasion required.

"Mr. Paris yesterday received the commands of the Queen to attend at the Palace this morning with his picture of the Coronation, when her Majesty has signified her intention to sit to him for the finishing of her portrait."—*Court Circular,* April 3.

"Mr. E. T. Parris had the honour yesterday of submitting his grand Coronation picture to her Majesty's approbation, and was honoured with a final sitting."—*Court Circular,* April 4.

It would be impossible to insert in this prospectus all the eulogiums which this superb production of art elicited from the leading Journals, during the few days it was on view at the Publisher's, MR. MOON ; but the following extracts are presumed to be worthy of public attention :—

"The fact that the likenesses are correct, will greatly enhance the value of the picture, as an historical document. Mr. Moon has secured the talents of one of the first engravers in the country to multiply this picture ; and it is creditable to his enterprise, to have spared no expense to render its publication worthy the present state of the art."—*Times.*

"Mr. Parris, an artist of vast power and exquisite taste, and whose rising merits early in his career attracted the notice of that judicious and munificent patron of the arts, Sir Robert Peel, has in this Coronation picture so completely excelled himself, as to establish his claim to be placed very high indeed on the list of our native artists. We cannot conceive a picture better calculated for engraving, or more certainly destined to take its place in every collection of value or importance."—*John Bull.*

"A very interesting historical work of art, which is so disposed and constructed that it cannot fail of engraving with fine effect."—*Morning Post.*

"The composition is skilfully managed."—*Morning Chronicle.*

"The picture has evidently been painted with great care and exactness."—*Morning Herald.*

"One of the most superb works of art, and every way worthy of the scene it represents."—*Globe.*

"This production entitles Mr. Parris to the very greatest praise : its merits will always distinguish it as one of the best historical pictures on record. The grouping of the women is as tasteful as it is skilful ; while their exquisite loveliness lends a relieving grace to the picture."—*Court Journal.*

"When we heard that Mr. Parris had undertaken to paint a picture of the late Coronation, we felt persuaded that it was just the kind of subject to which the peculiar talents and qualifications of that able and tasteful artist were calculated to do justice. The result has proved that our anticipation was well founded."—*Literary Gazette.*

Among the numerous Subscribers whose Names already honour the Subscription List for this grand National Engraving, are the following Illustrious Personages :—

Her Majesty the Queen	Her Grace the Duchess of Sutherland
Her Majesty the Queen Dowager	His Grace the Duke of Norfolk
His Majesty the King of Hanover	His Grace the Duke of Devonshire
His Majesty the King of Belgium	His Grace the Duke of Bedford
His Majesty the King of the French	His Grace the Duke of Sutherland
Her Royal Highness the Duchess of Kent	His Grace the Duke of Northumberland
Her Royal Highness the Princess Hohenlohe	Her Grace the Duchess of Northumberland
His Royal Highness the Duke of Sussex	His Grace the Duke of Buccleuch
Her Royal Highness the Duchess of Gloucester	His Grace the Duke of Somerset
His Royal Highness the Prince of Leinengen	His Grace the Duke of Hamilton
His Royal Highness the Duke de Nemours	The Right Honourable Lord Rolle
His Grace the Archbishop of Canterbury	The Right Honourable Viscount Palmerston

---

Now Ready,

CHALON'S PORTRAIT OF THE QUEEN.

ON A REDUCED SIZE, HALF LENGTH,

From the celebrated Whole-length Picture by that eminent Painter. The unprecedented popularity of the large Plate has induced the Publisher to submit the above Engraving, in the highest style of Art, by Mr. WAGSTAFF.

Price to Subscribers :—Prints, 1*l.* 1*s.* ; Proofs, 2*l.* 2*s.* ; India Proofs, 3*l.* 3*s.* ; Before Letters, 4*l.* 4*s.*

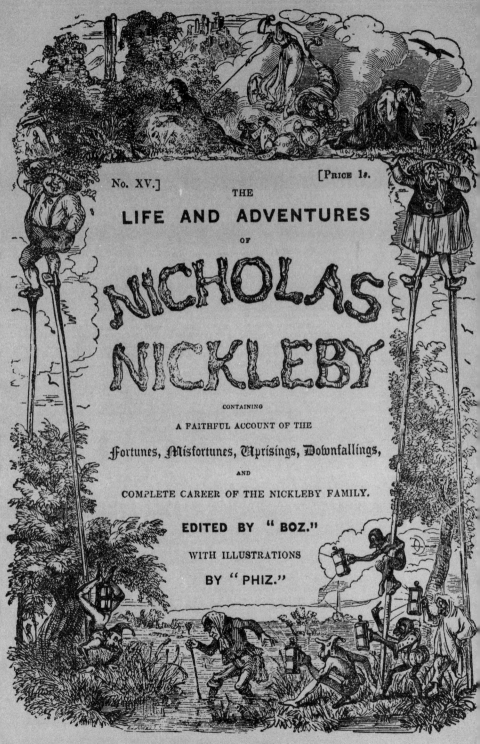

No. XV.]

[Price 1s.

THE

LIFE AND ADVENTURES

OF

NICHOLAS NICKLEBY

CONTAINING

A FAITHFUL ACCOUNT OF THE

Fortunes, Misfortunes, Uprisings, Downfallings,

AND

COMPLETE CAREER OF THE NICKLEBY FAMILY.

EDITED BY "BOZ."

WITH ILLUSTRATIONS

BY "PHIZ."

LONDON: CHAPMAN AND HALL, 186, STRAND.

No. XV.—JUNE 1, 1839.

THE
NICKLEBY ADVERTISER.

NEW AND INTERESTING JUVENILE BOOKS.

BINGLEY'S STORIES ABOUT HORSES, illustrative of their Intelligence, Fidelity, and Docility. With Twelve Engravings on Steel. 4s. neatly bound. *Just ready.*

2. BINGLEY'S TALES OF SHIPWRECKS and Disasters at Sea, including the Wreck of the Forfarshire and other recent Losses. With Eight striking Plates. 4s. bound.

3. BINGLEY'S STORIES ABOUT INSTINCT, illustrative of the Characters and Habits of Animals. Engravings after Landseer. Neatly bound, 4s.

4. BINGLEY'S STORIES ABOUT DOGS, illustrative of their Fidelity and Sagacity. Engravings after Landseer. A new Edition, neatly bound, 4s.

5. PETER PARLEY'S VISIT TO LONDON DURING THE CORONATION, in which he describes that splendid Ceremony, and tells his Young Friends many interesting Anecdotes of the Queen, &c. Illustrated with Six Coloured Plates of the Principal Scenes. Handsomely bound, 4s.

6. TALES OF ENTERPRISE, for the amusement of Youth. With Engravings, neatly bound, 2s. 6d.

Charles Tilt, Fleet Street.

CURVATURE OF THE SPINE.

AN ADDRESS TO PARENTS and to Ladies conducting Schools, on Curvature of the Spine, and on the Physical Education of Young Ladies. By R. KINGDON, M.D. & M.R.C.S. Embellished with several Plates. 18mo, 1s.

Published by Houlston and Hughes, 154, Strand.

Publishing in Weekly Numbers, price Twopence, and in Monthly Parts,

THE LONDON SATURDAY JOURNAL ; a cheap Weekly Periodical, whose object is to promote the moral and social improvement of the people.

" It is at once the best and cheapest publication of its class extant."—*United Service Gazette.*

" Of all the cheap periodical literature of the day, this publication is the cheapest."—*Manchester Courier.*

" It is as entertaining and instructive a periodical as we ever met with : much more so, in fact, than many of much higher pretensions and greater cost. The utile dulci is most admirably combined."—*Berwick Warder.*

" This periodical is printed with much neatness and care ; and, judging by the ability displayed in the numbers already published, we consider it will prove a valuable addition to the cheap and useful literature of the day."—*Birmingham Herald.*

London : Wm. Smith, 113, Fleet-street ; Fraser and Co. Edinburgh ; Curry and Co., Dublin.

Third Edition, price 5s. cloth (originally published as LETTERS TO BROTHER JOHN).

JOHNSON ON LIFE, HEALTH, and DISEASE. Explaining familiarly the severa Organs which compose the Human Body, showing the cause of disease, and how it may be avoided. " The rules are few, but they are golden ones."—*Metrop. Mag.*
" Here is a very clever and useful work."—*Dispatch.*
" The author has done society much service."—*Chronicle.*
Published by G. F. Cooper, 57, Carey-street ; T. W. Southgate, Fleet-street ; and Simpkin and Co. Also, lately published, JENNINGS & HECKFORD'S COSTS as Allowed on TAXATION. Price 5s. cloth.

Just published, in 18mo, with Portrait of Codrington, and Vignette, price 5s. in cloth,

BRITISH NAVAL BIOGRAPHY:

Comprising the Lives of the most distinguished Admirals, from Howard to Codrington ; with an outline of the Naval History of England, from the earliest period to the present time.

BOTANY.

In one vol. 12mo, with 155 Figures, price 10s. 6d. in cloth, Fourth Edition,

WITHERING'S SYSTEMATIC ARRANGEMENT OF BRITISH PLANTS.

Condensed and brought down to the present period ; with an Introduction to the Study of Botany. By WILLIAM MACGILLIVRAY, A.M.

This work comprises descriptions of the Plants of Great Britain and Ireland, given sufficiently full to enable the young botanist to determine every species that might come in his way without the assistance of others.

In one vol. 12mo, with 214 Figures, price 9s. in cloth,

SIR J. E. SMITH'S

INTRODUCTION TO PHYSIOLOGICAL AND SYTEMATIC BOTANY.

Edited by WILLIAM MACGILLIVRAY, A.M.

The utility of this work has been amply evinced by the number of editions which it has gone through ; the Editor has only considered it necessary to add a chapter, containing some remarks on the natural system.

In a few days will be published, with Plates and numerous Woodcuts, Vol. II. Part 1, price 12s., of

MACGILLIVRAY'S HISTORY OF BRITISH BIRDS.

This Part contains a detailed description of the forms, habits, and distribution of all the BRITISH SONG BIRDS properly so called, including the Thrushes, Piper, Oriole, Larks, Pipets, Wagtails, Stonechats, Redstarts, Nightingale Warbles, Titmice, and other genera.

" I consider this the best work on British Ornithological science with which I am acquainted."—*J. J. Audubon.*

London : SCOTT, WEBSTER, and GEARY, Charterhouse-square.

DIAMINE.

This name (derived from Διαμενω) is applied to the purest and most permanent chemical compounds yet discovered for **BLACK AND RED WRITING INKS.** They are rapidly superseding all others, and are to be had of every respectable Stationer.

The Trade supplied from the Diamine Works, 12, Wilson Street, Finsbury.

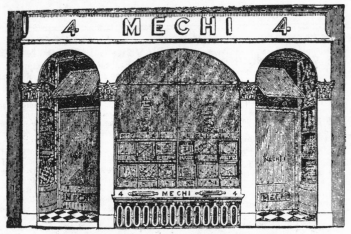

LEADENHALL STREET, LONDON.

MECHI'S NOVEL AND SPLENDID
PAPIER MACHÉ ARTICLES,

CONSISTING OF

TEA TRAYS, TEA CADDIES, LADIES' WORK, CAKE, AND NOTE BASKETS, CARD CASES, CARD POOLS, FRUIT PLATES, FRUIT BASKETS, NETTING BOXES, HAND SCREENS, CARD RACKS, CHESS BOARDS.

LADIES' COMPANIONS, or Work Cases 15*s*. to 2*l*.

LADIES' CARD CASES, in Pearl, Ivory, and Tortoiseshell . . . . . 10*s*. to 5*l*. each.

LADIES' WORK BOXES . 25*s*. fo 10 Guineas.

LADIES' DRESSING CASES 2*l*. 10*s*. to 50 Guineas.

LADIES' SCOTCH WORK BOXES at all prices.

LADIES' ROSEWOOD AND MAHOGANY DESKS 12*s*. 6*d*. to 10 Guineas.

LADIES' MOROCCO AND RUSSIA LEATHER WRITING CASES . . . . 5*s*. to 5*l*.

LADIES' ENVELOPE CASES, various prices.

LADIES' TABLE INKSTANDS, made of British Coal (quite a novelty) . . . 7*s*. 6*d*. to 30*s*.

LADIES' SCOTCH TOOTH-PICK CASES.

LADIES' IVORY AND TORTOISESHELL HAIR BRUSHES . . . at 2*l*. to 5*l*. per Pair.

LADIES' SCENT AND TOILET BOTTLES in great variety.

LADIES' SCOTCH TEA CADDIES . 21*s*. to 40*s*.

LADIES' PLAYING CARD BOXES . 30*s*. to 5*l*.

LADIES' JAPAN DRESSING CASES 7*s*. to 15*s*.

LADIES' TORTOISESHELL DRESSING & SIDE COMBS.

LADIES' HAND GLASSES.

LADIES' PATENT INSTANTANEOUS PEN-MAKERS . . . . 10*s*. 6*d*. and 12*s*. 6*d*.

LADIES' ELEGANT PENKNIVES AND SCISSORS 5*s*. to 30*s*.

INVENTOR OF THE PATENT CASTELLATED TOOTH BRUSHES.

INVENTOR OF THE MECHIAN PORTABLE DRESSING CASES.

MISCELLANEOUS.

BAGATELLE TABLES	£3 10 to 5 0	**POPE JOAN BOARDS**	£0 13 to 1 0
BACKGAMMON TABLES	1 0 to 5 10	**IVORY CHESSMEN** .	1 1 to 10 10
CHESS BOARDS . .	0 4 to 3 0	**BONE & WOOD DITTO**	Various Prices.

WHIST MARKERS, COUNTERS, &c.

GENT.'S DRESSING CASES, in Wood 2*l*. to 50*l*.

GENT.'S LEATHER DRESSING CASES 25*s*. to 24*l*.

GENT.'S WRITING DESKS, in Wood 30*s*. to 16*l*.

GENT.'S LEATHER WRITING DESKS 24*s*. 6*d*. to 5*l*.

GENT.'S WRITING & DRESSING CASE COMBINED . . . . . 5*l*. to 16*l*.

GENT.'S POCKET BOOKS WITH INSTRUMENTS 20*s*. to 40*s*.

GENT.'S ELEGANT CASES OF RAZORS 12*s*. to 3*l*.

GENT.'S SEVEN DAY RAZORS, in Fancy Woods 25*s*. to 5*l*.

GENT.'S RAZOR STROPS . 2*s*. to 30*s*.

GENT.'S SPORTING KNIVES . 12*s*. to 5*l*.

GENT.'S FANCY PENKNIVES . 5*s*. to 15*s*.

GENT.'S PEARL AND SHELL POCKET COMBS 3*s*. 6*d*. to 15*s*.

GENT.'S SCOTCH CIGAR BOXES 3*s*. 6*d*. to 40*s*.

GENT.'S COAL AND EBONY INKSTANDS 7*s*. 6*d*. to 50*s*.

GENT.'S IVORY AND FANCY WOOD HAIR BRUSHES . . . 20*s*. to 3*l*. 10*s*.

GENT.'S SETS OF BRUSHES in Russia Cases 25*s*. to 4*l*. 10*s*.

GENT.'S SILVER AND IVORY SHAVING BRUSHES In elegant Patterns.

GENT.'S SILVER AND SHELL TABLETS.

MECHI,   MECHI,

Submits, to public inspection, his Manufactures, as being of the finest quality this kingdom can produce, and at moderate prices.

A large Stock of Table Cutlery, Plated Tea and Coffee Services, Dish Covers, Hash Covers, &c.

CHINA, GLASS, EARTHENWARE, LAMPS, TRAYS, &c.

The most extensive general Stock in the metropolis in the above branches, may be inspected at the Show Rooms of

Newington and Sander, Nos. 319 and 320, High Holborn,

Opposite Gray's Inn. TABLE and DESSERT SERVICES, TEA SETTS, Toilet Setts, Fancy Jugs, and every description of coarse stone and earthenware for household purposes; ORNAMENTAL CHINA, Glass Dishes, Centres, Vases, Jugs, Decanters, Wine, Champagne and Claret Glasses, &c.; DRAWING-ROOM or SUSPENDING LAMPS, Table Lamps, Hall Lanterns, Palmer's patent Candle Lamps, in Bronze and Or-molu, CHANDELIERS, Lustres, Girandoles; TEA TRAYS in PAPIER MACHE or metal bodies, &c. &c. The above may be had, either plain or richly finished; but in either case, every article will be warranted good of its kind. As a scale of prices can convey but little information without a view of the goods, N. & S. will feel much pleasure in conducting Heads of Families through their Show Rooms. Parties favouring them with a visit will not be importuned to make purchases. Goods for the country are carefully packed. Patterns sent to any part of the Town by addressing as above.

HEAL & SON'S FRENCH MATTRESSES.

The universally acknowledged superiority of the FRENCH MATTRESS arises from the quality of the material of which they are made, and not, as is sometimes supposed, from the difference in the workmanship. The French Mattress is made of long Fleece Wool, and therefore but little work is requisite, leaving to the Wool the whole of its softness and elasticity; whereas even the best of English Wool Mattresses are made of the combings from blankets, and other manufactured goods, and a great deal more work is necessarily required to keep the material together; and when (as is now very frequently done) Mattresses are made in imitation of the French of this short Wool, they soon wear lumpy and out of condition. HEAL and SON'S FRENCH MATTRESSES, of which they make no second quality, are quite equal to the best that are made in Paris; also genuine Spring Mattresses, of the most approved construction; and being exclusively Manufacturers of Bedding, they are enabled to offer the above as well as Feather Beds, Horse-Hair Mattresses, Blankets, Quilts, and every article of Bedding on the very best terms. Old Bedding re-made, and mothy Bedding effectually cured.—Terms, net Cash on Delivery.—F. HEAL & SON, Bedding Manufacturers, 203, Tottenham Court Road.

BY HER MAJESTY'S ROYAL LETTERS PATENT.

HEELEY AND SONS' JOINTED TROWSERS STRAPS.

JAMES HEELEY and SONS beg to announce that they have completed their newly-invented Patent Jointed Trowsers Straps, which surpass in neatness, durability, and general appearance, every other description of Straps, and may be procured from all respectable houses. The Patentees submit the same with confidence to the Gentry and Public, feeling assured that their superiority will obtain them a preference wherever they are known.

Mount-street, Birmingham.

TROUSER-STRAPS SUPERSEDED

BY

THE DOUDNEY SPRING.

An entirely new, and the most complete mode of fastening the bottoms of Trousers, without anything passing under the feet. It is perfectly simple in its construction; and in durability, neatness, and effect, is very far superior to straps. One set is sufficient for any number of Trousers, to which no buttons, or other appendages of any kind are sewn, which renders it pre-eminently desirable where washing is necessary. It is adjusted in one minute, and fastened or unfastened in a moment, without soiling the hands, in the dirtiest weather. By extending its action along a great portion of the very edge of the Trouser, they are drawn down equally all round, and held close to the heel and sides of the foot, which cannot be attained when buttons are used, because they draw on single points, and cause projections at the sides. It is adapted to all kinds of Trousers, Gaiters, and Leggings, and all descriptions of boots and shoes. No. 1, for general purposes, are now ready; succeeding varieties will follow as quickly as possible. The Doudney Springs are sold on Cards, bearing the inventor's Autograph, at SIXPENCE PER SET; and may be obtained in the Country through any respectable Bookseller.——For an explanation of the Principles on which this is constructed, GEORGE D. DOUDNEY respectfully refers Gentlemen to his Advertisement in Blackwood, and the other leading Magazines of last year; and to his Pamphlet and Price Sheet, (which is forwarded by post, on application), for a more detailed list of his charges, adding only a few Items, which will, perhaps, be sufficient to convince Gentlemen that very great advantages are obtainable by paying for their Clothes on delivery, instead of taking credit.

ANDROMETER.

Dress Coats.
Elegantly lined with Silk, including extra Silk,
£2 5 0

Best Quality,
Richly trimmed with Silk
£2 18 0

Frock Coats,
Richly trimmed with Silk
£2 10 0

Trousers.
Excellent Buckskin and Cassimere,
ONE GUINEA.
The best qualities 25 and 28s.

Waistcoats.
Scarlet, Silk Jacquards, & Cassimere,
HALF-A-GUINEA.
Or, Three for 1 10 0

Contracts by the Year.
3 Suits per Ann.—1 First-rate & 2 excellent Business Suits, for 10 guineas,
The Old Suits to be returned. See the Pamphlet for other estimates.

Ladies' Habits,
Elegantly finished,
3 3 0

Liveries,
Plain Suit,
3 3 0

New Caglioni,
Fishing or Shooting Coat,
1 1 0

Washing Waistcoats.
7s. each, or 3 for £1.

Washing Trousers.
Of the various Fashionable Materials,
10s. 6d. a pair, or 3 pr. for 30s.

Regimentals and Naval Uniforms.

COUNTRY GENTLEMEN, who forward their addresses, are waited on by the Traveller.

METROPOLITAN BRITISH & FOREIGN CLOTHING ESTABLISHMENT,

97, FLEET STREET, LONDON.

MOST IMPORTANT INFORMATION.
BY HIS MAJESTY'S ROYAL LETTERS PATENT.
33, GERRARD STREET, SOHO.

G. MINTER begs to inform the Nobility, Gentry, &c., that he has invented an EASY CHAIR, that will recline and elevate, of itself, into an innumerable variety of positions, without the least trouble or difficulty to the occupier; and there being no machinery, rack, catch, or spring, it is only for persons sitting in the chair. merely to wish to recline or elevate themselves, and the seat and back take any desired inclination, without requiring the least assistance or exertion whatever, owing to the weight on the seat acting as a counterbalance to the pressure against the back by the application of a self-adjusting leverage; and for which G. M. has obtained his Majesty's Letters Patent. G. M. particularly recommends this invention to Invalids, or to those who may have lost the use of their hands or legs, as they are by it enabled to vary their position without requiring the use of either to obtain that change of position, from its endless variety, so necessary for the relief and comfort of the afflicted.

The Chair is made by the Inventor only, at his Wholesale Cabinet and Upholstery Manufactory, 33, Gerrard-street, Soho. G. M. is confident an inspection only is required to be convinced of its superiority over all others.

Merlin, Bath, Brighton, and every other description of Garden Wheel Chairs, much improved by G. Minter, with his self-acting reclining backs, so as to enable an invalid to lie at full length. Spinal Carriages, Portable Carriage Chairs, Water Beds, and every article for the comfort of the invalid.

ENGLISH GOLD WATCHES.—A. B. SAVORY & SONS, Watchmakers, No. 9, Cornhill, London, opposite the Bank of England, submit for selection a very large STOCK of GOLD WATCHES, the whole of which are made and finished under the careful inspection of experienced workmen on their own premises, and each warranted for correct performance.

SIZE FOR LADIES.

Fine Vertical Watches, jewelled, in engine-turned gold cases, and gold dials, warranted .... £ 10 10 0

Fine Vertical Watches, jewelled, with double-backed engine-turned gold cases, and gold dials, warranted .... £ 12 12 0

Patent Detached Lever Watches, jewelled in four holes, with double-backed gold cases, and gold dials, warranted .... £ 14 14 0

SIZE FOR GENTLEMEN.

Patent Detached Lever Watches, jewelled in four holes, seconds, and double-backed gold cases, warranted................... £ 14 14 0

Patent Detached Lever Watches, capped, jewelled in six holes, seconds, double-backed gold cases and enamel dials, warranted. £ 17 17 0

Patent Detached Lever Watches, capped, jewelled in six holes, seconds, double-backed gold cases and gold dials, warranted .. £ 21 0 0

Either of the Gentlemen's Watches may be had in gold hunting cases for £ 3 3s. each extra.

N.B. Second-hand Watches purchased in exchange.

REFORM YOUR TAILORS' BILLS!

LADIES' ELEGANT
RIDING HABITS.

Summer Cloth	£3	4 0
Ladies' Cloth	4	4 0
Saxony Cloth	5	5 0

GENTLEMAN'S

Superfine Dress Coat	2	7 6
Extra Saxony, the best that is made	2	15 0
Superfine Frock Coat, silk facings	2	10 0
Buckskin Trousers	1	1 0
Cloth or double-milled Cassimere ditto - 17s. 6d. to	1	5 0
New Patterns, Summer Trousers, 10s. 6d. per pr. or 3 pr.	1	10 0
Summer Waistcoats, 7s.; or 3,	1	0 0
Splendid Silk Valencia Dress Waistcoats, 10s. 6d. each, or 3,	1	10 0

FIRST-RATE
BOYS' CLOTHING.

Skeleton Dresses	£0	15 0
Tunic and Hussar Suits,	1	10 0
Camlet Cloaks	0	8 6
Cloth Cloaks	0	15 6

GENTLEMAN'S

Morning Coats and Dressing Gowns	0	18 0
Petersham Great Coats and Pilot P Jackets, bound, and Velvet Collar	1	10 0
Camlet Cloak, lined all through	1	1 0
Cloth Opera Cloak	1	10 0
Army Cloth Blue Spanish Cloak, 9½ yards round	2	10 0
Super Cloth ditto	3	3 0
Cloth or Tweed Fishing or Travelling Trousers	0	13 6

THE CELEBRITY THE

CITY CLOTHING ESTABLISHMENT

Has so many years maintained, being the

BEST AS WELL AS THE CHEAPEST HOUSE,

Renders any Assurance as to STYLE and QUALITY unnecessary. The NOBILITY and GENTRY are invited to the

SHOW-ROOMS, TO VIEW THE IMMENSE & SPLENDID STOCK.

The numerous Applications for

REGIMENTALS & NAVAL UNIFORMS,

Have induced E. P. D. & SON to make ample Arrangements for an extensive Business in this particular Branch; a perusal of their List of Prices (which can be had gratis) will show the EXORBITANT CHARGES to which OFFICERS OF THE ARMY AND NAVY HAVE SO LONG BEEN SUBJECTED.

CONTRACTS BY THE YEAR,

Originated by E. P. D. & SON, are universally adopted by CLERGYMEN and PROFESSIONAL GENTLEMEN, as being MORE REGULAR and ECONOMICAL. THE PRICES ARE THE LOWEST EVER OFFERED:—

Two Suits per Year, Superfine,	7 7—Extra Saxony, the best that is made,	8 5
Three Suits per Year, ditto	10 17—Extra Saxony, ditto	12 6
Four Suits per Year, ditto	14 6—Extra Saxony, ditto	15 18

(THE OLD SUITS TO BE RETURNED.)

Capital Shooting Jackets, 21s. The new Waterproof Cloak, 21s.

COUNTRY GENTLEMEN,

Preferring their Clothes Fashionably made, at a FIRST-RATE LONDON HOUSE, are respectfully informed, that by a Post-paid Application, they will receive a Prospectus explanatory of the System of Business, Directions for Measurement, and a Statement of Prices. Or if Three or Four Gentlemen unite, one of the Travellers will be dispatched immediately to wait on them.

STATE LIVERIES SPLENDIDLY MADE.
Footman's Suit of Liveries, £3 3. Scarlet Hunting Coat, £3 3

E. P. DOUDNEY AND SON,
49, LOMBARD-STREET. 1784.
Established

CHAPTER XLVI.

THROWS SOME LIGHT UPON NICHOLAS'S LOVE; BUT WHETHER FOR
GOOD OR EVIL THE READER MUST DETERMINE.

AFTER an anxious consideration of the painful and embarrassing
position in which he was placed, Nicholas decided that he ought to
lose no time in frankly stating it to the kind brothers. Availing himself
of the first opportunity of being alone with Mr. Charles Cheeryble at
the close of next day, he accordingly related Smike's little history, and
modestly but firmly expressed his hope that the good old gentleman
would, under such circumstances as he described, hold him justified in
adopting the extreme course of interfering between parent and child, and
upholding the latter in his disobedience; even though his horror and
dread of his father might seem, and would doubtless be represented as,
a thing so repulsive and unnatural, as to render those who countenanced
him in it, fit objects of general detestation and abhorrence.

" So deeply-rooted does this horror of the man appear to be," said
Nicholas, " that I can hardly believe he really is his son. Nature
does not seem to have implanted in his breast one lingering feeling of
affection for him, and surely she can never err."

" My dear sir," replied brother Charles, " you fall into the very
common mistake of charging upon Nature, matters with which she has
not the smallest connexion, and for which she is in no way responsible.
Men talk of nature as an abstract thing, and lose sight of what is
natural while they do so. Here is a poor lad who has never felt a
parent's care, who has scarcely known anything all his life but suffering
and sorrow, presented to a man who he is told is his father, and whose
first act is to signify his intention of putting an end to his short term of
happiness: of consigning him to his old fate, and taking him from the
only friend he has ever had—which is yourself. If Nature, in such a
case, put into that lad's breast but one secret prompting which urged
him towards his father and away from you, she would be a liar and an
idiot."

Nicholas was delighted to find that the old gentleman spoke so
warmly, and in the hope that he might say something more to the same
purpose made no reply.

" The same mistake presents itself to me, in one shape or other,
at every turn," said brother Charles. " Parents who never showed
their love, complain of want of natural affection in their children—children who never showed their duty, complain of want of natural feeling
in their parents—law-makers who find both so miserable that their
affections have never had enough of life's sun to develop them, are loud
in their moralisings over parents and children too, and cry that the very
ties of nature are disregarded. Natural affections and instincts, my dear

sir, are the most beautiful of the Almighty's works, but like other beautiful works of His, they must be reared and fostered, or it is as natural that they should be wholly obscured, and that new feelings should usurp their place, as it is that the sweetest productions of the earth, left untended, should be choked with weeds and briars. I wish we could be brought to consider this, and remembering natural obligations a little more at the right time, talk about them a little less at the wrong one."

After this, brother Charles, who had talked himself into a great heat, stopped to cool a little, and then continued :—

"I dare say you are surprised, my dear sir, that I have listened to your recital with so little astonishment. That is easily explained—your uncle has been here this morning."

Nicholas coloured, and drew back a step or two.

"Yes," said the old gentleman, tapping his desk emphatically, "here —in this room. He would listen neither to reason, feeling, nor justice. But brother Ned was hard upon him—brother Ned, sir, might have melted a paving-stone."

"He came to——" said Nicholas.

"To complain of you," returned brother Charles, "to poison our ears with calumnies and falsehoods ; but he came on a fruitless errand, and went away with some wholesome truths in his ear besides. Brother Ned, my dear Mr. Nickleby—brother Ned, sir, is a perfect lion. So is Tim Linkinwater—Tim is quite a lion. We had Tim in to face him at first, and Tim was at him, sir, before you could say ' Jack Robinson.' "

"How can I ever thank you, for all the deep obligations you impose upon me every day ?" said Nicholas.

"By keeping silence upon the subject, my dear sir," returned brother Charles. "You shall be righted. At least you shall not be wronged. Nobody belonging to you shall be wronged. They shall not hurt a hair of your head, or the boy's head, or your mother's head, or your sister's head. I have said it, brother Ned has said it, Tim Linkinwater has said it. We have all said it, and we'll all do it. I have seen the father—if he is the father—and I suppose he must be. He is a barbarian and a hypocrite, Mr. Nickleby. I told him, ' You are a barbarian, sir.' I did. I said, ' You're a barbarian, sir.' And I'm glad of it— I am *very* glad I told him he was a barbarian—very glad, indeed !"

By this time brother Charles was in such a very warm state of indignation, that Nicholas thought he might venture to put in a word, but the moment he essayed to do so, Mr. Cheeryble laid his hand softly upon his arm, and pointed to a chair.

"The subject is at an end for the present," said the old gentleman, wiping his face. "Don't revive it by a single word. I am going to speak upon another subject—a confidential subject, Mr. Nickleby. We must be cool again, we must be cool."

After two or three turns across the room he resumed his seat, and drawing his chair nearer to that on which Nicholas was seated, said—

"I am about to employ you, my dear sir, on a confidential and delicate mission."

" You might employ many a more able messenger, sir," said Nicholas, " but a more trustworthy or zealous one, I may be bold to say, you could not find."

" Of that I am well assured," returned brother Charles, " well assured. You will give me credit for thinking so, when I tell you, that the object of this mission is a young lady."

" A young lady, sir !" cried Nicholas, quite trembling for the moment with his eagerness to hear more.

" A very beautiful young lady," said Mr. Cheeryble, gravely.

" Pray go on, sir," returned Nicholas.

" I am thinking how to do so," said brother Charles—sadly, as it seemed to his young friend, and with an expression allied to pain. " You accidentally saw a young lady in this room one morning, my dear sir, in a fainting fit. Do you remember ? Perhaps you have forgotten——"

" Oh no," replied Nicholas, hurriedly. " I—I—remember it very well indeed."

" *She* is the lady I speak of," said brother Charles. Like the famous parrot, Nicholas thought a great deal but was unable to utter a word.

" She is the daughter," said Mr. Cheeryble, " of a lady who, when she was a beautiful girl herself, and I was very many years younger, I—it seems a strange word for me to utter now—I loved very dearly. You will smile, perhaps, to hear a grey-headed man talk about such things : you will not offend me, for when I was as young as you, I dare say I should have done the same."

" I have no such inclination, indeed," said Nicholas.

" My dear brother Ned," continued Mr. Cheeryble, " was to have married her sister, but she died. She is dead too now, and has been for many years. She married—her choice ; and I wish I could add that her after-life was as happy, as God knows I ever prayed it might be !"

A short silence intervened, which Nicholas made no effort to break.

" If trial and calamity had fallen as lightly on his head, as in the deepest truth of my own heart I ever hoped (for her sake) it would, his life would have been one of peace and happiness," said the old gentleman, calmly. " It will be enough to say that this was not the case—that she was not happy—that they fell into complicated distresses and difficulties—that she came, twelve months before her death, to appeal to my old friendship ; sadly changed, sadly altered, broken-spirited from suffering and ill usage, and almost broken-hearted. He readily availed himself of the money which, to give her but one hour's peace of mind, I would have poured out as freely as water— nay, he often sent her back for more—and yet even while he squandered it, he made the very success of these, her applications to me, the ground-work of cruel taunts and jeers, protesting that he knew she thought with bitter remorse of the choice she had made, that she had married him from motives of interest and vanity (he was a gay young man with great friends about him when she chose him for her husband),

and venting in short upon her, by every unjust and unkind means, the bitterness of that ruin and disappointment which had been brought about by his profligacy alone.   In those times this young lady was a mere child.   I never saw her again until that morning when you saw her also, but my nephew, Frank————"

Nicholas started, and indistinctly apologising for the interruption, begged his patron to proceed.

" My nephew, Frank, I say," resumed Mr. Cheeryble, " encountered her by accident, and lost sight of her almost in a minute afterwards, within two days after he returned to England.   Her father lay in some secret place to avoid his creditors, reduced, between sickness and poverty, to the verge of death, and she, a child,—we might almost think, if we did not know the wisdom of all Heaven's decrees—who should have blessed a better man, was steadily braving privation, degradation, and every thing most terrible to such a young and delicate creature's heart, for the purpose of supporting him.   She was attended, sir," said brother Charles, " in these reverses, by one faithful creature, who had been, in old times, a poor kitchen wench in the family, who was then their solitary servant, but who might have been, for the truth and fidelity of her heart—who might have been—ah! the wife of Tim Linkinwater himself, sir!"

Pursuing this encomium upon the poor follower with such energy and relish as no words can describe, brother Charles leant back in his chair, and delivered the remainder of his relation with greater composure.

It was in substance this :—That proudly resisting all offers of permanent aid and support from her late mother's friends, because they were made conditional upon her quitting the wretched man, her father, who had no friends left, and shrinking with instinctive delicacy from appealing in their behalf to that true and noble heart which he hated, and had, through its greatest and purest goodness, deeply wronged by misconstruction and ill report, this young girl had struggled alone and unassisted to maintain him by the labour of her hands.   That through the utmost depths of poverty and affliction she had toiled, never turning aside for an instant from her task, never wearied by the petulant gloom of a sick man sustained by no consoling recollections of the past or hopes of the future ; never repining for the comforts she had rejected, or bewailing the hard lot she had voluntarily incurred. That every little accomplishment she had acquired in happier days had been put into requisition for this purpose, and directed to this one end. That for two long years, toiling by day and often too by night, working at the needle, the pencil, and the pen, and submitting, as a daily governess, to such caprices and indignities as women (with daughters too) too often love to inflict upon their own sex when they serve in such capacities, as though in jealousy of the superior intelligence which they are necessitated to employ,—indignities, in ninety-nine cases out of every hundred, heaped upon persons immeasurably and incalculably their betters, but outweighing in comparison any that the most heartless blackleg would put upon his groom—that for two long years, by dint of labouring in all these capacities and wearying in none, she had not succeeded in the sole aim and object of her life, but that, overwhelmed by accumulated difficulties and disappointments, she had been compelled to seek out her mother's old friend, and, with a bursting heart, to confide in him at last.

"If I had been poor," said brother Charles, with sparkling eyes; "If I had been poor, Mr. Nickleby, my dear sir, which thank God I am not, I would have denied myself—of course anybody would under such circumstances—the commonest necessaries of life, to help her. As it is, the task is a difficult one. If her father were dead, nothing could be easier, for then she should share and cheer the happiest home that brother Ned and I could have, as if she were our child or sister. But he is still alive. Nobody can help him—that has been tried a thousand times; he was not abandoned by all without good cause, I know."

"Cannot she be persuaded to——" Nicholas hesitated when he had got thus far.

"To leave him?" said brother Charles. "Who could entreat a child to desert her parent? Such entreaties, limited to her seeing him occasionally, have been urged upon her—not by me—but always with the same result."

"Is he kind to her?" said Nicholas. "Does he requite her affection?"

"True kindness, considerate self-denying kindness, is not in his nature," returned Mr. Cheeryble. "Such kindness as he knows, he regards her with, I believe. The mother was a gentle, loving, confiding creature, and although he wounded her from their marriage till her death as cruelly and wantonly as ever man did, she never ceased to love him. She commended him on her death-bed to her child's care. Her child has never forgotten it, and never will."

"Have you no influence over him?" asked Nicholas.

"I, my dear sir! The last man in the world. Such is his jealousy and hatred of me, that if he knew his daughter had opened her heart to me, he would render her life miserable with his reproaches; although —this is the inconsistency and selfishness of his character—although if he knew that every penny she had came from me, he would not relinquish one personal desire that the most reckless expenditure of her scanty stock could gratify."

"An unnatural scoundrel!" said Nicholas, indignantly.

"We will use no harsh terms," said brother Charles, in a gentle voice; "but accommodate ourselves to the circumstances in which this young lady is placed. Such assistance as I have prevailed upon her to accept, I have been obliged, at her own earnest request, to dole out in the smallest portions, lest he, finding how easily money was procured, should squander it even more lightly than he is accustomed to do. She has come to and fro, to and fro, secretly and by night, to take even this; and I cannot bear that things should go on in this way, Mr. Nickleby—I really cannot bear it."

Then it came out by little and little, how that the twins had been revolving in their good old heads manifold plans and schemes for helping this young lady in the most delicate and considerate way, and so that her father should not suspect the source whence the aid was derived; and how they had at last come to the conclusion, that the best course would be to make a feint of purchasing her little drawings and ornamental work at a high price, and keeping up a constant demand for the same. For the furtherance of which end and object it was necessary that somebody should represent the dealer in such commodities, and after great deliberation they had pitched upon Nicholas to support this character.

"He knows me," said brother Charles, "and he knows my brother Ned. Neither of us would do. Frank is a very good fellow—a very fine fellow—but we are afraid that he might be a little flighty and thoughtless in such a delicate matter, and that he might, perhaps—that he might, in short, be too susceptible (for she is a beautiful creature, Sir; just what her poor mother was), and falling in love with her before he well knew his own mind, carry pain and sorrow into that innocent breast, which we would be the humble instruments of gradually making happy. He took an extraordinary interest in her fortunes when he first happened to encounter her; and we gather from the inquiries we have made of him, that it was she in whose behalf he made that turmoil which led to your first acquaintance."

Nicholas stammered out that he had before suspected the possibility of such a thing; and in explanation of its having occurred to him, described when and where he had seen the young lady himself.

"Well; then you see," continued brother Charles, "that *he* wouldn't do. Tim Linkinwater is out of the question; for Tim, Sir, is such a tremendous fellow, that he could never contain himself, but would go to loggerheads with the father before he had been in the place five minutes. You don't know what Tim is, Sir, when he is roused by anything that appeals to his feelings very strongly—then he is terrific, Sir, is Tim Linkinwater—absolutely terrific. Now, in you we can repose the strictest confidence; in you we have seen—or at least *I* have seen, and that's the same thing, for there's no difference between me and my brother Ned, except that he is the finest creature that ever lived, and that there is not, and never will be, anybody like him in all the world —in you we have seen domestic virtues and affections, and delicacy of feeling, which exactly qualify you for such an office. And you are the man, Sir."

"The young lady, Sir," said Nicholas, who felt so embarrassed that he had no small difficulty in saying anything at all—"Does—is—is she a party to this innocent deceit?"

"Yes, yes," returned Mr. Cheeryble; "at least she knows you come from us; she does *not* know, however, but that we shall dispose of these little productions that you'll purchase from time to time; and, perhaps, if you did it very well (that is, *very* well indeed), perhaps she might be brought to believe that we—that we made a profit of them. Eh?—Eh?"

In this guileless and most kind simplicity, brother Charles was so happy, and in this possibility of the young lady being led to think that she was under no obligation to him, he evidently felt so sanguine and had so much delight, that Nicholas would not breathe a doubt upon the subject.

All this time, however, there hovered upon the tip of his tongue a confession that the very same objections which Mr. Cheeryble had stated to the employment of his nephew in this commission applied with at least equal force and validity to himself, and a hundred times had he been upon the point of avowing the real state of his feelings, and entreating to be released from it. But as often, treading upon the heels of this impulse, came another which urged him to refrain, and to keep his secret to his own breast. "Why should I," thought Nicholas, "why should I throw difficulties in the way of this benevolent and high-minded design? What if I do love and reverence this good and lovely creature—should I not appear a most arrogant and shallow coxcomb if I gravely represented that there was any danger of her falling in love with me? Besides, have I no confidence in myself? Am I not now bound in honour to repress these thoughts? Has not this excellent man a right to my best and heartiest services, and should any considerations of self deter me from rendering them?"

Asking himself such questions as these, Nicholas mentally answered with great emphasis "No!" and persuading himself that he was a most conscientious and glorious martyr, nobly resolved to do what, if he had examined his own heart a little more carefully, he would have found, he could not resist. Such is the sleight of hand by which we juggle with ourselves, and change our very weaknesses into stanch and most magnanimous virtues!

Mr. Cheeryble, being of course wholly unsuspicious that such reflections were presenting themselves to his young friend, proceeded to give him the needful credentials and directions for his first visit, which was to be made next morning; and all preliminaries being arranged, and the strictest secrecy enjoined, Nicholas walked home for the night very thoughtfully indeed.

The place to which Mr. Cheeryble had directed him was a row of mean and not over-cleanly houses, situated within "the rules" of the King's Bench Prison, and not many hundred paces distant from the obelisk in Saint George's Fields. The Rules are a certain liberty adjoining the prison, and comprising some dozen streets in which debtors who can raise money to pay large fees, from which their creditors do *not* derive any benefit, are permitted to reside by the wise provisions of the same enlightened laws which leave the debtor who can raise no money to starve in jail, without the food, clothing, lodging, or warmth, which are provided for felons convicted of the most atrocious crimes that can disgrace humanity. There are many pleasant fictions of the law in constant operation, but there is not one so pleasant or practically humorous as that which supposes every man to be of equal value in its impartial eye, and the benefits of all laws to be equally attainable by all men, without the smallest reference to the furniture of their pockets.

To the row of houses indicated to him by Mr. Charles Cheeryble, Nicholas directed his steps, without much troubling his head with such matters as these; and at this row of houses—after traversing a very dirty and dusty suburb, of which minor theatricals, shell-fish, ginger-beer, spring vans, green-grocery, and brokers' shops, appeared to compose the main and most prominent features—he at length arrived with a palpitating heart. There were small gardens in front which, being wholly neglected in all other respects, served as little pens for the dust to collect in, until the wind came round the corner and blew it down the road. Opening the rickety gate which, dangling on its broken hinges before one of these, half admitted and half repulsed the visitor, Nicholas knocked at the street door with a faltering hand.

It was in truth a shabby house outside, with very dim parlour windows and very small show of blinds, and very dirty muslin curtains dangling across the lower panes on very loose and limp strings. Neither, when the door was opened, did the inside appear to belie the outward promise, as there was faded carpeting on the stairs and faded oil-cloth in the passage; in addition to which discomforts a gentleman Ruler was smoking hard in the front parlour (though it was not yet noon), while the lady of the house was busily engaged in turpentining the disjointed fragments of a tent-bedstead at the door of the back parlour, as if in preparation for the reception of some new lodger who had been fortunate enough to engage it.

Nicholas had ample time to make these observations while the little boy, who went on errands for the lodgers, clattered down the kitchen stairs and was heard to scream, as in some remote cellar, for Miss Bray's servant, who, presently appearing and requesting him to follow her, caused him to evince greater symptoms of nervousness and disorder than so natural a consequence of his having inquired for that young lady would seem calculated to occasion.

Up-stairs he went, however, and into a front room he was shown, and there, seated at a little table by the window, on which were drawing materials with which she was occupied, sat the beautiful girl who had so engrossed his thoughts, and who, surrounded by all the new and strong interest which Nicholas attached to her story, seemed now, in his eyes, a thousand times more beautiful than he had ever yet supposed her.

But how the graces and elegancies which she had dispersed about the poorly-furnished room, went to the heart of Nicholas! Flowers, plants, birds, the harp, the old piano whose notes had sounded so much sweeter in bygone times—how many struggles had it cost her to keep these two last links of that broken chain which bound her yet to home! With every slender ornament, the occupation of her leisure hours, replete with that graceful charm which lingers in every little tasteful work of woman's hands, how much patient endurance and how many gentle affections were entwined! He felt as though the smile of Heaven were on the little chamber; as though the beautiful devotion of so young and weak a creature, had shed a ray of its own on the inanimate things around and made them beautiful as itself; as

Nicholas makes his first visit to M^r. Bray.

though the halo with which old painters surround the bright angels of a sinless world played about a being akin in spirit to them, and its light were visibly before him.

And yet Nicholas was in the rules of the King's Bench Prison! If he had been in Italy indeed, and the time had been sunset, and the scene a stately terrace;—but, there is one broad sky over all the world, and whether it be blue or cloudy, the same heaven beyond it, so, perhaps, he had no need of compunction for thinking as he did.

It is not to be supposed that he took in everything at one glance, for he had as yet been unconscious of the presence of a sick man propped up with pillows in an easy-chair, who moving restlessly and impatiently in his seat, attracted his attention.

He was scarce fifty, perhaps, but so emaciated as to appear much older. His features presented the remains of a handsome countenance, but one in which the embers of strong and impetuous passions were easier to be traced than any expression which would have rendered a far plainer face much more prepossessing. His looks were very haggard, and his limbs and body literally worn to the bone, but there was something of the old fire in the large sunken eye notwithstanding, and it seemed to kindle afresh as he struck a thick stick, with which he seemed to have supported himself in his seat, impatiently on the floor twice or thrice, and called his daughter by her name.

"Madeline, who is this—what does anybody want here—who told a stranger we could be seen? What is it?"

"I believe—— " the young lady began, as she inclined her head with an air of some confusion, in reply to the salutation of Nicholas.

"You always believe," returned her father, petulantly. "What is it?"

By this time Nicholas had recovered sufficient presence of mind to speak for himself, so he said (as it had been agreed he should say) that he had called about a pair of hand-screens, and some painted velvet for an ottoman, both of which were required to be of the most elegant design possible, neither time nor expense being of the smallest consideration. He had also to pay for the two drawings, with many thanks, and, advancing to the little table, he laid upon it a bank note, folded in an envelope and sealed.

"See that the money is right, Madeline," said the father, "open the paper, my dear."

"It's quite right, papa, I am sure."

"Here!" said Mr. Bray, putting out his hand, and opening and shutting his bony fingers with irritable impatience. "Let me see. What are you talking about, Madeline—you're sure—how can you be sure of any such thing—five pounds—well, is *that* right?"

"Quite," said Madeline, bending over him. She was so busily employed in arranging the pillows that Nicholas could not see her face, but as she stooped he thought he saw a tear fall.

"Ring the bell, ring the bell," said the sick man, with the same nervous eagerness, and motioning towards it with such a quivering hand that the bank note rustled in the air. "Tell her to get it changed

—to get me a newspaper—to buy me some grapes—another bottle of the wine that I had last week—and—and—I forget half I want just now, but she can go out again. Let her get those first—those first. Now, Madeline my love, quick, quick! Good God, how slow you are!"

"He remembers nothing that *she* wants!" thought Nicholas. Perhaps something of what he thought was expressed in his countenance, for the sick man turning towards him with great asperity, demanded to know if he waited for a receipt.

"It is no matter at all," said Nicholas.

"No matter! what do you mean, sir?" was the tart rejoinder. "No matter! Do you think you bring your paltry money here as a favour or a gift; or as a matter of business, and in return for value received? D—n you, sir, because you can't appreciate the time and taste which are bestowed upon the goods you deal in, do you think you give your money away? Do you know that you are talking to a gentleman, sir, who at one time could have bought up fifty such men as you and all you have? What do you mean?"

"I merely mean that as I shall have many dealings with this lady, if she will kindly allow me, I will not trouble her with such forms," said Nicholas.

"Then *I* mean, if you please, that we'll have as many forms as we can," returned the father. "My daughter, sir, requires no kindness from you or anybody else. Have the goodness to confine your dealings strictly to trade and business, and not to travel beyond it. Every petty tradesman is to begin to pity her now, is he? Upon my soul! Very pretty. Madeline, my dear, give him a receipt; and mind you always do so."

While she was feigning to write it, and Nicholas was ruminating upon the extraordinary, but by no means uncommon character thus presented to his observation, the invalid, who appeared at times to suffer great bodily pain, sank back in his chair and moaned out a feeble complaint that the girl had been gone an hour, and that everybody conspired to goad him.

"When," said Nicholas, as he took the piece of paper, "when shall I—call again?"

This was addressed to the daughter, but the father answered immediately—

"When you're requested to call, sir, and not before. Don't worry and persecute. Madeline, my dear, when is this person to call again?"

"Oh, not for a long time—not for three or four weeks—it is not necessary, indeed—I can do without," said the young lady, with great eagerness.

"Why, how are we to do without?" urged her father, not speaking above his breath. "Three or four weeks, Madeline! Three or four weeks!"

"Then sooner—sooner, if you please," said the young lady, turning to Nicholas.

"Three or four weeks!" muttered the father. "Madeline, what on earth—do nothing for three or four weeks!"

"It is a long time, ma'am," said Nicholas.

"*You* think so, do you?" retorted the father, angrily. "If I chose to beg, sir, and stoop to ask assistance from people I despise, three or four months would not be a long time—three or four years would not be a long time. Understand, sir, that is if I chose to be dependent; but as I don't, you may call in a week."

Nicholas bowed low to the young lady and retired, pondering upon Mr. Bray's ideas of independence, and devoutly hoping that there might be few such independent spirits as he mingling with the baser clay of humanity.

He heard a light footstep above him as he descended the stairs, and looking round saw that the young lady was standing there, and glancing timidly towards him, seemed to hesitate whether she should call him back or no. The best way of settling the question was to turn back at once, which Nicholas did.

"I don't know whether I do right in asking you, sir," said Madeline, hurriedly, "but pray—pray—do not mention to my poor mother's dear friends what has passed here to-day. He has suffered much, and is worse this morning. I beg you, sir, as a boon, a favour to myself."

"You have but to hint a wish," returned Nicholas fervently, "and I would hazard my life to gratify it."

"You speak hastily, sir."

"Truly and sincerely," rejoined Nicholas, his lips trembling as he formed the words, "if ever man spoke truly yet. I am not skilled in disguising my feelings, and if I were, I could not hide my heart from you. Dear madam, as I know your history, and feel as men and angels must who hear and see such things, I do entreat you to believe that I would die to serve you."

The young lady turned away her head, and was plainly weeping.

"Forgive me," said Nicholas, with respectful earnestness, "if I seem to say too much, or to presume upon the confidence which has been intrusted to me. But I could not leave you as if my interest and sympathy expired with the commission of the day. I am your faithful servant, humbly devoted to you from this hour—devoted in strict truth and honour to him who sent me here, and in pure integrity of heart, and distant respect for you. If I meant more or less than this, I should be unworthy his regard, and false to the very nature that prompts the honest words I utter."

She waved her hand, entreating him to be gone, but answered not a word. Nicholas could say no more, and silently withdrew. And thus ended his first interview with Madeline Bray.

CHAPTER XLVII.

MR. RALPH NICKLEBY HAS SOME CONFIDENTIAL INTERCOURSE WITH
ANOTHER OLD FRIEND.   THEY CONCERT BETWEEN THEM A PRO-
JECT, WHICH PROMISES WELL FOR BOTH.

"THERE go the three quarters past!" muttered Newman Noggs,
listening to the chimes of some neighbouring church, "and my dinner
time's two.   He does it on purpose.   He makes a point of it.   It's
just like him."

It was in his own little den of an office and on the top of his official
stool that Newman thus soliloquised; and the soliloquy referred, as
Newman's grumbling soliloquies usually did, to Ralph Nickleby.

"I don't believe he ever had an appetite," said Newman, "except
for pounds, shillings, and pence, and with them he's as greedy as a wolf.
I should like to have him compelled to swallow one of every English coin.
The penny would be an awkward morsel—but the crown—ha! ha!"

His good humour being in some degree restored by the vision of
Ralph Nickleby swallowing, perforce, a five-shilling-piece, Newman
slowly brought forth from his desk one of those portable bottles,
currently known as pocket-pistols, and shaking the same close to his
ear so as to produce a rippling sound very cool and pleasant to listen
to, suffered his features to relax, and took a gurgling drink, which
relaxed them still more.   Replacing the cork he smacked his lips twice
or thrice with an air of great relish, and, the taste of the liquor having
by this time evaporated, recurred to his grievances again.

"Five minutes to three," growled Newman, "it can't want more by
this time; and I had my breakfast at eight o'clock, and *such* a breakfast! and my right dinner time two!   And I might have a nice little
bit of hot roast meat spoiling at home all this time—how does *he* know
I haven't!   'Don't go till I come back,' 'Don't go till I come back,'
day after day.   What do you always go out at my dinner time for
then—eh?   Don't you know it's nothing but aggravation—eh?"

These words, though uttered in a very loud key, were addressed to
nothing but empty air.   The recital of his wrongs, however, seemed
to have the effect of making Newman Noggs desperate; for he flattened
his old hat upon his head, and drawing on the everlasting gloves,
declared with great vehemence, that come what might, he would go to
dinner that very minute.

Carrying this resolution into instant effect, he had advanced as far
as the passage, when the sound of the latch-key in the street door
caused him to make a precipitate retreat into his own office again.

"Here he is," growled Newman, "and somebody with him.   Now
it'll be 'Stop till this gentleman's gone.'   But I wont—that's flat."

So saying, Newman slipped into a tall empty closet which opened
with two half doors, and shut himself up; intending to slip out directly
Ralph was safe inside his own room.

The Consultation.

" Noggs," cried Ralph, "where is that fellow—Noggs."
But not a word said Newman.

"The dog has gone to his dinner, though I told him not," muttered Ralph, looking into the office and pulling out his watch. "Humph! You had better come in here, Gride. My man's out, and the sun is hot upon my room. This is cool and in the shade, if you don't mind roughing it."

" Not at all, Mr. Nickleby, oh not at all. All places are alike to me, sir. Ah! very nice indeed. Oh! very nice!"

The person who made this reply was a little old man, of about seventy or seventy-five years of age, of a very lean figure, much bent, and slightly twisted. He wore a grey coat with a very narrow collar, an old-fashioned waistcoat of ribbed black silk, and such scanty trowsers as displayed his shrunken spindle-shanks in their full ugliness. The only articles of display or ornament in his dress, were a steel watch-chain to which were attached some large gold seals; and a black ribbon into which, in compliance with an old fashion scarcely ever observed in these days, his grey hair was gathered behind. His nose and chin were sharp and prominent, his jaws had fallen inwards from loss of teeth, his face was shrivelled and yellow, save where the cheeks were streaked with the colour of a dry winter apple; and where his beard had been, there lingered yet a few grey tufts which seemed, like the ragged eyebrows, to denote the badness of the soil from which they sprung. The whole air and attitude of the form, was one of stealthy cat-like obsequiousness; the whole expression of the face was concentrated in a wrinkled leer, compounded of cunning, lecherousness, slyness, and avarice.

Such was old Arthur Gride, in whose face there was not a wrinkle, in whose dress there was not one spare fold or plait, but expressed the most covetous and griping penury, and sufficiently indicated his belonging to that class of which Ralph Nickleby was a member. Such was old Arthur Gride, as he sat in a low chair looking up into the face of Ralph Nickleby, who, lounging upon the tall office stool, with his arms upon his knees, looked down into his,—a match for him on whatever errand he had come.

" And how have you been?" said Gride, feigning great interest in Ralph's state of health. "I haven't seen you for—oh! not for—"

" Not for a long time," said Ralph, with a peculiar smile, importing that he very well knew it was not on a mere visit of compliment that his friend had come. " It was a narrow chance that you saw me now, for I had only just come up to the door as you turned the corner."

" I am very lucky," observed Gride.

" So men say," replied Ralph, drily.

The older money-lender wagged his chin and smiled, but he originated no new remark, and they sat for some little time without speaking. Each was looking out to take the other at a disadvantage.

" Come, Gride," said Ralph, at length ; " what's in the wind to-day?"

" Aha! you're a bold man, Mr. Nickleby," cried the other, apparently very much relieved by Ralph's leading the way to business. " Oh dear, dear, what a bold man you are!"

"Why, you have a sleek and slinking way with you that makes me seem so by contrast," returned Ralph. "I don't know but that yours may answer better, but I want the patience for it."

"You were born a genius, Mr. Nickleby," said old Arthur. "Deep, deep, deep. Ah!"

"Deep enough," retorted Ralph, "to know that I shall need all the depth I have, when men like you begin to compliment. You know I have stood by when you fawned and flattered other people, and I remember pretty well what *that* always led to."

"Ha, ha, ha," rejoined Arthur, rubbing his hands. "So you do, so you do, no doubt. Not a man knows it better. Well, it's a pleasant thing now to think that you remember old times. Oh dear!"

"Now then," said Ralph, composedly; "what's in the wind, I ask again—what is it?"

"See that now!" cried the other. "He can't even keep from business while we're chatting over bygones! Oh dear, dear, what a man it is!"

"*Which* of the bygones do you want to revive?" said Ralph. "One of them, I know, or you wouldn't talk about them."

"He suspects even me!" cried old Arthur, holding up his hands. "Even me—oh dear, even me. What a man it is! Ha, ha, ha! What a man it is! Mr. Nickleby against all the world—there's nobody like him. A giant among pigmies—a giant—a giant!"

Ralph looked at the old dog with a quiet smile as he chuckled on in this strain, and Newman Noggs in the closet felt his heart sink within him as the prospect of dinner grew fainter and fainter.

"I must humour him though," cried old Arthur; "he must have his way—a wilful man, as the Scotch say—well, well, they're a wise people, the Scotch—he will talk about business, and won't give away his time for nothing. He's very right. Time is money—time is money."

"He was one of us who made that saying, I should think," said Ralph. "Time is money, and very good money too, to those who reckon interest by it. Time *is* money! Yes, and time costs money—it's rather an expensive article to some people we could name, or I forget my trade."

In rejoinder to this sally, old Arthur again raised his hands, again chuckled, and again ejaculated "What a man it is!" which done, he dragged the low chair a little nearer to Ralph's high stool, and looking upwards into his immoveable face, said,

"What would you say to me, if I was to tell you that I was—that I was—going to be married?"

"I should tell you," replied Ralph, looking coldly down upon him, "that for some purpose of your own you told a lie, and that it wasn't the first time and wouldn't be the last; that I wasn't surprised and wasn't to be taken in."

"Then I tell you seriously that I am," said old Arthur.

"And *I* tell you seriously," rejoined Ralph, "what I told you this minute. Stay. Let me look at you. There's a liquorish devilry in your face—what is this?"

" I wouldn't deceive *you*, you know," whined Arthur Gride; " I couldn't do it, I should be mad to try. I—I—to deceive Mr. Nickleby! The pigmy to impose upon the giant. I ask again—he, he, he!— what should you say to me if I was to tell you that I was going to be married?"

" To some old hag?" said Ralph.

" No, no," cried Arthur, interrupting him, and rubbing his hands in an ecstacy. " Wrong, wrong again. Mr. Nickleby for once at fault— out, quite out! To a young and beautiful girl; fresh, lovely, bewitch- ing, and not nineteen. Dark eyes—long eyelashes—ripe and ruddy lips that to look at is to long to kiss—beautiful clustering hair that one's fingers itch to play with—such a waist as might make a man clasp the air involuntarily, thinking of twining his arm about it—little feet that tread so lightly they hardly seem to walk upon the ground— to marry all this, sir,—this—hey, hey!"

" This is something more than common drivelling," said Ralph, after listening with a curled lip to the old sinner's raptures. " The girl's name?"

" Oh deep, deep! See now how deep that is!" exclaimed old Arthur. " He knows I want his help, he knows he can give it me, he knows it must all turn to his advantage, he sees the thing already. Her name—is there nobody within hearing?"

" Why, who the devil should there be?" retorted Ralph, testily.

" I didn't know but that perhaps somebody might be passing up or down the stairs," said Arthur Gride, after looking out at the door and carefully re-closing it; " or but that your man might have come back and might have been listening outside—clerks and servants have a trick of listening, and I should have been very uncomfortable if Mr. Noggs—"

" Curse Mr. Noggs," said Ralph, sharply, " and go on with what you have to say."

" Curse Mr. Noggs, by all means," rejoined old Arthur; " I am sure I have not the least objection to that. Her name is—"

" Well," said Ralph, rendered very irritable by old Arthur's pausing again, " what is it?"

" Madeline Bray."

Whatever reasons there might have been—and Arthur Gride ap- peared to have anticipated some—for the mention of this name pro- ducing an effect upon Ralph, or whatever effect it really did produce upon him, he permitted none to manifest itself, but calmly repeated the name several times, as if reflecting when and where he had heard it before.

" Bray," said Ralph. " Bray—there was young Bray of—no, he never had a daughter."

" You remember Bray?" rejoined Arthur Gride.

" No," said Ralph, looking vacantly at him.

" Not Walter Bray! The dashing man, who used his handsome wife so ill?"

" If you seek to recal any particular dashing man to my recollection by such a trait as that," said Ralph, shrugging his shoulders, " I shall confound him with nine-tenths of the dashing men I have ever known."

" Tut, tut. That Bray who is now in the rules of the Bench," said old Arthur. " You can't have forgotten Bray. Both of us did business with him. Why, he owes you money—"

" Oh *him!*" rejoined Ralph. " Ay, ay. Now you speak. Oh! It's *his* daughter, is it ?"

Naturally as this was said, it was not said so naturally but that a kindred spirit like old Arthur Gride might have discerned a design upon the part of Ralph to lead him on to much more explicit statements and explanations than he would have volunteered, or than Ralph could in all likelihood have obtained by any other means. Old Arthur, however, was so intent upon his own designs, that he suffered himself to be over-reached, and had no suspicion but that his good friend was in earnest.

" I knew you couldn't forget him, when you came to think for a moment," he said.

" You were right," answered Ralph. " But old Arthur Gride and matrimony is a most anomalous conjunction of words; old Arthur Gride and dark eyes and eyelashes, and lips that to look at is to long to kiss, and clustering hair that he wants to play with, and waists that he wants to span, and little feet that don't tread upon anything—old Arthur Gride and such things as these is more monstrous still; but old Arthur Gride marrying the daughter of a ruined ' dashing man' in the rules of the Bench, is the most monstrous and incredible of all. Plainly, friend Arthur Gride, if you want any help from me in this business (which of course you do, or you would not be here), speak out, and to the purpose. And, above all, don't talk to me of its turning to my advantage, for I know it must turn to yours also, and to a good round tune too, or you would have no finger in such a pie as this."

There was enough acerbity and sarcasm not only in the matter of Ralph's speech, but in the tone of voice in which he uttered it, and the looks with which he eked it out, to have fired even the ancient usurer's cold blood and flushed even his withered cheek. But he gave vent to no demonstration of anger, contenting himself with exclaiming as before, " What a man it is !" and rolling his head from side to side, as if in unrestrained enjoyment of his freedom and drollery. Clearly observing, however, from the expression in Ralph's features, that he had best come to the point as speedily as might be, he composed himself for more serious business, and entered upon the pith and marrow of his negotiation.

First, he dwelt upon the fact that Madeline Bray was devoted to the support and maintenance, and was a slave to every wish, of her only parent, who had no other friend on earth ; to which Ralph rejoined that he had heard something of the kind before, and that if she had known a little more of the world, she wouldn't have been such a fool.

Secondly, he enlarged upon the character of her father, arguing, that even taking it for granted that he loved her in return with the utmost affection of which he was capable, yet he loved himself a great deal better; which Ralph said it was quite unnecessary to say anything more about, as that was very natural, and probable enough.

And, thirdly, old Arthur premised that the girl was a delicate and beautiful creature, and that he had really a hankering to have her for his wife. To this Ralph deigned no other rejoinder than a harsh smile, and a glance at the shrivelled old creature before him, which were, however, sufficiently expressive.

"Now," said Gride, "for the little plan I have in my mind to bring this about; because, I haven't offered myself even to the father yet, I should have told you. But that you have gathered already? Ah! oh dear, oh dear, what an edged-tool you are!"

"Don't play with me then," said Ralph, impatiently. "You know the proverb."

"A reply always on the tip of his tongue!" cried old Arthur, raising his hands and eyes in admiration. "He is always prepared! Oh dear, what a blessing to have such a ready wit, and so much ready money to back it!" Then, suddenly changing his tone, he went on :—"I have been backwards and forwards to Bray's lodgings several times within the last six months. It is just half a year since I first saw this delicate morsel, and, oh dear, what a delicate morsel it is! But that is neither here nor there. I am his detaining creditor for seventeen hundred pounds."

"You talk as if you were the only detaining creditor," said Ralph, pulling out his pocket-book. "I am another for nine hundred and seventy-five pounds, four and threepence."

"The only other, Mr. Nickleby," said old Arthur, eagerly. "The only other. Nobody else went to the expense of lodging a detainer, trusting to our holding him fast enough, I warrant you. We both fell into the same snare—oh, dear, what a pitfall it was; it almost ruined me! And lent him our money upon bills, with only one name besides his own, which to be sure everybody supposed to be a good one, and was as negotiable as money, but which turned out—you know how. Just as we should have come upon him, he died insolvent. Ah! it went very nigh to ruin me, that loss did!"

"Go on with your scheme," said Ralph. "It's of no use raising the cry of our trade just now; there's nobody to hear us."

"It's always as well to talk that way," returned old Arthur, with a chuckle, "whether there's anybody to hear us or not. Practice makes perfect, you know. Now, if I offer myself to Bray as his son-in-law, upon one simple condition that the moment I am fast married he shall be quietly released, and have an allowance to live just t'other side the water like a gentleman (he can't live long, for I have asked his doctor, and he declares that his complaint is one of the Heart and it is impossible), and if all the advantages of this condition are properly stated and dwelt upon to him, do you think he could resist me? And if he could not resist *me*, do you think his daughter could resist *him?* Shouldn't I have her Mrs. Arthur Gride—pretty Mrs. Arthur Gride —a tit-bit—a dainty chick—shouldn't I have her Mrs. Arthur Gride in a week, a month, a day—any time I chose to name?"

" Go on," said Ralph, nodding his head deliberately, and speaking in a tone whose studied coldness presented a strange contrast to the rapturous squeak to which his friend had gradually mounted. " Go on. You didn't come here to ask me that."

" Oh dear, how you talk !" cried old Arthur, edging himself closer still to Ralph. " Of course, I didn't—I don't pretend I did ! I came to ask what you would take from me, if I prospered with the father, for this debt of yours—five shillings in the pound—six and eightpence —ten shillings ? I *would* go as far as ten for such a friend as you, we have always been on such good terms, but you won't be so hard upon me as that, I know. Now, will you ?"

" There's something more to be told," said Ralph, as stony and immovable as ever.

" Yes, yes, there is, but you won't give me time," returned Arthur Gride. " I want a backer in this matter—one who can talk, and urge, and press a point, which you can do as no man can. I can't do that, for I am a poor, timid, nervous creature. Now, if you get a good composition for this debt, which you long ago gave up for lost, you'll stand my friend, and help me. Won't you ?"

" There's something more," said Ralph.

" No, no, indeed," cried Arthur Gride.

" Yes, yes, indeed. I tell you yes," said Ralph.

" Oh !" returned old Arthur, feigning to be suddenly enlightened. " You mean something more, as concerns myself and my intention. Ay, surely, surely. Shall I mention that ?"

" I think you had better," rejoined Ralph, drily.

" I didn't like to trouble you with that, because I supposed your interest would cease with your own concern in the affair," said Arthur Gride. " That's kind of you to ask. Oh dear, how very kind of you ! Why, supposing I had a knowledge of some property—some little property—very little—to which this pretty chick was entitled ; which nobody does or can know of at this time, but which her husband could sweep into his pouch, if he knew as much as I do, would that account for—"

" For the whole proceeding," rejoined Ralph, abruptly. " Now, let me turn this matter over, and consider what I ought to have if I should help you to success."

" But don't be hard," cried old Arthur, raising his hands with an imploring gesture, and speaking in a tremulous voice. " Don't be too hard upon me. It's a very small property, it is indeed. Say the ten shillings, and we'll close the bargain. It's more than I ought to give, but you're so kind—shall we say the ten ? Do now, do."

Ralph took no notice of these supplications, but sat for three or four minutes in a brown study, looking thoughtfully at the person from whom they proceeded. After sufficient cogitation he broke silence, and it certainly could not be objected that he used any needless circumlocution, or failed to speak directly to the purpose.

" If you married this girl without me," said Ralph, " you must pay my debt in full, because you couldn't set her father free otherwise. It's plain, then, that I must have the whole amount, clear of all deduction or incumbrance, or I should lose from being honoured with your confidence, instead of gaining by it. That's the first article of the treaty. For the second, I shall stipulate that for my trouble in negotiation and persuasion, and helping you to this fortune, I have five hundred pounds—that's very little, because you have the ripe lips, and the clustering hair, and what not, all to yourself. For the third and last article, I require that you execute a bond to me, this day, binding yourself in the payment of these two sums, before noon of the day of your marriage with Madeline Bray. You have told me I can urge and press a point. I press this one, and will take nothing less than these terms. Accept them if you like. If not, marry her without me if you can. I shall still get my debt."

To all entreaties, protestations, and offers of compromise between his own proposals and those which Arthur Gride had first suggested, Ralph was deaf as an adder. He would enter into no further discussion of the subject, and while old Arthur dilated upon the enormity of his demands and proposed modifications of them, approaching by degrees nearer and nearer to the terms he resisted, sat perfectly mute, looking with an air of quiet abstraction over the entries and papers in his pocket-book. Finding that it was impossible to make any impression upon his stanch friend, Arthur Gride, who had prepared himself for some such result before he came, consented with a heavy heart to the proposed treaty, and upon the spot filled up the bond required (Ralph kept such instruments handy), after exacting the condition that Mr. Nickleby should accompany him to Bray's lodgings that very hour, and open the negotiation at once, should circumstances appear auspicious and favourable to their designs.

In pursuance of this last understanding the worthy gentlemen went out together shortly afterwards, and Newman Noggs emerged, bottle in hand, from the cupboard, out of the upper door of which, at the imminent risk of detection, he had more than once thrust his red nose when such parts of the subject were under discussion as interested him most.

"I have no appetite now," said Newman, putting the flask in his pocket. "I've had *my* dinner."

Having delivered this observation in a very grievous and doleful tone, Newman reached the door in one long limp, and came back again in another.

"I don't know who she may be, or what she may be," he said; "but I pity her with all my heart and soul; and I can't help her, nor can I any of the people against whom a hundred tricks—but none so vile as this—are plotted every day! Well, that adds to my pain, but not to theirs. The thing is no worse because I know it, and it tortures me as well as them. Gride and Nickleby! Good pair for a curricle—oh roguery! roguery! roguery!"

With these reflections, and a very hard knock on the crown of his unfortunate hat at each repetition of the last word, Newman Noggs, whose brain was a little muddled by so much of the contents of the

pocket-pistol as had found their way there during his recent conceal-
ment, went forth to seek such consolation as might be derivable from
the beef and greens of some cheap eating-house.

Meanwhile the two plotters had betaken themselves to the same
house whither Nicholas had repaired for the first time but a few
mornings before, and having obtained access to Mr. Bray, and found
his daughter from home, had, by a train of the most masterly ap-
proaches that Ralph's utmost skill could frame, at length laid open the
real object of their visit.

"There he sits, Mr. Bray," said Ralph, as the invalid, not yet
recovered from his surprise, reclined in his chair, looking alternately
at him and Arthur Gride. " What if he has had the ill fortune to be
one cause of your detention in this place—I have been another ; men
must live ; you are too much a man of the world not to see that in
its true light. We offer the best reparation in our power. Reparation !
Here is an offer of marriage, that many a titled father would leap at,
for his child. Mr. Arthur Gride, with the fortune of a prince. Think
what a haul it is !"

" My daughter, sir," returned Bray, haughtily, " as *I* have brought
her up, would be a rich recompense for the largest fortune that a man
could bestow in exchange for her hand."

" Precisely what I told you," said the artful Ralph, turning to his
friend, old Arthur. " Precisely what made me consider the thing so
fair and easy. There is no obligation on either side. You have
money, and Miss Madeline has beauty and worth. She has youth, you
have money. She has not money, you have not youth. Tit for tat—
quits—a match of Heaven's own making !"

" Matches are made in Heaven, they say," added Arthur Gride,
leering hideously at the father-in-law he wanted. " If we are married,
it will be destiny, according to that."

" Then think, Mr. Bray," said Ralph, hastily substituting for this
argument considerations more nearly allied to earth, " Think what
a stake is involved in the acceptance or rejection of these proposals of
my friend—"

" How can I accept or reject," interrupted Mr. Bray, with an
irritable consciousness that it really rested with him to decide. " It is
for my daughter to accept or reject ; it is for my daughter. You
know that."

" True," said Ralph, emphatically ; " but you have still the power
to advise ; to state the reasons for and against ; to hint a wish."

" To hint a wish, sir !" returned the debtor, proud and mean by
turns, and selfish at all times. " I am her father, am I not ? Why
should I hint, and beat about the bush ? Do you suppose, like her
mother's friends and my enemies—a curse upon them all—that there
is anything in what she has done for me but duty, sir, but duty ? Or
do you think that my having been unfortunate is a sufficient reason
why our relative positions should be changed, and that she should command and I should obey ? Hint a wish, too ! Perhaps you think
because you see me in this place and scarcely able to leave this chair

without assistance, that I am some broken-spirited dependent creature, without the courage or power to do what I may think best for my own child. Still the power to hint a wish! I hope so!"

" Pardon me," returned Ralph, who thoroughly knew his man, and had taken his ground accordingly; "you do not hear me out. I was about to say, that your hinting a wish—even hinting a wish—would surely be equivalent to commanding."

" Why, of course it would," retorted Mr. Bray, in an exasperated tone. " If you don't happen to have heard of the time, sir, I tell you that there was a time, when I carried every point in triumph against her mother's whole family, although they had power and wealth on their side—by my will alone."

" Still," rejoined Ralph, as mildly as his nature would allow him, " you have not heard me out. You are a man yet qualified to shine in society, with many years of life before you—that is, if you lived in freer air, and under brighter skies, and chose your own companions. Gaiety is your element, you have shone in it before. Fashion and freedom for you. France, and an annuity that would support you there in luxury, would give you a new lease of life—transfer you to a new existence. The town rang with your expensive pleasures once, and you could blaze upon a new scene again, profiting by experience, and living a little at others' cost, instead of letting others live at yours. What is there on the reverse side of the picture? What is there? I don't know which is the nearest church-yard, but a gravestone there, wherever it is, and a date—perhaps two years hence, perhaps twenty. That's all."

Mr. Bray rested his elbow on the arm of his chair, and shaded his face with his hand.

" I speak plainly," said Ralph, sitting down beside him, " because I feel strongly. It's my interest that you should marry your daughter to my friend Gride, because then he sees me paid—in part, that is. I don't disguise it. I acknowledge it openly. But what interest have you in recommending her to such a step? Keep that in view. She might object, remonstrate, shed tears, talk of his being too old, and plead that her life would be rendered miserable. But what is it now?"

Several slight gestures on the part of the invalid, showed that these arguments were no more lost upon him, than the smallest iota of his demeanour was upon Ralph.

" What is it now, I say," pursued the wily usurer, " or what has it a chance of being? If you died, indeed, the people you hate would make her happy. But can you bear the thought of that?"

" No!" returned Bray, urged by a vindictive impulse he could not repress.

" I should imagine not, indeed!" said Ralph, quietly. " If she profits by anybody's death," this was said in a lower tone, " let it be by her husband's—don't let her have to look back to yours, as the event from which to date a happier life. Where is the objection? Let me hear it stated. What is it? That her suitor is an old man. Why, how often do men of family and fortune, who haven't your excuse, but have all the means and superfluities of life within their reach—how often do they marry their daughters to old men, or (worse still) to young men without heads or hearts, to tickle some idle ,vanity, strengthen some family interest, or secure some seat in Parliament! Judge for her, sir, judge for her. You must know best, and she will live to thank you."

"Hush! hush!" cried Mr. Bray, suddenly starting up, and covering Ralph's mouth with his trembling hand. " I hear her at the door!"

There was a gleam of conscience in the shame and terror of this hasty action, which, in one short moment, tore the thin covering of sophistry from the cruel design, and laid it bare in all its meanness and heartless deformity. The father fell into his chair pale and trembling; Arthur Gride plucked and fumbled at his hat, and durst not raise his eyes from the floor; even Ralph crouched for the moment like a beaten hound, cowed by the presence of one young innocent girl!

The effect was almost as brief as sudden. Ralph was the first to recover himself, and observing Madeline's looks of alarm, entreated the poor girl to be composed, assuring her that there was no cause for fear.

"A sudden spasm," said Ralph, glancing at Mr. Bray. "He is quite well now."

It might have moved a very hard and worldly heart to see the young and beautiful creature, whose certain misery they had been contriving but a minute before, throw her arms about her father's neck, and pour forth words of tender sympathy and love, the sweetest a father's ear can know, or child's lips form. But Ralph looked coldly on; and Arthur Gride, whose bleared eyes gloated only over the outward beauties, and were blind to the spirit which reigned within, evinced—a fantastic kind of warmth certainly, but not exactly that kind of warmth of feeling which the contemplation of virtue usually inspires.

"Madeline," said her father, gently disengaging himself, " it was nothing."

"But you had that spasm yesterday, and it is terrible to see you in such pain. Can I do nothing for you?"

"Nothing just now. Here are two gentlemen, Madeline, one of whom you have seen before. She used to say," added Mr. Bray, addressing Arthur Gride, "that the sight of you always made me worse. That was natural, knowing what she did, and only what she did, of our connexion and its results. Well, well. Perhaps she may change her mind on that point; girls have leave to change their minds, you know. You are very tired, my dear."

"I am not, indeed."

"Indeed you are. You do too much."

"I wish I could do more."

"I know you do, but you over-task your strength. This wretched life, my love, of daily labour and fatigue, is more than you can bear, I am sure it is. Poor Madeline!"

With these and many more kind words, Mr. Bray drew his daughter to him and kissed her cheek affectionately. Ralph, watching him sharply and closely in the mean time, made his way towards the door, and signed to Gride to follow him.

" You will communicate with us again ?" said Ralph.

" Yes, yes," returned Mr. Bray, hastily thrusting his daughter aside. " In a week. Give me a week."

" One week," said Ralph, turning to his companion, " from to-day. Good morning. Miss Madeline, I kiss your hand."

" We will shake hands, Gride," said Mr. Bray, extending his, as old Arthur bowed. " You mean well, no doubt. I am bound to say so now. If I owed you money, that was not your fault. Madeline, my love—your hand here."

" Oh dear ! If the young lady would condescend—only the tips of her fingers"—said Arthur, hesitating and half retreating.

Madeline shrunk involuntarily from the goblin figure, but she placed the tips of her fingers in his hand and instantly withdrew them. After an ineffectual clutch, intended to detain and carry them to his lips, old Arthur gave his own fingers a mumbling kiss, and with many amorous distortions of visage went in pursuit of his friend, who was by this time in the street.

" What does he say, what does he say—what does the giant say to the pigmy ?" inquired Arthur Gride, hobbling up to Ralph.

" What does the pigmy say to the giant ?" rejoined Ralph, elevating his eyebrows and looking down upon his questioner.

" He doesn't know what to say," replied Arthur Gride. " He hopes and fears. But is she not a dainty morsel ?"

" I have no great taste for beauty," growled Ralph.

" But I have," rejoined Arthur, rubbing his hands. " Oh dear ! How handsome her eyes looked when she was stooping over him— such long lashes—such delicate fringe ! She—she—looked at me so soft."

" Not over-lovingly, I think ?" said Ralph. " Did she ?"

" Do you think not ?" replied old Arthur. " But don't you think it can be brought about—don't you think it can ?"

Ralph looked at him with a contemptuous frown, and replied with a sneer, and between his teeth—

" Did you mark his telling her she was tired and did too much, and over-tasked her strength ?"

" Ay, ay. What of it ?"

" When do you think he ever told her that before ? The life is more than she can bear. Yes, yes. He'll change it for her."

" D'ye think it's done ?" inquired old Arthur, peering into his companion's face with half-closed eyes.

" I am sure it's done," said Ralph. " He is trying to deceive himself, even before our eyes, already—making believe that he thinks of her good and not his own—acting a virtuous part, and so considerate and affectionate, sir, that the daughter scarcely knew him. I saw a tear of surprise in her eye. There'll be a few more tears of surprise there before long, though of a different kind. Oh ! we may wait with confidence for this day week."

CHAPTER XLVIII.

BEING FOR THE BENEFIT OF MR. VINCENT CRUMMLES, AND POSITIVELY
HIS LAST APPEARANCE ON THIS STAGE.

It was with a very sad and heavy heart, oppressed by many painful
ideas, that Nicholas retraced his steps eastward and betook himself to
the counting-house of Cheeryble Brothers. Whatever the idle hopes
he had suffered himself to entertain, whatever the pleasant visions
which had sprung up in his mind and grouped themselves round the
fair image of Madeline Bray, they were now dispelled, and not a vestige
of their gaiety and brightness remained.

It would be a poor compliment to Nicholas's better nature, and one
which he was very far from deserving, to insinuate that the solution,
and such a solution, of the mystery which had seemed to surround
Madeline Bray, when he was ignorant even of her name, had damped his
ardour or cooled the fervour of his admiration. If he had regarded her
before, with such a passion as young men attracted by mere beauty
and elegance may entertain, he was now conscious of much deeper and
stronger feelings. But, reverence for the truth and purity of her heart,
respect for the helplessness and loneliness of her situation, sympathy
with the trials of one so young and fair, and admiration of her great
and noble spirit, all seemed to raise her far above his reach, and, while
they imparted new depth and dignity to his love, to whisper that it
was hopeless.

" I will keep my word, as I have pledged it to her," said Nicholas,
manfully. " This is no common trust that I have to discharge, and I
will perform the double duty that is imposed upon me most scrupulously and strictly. My secret feelings deserve no consideration in
such a case as this, and they shall have none."

Still, there were the secret feelings in existence just the same, and in
secret Nicholas rather encouraged them than otherwise; reasoning (if
he reasoned at all) that there they could do no harm to anybody but
himself, and that if he kept them to himself from a sense of duty, he
had an additional right to entertain himself with them as a reward for
his heroism.

All these thoughts, coupled with what he had seen that morning
and the anticipation of his next visit, rendered him a very dull
and abstracted companion; so much so, indeed, that Tim Linkinwater
suspected he must have made the mistake of a figure somewhere, which
was preying upon his mind, and seriously conjured him, if such were
the case, to make a clean breast and scratch it out, rather than have
his whole life embittered by the tortures of remorse.

But in reply to these considerate representations, and many others
both from Tim and Mr. Frank, Nicholas could only be brought to
state that he was never merrier in his life; and so went on all day, and
so went towards home at night, still turning over and over again the

same subjects, thinking over and over again the same things, and arriving over and over again at the same conclusions.

In this pensive, wayward, and uncertain state, people are apt to lounge and loiter without knowing why, to read placards on the walls with great attention and without the smallest idea of one word of their contents, and to stare most earnestly through shop-windows at things which they don't see. It was thus that Nicholas found himself poring with the utmost interest over a large play-bill hanging outside a Minor Theatre which he had to pass on his way home, and reading a list of the actors and actresses who had promised to do honour to some approaching benefit, with as much gravity as if it had been a catalogue of the names of those ladies and gentlemen who stood highest upon the Book of Fate, and he had been looking anxiously for his own. He glanced at the top of the bill, with a smile at his own dulness, as he prepared to resume his walk, and there saw announced, in large letters with a large space between each of them, " Positively the last appearance of Mr. Vincent Crummles of Provincial Celebrity !!!"

" Nonsense !" said Nicholas, turning back again. " It can't be."

But there it was. In one line by itself was an announcement of the first night of a new melo-drama ; in another line by itself was an announcement of the last six nights of an old one; a third line was devoted to the re-engagement of the unrivalled African Knife-swallower, who had kindly suffered himself to be prevailed upon to forego his country engagements for one week longer ; a fourth line announced that Mr. Snittle Timberry, having recovered from his late severe indisposition, would have the honour of appearing that evening ; a fifth line said that there were " Cheers, Tears, and Laughter !" every night ; a sixth, that that was positively the last appearance of Mr. Vincent Crummles of Provincial Celebrity.

" Surely it must be the same man," thought Nicholas. " There can't be two Vincent Crummleses."

The better to settle this question he referred to the bill again, and finding that there was a Baron in the first piece, and that Roberto (his son) was enacted by one Master Crummles, and Spaletro (his nephew) by one Master Percy Crummles—*their* last appearances—and that, incidental to the piece, was a characteristic dance by the characters, and a castanet pas seul by the Infant Phenomenon—*her* last appearance— he no longer entertained any doubt ; and presenting himself at the stage door, and sending in a scrap of paper with " Mr. Johnson " written thereon in pencil, was presently conducted by a Robber, with a very large belt and buckle round his waist, and very large leather gauntlets on his hands, into the presence of his former manager.

Mr. Crummles was unfeignedly glad to see him, and starting up from before a small dressing-glass, with one very bushy eyebrow stuck on crooked over his left eye, and the fellow eyebrow and the calf of one of his legs in his hand, embraced him cordially; at the same time observing, that it would do Mrs. Crummles's heart good to bid him good-bye before they went.

" You were always a favourite of hers, Johnson," said Crummles, "always were from the first. I was quite easy in my mind about you from that first day you dined with us. One that Mrs. Crummles took a fancy to, was sure to turn out right. Ah! Johnson, what a woman that is!"

"I am sincerely obliged to her for her kindness in this and all other respects," said Nicholas. "But where are you going, that you talk about bidding good-bye?"

"Haven't you seen it in the papers?" said Crummles, with some dignity.

"No," replied Nicholas.

"I wonder at that," said the manager. "It was among the varieties. I had the paragraph here somewhere—but I don't know—oh, yes, here it is."

So saying, Mr. Crummles, after pretending that he thought he must have lost it, produced a square inch of newspaper from the pocket of the pantaloons he wore in private life (which, together with the plain clothes of several other gentlemen, lay scattered about on a kind of dresser in the room), and gave it to Nicholas to read:—

"The talented Vincent Crummles, long favourably known to fame as a country manager and actor of no ordinary pretensions, is about to cross the Atlantic on a histrionic expedition. Crummles is to be accompanied, we hear, by his lady and gifted family. We know no man superior to Crummles in his particular line of character, or one who, whether as a public or private individual, could carry with him the best wishes of a larger circle of friends. Crummles is certain to succeed."

"Here's another bit," said Mr. Crummles, handing over a still smaller scrap. "This is from the notices to correspondents, this one."

Nicholas read it aloud. "'Philo Dramaticus.—Crummles, the country manager and actor, cannot be more than forty-three, or forty-four years of age. Crummles is NOT a Prussian, having been born at Chelsea.' Humph!" said Nicholas, "that's an odd paragraph."

"Very," returned Crummles, scratching the side of his nose, and looking at Nicholas with an assumption of great unconcern. "I can't think who puts these things in. _I_ didn't."

Still keeping his eye on Nicholas, Mr. Crummles shook his head twice or thrice with profound gravity, and remarking, that he could not for the life of him imagine how the newspapers found out the things they did, folded up the extracts and put them in his pocket again.

"I am astonished to hear this news," said Nicholas. "Going to America! You had no such thing in contemplation when I was with you."

"No," replied Crummles, "I hadn't then. The fact is, that Mrs. Crummles—most extraordinary woman, Johnson"—here he broke off and whispered something in his ear.

"Oh!" said Nicholas, smiling. "The prospect of an addition to your family?"

"The seventh addition, Johnson," returned Mr. Crummles, solemnly. "I thought such a child as the Phenomenon must have been a closer;

but it seems we are to have another. She is a very remarkable woman."

" I congratulate you," said Nicholas, " and I hope this may prove a phenomenon too."

" Why, it's pretty sure to be something uncommon, I suppose," rejoined Mr. Crummles. " The talent of the other three is principally in combat and serious pantomime. I should like this one to have a turn for juvenile tragedy ; I understand they want something of that sort in America very much. However, we must take it as it comes. Perhaps it may have a genius for the tight-rope. It may have any sort of genius, in short, if it takes after its mother, Johnson, for she is an universal genius ; but, whatever its genius is, that genius shall be developed."

Expressing himself after these terms, Mr. Crummles put on his other eyebrow, and the calves of his legs, and then put on his legs, which were of a yellowish flesh-colour, and rather soiled about the knees, from frequent going down upon those joints, in curses, prayers, last struggles, and other strong passages.

While the ex-manager completed his toilet, he informed Nicholas that as he should have a fair start in America, from the proceeds of a tolerably good engagement which he had been fortunate enough to obtain, and as he and Mrs. Crummles could scarcely hope to act for ever—not being immortal, except in the breath of Fame and in a figurative sense—he had made up his mind to settle there permanently, in the hope of acquiring some land of his own which would support them in their old age, and which they could afterwards bequeath to their children. Nicholas, having highly commended this resolution, Mr. Crummles went on to impart such further intelligence relative to their mutual friends as he thought might prove interesting ; informing Nicholas, among other things, that Miss Snevellici was happily married to an affluent young wax-chandler who had supplied the theatre with candles, and that Mr. Lillyvick didn't dare to say his soul was his own, such was the tyrannical sway of Mrs. Lillyvick, who reigned paramount and supreme.

Nicholas responded to this confidence on the part of Mr. Crummles, by confiding to him his own name, situation, and prospects, and informing him in as few general words as he could, of the circumstances which had led to their first acquaintance. After congratulating him with great heartiness on the improved state of his fortunes, Mr. Crummles gave him to understand that next morning he and his were to start for Liverpool, where the vessel lay which was to carry them from the shores of England, and that if Nicholas wished to take a last adieu of Mrs. Crummles, he must repair with him that night to a farewell-supper, given in honour of the family at a neighbouring tavern ; at which Mr. Snittle Timberry would preside, while the honours of the vice chair would be sustained by the African Swallower.

The room being by this time very warm and somewhat crowded, in consequence of the influx of four gentlemen, who had just killed each other in the piece under representation, Nicholas accepted the invitation, and promised to return at the conclusion of the performances ; preferring the cool air and twilight out of doors to the mingled perfume of gas, orange-peel, and gunpowder, which pervaded the hot and glaring theatre.

He availed himself of this interval to buy a silver snuff-box—the best his funds would afford—as a token of remembrance for Mr. Crummles, and having purchased besides a pair of ear-rings for Mrs. Crummles, a necklace for the Phenomenon, and a flaming shirt-pin for each of the young gentlemen, he refreshed himself with a walk, and returning a little after the appointed time, found the lights out, the theatre empty, the curtain raised for the night, and Mr. Crummles walking up and down the stage expecting his arrival.

" Timberry won't be long," said Mr. Crummles. " He played the audience out to-night. He does a faithful black in the last piece, and it takes him a little longer to wash himself."

" A very unpleasant line of character, I should think ? " said Nicholas.

" No, I don't know," replied Mr. Crummles ; " it comes off easily enough, and there's only the face and neck. We had a first-tragedy man in our company once, who, when he played Othello, used to black himself all over. But that's feeling a part and going into it as if you meant it ; it isn't usual—more's the pity."

Mr. Snittle Timberry now appeared, arm in arm with the African Swallower, and, being introduced to Nicholas, raised his hat half-a-foot, and said he was proud to know him. The Swallower said the same, and looked and spoke remarkably like an Irishman.

" I see by the bills that you have been ill, sir," said Nicholas to Mr. Timberry. " I hope you are none the worse for your exertions to-night ? "

Mr. Timberry in reply, shook his head with a gloomy air, tapped his chest several times with great significancy, and drawing his cloak more closely about him, said, " But no matter—no matter. Come ! "

It is observable that when people upon the stage are in any strait involving the very last extremity of weakness and exhaustion, they invariably perform feats of strength requiring great ingenuity and muscular power. Thus, a wounded prince or bandit-chief, who is bleeding to death and too faint to move, except to the softest music (and then only upon his hands and knees), shall be seen to approach a cottage door for aid, in such a series of writhings and twistings, and with such curlings up of the legs, and such rollings over and over, and such gettings up and tumblings down again, as could never be achieved save by a very strong man skilled in posture-making. And so natural did this sort of performance come to Mr. Snittle Timberry, that on their way out of the theatre and towards the tavern where the supper was to be holden, he testified the severity of his recent indisposition and its wasting effects upon the nervous system, by a series of gymnastic per- formances, which were the admiration of all witnesses.

" Why this is indeed a joy I had not looked for ! " said Mrs. Crummles, when Nicholas was presented.

"Nor I," replied Nicholas. "It is by a mere chance that I have this opportunity of seeing you, although I would have made a great exertion to have availed myself of it."

"Here is one whom you know," said Mrs. Crummles, thrusting forward the Phenomenon in a blue gauze frock, extensively flounced, and trowsers of the same; "and here another—and another," presenting the Masters Crummleses. "And how is your friend, the faithful Digby?"

"Digby!" said Nicholas, forgetting at the instant that this had been Smike's theatrical name. "Oh yes. He's quite—what am I saying? —he is very far from well."

"How!" exclaimed Mrs. Crummles, with a tragic recoil.

"I fear," said Nicholas, shaking his head, and making an attempt to smile, "that your better-half would be more struck with him now, than ever."

"What mean you?" rejoined Mrs. Crummles, in her most popular manner. "Whence comes this altered tone?"

"I mean that a dastardly enemy of mine has struck at me through him, and that while he thinks to torture me, he inflicts on him such agonies of terror and suspense as——You will excuse me, I am sure," said Nicholas, checking himself. "I should never speak of this, and never do, except to those who know the facts, but for a moment I forgot myself."

With this hasty apology, Nicholas stooped down to salute the Phenomenon, and changed the subject; inwardly cursing his precipitation, and very much wondering what Mrs. Crummles must think of so sudden an explosion.

That lady seemed to think very little about it, for the supper being by this time on table, she gave her hand to Nicholas and repaired with a stately step to the left hand of Mr. Snittle Timberry. Nicholas had the honour to support her, and Mr. Crummles was placed upon the chairman's right; the Phenomenon and the Masters Crummleses sustained the vice.

The company amounted in number to some twenty-five or thirty, being composed of such members of the theatrical profession, then engaged or disengaged in London, as were numbered among the most intimate friends of Mr. and Mrs. Crummles. The ladies and gentlemen were pretty equally balanced; the expenses of the entertainment being defrayed by the latter, each of whom had the privilege of inviting one of the former as his guest.

It was upon the whole a very distinguished party, for independently of the lesser theatrical lights who clustered on this occasion round Mr. Snittle Timberry, there was a literary gentleman present who had dramatised in his time two hundred and forty-seven novels as fast as they had come out—some of them faster than they had come out— and *was* a literary gentleman in consequence.

This gentleman sat on the left hand of Nicholas, to whom he was introduced by his friend the African Swallower, from the bottom of the table, with a high eulogium upon his fame and reputation.

" I am happy to know a gentleman of such great distinction," said Nicholas, politely.

" Sir," replied the wit, " you're very welcome, I'm sure. The honour is reciprocal, sir, as I usually say when I dramatise a book. Did you ever hear a definition of fame, sir ?"

" I have heard several," replied Nicholas, with a smile. " What is yours?"

" When I dramatise a book, sir," said the literary gentleman, " *that's* fame—for its author."

" Oh, indeed !" rejoined Nicholas.

" That's fame, sir," said the literary gentleman.

" So Richard Turpin, Tom King, and Jerry Abershaw, have handed down to fame the names of those on whom they committed their most impudent robberies ?" said Nicholas.

" I don't know anything about that, sir," answered the literary gentleman.

" Shakspeare dramatised stories which had previously appeared in print, it is true," observed Nicholas.

" Meaning Bill, sir ?" said the literary gentleman. " So he did. Bill was an adapter, certainly, so he was—and very well he adapted too—— considering."

" I was about to say," rejoined Nicholas, " that Shakspeare derived some of his plots from old tales and legends in general circulation ; but it seems to me, that some of the gentlemen of your craft at the present day, have shot very far beyond him—"

" You're quite right, sir," interrupted the literary gentleman, leaning back in his chair and exercising his toothpick. " Human intellect, sir, has progressed since his time—is progressing—will progress—"

" Shot beyond him, I mean," resumed Nicholas, " in quite another respect, for, whereas he brought within the magic circle of his genius, traditions peculiarly adapted for his purpose, and turned familiar things into constellations which should enlighten the world for ages, you drag within the magic circle of your dulness, subjects not at all adapted to the purposes of the stage, and debase as he exalted. For instance, you take the uncompleted books of living authors, fresh from their hands, wet from the press, cut, hack, and carve them to the powers and capacities of your actors, and the capability of your theatres, finish unfinished works, hastily and crudely vamp up ideas not yet worked out by their original projector, but which have doubtless cost him many thoughtful days and sleepless nights ; by a comparison of incidents and dialogue, down to the very last word he may have written a fortnight before, do your utmost to anticipate his plot—all this without his permission, and against his will ; and then, to crown the whole proceeding, publish in some mean pamphlet, an unmeaning farrago of garbled extracts from his work, to which you put your name as author, with the honourable distinction annexed, of having perpetrated a hundred other outrages of the same description. Now, show me the distinction between such pilfering as this, and picking a man's pocket in the street : unless, indeed, it be, that the legislature has a regard for pocket handkerchiefs, and leaves men's brains, except when they are knocked out by violence, to take care of themselves."

"Men must live, sir," said the literary gentleman, shrugging his shoulders.

"That would be an equally fair plea in both cases," replied Nicholas; "but if you put it upon that ground, I have nothing more to say, than, that if I were a writer of books, and you a thirsty dramatist, I would rather pay your tavern score for six months—large as it might be—than have a niche in the Temple of Fame with you for the humblest corner of my pedestal, through six hundred generations."

The conversation threatened to take a somewhat angry tone when it had arrived thus far, but Mrs. Crummles opportunely interposed to prevent its leading to any violent outbreak, by making some inquiries of the literary gentleman relative to the plots of the six new pieces which he had written by contract to introduce the African Knife-swallower in his various unrivalled performances. This speedily engaged him in an animated conversation with that lady, in the interest of which, all recollection of his recent discussion with Nicholas very quickly evaporated.

The board being now clear of the more substantial articles of food, and punch, wine, and spirits being placed upon it and handed about, the guests, who had been previously conversing in little groups of three or four, gradually fell off into a dead silence, while the majority of those present, glanced from time to time at Mr. Snittle Timberry, and the bolder spirits did not even hesitate to strike the table with their knuckles, and plainly intimate their expectations, by uttering such encouragements as "Now, Tim," "Wake up, Mr. Chairman," "All charged, sir, and waiting for a toast," and so forth.

To these remonstrances, Mr. Timberry deigned no other rejoinder than striking his chest and gasping for breath, and giving many other indications of being still the victim of indisposition—for a man must not make himself too cheap either on the stage or off—while Mr. Crummles, who knew full well that he would be the subject of the forthcoming toast, sat gracefully in his chair with his arm thrown carelessly over the back, and now and then lifted his glass to his mouth and drank a little punch, with the same air with which he was accustomed to take long draughts of nothing, out of the pasteboard goblets in banquet scenes.

At length Mr. Snittle Timberry rose in the most approved attitude, with one hand in the breast of his waistcoat and the other on the nearest snuff-box, and having been received with great enthusiasm, proposed, with abundance of quotations, his friend Mr. Vincent Crummles: ending a pretty long speech by extending his right hand on one side and his left on the other, and severally calling upon Mr. and Mrs. Crummles to grasp the same. This done, Mr. Vincent Crummles returned thanks, and that done, the African Swallower proposed Mrs. Vincent Crummles, in affecting terms. Then were heard loud moans and sobs from Mrs. Crummles and the ladies, despite of which that heroic woman insisted upon returning thanks herself, which she did, in a manner and in a speech which has never been surpassed and seldom equalled. It then became the duty of Mr. Snittle Timberry to give the young Crummleses, which he did; after which Mr. Vincent Crummles, as their father, addressed the company in a supplementary speech, enlarging on their virtues, amiabilities, and excellences, and wishing that they were the sons and daughter of every lady and gentleman present. These solemnities having been succeeded by a decent interval, enlivened by musical and other entertainments, Mr. Crummles proposed that ornament of the profession, Mr. Snittle Timberry ; and at a little later period of the evening, the health of that other ornament of the profession, the African Swallower—his very dear friend, if he would allow him to call him so ; which liberty (there being no particular reason why he should not allow it) the African Swallower graciously permitted. The literary gentleman was then about to be drunk, but it being discovered that he had been drunk for some time in another acceptation of the term, and was then asleep on the stairs, the intention was abandoned, and the honour transferred to the ladies. Finally, after a very long sitting, Mr. Snittle Timberry vacated the chair, and the company with many adieus and embraces dispersed.

Nicholas waited to the last to give his little presents. When he had said good-bye all round and came to Mr. Crummles, he could not but mark the difference between their present separation and their parting at Portsmouth. Not a jot of his theatrical manner remained ; he put out his hand with an air which, if he could have summoned it at will, would have made him the best actor of his day in homely parts, and when Nicholas shook it with the warmth he honestly felt, appeared thoroughly melted.

" We were a very happy little company, Johnson," said poor Crummles. " You and I never had a word. I shall be very glad to-morrow morning to think that I saw you again, but now I almost wish you hadn't come."

Nicholas was about to return a cheerful reply, when he was greatly disconcerted by the sudden apparition of Mrs. Grudden, who it seemed had declined to attend the supper in order that she might rise earlier in the morning, and who now burst out of an adjoining bedroom, habited in very extraordinary white robes : and throwing her arms about his neck, hugged him with great affection.

" What ! Are you going too ?" said Nicholas, submitting with as good a grace as if she had been the finest young creature in the world.

" Going ?" returned Mrs. Grudden. " Lord ha' mercy, what do you think they'd do without me ?"

Nicholas submitted to another hug with even a better grace than before, if that were possible, and waving his hat as cheerfully as he could, took farewell of the Vincent Crummleses.

MR. ADOLPHUS'S
HISTORY OF ENGLAND.

Three volumes of this work, comprising the reign of George the third, from its commencement, to the termination of the American war, appeared in 1802, and in 1817, a fourth edition was published. To the merits of this work, the public, in purchasing four large editions, and most distinguished persons of all ranks, bore ample testimony.

The author always had it sincerely at heart, to continue the narrative to the end of the reign, and has now prepared his work for publication. The momentous events which occurred, and the striking personages who have appeared in that, perhaps, the most extraordinary period in the annals of man, have required thought and laborious investigation. The acts of the brave, the deliberations of the wise, the rashness of pretenders, the guilt of traitors, have taken their turns in rapid succession, and results have been produced, such as no antecedent history, of a similar period, can equal

Mr. Adolphus is now enabled to propose the republication of the three earlier volumes, with many important corrections and additions, and a continuation to the conclusion of the reign of George the third.

This entire work will form eight octavo volumes of larger contents than those which have already appeared.

The author omits making any professions as to the manner in which this History will be written. On the first three volumes, the favorable opinion of all classes has been pronounced; the same, or even greater industry, has been used in collecting and arranging materials for the improvement of those volumes, and the composition of the remainder; and the same candour and impartiality, which are admitted to be the characteristics of those volumes, have been earnestly and faithfully maintained in the continuation.

It has been proposed to publish this work by subscription, at five pounds for the whole, to be paid in advance; and to that form, very liberal aid has been afforded by the Royal Family, by members of both houses of parliament, by Judges, and eminent persons in the legal profession, by the clergy, and by gentlemen of high respectability in other stations in life. It is still proposed to receive names on that footing; and others, who prefer such a mode, may subscribe at fourteen shillings a volume, to be paid on delivery.

Subscriptions, with addresses, are received by Mr. John Lee, Bookseller, No. 440, West Strand, where a list of subscribers may be seen.

John Such, Printer, 9, Dove Court, King William Street, City, London.

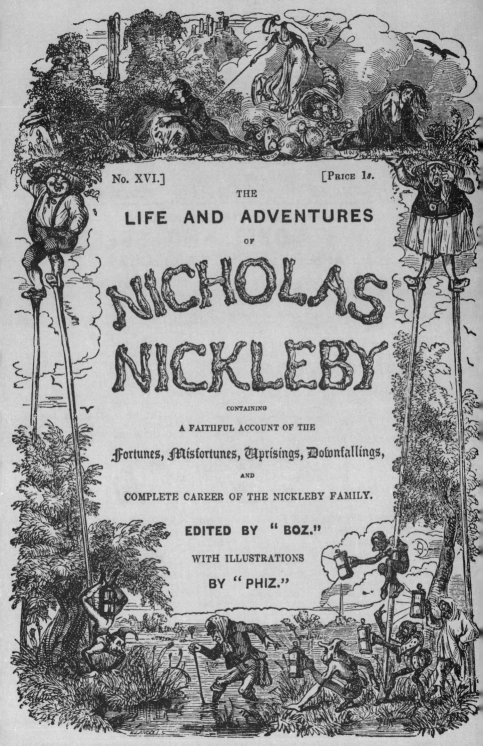

No. XVI.]   [Price 1s.

THE

LIFE AND ADVENTURES

OF

NICHOLAS NICKLEBY

CONTAINING

A FAITHFUL ACCOUNT OF THE

Fortunes, Misfortunes, Uprisings, Downfallings,

AND

COMPLETE CAREER OF THE NICKLEBY FAMILY.

EDITED BY "BOZ."

WITH ILLUSTRATIONS

BY "PHIZ."

LONDON: CHAPMAN AND HALL, 186, STRAND.

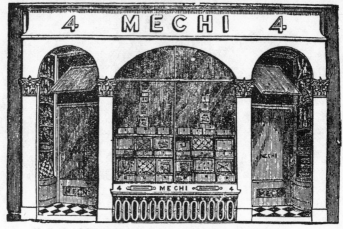
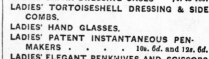

MAXWELL'S LIFE OF WELLINGTON.

Now ready, Part II. of the

LIFE OF HIS GRACE FIELD-MARSHAL THE DUKE OF WELLINGTON, K.G. &c. &c.

BY THE

AUTHOR OF "STORIES OF WATERLOO," "BIVOUAC," "VICTORIES OF THE BRITISH ARMY," &c.

Part II. will be beautifully embellished by

A PORTRAIT OF THE "MARQUIS WELLESLEY," by SIR THOMAS LAWRENCE, engraved on Steel expressly for the Work.

"COLONEL MAXWELL'S LAST CHARGE AT ASSYE," from an Original Painting, by A. COOPER, R.A.

A MAP OF THE "SEAT OF WAR IN INDIA."

COLOURED PLANS OF THE "BATTLES OF ASSYE AND ARGAUM."

And a number of beautiful Wood Engravings, illustrative of Oriental and European Warfare.

London: A. H. BAILY and Co., 83, Cornhill.

NEARLY ready, A *THIRD* PREFACE to a book advertised by Messrs. CHARLES KNIGHT & Co., under the fallacious title of "A TREATISE ON WOOD ENGRAVING, HISTORICAL AND PRACTICAL; with upwards of 300 Illustrations, engraved on wood, by JOHN JACKSON;" giving an account of Mr. Jackson's *actual* share in the Composition and Illustration of that work, and restoring the passages suppressed by Mr. Knight. With remarks on LITERARY AND ARTISTIC *Conveyance.* In a Letter to STEPHEN OLIVER,

By WM. A. CHATTO, Author of the Historical Portion of the Work, comprising the first Seven Chapters, and the *Writer* of the whole, as originally printed.

"Convey, the wise call it."—MERRY WIVES OF WINDSOR, Act I., Scene 3.

"——— When the ayerie traine
Their well-knowne plumes shall challenge back againe,
The naked daw a general game shall be,
Spoiled of his grace and pilfered braverie."—HIVE OF HONIE COMBES, 1631.

Preparing for immediate publication, In Monthly Parts (each containing Two splendid Maps on super-royal 4to, executed in the first style of art), price only 1*s.* plain, or 1*s.* 6*d.* coloured,

GILBERT'S MODERN ATLAS;

GEOGRAPHICAL, HISTORICAL, COMMERCIAL, AND DESCRIPTIVE;

WITH

COPIOUS AND ORIGINAL DESCRIPTIVE LETTER-PRESS, BY HENRY INCE, M.A.

The Proprietor is determined this shall be the best and cheapest Atlas ever published; that it shall form an important accession to the desk of the counting-house, the library of the student, and an ornament to the fashionable boudoir. To be completed in Twenty-five Parts, containing 50 steel-plate Maps, engraved expressly for this Work, and about 300 pages of letter-press.

GRATTAN and GILBERT, 51, Paternoster Row.

SMEATON'S Superior Theory of Toothed Wheel-works;

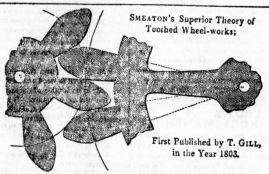

First Published by T. GILL, in the Year 1803.

Just published, in 1 vol. 8vo, price 5*s.* in boards,

GILL'S MACHINERY IMPROVED,

ITS FRICTION REDUCED, ITS POWERS INCREASED, & ITS DURABILITY PROMOTED.

This work, the publication of which has been unavoidably delayed, in order to receive valuable Improvements and Additions, and which is copiously illustrated by numerous Figures, engraved upon steel, copper, and wood, will be found chiefly to treat upon, and to give the favourable results of fifty years' experience, in large Mill-works, constructed upon SMEATON's improved plans of Toothed Wheel-works, and in the Pivots and their Bearings. It will form the first volume of a series of Thirty Scientific Treatises, all at 5*s.* each—which will be published, as completed, by THOMAS GILL, Confidential Consulting and Advising Engineer, and Patent Solicitor, at his Patent Soliciting and Publishing Offices No. 125, Central Strand, opposite to the Lyceum Theatre, London: and sold by all the principal Booksellers, Newsmen, and Manufacturers of Engines, Lathes, Tools, Optical and Philosophical Instrument-makers, &c., in this and foreign countries.

IMPORTANT CASE.

MR. JAMES MORISON,

PRESIDENT OF THE BRITISH COLLEGE OF HEALTH, NEW ROAD,

Begs to lay before the Public the following important case of Scrofula, forwarded to him by Mrs. Beanham, his Agent for Dorset and Somerset, and which is attested by the Rev. C. W. H. Evered, Rector of Exton.

Crewkerne, May 30th, 1839.

Sir,—I have much pleasure in forwarding to you, for publication, at the express wish of the undersigned, the following most extraordinary proof of the efficacy of your medicines, in the cure of a case of Scrofula, which, under the usual treatment being deemed incurable, had defied all probability of ever being eradicated.

I beg to observe that the writer, Henry Howe, is an entire stranger to me, that he has sent me this, his own statement, quite unsolicited, written and signed by himself, and as it is attested by the resident Clergyman of the Village, I humbly presume that its authenticity cannot and will not be doubted.

I remain, Sir, yours, ever faithfully,   HARRIET BEANHAM.

HENRY HOWE'S STATEMENT OF HIS OWN CASE.

I first had a swelling in my side, in the latter part of February, 1830, and applied to Dr. Welbank, of London, whose prescriptions I took many weeks, and in the month of June following he lanced my side and thumb. I left London July 1st, and came home to Orchard, when I drank, as I was ordered, sassafras, sarsaparilla, and root liquorice, during a long time; after which I drank dandelion and dock roots several weeks. In August I removed to Halscombe, where I took medicines six or seven weeks, which were prescribed to me by Mr. Collins. In the latter part of September I returned to Orchard, and finding myself no better was induced to try Dr. Green's Drops, and consulted Mr. Titticutt, who put a seton into my knee; this was a little before Christmas. After suffering a long time, I was persuaded to try Mr. Churchill's Medicines, and applied his Ointment to my wounds sixteen weeks. Finding no benefit, I applied to Dr. Chorley, and took his prescriptions,—March 10th, 1831, came home to Halscombe, and was ordered to drink lime water, and apply fresh butter to my wounds. After trying this in vain, I consulted Dr. Baker, taking his prescriptions, and applying mercurial ointment to my wounds, with lotions and herb poultices to the swellings. My increased sufferings led me to apply again to Dr. Collins and Dr. Sully; I took their prescriptions ten weeks, applying poultices, Poor Man's Friend, and caustic, to the wounds, but without any benefit. Afterwards had recourse again to Dr. Green's Drops, with poultices and Poor Man's Friend, but these and many other remedies were all in vain. I despaired of ever finding relief from my sufferings, when at Christmas, 1832, MORISON'S UNIVERSAL MEDICINES were recommended to me, and I took them in doses from four to twenty-two pills each day—after taking them about three weeks my pains were greatly abated, and I was enabled to turn in my bed and change from side to side, which I had not been able to do during twenty months before, from the dreadful state of my wounds. By continuing these Pills every day during twelve months, I was able to get up and walk about with my crutches—a blessing which it was never expected I should enjoy—I had tried every Doctor within many miles, and it cost me scores of pounds to no good purpose—they all said no medicine could do me any good. I do believe if I had known these UNIVERSAL MEDICINES a year and a half before, I should never have been a cripple; but I am thankful to God that I now know them, and that I have experienced such unexpected good from his medicines. I am bound in gratitude to Mr. Morison to make this as public as possible.

I well know that a person must not be afraid to take any number of these Pills, the more they take, in such a case as mine, the more good they will do. They have not cost me £5 during the time I have taken them. I am now without any pain, have a good appetite, and sleep well, being in the enjoyment of perfect health, and have been for the last eighteen months. All my wounds are healed, but the scars can testify what I have suffered—these still remain, but I need neither crutch nor stick, and am able to work in my garden, and at my various employments. I send this to Mrs. Beanham, General Agent for Somerset and Dorset, and request her to publish it for the good of the afflicted.

Witness my hand,   (Signed)   HENRY HOWE,
                                     Landlord of the Rock Inn, Exton, Somerset.

Witnessed by
The Rev. C. W. H. EVERED, Rector of Exton.
And by JAMES YOUNG.

April 24th, 1839.

CAUTION.

BEWARE OF COUNTERFEITS.—See that the words "MORISON'S UNIVERSAL MEDICINES" be engraved on the Government Stamp, in white letters upon a red ground, without which, none can be genuine.

BEAUFOY AND Co., SOUTH LAMBETH, LONDON.

BEAUFOY'S INSTANT CURE

FOR THE

TOOTHACHE.

THE GENUINE PACKAGES CONTAIN
A FAC-SIMILE
OF ONE OR THE OTHER OF THESE
VIGNETTES.

SOLD BY MOST RESPECTABLE DRUGGISTS, WITH AMPLE DIRECTIONS FOR USE,
In Bottles, Price 1s. 1½d each. Stamp included.

BEAUFOY AND CO., SOUTH LAMBETH, LONDON.

TRUE ECONOMY

Is best consulted by an inspection of the Elegant and Extensive Stock at the Establishment of

THOMAS FOX,

UPHOLDER BY APPOINTMENT

93, BISHOPSGATE STREET WITHIN,

which in combination of quality and price cannot be excelled.

BISHOPSGATE PLATE GLASS WAREHOUSE.

The late scientific improvements in the manufacture of PLATE GLASS, now enables all parties to embellish with this splendid article of internal and external decoration; and from its greatly improved quality and considerable reduction in cost, will be found, for Windows, Conservatories, &c., a most elegant substitute for the Glass in general use, and comparatively more economical.

HANDSOME COTTAGE CHIMNEY GLASSES
From £5. upwards.

ELEGANT LOOKING GLASSES

For the Drawing or Dining Room, the Boudoir, &c., with richly-ornamented Gold Frames; also CHEVAL and TOILET GLASSES, in every variety.

In consequence of the increasing demand at this Establishment for

STAINED AND ORNAMENTAL GLASS,

Rich specimens in every style are now exhibited, and by the recent engagement of the first Artists in the Trade, works of any magnitude can be executed with facility, at prices much below the usual charge.

BISHOPSGATE STREET WITHIN, LONDON.

LONDON : BRADBURY AND EVANS, PRINTERS, WHITEFRIARS.

CHAPTER XLIX.

CHRONICLES THE FURTHER PROCEEDINGS OF THE NICKLEBY FAMILY,
AND THE SEQUEL OF THE ADVENTURE OF THE GENTLEMAN IN THE
SMALL-CLOTHES.

WHILE Nicholas, absorbed in the one engrossing subject of interest
which had recently opened upon him, occupied his leisure hours with
thoughts of Madeline Bray, and, in execution of the commissions which
the anxiety of Brother Charles in her behalf imposed upon him, saw
her again and again, and each time with greater danger to his peace of
mind and a more weakening effect upon the lofty resolutions he had
formed, Mrs. Nickleby and Kate continued to live in peace and quiet,
agitated by no other cares than those which were connected with certain
harassing proceedings taken by Mr. Snawley for the recovery of his son,
and their anxiety for Smike himself, whose health, long upon the wane,
began to be so much affected by apprehension and uncertainty as sometimes to occasion both them and Nicholas considerable uneasiness, and
even alarm.

It was no complaint or murmur on the part of the poor fellow himself that thus disturbed them. Ever eager to be employed in such
slight services as he could render, and always anxious to repay his benefactors with cheerful and happy looks, less friendly eyes might have
seen in him no cause for any misgiving. But there were times—and
often too—when the sunken eye was too bright, the hollow cheek too
flushed, the breath too thick and heavy in its course, the frame too
feeble and exhausted, to escape their regard and notice.

There is a dread disease which so prepares its victim, as it were, for
death; which so refines it of its grosser aspect, and throws around
familiar looks unearthly indications of the coming change—a dread
disease, in which the struggle between soul and body is so gradual,
quiet, and solemn, and the result so sure, that day by day, and grain
by grain, the mortal part wastes and withers away, so that the spirit
grows light and sanguine with its lightening load and feeling immor-
tality at hand, deems it but a new term of mortal life—a disease in
which death and life are so strangely blended, that death takes the
glow and hue of life, and life the gaunt and grisly form of death—a
disease which medicine never cured, wealth warded off, or poverty could
boast exemption from—which sometimes moves in giant strides, and
sometimes at a tardy sluggish pace, but, slow or quick, is ever sure and
certain.

It was with some faint reference in his own mind to this disorder,
though he would by no means admit it, even to himself, that Nicholas
had already carried his faithful companion to a physician of great
repute. There was no cause for immediate alarm, he said. There

were no present symptoms which could be deemed conclusive. The constitution had been greatly tried and injured in childhood, but still it *might* not be—and that was all.

But he seemed to grow no worse, and as it was not difficult to find a reason for these symptoms of illness in the shock and agitation he had recently undergone, Nicholas comforted himself with the hope that his poor friend would soon recover. This hope his mother and sister shared with him ; and as the object of their joint solicitude seemed to have no uneasiness or despondency for himself, but each day answered with a quiet smile that he felt better than he had upon the day before, their fears abated, and the general happiness was by degrees restored.

Many and many a time in after years did Nicholas look back to this period of his life, and tread again the humble quiet homely scenes that rose up as of old before him. Many and many a time, in the twilight of a summer evening, or beside the flickering winter's fire—but not so often or so sadly then—would his thoughts wander back to these old days, and dwell with a pleasant sorrow upon every slight remembrance which they brought crowding home. The little room in which they had so often sat long after it was dark, figuring such happy futures—Kate's cheerful voice and merry laugh ; and how, if she were from home they used to sit and watch for her return, scarcely breaking silence but to say how dull it seemed without her—the glee with which poor Smike would start from the darkened corner where he used to sit, and hurry to admit her, and the tears they often saw upon his face, half wondering to see them too and he so pleased and happy—every little incident, and even slight words and looks of those old days, little heeded then, but well remembered when busy cares and trials were quite forgot, came fresh and thick before him many and many a time, and, rustling above the dusty growth of years, came back green boughs of yesterday.

But there were other persons associated with these recollections, and many changes came about before they had being—a necessary reflection for the purposes of these adventures, which at once subside into their accustomed train, and shunning all flighty anticipations or wayward wanderings, pursue their steady and decorous course.

If the Brothers Cheeryble, as they found Nicholas worthy of trust and confidence, bestowed upon him every day some new and substantial mark of kindness, they were not less mindful of those who depended on him. Various little presents to Mrs. Nickleby—always of the very things they most required—tended in no slight degree to the improvement and embellishment of the cottage. Kate's little store of trinkets became quite dazzling ; and for company——! If Brother Charles and Brother Ned failed to look in for at least a few minutes every Sunday, or one evening in the week, there was Mr. Tim Linkinwater (who had never made half-a-dozen other acquaintances in all his life, and who took such delight in his new friends as no words can express) constantly coming and going in his evening walks, and stopping to rest ; while Mr. Frank Cheeryble happened, by some strange conjunction of circumstances, to be passing the door on some business or other at least three nights in the week.

" He is the most attentive young man *I* ever saw, Kate," said Mrs. Nickleby to her daughter, one evening when this last-named gentleman had been the subject of the worthy lady's eulogium for some time, and Kate had sat perfectly silent.

" Attentive, mama!" rejoined Kate.

" Bless my heart, Kate!" cried Mrs. Nickleby, with her wonted suddenness, " what a colour you have got; why, you're quite flushed!"

" Oh, mama! what strange things you fancy."

" It wasn't fancy, Kate, my dear, I'm certain of that," returned her mother. " However, it's gone now at any rate, so it don't much matter whether it was or not. What was it we were talking about? Oh! Mr. Frank. I never saw such attention in *my* life, never."

" Surely you are not serious," returned Kate, colouring again; and this time beyond all dispute.

" Not serious!" returned Mrs. Nickleby; " why shouldn't I be serious? I'm sure I never was more serious. I will say that his politeness and attention to me is one of the most becoming, gratifying, pleasant things I have seen for a very long time. You don't often meet with such behaviour in young men, and it strikes one more when one does meet with it."

" Oh! attention to *you*, mama," rejoined Kate quickly—" oh yes."

" Dear me, Kate," retorted Mrs. Nickleby, " what an extraordinary girl you are. Was it likely I should be talking of his attention to anybody else? I declare I'm quite sorry to think he should be in love with a German lady, that I am."

" He said very positively that it was no such thing, mama," returned Kate. " Don't you remember his saying so that very first night he came here? Besides," she added, in a more gentle tone, " why should *we* be sorry if it is the case? What is it to us, mama?"

" Nothing to *us*, Kate, perhaps," said Mrs. Nickleby emphatically; " but something to *me*, I confess. I like English people to be thorough English people, and not half English and half I don't know what. I shall tell him point-blank next time he comes, that I wish he would marry one of his own countrywomen; and see what he says to that."

" Pray don't think of such a thing, mama," returned Kate hastily; " not for the world. Consider—how very——."

" Well, my dear, how very what!" said Mrs. Nickleby, opening her eyes in great astonishment.

Before Kate had returned any reply, a queer little double-knock announced that Miss La Creevy had called to see them; and when Miss La Creevy presented herself, Mrs. Nickleby, though strongly disposed to be argumentative on the previous question, forgot all about it in a gush of supposes about the coach she had come by; supposing that the man who drove must have been either the man in the shirt-sleeves or the man with the black eye; that whoever he was, he hadn't found that parasol she left inside last week; that no doubt they had stopped a long while at the Halfway House, coming down; or that perhaps being full, they had come straight on; and lastly, that they surely must have passed Nicholas on the road.

" I saw nothing of him," answered Miss La Creevy ; " but I saw that dear old soul Mr. Linkinwater."

" Taking his evening walk, and coming on to rest here before he turns back to the city, I'll be bound !" said Mrs. Nickleby.

" I should think he was," returned Miss La Creevy; " especially as young Mr. Cheeryble was with him."

" Surely that is no reason why Mr. Linkinwater should be coming here," said Kate.

" Why I think it is, my dear," said Miss La Creevy. " For a young man Mr. Frank is not a very great walker; and I observe that he generally falls tired, and requires a good long rest, when he has come as far as this. But where is my friend ?" said the little woman, looking about, after having glanced slyly at Kate. " He has not been run away with again, has he ? "

" Ah ! where is Mr. Smike ?" said Mrs. Nickleby ; " he was here this instant."

Upon further inquiry, it turned out, to the good lady's unbounded astonishment, that Smike had that moment gone up-stairs to bed.

" Well now," said Mrs. Nickleby, " he is the strangest creature ! Last Tuesday—was it Tuesday ? Yes to be sure it was ; you recollect, Kate, my dear, the very last time young Mr. Cheeryble was here—last Tuesday night he went off in just the same strange way, at the very moment the knock came to the door. It cannot be that he don't like company, because he is always fond of people who are fond of Nicholas, and I am sure young Mr. Cheeryble is. And the strangest thing is, that he does not go to bed ; therefore it cannot be because he is tired. I know he doesn't go to bed, because my room is the next one, and when I went up-stairs last Tuesday, hours after him, I found that he had not even taken his shoes off; and he had no candle, so he must have sat moping in the dark all the time. Now, upon my word," said Mrs. Nickleby, " when I come to think of it, that's very extraordinary!"

As the hearers did not echo this sentiment, but remained profoundly silent, either as not knowing what to say, or as being unwilling to interrupt, Mrs. Nickleby pursued the thread of her discourse after her own fashion.

" I hope," said that lady, " that this unaccountable conduct may not be the beginning of his taking to his bed and living there all his life, like the Thirsty Woman of Tutbury, or the Cock-lane Ghost, or some of those extraordinary creatures. One of them had some connexion with our family. I forget, without looking back to some old letters I have up-stairs, whether it was my great-grandfather who went to school with the Cock-lane ghost, or the Thirsty Woman of Tutbury who went to school with my grandmother. Miss La Creevy, you know, of course. Which was it that didn't mind what the clergyman said ? The Cock-lane Ghost or the Thirsty Woman of Tutbury ? "

" The Cock-lane Ghost, I believe."

" Then I have no doubt," said Mrs. Nickleby, " that it was with him my great-grandfather went to school ; for I know the master of his school was a dissenter, and that would in a great measure account for

the Cock-lane Ghost's behaving in such an improper manner to the
clergyman when he grew up. Ah! Train up a Ghost—child, I
mean——."

Any further reflections on this fruitful theme were abruptly cut short
by the arrival of Tim Linkinwater and Mr. Frank Cheeryble; in the
hurry of receiving whom, Mrs. Nickleby speedily lost sight of everything else.

"I am so sorry Nicholas is not at home," said Mrs. Nickleby.
"Kate, my dear, you must be both Nicholas and yourself."

"Miss Nickleby need be but herself," said Frank. "I—if I may
venture to say so—oppose all change in her."

"Then at all events she shall press you to stay," returned Mrs.
Nickleby. "Mr. Linkinwater says ten minutes, but I cannot let you
go so soon; Nicholas would be very much vexed, I am sure. Kate,
my dear ——."

In obedience to a great number of nods and winks and frowns of
extra significance, Kate added her entreaties that the visitors would
remain; but it was observable that she addressed them exclusively to
Tim Linkinwater; and there was, besides, a certain embarrassment in
her manner, which, although it was as far from impairing its graceful
character as the tinge it communicated to her cheek was from dimi-
nishing her beauty, was obvious at a glance even to Mrs. Nickleby. Not
being of a very speculative character, however, save under circumstances when her speculations could be put into words and uttered
aloud, that discreet matron attributed the emotion to the circumstance
of her daughter's not happening to have her best frock on—" though I
never saw her look better, certainly," she reflected at the same time.
Having settled the question in this way, and being most complacently
satisfied that in this, as in all other instances, her conjecture could not
fail to be the right one, Mrs. Nickleby dismissed it from her thoughts,
and inwardly congratulated herself on being so shrewd and knowing.

Nicholas did not come home, nor did Smike re-appear; but neither
circumstance, to say the truth, had any great effect upon the little
party, who were all in the best humour possible. Indeed, there sprung
up quite a flirtation between Miss La Creevy and Tim Linkinwater,
who said a thousand jocose and facetious things, and became, by degrees,
quite gallant, not to say tender. Little Miss La Creevy on her part was
in high spirits, and rallied Tim on having remained a bachelor all his
life, with so much success, that Tim was actually induced to declare,
that if he could get anybody to have him, he didn't know but
what he might change his condition even yet. Miss La Creevy
earnestly recommended a lady she knew who would exactly suit Mr.
Linkinwater, and had a very comfortable property of her own; but this
latter qualification had very little effect upon Tim, who manfully
protested that fortune would be no object with him, but that true worth
and cheerfulness of disposition were what a man should look for in a
wife, and that if he had these he could find money enough for the
moderate wants of both. This avowal was considered so honourable to
Tim, that neither Mrs. Nickleby nor Miss La Creevy could sufficiently
extol it; and stimulated by their praises, Tim launched out into several

other declarations also manifesting the disinterestedness of his heart, and a great devotion to the fair sex, which were received with no less approbation. This was done and said with a comical mixture of jest and earnest, and, leading to a great amount of laughter, made them very merry indeed.

Kate was commonly the life and soul of the conversation at home; but she was more silent than usual upon this occasion—perhaps because Tim and Miss La Creevy engrossed so much of it—and keeping aloof from the talkers, sat at the window watching the shadows as the evening closed in, and enjoying the quiet beauty of the night, which seemed to have scarcely less attractions for Frank, who first lingered near and then sat down beside her. No doubt there are a great many things to be said appropriate to a summer evening, and no doubt they are best said in a low voice, as being most suitable to the peace and serenity of the hour; long pauses, too, at times, and then an earnest word or so, and then another interval of silence which somehow does not seem like silence either, and perhaps now and then a hasty turning away of the head, or drooping of the eyes towards the ground—all these minor circumstances, with a disinclination to have candles introduced and a tendency to confuse hours with minutes, are doubtless mere influences of the time, as many lovely lips can clearly testify. Neither is there the slightest reason why Mrs. Nickleby should have expressed surprise when—candles being at length brought in—Kate's bright eyes were unable to bear the light which obliged her to avert her face, and even to leave the room for some short time; because when one has sat in the dark so long, candles *are* dazzling, and nothing can be more strictly natural than that such results should be produced, as all well-informed young people know. For that matter, old people know it too or did know it once, but they forget these things sometimes, and more's the pity.

The good lady's surprise, however, did not end here. It was greatly increased when it was discovered that Kate had not the least appetite for supper: a discovery so alarming that there is no knowing in what unaccountable efforts of oratory Mrs. Nickleby's apprehensions might have been vented, if the general attention had not been attracted at the moment by a very strange and uncommon noise, proceeding, as the pale and trembling servant-girl affirmed, and as everybody's sense of hearing seemed to affirm also, "right down" the chimney of the adjoining room.

It being quite plain to the comprehension of all present that, however extraordinary and improbable it might appear, the noise did nevertheless proceed from the chimney in question; and the noise (which was a strange compound of various shuffling, sliding, rumbling, and struggling sounds, all muffled by the chimney) still continuing, Frank Cheeryble caught up a candle, and Tim Linkinwater the tongs, and they would have very quickly ascertained the cause of this disturbance if Mrs. Nickleby had not been taken very faint, and declined being left behind on any account. This produced a short remonstrance, which terminated in their all proceeding to the troubled chamber in a body, excepting only Miss La Creevy, who, as the servant-girl volunteered a confession of

Mysterious appearance of the Gentleman in the small clothes.

having been subject to fits in her infancy, remained with her to give the alarm and apply restoratives, in case of extremity.

Advancing to the door of the mysterious apartment, they were not a little surprised to hear a human voice, chaunting with a highly elaborated expression of melancholy, and in tones of suffocation which a human voice might have produced from under five or six feather-beds of the best quality, the once popular air of " Has she then failed in her truth, the beautiful maid I adore !" Nor, on bursting into the room without demanding a parley, was their astonishment lessened by the discovery that these romantic sounds certainly proceeded from the throat of some man up the chimney, of whom nothing was visible but a pair of legs, which were dangling above the grate, apparently feeling with extreme anxiety for the top bar whereon to effect a landing.

A sight so unusual and unbusiness-like as this completely paralysed Tim Linkinwater, who, after one or two gentle pinches at the stranger's ancles, which were productive of no effect, stood clapping the tongs together as if he were sharpening them for another assault, and did nothing else.

" This must be some drunken fellow," said Frank. " No thief would announce his presence thus."

As he said this with great indignation, he raised the candle to obtain a better view of the legs, and was darting forward to pull them down with very little ceremony, when Mrs. Nickleby, clasping her hands, uttered a sharp sound something between a scream and an exclamation, and demanded to know whether the mysterious limbs were not clad in small-clothes and grey worsted stockings, or whether her eyes had deceived her.

" Yes," cried Frank, looking a little closer. " Small-clothes certainly, and—and—rough grey stockings, too. Do you know him, ma'am ?"

" Kate, my dear," said Mrs. Nickleby, deliberately sitting herself down in a chair with that sort of desperate resignation which seemed to imply that now matters had come to a crisis, and all disguise was useless, " you will have the goodness, my love, to explain precisely how this matter stands. I have given him no encouragement—none whatever—not the least in the world. You know that, my dear, perfectly well. He was very respectful—exceedingly respectful—when he declared, as you were a witness to ; still at the same time, if I am to be persecuted in this way, if vegetable what's-his-names and all kinds of garden-stuff are to strew my path out of doors, and gentlemen are to come choking up our chimneys at home, I really don't know—upon my word I do *not* know—what is to become of me. It's a very hard case—harder than anything I was ever exposed to before I married your poor dear papa, though I suffered a good deal of annoyance then — but that, of course, I expected, and made up my mind for. When I was not nearly so old as you, my dear, there was a young gentleman who sat next us at church, who used almost every Sunday to cut my name in large letters in the front of his pew while the sermon was going on. It was gratifying, of course, naturally so, but still it was an annoyance, because the pew was in a very conspicuous place, and he was several times publicly taken out by the beadle for doing it.   But that was nothing to this.   This is a great deal worse, and a great deal more embarrassing.   I would rather, Kate, my dear," said Mrs. Nickleby, with great solemnity, and an effusion of tears—" I would rather, I declare, have been a pig-faced lady, than be exposed to such a life as this!"

Frank Cheeryble and Tim Linkinwater looked, in irrepressible astonishment, first at each other and then at Kate, who felt that some explanation was necessary, but who, between her terror at the apparition of the legs, her fear lest their owner should be smothered, and her anxiety to give the least ridiculous solution of the mystery that it was capable of bearing, was quite unable to utter a single word.

" He gives me great pain," continued Mrs. Nickleby, drying her eyes —" great pain; but don't hurt a hair of his head, I beg.   On no account hurt a hair of his head."

It would not, under existing circumstances, have been quite so easy to hurt a hair of the gentleman's head as Mrs. Nickleby seemed to imagine, inasmuch as that part of his person was some feet up the chimney, which was by no means a wide one.   But as all this time he had never left off singing about the bankruptcy of the beautiful maid in respect of truth, and now began not only to croak very feebly, but to kick with great violence as if respiration became a task of difficulty, Frank Cheeryble without further hesitation pulled at the shorts and worsteds with such heartiness as to bring him floundering into the room with greater precipitation than he had quite calculated upon.

" Oh! yes, yes," said Kate, directly the whole figure of the singular visitor appeared in this abrupt manner.   " I know who it is.   Pray don't be rough with him.   Is he hurt?   I hope not—oh, pray see if he is hurt."

" He is not, I assure you," replied Frank, handling the object of his surprise, after this appeal, with sudden tenderness and respect.   " He is not hurt in the least."

" Don't let him come any nearer," said Kate, retiring as far as she could.

" No no, he shall not," rejoined Frank.   " You see I have him secure here.   But may I ask you what this means, and whether you expected this old gentleman?"

" Oh, no," said Kate, " of course not; but he—mama does not think so, I believe—but he is a mad gentleman who has escaped from the next house, and must have found an opportunity of secreting himself here."

" Kate," interposed Mrs. Nickleby, with a severe dignity, " I am surprised at you."

" Dear mama——" Kate gently remonstrated.

" I am surprised at you," repeated Mrs. Nickleby; " upon my word, Kate, I am quite astonished that you should join the persecutors of this unfortunate gentleman, when you know very well that they have the basest designs upon his property, and that that is the whole secret of it.   It would be much kinder of you, Kate, to ask Mr. Linkinwater or Mr. Cheeryble to interfere in his behalf, and see him righted.   You ought not to allow your feelings to influence you ; it's not right—very far from it. What should my feelings be, do you suppose ? If anybody ought to be indignant, who is it ? I, of course, and very properly so. Still, at the same time, I wouldn't commit such an injustice for the world. No," continued Mrs. Nickleby, drawing herself up, and looking another way with a kind of bashful stateliness; " this gentleman will understand me when I tell him that I repeat the answer I gave him the other day, —that I always will repeat it, though I do believe him to be sincere when I find him placing himself in such dreadful situations on my account—and that I request him to have the goodness to go away directly, or it will be impossible to keep his behaviour a secret from my son Nicholas. I am obliged to him, very much obliged to him, but I cannot listen to his addresses for a moment. It's quite impossible."

While this address was in course of delivery, the old gentleman, with his nose and cheeks embellished with large patches of soot, sat upon the ground with his arms folded, eyeing the spectators in profound silence, and with a very majestic demeanour. He did not appear to take the smallest notice of what Mrs. Nickleby said, but when she ceased to speak he honoured her with a long stare, and inquired if she had quite finished.

" I have nothing more to say," replied that lady modestly. " I really cannot say anything more."

" Very good," said the old gentleman, raising his voice, " then bring in the bottled lightning, a clean tumbler, and a corkscrew."

Nobody executing this order, the old gentleman, after a short pause, raised his voice again and demanded a thunder sandwich. This article not being forthcoming either, he requested to be served with a fricassee of boot-tops and gold-fish sauce, and then laughing heartily, gratified his hearers with a very long, very loud, and most melodious bellow.

But still Mrs. Nickleby, in reply to the significant looks of all about her, shook her head as though to assure them that she saw nothing whatever in all this, unless, indeed, it were a slight degree of eccentricity. She might have remained impressed with these opinions down to the latest moment of her life, but for a slight train of circumstances, which, trivial as they were, altered the whole complexion of the case.

It happened that Miss La Creevy, finding her patient in no very threatening condition and being strongly impelled by curiosity to see what was going forward, bustled into the room while the old gentleman was in the very act of bellowing. It happened, too, that the instant the old gentleman saw her, he stopped short, skipped suddenly on his feet, and fell to kissing his hand violently : a change of demeanour which almost terrified the little portrait-painter out of her senses, and caused her to retreat behind Tim Linkinwater with the utmost expedition.

" Aha !" cried the old gentleman, folding his hands, and squeezing them with great force against each other. " I see her now ; I see her now. My love, my life, my bride, my peerless beauty. She is come at last—at last—and all is gas and gaiters !"

Mrs. Nickleby looked rather disconcerted for a moment, but imme-diately recovering, nodded to Miss La Creevy and the other spectators several times, and frowned, and smiled gravely, giving them to understand that she saw where the mistake was, and would set it all to rights in a minute or two.

"She is come!" said the old gentleman, laying his hand upon his heart. "Cormoran and Blunderbore! She is come! All the wealth I have is hers if she will take me for her slave. Where are grace beauty and blandishments like those? In the Empress of Madagascar? No. In the Queen of Diamonds? No. In Mrs. Rowland, who every morning bathes in Kalydor for nothing? No. Melt all these down into one, with the three Graces, the nine Muses, and fourteen biscuit-bakers' daughters from Oxford-street, and make a woman half as lovely. Pho! I defy you."

After uttering this rhapsody, the old gentleman snapped his fingers twenty or thirty times, and then subsided into an ecstatic contemplation of Miss La Creevy's charms. This affording Mrs. Nickleby a favourable opportunity of explanation, she went about it straight.

"I am sure," said the worthy lady, with a prefatory cough, "that it's a great relief under such trying circumstances as these, to have anybody else mistaken for me—a very great relief; and it's a circumstance that never occurred before, although I have several times been mistaken for my daughter Kate. I have no doubt the people were very foolish and perhaps ought to have known better, but still they did take me for her, and of course that was no fault of mine and it would be very hard indeed if I was to be made responsible for it. However, in this instance, of course I must feel that I should do exceedingly wrong if I suffered anybody—especially anybody that I am under great obligations to—to be made uncomfortable on my account, and therefore I think it my duty to tell that gentleman that he is mistaken—that I am the lady who he was told by some impertinent person was niece to the Council of Paving-stones, and that I do beg and intreat of him to go quietly away, if it's only for"—here Mrs. Nickleby simpered and hesitated—"for _my_ sake."

It might have been expected that the old gentleman would have been penetrated to the heart by the delicacy and condescension of this appeal, and that he would at least have returned a courteous and suitable reply. What, then, was the shock which Mrs. Nickleby received, when, accosting _her_ in the most unmistakeable manner, he replied in a loud and sonorous voice—" Avaunt——Cat!"

"Sir!" cried Mrs. Nickleby, in a faint tone.

"Cat!" repeated the old gentleman. "Puss, Kit, Tit, Grimalkin, Tabby, Brindle—Whoosh!" with which last sound, uttered in a hissing manner between his teeth, the old gentleman swung his arms violently round and round, and at the same time alternately advanced on Mrs. Nickleby, and retreated from her, in that species of savage dance with which boys on market-days may be seen to frighten pigs, sheep, and other animals, when they give out obstinate indications of turning down a wrong street.

Mrs. Nickleby wasted no words, but uttered an exclamation of horror and surprise, and immediately fainted away.

"I'll attend to mama," said Kate, hastily; "I am not at all frightened. But pray take him away; pray take him away."

Frank was not at all confident of his power of complying with this request, until he bethought himself of the stratagem of sending Miss La Creevy on a few paces in advance, and urging the old gentleman to follow her. It succeeded to a miracle; and he went away in a rapture of admiration, strongly guarded by Tim Linkwater on one side, and Frank himself on the other.

"Kate," murmured Mrs. Nickleby, reviving when the coast was clear, "is he gone?"

She was assured that he was.

"I shall never forgive myself, Kate," said Mrs. Nickleby; "Never! That gentleman has lost his senses, and *I* am the unhappy cause."

"*You* the cause!" said Kate, greatly astonished.

"I, my love," replied Mrs. Nickleby, with a desperate calmness. "You saw what he was the other day; you see what he is now. I told your brother, weeks and weeks ago, Kate, that I hoped a disappointment might not be too much for him. You see what a wreck he is. Making allowance for his being a little flighty, you know how rationally, and sensibly, and honourably he talked, when we saw him in the garden. You have heard the dreadful nonsense he has been guilty of this night, and the manner in which he has gone on with that poor unfortunate little old maid. Can anybody doubt how all this has been brought about!"

"I should scarcely think they could," said Kate mildly.

"*I* should scarcely think so, either," rejoined her mother. "Well! if I am the unfortunate cause of this, I have the satisfaction of knowing that I am not to blame. I told Nicholas—I said to him, ' Nicholas, my dear, we should be very careful how we proceed.' He would scarcely hear me. If the matter had only been properly taken up at first, as I wished it to be——. But you are both of you so like your poor papa. However, I have *my* consolation, and that should be enough for me!"

Washing her hands, thus, of all responsibility under this head, past, present, or to come, Mrs. Nickleby kindly added that she hoped her children might never have greater cause to reproach themselves than she had, and prepared herself to receive the escort, who soon returned with the intelligence that the old gentleman was safely housed, and that they found his custodians, who had been making merry with some friends, wholly ignorant of his absence.

Quiet being again restored, a delicious half hour—so Frank called it in the course of subsequent conversation with Tim Linkinwater as they were walking home—a delicious half hour was spent in conversation, and Tim's watch at length apprising him that it was high time to depart, the ladies were left alone, though not without many offers on the part of Frank to remain until Nicholas arrived, no matter what hour of the night it might be, if, after the late neighbourly irruption, they entertained the least fear of being left to themselves. As their freedom from all further apprehension, however, left no pretext for his insisting on mounting guard, he was obliged to abandon the citadel, and to retire with the trusty Tim.

Nearly three hours of silence passed away, and Kate blushed to find when Nicholas returned, how long she had been sitting alone occupied with her own thoughts.

" I really thought it had not been half an hour," she said.

" They must have been pleasant thoughts, Kate," rejoined Nicholas gaily, " to make time pass away like that. What were they now?"

Kate was confused ; she toyed with some trifle on the table—looked up and smiled—looked down and dropped a tear.

" Why, Kate," said Nicholas, drawing his sister towards him and kissing her, " let me see your face. No? Ah! that was but a glimpse ; that's scarcely fair. A longer look than that, Kate. Come —and I'll read your thoughts for you."

There was something in this proposition, albeit it was said without the slightest consciousness or application, which so alarmed his sister, that Nicholas laughingly changed the subject to domestic matters, and thus gathered by degrees as they left the room and went up-stairs together, how lonely Smike had been all night—and by very slow degrees, too, for on this subject also Kate seemed to speak with some reluctance.

" Poor fellow," said Nicholas, tapping gently at his door, " what can be the cause of all this !"

Kate was hanging on her brother's arm, and the door being quickly opened, had not time to disengage herself, before Smike, very pale and haggard, and completely dressed, confronted them.

" And have you not been to bed?" said Nicholas.

" N—n—no," was the reply.

Nicholas gently detained his sister, who made an effort to retire ; and asked, " Why not?"

" I could not sleep," said Smike, grasping the hand which his friend extended to him.

" You are not well ?" rejoined Nicholas.

" I am better, indeed—a great deal better," said Smike quickly.

" Then why do you give way to these fits of melancholy?" inquired Nicholas, in his kindest manner ; " or why not tell us the cause? You grow a different creature, Smike."

" I do ; I know I do," he replied. " I will tell you the reason one day, but not now. I hate myself for this ; you are all so good and kind. But I cannot help it. My heart is very full ;—you do not know how full it is."

He wrung Nicholas's hand before he released it ; and glancing for a moment at the brother and sister as they stood together, as if there were something in their strong affection which touched him very deeply, withdrew into his chamber, and was soon the only watcher under that quiet roof.

CHAPTER L.

INVOLVES A SERIOUS CATASTROPHE.

THE little race-course at Hampton was in the full tide and height of its gaiety, the day as dazzling as day could be, the sun high in the cloudless sky and shining in its fullest splendour. Every gaudy colour that fluttered in the air from carriage seat and garish tent top, shone out in its gaudiest hues. Old dingy flags grew new again, faded gilding was re-burnished, stained rotten canvas looked a snowy white; the very beggars' rags were freshened up, and sentiment quite forgot its charity in its fervent admiration of poverty so picturesque.

It was one of those scenes of life and animation, caught in its very brightest and freshest moments, which can scarcely fail to please; for if the eye be tired of show and glare, or the ear be weary with a ceaseless round of noise, the one may repose, turn almost where it will, on eager happy and expectant faces, and the other deaden all consciousness of more annoying sounds in those of mirth and exhilaration. Even the sun-burnt faces of gipsy children, half naked though they be, suggest a drop of comfort. It is a pleasant thing to see that the sun has been there to know that the air and light are on them every day, to feel that they *are* children and lead children's lives; that if their pillows be damp, it is with the dews of Heaven, and not with tears; that the limbs of their girls are free, and that they are not crippled by distortions, imposing an unnatural and horrible penance upon their sex; that their lives are spent from day to day at least among the waving trees, and not in the midst of dreadful engines which make young children old before they know what childhood is, and give them the exhaustion and infirmity of age, without, like age, the privilege to die. God send that old nursery tales were true, and that gipsies stole such children by the score!

The great race of the day had just been run; and the close lines of people on either side of the course suddenly breaking up and pouring into it, imparted a new liveliness to the scene, which was again all busy movement. Some hurried eagerly to catch a glimpse of the winning horse, others darted to and fro searching no less eagerly for the carriages they had left in quest of better stations. Here a little knot gathered round a pea and thimble table to watch the plucking of some unhappy greenhorn, and there another proprietor with his confederates in various disguises—one man in spectacles, another with an eye-glass and a stylish hat, a third dressed as a farmer well to do in the world, with his top-coat over his arm and his flash notes in a large leathern pocket-book, and all with heavy-handled whips to represent most innocent country fellows who had trotted there on horseback—sought, by loud and noisy talk and pretended play, to entrap some unwary customer, while the gentlemen confederates (of more villanous aspect still, in clean linen and good clothes,) betrayed their close interest in the concern by the anxious furtive glance they cast on all new comers. These would be hanging on the outskirts of a wide circle of people assembled round some itinerant juggler, opposed in his turn by a noisy band of music, or the classic game of "Ring the Bull," while ventriloquists holding dialogues with wooden dolls, and fortune-telling women smothering the cries of real babies, divided with them, and many more, the general attention of the company. Drinking-tents were full, glasses began to clink in carriages, hampers to be unpacked, tempting provisions to be set forth, knives and forks to rattle, champagne corks to fly, eyes to brighten that were not dull before, and pickpockets to count their gains during the last heat. The attention so recently strained on one object of interest, was now divided among a hundred; and look where you would, was a motley assemblage of feasting, laughing, talking, begging, gambling, and mummery.

Of the gambling-booths there was a plentiful show, flourishing in all the splendour of carpeted ground, striped hangings, crimson cloth, pinnacled roofs, geranium pots, and livery servants. There were the Stranger's club-house, the Athenæum club-house, the Hampton club-house, the Saint James's club-house, and half-a-mile of club-houses to play in; and there was rouge-et-noir, French hazard, and La Merveille, to play at. It is into one of these booths that our story takes its way.

Fitted up with three tables for the purposes of play, and crowded with players and lookers on, it was—although the largest place of the kind upon the course—intensely hot, notwithstanding that a portion of the canvas roof was rolled back to admit more air, and there were two doors for a free passage in and out. Excepting one or two men who—each with a long roll of half-crowns, chequered with a few stray sovereigns, in his left hand—staked their money at every roll of the ball with a business-like sedateness which showed that they were used to it, and had been playing all day and most probably all the day before, there was no very distinctive character about the players, who were chiefly young men apparently attracted by curiosity, or staking small sums as part of the amusement of the day, with no very great interest in winning or losing. There were two persons present, however, who, as peculiarly good specimens of a class, deserve a passing notice.

Of these, one was a man of six or eight and fifty, who sat on a chair near one of the entrances of the booth, with his hands folded on the top of his stick and his chin appearing above them. He was a tall, fat, long-bodied man, buttoned up to the throat in a light green coat, which made his body look still longer than it was, and wore besides drab breeches and gaiters, a white neckerchief, and a broad-brimmed white hat. Amid all the buzzing noise of the games and the perpetual passing in and out of people, he seemed perfectly calm and abstracted, without the smallest particle of excitement in his composition. He exhibited no indication of weariness, nor, to a casual observer, of interest either. There he sat, quite still and collected. Sometimes, but very rarely, he nodded to some passing face, or beckoned to a waiter to obey a call from one of the tables. The next instant he subsided into his old state. He might have been some profoundly deaf old gentleman, who had come in to take a rest, or he might have been patiently waiting for a friend without the least consciousness of anybody's presence, or fixed in a trance, or under the influence of opium. People turned round and looked at him ; he made no gesture, caught nobody's eye,—let them pass away, and others come on and be succeeded by others, and took no notice. When he did move, it seemed wonderful how he could have seen anything to occasion it. And so, in truth, it was. But there was not a face that passed in or out this man failed to see, not a gesture at any one of the three tables that was lost upon him, not a word spoken by the bankers but reached his ear, not a winner or loser he could not have marked ; and he was the proprietor of the place.

The other presided over the *rouge-et-noir* table. He was probably some ten years younger, and was a plump, paunchy, sturdy-looking fellow, with his under lip a little pursed from a habit of counting money inwardly as he paid it, but with no decidedly bad expression in his face, which was rather an honest and jolly one than otherwise. He wore no coat, the weather being hot, and stood behind the table with a huge mound of crowns and half-crowns before him, and a cash-box for notes. This game was constantly playing. Perhaps twenty people would be staking at the same time. This man had to roll the ball, to watch the stakes as they were laid down, to gather them off the colour which lost, to pay those who won, to do it all with the utmost despatch, to roll the ball again, and to keep this game perpetually alive. He did it all with a rapidity absolutely marvellous ; never hesitating, never making a mistake, never stopping, and never ceasing to repeat such unconnected phrases as the following, which, partly from habit, and partly to have something appropriate and business-like to say, he constantly poured out with the same monotonous emphasis, and in nearly the same order, all day long :—

" Rooge-a-nore from Paris gentlemen, make your game and back your own opinions—any time while the ball rolls—rooge-a-nore from Paris gentlemen, it's a French game, gentlemen, I brought it over myself I did indeed !—rooge-a-nore from Paris—black wins—black —stop a minute, sir, and I'll pay you directly—two there, half a pound there, three there—and one there—gentlemen, the ball's a rolling—any time, sir, while the ball rolls—the beauty of this game is, that you can double your stakes or put down your money, gentlemen, any time while the ball rolls—black again—black wins—I never saw such a thing—I never did in all my life, upon my word I never did ; if any gentleman had been backing the black in the last five minutes he must have won five-and-forty pound in four rolls of the ball, he must indeed—Gentlemen, we've port, sherry, cigars, and most excellent champagne. Here, wai-ter, bring a bottle of champagne, and let's have a dozen or fifteen cigars here—and let's be comfortable, gentlemen—and bring some clean glasses—any time while the ball rolls—I lost one hundred and thirty-seven pound yesterday,

gentlemen, at one roll of the ball: I did indeed!—how do you do, sir,"
(recognising some knowing gentleman without any halt or change of
voice, and giving a wink so slight that it seems an accident) " will
you take a glass of sherry, sir—here wai-ter, bring a clean glass, and
hand the sherry to this gentleman—and hand it round, will you waiter
—this is the rooge-a-nore from Paris, gentlemen—any time while the
ball rolls—gentlemen, make your game, and back your own opinions—
it's the rooge-a-nore from Paris, quite a new game, I brought it over
myself, I did indeed—gentlemen, the ball's a rolling!"

This officer was busily plying his vocation when half-a-dozen
persons sauntered through the booth, to whom—but without stopping
either in his speech or work—he bowed respectfully, at the same time
directing by a look the attention of a man beside him to the tallest
figure in the group, in recognition of whom the proprietor pulled off
his hat. This was Sir Mulberry Hawk, with whom were his friend
and pupil, and a small train of gentlemanly-dressed men, of characters
more doubtful than obscure.

The proprietor, in a low voice, bade Sir Mulberry good day. Sir
Mulberry, in the same tone, bade the proprietor go to the devil, and
turned to speak with his friends.

There was evidently an irritable consciousness about him that he
was an object of curiosity on this first occasion of showing himself
in public after the accident that had befallen him; and it was easy to
perceive that he appeared on the race-course, that day, more in the
hope of meeting with a great many people who knew him, and so
getting over as much as possible of the annoyance at once, than with
any purpose of enjoying the sport. There yet remained a slight scar
upon his face, and whenever he was recognised, as he was almost every
minute by people sauntering in and out, he made a restless effort to
conceal it with his glove, showing how keenly he felt the disgrace he
had undergone.

" Ah! Hawk," said one very sprucely-dressed personage in a New-
market coat, a choice neckerchief, and all other accessories of the most
unexceptionable kind. " How d'ye do, old fellow?"

This was a rival trainer of young noblemen and gentlemen, and the
person of all others whom Sir Mulberry most hated and dreaded to
meet. They shook hands with excessive cordiality.

" And how are you now, old fellow, hey?"

" Quite well, quite well," said Sir Mulberry.

" That's right," said the other. " How d'ye do, Verisopht? He's a
little pulled down, our friend here—rather out of condition still, hey?"

It should be observed that the gentleman had very white teeth, and
that when there was no excuse for laughing, he generally finished with
the same monosyllable, which he uttered so as to display them.

" He's in very good condition, there's nothing the matter with him,"
said the young man carelessly.

" Upon my soul I'm glad to hear it," rejoined the other. " Have
you just returned from Brussels?"

" We only reached town late last night," said Lord Frederick. Sir

Mulberry turned away to speak to one of his own party, and feigned not to hear.

" Now, upon my life," said the friend, affecting to speak in a whisper, " it's an uncommonly bold and game thing in Hawk to show himself so soon. I say it advisedly, there's a vast deal of courage in it. You see he has just rusticated long enough to excite curiosity, and not long enough for men to have forgotten that deuced unpleasant—by the bye —you know the rights of the affair, of course. Why did you never give those confounded papers the lie ? I seldom read the papers, but I looked in the papers for that, and may I be——"

" Look in the papers," interrupted Sir Mulberry, turning suddenly round—" to-morrow—no, next day, will you ?"

" Upon my life, my dear fellow, I seldom or never read the papers," said the other, shrugging his shoulders, " but I will at your recommendation. What shall I look for, hey ?"

" Good day," said Sir Mulberry, turning abruptly on his heel, and drawing his pupil with him. Falling again into the loitering careless pace at which they had entered, they lounged out arm in arm.

" I won't give him a case of murder to read," muttered Sir Mulberry with an oath ; " but it shall be something very near it, if whip-cord cuts and bludgeons bruise."

His companion said nothing, but there was that in his manner which galled Sir Mulberry to add, with nearly as much ferocity as if his friend had been Nicholas himself,

" I sent Jenkins to Nickleby before eight o'clock this morning. He's a staunch one; he was back with me before the messenger. I had it all from him in the first five minutes. I know where this hound is to be met with—time and place both. But there's no need to talk ; to-morrow will soon be here."

" And wha-at's to be done to-morrow ?" inquired Lord Frederick.

Sir Mulberry Hawk honoured him with an angry glance, but condescended to return no verbal answer to this inquiry, and both walked sullenly on as though their thoughts were busily occupied, until they were quite clear of the crowd, and almost alone, when Sir Mulberry wheeled round to return.

" Stop," said his companion, " I want to speak to you—in earnest. Don't turn back. Let us walk here a few minutes."

" What have you to say to me, that you could not say yonder as well as here ?" returned his Mentor, disengaging his arm.

" Hawk," rejoined the other, " tell me ; I must know—"

" *Must* know," interrupted the other disdainfully. " Whew ! Go on. If you must know, of course there's no escape for me. Must know !"

" Must ask then," returned Lord Frederick, " and must press you for a plain and straight-forward answer—is what you have just said only a mere whim of the moment, occasioned by your being out of humour and irritated, or is it your serious intention, and one that you have actually contemplated ?"

" Why, don't you remember what passed on the subject one night, when I was laid up with a broken limb?" said Sir Mulberry, with a sneer.

" Perfectly well."

" Then take that for an answer, in the devil's name," replied Sir Mulberry, " and ask me for no other."

Such was the ascendancy he had acquired over his dupe, and such the latter's general habit of submission, that, for the moment, the young man seemed half-afraid to pursue the subject. He soon overcame this feeling, however, if it had restrained him at all, and retorted angrily :

" If I remember what passed at the time you speak of, I expressed a strong opinion on this subject, and said that with my knowledge or consent, you never should do what you threaten now."

" Will you prevent me ? " asked Sir Mulberry, with a laugh.

" Ye-es, if I can ; " returned the other, promptly.

" A very proper saving clause, that last," said Sir Mulberry ; " and one you stand in need of. Oh ! look to your own business, and leave me to look to mine."

" This *is* mine," retorted Lord Frederick. " I make it mine ; I will make it mine. It's mine already. I am more compromised than I should be, as it is."

" Do as you please, and what you please, for yourself," said Sir Mulberry, affecting an easy good humour. " Surely that must content you ! Do nothing for me ; that's all. I advise no man to interfere in proceedings that I choose to take, and I am sure you know me better than to do so. The fact is, I see, you mean to offer me advice. It is well meant, I have no doubt, but I reject it. Now, if you please, we will return to the carriage. I find no entertainment here, but quite the reverse, and if we prolonged this conversation we might quarrel, which would be no proof of wisdom in either you or me."

With this rejoinder, and waiting for no further discussion, Sir Mulberry Hawk yawned, and very leisurely turned back.

There was not a little tact and knowledge of the young lord's disposition in this mode of treating him. Sir Mulberry clearly saw that if his dominion were to last, it must be established now. He knew that the moment he became violent, the young man would become violent too. He had many times been enabled to strengthen his influence when any circumstance had occurred to weaken it, by adopting this cool and laconic style, and he trusted to it now, with very little doubt of its entire success.

But while he did this, and wore the most careless and indifferent deportment that his practised arts enabled him to assume, he inwardly resolved not only to visit all the mortification of being compelled to suppress his feelings, with additional severity upon Nicholas, but also to make the young lord pay dearly for it one day in some shape or other. So long as he had been a passive instrument in his hands, Sir Mulberry had regarded him with no other feeling than contempt ; but now that he presumed to avow opinions in opposition to his, and even to turn upon him with a lofty tone and an air of superiority, he began to hate him. Conscious that in the vilest and most worthless sense of the term, he was dependent upon the weak young lord, Sir Mulberry could the less brook humiliation at his hands, and when he began to dislike him he measured his dislike—as men often do—by the extent of the injuries he had inflicted upon its object. When it is remembered that Sir Mulberry Hawk had plundered, duped, deceived, and fooled his pupil in every possible way, it will not be wondered at that beginning to hate him, he began to hate him cordially.

On the other hand, the young lord having thought—which he very seldom did about anything—having thought, and seriously too, upon the affair with Nicholas, and the circumstances which led to it, had arrived at a manly and honest conclusion. Sir Mulberry's coarse and insulting behaviour on the occasion in question had produced a deep impression on his mind ; a strong suspicion of his having led him on to pursue Miss Nickleby for purposes of his own, had been lurking there for some time ; he was really ashamed of his share in the transaction, and deeply mortified by the misgiving that he had been gulled. He had had sufficient leisure to reflect upon these things during their late retirement, and at times when his careless and indolent nature would permit, had availed himself of the opportunity. Slight circumstances too had occurred to increase his suspicion. It wanted but a very slight circumstance to kindle his wrath against Sir Mulberry, and this his disdainful and insolent tone in their recent conversation (the only one they had held upon the subject since the period to which Sir Mulberry referred) effected.

Thus they rejoined their friends, each with causes of dislike against the other rankling in his breast, and the young man haunted besides with thoughts of the vindictive retaliation which was threatened against Nicholas, and the determination to prevent it by some strong step, if possible. But this was not all. Sir Mulberry, conceiving that he had silenced him effectually, could not suppress his triumph, or forbear from following up what he conceived to be his advantage. Mr. Pyke was there, and Mr. Pluck was there, and Colonel Chouser, and other gentlemen of the same caste, and it was a great point for Sir Mulberry to show them that he had not lost his influence. At first the young lord contented himself with a silent determination to take measures for withdrawing himself from the connection immediately. By degrees he grew more angry, and was exasperated by jests and familiarities which a few hours before would have been a source of amusement to him. This did not serve him, for at such bantering or retort as suited the company, he was no match for Sir Mulberry. Still no violent rupture took place, and they returned to town, Messrs. Pyke and Pluck and other gentlemen frequently protesting on the way thither, that Sir Mulberry had never been in such tip-top spirits in all his life.

They dined together sumptuously. The wine flowed freely, as indeed it had done all day. Sir Mulberry drank to recompense himself for his recent abstinence, the young lord to drown his indignation, and the remainder of the party because the wine was of the best and they had nothing to pay. It was nearly midnight when they rushed out, wild, burning with wine, their blood boiling, and their brains on fire, to the gaming-table.

Here they encountered another party, mad like themselves. The excitement of play, hot rooms, and glaring lights, was not calculated to allay the fever of the time. In that giddy whirl of noise and confusion the men were delirious. Who thought of money, ruin, or the morrow, in the savage intoxication of the moment? More wine was called for, glass after glass was drained, their parched and scalding mouths were cracked with thirst. Down poured the wine like oil on blazing fire. And still the riot went on—the debauchery gained its height—glasses were dashed upon the floor by hands that could not carry them to lips, oaths were shouted out by lips which could scarcely form the words to vent them in; drunken losers cursed and roared; some mounted on the tables, waving bottles above their heads and bidding defiance to the rest; some danced, some sang, some tore the cards and raved. Tumult and frenzy reigned supreme; when a noise arose that drowned all others, and two men, seizing each other by the throat, struggled into the middle of the room.

A dozen voices, until now unheard, called aloud to part them. Those who had kept themselves cool to win, and who earned their living in such scenes, threw themselves upon the combatants, and forcing them asunder, dragged them some space apart.

"Let me go!" cried Sir Mulberry, in a thick hoarse voice; "he struck me! Do you hear? I say, he struck me. Have I a friend here? Who is this? Westwood. Do you hear me say he struck me!"

"I hear, I hear," replied one of those who held him. "Come away for to-night."

"I will not, by G—" he replied, fiercely. "A dozen men about us saw the blow."

"To-morrow will be ample time," said the friend.

"It will not be ample time!" cried Sir Mulberry, gnashing his teeth. "To-night—at once—here!" His passion was so great that he could not articulate, but stood clenching his fist, tearing his hair, and stamping upon the ground.

"What is this, my lord?" said one of those who surrounded him. "Have blows passed?"

"*One* blow has," was the panting reply. "I struck him—I proclaim it to all here. I struck him, and he well knows why. I say with him, let this quarrel be adjusted now. Captain Adams," said the young lord, looking hurriedly about him, and addressing one of those who had interposed, "Let me speak with you, I beg."

The person addressed stepped forward, and, taking the young man's arm, they retired together, followed shortly afterwards by Sir Mulberry and his friend.

It was a profligate haunt of the worst repute, and not a place in which such an affair was likely to awaken any sympathy for either party, or to call forth any further remonstrance or interposition. Elsewhere its further progress would have been instantly prevented, and time allowed for sober and cool reflection; but not there. Disturbed

The last brawl between Sir Mulbery and his pupil.

in their orgies, the party broke up ; some reeled away with looks of tipsy gravity, others withdrew noisily discussing what had just occurred ; the gentlemen of honour who lived upon their winnings remarked to each other as they went out that Hawk was a good shot; and those who had been most noisy fell fast asleep upon the sofas, and thought no more about it.

Meanwhile the two seconds, as they may be called now, after a long conference, each with his principal, met together in another room. Both utterly heartless, both men upon town, both thoroughly initiated in its worst vices, both deeply in debt, both fallen from some higher estate, both addicted to every depravity for which society can find some genteel name and plead its most depraving conventionalities as an excuse, they were naturally gentlemen of most unblemished honour themselves, and of great nicety concerning the honour of other people.

These two gentlemen were unusually cheerful just now, for the affair was pretty certain to make some noise, and could scarcely fail to enhance their reputations considerably.

" This is an awkward affair, Adams," said Mr. Westwood, drawing himself up.

" Very," returned the captain ; " a blow has been struck, and there is but one course, *of* course."

" No apology, I suppose ? " said Mr. Westwood.

" Not a syllable, sir, from my man, if we talk till doomsday," returned the captain. " The original cause of dispute, I understand, was some girl or other, to whom your principal applied certain terms, which Lord Frederick, defending the girl, repelled. But this led to a long recrimination upon a great many sore subjects, charges, and counter-charges. Sir Mulberry was sarcastic ; Lord Frederick was excited, and struck him in the heat of provocation, and under circumstances of great aggravation. That blow, unless there is a full retraction on the part of Sir Mulberry, Lord Frederick is ready to justify."

" There is no more to be said," returned the other, " but to settle the hour and the place of meeting. It's a responsibility ; but there is a strong feeling to have it over : do you object to say at sunrise ? "

" Sharp work," replied the captain, referring to his watch ; . " however, as this seems to have been a long time brooding, and negotiation is only a waste of words—no."

" Something may possibly be said out of doors after what passed in the other room, which renders it desirable that we should be off without delay, and quite clear of town," said Mr. Westwood. " What do you say to one of the meadows opposite Twickenham, by the river-side ? "

The captain saw no objection.

" Shall we join company in the avenue of trees which leads from Petersham to Ham House, and settle the exact spot when we arrive there ? " said Mr. Westwood.

To this the captain also assented. After a few other preliminaries, equally brief, and having settled the road each party should take to avoid suspicion, they separated.

" We shall just have comfortable time, my lord," said the captain, when he had communicated the arrangements, "to call at my rooms for a case of pistols, and then jog coolly down. If you will allow me to dismiss your servant, we'll take my cab, for yours, perhaps, might be recognised."

What a contrast, when they reached the street, to the scene they had just left! It was already daybreak. For the flaring yellow light within, was substituted the clear, bright, glorious morning ; for a hot, close atmosphere, tainted with the smell of expiring lamps, and reeking with the steams of riot and dissipation, the free, fresh, wholesome air. But to the fevered head on which that cool air blew, it seemed to come laden with remorse for time mis-spent and countless opportunities neglected. With throbbing veins and burning skin, eyes wild and heavy, thoughts hurried and disordered, he felt as though the light were a reproach, and shrunk involuntarily from the day as if he were some foul and hideous thing.

"Shivering?" said the captain. "You are cold."

"Rather."

"It does strike cool, coming out of those hot rooms. Wrap that cloak about you. So, so ; now we're off."

They rattled through the quiet streets, made their call at the captain's lodgings, cleared the town, and emerged upon the open road, without hindrance or molestation.

Fields, trees, gardens, hedges, everything looked very beautiful ; the young man scarcely seemed to have noticed them before, though he had passed the same objects a thousand times. There was a peace and serenity upon them all strangely at variance with the bewilderment and confusion of his own half-sobered thoughts, and yet impressive and welcome. He had no fear upon his mind ; but as he looked about him he had less anger, and though all old delusions, relative to his worthless late companion, were now cleared away, he rather wished he had never known him than thought of its having come to this.

The past night, the day before, and many other days and nights beside, all mingled themselves up in one unintelligible and senseless whirl ; he could not separate the transactions of one time from those of another. Last night seemed a week ago, and months ago were as last night. Now the noise of the wheels resolved itself into some wild tune in which he could recognise scraps of airs he knew, and now there was nothing in his ears but a stunning and bewildering sound like rushing water. But his companion rallied him on being so silent, and they talked and laughed boisterously. When they stopped he was a little surprised to find himself in the act of smoking, but on reflection he remembered when and where he had taken the cigar.

They stopped at the avenue gate and alighted, leaving the carriage to the care of the servant, who was a smart fellow, and nearly as well accustomed to such proceedings as his master. Sir Mulberry and his friend were already there, and all four walked in profound silence up the aisle of stately elm trees, which, meeting far above their heads, formed a long green perspective of gothic arches, terminating like some old ruin in the open sky.

After a pause, and a brief conference between the seconds, they at length turned to the right, and taking a track across a little meadow, passed Ham House and came into some fields beyond. In one of these they stopped. The ground was measured, some usual forms gone through, the two principals were placed front to front at the distance agreed upon, and Sir Mulberry turned his face towards his young adversary for the first time. He was very pale—his eyes were bloodshot, his dress disordered, and his hair dishevelled,—all most probably the consequences of the previous day and night. For the face, it expressed nothing but violent and evil passions. He shaded his eyes with his hand, gazed at his opponent stedfastly for a few moments, and then taking the weapon which was tendered to him, bent his eyes upon that, and looked up no more until the word was given, when he instantly fired.

The two shots were fired as nearly as possible at the same instant. In that instant the young lord turned his head sharply round, fixed upon his adversary a ghastly stare, and, without a groan or stagger, fell down dead.

" He's gone," cried Westwood, who, with the other second, had run up to the body, and fallen on one knee beside it.

" His blood on his own head," said Sir Mulberry. " He brought this upon himself, and forced it upon me."

"Captain Adams," cried Westwood, hastily, " I call you to witness that this was fairly done. Hawk, we have not a moment to lose. We must leave this place immediately, push for Brighton, and cross to France with all speed. This has been a bad business, and may be worse if we delay a moment. Adams, consult your own safety, and don't remain here ; the living before the dead—good bye."

With these words, he seized Sir Mulberry by the arm, and hurried him away. Captain Adams, only pausing to convince himself beyond all question of the fatal result, sped off in the same direction, to concert measures with his servant for removing the body, and securing his own safety likewise.

So died Lord Frederick Verisopht, by the hand which he had loaded with gifts and clasped a thousand times ; by the act of him but for whom and others like him he might have lived a happy man, and died with children's faces round his bed.

The sun came proudly up in all his majesty, the noble river ran its winding course, the leaves quivered and rustled in the air, the birds poured their cheerful songs from every tree, the short-lived butterfly fluttered its little wings ; all the light and life of day came on, and, amidst it all, and pressing down the grass whose every blade bore twenty tiny lives, lay the dead man, with his stark and rigid face turned upwards to the sky.

CHAPTER LI.

THE PROJECT OF MR. RALPH NICKLEBY AND HIS FRIEND APPROACH-
ING A SUCCESSFUL ISSUE, BECOMES UNEXPECTEDLY KNOWN TO
ANOTHER PARTY, NOT ADMITTED INTO THEIR CONFIDENCE.

In an old house, dismal dark and dusty, which seemed to have
withered, like himself, and to have grown yellow and shrivelled in
hoarding him from the light of day, as he had in hoarding his money,
lived Arthur Gride. Meagre old chairs and tables of spare and bony
make, and hard and cold as misers' hearts, were ranged in grim array
against the gloomy walls; attenuated presses, grown lank and lantern-
jawed in guarding the treasures they inclosed, and tottering, as though
from constant fear and dread of thieves, shrunk up in dark corners,
whence they cast no shadows on the ground, and seemed to hide
and cower from observation. A tall grim clock upon the stairs, with
long lean hands and famished face, ticked in cautious whispers, and
when it struck the time in thin and piping sounds, like an old man's
voice, rattled as if 'twere pinched with hunger.

No fireside couch was there, to invite repose and comfort. Elbow-
chairs there were, but they looked uneasy in their minds, cocked their
arms suspiciously and timidly, and kept upon their guard. Others
were fantastically grim and gaunt, as having drawn themselves up to
their utmost height, and put on their fiercest looks to stare all comers
out of countenance. Others again knocked up against their neighbours,
or leant for support against the wall, somewhat ostentatiously, as if
to call all men to witness that they were not worth the taking. The
dark square lumbering bedsteads seemed built for restless dreams; the
musty hangings to creep in scanty folds together, whispering among
themselves, when rustled by the wind, their trembling knowledge of the
tempting wares that lurked within the dark and tight-locked closets.

From out the most spare and hungry room in all this spare and
hungry house, there came one morning the tremulous tones of old
Gride's voice, as it feebly chirruped forth the fag end of some forgotten song, of which the burden ran

> Ta—ran—tan—too,
> Throw the old shoe,
> And may the wedding be lucky:

which he repeated in the same shrill quavering notes again and again,
until a violent fit of coughing obliged him to desist, and to pursue in
silence the occupation upon which he was engaged.

This occupation was to take down from the shelves of a worm-eaten
wardrobe, a quanty of frowsy garments, one by one; to subject each to
a careful and minute inspection by holding it up against the light, and
after folding it with great exactness, to lay it on one or other of two
little heaps beside him. He never took two articles of clothing out

together, but always brought them forth singly, and never failed to shut the wardrobe door and turn the key, between each visit to its shelves.

"The snuff-coloured suit," said Arthur Gride, surveying a threadbare coat, "Did I look well in snuff-colour? let me think."

The result of his cogitations appeared to be unfavourable, for he folded the garment once more, laid it aside, and mounted on a chair to get down another, chirping while he did so—

> Young, loving, and fair,
> Oh what happiness there!
> The wedding is sure to be lucky.

"They always put in ' young,' " said old Arthur, "but songs are only written for the sake of rhyme, and this is a silly one that the poor country people sang when I was a little boy. Though stop—young is quite right too—it means the bride—yes. He, he, he! It means the bride. Oh dear, that's good. That's very good. And true besides—quite true!"

In the satisfaction of this discovery he went over the verse again with increased expression and a shake or two here and there, and then resumed his employment.

"The bottle green," said old Arthur; "the bottle-green was a famous suit to wear, and I bought it very cheap at a pawnbroker's, and there was—he, he, he!—a tarnished shilling in the waistcoat pocket. To think that the pawnbroker shouldn't have known there was a shilling in it! I knew it; I felt it when I was examining the quality. Oh, what a dull dog! It was a lucky suit too, this bottle-green. The very day I put it on first, old Lord Mallowford was burnt to death in his bed, and all the post-obits fell in.   I'll be married in the bottle-green. Peg—Peg Sliderskew—I'll wear the bottle-green."

This call, loudly repeated twice or thrice at the room door, brought into the apartment a short, thin, weasen, blear-eyed old woman, palsy-stricken and hideously ugly, who, wiping her shrivelled face upon her dirty apron, inquired, in that subdued tone in which deaf people commonly speak :—

"Was that you a calling, or only the clock a striking?   My hearing gets so bad, I never know which is which ; but when I hear a noise I know it must be one of you, because nothing else ever stirs in the house."

"Me, Peg—me," said Arthur Gride, tapping himself on the breast to render the reply more intelligible.

"You, eh?" returned Peg.   "And what do *you* want?"

"I'll be married in the bottle-green," cried Arthur Gride.

"It's a deal too good to be married in, master," rejoined Peg, after a short inspection of the suit.   "Haven't you got anything worse than this?"

"Nothing that'll do," replied old Arthur.

"Why not do?" retorted Peg.   "Why don't you wear your every-day clothes like a man—eh?"

"They an't becoming enough, Peg," returned her master.

"Not what enough?" said Peg.

"Becoming."

"Becoming what?" said Peg sharply. "Not becoming too old to wear?"

Arthur Gride muttered an imprecation upon his housekeeper's deafness, as he roared in her ear:—

"Not smart enough: I want to look as well as I can."

"Look?" cried Peg. "If she's as handsome as you say she is, she won't look much at you, master, take your oath of that; and as to how you look yourself—pepper-and-salt, bottle-green, sky-blue, or tartan-plaid, will make no difference in you."

With which consolatory assurance, Peg Sliderskew gathered up the chosen suit, and folding her skinny arms upon the bundle, stood mouthing, and grinning, and blinking her watery eyes like an uncouth figure in some monstrous piece of carving.

"You're in a funny humour, an't you, Peg?" said Arthur, with not the best possible grace.

"Why, isn't it enough to make me?" rejoined the old woman. "I shall soon enough be put out, though, if anybody tries to domineer it over me, and so I give you notice, master. Nobody shall be put over Peg Sliderskew's head after so many years; you know that, and so I needn't tell you. That won't do for me—no, no, nor for you. Try that once and come to ruin—ruin—ruin."

"Oh dear, dear, I shall never try it," said Arthur Gride, appalled by the mention of the word, "not for the world. It would be very easy to ruin me; we must be very careful; more saving than ever with another mouth to feed. Only we—we mustn't let her lose her good looks, Peg, because I like to see 'em."

"Take care you don't find good looks come expensive," returned Peg, shaking her fore-finger.

"But she can earn money herself, Peg," said Arthur Gride, eagerly watching what effect his communication produced upon the old woman's countenance: "She can draw, paint, work all manner of pretty things for ornamenting stools and chairs: slippers, Peg, watch-guards, hair-chains, and a thousand little dainty trifles that I couldn't give you half the names of. Then she can play the piano, (and, what's more, she's got one,) and sing like a little bird. She'll be very cheap to dress and keep, Peg; don't you think she will?"

"If you don't let her make a fool of you, she may," returned Peg.

"A fool of me!" exclaimed Arthur. "Trust your old master not to be fooled by pretty faces, Peg; no, no, no—nor by ugly ones neither, Mrs. Sliderskew," he softly added by way of soliloquy.

"You're a saying something you don't want me to hear," said Peg; "I know you are."

"Oh dear! the devil's in this woman," muttered Arthur; adding with an ugly leer, "I said I trusted everything to you, Peg, that was all."

"You do that, master, and all your cares are over," said Peg approvingly.

" *When* I do that, Peg Sliderskew," thought Arthur Gride, " they will be."

Although he thought this very distinctly, he durst not move his lips lest the old woman should detect him. He even seemed half afraid that she might have read his thoughts, for he leered coaxingly upon her as he said aloud :—

" Take up all loose stitches in the bottle-green with the best black silk. Have a skein of the best, and some new buttons for the coat, and—this is a good idea, Peg, and one you'll like, I know—as I have never given her anything yet, and girls like such attentions, you shall polish up a sparkling necklace that I've got up stairs, and I'll give it her upon the wedding morning—clasp it round her charming little neck myself—and take it away again next day. He, he, he!—lock it up for her, Peg, and lose it. Who'll be made the fool of there, I wonder, to begin with—eh Peg ?"

Mrs. Sliderskew appeared to approve highly of this ingenious scheme, and expressed her satisfaction by various rackings and twitchings of her head and body, which by no means enhanced her charms. These she prolonged until she had hobbled to the door, when she exchanged them for a sour malignant look, and twisting her under-jaw from side to side, muttered hearty curses upon the future Mrs. Gride, as she crept slowly down the stairs, and paused for breath at nearly every one.

" She's half a witch, I think," said Arthur Gride, when he found himself again alone. " But she's very frugal, and she's very deaf ; her living costs me next to nothing, and it's no use her listening at keyholes for she can't hear. She's a charming woman—for the purpose ; a most discreet old housekeeper, and worth her weight in—copper."

Having extolled the merits of his domestic in these high terms, old Arthur went back to the burden of his song, and, the suit destined to grace his approaching nuptials being now selected, replaced the others with no less care than he had displayed in drawing them from the musty nooks where they had silently reposed for many years.

Startled by a ring at the door he hastily concluded this operation, and locked the press ; but there was no need for any particular hurry as the discreet Peg seldom knew the bell was rung unless she happened to cast her dim eyes upwards and to see it shaking against the kitchen ceiling. After a short delay, however, Peg tottered in, followed by Newman Noggs.

" Ah ! Mr. Noggs !" cried Arthur Gride, rubbing his hands. " My good friend, Mr. Noggs, what news do you bring for me ?"

Newman, with a stedfast and immovable aspect, and his fixed eye very fixed indeed, replied, suiting the action to the word, " A letter. From Mr. Nickleby. The bearer waits."

" Won't you take a—a—"

Newman looked up, and smacked his lips.

" A chair ? " said Arthur Gride.

" No," replied Newman. " Thank'ee."

Arthur opened the letter with trembling hands, and devoured its contents with the utmost greediness, chuckling rapturously over it and reading it several times before he could take it from before his eyes. So many times did he peruse and re-peruse it, that Newman considered it expedient to remind him of his presence.

"Answer," said Newman. "Bearer waits."

"True," replied old Arthur. "Yes—yes; I almost forgot, I do declare."

"I thought you were forgetting," said Newman.

"Quite right to remind me, Mr. Noggs. Oh, very right indeed," said Arthur. "Yes. I'll write a line. I'm—I'm—rather flurried, Mr. Noggs. The news is —"

"Bad?" interrupted Newman.

"No, Mr. Noggs, thank you ; good, good. The very best of news. Sit down, I'll get the pen and ink, and write a line in answer. I'll not detain you long, I know you're a treasure to your master, Mr. Noggs. He speaks of you in such terms sometimes, that, oh dear ! you'd be astonished. I may say that I do too, and always did. I always say the same of you."

"That's 'Curse Mr. Noggs with all my heart!' then, if you do," thought Newman, as Gride hurried out.

The letter had fallen on the ground. Looking carefully about him for an instant, Newman, impelled by curiosity to know the result of the design he had overheard from his office closet, caught it up and rapidly read as follows :

"Gride,

"I saw Bray again this morning, and proposed the day after to-morrow (as you suggested) for the marriage. There is no objection on his part, and all days are alike to his daughter. We will go together, and you must be with me by seven in the morning. I need not tell you to be punctual.

"Make no further visits to the girl in the meantime. You have been there of late much oftener than you should. She does not languish for you, and it might have been dangerous. Restrain your youthful ardour for eight-and-forty hours, and leave her to the father. You only undo what he does, and does well.

"Yours,
"RALPH NICKLEBY."

A footstep was heard without. Newman dropped the letter on the same spot again, pressed it with his foot to prevent its fluttering away, regained his seat in a single stride, and looked as vacant and unconscious as ever mortal looked. Arthur Gride, after peering nervously about him, spied it on the ground, picked it up, and sitting down to write, glanced at Newman Noggs, who was staring at the wall with an intensity so remarkable, that Arthur was quite alarmed.

"Do you see anything particular, Mr. Noggs?" said Arthur, trying to follow the direction of Newman's eyes—which was an impossibility, and a thing no man had ever done.

"Only a cobweb," replied Newman.

" Oh! is that all ?"

" No," said Newman. " There's a fly in it."

" There are a good many cobwebs here," observed Arthur Gride.

" So there are in our place," returned Newman ; " and flies, too."

Newman appeared to derive great entertainment from this repartee, and to the great discomposure of Arthur Gride's nerves produced a series of sharp cracks from his finger-joints, resembling the noise of a distant discharge of small artillery. Arthur succeeded in finishing his reply to Ralph's note, nevertheless, and at length handed it over to the eccentric messenger for delivery.

" That's it, Mr. Noggs," said Gride.

Newman gave a nod, put it in his hat, and was shuffling away, when Gride, whose doting delight knew no bounds, beckoned him back again, and said in a shrill whisper, and with a grin which puckered up his whole face, and almost obscured his eyes—

" Will you—will you take a little drop of something—just a taste ?"

In good fellowship (if Arthur Gride had been capable of it) Newman would not have drunk with him one bubble of the richest wine that was ever made ; but to see what he would be at, and to punish him as much as he could, he accepted the offer immediately.

Arthur Gride, therefore, again applied himself to the press, and from a shelf laden with tall Flemish drinking-glasses and quaint bottles, some with necks like so many storks, and others with square Dutch-built bodies and short fat apoplectic throats, took down one dusty bottle of promising appearance and two glasses of curiously small size.

" You never tasted this," said Arthur. " Its *eau-d'or*—golden water. I like it on account of its name. It's a delicious name. Water of gold, golden water ! Oh dear me, it seems quite a sin to drink it !"

As his courage appeared to be fast failing him, and he trifled with the stopper in a manner which threatened the dismissal of the bottle to its old place, Newman took up one of the little glasses and chinked it twice or thrice against the bottle, as a gentle reminder that he had not been helped yet. With a deep sigh Arthur Gride slowly filled it— though not to the brim—and then filled his own.

" Stop, stop ; don't drink it yet," he said, laying his hand on Newman's ; " it was given to me twenty years ago, and when I take a little taste, which is ve—ry seldom, I like to think of it beforehand and teaze myself. We'll drink a toast. Shall we have a toast, Mr. Noggs ?"

" Ah !" said Newman, eyeing his little glass impatiently. " Look sharp. Bearer waits."

" Why, then, I'll tell you what," tittered Arthur, " we'll drink— he, he, he !—we'll drink a lady."

" *The* ladies ?" said Newman.

" No, no, Mr. Noggs," replied Gride, arresting his hand, " *a* lady. You wonder to hear me say *a* lady—I know you do, I know you do. Here's little Madeline—that's the toast, Mr. Noggs—little Madeline !"

" Madeline !" said Newman ; inwardly adding, " and God help her !."

The rapidity and unconcern with which Newman dismissed his portion of the golden water had a great effect upon the old man, who sat upright in his chair and gazed at him open-mouthed, as if the sight had taken away his breath. Quite unmoved, however, Newman left him to sip his own at leisure, or to pour it back again into the bottle if he chose, and departed; after greatly outraging the dignity of Peg Sliderskew by brushing past her in the passage without a word of apology or recognition.

Mr. Gride and his housekeeper, immediately on being left alone, resolved themselves into a committee of ways and means, and discussed the arrangements which should be made for the reception of the young bride. As they were, like some other committees, extremely dull and prolix in debate, this history may pursue the footsteps of Newman Noggs, thereby combining advantage with necessity; for it would have been necessary to do so under any circumstances, and necessity has no law as all the world know.

" You've been a long time," said Ralph, when Newman returned.

" He was a long time," replied Newman.

" Bah!" cried Ralph impatiently. " Give me his note, if he gave you one; his message, if he didn't. And don't go away. I want a word with you, sir."

Newman handed in the note, and looked very virtuous and innocent while his employer broke the seal, and glanced his eye over it.

" He'll be sure to come!" muttered Ralph, as he tore it to pieces; " why of course I know he'll be sure to come. What need to say that? Noggs! Pray sir, what man was that with whom I saw you in the street last night ? "

" I don't know," replied Newman.

" You had better refresh your memory, sir," said Ralph with a threatening look.

" I tell you," returned Newman boldly, " that I don't know him at all. He came here twice and asked for you. You were out. He came again. You packed him off yourself. He gave the name of Brooker.

" I know he did," said Ralph; " what then?"

" What then? Why, then he lurked about and dogged me in the street. He follows me night after night, and urges me to bring him face to face with you, as he says he has been once, and not long ago either. He wants to see you face to face, he says, and you'll soon hear him out, he warrants."

" And what say you to that?" inquired Ralph, looking keenly at his drudge.

" That it's no business of mine, and I won't. I told him he might catch you in the street, if that was all he wanted, but no! that wouldn't do. You wouldn't hear a word there, he said. He must have you alone in a room with the door locked, where he could speak without fear, and you'd soon change your tone, and hear him patiently."

" An audacious dog!" Ralph muttered.

" That's all I know," said Newman. " I say again, I don't know what man he is. I don't believe he knows himself. You have seen him; perhaps you do."

" I think I do," replied Ralph.

" Well," retorted Newman, sulkily, " then don't expect me to know him too, that's all. You'll ask me next why I never told you this before. What would you say, if I was to tell you all that people say of you ? What do you call me when I sometimes do ? ' Brute, ass !' and snap at me like a dragon."

This was true enough, though the question which Newman anticipated was, in fact, upon Ralph's lips at the moment.

" He is an idle ruffian," said Ralph ; " a vagabond from beyond the sea where he travelled for his crimes, a felon let loose to run his neck into the halter ; a swindler, who has the audacity to try his schemes on me who know him well. The next time he tampers with you, hand him over to the police, for attempting to extort money by lies and threats,—d'ye hear ? and leave the rest to me. He shall cool his heels in jail a little time, and I'll be bound he looks for other folks to fleece when he comes out. You mind what I say, do you ?"

" I hear," said Newman.

" Do it then," returned Ralph, " and I'll reward you. Now, you may go."

Newman readily availed himself of the permission, and shutting himself up in his little office, remained there in very serious cogitation all day. When he was released at night, he proceeded with all the expedition he could use to the City, and took up his old position behind the pump, to watch for Nicholas—for Newman Noggs was proud in his way, and could not bear to appear as his friend before the brothers Cheeryble, in the shabby and degraded state to which he was reduced.

He had not occupied this position many minutes when he was rejoiced to see Nicholas approaching, and darted out from his ambuscade to meet him. Nicholas, on his part, was no less pleased to encounter his friend, whom he had not seen for some time, so their greeting was a warm one.

" I was thinking of you at that moment," said Nicholas.

" That's right," rejoined Newman, " and I of you. I couldn't help coming up to-night. I say, I think I'm going to find out something."

" And what may that be ?" returned Nicholas, smiling at this odd communication.

" I don't know what it may be, I don't know what it may not be," said Newman ; " it's some secret in which your uncle is concerned, but what, I've not yet been able to discover, although I have my strong suspicions. I'll not hint 'em now, in case you should be disappointed."

" *I* disappointed !" cried Nicholas ; " am I interested ?"

" I think you are," replied Newman. " I have a crotchet in my head that it must be so. I have found out a man, who, plainly knows more than he cares to tell at once, and he has already dropped such hints to me as puzzle me—I say, as puzzle me," said Newman, scratching his red nose into a state of violent inflammation, and staring at Nicholas with all his might and main meanwhile.

Admiring what could have wound his friend up to such a pitch of mystery, Nicholas endeavoured, by a series of questions, to elucidate the cause, but in vain. Newman could not be drawn into any more explicit statement, than a repetition of the perplexities he had already thrown out, and a confused oration, showing, How it was necessary to use the utmost caution ; how the lynx-eyed Ralph had already seen him in company with his unknown correspondent ; and how he had baffled the said Ralph by extreme guardedness of manner and ingenuity of speech, having prepared himself for such a contingency from the first.

Remembering his companion's propensity,—of which his nose, indeed, perpetually warned all beholders like a beacon,—Nicholas had drawn him into a sequestered tavern, and here they fell to reviewing the origin and progress of their acquaintance, as men sometimes do, and tracing out the little events by which it was most strongly marked, came at last to Miss Cecilia Bobster.

" And that reminds me," said Newman, " that you never told me the young lady's real name."

" Madeline !" said Nicholas.

" Madeline !" cried Newman ; " what Madeline ? Her other name —say her other name."

" Bray," said Nicholas, in great astonishment.

" It's the same !" shrieked Newman. " Sad story ? Can you stand idly by, and let that unnatural marriage take place without one attempt to save her ? "

" What do you mean ?" exclaimed Nicholas, starting up ; " marriage ! are you mad ? "

" Are you ? is she ? are you blind, deaf, senseless, dead ?" said Newman. " Do you know that within one day, by means of your uncle Ralph, she will be married to a man as bad as he, and worse, if worse there is ? Do you know that within one day she will be sacrificed, as sure as you stand there alive, to a hoary wretch—a devil born and bred, and grey in devils' ways ? "

" Be careful what you say," replied Nicholas, " for Heaven's sake be careful. I am left here alone, and those who could stretch out a hand to rescue her are far away. What is it that you mean ? "

" I never heard her name," said Newman, choking with his energy. " Why didn't you tell me ? How was I to know ? We might at least have had some time to think ! "

" What is it that you mean ? " cried Nicholas.

It was not an easy task to arrive at this information ; but after a great quantity of extraordinary pantomime which in no way assisted it, Nicholas, who was almost as wild as Newman Noggs himself, forced him down upon his seat and held him down until he began his tale.

Rage, astonishment, indignation, and a storm of passions rushed through the listener's heart as the plot was laid bare. He no sooner understood it all, than with a face of ashy paleness, and trembling in every limb, he darted from the house.

" Stop him !" cried Newman, bolting out in pursuit. " He'll be doing something desperate—he'll murder somebody—hallo ! there, stop him. Stop thief! stop thief ! "

Published this Day,

THE CHEAPEST TRAVELLING MAP EXTANT.

DARTON'S TRAVELLERS' GUIDE

THROUGH ENGLAND AND WALES,

And the principal parts of SCOTLAND, including ALL the RAILROADS, the Direct and Principal Cross Roads, Rivers, Canals, Cities, Market Towns, &c. &c., from the most recent Surveys. Size, 29 Inches by 25. Price 4s. 6d. Sheet, full Coloured ; in Case, for the Pocket, 7s.

Shortly will be ready,

SCOTLAND AND IRELAND,

Uniform with the above.

MODERN CHEAP MAPS.

Darton's Maps.

On a large sheet,—size, 28 by 23½ inches. On sheets, 2s. 6d. each. In a Case, 3s. 6d. On Canvas Rollers, and Varnished, 7s. 6d.

*Darton's Map of the World, in Hemispheres
*———— Europe, according to the last Treaty at Vienna
*———— Asia
*———— Africa
*———— America
" Decidedly the best Map of America published."—*Times.*

*Darton's England and Wales
*———— Ireland
———— British Islands
———— Diagrams of the Great Triangle in the trigonometrical Survey of England and Wales, with the Heights of the several Stations, and other remarkable Hills, &c.

Skeleton Maps, &c. to the above, containing over them the Lines of Latitude and Longitude, at 2s. each.

Darton's four-sheet Map of Europe.

Size 4 feet 2 inches by 4 feet 1 inch, 12s. 6d. in Sheets. In Case for the Library, 21s On Canvas, Roller, and Varnished, 26s.

Wilkinson's large four-sheet Maps,

Containing the latest Discoveries. Size, 4 feet 2 inches by 4 feet 1 inch.

ASIA, on 5 sheets, 10s. 6d. In Case, for the Library, 21s.
AFRICA, on 4 sheets, 10s. 6d. In Case, for the Library, 21s.
NORTH AND SOUTH AMERICA, on 4 sheets, 10s. 6d. In Case, for the Library, 12s.
The above, on Canvas, Roller, and Varnished, 25s. each.
The above correspond with Darton's Europe.

Darton's Outlined Maps.

FOR JUNIOR PUPILS TO FILL UP.

Printed on fine paper Size, 20½ inches by 16½ inches, 1s. each Map.

Eastern Hemisphere	Asia	England
Western Hemisphere	Africa	Scotland
Europe	America	Ireland

Key Maps, to the above, Coloured, on the same Scale, at the same Price.

These Maps are particularly adapted to Schools and Libraries. The great demand has induced the Publishers to reduce the price 30 per cent., which brings them to nearly 50 per cent. below most of the Maps of the same description which are now before the Public.

** Please Ask for " Darton's."

DARTON AND CLARK, HOLBORN HILL.

In square 16mo., neatly bound, and beautifully Illustrated, price 4s. 6d.,

THE THIRD AND FOURTH SERIES OF
THE BIBLE STORY BOOK.
BY THE REV. B. H. DRAPER.
WITH MANY ENGRAVINGS.

JOB IN HIS PROSPERITY.

In Royal 32mo., with numerous Anecdotes and Wood Cuts, price 2s., the Third Edition of

THE BOOK FOR THE LORD'S DAY,
FOR SCHOOLS AND FAMILIES.
BY THE REV. B. H. DRAPER.

In Royal 32mo., illustrated in a new style, price 3s.,

THE

BREAKFAST-TABLE COMPANION;
OR,
CHRISTIAN'S POCKET MISCELLANY.
DEDICATED TO THE REV. B. H. DRAPER, OF SOUTHAMPTON,
BY HIS DAUGHTER.

Appropriate Presents for the Young. Just Published by Darton and Clark,

Neatly Bound, in one thick volume, price 6s. 6d.,

THE JUVENILE NATURALIST;

OR,

WALKS IN SPRING, SUMMER, AUTUMN, AND WINTER.

BY THE REV. B. H. DRAPER.

𝔚𝔦𝔱𝔥 𝔖𝔱𝔢𝔢𝔩 𝔉𝔯𝔬𝔫𝔱𝔦𝔰𝔭𝔦𝔢𝔠𝔢 𝔞𝔫𝔡 𝔗𝔦𝔱𝔩𝔢-𝔭𝔞𝔤𝔢, 𝔞𝔫𝔡 𝔫𝔢𝔞𝔯𝔩𝔶 100 𝔈𝔫𝔤𝔯𝔞𝔳𝔦𝔫𝔤𝔰.

SUMMER.

THE PARLOUR BOOK;

OR,

FAMILIAR CONVERSATIONS ON SCIENCE AND THE ARTS.

BY WILLIAM MARTIN,

AUTHOR OF "THE CHRISTIAN LACON," EDITOR OF "THE EDUCATIONAL MAGAZINE,"
ETC., ETC.

WITH MANY BEAUTIFUL PLATES.

Square 16mo. Price 4s. 6d., in Fancy Wrapper.

" To direct the minds of youth to some of the most interesting phenomena of nature, they could hardly have a more attractive companion."—*Literary Gazette.*

" We advise all the young gentlemen to ask Papa for the Parlour Book as a present. The illustrations do great credit to the volume."—*Metropolitan Conservative Journal.*

" A beautiful book filled with good matter and excellent engravings."—*Family Magazine.*

"The author could not have employed his talents more laudably than in engaging the minds of children in the study of such important objects."—*Christian Reformer.*

THE BOOK OF QUADRUPEDS:

FOR THE AMUSEMENT AND INSTRUCTION OF YOUNG PEOPLE.

BY T. BILBY & R. RIDGWAY.

WITH ORIGINAL AND SELECTED ILLUSTRATIVE ANECDOTES.

BY W. R. MACDONALD.

Many beautiful Plates. Square 16mo.

POPULAR SCHOOL BOOKS.

THE MORAL AND INTELLECTUAL SCHOOL BOOK. By WILLIAM MARTIN. Royal 18mo. Embossed Roan, Price Four Shillings.

" This book is in reality a ' Reader.'—The Selections have a character about them adapted to the spirit of the times, and very different from the ' My Name is Norval,'—mode of the old School books."—*Spectator.*

" The Lessons lead to a thorough acquaintance with the English Language, and the Extracts from the Modern Poets with remarks on the writers, are well chosen to cultivate the taste, and improve the mind."—*Literary Gazette.*

THE MOTHER'S DICTIONARY. By MRS. JAMIESON (late Murphy). 18mo., bound. Price 3s. 6d.

" This little book is distinguished from other Dictionaries by the easy and familiar form of its definitions, and is peculiarly adapted to the purposes of domestic Education."

BROOKES' SCHOOL ATLAS; Comprising all the Modern Maps usually required in a Course of Elementary Instruction, according to the Best and Latest Authorities. With an Accurate Index. Price 6s.

** The only Modern School Atlas published with an Index, at 6s.

THE MORAL PRINCIPLES OF THE OLD AND NEW TESTAMENT, arranged in Lessons for the purposes of Education. By MRS. PETCH. 12mo., Cloth Lettered. Price 2s.

A CATECHISM of the HISTORY OF ENGLAND, from the Time of the Ancient Britons to the present Reign. By the Rev. T. WILSON. Price 9d.

BLAIR'S FIRST or MOTHER'S CATECHISM, containing Common Things necessary to be known at an Early Age. By the Rev. DAVID BLAIR, Author of the Second and Third Catechisms, " Why and Because," " Universal Preceptor," " Grammar of Natural Philosophy," &c. The Eighty-first Edition, carefully revised and corrected, with valuable additions. Price 9d.

BLAIR'S SECOND or MOTHER'S CATECHISM, being a Sequel to the First Catechism, Treating of other Subjects proper to be known at an early Age. By the Rev. DAVID BLAIR, Author of the First and Third Catechisms, &c. &c. Carefully revised and corrected, with valuable Additions. Price 9d.

BLAIR'S THIRD or MOTHER'S CATECHISM, being a Sequel to the Second Catechism, treating of other Subjects proper to be known at an early Age. By the Rev. DAVID BLAIR, Author of the First and Second Catechisms, &c. &c. Carefully revised and corrected, with valuable Additions. Price 9d.

THE GOSPEL PREACHED TO BABES:

PRINCIPALLY IN WORDS OF ONE AND TWO SYLLABLES.

With above Forty Engravings. Price 1s. 6d.

With numerous Illustrative Plates, and Gilt Edges, price 1s. 6d.,

THE LITTLE BOOK OF BOTANY; or, Familiar Exposition of

Botanical Science, simplified and written expressly for Young Botanists. By DANIEL COOPER, A.L.S., Curator to the Botanical Society of London, &c.

36mo., Plates, and Gilt Edges, Price 1s. 6d.,

THE LITTLE BOOK OF ANIMALS; or, Select and amusing Anec-

dotes of various Animals.

THE LITTLE READER: A Collection of Reading Lessons, in Prose.

THE LITTLE BOOK FOR LITTLE READERS; a Selection

of Poems ; and

THE CHILD'S FIRST BOOK OF MANNERS:

By the Editor of "The Parting Gift." Royal 36mo. Cloth, Gilt Edges. 1s. 6d. each.

" These two little books are equally bijoux as specimens of typography. They are on tinted paper, and are altogether got up in a superior style."—*Metropolitan.*

THE LITTLE MINERALOGIST ; or, First Book of Mineralogy ; and

THE LITTLE CONCHOLOGIST : A Guide to the Classification of

Shells. By the Rev. T. WILSON. Gilt Edges, Coloured Frontispiece, and several Copper Plates. Price 1s. each.

THE ARCHBISHOP'S DAUGHTER : A Tale of the Sixteenth

Century. By DIDYMUS. Plates. Square 16mo. Fancy Wrapper. Price 1s. 6d.

PUBLISHED BY DARTON AND CLARK.

UNIVERSAL EDUCATION,

FOUNDED UPON A PERFECT

SCIENCE OF MIND,

Which must be Introduced into every Seminary in the World!

BY THOMAS WIRGMAN, ESQ

AUTHOR OF THE FOLLOWING WORKS.

GRAMMAR OF THE FIVE SENSES,

" For the Use of Schools," in Dialogues, with Illustrative Wood-cuts ; forming the first step to a perfect

" PHILOSOPHY OF MIND."

Price 6s.

"This work proceeds with the education of infants on the only sure basis—the Education of the Five Senses. On this he founds his "*moral training.*"—*Educational Magazine.*

UNIVERSAL PICTURE LESSONS

OF THE

FIVE SENSES;

FOR INFANT, NATIONAL, AND NORMAL SCHOOLS:

Being delineations of the Hand, the Eye, the Ear, the Tongue, and the Nose. Awakening the Infant mind to the distinct operations of these " *Five Organs of Sense,*" really forms the First Step to " Education," and enables the Teacher to show the Pupil how all the physical sciences—Mechanics, Optics, Acoustics, Gastronomy, Odoration—have their origin in the Five Senses. Make the blind man a Dyer, and the deaf man an Organist.

Price 6d. ; mounted, 1s. 3d. each.

"These Picture Lessons correspond with the " GRAMMAR of the FIVE SENSES " We particularly recommend them to the notice of all infant teachers ; for they really form the FIRST STEP to all " education."—*Educational Magazine.*

CARDS OF THE FIVE SENSES,

Explanatory of their Uses, and their Division into *Two Kinds,* which establish for ever strict definitions of those all-important notions,

TIME and SPACE.

Price 1s.

" These will be found very fascinating for children, *being coloured,* and will early introduce them to the value of these all-important organs."—*Infant Teacher.*

PUBLISHED BY DARTON AND CLARK.

BRITISH EUCLID,

WHICH ESTABLISHES THE "TWENTY ELEMENTS" OF THE MIND.

Price 6d.

"The definitions in this work are strictly sound, and the reasoning is mathematical."—*Educational Magazine.*

MENTAL PHILOSOPHY.

A PRESENT FOR EVERY GOOD BOY AND GIRL

IN ALL THE

"INFANT SCHOOLS"

THROUGHOUT THE KINGDOM;

WITH A SONG OF THE FIVE SENSES.

Price 4s. 6d. per 100, or 2l. per 1,000.

"An amusing little work, which contains more philosophy than meets the eye."—*Universal Magazine.*

THE SONGS OF

SENSE, UNDERSTANDING, REASON.

SET TO MUSIC,

With Beautiful Coloured Frontispieces, explanatory of the

"SCIENCE OF MIND."

Price 1s. each.

DIVARICATION of the NEW TESTAMENT

INTO

DOCTRINE and HISTORY,

With gold Title-pages on a blue ground,—a perfect bijou,

WITH

AN ENGRAVING ON STEEL,

Representing the Crucifixion ; and over the Head of the Dying Redeemer, in a circle, one-eighth of an inch in diameter,

IS PLACED

THE LORD'S PRAYER.

Second edition. Price 21s. in fancy boards ; 1l. 11s. 6d. elegantly bound in calf, gilt edges, and highly embellished.

"This work is a masterpiece.—Probably no man in the world besides the Author could have produced it ; and a hundred generations will pass away before men generally are wise enough to understand its multifarious contents. It blends all discordant sects into one ; and thus establishes ' PRIMITIVE CHRISTIANITY' in its pristine vigour."—*Christian Advocate.*

THE DUBLIN DISCUSSION.—CHURCH EDITION.

LONDON: RICHARD GROOMBRIDGE, 6, PANYER ALLEY, PATERNOSTER ROW.
CARSON, ROBERTSON, and BLEAKLEY, Dublin.

In Octavo, price 7s. 6d.

THE AUTHENTICATED REPORT

(Signed by Mr. Gregg and his Special Reporters)

OF THE

DISCUSSION

WHICH TOOK PLACE IN THE ROUND ROOM OF THE ROTUNDA, DUBLIN, ON THE 29th
OF MAY, 1838, AND EIGHT FOLLOWING DAYS,

BETWEEN

THE REV. T. D. GREGG, A.M.,

MINISTER OF THE FREE CHURCH, SWIFT'S ALLEY, DUBLIN,

AND THE REV. THOMAS MAGUIRE, P.P.

OF BALLINAMORE.

It is necessary to inform the Public, that inasmuch as a disagreement arose between the parties, there is no *joint* Edition of the Discussion. The Protestant Edition is not signed by Mr. Maguire; nor is the Roman Catholic Edition signed by Mr. Gregg. A reference to the Correspondence will clearly explain the reasons why.

This Edition has a copious Index, which will enable the reader at once to turn to the arguments advanced on both sides, and the answers given. The Propositions argued were as follow:—

MR. GREGG'S PROPOSITIONS.

" *First.*—I assert that the United Church of England and Ireland is the Church of Christ, Holy, Catholic, and Apostolic, in these Kingdoms; that it knows the true road to Heaven, points it out to its followers, and that its blessed fruits are the holiness and happiness of those with whom it prevails."

" *Second.*—I assert that the Roman Catholic Church is the Church of Antichrist, unholy and apostate, that it does not know, and does not teach the way to heaven; that it conducts its followers in the broad road which lendeth to destruction; that it brings down the curse of God upon every country where it prevails; that it is the mother of abominations, the plague and pest of the human race; that it will be destroyed by the signal vengeance of the Most High, and that the very first duty of every member of it is, instantly to come out of it, that he be not a partaker at once of its sins and of its plagues."—*Mr. Gregg's Letter.*

MR. MAGUIRE'S PROPOSITION.

" The comparative claims of the two great rival Churches to unity, sanctity, catholicity, and apostolicity, are now in a promising way of being fairly, fully, equally, and searchingly discussed. Your two propositions are already before the public. These you undertake to *prove*, I to *disprove*."—*Mr. Maguire's Letter.*

Opinions of the Press on the Discussion.

From the Derry Sentinel.

No event which has occurred for many years should yield the Protestants of Ireland more genuine, more solemn satisfaction, than the controversy between the Reverends T. D. Gregg and T. Maguire. No doubt the spirit of some will be chafed, particularly among the ignorant and bigoted; but the controversy will lead also to thoughtful inquiry, and many a deluded Roman Catholic will be taught by it to "search the Scriptures," and to abandon a system which substitutes a round of formal empty services with all the trumpery of beads, holy water, scapulars, cords, and relics, for that spiritual worship which God has declared that he will alone receive, and which is the only worship worthy a rational and immortal being. Yes, this controversy will lighten the moral gloom that rests on our country, and the Sun of Righteousness will penetrate the mists of superstition, until, by degrees, he shall shine more and more unto the perfect day.

From the Leinster Express.

Since the days of the great German Reformer, when the voice of truth was heard assailing her doctrines from the cloister of Wittemberg, the Papal Church never met a more potent adversary than the Rev. Mr. Gregg. He chased his subtle adversary through all the labyrinths of wily arguments and slippery evasions. No perversion could foil, no declamation disconcert him—no smooth and specious but false gloss of reason could deceive him. He drove his adversary from his different positions, and then followed him with the greatest perseverance and pertinacity through the perplexing doubles of a peculiar sophistry, defeating every attempt and artifice to elude his immitigable pursuit. Mr. Gregg's answer to Mr. Maguire, when the latter defied him to prove the authenticity of the Bible, is, we think, one of the severest and most solemn specimens of eloquent rebuke we have ever read; and we are sure it will take a long time to erase the effects of his exposure of that canonized —— Dens from the public mind. The marble, the statuary, and graven silver of the sculptor could not last as long. Mr. Gregg undertook the discussion under the most discouraging circumstances, and we cannot too much admire the honest confidence that made him hold out against all the cold dissuasion of distrustful friends. His conduct on that occasion not a little resembled that of Luther, who, when advised not to go to the diet of Worms, resolutely declared that he would go, " though there were as many devils there as tiles on the houses."

CLARKE, PRINTERS, SILVER STREET, FALCON SQUARE, LONDON.

From the Kilkenny Moderator.

The late discussion has inflicted a wound on the side of Popery, from the effects of which she will take some time to recover. It is admitted on all hands, that Mr. Maguire is an able casuist, but when opposed to the champion of truth, who wielded his weapons with consummate skill and ingenuity, he was utterly confounded. Indeed the merciless exposure of the superstitions of the apostate Church struck the priests with such dismay as to induce them to quit the field. Mr. Gregg laid the system open in all its naked deformity. The great champion of Popery is now laid low. We shall hear no more of his perigrinations to Glasgow, or of his challenges to the Protestant clergy ; and we should not be surprised if the confession box were in future carefully guarded, if not voted useless, after Mr. Gregg's exposure of its contents. We have had a great victory.

From the Drogheda Conservative.

The discussion between the Rev. Mr. Gregg, and Father Tom Maguire has come to a close — the champion of mother Church having fled the field, conscious that in his opponent he had caught a tartar. As it is, we are convinced that Popery has received a blow in the recent discussion, which it will never recover in this country.

From the Londonderry Standard.

The most extraordinary discussion perhaps ever witnessed—that which recently occupied the public mind—has come to a close. A victory more complete we could not have wished for. Mr. Gregg proved himself a very David against the Popish Goliath. He had no mercy on the apostate church—he dealt his blows one after another with a force and pertinacity which astonished while it stupified his adversary. People could scarce believe their ears while the Protestant champion uttered the tremendous truths of Christianity before those who only knew them through the mist and shadow of Roman dogmatism. It almost appeared as if this brilliant disputant had been raised up for the overthrow of Popery in this country, at least he spoke as if he thought so. His denunciations of the apostate Church and its theologians were terrific. Even in the poorest weapon of the controversialist, that of personal sarcasm, he was mmeasurably more skilful than his opponent.

From the Westmeath Guardian.

The issue of the contest between the two churches will naturally benefit the cause of truth, and should be hailed with satisfaction and delight by every friend of civil and religious liberty. Mr. Maguire left the field in possession of his opponent. He was foiled in argument, defeated in all his false positions, and driven out of all his resources.

From the Fermanagh Reporter.

Mr. Gregg's services in the cause of truth are become duly appreciated. The vulgar abuse which the radical press is heaping on him is grateful to the ears of protestants, who can see that there would be little of this passionate ebullition of spleen if they did not smart under the mortification of defeat, on the same principle that children seldom cry until they are hurt. In the chief towns meetings have been held and complimentary resolutions and addresses are showering upon him. Every good man and true will lose no time in coming forward and adding the weight of his individual testimony, to the general feeling of rational gratitude with which Mr. Gregg's efforts deserve to be greeted.

From the Cork Constitution.

Mr. Gregg has done good service to the cause of truth. Brushing aside the sophisms by which an ingenious and accomplished disputant endeavoured to mislead him, he stood unflinchingly by the oracles of God—refused all recognition of the phantasies of Rome, and, rending the veil from the " mystery of iniquity," made such an exposure of the foulness it concealed, as that the very " sons whom she had brought up" stood aghast at the impurities of their delinquent mother.

From the Sligo Journal.

We have read with deep interest the important discussion between Messrs. Gregg and Maguire, but forbore any comment upon the proceedings until we should ascertain the result. Mr. Gregg has now, it must be acknowledged even by the opposing party, been gloriously triumphant over the celebrated champion of Popery, both in the soundness of his logic, the power of his argument, the uncompromising boldness with which he assailed the mysterious system, and unbending determination to expose the fallacy of her superstition to the last. It is needless to make the slightest allusion to the manner in which the discussion terminated. We congratulate Mr. Gregg upon the victory. It is well that an extinguisher has been put on Mr. Maguire's vauntings.

Birmingham Advertiser.

As we confidently anticipated, the interesting discussion in Dublin has terminated in the complete triumph of the Rev. Mr. Gregg. Never was Popery so completely exposed in any similar controversy—never was Protestantism more nobly or successfully vindicated. The sudden and unexpected retirement of Father Maguire from the arena is sufficient evidence of the utter frustration of the cause which he advocated.

Felix Farley's Bristol Journal.

It has been out of our power to give any report of the very interesting discussion which has taken place at Dublin between the Rev. Mr. Gregg and Father Maguire ; but we rejoice to say, that Protestantism has achieved a splendid triumph, in the person of Mr. Gregg, over the errors of Popery, as represented by the celebrated champion of the Romish Church.

Wakefield Journal.

Previous to the commencement of the discussion, the Protestants trembled for the fate of their champion, fearful that he might not be equal to an encounter with his celebrated antagonist. But the first day's controversy relieved the minds of the Protestants of all their fears. Their champion exhibited talent and eloquence of the first order, an intimate acquaintance with every thing bearing upon the subject in debate, and a skill in bringing forward the stores of learning he possessed, which astonished his auditory. It is not to be concealed that the eloquent speeches of Mr. Gregg have inflicted the severest blow upon the cause of Romanism which it has yet received.

Newcastle Journal.

An interesting discussion has taken place in Dublin, between the Rev. T. D. Gregg and the Rev. Father Maguire, on the doctrines of the Popish Church, and has terminated in the complete discomfiture of the latter. Never was a greater victory achieved than on this occasion, and the effect of it will be felt through the length and breadth of the enslaved dominions of Popery. The controversy was protracted for nine days, and was unexpectedly concluded, in consequence of the Rev. Father being unable any longer to sustain the well-directed artillery of his successful opponent.

Limerick Standard.

Universally admitted as it now is, that the victory obtained by Mr. Gregg has been the most triumphant and complete that has been achieved in late years, it becomes our bounden duty to offer up our thanks, in the first place, to Him who so graciously enabled his servant to combat with success against the powers of darkness.

Bath Chronicle.

The discussion came to an end on Thursday last, by Mr. Maguire declining to prolong it. A wish to prevent public excitement was assigned as the reason for bringing the matter to a conclusion, but this has deceived nobody. The public of Dublin agree that the discomfiture of the Priest has been complete. These uncloakings of the dark doings of Popery cannot but be productive of the greatest good. There are, we are aware, well-meaning Protestants, who are opposed to such discussions, as creating, they say, irritation on religious subjects. But these individuals effectually play the game of the Papistical priesthood, whose object is to mine in undisturbed secrecy, until they think they may boldly operate in open day, and who for the present dread nothing so much as the result of free enquiry. To appeal to a Protestant in favour of religious liberty is to take him on his most accessible side; but to consider that it is inconsistent with liberty of conscience to lay bare the iniquities of a system, the tendency of which is to cripple all liberty, whether civil or religious, is a most fatal error.

From the Liverpool Standard.

The discussion has more than realized the most sanguine expectations of the friends of true and unadulterated Christianity. Day after day did Mr. Gregg meet the cavils and demolish the sophistries of his crafty opponent. The word of truth has proved indeed a powerful weapon in the hands of the admirable champion of Protestantism. Fears were entertained when he entered the arena with so accomplished a logician and so eloquent a speaker as the doughty priest Maguire; but we are proud to say that Mr. Gregg has proved himself in every respect more than a match for his opponent.

We sincerely hope that the proceedings of this triumphant discussion may shortly be published, so as to be accessible to all classes of the community. We are sure that much good may be done by their dissemination in England.

Second Notice.

That Mr. Gregg has acquitted himself with zeal, energy, and talent in the course of this protracted discussion, is evident;—but who or what has triumphed? Is it merely Mr. Gregg that has achieved a victory over his subtle and crafty opponent? Is it merely the personal triumph of one out of two acute logicians or accomplished scholars? No! It is a far greater victory than this. It is the triumph of the purity of Protestantism over the complicated abominations of Popery. It is the triumph of truth over error, and Christian knowledge over sottish superstition, of charity over bigotry, of the immutable Word of God over the cunningly-devised fables of the Church of Rome. The effects of this glorious victory will be long felt, in Ireland especially, and throughout the whole extent of the usurped dominion of the Papacy. A spirit of inquiry has been already generated which cannot but lead to the most satisfactory results.

From the Dublin Record, during the discussion.

Let our report go forth as it stands. We appeal to it without a moment's hesitation, as affording a noble and convincing evidence of the clear and manifest triumph of truth during, and at the end of, those two days of trial. The Lord has blessed the work in the hands of his servant, and the prayers of his believing people have been manifestly answered. Thus far the battle has gone gloriously for us, and a great victory has been achieved. In Mr. Maguire, we perceive all his accustomed fluency and readiness; and on the first day at least, we might add, his usual confidence also. Of our friend Mr. Gregg, we cannot possibly speak in the frigid terms of supervising criticism; and we must not give way to those expressions of pleasure and satisfaction, at the manner in which he has been enabled thus far to perform his great work.

Second Notice.

The farther progress of this contest leaves us nothing to wish for. The Goliath of Irish Popery has been brought low; so low, that all that can be said of him is that he is alive. The [newspaper] reports, with all our care, give no adequate idea of the clearness of argument, the perspicuity of style, the point, vigour, and decision of our admirable champion, for such we gladly hail him. The priests of the apostasy all feel it deeply. God has sent upon them a strong delusion in provoking this controversy; and they are trembling for the consequences. They see what an exposure they have brought upon themselves; they see what an able champion of the truth it has pleased God to raise up; they perceive what a tremendous castigation he has inflicted on their (as they vainly hoped) indomitable hero; and perceiving how admirably our advocate has used every opportunity, not merely to overturn error, but to impress truth—not to

ensure a conquest merely, but to effect a conversion, the terrific result yawns before them, they feel keenly and sorely that their craft is in danger.

Our present conviction is, that the Rev. Mr. Gregg has, by God's permission, struck a blow in Ireland, which will be felt in its remotest corner—a deadly blow at the head of the beast.

Third Notice, at the conclusion of the discussion.

It is quite unnecessary to exert any little weight that our opinion may have with our readers, in order to convince them of the reality of the signal victory we have obtained in this remarkable, and as we trust it will long be, this memorable controversy. We have an immediate and palpable victory, felt, we are sure, and admitted by Roman Catholics themselves; and felt too, and acknowledged, by protestants also, we trust, in a Christian spirit of joy and thankfulness. Mr. Gregg has occupied a place, and performed a great undertaking, for which he has showed himself eminently qualified, and to which he seems to have been called in the providence of God. We cannot speak too highly of the ability and the spirit with which he has executed his task. It was nobly done in the Lord's strength, from first to last. As to Popery and its priests, never, we believe, were they so powerfully exposed,—never, certainly, were they shown up with such uncompromising severity in the presence of hundreds of Roman Catholics.

Liverpool Mail.

We refrain, through want of space, from attempting any report of the Dublin Controversy, which has so intensely engaged public attention. Our readers, however, know, that the Church of Rome had for its redoubted champion on the occasion the famous Father Thomas Maguire; and that the Protestant Church of this land was defended by the Rev. T. D. Gregg, of Swift Alley Church, Dublin. They perhaps know that the discussion terminated rather abruptly, by the Romanists withdrawing their champion—by Father Thomas's hasty retreat from the field, a disappointed priest, and a discomfited chevalier. The letter which is found in our columns to-day has been extorted from Mr. Gregg, in consequence of Mr. Maguire persevering in denying his defeat. It is written in good, old, stiff, uncompromising Saxon, and inflicts a terrible castigation on the monk. We make bold to say, that nothing has been penned like to it since the days of Luther, Calvin, and John Knox.

Mr. Gregg took his stand (to use his own expression) "on the platform of the Holy Catholic Church," and that was vantage ground, from which the boldest efforts of the Popish champion could not drive him. He never deserted that ground for an instant. Father Tom felt his difficulty. He was not to be scared by a bubble which would erect every individual token into a tribunal which could roll the thunders of the Vatican; but when Mr. Gregg proceeded to show, step by step, the encroachments of Papal Rome and the Catholicity of Reformed England, then did the priest of the intruding faith quail under his well-administered lash, and retired vanquished from the contest. Mr. Gregg, by keeping his ground, made every blow tell—there was no recoil—there were no suicidal stabs. If any good is to come of our controversy with Rome, it must be conducted with a due regard to the authority of that one Holy Catholic and Apostolic Church of which we express our belief in the Nicene Creed.

From the Carlow Sentinel.

We have attentively perused the discussion between Messrs. Gregg and Maguire; and we believe we may add that, since the Reformation, the power of our liege Lord the Pope never received so fatal a blow in Ireland. Mr. Maguire, the great Goliath of the Irish priesthood, was prostrated—in fact, with him it was a continued scene of shifting and manœuvring to evade the force of truth, powerfully brought to bear upon the superstitions he vainly defended. He fled for refuge to the fathers of the Church, and occasionally attempted to shelter himself beneath the wings of Dr. Jeremy Taylor, Thorndyke, and Protestant divines, but he was hunted out of every position by his powerful opponent, who grappled with every sophism with a vigour and strength of reasoning which astonished him.

The closing scene is extremely fine, if not dramatic—to behold priestcraft stripped of every tattered garment, and exhibited to the gaze of the astonished multitude, was a scene both novel and interesting. To see the consecrated trumpery, beads, holy cords, gospels, hair shirts, knee bones, holy candles, and so forth, laughed at even by the Roman Catholics, is a circumstance which appears to us to force Popery to a crisis. The astonishment of the priests may well be conceived when husbands, fathers, and brothers, were led into the secrets of Peter Dens—when the mysteries of the Confessional were exposed to public view.

From the Dublin Evening Mail.

The discussion between the Rev. Tresham D. Gregg and the Rev. Thomas Maguire has come to a close. The Roman Catholic party have formally declined to continue the controversy—the most interesting and probably the most important discussion which our times have witnessed. We feel a pleasing triumph in using the liberty we enjoy, and expressing our entire contentment with the whole proceeding.

The dissenter is not a separatist from the Church of Rome. He has come forth out of the bosom of the Church of England, and with *her* is his *immediate* controversy. His quarrel with Rome is but *mediate*—nay, remote; and his position requires him to justify nothing of his own institutions or faith, until first the Church of England has justified her secession and his inclusively. The true quarrel is between the member of the Anglican Church and the member of the Church of Rome; and therefore, entering into the argument on this ground, Mr. Gregg occupied the very position which enabled him to wield the spiritual sword, that is the Word of God, with its full effect. He stood upon the foundations of the Church, and on her acknowledged and recognised formulæ and laws; and he was thence enabled to use all her constitutional weapons with advantage. The Bible is the charter, the *constitution* of the established Church —of the Church of God—and, in Mr. Gregg's position, his appeal to its authority, his voucher for its genuiness and authenticity, and his confidence in its true interpretation, were as consclusive as they were easy and free from cavil.

From the Manchester Courier.

The discussion on the tenets of the Protestant and Romish religions, between the Rev. T. D. Gregg, A. M., and the Rev. T. Maguire, is likely to result in the utter confusion and defeat of the Romish party. Mr. Maguire cannot fail to have convinced every rational mind that he is fully sensible of the disadvantageous position in which he has been placed by his astute and talented opponent.

Since writing the above, the success of the latter gentleman has been so complete as to render it impera-tive on the civil authorities to cause him to be escorted to the place of disputation by the police patrol, in order to protect him from threatened violence.

We think the Roman Catholics have exercised a sound discretion in putting a stop to the discussion: we hope they may profit by the lesson that has been read to them.

From the Church of England Gazette.

The discussion in Dublin between our old friend, the Rev. T. D. Gregg, and Father Maguire, has terminated; and it is agreed on all hands that the priest of the Ancient Catholic Faith has gloriously triumphed over the wily advocate of the new and degrading religion known by the name of Popery. The matter will not end with the Dublin discussion; it will be followed up, not only in Dublin, but in England, with a power and energy which will make Popery quail, and skulk in the dark places of the earth. We congratulate Mr. Gregg on the success of his important struggle, and on the feeling which has been manifested towards him by his brethren.

For further notices, see the *Achill Herald*, the *Evening Packet*, *Warder*, *Protestant Guardian*, &c. &c. &c.

REV. T. D. GREGG'S CONTROVERSIAL WORKS.

The WITNESS, showing that POPERY is a great foretold APOSTACY—that nothing but the prevalence of the Holy Catholic Religion, through the co-operation of Church and State, can bless the Country—that therefore the Papists must be excluded from Parliament—that they can be, and the way how. By the Rev. T. D. GREGG, A.M. Complete in 1 vol. 4to, price 10s.

MEDE'S APOSTACY of the LATTER TIMES; with an Introduction, by the Rev. T. D. GREGG, on the Mode of maintaining the Roman Catholic Controversy.

In the introduction to this work, which was published some time before the discussion, Mr. Gregg shows, that the ordinary method of maintaining the controversy with the Roman Catholics can lead to no satisfactory result. He lays down a new system. It was that on which he acted on the important occasion referred to. Price 4s. 6d.

LETTERS TO J. E. GORDON, Esq. *Price* 2s.

The APOSTACY of the ROMAN CATHOLIC CHURCH clearly demon-strated, by the Rev. T. D. GREGG. This work summarily exhibits the argument which Mr. GREGG developed in the discussion. Price Sixpence.

POPERY the CURSE of IRELAND; being a Speech of the Rev. T. D. GREGG, delivered in the City of Limerick, in which he states the practicable mode of rooting Popery out of Ireland. Price Twopence.

Clarke, Printers, Silver Street, Falcon Square, London.

THE

MEDICAL CASKET:

DEDICATED, BY PERMISSION, TO

HIS ROYAL HIGHNESS THE DUKE OF SUSSEX.

(ABRIDGED.)

BEING A CONCISE SUMMARY OF

IMPORTANT INFORMATION

FOR THE DYSPEPTIC AND NERVOUS,

ON

INDIGESTION

AND ITS CONSEQUENCES,

NERVOUS AND BILIOUS COMPLAINTS,

DIET AND REGIMEN, &c.:

WITH

OBSERVATIONS

ON THE COMBINED PROPERTIES OF

QUININE WITH CAMPHOR, ETC.,

AS A RESTORATIVE REMEDY IN ALL CASES OF DISORDER IN THE
STOMACH AND THE NERVES, OCCASIONED BY INTERRUPTION
OF THE DIGESTIVE PROCESS:

THE DISCOVERY OF

DR. FLEMMING.

LONDON:

PRINTED BY W. TYLER, BOLT COURT, FLEET STREET.

PUBLISHED FOR THE AUTHOR, (HENRY CONGREVE, PECKHAM),

BY HANNAY AND DIETRICHSEN, 63, OXFORD - STREET, LONDON.

PRICE TWO PENCE.

PREFACE.

THE stomach and digestive organs form so important a part of the animal system, and are so intimately connected with every part of it, that in no case can they with safety be disregarded.

Indigestion, and the various consequences arising from it, known by the terms of Nervous and Bilious Complaints, proceed chiefly and immediately from loss of tone in the stomach, debility of its digestive organs, and want of energy in the nervous system; and there is no disorder which pervades the human frame, in which it does not constitute a prominent symptom.

That this complicated source of evils prevails, in a greater or less degree, in every individual, is beyond doubt. The most numerous class of diseases incident to life, and particularly of those who are verging to its decline, evidently emanate from failure of the powers, or disorder in the stomach and its dependences; and it is equally certain, that the first origin of infirmity may be traced to the effects arising from imperfectly digested food, produced either by excesses and intemperate habits, or from natural debility in that organ. When the powers of the stomach gradually decline, it is of essential importance carefully to examine into the habits of diet, and other causes, which have induced the evil, and to counteract the train of consequences which follow, by suitable food and medicine, without delay.

The great object aimed at in this treatise is to condense, within the compass of a few pages, all the information which, in most cases, is necessary to be attained. The principal causes which affect health, and induce disease, are shortly explained, with a view to render every person acquainted with himself, and consequently more capable of preserving his health unimpaired, or to regain it when it has suffered dilapidation.

Diet and regimen are always of importance, but especially so to the dyspeptic, to assist proper remedies in fulfilling their curative intentions; and it is presumed that the observations on this subject, which are superadded to the work, will prove generally and essentially useful to such, and that their importance will become practically exemplified in their individual experience.

The observations (p. 15) on the combined proportions of *Quinine* (a preparation from the finest Peruvian Bark, in a highly concentrated state, forming an elegant tonic and febrifuge medicine) with Camphor, and other newly discovered aperients and stomachics, by Dr. Flemming, as a remedy for all disorders consequent on impeded digestion, are equally important, and the Author confidently affirms his belief that a more valuable compound has never on any former occasion been introduced to public notice and attention.

HENRY CONGREVE.

Peckham.

MEDICAL CASKET.

OBSERVATIONS ON
INDIGESTION AND ITS CONSEQUENCES,
DENOMINATED
NERVOUS AND BILIOUS COMPLAINTS, &c.

PERHAPS no disease is less understood than that which most frequently invades the system, called Indigestion, and generally known by the vague appellation of Nervous and Bilious complaints, though none is of greater importance, whether we regard its consequences, or connexion with other diseases.

Indigestion is a complaint, from the consequences of which a great majority of the inhabitants of this island more or less suffer. Indeed, no individual is exempt from interruptions of the digestive process; and as the evils arising from this fertile source are extremely various, and often pregnant with considerable danger, the causes should be diligently investigated, with a view to interpose a counteractive.

This complaint commences in apparently unimportant deviations from health; it gradually assumes a more complicated character, and in the issue so undermines and weakens the powers of the system, as to render it very susceptible of every other malady.

The certain and direct results of this disorder are: Headache, Soreness of the Mouth, Hysteric Fits, St. Vitus's Dance, Epilepsy, Scrofulous complaints, Diabetes, Gravel, Gout and Rheumatism, Rickets, Worms, &c., and other disorders incident to the weakly sex.

The symptoms that immediately arise from undigested food, or from the foulness of the stomach, which causes the disease called Indigestion, are Flatulence, Distension of the Stomach and Bowels, Spasms, Periodical Pains, Giddiness, and Swimming of the Head, Costiveness, Loss of Memory, Weakness of Sight, Atoms flitting before the Eyes, Loss of Appetite, Heartburn, Acidity, and Putrescent Eructations. They occasion much uneasiness, but do not, at first, materially affect the general health. Owing to negligence in the early application of a remedial agent, the stomach and the digestive organs suffer considerable derangement. The alimentary canal partakes of the disease. The mouth in the morning contracts a disagreeable taste, and the tongue is incrusted with fur ; and, notwithstanding every effort to prevent it, the breath will acquire an offensive taint, which is a pretty certain indication that there exists in the stomach great disorder. The quantity and quality of the secretions of the intestines also become disordered, in a corresponding degree. The bowels cease to act with their accustomed energy, and are frequently distended and tense, especially after a meal. In some cases there is a total disrelish for food, although the appetite be not greatly impaired. Nausea, and bilious ejections, often occur in the morning, with those who are intemperate ; and, when the constitution has been undermined or ruined by dissipated habits, incessant thirst, fever, vitiated appetite, debility, difficulty of breathing, pallid countenance, and dropsy, usually ensue.

The stomach is one of the principal, and a most important organ of digestion. It is extremely liable to disorder ; and, of all the diseases which pervade the human frame, none are more prevalent than those which affect the stomach and bowels, or, when they are neglected or improperly treated, more fatal ; for, in such cases, they generally terminate in obstinate chronic maladies, which are frequently obstinately proof against the power of medicine or art to cure. And, on the other hand, there are but few diseases, whether chronic or acute, which do not in some degree affect these organs.

Between the stomach and other parts of the body there exists a powerful sympathy, and direct communication. That organ being the great source of nutriment, and amply supplied with nerves—the only medium of sensation—maintains a mutual intercourse with every other part ; first, by supplying the blood with chyle ; and secondly, by conveying its nervous sympathy throughout the whole, from which impressions are communicated to the brain, and through the entire corporeal system ; hence so extensive and extraordinary an influence is manifest therein, that there are but few, if any, diseases in which these organs are not affected to a great degree.

The health and welfare of the body, and the efficacy of such medicinal substances which are calculated to relieve its maladies, mainly depend upon the state and condition of the stomach, for in that organ their power and influence are first exerted ; and although some of these means may act as alteratives, universally, in a manner peculiar to their own nature, their operation will be regulated and diversified as the sensibility and the irritation then existing in the stomach may direct. This circumstance, in the treatment of diseases, has not always obtained the attention which its importance has demanded.

The firm texture and strength of the solids, or weakness of the animal economy, and the regularity of its functions, especially those of the stomach, evidently depend on the exertion of nervous power, which, from various sudden and accidental causes, becomes increased or diminished accordingly; hence we observe, that pure and uncontaminated air, and those medicines which brace the solids, materially add to the corporal vigour ; and wine, or beverages of a warm and cordial nature, when partaken in moderate supplies, as such, administer a temporary invigorating quality to that organ, and not only communicate bodily strength, but mental fortitude, by an increase of nervous energy thereto. Of a like nature is camphor, among medicinal agents, which in minute doses, properly combined,[*] gently stimulates, and proves reviving to the system. But, on the contrary, a moist, damp, cold, contaminated, and relaxing air; long abstinence from food, disquietude of mind, and extreme application to studious pursuits, invariably diminish the natural solidity of the structure, greatly impair digestion, and in the issue, superinduce the multifarious calamities which characterise or mark diseases of the chronic species.

As a particular evidence of the general and immediate communication which the stomach maintains with other parts of the bodily frame, may be stated, the sudden relief which has frequently been obtained from the tormenting pangs of toothache by an opiate, taken into the stomach, before it

* See page 15.

could possibly accomplish that object through the circulation of the blood. This testimony is conclusive. Moreover, the trembling hand of the inebriate becomes more steady, for a time, from a repetition of the cordial dram, which is effected or produced solely by the stimulative and invigorating power of that beverage upon the nerves, so abundant in that organ. Violent emotions of the mind invariably disorder the stomach; and a diseased state of that important repository will also materially affect the mind, and beget Languor, Lassitude, Despondency, and Hypochondriacal complaints.

The intimate and mutual intercourse which subsists between the body and mind is, therefore, evident; and that they alternately communicate their sensations to each other through the sympathy of the stomach, with different parts of the animal system, is equally demonstrated. Local disorders of the stomach at length affect the constitution, and beget chronic diseases, arising from Indigestion, and the incorporation of crude chyle with the blood, by which it becomes so much impoverished, that it is rendered unfit, as a source of nourishment, and consequently, Gout, Scurvy, Dropsy, Consumption, and various painful affections, follow in the train.

The official duties consigned to the stomach are of great importance in the animal economy. They consist principally in the preparation of the food deposited therein for the support and nourishment of the body; and the health of every organ necessarily depends on the proper fulfilment of their task. A fluid is secreted in this organ which possesses an astonishing power of assimilating and digesting the food. When this process is completed, the digested mass is propelled forwards by a gently-acting force into the intestinal canal, and speedily intermingles with the bile and other fluids secreted by the liver, which aid in that work. At length the food is reduced to the smoothest and most nicely-mixed pulp, in which state it is found in the smaller intestines, on the inner surface of which are innumerable minute vessels, that perform the functions of absorption, and carry off the nutritious part of the food, called chyle, to certain glandular bodies situated on the surface of the membrane which connects the intestines together. The chyle, being detained here for some time, is at length brought, by various channels, towards one ultimate vessel, denominated the thoracic duct; and this vessel pours its contents into the general mass of blood; and thus the nourishment of the body is accomplished. If the chyle, or the digestive fluid, be disordered, the body cannot be sufficiently nourished and supported; the nervous system will, consequently, become seriously affected; the secretions of the whole frame must be obstructed, and the vital fluid con-

taminated and impure. The result is, that fevers, febrile symptoms, general irritation, great exhaustion of the vital powers, emaciation of the whole body, and a retinue of complicated disorders, which resist the ordinary means of cure, ensue.

Moreover, the lungs, being also deprived of their healthy nutriment, sustain structural derangement, and inflammation and tubercles follow. Ulceration of the lungs may, however, exist from an early period; but it is very obvious that their growth is advanced by the causes just assigned. The lungs being encumbered by their obstruction, endeavour to throw it off by cough, and thus violent effort of the muscles of the thorax, pain, restless nights, &c. are occasioned; and all the increased symptoms which mark consumption rapidly succeed.

It therefore appears obvious, that none of the various parts of which the body is composed require equal care and attention as the stomach, both as it regards the avoidance of those substances of a deleterious nature, which would excite nausea or acidity in that organ, create debility in the digestive powers, and enervate its nerves; or, when that state has been induced, to restore it to its natural vigour by a timely and judicious recourse to strengthening remedies.

Whatever depresses or enervates the nervous power and influence, transmitted to the stomach, weakens the digestive action. Mental agitation, ardent study, habits of indolence, profuse evacuations, the abuse of intoxicating liquors, the too liberal use of warm diluting beverages, over-distension of the stomach, deficient secretion of bile, or gastric juice, liver complaints, hysterical and nervous disorders, want of exercise, &c., are primary causes of indigestion, and debility in the nervous system.

One of the greatest causes of the frequency of indigestion in this country, is the abuse of vinous liquors, and full meals of animal food, savoury dishes, &c., which keep the stomach in a perpetual state of irritability. In this morbid condition of that organ, it is impossible that the food can be properly digested. The animal fat becomes rancid; and the vegetable matter and vinous liquids, with which the stomach is overladen, rapidly run into acetous fermentation, occasioning heartburn, flatulence, great oppression, and general excitement, and subsequently languor, throughout the nervous economy. It is, perhaps, fortunate for the patient that digestion is thus impeded; for if all the food taken into the stomach were assimilated, the system would soon become in such a state of plethora, that sudden death must inevitably ensue. There is no doubt that numerous cases of Apoplexy, which terminate fatally, arise from that source and that alone.

The cases of Indigestion which occur in the higher classes of society from these causes are very general, and are aggravated by the late hours in which they dine. It is utterly impossible that the superabundance of food which is then partaken, over and above the requirements of nature, can be properly masticated ; and, instead of being allowed to remain in the stomach a sufficient time to be acted on by the gastric juice, the liquid is forced into the intestines by the extra supplies, and by the occasional contraction of that organ, from the stimulus of condiments and wine. With an over-distended stomach, and a brain unduly excited by wine, the epicure retires to rest ; but, instead of enjoying sound and refreshing sleep, he is harassed by disturbing dreams, and in consequence of the irritation of the brain, produced by the unnatural commotion in the stomach and the intestines, he passes a restless night. In the morning he arises with a countenance pale and lowering, with a mind dejected, an appetite impaired ; and is flatulent to a great degree. To take breakfast he has but little inclination ; but to dissipate *ennui*, and prepare for another meal, he visits the confectioner's, takes a jelly and a cordial, which, by stimulating the stomach, momentarily resuscitates the system with a little vigour, and renders life tolerable until the arrival of the dinner hour, when a few glasses of wine again dissipate his uncomfortable feelings, and reprocure the requisite spirits for conversation. A constant recurrence to this pernicious practice will infallibly produce organic disease in the stomach, intestines, or liver, and a speedy termination of that career. The only rational treatment which can be employed to facilitate a recovery, in these cases, consists in the observance of a spare diet, without delay, with the use of *mild* laxative and tonic medicines ; and above all, abstaining from a repetition of these excesses ; for it is certain that the organic diseases of the stomach, liver, and lungs, and complaints of the head, of which four-fifths of the inhabitants of this island die, are occasioned by unduly stimulating and overloading the stomach, to the serious depression of its energies.

In complaints of the stomach, accompanied with impaired appetite, flatulent eructations, acidity, and heartburn, not only is a confined state of the bowels with giddiness, obscurity of vision, deafness, and fluttering or palpitations of the heart, painfully manifest, but great irritability, despondency, and mental anxieties are depicted in the countenance ; fatigue and perspiration result from the slightest exercise, and sleepless nights, disturbed dreams, oppression on the chest, and in numerous instances pains in the stomach follow in the train.

The sensation called heartburn, from which so many patients suffer, generally proceeds from debility of the stomach, or the frequent use of acid food, owing to its fermentation. Heartburn is an uneasy sensation of heat about the pit of the stomach, which is sometimes attended with flatulence, difficulty of breathing, and an inclination to vomit. Those who are subject to that affection should avoid all fat substances, acids, &c. Violent exercise after a full meal is also injurious. If this disorder arise, as it generally does, from Indigestion, rhubarb, calcined magnesia, and Peruvian bark, or quinine, combined with stomachic bitters, as strengtheners, may be taken with advantage.

Of late years it has become fashionable to term all disorders of the stomach *bilious*, and even complaints of remote parts of the body, as sympathetic of affections of the liver. If a patient complain of nausea, according to their notions it is produced by bile ; and even acid eructations are termed bilious, although bile is conveyed into the upper portion of the intestines, called the duodenum, and not into the stomach.

The popular disease denominated *bilious*, is distinguished by impaired appetite, sense of thirst, or a clammy sensation in the mouth, sallow skin, restless nights, irritability of temper, and moral depression, originating in disordered digestion, and an inadequate exertion of the peristaltic or undulatory power of the intestines. That bile really prevails in these circumstances, is easily to be conceived, as the usual supply of that fluid is furnished by the hepatic secretion, or the secretions of the liver, and for the want of its being seasonably and sufficiently appropriated in carrying on the process of digestion, it necessarily superabounds in quantity. Sometimes, indeed, on these occasions, it acts as a vigorous cathartic, inducing copious bilious discharges from the bowels ; at other times, when the stomach is drawn into sympathy by the stimulant effects on the duodenum, an inverted action of the peristaltic power causes it to retrograde into that viscus, and to be ejected by vomiting. Thus the effects of indigestion and constipation are mistaken for morbid causes, instead of which they result from a derangement of the first passages, which will require to be adjusted, by invigorating measures, before the bilious consequences can be either corrected or remedied.

To accomplish this desirable object, dietetic regulation (according to the advice hereafter submitted to invalids on Diet, &c.) prohibiting substances and aliment that do not readily digest, and keeping the bowels soluble by mild aperients, blended with a strengthening remedy (as gentian, chirayita, essential salt of round-leaf cornel, best Turkey rhubarb, and bark, but especially its elegant preparation, quinine*) will cause

* See the close of this Treatise, on the properties of Quinine, as a tonic and febrifuge remedy.

the bilious fluid to be regularly occupied in its natural uses, and prevent its unemployed redundancy, and the disturbed state of the alimentary canal, by which it is occasionally ejected, both by vomiting and purging.

Chronic inflammation of the liver is also peculiarly marked by symptoms of dyspepsia, or indigestion, loss of appetite, flatulence, lowness of spirits, headache, debility, sense of fulness, and distension of the stomach. It comes on so gradually, and its symptoms at commencement are so obscure. that the complaint remains long unattended to. At length the general health suffers. An obtuse pain in the region of the liver and back ensues. The countenance assumes a yellow tinge, and inactivity, great dejection of spirits, obstinate costiveness, dropsy, and jaundice, follow. In these cases, one of the chief indications of cure is the continued use of bitter tonics, with aperients. The acute species of this complaint is ushered in with a sense of chilliness; pain in the chest and left side; dry cough; shortness of breath; pain in the right shoulder; jaundice; costiveness; or a relaxed state of the bowels.

Whenever the causes which produce languor and inactivity in the system, loathing of food, flatulence, acidities in the stomach and bowels, and a constipated habit, are long neglected, an overflowing or excess of bile, generally known by the name of jaundice, will occur. Purgatives have been used in these cases with success, but they always answer best, especially with weakly patients, when they are administered with strengthening bitters, and deobstruents; because it is necessary to obtain a return of appetite and vigour to the digestive powers, with regular stools of a proper character, and a soluble state of the bowels. Calomel has, of late, been exhibited very freely in these cases, with a view to restore the interrupted passage of the bile through the duct. This course is certainly objectionable, in a great majority of instances. Those individuals who are, however, prepossessed with a high opinion of its properties, and have hitherto experienced no ill effects from its occasional use, should take a sufficient dose of an aperient and strengthening medicine on the following morning. Many physicians, who are partial to the use of Mercury, combine it with Cinchona, or Peruvian Bark, or Quinine, in order to obviate or counteract any injurious consequences which might follow the latter, and to promote and regulate a beneficial operation.

In the preternatural secretions of bile, which are observed in Cholera-Morbus, wherein extreme debility is peculiarly manifest, which state of the system greatly favours the disposition to spasmodic affections, Bark, in any form, may be taken with advantage, to promote the strength of the stomach and intestines, especially so when it is conjoined with a mild cordial, as Camphor, and a deobstruent, to correct the spasms and to break down the coagulation of the blood, and consequently to restore its free and uninterrupted circulation, an obstruction to which is admitted by all to be the real cause of that afflicting malady.

Perhaps no sensation is more distressing, or more generally complained of, than headache. Bilious, or sick headache, nervous, rheumatic, and plethoric, are the species of that disorder, which prevail much in this country. The head holds a particular sympathy with the stomach, and in most cases, its numerous symptoms are occasioned by Indigestion. Bilious headache commences in the temples, and extends its influence over the whole head, producing therein a sense of weight and great uneasiness. It is usually induced by irregular habits and sedentary life, atmospheric heat, violent exercise, and a constipated state, or torpidity of the bowels. Nervous headache is attended by symptoms of acute pain in the forehead and temples, and giddiness of the head. The patient generally complains of cold, as though cold water were trickling down his back. Females are most subject to this disorder. When it is occasioned by Indigestion, (as is usually the case), it must be removed by appropriate remedies. This species of headache being frequently the consequence of debility—a state which the nervous system has sustained, attention must be directed to a reproduction of a healthy action. With this view, tonic medicines, blended with those of a stimulating kind, as bark and aromatics, are most appropriate. At the same time, a nutritious, generous, and invigorating diet, with a moderate portion of Madeira, will be advisable. Rheumatic headache is also very prevalent. The pains are periodical. In many instances they intermit, and cease abruptly, without occasioning any peculiar sensation. This disorder ebbs and flows according to the changes of the weather. Warmth, and the use of warm aperient or purgative medicines, is generally the only requisite treatment the case demands. Every person who is liable to that affection, should constantly wear flannel next the skin. There is also a Plethoric headache, which is very common. It arises from fulness of the vessels of the brain. Those whose employments occasion much stooping, are greatly affected with this species of the complaint. The bowels should be well moved by a suitable aperient, taking care to keep the head cool, and the feet warm, and to avoid excesses of every kind.

When Indigestion is produced by an increased excitement of the stomach, the circulating fluids are accelerated in their course by a full meal, the heat of the body is much augmented, the face flushed, the head confused, the palms of the hands and feet hot and dry; and the patient, in general, is very restless and nervous until that organ is quieted by the tranquillizing effects of a cup of tea or coffee, which, by creating perspiration, reduces the temperature of the body, and consequently the excitement. A frequent recurrence of this stimulus invariably begets serious debility; which, when it does exist, must be alleviated and removed by desisting from luxurious or pernicious habits, and by the exhibition of restorative and strengthening medicines to invigorate the stomach and alimentary tube, and to promote a good digestion, the only means by which a nutritious chyle can be obtained, and the body be preserved in a sound and healthy state. It must however be remarked that, when, from a long continuance of Indigestion, very great and general debility, and ultimately dropsy, is induced; or when organic affections of the stomach, as ulceration, &c. has commenced, such remedies may and will alleviate, but a radical and permanent cure cannot invariably be relied on; and in every such case, greater perseverance with the means referred to, is indispensable.

Literary men and others, of sedentary habits, soon become subject to dyspeptic disorders, to affections of the kidneys, and urinary passages, to constipation, piles, &c., pains in the stomach, nervous palpitations, and pulmonary consumption. Amongst the disorders which depend upon over-exertion of the mental faculties, melancholy, lowness of spirits, headache, apoplexy, palsy, inflammatory affections of the brain, &c., hold a prominent position. These evils may, in a great measure, be prevented by moderate diet and regimen, by avoiding excesses of every description, by proper exercise in the open air, by early rising, by sufficient, but not too much sleep, and by attention to the digestive powers. Derangement of these organs ought to be watched with care, and a confined state of the bowels carefully guarded against, and corrected by the timely use of the aperient combined with tonics, recommended at the close of this work.

In incipient, as well as confirmed diseases, the calls of nature should be assiduously regarded, since her dictates, whether they relate to warmth, or cold, sleep, excitement, abstinence, or nourishment, &c., are hardly ever erroneous or improper; but more especially so, as it regards her customary evacuations. The superfluous humours and putrid particles, which are conveyed into the system through the cutaneous pores, and which arise therein from undigested food, pass off by the common outlets of nature; but, when these obnoxious principles are long retained, they enter the circulating fluids, and imperceptibly produce fevers and other alarming complaints, which break out on taking the slightest cold.

To the female, whose constitution is naturally of a more delicate formation than the other sex, these admonitions will apply with peculiar force. At particular periods, they are subject to painful and critical vicissitudes, which demand vigilant attention. A sedentary life, and exposures to cold damp air, must then be equally avoided. When the bowels are constipated, it will be wise to interpose a remedy, and wrong to neglect the means of inducing a regular action in them. It is much to be deplored that this prolific source of evils is very general in seminaries and boarding-schools, where young ladies are deprived of the advantages of maternal solicitude and watchfulness. It is not unusual to be informed by those who have arrived at the ages between twelve and sixteen years, that their bowels have been confined for many days, without, however, occasioning any material inconvenience. Although a constipated state of the bowels is not necessarily a disease, it may be considered, at certain periods of life, highly inimical to health, or favouring a disease to which the system is pre-disposed. It is of great consequence in females at the age of fourteen, to maintain the vitality of the abdominal viscera, by the use of mild aperient medicines combined with tonics, (always avoiding drastic cathartics, which produce too much commotion in the system,) for if they be allowed to continue in a state of sluggishness, irregularities ensue, a determination to the lungs is produced, which, if neglected, lays the foundation of organic diseases of an obstinate nature, and very difficult of cure.

Inactivity is also very destructive to health. The confinement of females especially, injures their figure and the natural bloom of their complexion; relaxes their solids, enervates their minds, and disorders all the functions of the body. To this cause is owing the serious debility of the system, and the stomach in particular, with impaired digestion, which but too frequently prevails.

Closely allied to this disorder is hypochondriasis, better known by the appellation of lowness of spirits, vapours, &c., but perfectly distinguishable from it, by the languor, listlessness, want of resolution, inactivity, and fearful apprehensions, which ever characterize these affections. It would, indeed, occupy many pages to specify and define the numerous symptoms which attend this complaint; but in reality, and in a great majority of cases, it is merely an affection of the mind diversified. Attention should be directed to excite the nervous energy, both mentally and physically; mentally, by cheerful society and change of scenery; physically, by small and often-repeated doses of some gentle cordial and stimulating aperient and tonic, in combination, as Camphor in minute doses, merely sufficient to rouse the nervous power, with Bark, or its elegant preparation, Quinine, &c., in order to strengthen the parts, and remove, as remotely as possible, all those symptoms which aggravate the disorder.

A fine, or dull day, and the atmospheric changes which distinguish our variable climate, have a marked influence on the nervous system, and especially so in those whose nerves have been weakened by previous shocks. Foreign substances dissolved in, or combined with the moisture of the air, operate immediately on the nerves, and produce great debility therein; and become a fruitful source of disease, especially of the febrile species, in proportion to the depression of their vital power; which fact at once directs to the employment of mild stimulating and corroborating remedies. with a gently-acting aperient, sufficient to induce a regular movement in the bowels, and to remove the morbid matter which this oppressive and obnoxious effluvia, in a greater or less degree, invariably generates, for, without such means, that affection in the viscera denominated dysentery, or a preternatural relaxation of the intestines, and consequent debility or weakness in the solids, will assuredly ensue.

Moreover the stomach and bowels of the hypochondriac, nervous, and hysterical, are often much affected by spasms, particularly after eating, arising from a thick and glutinous mucus lodged therein, and especially the intestines. Owing to this collection of viscous slime in the stomach, adhering firmly to its inner surface, and blocking up the vessels, a due motion of the nervous fluid is prevented, and loss of appetite and lowness of spirits usually ensue. The best remedy in such cases is that which will incite and attenuate the obstructing matter, and (by operating throughout the alimentary tube) convey it away from the remotest parts of the body, with the attendant vitiated humours;* for, if they are suffered to remain in undisturbed possession, they gain such an ascendency, that the corporeal structure is subject to all the worst consequences resulting from indigestion, general nervousness, and debility, and the disorders of the system before enumerated.

Febrile symptoms more or less accompany every disorder. Their approach is ushered in by some extraordinary agitation in the system. Languors, loss of strength, flying pains, dreams, &c., denote somewhat morbid acting on the nerves; but if these are attended with nausea at the stomach, chills, and alternate glows, or sweats, some acute

* See Chapter on the properties of Quinine and Camphor, p. 60, wherein the most efficient means are stated.

malady is much to be apprehended. Indeed, chills, (except after meals and evacuations,) as they come by contraction of the skin, and a general spasm throughout the system, from debility or irritation, always import a degree of danger. From these indications of acute diseases, caution ought to take the alarm; and as it is easier to prevent, than effect a cure, it would be most advisable to arm and oppose their first advances, by recourse to corroborating measures.

A strong and full habit (indicated by the hardness and rapidity of the pulse, in which the force of the circulation is greater than ordinary), tends greatly to the production of inflammatory and febrile complaints; and often convulsions and epilepsy ensue. The opposite extreme—a state of relaxation of the habit, where the vital powers are languid and imperfect, exposes the body to an invasion by every nervous disorder, to obstructions, to dropsy, and scurvy, and renders it very liable to the attacks of intermittent, nervous, bilious, and putrid fevers; and if there be at the same time a superfluous quantity of half stagnant, inactive fluids in the constitution, the danger is in all respects augmented by it. In these cases, and in cases of Indigestion arising from relaxation of the stomach, and direct debility of the nervous frame, such a remedy as we have before alluded to should be taken, and continued without intermission, until symptoms of amendment appear, and health be fully re-established.

The stomach and bowels of those who are asthmatic, are extremely susceptible to disorder, particularly those who are subject to the spasmodic form of the disease. Those persons are generally harassed, even in the intervals between the fits, by spasms and colicky pains, flatulence, loss of appetite, an irregular state of the bowels, and unrefreshing sleep. The stomach and the lungs being supplied by the same nerves, the irritation of the lungs (from which arises frequent fits of coughing, called stomach coughs) doubtless proceeds from the state of the *digestive organs.* Neglected or confirmed dyspepsia, has an obvious influence in predisposing to asthma. This disease may also be produced, or rather a paroxysm may be occasioned in those subject to its attacks, by whatever deranges the healthy functions of the digestive organs, and particularly if it occasion acid or acrid and irritating eructations, or heartburn, flatulent or inordinate distension of the stomach. Asthma is occasioned in the female by hysterical affections; by great obesity; by the suppression of accustomed evacuations, and from plethora or a fulness of blood in the corporeal frame. Amidst the most common complications of this distressing malady may be mentioned, catarrh or cold, and harassing cough, indigestion, lowness of spirits, hysterical complaints, &c., as especially requiring prompt attention. Indigestion and nervous debility not only accompany asthma, but generally precede an attack, which circumstance clearly demonstrates the validity of the doctrine before advanced, that between the stomach and the lungs, as well as the other parts of the animal system, there exists a mutual and never-failing sympathy. It will therefore be palpably evident, that the condition of the digestive organs, and the nerves of the stomach, require vigilant attention, and if impaired, the immediate application of an antidote. With a view to relieve the spasms occasioned by the attacks, and in many cases to prevent their recurrence, Camphor is one of the most *generally* beneficial antispasmodics and anodynes which can be administered, and when judiciously exhibited, applicable to nearly all the forms and complications of the disease, especially the nervous species of it. Stomachic aperients, given in combination with tonics, antispasmodics, and deobstruents, (to remove obstructing matter from the vessels,) to the extent of merely promoting the digestive, assimilating, secreting, and excreting functions, are particularly beneficial. The use of Bark or Quinine invariably does good in these cases. The food partaken should be light, farinaceous, and digestible; and taken in small quantities each time, never exceeding the powers of the stomach to manage with facility.

In atrophy, or that depraved habit of the body, and of the constitution which affects the solids, the circulating fluids and the secretions, the chief characteristics of which are, want of vigour and vital cohesion of the soft solids, with defective digestion, diminished animal warmth, general languor, and deficient strength or activity, &c., in which case the food is not sufficiently assimilated and prepared for digestion, the circulating fluid does not undergo the requisite change resulting from nervous influence, and the action of the viscera, and the secreting functions are imperfectly performed, whereby the mass of blood becomes impoverished or impure, the development of the nervous and muscular systems are feebly executed, and ultimately the whole body is more or less depraved. In these cases, in which *dyspeptic* symptoms are painfully manifest, light nutritious food, in small supplies, healthy air, or change of air, with gentle or regular exercise, without fatiguing the body, should be taken, with the use of medicinal agents of tonic, deobstruent, and opening properties, to promote the functions of the secreting organs, and pleasant mental occupation. This end is better attained by adopting measures to benefit the general health, and to increase the action of the stomach and bowels by mild aperients and stomachics, than by the occasional use of very active and debilitating cathartics; which, however, operate more effectually and much more beneficially when they are associated with bitters and tonics.

In the treatment of these complaints, and the effects arising from them, the first and chief object should be to produce healthy digestion, and to keep up a regular action of the intestines; and when these are effected, a state of system follows, which is very unfavourable to a great variety of diseases. These intentions are best accomplished by bitter tonics, aperients, antispasmodics, and deobstruents, in combination with each other, for the purpose of removing obstructions in the liver, spleen, mesentery, &c.; which impediment to the due and uniform circulation of the fluids, produces languor and debility in the constitution. This is the true way to subdue the evil, and the only safe and salutary mode in which medicine can be prepared to prove successful. If the causes which relax the habit and induce debility, inevitably bring on every species of nervous disorder, indigestion, and its train of painful consequences; it follows as a matter of course, that from whatever source such a state of complicated indisposition arises, the general principle of cure is, that of strengthening and giving tone to the digestive apparatus; of invigorating the alimentary canal and the whole nervous system, and to promote the various secretions; of supplying vigour to the solids, and producing a free and equal motion of the fluids.

Dietetic regulation should be observed by those who have long neglected the faithful admonitions of this most important part of the animal structure, the stomach, with the interposition of medicine to promote its strength and tranquillity, and to yield support to the system at large, in order to beget a beneficial influence on all its parts, and greatly induce and advance the welfare of the whole.

ON DIET AND REGIMEN.

The suitableness of diet, and the preventive art of medicine, are always worthy the peculiar attention of the debilitated; but, when the functions of the stomach are disturbed, or the digestive apparatus is weakened, as is frequently the case in the declining stages of life, the wholesome regulation of diet, exercise, air, and clothing is, generally speaking, of greater importance than is usually imagined.

Every person inherits a peculiarity of the stomach, or of the nervous temperament, and is, in some degree, influenced by the force of custom and habit; consequently, that regimen which is suited to one person proves detrimental to another. Indeed, scarcely two professional men agree on the subject; for, while one strenuously advocates a vegetable diet, another contends that it is improper, and that an animal diet is best; while a third more rationally concludes, that a due admixture of animal and vegetable sustenance is most conducive to the healthy structure of the body.

Those who are too scrupulously governed by the dictates of writers on dietetics, in what they partake, are often observed to be unhealthy. The modern treatises on this subject are too well calculated to render those who follow their instructions a prey to a host of nervous feelings. The constitution undergoes certain changes at different periods of life; and it not unfrequently occurs that articles of diet, which during the period of youth or manhood created disorder in the stomach, and greatly disturbed the general health, agree well after the age of fifty. No person in health, or even when suffering from chronic malady, will reject that food, &c., which is evidently congenial to his stomach, merely because others have pronounced it unwholesome and hard of digestion, without assigning satisfactory reasons for such objections. Generally speaking, that sustenance which is most pleasant to the palate, sits comfortable on the stomach, and is easily digested, unless some disturbance in that organ had previously existed, when a suitable remedy should be applied to correct it.

In the selection of articles of diet, peculiarity of the stomach must have its due measure of consideration; but, nothing is more to be deprecated than excesses in eating; especially so of that which is difficult of digestion, and devoid of nutritious matter, because all such excesses derange the stomach and oppress the system, and consequently become a fruitful source of disease. It should ever be borne in mind, that a moderate meal, well digested, yields more nourishment than a larger one, which is not perfectly so, and of course it proves more wholesome.

There are three distinct processes of digestion, each of which is indispensable to the maintenance of health. The first and most important one is performed by the teeth. It consists in separating the fibres of meat and vegetables; or in other words, properly masticating the solid food, and well blending it with saliva, which possesses a solvent property. Hence, it will appear evident, by the important office they have to fulfil, that they are of great value in the animal economy, and that the utmost care should be taken, not only to prevent their decay, but to cherish the gums, which serve to embrace them with the requisite degree of firmness for that purpose. That many cases of indigestion and disordered stomach originate from insufficient mastication of the food is beyond all question; for, without that operation is properly performed by the teeth, the salivary glands will not yield the portion of fluid called saliva, necessary to be intimately blended and intermingled with the food, which can only be accomplished by the act of chewing; the stomach will be subject to the tribute of double labour, and consequently its powers must ultimately be weakened and impaired; the food, from imperfect mastication, and the want of the solvent principle induced by the act, will attain a degree of putrescency and acidity in that organ, before the gastric juice which flows to it can properly prepare it for the important changes it has to undergo;—hence the prevalence of offensive breath, flatulence, acidity, irregular bowels, headache, &c.

The second process of digestion is performed in the stomach, where the food is concocted by the combination of heat and humidity, and reduced to a proper consistence and temperature for the tender bowels. The third process is carried on in the duodenum, or the first passages, by the acrimonious, but salutary juice, called gall, transfused from the gall-bladder upon the advancing aliment, which dissolves its remaining viscidities, scours the passages of the intestines, and keeps all its fine apertures clear. The stomach, situated in the centre of the system, is certainly one of the most important organs of the body; for, in that repository, the nutritious parts of the food are separated from that which is useless, and changed into a milky substance; and this important fluid being conveyed into the mass of blood by numerous vessels, participates of and becomes the vital principle, called blood; on the pure and healthy state of which, greatly depends the healthy structure of the body. Hence the importance of rigid observance of the reasonable admonitions and requirements of that organ; on the one hand, to be careful not to offend it by undue and injurious indulgences; and on the other, to obey its rational demands by partaking moderately of such articles that are necessary for the support of the system, and for the supply of that vital fluid—the blood, which is perpetually wasting, in order to sustain and uphold the vigour of the whole.

We have said that to a disordered condition of the stomach almost all disorders may be traced. This doctrine was maintained by the learned Abernethy, who was peculiarly successful in curing diseases by acting on the stomach. He considered that this organ has a great influence on the health, and his knowledge and experience of the propensities in individuals to violate its moderate demands by various unwarrantable excesses, induced him to require in his patients an observance of abstinence, or those very limited supplies, which subjected him in after life to the charges of singularity.

That the stomach has a great influence on other parts of the body, by sympathy, is evident from the fact which experience has long established—that the deranged state of that organ must be first corrected, before any wound of the body will heal; it will therefore be manifest, that the stomach and duodenum may perform their office efficiently, the first and second processes should be well fulfilled; and, that the latter may do its duties as they ought to be, the first process—mastication in the mouth, must be efficiently accomplished.

But, in elderly people and others, who are deprived of their teeth, and consequently unable to fulfil the duties of mastication, it is most important to cut the meat very fine, and to press it well between the gums, in the same manner as chewing, so as to induce a flow of saliva to incorporate with it; for that fluid, as a solvent, is of great consequence to the promotion of digestion. When this calamity has occurred, the individual should select, and give a decided preference to the interior part of roasted or boiled mutton, lamb, or beef, containing the red gravy, as yielding the most nutritious properties. The fibres of external parts, being rendered too tense and hard by much roasting or boiling, should be rejected. Veal and pork, and the meat of young animals, of course require more cooking.

OF ANIMAL FOOD.

Animal food, when sufficiently masticated, being more digestible than vegetable, as also more grateful to the palate, seems to indicate that such food is most congenial to the human system. An entirely vegetable diet may be best adapted to those subjects who are predisposed to pulmonary consumption and to inflammatory affections; but, generally speaking, the most healthy are those who partake of an equal, or greater portion of animal, than of vegetable food.

A few remarks on the articles of food supplied from the animal and vegetable kingdoms, from which the human race select their sustenance, will suffice as a general guide to what is most proper, both to the invalid and those who are in the enjoyment of perfect health.

Debilitated subjects, or those who are advanced in life, whose digestive powers are weak, will find that the internal parts of tender beef and mutton, when roasted or moderately boiled, so as to contain the red gravy, will easily digest; and it is as readily converted into chyle, as the food of younger animals, which requires more cooking.

Stewed meat is certainly made more tender by that mode of cooking, but its nutritious part is lost by the process, and the liquor becomes so much impregnated with the jelly, as to oppress the stomach, and to require a considerable degree of seasoning to render it at all digestible, especially to invalids. It is, therefore, a most inconvenient practice to commence the dinner-meal with it, as is the usual custom. A moderate portion of hare, rabbit, pigeon, fowl, turkey, pheasant, and other birds, without sauce or seasoning, and a little cayenne, or black or white pepper, and salt, to promote their digestion, will generally agree with a weakly stomach. Uncooked oysters, with pepper and vinegar, digest easily, and afford much nourishment. Some kinds of fish, as salmon, turbot, soles, and whitings, are nourishing, and with cayenne pepper are digestible.

New milk from the cow, mixed with biscuits, arrow-root, sago, &c., or cow's milk alone, with the addition of one or two table-spoonfuls of lime water (to prevent its coagulation in the stomach) to a pint of the milk, with a small quantity of nutmeg or ginger, will be found grateful, and digest easy. Cheese, being of a firm and indigestible texture, should be carefully avoided by the dyspeptic, and those who are the subjects of debility.

OF VEGETABLE FOOD.

The vegetable food generally partaken, consists of wheat, peas and beans, salads, roots and fruits. Wheat, divested of its cortical part called bran, produces a strong and mucilaginous matter of a very nutritious nature, which, when it is light, well fermented, and sufficiently baked, and in every respect properly prepared, will generally agree with the stomach, taken in moderation; but it ought not to be eaten when new, or until the following day, because new bread dilates, and uniformly oppresses it. Rice, with spices, &c., well boiled or baked, is nourishing and readily digested. The Indians, who are a healthy race, subsist almost entirely upon it. What are called Abernethy biscuits, containing sugar and spice, and well baked, are preferable to bread in a great variety of cases, particularly for invalids, and more especially so when taken for supper.

Peas and beans, cabbage, cauliflowers, and vegetables of that class, do not well digest in a weakly stomach; and, when they are not properly blended with pepper and salt, distend the stomach; but this objection may be considerably obviated and overcome by taking at the same time a small portion of tender and well-cured bacon. All green and raw vegetables disorder the alimentary canal, and become highly injurious to dyspeptic, and elderly, or debilitated subjects, on which account they should be avoided.

Turnips, carrots, parsnips, artichokes of the Jerusalem species, celery, radishes, onions, &c., sit heavily on some stomachs, (especially the latter,) however well they have been seasoned. A good mealy potato, either roasted or cooked by steam, and well mashed up with a little butter, salt, and pepper, not only agrees best with the stomach, and digests better than any other vegetable, but contributes to the substantial support and nourishment of the system.

Ripe fruit may be eaten in moderate quantities, without inconvenience to the stomach of the debilitated; but when the bowels are irritable or relaxed, fruits, either roasted, baked, or boiled, or taken raw, are improper, because their acidity tends to aggravate the evil. Condiments and pastry are also liable to many objections, for reasons which, have already been assigned.

OF WINES, MALT LIQUORS, AND SPIRITS.

Many volumes have been written on the salubrious and insalubrious qualities of wines, &c., but all the information of interest to the public may be condensed within a very narrow space. The salubrity of wine much depends on a proper fermentation, or a decomposition of the saccharine matter of the juice of the fruit. The spirituous principle is strong or weak, according to the richness of the juice; and when the saccharine matter is abundant, the process of fermentation should be continued longer accordingly. When wine is not well fermented, it soon becomes converted into acid in the stomach, particularly in those of a feverish or gouty habit. As a general observation, it may be stated, that no wine is fit for use before it has been preserved in a close vessel until that process is complete, and the acid be either deposited or decomposed.

Wine, taken in moderation, is salutary to the system, but when repeatedly drank in excess, it produces a state of permanent irritation. The effects such abuses occasion are general Nervousness, Irritability, Hypochondriasis, Melancholy, and Maniacal Affections, which often terminate fatally in inflammation of the bowels, or of dropsy. As a medicinal agent, the rich and the poor, the monarch and the peasant, alike value it as a panacea; and it is frequently prescribed in proper quantities by the physician, during the recovery from typhus and continued fevers, yellow fever, the blue stages of cholera, and in all cases of debility, unaccompanied by inflammation, or after severe hemorrhages of blood, in scrofula, scurvy, &c. But in acceleration of the circulation in cases of fevers, in acute inflammations, and in diseases of the heart and large blood-vessels, and in cases where there is a manifest tendency to determination of blood to the brain, wine is improper.

Wine is very useful to all persons in health, especially to those whose occupations require much mental or corporeal exertion. When it is taken medicinally, for the purpose of invigorating the stomach,

the addition of a small quantity of brandy renders it more salubrious: but to those who are inclined to too free an indulgence in that luxury, that addition would prove injurious.

White wines possess a stimulating quality only; but Port, or Red Wine, is stimulating and astringent, on which account some of the faculty prefer it in cases of debility, but generally it does not agree with the stomach so well as White wine, because the astringent principle is but partially derived from the grape, and to logwood or rhatany root is it chiefly indebted for its astringent quality; and, certainly, to those of a sanguineous and nervous temperament, White is most to be preferred.

A glass or two of Champaign, with a little brandy, will generally agree best with weakly subjects. Hock and Rhenish wines, being the least powerful and heating, are best calculated for hot weather. Thin and weak wines, and all sweet wines, not well made, are liable to objections to weakly stomachs, from their tendency to acidity. Burgundy, *good* Sherry, and Madeira, are more cordial than acid wines, and may be used in moderation.

MALT LIQUORS.

The salubrity of all malt liquors, likewise, depends on their having been properly fermented, and impregnated with the qualities of the hop. New malt liquor, like new wine, rapidly enters into a state of acetous fermentation, even in the stomach of a healthy person, in consequence of the vinous state being incomplete. It is an excellent custom to bottle ale or beer when the vinous fermentation is completed, because the fixed air which that liquid disengages in the stomach, acts beneficially on that organ; which advantage is entirely lost by drawing it from a large butt or cask. From ten to twenty grains of carbonate of soda, added to a tumbler of ale, as its acidity or staleness may direct, renders it more agreeable and wholesome.

In the choice of malt liquor, as well as wine, every person should consult his temperament, and the peculiarities of his stomach, which will best point out what will prove most congenial with his constitution, and most promote his health; and then he will seldom commit a serious error.

SPIRITUOUS LIQUORS, ETC.

When a spirit is taken as a beverage, it should always be diluted with water, and a little fine loaf-sugar be added to blunt its acrimony, and to prevent its injurious action on the mucous membrane of the stomach. All spirits are rendered more wholesome by incorporating with them an aromatic, as nutmeg, ginger, &c. For elderly or weakly persons, brandy diluted with water is certainly preferable to any wine. If water, or very weak brandy and water, be drank cold during dinner, a small quantity of warm brandy-and-water, with sugar and nutmeg, taken about an hour afterwards, will promote digestion, and of course prove beneficial. Spirits and water, taken cold, is not so likely to injure the stomach as when taken warm; but former habits and customs, and peculiarities of the stomach, must constitute and form the rule of direction.

That the principal points contained in the foregoing observations may be productive of the desired impressions on the mind, and particularly of the dyspeptic, for whose special benefit they are advanced, we shall superadd a few concise remarks on the kind and description of food which should be partaken at each meal, deviations or alterations from which may be made or substituted as habit, custom, temperament, or peculiarity may indicate. In some cases a small quantity of food, taken frequently, will best agree with the individual; but, generally speaking, three, and at most four moderate meals a-day will suffice, and be as many as the stomach can properly'digest. We will commence with

BREAKFAST.

This meal should not be taken until the teeth and gums have been well washed.— Shortly after this ablution the stomach will be prepared for the reception of food. A little gentle exercise may be enjoyed previously, when the weather and other circumstances will permit, for the purpose of calling the stomach into action, and promoting circulation in the extremities, which proves a wise and beneficial practice.

The breakfast should consist of tea or coffee, cocoa or chocolate, giving preference to the latter as most nutritious; to which also may be added, bread and butter—the bread lightly buttered—or dry toast, or a thin slice of toasted bacon, in lieu of butter, an egg boiled three minutes, with a little salt and pepper.

Bacon, of good flavour, when well cured, is an excellent substitute for butter, because it gently stimulates the stomach, which the breakfast, more than any other meal, requires. Hot bread or rolls are generally injurious, for they distend and oppress that organ. The propriety of eating meat at that meal depends much on habit and temperament. When it does not disagree, it may be taken, as also may the other articles before specified. The lean of broiled mutton or pork, with pepper and salt, or roasted or boiled fowl, are in that case to be preferred. All raw vegetable substances being detrimental to weakly subjects, should be rejected.

DINNER.

To maintain a healthy and vigorous state of the stomach and the digestive organs, it is of great moment to consider, first, what kind of food agrees best and sits most easy on the stomach; secondly, to pay very particular attention to its quality; thirdly, to avoid too long an abstinence, and to guard against all excesses; and lastly, so to masticate it, that it may be properly prepared for the second course of digestion in the stomach. No definite and invariable rule can be laid down to direct and regulate the particular diet of every individual, because what will remain easy and readily digest in the stomach of some, will oppress others : but, as a general principle, it may be stated, that that food should be selected which is most nutritive, generous, and easy of digestion. Weakly or aged people should refrain, as much as possible, from partaking of thick mucilaginous soup, fish with sauce, green vegetables, and in fact, from all indigestible food and flatulent vegetables, pastry, sweetmeats, and fruits of a firm texture, as apples, &c., or eat of them very sparingly indeed; because they are highly improper articles of food for such subjects, on which account it would be better to abandon them altogether.

Roasted and boiled beef, lamb, mutton, not too much cooked, are perhaps the most generally approved dishes, because they seldom disagree with any one. Veal and pork, though very palatable when nicely cooked, are not so nutritious; yet they may be taken in moderate supplies occasionally, when well prepared, and when the flesh is young and fresh. Fish, and poultry of all kinds, hare or partridge, &c., may also be partaken, when they are young, tender, and good in quality, with mealy potatoes, and such other vegetables which experience has proved to be congenial to the stomach. With respect to puddings and pastry, those which contain nourishment, as rice, &c., either baked or boiled, should be preferred; but those made with ripe fruit and but little pastry, and a sufficient quantity of sugar or sweet sauce to destroy the acidity, may be also eaten, to complete the quantity nature requires on that occasion. And here we must again interpose a caution, and advise that whenever it is discovered that any of these articles materially affect the stomach, and consequently enervate the system, unless an excess is the real cause of that oppression, they should be scrupulously rejected; and this remark will especially apply to the dessert, which generally follows this important meal ; for the most lamentable consequences have resulted from that pernicious custom to those whose digestive powers are weak. With respect to liquids, some condemn their use during dinner; but experience demonstrates that it is better to intermingle a portion of liquid with the solid food, because it tends to separate in the stomach the fibres of meat, &c., which have not been sufficiently masticated in the mouth, so that the gastric juice needful for its digestion may the more readily flow to and be incorporated with it, for that purpose.

No custom is more injurious than that of partaking of a variety at one meal, and that frequently in large supplies. Soups, fish, fowl, roast or boiled meat, pastry, and cheese, with all their appendages, are often combined in one meal ; the consequence is, that flatulent eructations and the numerous effects arising from debility in the organs of digestion infallibly ensue. It would be much better for the health of such individuals, if they confined themselves to less variety ; a certain quantity of one or two plain articles would prove less injurious than two-thirds the proportion of a variety. To stipulate persons, under all circumstances, to quantity and particular kinds of food, would be improper ; age, constitution, situation, and exercise of individuals, must be taken into consideration, before any thing like a system can be laid down ; many contingent circumstances would intercept it ; for example, a robust agriculturist, or labourer in the country, who inhales the pure air, in his daily avocations, would naturally require more sustenance for the support of his animal frame than a mercantile man in the metropolis, who is confined to the atmosphere of his counting-house, and has but comparatively little corporeal exercise the greater part of the day : besides which, as has been observed, the quantity and kind of food which, from peculiarity, might suit some, would be equally detrimental to others.

The quality of food always demands especial and most minute attention ; and the utmost care should be observed to obtain the very best. It must be perfectly understood by every one who thinks upon the subject, that that animal whose flesh, at the period of its death, is diseased, and that meat which from long keeping has entered into the putrefactive state, are not only improper articles of diet, but highly hurtful to the system, because such disease in the food from which the human frame is supplied with blood, enters the circulation, and renders that fluid feverish and impure ; and amongst many other consequences, cutaneous affections arise, sometimes of an alarming nature, which have their sole origin in this unexpected cause.

No practice can be more prejudicial to the constitution than long abstinence from food. To this some mercantile men are much addicted. It not unfrequently occurs, that they partake of no sustenance whatever from the hour of breakfast until six or seven o'clock in the evening. We would warn such individuals of the sad tendency of that pernicious custom. The evil consequences may not immediately appear ; but maturer years will generally develop them, in the production of great debility of the digestive organs, accompanied by all the distressing effects arising from indigestion, and what are usually denominated bilious and nervous complaints.

The natural demands of the stomach should be regarded as the surest guide, and the habit will best regulate the necessary quantity ; but great care ought to be exercised not to eat more at one meal than the stomach will digest.

A custom is very prevalent in this country of taking hot tea and coffee immediately after dinner ; but it is certainly a bad one, because it is the surest way to impede digestion of the food previously taken that can be devised. The pleasurable excitement which that beverage produces on the nerves of the stomach is but transitory ; and that organ is consequently often oppressively distended with gas ; by reason of which it operates injuriously on the brain, and throughout the nervous system.

A cup of tea, with bread and butter, will be found refreshing, if taken about three hours afterwards, without proving at all detrimental or injurious.

SUPPER.

If supper ber eally necessary, (which cannot be the case with those who dine late, and who generally substitute tea or coffee in the evening,) it ought to be taken full an hour before going to bed, and should be light, and easy of digestion. An egg lightly boiled, or a piece of dry toast, with a small quantity of white wine negus, or a small tumbler of weak brandy-and-water,* will often secure a tranquil night, which would otherwise be restless. But in no meal is it more requisite to attend to habit, and peculiarity of stomach, than supper. When suppers disturb the rest, and prevent sleep, or occasion foulness of the mouth in the morning, it is always prudent to refrain from them. Aged people may take either biscuit-powder or arrow-root, thickened with milk, with the addition of brandy-and-water, nutmeg, and a little sugar ; or a well-baked biscuit may be taken alone.

EXERCISE AND AIR.

As it respects the exercise of the dyspeptic invalid, it may be observed, generally, that if walking occasion much fatigue, horse-exercise, enjoyed in moderation, will form the best substitute ; or exercise in a carriage may be preferred. A pure, dry, and temperate air should be selected, whenever it is practicable.

* See the article on Wine, &c., p. 12.

OBSERVATIONS ON
THE MEDICINAL PROPERTIES
OF
QUININE AND CAMPHOR,
IN COMBINATION.

In all cases of Indigestion, and what are designated nervous and bilious affections (from the effects of which very few individuals are entirely exempt), we have urged the great importance of preserving a proper action of the stomach and bowels, by the judicious use of remedies, combining tonic, aperient, antispasmodic, and deobstruent powers, for the purpose of giving the required tone, and tranquillizing the stomach at the same time, and removing obstructions, &c., and have deservedly extolled Sulphate of Quinine and Camphor, with other ingredients referred to, as medicines of considerable efficacy in such cases.

Quinine, or Sulphate of Quinine, and Camphor, are so well known and approved, that a *minute* description might be deemed superfluous. It is not, however, so fully understood that their valuable properties are promoted in combination with each other, when the due proportions are accurately ascertained; but it must be observed that every thing depends on the proportions of each remedy being properly adjusted and combined.

The medical virtues of Quinine may be summed up in a few words. In addition to its permanent tonic and febrifuge, it possesses also antispasmodic and antiseptic properties, and is undoubtedly superior to all other remedies in counteracting febrile action, and restoring vigour and strength to morbidly weakened habits. This essential salt is precipitated, in small quantities, from Cinchona or Peruvian Bark, and of course it is on that account more costly than the bark itself, and of greater value; because it concentrates within a small compass the necessary dose, and sits more easy on the stomach; while the considerable bulk of the powder of Cinchona, which is requisite to produce the desired effect, proves oppressive to that organ, and is often ejected from it accordingly.

Cinchona, or Peruvian Bark, and Quinine, have been found very efficacious in a great variety of fevers, and in all disorders attended by feverish symptoms. In spasms and periodical pains, hysterical affections, and in habitual and frequently-returning coughs, and pulmonary consumption, gout, rheumatism, &c., much advantage has attended its use. Combined with Camphor, its value is greatly increased, for by this incorporation of properties, that morbid sensibility of the nerves, attendant on diminished irritability of the muscles, &c., from which affection so many suffer, is reduced, and all the beneficial effects resulting from Quinine are abundantly promoted.

Camphor, also, is a well-known drug, of great efficacy in all nervous affections, arising from debility; but its value is not always duly appreciated, which may partly arise from the usual mode of administering it. In small doses, with Quinine, it acts as a mild cordial, and gentle stimulus to the nerves, reviving the spirits, without producing a subsequent counteraction, with debility: on which account it has been well recommended from an early age; and has been employed from the remotest period, with success, in all cases of nervous debility. This important eastern gum is also much prescribed in modern practice, for the purpose of alleviating pain and irritation in inflammatory and febrile diseases, rheumatism, and gout; and, blended with Quinine, it is esteemed a specific in hectic fever, and in the enlarged bowels to which children, at an early age, are subjected.

In numerous instances, particularly in those cases in which indigestion and nervous symptoms constitute and form prominent features, marked advantage has resulted from its use. When Quinine and Camphor are blended with a well-prepared extract from that valuable Asiatic drug, the *genuine* Turkey Rhubarb, with deobstruents of the vegetable class, and mild aperients, (such as will produce a laxative effect, without griping, or inducing debility, in the remotest degree,) the combination does not then nauseate the stomach; and not only does it prove generally beneficial, but it is applicable to almost every form of the disorder of which this volume treats; and of this character are the excellent Pills, from the prescription of Dr. Flemming, called " Dr. Flemming's Quinine and Camphor Pills."

TESTIMONIALS

In favour of Quinine and Camphor, &c., as contained in Dr. Flemming's Quinine and Camphor Pills, above alluded to.

The combination of *Quinine and Camphor*, with the other ingredients referred to in this pamphlet, which has recently been announced in this country under the appellation of " Dr. Flemming's Quinine and Camphor Pills," sustains a high character as a tonic, febrifuge, and aperient remedy; in consequence of which, it is deservedly patronised by a numerous class of dyspeptic and nervous subjects, with which this country, unhappily, abounds. In the course of considerable practice the value of this compound has been developed, in numerous cases of Indigestion and general nervousness of the system, Obstructions of the Liver, and Bilious Complaints; and in Asthmatic cases; and in fact, in all cases where the chief object is to produce healthy digestion, and to maintain the tone and strength, and a regular action of the intestines, the remedy will be found invaluable.

The following cases are from the most respectable sources:—

I.

EXTRACT FROM A LETTER.

"I have given Dr. Flemming's Quinine and Camphor Pills a fair trial. I consider their great merit consists in their mild and gentle operation; in inducing a healthy tone of stomach; creating an appetite, and relish of food; in promoting refreshing sleep, thereby dissipating morning languor, and general nervousness, to which I have been long subject—in short, in resuscitating the system."—(Extract from the communication of Christopher Bushman, Esq., No. 3, Addison-terrace, Notting-hill, Feb. 12, 1836.)

II.

A. M., Esq., a gentleman of high respectability, after having tried every other tonic remedy, to obtain relief from the consequences of Indigestion, with general nervousness and great debility, was rapidly restored to health by the Quinine and Camphor Pills of Dr. Flemming. The renovating effects of the Camphor upon his nervous system, he states to have been very beneficial and permanent.

III.

W. G., Esq., had been subject to great despondency and general languor for several years, attended with Nervous Headache, frequent palpitation of heart, occurring periodically. Colombo Root, Cascarilla Bark, Peruvian Bark, and other tonics, were administered by a skilful Physician, alone and combined with other remedies of the nervous class, but to no effect. The Quinine and Camphor Pills operated very beneficially in a short space of time, and produced in the issue permanent relief. He continued the use of the Quinine and Camphor Pills about a month.

IV.

J. L., aged 45, had experienced a recurrence of a truly distressing Nervous Headache, every three or four days, and for several years suffered much from bodily weakness and infirmity, and great depression of spirits. He was, at times, much affected by a sensation of noise in his ears, like that of the rumbling of chariot wheels at a distance, with dimness of sight. He had recourse to Dr. Flemming's Quinine and Camphor Pills, and by steadily persevering in their use, in small doses, he lost every symptom of his complaint.

V.

Mr. D., a gentleman, who closely applied himself to business, in an official situation, throughout the day, suffered much from periodical Headache, constipated bowels, flatulence, and the usual symptoms of Indigestion. He complained of great oppression at the stomach, and nausea, and painful sensations after eating, which were the consequences of a sedentary habit. A few doses of the Quinine and Camphor Pills only were sufficient to prove the value of the remedy; and although the symptoms have long since subsided, and altogether disappeared, he takes an occasional dose to prevent a recurrence of them.

VI.

A Gentleman, residing in the Metropolis, who had long endured violent attacks of Asthma, and whose stomach and bowels were extremely susceptible to disorder, occasioning spasms, flatulence, &c., arising from debility of the digestive organs, was advised to take a course of the Quinine and Camphor Pills prescribed by Dr. Flemming, in order to afford him the desired relief, it having been represented to him how beneficially Camphor frequently operates as an antispasmodic in such cases. It was truly astonishing how beneficially they acted in removing the obstructing matter from the vessels, imparting strength to the stomach and its organs of digestion, obviating a confined state of the bowels to which he was generally liable, and in promoting his general health.

VII.

H. R., Esq., had endured much from Indigestion, attended with considerable nausea, foul tongue, especially in the morning, impaired appetite, flatulence, acidity, sensations of great internal heat, confined bowels, giddiness, dimness of sight, deafness, fluttering and painful palpitations of heart, despondency, &c. He derived the most essential relief from the Quinine and Camphor Pills, in a very short period, and is now convalescent. He still continues to use the Pills, which he finds necessary to regulate and induce a regular action in the bowels.

Various other cases might be added, were it compatible with the design of this work, which would show how truly valuable is this remedy in all cases of Constipated Bowels, affections of the Nerves, Stomach and Liver Complaints, Obstructions of every kind, in either sex, and in those cases where, from debility of the organs of digestion, they do not properly fulfil their functions; but it is presumed that sufficient has been said to induce a trial in those who require the aid of medicine, and thereby to secure to them the desired benefit.

Directions for Use of
DR. FLEMMING'S QUININE AND CAMPHOR PILLS.

Two or three Pills taken at night, and repeated on the following morning, if necessary, is the usual dose, in ordinary cases, for an adult; but in many cases these Pills may be taken two or three times a day, and when a decided amendment is manifest, the number may be gradually reduced, and be continued until the recovery is complete. As a dinner-pill, one pill may be taken daily, one hour before that meal.

In all states of Indigestion, and when the uncomfortable sensations of the stomach point out the necessity of resorting to a remedy, the proper use of aperient or opening medicines, combined with tonics, and a mild stimulant (as, Camphor,) is ever of great importance, for the purpose of supporting a regular action in the bowels. In such cases, these Pills, in small and continued doses, will always be of service; and what must ever render them valuable is, that however long they may be taken, they never lose their aperient and invigorating efficacy, nor will they ever, like the drastic purgatives in general use, occasion irritability of the bowels, followed by debility.

Dr. Flemming's Quinine and Camphor Pills are prepared only by the Author, H. Congreve, High-street, Peckham, (late Shepherd's Bush,) from the Doctor's original recipe. They differ most essentially from every other preparation of Quinine, or Quinine and Camphor; and as the proportions of each ingredient contributes to the superior efficacy of this remedy, too much care cannot be taken to obtain the genuine sort.

They may be obtained, wholesale and retail, from the Proprietor's sole Wholesale Agents, Hannay and Dietrichsen, No. 63, Oxford-street, London; also of Ward, Pring, and Rawle, Dublin; G. and J. Raines, Leith-walk, Edinburgh; and retail of all Druggists and Patent Medicine Venders, in Boxes at 4s. 6d., 2s. 9d., and 1s. 1½d. each, including the Stamp, pasted on the outside of each Box, signed by the Proprietor's name, "HENRY CONGREVE," in his own hand-writing, which the purchaser should carefully observe, in order to detect counterfeit preparations.

They may also be had in family Bottles, at 11s. each, for exportation, in which their properties will be preserved unimpaired for any length of time.—The Boxes at 4s. 6d., and the Bottles at 11s. each, will contain a copy of this work, gratis.

Any Chemist or Medicine Vender, who either does not keep the Pills, or may be out of Stock, will obtain a Box or Bottle, or whatever quantity may be wanted, in a day or two, from London, on leaving the cash for the same, with an order to that effect.

₊ Ask for "Dr. Flemming's Quinine and Camphor Pills," prepared only by H. Congreve.

W. Tyler, Printer, Bolt-court, London.

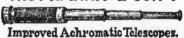

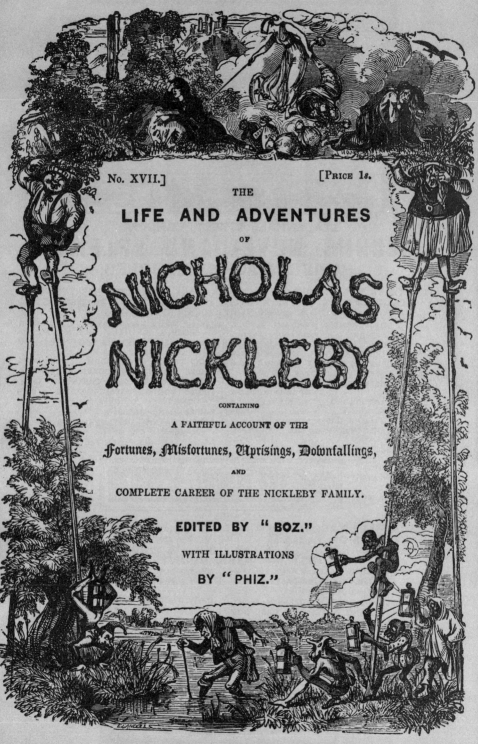

No. XVII.] [PRICE 1s.

THE
LIFE AND ADVENTURES
OF
NICHOLAS NICKLEBY

CONTAINING

A FAITHFUL ACCOUNT OF THE

Fortunes, Misfortunes, Uprisings, Downfallings,

AND

COMPLETE CAREER OF THE NICKLEBY FAMILY.

EDITED BY "BOZ."

WITH ILLUSTRATIONS

BY "PHIZ."

LONDON: CHAPMAN AND HALL, 186, STRAND.

LEADENHALL STREET, LONDON.

MECHI'S NOVEL AND SPLENDID
PAPIER MACHE ARTICLES,

CONSISTING OF

TEA TRAYS, TEA CADDIES, LADIES' WORK, CAKE, AND NOTE BASKETS, CARD
CASES, CARD POOLS, FRUIT PLATES, FRUIT BASKETS, NETTING BOXES,
HAND SCREENS, CARD RACKS, CHESS BOARDS.

LADIES' COMPANIONS, or Work Cases 15s. to 2l.
LADIES' CARD CASES, in Pearl, Ivory, and Tor-
toiseshell . . . . . 10s. to 5l. each.
LADIES' WORK BOXES . 25s. to 10 Guineas.
LADIES' DRESSING CASES 2l. 10s. to 50 Guineas.
LADIES' SCOTCH WORK BOXES at all prices.
LADIES' ROSEWOOD AND MAHOGANY DESKS
12s. 6d. to 10 Guineas.
LADIES' MOROCCO AND RUSSIA LEATHER
WRITING CASES . . . . . 5s. to 5l.
LADIES' ENVELOPE CASES, various prices.
LADIES' TABLE INKSTANDS, made of British Coal
(quite a novelty) . . . 7s. 6d. to 30s.
LADIES' SCOTCH TOOTH-PICK CASES.

LADIES' IVORY AND TORTOISESHELL HAIR
BRUSHES . . . at 2l. to 5l. per Pair.
LADIES' SCENT AND TOILET BOTTLES in great
variety.
LADIES' SCOTCH TEA CADDIES . 21s. to 40s.
LADIES' PLAYING CARD BOXES . 30s. to 5l.
LADIES' JAPAN DRESSING CASES 7s. to 15s.
LADIES' TORTOISESHELL DRESSING & SIDE
COMBS.
LADIES' HAND GLASSES.
LADIES' PATENT INSTANTANEOUS PEN-
MAKERS . . . . 10s. 6d. and 12s. 6d.
LADIES' ELEGANT PENKNIVES AND SCISSORS
5s. to 30s.

INVENTOR
OF THE PATENT
CASTELLATED
TOOTH BRUSHES.

TRY MECHI'S Magic STROP.

INVENTOR
OF THE MECHIAN
PORTABLE
DRESSING CASES.

MISCELLANEOUS.

BAGATELLE TABLES	£3 10 to 5 0		POPE JOAN BOARDS	£0 13 to 1 0		
BACKGAMMON TABLES	1 0 to 5 10		IVORY CHESSMEN	1 1 to 10 10		
CHESS BOARDS .	0 4 to 3 0		BONE & WOOD DITTO	Various Prices.		

WHIST MARKERS, COUNTERS, &c.

GENT.'S DRESSING CASES, in Wood 2l. to 50l.
GENT.'S LEATHER DRESSING CASES 25s. to 24l.
GENT.'S WRITING DESKS, in Wood 30s. to 16l.
GENT.'S LEATHER WRITING DESKS 24s. 6d. to 5l.
GENT.'S WRITING & DRESSING CASE COM-
BINED . . . . 5l. to 16l.
GENT.'S POCKET BOOKS WITH INSTRUMENTS
20s. to 40s.
GENT.'S ELEGANT CASES OF RAZORS 12s. to 3l.
GENT.'S SEVEN DAY RAZORS, in Fancy Woods
25s. to 5l.
GENT.'S RAZOR STROPS . 2s. to 30s.
GENT.'S SPORTING KNIVES . 12s. to 5l.

GENT.'S FANCY PENKNIVES . 5s. to 15s.
GENT.'S PEARL AND SHELL POCKET COMBS
3s. 6d. to 40s.
GENT.'S SCOTCH CIGAR BOXES 3s. 6d. to 40s.
GENT.'S COAL AND EBONY INKSTANDS
7s. 6d. to 50s.
GENT.'S IVORY AND FANCY WOOD HAIR
BRUSHES . . . . 20s. to 3l. 10s.
GENT.'S SETS OF BRUSHES in Russia Cases
25s. to 4l. 10s.
GENT.'S SILVER AND IVORY SHAVING BRUSHES
In elegant Patterns.
GENT.'S SILVER AND SHELL TABLETS.

MECHI,  4, LEADENHALL ST. LONDON. MECHI,

Submits, to public inspection, his Manufactures, as being of the finest quality this kingdom can produce, and
at moderate prices.
A large Stock of Table Cutlery, Plated Tea and Coffee Services, Dish Covers, Hash Covers, &c.

Just published, in super-royal 8vo, price One Shilling,

A THIRD PREFACE to a book advertised by Messrs. CHARLES KNIGHT & Co., under the fallacious title of "A TREATISE ON WOOD ENGRAVING, HISTORICAL AND PRACTICAL; with upwards of 300 Illustrations, engraved on wood, by JOHN JACKSON," giving an account of Mr. Jackson's *actual* share in the Composition and Illustration of that work, and restoring the passages suppressed by Mr. Knight. With remarks on LITERARY AND ARTISTIC *Conveyance.* In a Letter to STEPHEN OLIVER.

By WM. A. CHATTO, Author of the Historical Portion of the Work, comprising the first Seven Chapters, and the *Writer* of the whole, as originally printed.

" *Convey*, the wise call it."—MERRY WIVES OF WINDSOR, Act I., Scene 3.

" ———— When the ayerie traine
Their well-knowne plumes shall challenge back againe,
The naked daw a general game shall be,
Spoiled of his grace and pilfered braverie."—HIVE OF HONIE COMBES, 1631.

Printed for the Author by W. SPIERS, 399, Oxford Street, and to be had of all Booksellers.

MRS. TROLLOPE REFUTED.

On August 1, (to be completed in Ten Monthly Numbers, each with Two spirited Illustrations, at 1s.) No. I. of

MARY ASHLEY; OR, FACTS UPON FACTORIES.

BY FREDERICK MONTAGU.

London; H. JOHNSON, 49, Paternoster Row; BANCKS & Co., Manchester; and all Booksellers.

SIMPLICITY OF LIVING.

This day is published, considerably enlarged and improved, Third Edition, price 3s. 6d. cloth boards,

CURTIS ON HEALTH, IN INFANCY, YOUTH, MANHOOD, AND AGE;

Showing the best Means of prolonging Life and promoting Human Happiness.

CONTENTS:—

Physical, organic, and moral laws.
Infringement of these laws the cause of disease.
Care of the health in infancy and youth, its advantages in after-life.
Air, exercise, sleep, diet, regimen, clothing, bathing, &c.
Health of individuals greatly dependent on themselves.
Education—choice of a profession.
Training for longevity as practicable as training for athletic feats.
Adulteration of food—bread, wine, beer, &c.
Causes and seat of disease.
Rules for the sedentary and dyspeptic.

Indigestion, its effects upon hearing and sight.
Improvements of the metropolis in relation to health.—
The erection of fountains, opening of the squares to the public, &c.
The choice of watering-places.
Mental culture—tranquillity and excitement.
Insanity and suicidal monomania—increase and causes.
Love—marriage—influence on health, rules for.
List of eminent persons who have attained old age; the history of several of the oldest persons known, four of whom attained the ages of 164, 172, 185, and 207.

London: LONGMAN and Co., and H. RENSHAW, 356, Strand.
Of whom may be had, by the same Author,
A TREATISE on the DISEASES of the EAR, illustrated with Cases and Plates. Sixth Edition, price 7s. 6d. bds.
A TREATISE on the DISEASES of the EYE. Cases and Plates. Second Edition, 7s. 6d. bds.

HAMILTONIAN SYSTEM.

" We recommend those who wish to acquire a knowledge of Languages in the least time possible, to use the Books arranged with interlineal translations, by J. HAMILTON."

The *Edinburgh Review* ascribes to the Author of this System " the great merit of introducing translations made in invariable accordance with a strict *verbal analysis ;*" and it remarks, that " it is this peculiarity which renders them such invaluable instruments to the Learner."

The following Books, on the Hamiltonian System, are published at

SOUTER'S SCHOOL LIBRARY, 131, FLEET STREET.

LATIN.	s.	d.		s.	d.		s.	d.
Gospel of St. John	4	0	First Six Books of the Æneid	9	0	Verbs	2	0
Epitome Historiæ Sacræ	4	0	Ovid	7	0	GERMAN.		
Æsop's Fables	4	0	GREEK.			Edward in Scotland	4	6
Phædrus' Fables	4	0	Gospel of St. John	6	0	Gospel of St. John	4	0
Eutropius	4	0	Gospel of St. Matthew	7	6	Robinson der Jungere, 2 vols.	10	0
Aurelius Victor	4	0	Æsop's Fables	6	0	ITALIAN.		
Cornelius Nepos	6	6	Analecta Minora	6	0	Gospel of St. John	4	0
Selectæ è Profanis	10	0	Aphorisms of Hippocrates	9	0	Merope, by Alfieri	5	0
Cæsar's Commentaries, New Edition	9	0	FRENCH.			Notti Romane	6	6
			Elizabeth, Exiles of Siberia	3	0	Novelle Morali	4	0
Celsus de Medicina, 3 vols.	20	0	Florian's Fables, 12mo	2	6	Raccolta di Favole	5	6
Cicero's Four Orations	4	0	Frank, 2 Parts	1	6	Tasso's Jerusalem Delivered	5	6
Gregory's Conspectus, 2 vols.	16	0	Gospel of St. John	4	0	Verbs	2	0
Latin Verbs	2	0	Perrin's Fables	5	0	SPANISH.		
Sallust	7	6	Recueil Choisi	7	6	Gospel of St. John	4	0
			Telemachus	5	6			

The HISTORY, PRINCIPLES, and PRACTICE of the System 1 6

THE GOLDEN PERCH, 52, STRAND.

THE CHEAPEST RIDING-WHIP MANUFACTORY IN THE WORLD. Strong Riding Whips, 1s. each; Ladies' best Town-made, with Patent Braided Whalebone Handles, 5s.; Jockey size do. do., from 6s.; Ladies' do. do., with solid silver mountings, from 6s. 6d.; Jockey size, do. do., from 8s.; Ladies' do. da., with handsomely worked solid silver wire buttons, from 10s.; Jockey size do. do. do., from 12s. Can be selected from the largest assortment in London, or forwarded in answer to a post-paid letter, with a remittance, and exchanged if not approved of.

J. CHEEK, Golden Perch, 52, Strand.

EXCELLENT SUMMER BEVERAGE.

MIX smoothly two teaspoonfuls of ROBINSON'S PATENT BARLEY, in two tablespoonfuls of cold spring water, gradually adding three quarts of the same; boil it gently for ten minutes, and when cold, strain through muslin. It may be flavoured with the peel or juice of lemon, or sweetened according to taste. This has greatly superseded the use of other drinks at the dinner table.

Extract from a letter of a medical gentleman, in extensive practice, to the patentees:—

" The purity of your Patent Barley, and the facility by which a grateful beverage is obtained, has induced me for many years to recommend it to the use of my patients, the consequence is, both the affluent and the poor of my connexion have generally a supply of it. I have always found it of great use in allaying thirst in febrile diseases; and delicate stomachs have retained it, after having rejected all other fluids."

Prepared only by the Patentees, ROBINSON and BELLVILLE, Purveyors to the Queen, 64, Red Lion-street, Holborn; and sold retail by all respectable Druggists, Grocers, Oilmen, &c. in Town or Country.

HOSIERY.

POPE and Co. have removed from 28, Friday Street, to 4, *Waterloo Place, Pall Mall.*

THEY continue to manufacture every description of HOSIERY, in the old-fashioned substantial manner, the greatest attention being paid to *Elasticity and Durability.*—Orders and Patterns to be forwarded to 4, Waterloo Place, or to their manufactory, Mount Street, Nottingham.

NEEDLES.—" A great improvement in the manufacture of these important articles has recently been made by Mr. Walker, who has invented a needle possessing, with the most beautifully tapered form, an unusual and amazing strength, and, above all, a new finish, which prevents their great liability to rust, and enables them to work with a freedom hitherto unknown; they possess the greatest elasticity, yet the hardness and brilliant smoothness of their surface can be equalled only by that of a diamond."—*Court Journal, April 12, 1834.*—These unrivalled NEEDLES, which do not cut the thread, are put up in the usual manner, or in the Victoria cases, containing 100, 500, or 1,000 needles, either of which forms a most pleasing present. These cases are decorated in a variety of colours, with the following devices in relief, engraved by one of our first artists:—A HEAD OF HER MAJESTY, surrounded with an elegant scroll work; a bust of ditto; AN EQUESTRIAN FIGURE of ditto; a royal crown, surrounded with the shamrock, rose, and thistle, &c. The resemblance of OUR YOUTHFUL QUEEN is most striking, and universally admitted to be the best published. The name " H. Walker " on each label will prevent others of a different character being mistaken for them. Sold by almost every respectable dealer.—H. WALKER, 20, Maiden-lane, Wood-street.

TO EPICURES.

CROSSE and BLACKWELL'S celebrated SOHO SAUCE for Fish, Game, Steaks, Made Dishes, &c. DINMORE'S ESSENCE OF SHRIMPS, for every description of boiled and fried Fish. The above to be had of most Sauce Venders throughout the Kingdom, and wholesale at 11, King-street, Soho.

I. INDERWICK'S

WHOLESALE WAREHOUSES for every description of SMOKING APPARATUS, 58, Princes-street, Leicester-square, London, and vis-à-vis, La Sophien Mosch, Constantinople, Inventor and Patentee of the improved Persian Hookah for smoking through water, and part Proprietor of the Keff Kil, or better known as the Meerschaum Pits of the Crimea in Asia Minor, of which those beautiful Ecume de Mer Pipes are made, which, from the peculiar properties they possess of imbibing the oil of the tobacco and giving it a most delicious flavour, are so much esteemed and patronised by H. R. H. the Duke of Sussex, and the Nobility and Gentry.

I. I. begs respectfully to acquaint Tobacconists, Silversmiths, and others, that they may be supplied at all times with the undermentioned articles of the first quality:— Meerschaum and every description of Foreign Smoking Pipes, suitable in quality and price from the Prince to the Peasant. Snuff Boxes from every manufactory in Europe. Cigar Cases of every description, together with every article connected with the above line.

Sole Agent in London for the real Laurence Kirk Snuff Boxes.

Merchants or others going out to any of the new Settlements, supplied at the Continental prices.

NASCITUR FLAMMANS ET MORITUR FLAMMANS.

By the King's Royal Letters Patent.

JONES'S PROMETHEANS.—The advantages the Prometheans possess over all other instantaneous lights are their extreme simplicity and durability, as neither time nor climate can impair their original quality: they are composed of a small glass bulb hermetically sealed, containing about a quarter of a drop of sulphuric acid, encompassed by a composition of the chlorate of potash, enclosed in wax papers or wax tapers: the latter will burn sufficiently long to admit of sealing two or three letters. The Prometheans being pleasant to use, and never failing of their purpose, they are rendered nearly as cheap as the common Lucifers. To be had of all respectable chemists, &c., or at the Manufactory, 201, Strand.

FOR THE HAIR.—Patronised by her Majesty Queen Victoria, the Duchess of Kent, and adopted in most of the Noble Families in the Kingdom. DAWSON'S AUXILIAR, which restores Hair from baldness or greyness, and preserves its juvenile shade to the latest period of life: it imparts a beautifully lustrous appearance, with a graceful curl, to the most unsightly hair, eradicates dandriff, produces eyebrows and whiskers, and beautiful hair on children's heads. Price 3s. 6d., 7s., 10s. 6d., 15s., and 21s. per bottle.

Also, extensively used by the Army and Navy, DAWSON'S EXOPTABLE SHAVING SOAP, an important discovery, which produces an immediate lather that does not dry, and that softens the beard, and mollifies the skin, by which the operation is performed with the utmost facility and comfort; at 1s. each, or 10s. per dozen cakes.—Both the above articles are sold at the proprietor's only depot, 24, High Holborn, close to Gray's-Inn; and by all Medicine Vendors and Perfumers.—The great celebrity of the above articles has caused many unprincipled imitators; but the genuine are always enclosed in green envelopes, with the proprietor's signature. A great saving in the larger bottles.

MOST IMPORTANT INFORMATION.
BY HIS MAJESTY'S ROYAL LETTERS PATENT.
33, GERRARD STREET, SOHO.

G. MINTER begs to inform the Nobility, Gentry, &c., that he has invented an EASY CHAIR, that will recline and elevate, of itself, into an innumerable variety of positions, without the least trouble or difficulty to the occupier; and there being no machinery, rack, catch, or spring, it is only for persons sitting in the chair merely to wish to recline or elevate themselves, and the seat and back take any desired inclination, without requiring the least assistance or exertion whatever, owing to the weight on the seat acting as a counterbalance to the pressure against the back by the application of a self-adjusting leverage; and for which G. M. has obtained his Majesty's Letters Patent. G. M. particularly recommends this invention to Invalids, or to those who may have lost the use of their hands or legs, as they are by it enabled to vary their position without requiring the use of either to obtain that change of position, from its endless variety, so necessary for the relief and comfort of the afflicted.

The Chair is made by the Inventor only, at his Wholesale Cabinet and Upholstery Manufactory, 33, Gerrard-street, Soho. G. M. is confident an inspection only is required to be convinced of its superiority over all others.

Merlin, Bath, Brighton, and every other description of Garden Wheel Chairs, much improved by G. Minter, with his self-acting reclining backs, so as to enable an invalid to lie at full length. Spinal Carriages, Portable Carriage Chairs, Water Beds, and every article for the comfort of the invalid.

PALMER'S
IMPROVED PNEUMATIC
FILTERING MACHINES,
Of all sizes, for making and filtering Coffee
IN THE HIGHEST PERFECTION,
And for filtering quickly and without Waste,
WINES, LIQUEURS,
TINCTURES, ESSENCES, OILS, &c.
AND MAKE MOST VALUABLE AND RAPID
WATER FILTERS,
PRICES, 25*s*., 30*s*., 42*s*.. and upwards.

Manufactured and Sold by E. PALMER,
Chemical and Philosophical Instrument Maker,
103, NEWGATE STREET, LONDON.

N.B. Electrical and Electro-Magnetic Machines, Improved Galvanic Batteries, Air Pumps, Pneumatic Apparatus, Single and Compound Microscopes, and all kinds of Chemical and Philosophical Instruments of superior workmanship at very moderate prices. PALMER'S NEW CATALOGUE, with 120 Engravings, 1*s.* each.

WORKING MODELS OF STEAM ENGINES, AND ALL KINDS OF MACHINERY, MADE TO ORDER.

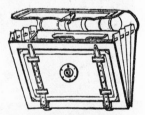

WOOD AND BARRETT,
247, TOTTENHAM COURT ROAD, NEAR OXFORD STREET,

Inform the Public that they confine themselves to the Manufacture of Kitchen Ranges, Hot Plates, Smoke Jacks, Hot Closets, Broiling Stoves, Stewing Stoves, Steam Tables, Steam Kettles, Warm Baths, Bell Hanging, Register Grates, Fender Grates, and Dr. Arnott's Thermometer Stoves, upon the best principle.

MOSLEY'S METALLIC PENS.

R. MOSLEY & CO. beg to call the attention of Mercantile Men, and the Public in general, to their superior Metallic Pens. They possess the highest degree of elasticity and flexibility, and are found perfectly free from all those inconveniences which have prevented so many persons making use of Metallic Pens.

Every description of writer may be suited, as these pens are manufactured of various qualities, degrees of hardness, &c. They may be had of all respectable Stationers throughout the kingdom.

Observe that every Pen is stamped, R. MOSLEY & CO. LONDON.

WHOLESALE AND FOR EXPORTATION.

V. R.

JOSEPH GILLOTT,
PATENT STEEL PEN MANUFACTURER,
59, NEWHALL STREET & GRAHAM STREET, BIRMINGHAM.

JOSEPH GILLOTT has been for nearly twenty years engaged in the manufacture of Steel Pens, and during that time has devoted his unceasing attention to the improving and perfecting this useful and necessary article: the result of his persevering efforts, and numerous experiments upon the properties of the metal used, has been the construction of a Pen upon a principle entirely new, combining all the advantages of the elasticity and fineness of the quill, with the durability of the metallic pen, and thus obviating the objections which have existed against the use of Steel Pens.

The Patentee is proud to acknowledge that a discerning public has paid the most gratifying tribute to his humble, though useful, labours, by a demand for his Pens far exceeding his highest expectations.——The number of Steel Pens manufactured at Joseph Gillott's works, from October, 1837, to October, 1838,

was 35,808,452
or 2,984,037 2-3rds dozens
or 248,669 gross, 9 dozen and 8 Pens.

This statement will show the estimation in which these Pens are held, and it is presumed will be an inducement to those who desire to have a really good article, at least to make a trial of Joseph Gillott's Pen.

☞ The universal celebrity of these Pens has induced certain disreputable Makers to foist upon the Public a spurious article, bearing the mis-spelled name of the Patentee and Sole Manufacturer, thus "GILOTT," by omitting the L; and in some instances the omission of the final T is resorted to, in order to retain the same SOUND as GILLOTT: but observe,

☞ NONE ARE GENUINE BUT THOSE MARKED IN FULL **JOSEPH GILLOTT**.

Sold by all Stationers and other respectable Dealers in Steel Pens throughout the Kingdom.

THOS. HARRIS & SON,
OPTICIANS TO THE ROYAL FAMILY,
OPPOSITE THE ENTRANCE TO
THE BRITISH MUSEUM, LONDON.

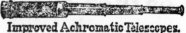

186, Strand.
August, 1839.

NEW WORK BY BOZ.

Messrs. Chapman & Hall have the pleasure of announcing that they have completed arrangements with Mr. Charles Dickens for the publication of

A NEW WORK,

ON AN ENTIRELY NEW PLAN.

The first number of this work will appear in March next.

COMPLETION OF NICHOLAS NICKLEBY.

Subscribers are informed that the last number of Nicholas Nickleby will contain a Portrait of the Author, engraved by Mr. Wm. Finden, from an original painting by D. Maclise, Esq., A.R.A.

Bradbury and Evans, Printers, Whitefriars.]

CHAPTER LII.

NICHOLAS DESPAIRS OF RESCUING MADELINE BRAY, BUT PLUCKS UP HIS
SPIRITS AGAIN, AND DETERMINES TO ATTEMPT IT. DOMESTIC INTEL-
LIGENCE OF THE KENWIGSES AND LILLYVICKS.

FINDING that Newman was determined to arrest his progress at any
hazard, and apprehensive that some well-intentioned passenger attracted
by the cry of "stop thief," might really lay violent hands upon his
person, and place him in a disagreeable predicament from which he
might have some difficulty in extricating himself, Nicholas soon
slackened his pace, and suffered Newman Noggs to come up with him,
which he did in so breathless a condition that it seemed impossible he
could have held out for a minute longer.

"I will go straight to Bray's," said Nicholas. "I will see this
man; and if there is one feeling of humanity lingering in his breast,
one spark of consideration for his own child, motherless and friendless
as she is, I will awaken it."

"You will not," replied Newman. "You will not, indeed."

"Then," said Nicholas, pressing onward, "I will act upon my first
impulse, and go straight to Ralph Nickleby."

"By the time you reach his house he will be in bed," said Newman.

"I'll drag him from it," cried Nicholas, fiercely.

"Tut, tut," said Noggs. "Be yourself."

"You are the best of friends to me, Newman," rejoined Nicholas
after a pause, and taking his hand as he spoke. "I have made head
against many trials, but the misery of another, and such misery is
involved in this one, that I declare to you I am rendered desperate, and
know not how to act."

In truth, it did seem a hopeless case. It was impossible to make
any use of such intelligence as Newman Noggs had gleaned when he
lay concealed in the closet. The mere circumstance of the compact
between Ralph Nickleby and Gride would not invalidate the marriage,
or render Bray averse to it, who, if he did not actually know of the
existence of some such understanding, doubtless suspected it. What
had been hinted with reference to some fraud on Madeline, had been
put with sufficient obscurity by Arthur Gride, but coming from
Newman Noggs, and obscured still further by the smoke of his pocket
pistol, it became wholly unintelligible and involved in utter darkness.

"There seems no ray of hope," said Nicholas.

"The greater necessity for coolness, for reason, for consideration, for
thought," said Newman, pausing at every alternate word, to look
anxiously in his friend's face. "Where are the brothers?"

"Both absent on urgent business, as they will be for a week to
come."

" Is there no way of communicating with them? no way of getting one of them here by to-morrow night?"

" Impossible!" said Nicholas, " the sea is between us and them. With the fairest winds that ever blew, to go and return would take three days and nights."

" Their nephew—" said Newman, " their old clerk."

" What could either do that I cannot?" rejoined Nicholas. " With reference to them especially, I am enjoined to the strictest silence on this subject. What right have I to betray the confidence reposed in me, when nothing but a miracle can prevent this monstrous sacrifice?"

" Think," urged Newman. " Is there no way?"

" There is none," said Nicholas, in utter dejection. " Not one. The father urges—the daughter consents. These demons have her in their toils ; legal right, might, power, money, and every influence are on their side. How can I hope to save her?"

" Hope to the last," said Newman, clapping him on the back. " Always hope, that's a dear boy. Never leave off hoping, it don't answer. Do you mind me, Nick? it don't answer. Don't leave a stone unturned. It's always something to know you've done the most you could. But don't leave off hoping, or it's of no use doing anything. Hope, hope, to the last!"

Nicholas needed encouragement, for the suddenness with which intelligence of the two usurers' plans had come upon him, the little time which remained for exertion, the probability, almost amounting to certainty itself, that a few hours would place Madeline Bray for ever beyond his reach, consign her to unspeakable misery, and perhaps to an untimely death : all this quite stunned and overwhelmed him. Every hope connected with her that he had suffered himself to form, or had entertained unconsciously, seemed to fall at his feet withered and dead. Every charm with which his memory or imagination had surrounded her, presented itself before him only to heighten his anguish and add new bitterness to his despair. Every feeling of sympathy for her forlorn condition, and of admiration for her heroism and fortitude, aggravated the indignation which shook him in every limb, and swelled his heart almost to bursting.

But if Nicholas's own heart embarrassed him, Newman's came to his relief. There was so much earnestness in his remonstrance, and such sincerity and fervour in his manner, odd and ludicrous as it always was, that it imparted to Nicholas new firmness, and enabled him to say, after he had walked on for some little way in silence,

" You read me a good lesson, Newman, and I will profit by it. One step at least I may take, am bound to take indeed, and to that I will apply myself to-morrow."

" What is that?" asked Noggs, wistfully. " Not to threaten Ralph? Not to see the father?"

" To see the daughter, Newman," replied Nicholas. " To do what after all is the utmost that the brothers could do if they were here, as Heaven send they were! To reason with her upon this hideous union, to point out to her all the horrors to which she is hastening ; rashly, it may be, and without due reflection. To entreat her at least to pause. She can have had no counsellor for her good; and perhaps even I may move her so far yet, though it is the eleventh hour, and she upon the very brink of ruin."

" Bravely spoken!" said Newman. " Well done, well done! Yes. Very good."

" And I do declare," cried Nicholas, with honest enthusiasm, " that in this effort I am influenced by no selfish or personal considerations, but by pity for her and detestation and abhorrence of this heartless scheme; and that I would do the same were there twenty rivals in the field, and I the last and least favoured of them all."

" You would, I believe," said Newman. " But where are you hurrying now?"

" Homewards," answered Nicholas. " Do you come with me, or shall I say good night?"

" I'll come a little way if you will but walk, not run," said Noggs.

" I cannot walk to-night, Newman," returned Nicholas, hurriedly. " I must move rapidly, or I could not draw my breath. I'll tell you what I've said and done to-morrow!"

Without waiting for a reply, he darted off at a rapid pace, and plunging into the crowds which thronged the street, was quickly lost to view.

" He's a violent youth at times," said Newman, looking after him; " and yet I like him for it. There's cause enough now, or the deuce is in it. Hope! I *said* hope, I think! Ralph Nickleby and Gride with their heads together—and hope for the opposite party! Ho! ho!"

It was with a very melancholy laugh that Newman Noggs concluded this soliloquy, and it was with a very melancholy shake of the head and a very rueful countenance, that he turned about, and went plodding on his way.

This, under ordinary circumstances, would have been to some small tavern or dram-shop, that being his way in more senses than one; but Newman was too much interested and too anxious to betake himself even to this resource, and so, with many desponding and dismal reflections, went straight home.

It had come to pass that afternoon, that Miss Morleena Kenwigs had received an invitation to repair next day per steamer from Westminster Bridge unto the Eel-pie Island at Twickenham, there to make merry upon a cold collation, bottled-beer, shrub, and shrimps, and to dance in the open air to the music of a locomotive band, conveyed thither for the purpose: the steamer being specially engaged by a dancing-master of extensive connection for the accommodation of his numerous pupils, and the pupils displaying their appreciation of the dancing-master's services by purchasing themselves, and inducing their friends to do the like, divers light-blue tickets entitling them to join the expedition. Of these light-blue tickets, one had been presented by an ambitious neighbour to Miss Morleena Kenwigs, with an invitation to join her daughters; and Mrs. Kenwigs, rightly deeming that the honour of the family was involved in Miss Morleena's making the most splendid appearance possible on so short a notice, and testifying to the dancing-master that there were other dancing-masters besides him, and to all fathers and mothers present that other people's children could learn to be genteel besides theirs, had fainted away twice under the magnitude of her preparations, but upheld by a determination to sustain the family name or perish in the attempt, was still hard at work when Newman Noggs came home.

Now, between the italian-ironing of frills, the flouncing of trousers, the trimming of frocks, the faintings and the comings-to again incidental to the occasion, Mrs. Kenwigs had been so entirely occupied that she had not observed, until within half an hour before, that the flaxen tails of Miss Morleena's hair were in a manner run to seed ; and that unless she were put under the hands of a skilful hair-dresser, she never could achieve that signal triumph over the daughters of all other people, anything less than which would be tantamount to defeat. This discovery drove Mrs. Kenwigs to despair, for the hair-dresser lived three streets and eight dangerous crossings off. Morleena could not be trusted to go there alone, even if such a proceeding were strictly proper, of which Mrs. Kenwigs had her doubts ; Mr. Kenwigs had not returned from business ; and there was nobody to take her. So Mrs. Kenwigs first slapped Miss Kenwigs for being the cause of her vexation, and then shed tears.

" You ungrateful child ! " said Mrs. Kenwigs, " after I have gone through what I have this night for your good."

" I can't help it, ma," replied Morleena, also in tears ; " my hair *will* grow."

" Don't talk to me, you naughty thing ! " said Mrs. Kenwigs, " don't. Even if I was to trust you by yourself and you were to escape being run over, I know you'd run in to Laura Chopkins," who was the daughter of the ambitious neighbour, " and tell her what you're going to wear to-morrow, I know you would. You've no proper pride in yourself, and are not to be trusted out of sight for an instant."

Deploring the evil-mindedness of her eldest daughter in these terms, Mrs. Kenwigs distilled fresh drops of vexation from her eyes, and declared that she did believe there never was anybody so tried as she was. Thereupon Morleena Kenwigs wept afresh, and they bemoaned themselves together.

Matters were at this point as Newman Noggs was heard to limp past the door on his way up-stairs, when Mrs. Kenwigs, gaining new hope from the sound of his footsteps, hastily removed from her countenance as many traces of her late emotion as were effaceable on so short a notice ; and presenting herself before him, and representing their dilemma, entreated that he would escort Morleena to the hair-dresser's shop.

" I wouldn't ask you, Mr. Noggs," said Mrs. Kenwigs, " if I didn't know what a good, kind-hearted creature you are—no, not for worlds. I am a weak constitution, Mr. Noggs, but my spirit would no more let me ask a favour where I thought there was a chance of its being refused, than it would let me submit to see my children trampled down and trod upon by envy and lowness ! "

Newman was too good-natured not to have consented, even without this avowal of confidence on the part of Mrs. Kenwigs. Accordingly, a very few minutes had elapsed when he and Miss Morleena were on their way to the hair-dresser's.

It was not exactly a hair-dresser's; that is to say, people of a coarse and vulgar turn of mind might have called it a barber's, for they not only cut and curled ladies elegantly and children carefully, but shaved gentlemen easily. Still it was a highly genteel establishment—quite first-rate in fact—and there were displayed in the window, besides other elegancies, waxen busts of a light lady and a dark gentleman which were the admiration of the whole neighbourhood. Indeed, some ladies had gone so far as to assert, that the dark gentleman was actually a portrait of the spirited young proprietor, and the great similarity between their head-dresses—both wore very glossy hair with a narrow walk straight down the middle, and a profusion of flat circular curls on both sides—encouraged the idea. The better informed among the sex, however, made light of this assertion, for however willing they were (and they were very willing) to do full justice to the handsome face and figure of the proprietor, they held the countenance of the dark gentleman in the window to be an exquisite and abstract idea of masculine beauty, realised sometimes perhaps among angels and military men, but very rarely embodied to gladden the eyes of mortals.

It was to this establishment that Newman Noggs led Miss Kenwigs in safety, and the proprietor knowing that Miss Kenwigs had three sisters, each with two flaxen tails, and all good for sixpence a-piece once a month at least, promptly deserted an old gentleman whom he had just lathered for shaving, and handing him over to the journeyman, (who was not very popular among the ladies, by reason of his obesity and middle age) waited on the young lady himself.

Just as this change had been effected, there presented himself for shaving, a big, burly, good-humoured coal-heaver with a pipe in his mouth, who drawing his hand across his chin, requested to know when a shaver would be disengaged.

The journeyman to whom this question was put looked doubtfully at the young proprietor, and the young proprietor looked scornfully at the coal-heaver, observing at the same time—

" You won't get shaved here, my man."

" Why not ? " said the coal-heaver.

" We don't shave gentlemen in your line," remarked the young proprietor.

" Why, I see you a shaving of a baker when I was a looking through the winder, last week," said the coal-heaver.

" It's necessary to draw the line somewheres my fine feller," replied the principal. " We draw the line there. We can't go beyond bakers. If we was to get any lower than bakers our customers would desert us, and we might shut up shop. You must try some other establishment, sir. We couldn't do it here."

The applicant stared, grinned at Newman Noggs, who appeared highly entertained, looked slightly round the shop as if in depreciation of the pomatum pots and other articles of stock, took his pipe out of his mouth and gave a very loud whistle, and then put it in again, and walked out.

The old gentleman who had just been lathered, and who was sitting in a melancholy manner with his face turned towards the wall, appeared quite unconscious of this incident, and to be insensible to everything around him in the depth of a reverie—a very mournful one, to judge from the sighs he occasionally vented—in which he was absorbed. Affected by this example, the proprietor began to clip Miss Kenwigs, the journeyman to scrape the old gentleman, and Newman Noggs to read last Sunday's paper, all three in silence; when Miss Kenwigs uttered a shrill little scream, and Newman raising his eyes, saw that it had been elicited by the circumstance of the old gentleman turning his head, and disclosing the features of Mr. Lillyvick the collector.

The features of Mr. Lillyvick they were, but strangely altered. If ever an old gentleman had made a point of appearing in public, shaved close and clean, that old gentleman was Mr. Lillyvick. If ever a collector had borne himself like a collector, and assumed before all men a solemn and portentous dignity as if he had the world on his books and it was all two quarters in arrear, that collector was Mr. Lillyvick. And now, there he sat with the remains of a beard at least a week old encumbering his chin, a soiled and crumpled shirt-frill crouching as it were upon his breast instead of standing boldly out; a demeanour so abashed and drooping, so despondent, expressive of such humiliation, grief, and shame, that if the souls of forty unsubstantial housekeepers all of whom had had their water cut off for non-payment of the rate, could have been concentrated in one body, that one body could hardly have expressed such mortification and defeat as were now expressed in the person of Mr. Lillyvick the collector.

Newman Noggs uttered his name, and Mr. Lillyvick groaned, then coughed to hide it. But the groan was a full-sized groan, and the cough was but a wheeze.

" Is anything the matter ? " said Newman Noggs.

" Matter, Sir ! " cried Mr. Lillyvick. " The plug of life is dry, Sir, and but the mud is left."

This speech—the style of which Newman attributed to Mr. Lillyvick's recent association with theatrical characters—not being quite explanatory, Newman looked as if he were about to ask another question, when Mr. Lillyvick prevented him by shaking his hand mournfully, and then waving his own.

" Let me be shaved," said Mr. Lillyvick. " I shall be done before Morleena—it *is* Morleena, isn't it ? "

" Yes," said Newman.

" Kenwigses have got a boy, haven't they ? " inquired the collector. Again Newman said " Yes."

" Is it a nice boy ? " demanded the collector.

" It ain't a very nasty one," returned Newman, rather embarrassed by the question.

Great excitement of Miss Kenwigs at the hair dressers shop.

" Susan Kenwigs used to say," observed the collector, " that if ever she had another boy, she hoped it might be like me. Is this one like me, Mr. Noggs?"

This was a puzzling inquiry, but Newman evaded it by replying to Mr. Lillyvick, that he thought the baby might possibly come like him in time.

" I should be glad to have somebody like me, somehow," said Mr. Lillyvick, " before I die."

" You don't mean to do that yet awhile?" said Newman.

Unto which Mr. Lillyvick replied in a solemn voice, " Let me be shaved ;" and again consigning himself to the hands of the journeyman, said no more.

This was remarkable behaviour, and so remarkable did it seem to Miss Morleena, that that young lady, at the imminent hazard of having her ear sliced off, had not been able to forbear looking round some score of times during the foregoing colloquy. Of her, however, Mr. Lillyvick took no notice, rather striving (so, at least, it seemed to Newman Noggs) to evade her observation, and to shrink into himself whenever he attracted her regards. Newman wondered very much what could have occasioned this altered behaviour on the part of the collector; but philosophically reflecting that he would most likely know sooner or later, and that he could perfectly afford to wait, he was very little disturbed by the singularity of the old gentleman's deportment.

The cutting and curling being at last concluded, the old gentleman, who had been some time waiting, rose to go, and walking out with Newman and his charge, took Newman's arm, and proceeded with them for some time without making any observation. Newman, who in power of taciturnity was excelled by few people, made no attempt to break silence, and so they went on until they had very nearly reached Miss Morleena's home, when Mr. Lillyvick said—

" Were the Kenwigses very much overpowered, Mr. Noggs, by that news?"

" What news?" returned Newman.

" That about—my—being——"

" Married?" suggested Newman.

" Ah !" replied Mr. Lillyvick, with another groan—this time not even disguised by a wheeze.

" It made ma cry when she knew it," interposed Miss Morleena, "but we kept it from her for a long time; and pa was very low in his spirits, but he is better now; and I was very ill, but I am better too."

" Would you give your great-uncle Lillyvick a kiss if he was to ask you, Morleena?" said the collector, with some hesitation.

" Yes,—uncle Lillyvick, I would," returned Miss Morleena, with the energy of both her parents combined; " but not aunt Lillyvick. She's not an aunt of mine, and I'll never call her one."

Immediately upon the utterance of these words, Mr. Lillyvick caught Miss Morleena up in his arms and kissed her, and being by this time at the door of the house where Mr. Kenwigs lodged (which, as has been before-mentioned, usually stood wide open), he walked straight up into Mr. Kenwigs' sitting-room, and put Miss Morleena down in the midst. Mr. and Mrs. Kenwigs were at supper. At sight of their perjured relative, Mrs. Kenwigs turned faint and pale, and Mr. Kenwigs rose majestically.

" Kenwigs," said the collector, " shake hands."

" Sir," said Mr. Kenwigs, " the time has been when I was proud to shake hands with such a man as that man as now surweys me. The time has been, Sir," said Mr. Kenwigs, " when a wisit from that man has excited in me and my family's boozums sensations both nateral and awakening. But now I look upon that man with emotions totally surpassing everythink, and I ask myself where is his /honour, where is his straight-for'ardness, and where is his human natur."

" Susan Kenwigs," said Mr. Lillyvick, turning humbly to his niece, " don't you say anything to me ?"

" She is not equal to it, Sir," said Mr. Kenwigs, striking the table emphatically. " What with the nursing of a healthy babby, and the reflections upon your cruel conduct, four pints of malt liquor a day is hardly able to sustain her."

" I am glad," said the poor collector meekly, " that the baby is a healthy one. I am very glad of that."

This was touching the Kenwigses on their tenderest point. Mrs. Kenwigs instantly burst into tears, and Mr. Kenwigs evinced great emotion.

" My pleasantest feeling all the time that child was expected," said Mr. Kenwigs, mournfully, " was a thinking, ' if it's a boy, as I hope it may be, for I have heard it's uncle Lillyvick say again and again he would perfer our having a boy next—if it's a boy, what will his uncle Lillyvick say—what will he like him to be called—will he be Peter, or Alexander, or Pompey, or Diorgeenes, or what will he be ? ' and now when I look at him—a precious, unconscious, helpless infant, with no use in his little arms but to tear his little cap, and no use in his little legs but to kick his little self—when I see him a-lying on his mother's lap cooing and cooing, and in his innocent state almost a choking himself with his little fist—when I see him such a infant as he is, and think that that uncle Lillyvick, as was once a going to be so fond of him has withdrawed himself away, such a feeling of wengeance comes over me as no language can depicter, and I feel as if even that holy babe was a telling me to hate him."

This affecting picture moved Mrs. Kenwigs deeply. After several imperfect words which vainly attempted to struggle to the surface, but were drowned and washed away by the strong tide of her tears, she spake.

" Uncle," said Mrs. Kenwigs, " to think that you should have turned your back upon me and my dear children, and upon Kenwigs which is the author of their being—you who was once so kind and affectionate, and who, if anybody had told us such a thing of, we should have withered with scorn like lightning—you that little Lillyvick our first and earliest boy was named after at the very altar—oh gracious ! "

"Was it money that we cared for?" said Mr. Kenwigs. "Was it property that we ever thought of?"

"No," cried Mrs. Kenwigs, "I scorn it."

"So do I," said Mr. Kenwigs, "and always did."

"My feelings have been lancerated," said Mrs. Kenwigs, "my heart has been torn asunder with anguish, I have been thrown back in my confinement, my unoffending infant has been rendered uncomfortable and fractious, Morleena has pined herself away to nothing; all this I forget and forgive, and with you, uncle, I never can quarrel. But never ask me to receive *her*—never do it, uncle. For I will not, I will not, I won't, I won't, I won't—"

"Susan, my dear," said Mr. Kenwigs, "consider your child."

"Yes," shrieked Mrs. Kenwigs, "I will consider my child! I will consider my child! my own child, that no uncles can deprive me of, my own hated, despised, deserted, cut-off little child." And here the emotions of Mrs. Kenwigs became so violent that Mr. Kenwigs was fain to administer hartshorn internally and vinegar externally, and to destroy a staylace, four petticoat strings, and several small buttons.

Newman had been a silent spectator of this scene, for Mr. Lillyvick had signed to him not to withdraw, and Mr. Kenwigs had further solicited his presence by a nod of invitation. When Mrs. Kenwigs had been in some degree restored, and Newman, as a person possessed of some influence with her, had remonstrated and begged her to compose herself, Mr. Lillyvick said in a faltering voice:

"I never shall ask anybody here to receive my——I needn't mention the word, you know what I mean. Kenwigs and Susan, yesterday was a week she eloped with a half-pay captain."

Mr. and Mrs. Kenwigs started together.

"Eloped with a half-pay captain," repeated Mr. Lillyvick, "basely and falsely eloped with a half-pay captain—with a bottle-nosed captain that any man might have considered himself safe from. It was in this room," said Mr. Lillyvick, looking sternly round, "that I first see Henrietta Petowker. It is in this room that I turn her off for ever."

This declaration completely changed the whole posture of affairs. Mrs. Kenwigs threw herself upon the old gentleman's neck, bitterly reproaching herself for her late harshness, and exclaiming if she had suffered, what must his sufferings have been! Mr. Kenwigs grasped his hand and vowed eternal friendship and remorse. Mrs. Kenwigs was horror-stricken to think that she should ever have nourished in her bosom such a snake, adder, viper, serpent, and base crocodile as Henrietta Petowker. Mr. Kenwigs argued that she must have been bad indeed not to have improved by so long a contemplation of Mrs. Kenwigs's virtue. Mrs. Kenwigs remembered that Mr. Kenwigs had often said that he was not quite satisfied of the propriety of Miss Petowker's conduct, and wondered how it was that she could have been blinded by such a wretch. Mr. Kenwigs remembered that he had had his suspicions, but did not wonder why Mrs. Kenwigs had not had hers, as she was all chastity, purity, and truth, and Henrietta all baseness, falsehood, and deceit. And Mr. and Mrs. Kenwigs both said with strong feeling and tears of sympathy, that everything happened for the best, and conjured the good collector not to give way to unavailing grief, but to seek consolation in the society of those affectionate relations whose arms and hearts were ever open to him.

" Out of affection and regard for you, Susan and Kenwigs," said Mr. Lillyvick, " and not out of revenge and spite against her, for she is below it, I shall to-morrow morning settle upon your children, and make payable to the survivors of them when they come of age or marry, that money that I once meant to leave 'em in my will. The deed shall be executed to-morrow, and Mr. Noggs shall be one of the witnesses. He hears me promise this, and he shall see it done."

Overpowered by this noble and generous offer, Mr. Kenwigs, Mrs. Kenwigs, and Miss Morleena Kenwigs all began to sob together, and the noise of their sobbing communicating itself to the next room, where the children lay a-bed, and causing them to cry too, Mr. Kenwigs rushed wildly in and bringing them out in his arms by two and two, tumbled them down in their nightcaps and gowns at the feet of Mr. Lillyvick, and called upon them to thank and bless him.

" And now," said Mr. Lillyvick, when a heart-rending scene had ensued and the children were cleared away again, " Give me some supper. This took place twenty mile from town. I came up this morning, and have been lingering about all day without being able to make up my mind to come and see you. I humoured her in everything, she had her own way, she did just as she pleased, and now she has done this. There was twelve teaspoons and twenty-four pound in sovereigns—I missed them first—it's a trial—I feel I shall never be able to knock a double knock again when I go my rounds—don't say anything more about it, please—the spoons were worth—never mind— never mind ! "

With such muttered outpourings as these, the old gentleman shed a few tears, but they got him into the elbow-chair and prevailed upon him, without much pressing, to make a hearty supper, and by the time he had finished his first pipe and disposed of half-a-dozen glasses out of a crown bowl of punch, ordered by Mr. Kenwigs in celebration of his return to the bosom of his family, he seemed, though still very humble, quite resigned to his fate, and rather relieved than otherwise by the flight of his wife.

" When I see that man," said Mr. Kenwigs, with one hand round Mrs. Kenwigs's waist, his other hand supporting his pipe (which made him wink and cough very much, for he was no smoker) and his eyes on Morleena, who sat upon her uncle's knee, " when I see that man a mingling once again in the spear which he adorns, and see his affections deweloping themselves in legitimate sitiwations, I feel that his natur is as elewated and expanded as his standing afore society as a public character is unimpeached, and the woices of my infant children purvided for in life, seem to whisper to me softly, ' This is an ewent at which Evins itself looks down ! ' "

CHAPTER LIII.

CONTAINING THE FURTHER PROGRESS OF THE PLOT CONTRIVED BY
MR. RALPH NICKLEBY AND MR. ARTHUR GRIDE.

WITH that settled resolution and steadiness of purpose to which
extreme circumstances so often give birth, acting upon far less excitable
and more sluggish temperaments than that which was the lot of
Madeline Bray's admirer, Nicholas started, at dawn of day, from the
restless couch which no sleep had visited on the previous night, and
prepared to make that last appeal by whose slight and fragile thread
her only remaining hope of escape depended.

Although to restless and ardent minds, morning may be the fitting
season for exertion and activity, it is not always at that time that hope
is strongest or the spirit most sanguine and buoyant. In trying and
doubtful positions, use, custom, a steady contemplation of the difficulties which surround us, and a familiarity with them, imperceptibly
diminish our apprehensions and beget comparative indifference, if not
a vague and reckless confidence in some relief, the means or nature of
which we care not to foresee. But when we come fresh upon such
things in the morning, with that dark and silent gap between us and
yesterday, with every link in the brittle chain of hope to rivet afresh,
our hot enthusiasm subdued, and cool calm reason substituted in its
stead, doubt and misgiving revive. As the traveller sees farthest by
day, and becomes aware of rugged mountains and trackless plains which
the friendly darkness had shrouded from his sight and mind together,
so the wayfarer in the toilsome path of human life sees with each returning sun some new obstacle to surmount, some new height to be
attained ; distances stretch out before him which last night were scarcely
taken into account, and the light which gilds all nature with its cheerful beams, seems but to shine upon the weary obstacles which yet lie
strewn between him and the grave.

So thought Nicholas, when, with the impatience natural to a situation like his, he softly left the house, and feeling as though to remain
in bed were to lose most precious time, and to be up and stirring were
in some way to promote the end he had in view, he wandered into London,
although perfectly well knowing that for hours to come he could not
obtain speech with Madeline, and could do nothing but wish the inter-
vening time away.

And even now, as he paced the streets and listlessly looked round on
the gradually increasing bustle and preparation for the day, everything
appeared to yield him some new occasion for despondency. Last night
the sacrifice of a young, affectionate, and beautiful creature to such a
wretch and in such a cause, had seemed a thing too monstrous to
succeed, and the warmer he grew the more confident he felt that some
interposition must save her from his clutches. But now, when he

thought how regularly things went on from day to day in the same unvarying round—how youth and beauty died, and ugly griping age lived tottering on—how crafty avarice grew rich, and manly honest hearts were poor and sad—how few they were who tenanted the stately houses, and how many those who lay in noisome pens, or rose each day and laid them down at night, and lived and died, father and son, mother and child, race upon race, and generation upon generation, without a home to shelter them or the energies of one single man directed to their aid —how in seeking, not a luxurious and splendid life, but the bare means of a most wretched and inadequate subsistence, there were women and children in that one town, divided into classes, numbered and estimated as regularly as the noble families and folks of great degree, and reared from infancy to drive most criminal and dreadful trades—how ignorance was punished and never taught—how jail-door gaped and gallows loomed for thousands urged towards them by circumstances darkly curtaining their very cradles' heads, and but for which they might have earned their honest bread and lived in peace—how many died in soul, and had no chance of life—how many who could scarcely go astray, be they vicious as they would, turned haughtily from the crushed and stricken wretch who could scarce do otherwise, and who would have been a greater wonder had he or she done well, than even they, had they done ill—how much injustice, and misery, and wrong there was, and yet how the world rolled on from year to year, alike careless and indifferent, and no man seeking to remedy or redress it :—when he thought of all this, and selected from the mass the one slight case on which his thoughts were bent, he felt indeed that there was little ground for hope, and little cause or reason why it should not form an atom in the huge aggregate of distress and sorrow, and add one small and unimportant unit to swell the great amount.

But youth is not prone to contemplate the darkest side of a picture it can shift at will. By dint of reflecting on what he had to do and reviving the train of thought which night had interrupted, Nicholas gradually summoned up his utmost energy, and by the time the morning was sufficiently advanced for his purpose, had no thought but that of using it to the best advantage. A hasty breakfast taken, and such affairs of business as required prompt attention disposed of, he directed his steps to the residence of Madeline Bray, whither he lost no time in arriving.

It had occurred to him that very possibly the young lady might be denied, although to him she never had been; and he was still pondering upon the surest method of obtaining access to her in that case, when, coming to the door of the house, he found it had been left ajar—probably by the last person who had gone out. The occasion was not one upon which to observe the nicest ceremony ; therefore, availing himself of this advantage, Nicholas walked gently up stairs and knocked at the door of the room into which he had been accustomed to be shown. Receiving permission to enter from some person on the other side, he opened the door and walked in.

Bray and his daughter were sitting there alone. It was nearly three weeks since he had seen her last, but there was a change in the lovely girl before him which told Nicholas, in startling terms, what mental suffering had been compressed into that short time. There are no words which can express, nothing with which can be compared, the perfect pallor, the clear transparent cold ghastly whiteness, of the beautiful face which turned towards him when he entered. Her hair was a rich deep brown, but shading that face, and straying upon a neck that rivalled it in whiteness, it seemed by the strong contrast raven black. Something of wildness and restlessness there was in the dark eye, but there was the same patient look, the same expression of gentle mournfulness which he well remembered, and no trace of a single tear. Most beautiful— more beautiful perhaps in appearance than ever—there was something in her face which quite unmanned him, and appeared far more touching than the wildest agony of grief. It was not merely calm and composed, but fixed and rigid, as though the violent effort which had summoned that composure beneath her father's eye, while it mastered all other thoughts, had prevented even the momentary expression they had communicated to the features from subsiding, and had fastened it there as an evidence of its triumph.

The father sat opposite to her—not looking directly in her face, but glancing at her as he talked with a gay air which ill disguised the anxiety of his thoughts. The drawing materials were not on their accustomed table, nor were any of the other tokens of her usual occupations to be seen. The little vases which he had always seen filled with fresh flowers, were empty or supplied only with a few withered stalks and leaves. The bird was silent. The cloth that covered his cage at night was not removed. His mistress had forgotten him.

There are times when the mind being painfully alive to receive impressions, a great deal may be noted at a glance. This was one, for Nicholas had but glanced round him when he was recognised by Mr. Bray, who said impatiently,

"Now, Sir, what do you want? Name your errand here quickly if you please, for my daughter and I are busily engaged with other and more important matters than those you come about. Come, Sir, address yourself to your business at once."

Nicholas could very well discern that the irritability and impatience of this speech were assumed, and that Bray in his heart was rejoiced at any interruption which promised to engage the attention of his daughter. He bent his eyes involuntarily upon the father as he spoke, and marked his uneasiness, for he coloured directly and turned his head away.

The device, however, so far as it was a device for causing Madeline to interfere, was successful. She rose, and advancing towards Nicholas paused half way, and stretched out her hand as expecting a letter.

"Madeline," said her father impatiently, "my love, what are you doing?"

"Miss Bray expects an enclosure perhaps," said Nicholas, speaking very distinctly, and with an emphasis she could scarcely misunderstand. "My employer is absent from England, or I should have brought a letter with me. I hope she will give me time—a little time—I ask a very little time."

"If that is all you come about, Sir," said Mr. Bray, "you may make yourself easy on that head. Madeline, my dear, I didn't know this person was in your debt?"

"A—a trifle I believe," returned Madeline, faintly.

"I suppose you think now," said Bray, wheeling his chair round and confronting Nicholas, "that but for such pitiful sums as you bring here because my daughter has chosen to employ her time as she has, we should starve?"

"I have not thought about it," returned Nicholas.

"You have not thought about it!" sneered the invalid. "You know you have thought about it, and have thought that and think so every time you come here. Do you suppose, young man, that I don't know what little purse-proud tradesmen are, when through some fortunate circumstances they get the upper hand for a brief day—or think they get the upper hand—of a gentleman?"

"My business," said Nicholas respectfully, "is with a lady."

"With a gentleman's daughter, Sir," returned the sick man, "and the pettifogging spirit is the same. But perhaps you bring *orders* eh? Have you any fresh *orders* for my daughter, Sir?"

Nicholas understood the tone of triumph and the sneer in which this interrogatory was put, but remembering the necessity of supporting his assumed character, produced a scrap of paper purporting to contain a list of some subjects for drawings which his employer desired to have executed; and with which he had prepared himself in case of any such contingency.

"Oh!" said Mr. Bray. "These are the orders, are they?"

"Since you insist upon the term, Sir—yes," replied Nicholas.

"Then you may tell your master," said Bray, tossing the paper back again with an exulting smile, "that my daughter—Miss Madeline Bray—condescends to employ herself no longer in such labours as these; that she is not at his beck and call as he supposes her to be; that we don't live upon his money as he flatters himself we do; that he may give whatever he owes us to the first beggar that passes his shop, or add it to his own profits next time he calculates them; and that he may go to the devil, for me. That's my acknowledgment of his orders, Sir!"

"And this is the independence of a man who sells his daughter as he has sold that weeping girl!" thought Nicholas indignantly.

The father was too much absorbed with his own exultation to mark the look of scorn which for an instant Nicholas would not have suppressed had he been upon the rack. "There," he continued, after a short silence, "you have your message and can retire—unless you have any further—ha!—any further orders."

"I have none," said Nicholas sternly; "neither in consideration of the station you once held, have I used that or any other word which, however harmless in itself, could be supposed to imply authority on my part or dependence on yours. I have no orders, but I have fears—fears that I will express, chafe as you may—fears that you may be consigning that young lady to something worse than supporting you by the labour of her hands, had she worked herself dead. These are my fears, and these fears I found upon your own demeanour. Your conscience will tell you, Sir, whether I construe it well or not."

" For Heaven's sake!" cried Madeline, interposing in alarm between them. " Remember, Sir, he is ill."

" Ill!" cried the invalid, gasping and catching for breath. " Ill! Ill! I am bearded and bullied by a shop-boy, and she beseeches him to pity me and remember I am ill!"

He fell into a paroxysm of his disorder, so violent that for a few moments Nicholas was alarmed for his life; but finding that he began to recover, he withdrew, after signifying by a gesture to the young lady that he had something important to communicate, and would wait for her outside the room. He could hear that the sick man came gradually but slowly to himself, and that without any reference to what had just occurred, as though he had no distinct recollection of it as yet, he requested to be left alone.

" Oh!" thought Nicholas, " that this slender chance might not be lost, and that I might prevail if it were but for one week's time and re-consideration!"

" You are charged with some commission to me, Sir," said Madeline, presenting herself in great agitation. " Do not press it now, I beg and pray you. The day after to-morrow—come here then."

" It will be too late—too late for what I have to say," rejoined Nicholas, " and you will not be here. Oh, Madam, if you have but one thought of him who sent me here, but one last lingering care for your own peace of mind and heart, I do for God's sake urge you to give me a hearing."

She attempted to pass him, but Nicholas gently detained her.

" A hearing," said Nicholas. " I ask you but to hear me—not me alone, but him for whom I speak, who is far away and does not know your danger. In the name of Heaven hear me."

The poor attendant with her eyes swollen and red with weeping stood by, and to her Nicholas appealed in such passionate terms that she opened a side-door, and supporting her mistress into an adjoining room beckoned Nicholas to follow them.

" Leave me, Sir, pray," said the young lady.

" I cannot, will not leave you thus," returned Nicholas. " I have a duty to discharge, and either here or in the room from which we have just now come, at whatever risk or hazard to Mr. Bray, I must beseech you to contemplate again the fearful course to which you have been impelled."

" What course is this you speak of, and impelled by whom, Sir?" demanded the young lady, with an effort to speak proudly.

" I speak of this marriage," returned Nicholas, " of this marriage, fixed for to-morrow by one who never faltered in a bad purpose, or lent his aid to any good design; of this marriage, the history of which is known to me, better, far better, than it is to you. I know what web is wound about you. I know what men they are from whom these schemes have come. You are betrayed, and sold for money—for gold, whose every coin is rusted with tears, if not red with the blood of ruined men, who have fallen desperately by their own mad hands."

" You say you have a duty to discharge," said Madeline, firmly, " and so have I. And with the help of Heaven I will perform it."

" Say rather with the help of devils," replied Nicholas, " with the help of men, one of them your destined husband, who are——"

" I must not hear this," cried the young lady, striving to repress a shudder, occasioned, as it seemed, even by this slight allusion to Arthur Gride. " This evil, if evil it is, has been of my own seeking. I am impelled to this course by no one, but follow it of my own free will. You see I am not constrained or forced by menace and intimidation. Report this," said Madeline, " to my dear friend and benefactor, and taking with you my prayers and thanks for him and for yourself, leave me for ever."

" Not until I have besought you, with all the earnestness and fervour by which I am animated," cried Nicholas, " to postpone this marriage for one short week. Not until I have besought you to think more deeply than you can have done, influenced as you are, upon the step you are about to take. Although you cannot be fully conscious of the villany of this man to whom you are about to give your hand, some of his deeds you know. You have heard him speak, and looked upon his face—reflect, reflect before it is too late, on the mockery of plighting to him at the altar, faith in which your heart can have no share—of uttering solemn words, against which nature and reason must rebel—of the degradation of yourself in your own esteem, which must ensue, and must be aggravated every day as his detested character opens upon you more and more. Shrink from the loathsome companionship of this foul wretch as you would from corruption and disease. Suffer toil and labour if you will, but shun him, shun him, and be happy. For, believe me, that I speak the truth, the most abject poverty, the most wretched condition of human life, with a pure and upright mind, would be happiness to that which you must undergo as the wife of such a man as this !"

Long before Nicholas ceased to speak, the young lady buried her face in her hands, and gave her tears free way. In a voice at first inarticulate with emotion, but gradually recovering strength as she proceeded, she answered him,

" I will not disguise from you, Sir—though perhaps I ought—that I have undergone great pain of mind, and have been nearly broken-hearted since I saw you last. I do *not* love this gentleman; the difference between our ages, tastes, and habits, forbids it. This he knows, and knowing, still offers me his hand. By accepting it, and by that step alone, I can release my father who is dying in this place, prolong his life, perhaps, for many years, restore him to comfort—I may almost call it affluence—and relieve a generous man from the burden of assisting one by whom, I grieve to say, his noble heart is little understood.

Do not think so poorly of me as to believe that I feign a love I do not feel. Do not report so ill of me, for *that* I could not bear. If I cannot in reason or in nature love the man who pays this price for my poor hand, I can discharge the duties of a wife: I can be all he seeks in me, and will. He is content to take me as I am. I have passed my word, and should rejoice, not weep, that it is so—I do. The interest you take in one so friendless and forlorn as I, the delicacy with which you have discharged your trust, the faith you have kept with me, have my warmest thanks, and while I make this last feeble acknowledgment, move me to tears, as you see. But I do not repent, nor am I unhappy. I am happy in the prospect of all I can achieve so easily, and shall be more so when I look back upon it, and all is done, I know."

" Your tears fall faster as you talk of happiness," said Nicholas, " and you shun the contemplation of that dark future which must come laden with so much misery to you. Defer this marriage for a week—for but one week."

" He was talking, when you came upon us just now, with such smiles as I remember to have seen of old, and have not seen for many and many a day, of the freedom that was to come to-morrow," said Madeline, with momentary firmness, " of the welcome change, the fresh air; all the new scenes and objects that would bring fresh life to his exhausted frame. His eye grew bright, and his face lightened at the thought. I will not defer it for an hour."

" These are but tricks and wiles to urge you on," cried Nicholas.

" I'll hear no more," said Madeline, hurriedly, " I have heard too much—more than I should—already. What I have said to you, Sir, I have said as to that dear friend to whom I trust in you honourably to repeat it. Some time hence when I am more composed and reconciled to my new mode of life, if I should live so long, I will write to him. Meantime, all holy angels shower their blessings on his head, and prosper and preserve him."

She was hurrying past Nicholas, when he threw himself before her, and implored her to think but once again upon the fate to which she was precipitately hastening.

" There is no retreat," said Nicholas, in an agony of supplication " no withdrawing; all regret will be unavailing, and deep and bitter it must be. What can I say that will induce you to pause at this last moment! What can I do to save you !"

" Nothing," she incoherently replied. " This is the hardest trial I have had. Have mercy on me, Sir, I beseech, and do not pierce my heart with such appeals as these. I—I hear him calling; I—I—must not, will not, remain here for another instant."

" If this were a plot," said Nicholas, with the same violent rapidity with which she spoke, " a plot, not yet laid bare by me, but which, with time, I might unravel, if you were (not knowing it) entitled to fortune of your own, which being recovered, would do all that this marriage can accomplish, would you not retract ?"

" No, no, no !—it is impossible ; it is a child's tale, time would bring his death. He is calling again.'

" It may be the last time we shall ever meet on earth," said Nicholas,
" it may be better for me that we should never meet more."

" For both—for both," replied Madeline, not heeding what she said.
" The time will come when to recal the memory of this one interview
might drive me mad. Be sure to tell them that you left me calm and
happy. And God be with you, Sir, and my grateful heart and
blessing!"

She was gone, and Nicholas, staggering from the house, thought of
the hurried scene which had just closed upon him, as if it were the
phantom of some wild, unquiet dream. The day wore on; at night,
having been enabled in some measure to collect his thoughts, he issued
forth again.

That night, being the last of Arthur Gride's bachelorship, found
him in tip-top spirits and great glee. The bottle-green suit had been
brushed ready for the morrow. Peg Sliderskew had rendered the
accounts of her past housekeeping; the eighteenpence had been rigidly
accounted for (she was never trusted with a larger sum at once, and
the accounts were not usually balanced more than twice a-day), every
preparation had been made for the coming festival, and Arthur might
have sat down and contemplated his approaching happiness, but that
he preferred sitting down and contemplating the entries in a dirty old
vellum-book with rusty clasps.

" Well-a-day!" he chuckled, as sinking on his knees before a
strong chest screwed down to the floor, he thrust in his arm nearly up
to the shoulder, and slowly drew forth this greasy volume, " Well-a-
day now, this is all my library, but it's one of the most entertaining
books that were ever written; it's a delightful book, and all true and
real—that's the best of it—true as the Bank of England, and real as
its gold and silver. Written by Arthur Gride—he, he, he! None of
your story-book writers will ever make as good a book as this, I
warrant me. It's composed for private circulation—for my own particular reading, and nobody else's. He, he!"

Muttering this soliloquy, Arthur carried his precious volume to the
table, and adjusting it upon a dusty desk, put on his spectacles, and
began to pore among the leaves.

" It's a large sum to Mr. Nickleby," he said, in a dolorous voice.
" Debt to be paid in full, nine hundred and seventy-five, four, three,
Additional sum as per bond five hundred pound. One thousand, four
hundred and seventy-five pounds, four shillings, and threepence,
to-morrow at twelve o'clock. On the other side though, there's the
per contra by means of this pretty chick. But again there's the
question whether I mightn't have brought all this about myself.
' Faint heart never won fair lady.' Why was my heart so faint?
Why didn't I boldly open it to Bray myself, and save one thousand
four hundred and seventy-five, four, three!"

These reflections depressed the old usurer so much as to wring a
feeble groan or two from his breast, and cause him to declare with
uplifted hands that he would die in a workhouse. Remembering
on further cogitation, however, that under any circumstances he

must have paid, or handsomely compounded for, Ralph's debt, and being by no means confident that he would have succeeded had he undertaken his enterprise alone, he regained his equanimity, and chattered and mowed over more satisfactory items until the entrance of Peg Sliderskew interrupted him.

"Aha, Peg!" said Arthur, "what is it? What is it now, Peg?"

"It's the fowl," replied Peg, holding up a plate containing a little —a very little one—quite a phenomenon of a fowl—so very small and skinny.

"A beautiful bird!" said Arthur, after inquiring the price, and finding it proportionate to the size. "With a rasher of ham, and an egg made into sauce, and potatoes, and greens, and an apple-pudding, Peg, and a little bit of cheese, we shall have a dinner for an emperor. There'll only be she and me—and you, Peg, when we've done—nobody else."

"Don't you complain of the expense afterwards," said Mrs. Sliderskew, sulkily.

"I'm afraid we must live expensively for the first week," returned Arthur, with a groan, "and then we must make up for it. I won't eat more than I can help, and I know you love your old master too much to eat more than *you* can help, don't you, Peg?"

"Don't I what?" said Peg.

"Love your old master too much—"

"No, not a bit too much," said Peg.

"Oh dear, I wish the devil had this woman!" cried Arthur— "love him too much to eat more than you can help at his expense."

"At his what?" said Peg.

"Oh dear! she can never hear the most important word, and hears all the others!" whined Gride. "At his expense—you catamaran."

The last-mentioned tribute to the charms of Mrs. Sliderskew being uttered in a whisper, that lady assented to the general proposition by a harsh growl, which was accompanied by a ring at the street-door.

"There's the bell," said Arthur.

"Ay, ay; I know that," rejoined Peg.

"Then why don't you go?" bawled Arthur.

"Go where?" retorted Peg. "I ain't doing any harm here, am I?"

Arthur Gride in reply repeated the word "bell" as loud as he could roar, and his meaning being rendered further intelligible to Mrs. Sliderskew's dull sense of hearing by pantomime expressive of ringing at a street-door, Peg hobbled out, after sharply demanding why he hadn't said there was a ring before, instead of talking about all manner of things that had nothing to do with it, and keeping her half-pint of beer waiting on the steps.

"There's a change come over you, Mrs. Peg," said Arthur, following her out with his eyes. "What it means I don't quite know, but if it lasts we shan't agree together long, I see. You are turning crazy, I think, and if you are you must take yourself off, Mrs. Peg—or be taken off. All's one to me." Turning over the leaves of his book as he muttered this, he soon lighted upon something which attracted his attention, and forgot Peg Sliderskew and everything else in the engrossing interest of its pages.

The room had no other light than that which it derived from a dim and dirt-clogged lamp, whose lazy wick, being still further obscured by a dark shade, cast its feeble rays over a very little space, and left all beyond in heavy shadow. This, the money-lender had drawn so close to him, that there was only room between it and himself for the book over which he bent; and as he sat with his elbows on the desk, and his sharp cheek-bones resting on his hands, it only served to bring out his hideous features in strong relief, together with the little table at which he sat, and to shroud all the rest of the chamber in a deep sullen gloom. Raising his eyes and looking vacantly into this gloom as he made some mental calculation, Arthur Gride suddenly met the fixed gaze of a man.

"Thieves! thieves!" shrieked the usurer, starting up and folding his book to his breast, "robbers! murder!"

"What is the matter?" said the form, advancing.

"Keep off!" cried the trembling wretch. "Is it a man or a—a—"

"For what do you take me, if not for a man?" was the disdainful inquiry.

"Yes, yes," cried Arthur Gride, shading his eyes with his hand, "it is a man, and not a spirit. It is a man. Robbers! robbers!"

"For what are these cries raised—unless indeed you know me, and have some purpose in your brain?" said the stranger, coming close up to him. "I am no thief, fellow."

"What then, and how come you here?" cried Gride, somewhat reassured, but still retreating from his visitor, "what is your name, and what do you want?"

"My name you need not know," was the reply. "I came here because I was shown the way by your servant. I have addressed you twice or thrice, but you were too profoundly engaged with your book to hear me, and I have been silently waiting until you should be less abstracted. What I want I will tell you, when you can summon up courage enough to hear and understand me."

Arthur Gride venturing to regard his visitor more attentively, and perceiving that he was a young man of good mien and bearing, returned to his seat, and muttering that there were bad characters about, and that this, with former attempts upon his house, had made him nervous, requested his visitor to sit down. This however he declined.

"Good God! I don't stand up to have you at an advantage," said Nicholas (for Nicholas it was), as he observed a gesture of alarm on the part of Gride. "Listen to me. You are to be married to-morrow morning."

"N—n—no," rejoined Gride. "Who said I was? How do you know that?"

"No matter how," replied Nicholas, "I know it. The young lady who is to give you her hand hates and despises you. Her blood runs cold at the mention of your name—the vulture and the lamb, the rat and the dove, could not be worse matched than you and she. You see I know her."

Gride looked at him as if he were petrified with astonishment, but did not speak, perhaps lacking the power.

"You and another man, Ralph Nickleby by name, have hatched this plot between you," pursued Nicholas, "you pay him for his share in bringing about this sale of Madeline Bray. You do. A lie is trembling on your lips, I see."

He paused, but Arthur making no reply, resumed again.

"You pay yourself by defrauding her. How or by what means—for I scorn to sully her cause by falsehood or deceit—I do not know; at present I do not know, but I am not alone or single-handed in this business. If the energy of man can compass the discovery of your fraud and treachery before your death—if wealth, revenge, and just hatred can hunt and track you through your windings—you will yet be called to a dear account for this. We are on the scent already—judge you, that know what we do not, when we shall have you down."

He paused again, and still Arthur Gride glared upon him in silence.

"If you were a man to whom I could appeal with any hope of touching his compassion or humanity," said Nicholas, "I would urge upon you to remember the helplessness, the innocence, the youth of this lady, her worth and beauty, her filial excellence, and last, and more than all as concerning you more nearly, the appeal she has made to your mercy and your manly feeling. But I take the only ground that can be taken with men like you, and ask what money will buy you off. Remember the danger to which you are exposed. You see I know enough to know much more with very little help. Bate some expected gain, for the risk you save, and say what is your price."

Old Arthur Gride moved his lips, but they only formed an ugly smile and were motionless again.

"You think," said Nicholas, "that the price would not be paid. Miss Bray has wealthy friends who would coin their hearts to save her in such a strait as this. Name your price, defer these nuptials for but a few days, and see whether those I speak of shrink from the payment. Do you hear me?"

When Nicholas began, Arthur Gride's impression was that Ralph Nickleby had betrayed him; but as he proceeded he felt convinced that however he had come by the knowledge he possessed, the part he acted was a genuine one, and that with Ralph he had no concern. All he seemed to know for certain was, that he, Gride, paid Ralph's debt, but that to anybody who knew the circumstances of Bray's detention—even to Bray himself on Ralph's own statement—must be perfectly notorious. As to the fraud on Madeline herself, his visitor knew so little about its nature or extent, that it might be a lucky guess or a hap-hazard accusation, and whether or no, he had clearly no key to the mystery, and could not hurt him who kept it close within his own breast. The allusion to friends and the offer of money Gride held to be mere empty vapouring for purposes of delay. "And even if money were to be had," thought Arthur Gride, as he glanced at Nicholas, and trembled with passion at his boldness and audacity,

"I'd have that dainty chick for my wife, and cheat *you* of her, young smooth-face."

Long habit of weighing and noting well what clients said, and nicely balancing chances in his mind and calculating odds to their faces, without the least appearance of being so engaged, had rendered Gride quick in forming conclusions and arriving, from puzzling, intricate, and often contradictory premises, at very cunning deductions. Hence it was that as Nicholas went on he followed him closely with his own constructions, and when he ceased to speak was as well prepared as if he had deliberated for a fortnight.

"I hear you," he cried, starting from his seat, casting back the fastenings of the window-shutters, and throwing up the sash. "Help here! Help! Help!"

"What are you doing!" said Nicholas, seizing him by the arm.

"I'll cry robbers, thieves, murder, alarm the neighbourhood, struggle with you, let loose some blood, and swear you came to rob me if you don't quit my house," replied Gride, drawing in his head with a frightful grin, "I will."

"Wretch!" cried Nicholas.

"*You'll* bring your threats here, will you?" said Gride, whom jealousy of Nicholas and a sense of his own triumph had converted into a perfect fiend. "You, the disappointed lover—oh dear! He! he! he!—but you shan't have her, nor she you. She's my wife, my fond doting little wife. Do you think she'll miss you? Do you think she'll weep? I shall like to see her weep—I shan't mind it. She looks prettier in tears."

"Villain!" said Nicholas, choking with his rage.

"One minute more," cried Arthur Gride, "and I'll rouse the street with such screams as, if they were raised by anybody else, should wake me even in the arms of pretty Madeline."

"You base hound!" said Nicholas, "if you were but a younger man——"

"Oh yes!" sneered Arthur Gride, "if I was but a younger man it wouldn't be so bad, but for me, so old and ugly—to be jilted by little Madeline for me!"

"Hear me," said Nicholas, "and be thankful I have enough command over myself not to fling you into the street, which no aid could prevent my doing if I once grappled with you. I have been no lover of this lady's. No contract or engagement, no word of love, has ever passed between us. She does not even know my name."

"I'll ask it for all that—I'll beg it of her with kisses," said Arthur Gride. "Yes, and she'll tell me, and pay them back, and we'll laugh together, and hug ourselves—and be very merry—when we think of the poor youth that wanted to have her, but couldn't, because she was bespoke by me."

This taunt brought such an expression into the face of Nicholas, that Arthur Gride plainly apprehended it to be the forerunner of his putting his threat of throwing him into the street in immediate execution, for he thrust his head out of the window, and holding tight on with both hands, raised a pretty brisk alarm. Not thinking it necessary to abide the issue of the noise, Nicholas gave vent to an indignant defiance, and stalked from the room and from the house. Arthur Gride watched him across the street, and then drawing in his head, fastened the window as before, and sat down to take breath.

" If she ever turns pettish or ill-humoured, I'll taunt her with that spark," he said, when he had recovered. " She'll little think I know about him, and if I manage it well, I can break her spirit by this means and have her under my thumb. I'm glad nobody came. I didn't call too loud. The audacity to enter my house, and open upon me!—But I shall have a very good triumph to-morrow, and he'll be gnawing his fingers off, perhaps drown himself, or cut his throat! I shouldn't wonder! That would make it quite complete, that would— quite."

When he had become restored to his usual condition by these and other comments on his approaching triumph, Arthur Gride put away his book, and having locked up the chest with great caution, descended into the kitchen to warn Peg Sliderskew to bed, and to scold her for having afforded such ready admission to a stranger.

The unconscious Peg, however, not being able to comprehend the offence of which she had been guilty, he summoned her to hold the light while he made a tour of the fastenings, and secured the street-door with his own hands.

" Top bolt," muttered Arthur, fastening as he spoke, " bottom bolt —chain—bar—double-lock—and key out to put under my pillow— so if any more rejected admirers come, they may come through the keyhole. And now I'll go to sleep till half-past five, when I must get up to be married, Peg."

With that, he jocularly tapped Mrs. Sliderskew under the chin, and appeared, for the moment, inclined to celebrate the close of his bachelor days by imprinting a kiss on her shrivelled lips. Thinking better of it, however, he gave her chin another tap in lieu of that warmer fami- liarity, and stole away to bed.

CHAPTER LIV.

THE CRISIS OF THE PROJECT AND ITS RESULT.

THERE are not many men who lie abed too late or oversleep them- selves on their wedding morning. A legend there is of somebody remarkable for absence of mind, who opened his eyes upon the day which was to give him a young wife, and forgetting all about the matter, rated his servants for providing him with such fine clothes as had been prepared for the festival. There is also a legend of a young gentleman who, not having before his eyes the fear of the canons of the church for such cases made and provided, conceived a passion for his grandmama. Both cases are of a singular and special kind, and it is very doubtful whether either can be considered as a precedent likely to be extensively followed by succeeding generations.

Arthur Gride had enrobed himself in his marriage garments of bottle-green, a full hour before Mrs. Sliderskew, shaking off her more heavy slumbers, knocked at his chamber door; and he had hobbled down stairs in full array and smacked his lips over a scanty taste of his favourite cordial, ere that delicate piece of antiquity enlightened the kitchen with her presence.

"Faugh!" said Peg, grubbing, in the discharge of her domestic functions, among a scanty heap of ashes in the rusty grate, "Wedding indeed! A precious wedding! He wants somebody better than his old Peg to take care of him, does he? And what has he said to me many and many a time to keep me content with short food, small wages, and little fire? 'My will, Peg! my will!' says he, 'I'm a bachelor—no friends—no relations, Peg.' Lies! And now he's to bring home a new mistress, a baby-faced chit of a girl—if he wanted a wife, the fool, why couldn't he have one suitable to his age and that knew his ways? She won't come in my way, he says. No, that she won't, but you little think why, Arthur boy."

While Mrs. Sliderskew, influenced possibly by some lingering feelings of disappointment and personal slight occasioned by her old master's preference for another, was giving loose to these grumblings below-stairs, Arthur Gride was cogitating in the parlour upon what had taken place last night.

"I can't think how he can have picked up what he knows," said Arthur, "unless I have committed myself—let something drop at Bray's, for instance, which has been overheard. Perhaps I may. I shouldn't be surprised if that was it. Mr. Nickleby was often angry at my talking to him before we got outside the door. I mustn't tell him that part of the business, or he'll put me out of sorts and make me nervous for the day."

Ralph was universally looked up to and recognised among his fellows as a superior genius, but upon Arthur Gride his stern unyielding character and consummate art had made so deep an impression, that he was actually afraid of him. Cringing and cowardly to the core by nature, Arthur Gride humbled himself in the dust before Ralph Nickleby, and even when they had not this stake in common, would have licked his shoes and crawled upon the ground before him rather than venture to return him word for word, or retort upon him in any other spirit than that of the most slavish and abject sycophancy.

To Ralph Nickleby's, Arthur Gride now betook himself according to appointment, and to Ralph Nickleby he related how that last night some young blustering blade, whom he had never seen, forced his way into his house and tried to frighten him from the proposed nuptials :— told in short, what Nicholas had said and done, with the slight reser-vation upon which he had determined.

"Well, and what then?" said Ralph.

" Oh ! nothing more," rejoined Gride.

" He tried to frighten you ? " said Ralph, disdainfully, " and you *were* frightened I suppose, is that it ? "

" I frightened him by crying thieves and murder," replied Gride. " Once I was in earnest, I tell you that, for I had more than half a mind to swear he uttered threats and demanded my life or my money."

" Oho ! " said Ralph, eyeing him askew. " Jealous too ! "

" Dear now, see that ! " cried Arthur, rubbing his hands and affecting to laugh.

" Why do you make those grimaces, man ? " said Ralph, harshly, " you *are* jealous—and with good cause I think."

" No, no, no,—not with good cause, hey ? You don't think with good cause, do you ? " cried Arthur, faltering, " Do you though— hey ? "

" Why, how stands the fact ? " returned Ralph. " Here is an old man about to be forced in marriage upon a girl, and to this old man there comes a handsome young fellow—you said he was handsome, didn't you ? "

" No ! " snarled Arthur Gride.

" Oh ! " rejoined Ralph, " I thought you did. Well, handsome or not handsome, to this old man there comes a young fellow who casts all manner of fierce defiances in his teeth—gums I should rather say— and tells him in plain terms that his mistress hates him. What does he do that for ? Philanthropy's sake ? "

" Not for love of the lady," replied Gride, " for he said that no word of love—his very words—had ever passed between 'em."

" He said ! " repeated Ralph, contemptuously. " But I like him for one thing, and that is his giving you this fair warning to keep your— what is it ? Tit-tit or dainty chick—which ?—under lock and key. Be careful, Gride, be careful. It's a triumph too to tear her away from a gallant young rival ; a great triumph for an old man. It only remains to keep her safe when you have her—that's all."

" What a man it is ! " cried Arthur Gride, affecting in the extremity of his torture to be highly amused. And then he added, anxiously, " Yes ; to keep her safe, that's all. And that isn't much, is it ? "

" Much ! " said Ralph, with a sneer. " Why, everybody knows what easy things to understand and to control, women are. But come, it's very nearly time for you to be made happy. You'll pay the bond now I suppose, to save us trouble afterwards."

" Oh what a man you are ! " croaked Arthur.

" Why not ? " said Ralph. " Nobody will pay you interest for the money, I suppose, between this and twelve o'clock, will they ? "

" But nobody would pay you interest for it either, you know," returned Arthur, leering at Ralph with all the cunning and slyness he could throw into his face.

" Besides which," said Ralph, suffering his lip to curl into a smile, " you haven't the money about you, and you weren't prepared for this or you'd have brought it with you, and there's nobody you'd so much like to accommodate as me. I see. We trust each other in about an equal degree. Are you ready?"

Gride, who had done nothing but grin, and nod, and chatter, during this last speech of Ralph's, answered in the affirmative, and producing from his hat a couple of large white favours, pinned one on his breast, and with considerable difficulty induced his friend to do the like. Thus accoutred they got into a hired coach which Ralph had in waiting, and drove to the residence of the fair and most wretched bride.

Gride, whose spirits and courage had gradually failed him more and more as they approached nearer and nearer to the house, was utterly dismayed and cowed by the mournful silence which pervaded it. The face of the poor servant-girl, the only person they saw, was disfigured with tears and want of sleep. There was nobody to receive or welcome them; and they stole up stairs into the usual sitting-room more like two burglars than the bridegroom and his friend.

" One would think," said Ralph, speaking in spite of himself in a low and subdued voice, " that there was a funeral going on here, and not a wedding."

" He, he!" tittered his friend, " you are so—so very funny!"

" I need be," remarked Ralph, drily, " for this is rather dull and chilling. Look a little brisker, man, and not so hang-dog like."

" Yes, yes, I will," said Gride. " But—but—you don't think she's coming just yet, do you?"

" Why, I suppose she'll not come till she is obliged," returned Ralph, looking at his watch, " and she has a good half hour to spare yet. Curb your impatience."

" I—I—am not impatient," stammered Arthur. " I wouldn't be hard with her for the world. Oh dear, dear, not on any account. Let her take her time—her own time. Her time shall be ours by all means."

While Ralph bent upon his trembling friend a keen look, which showed that he perfectly understood the reason of this great consideration and regard, a footstep was heard upon the stairs, and Bray himself came into the room on tiptoe, and holding up his hand with a cautious gesture as if there were some sick person near who must not be disturbed.

" Hush!" he said in a low voice. " She was very ill last night. I thought she would have broken her heart. She is dressed, and crying bitterly in her own room; but she's better, and quite quiet—that's everything."

" She is ready, is she?" said Ralph.

" Quite ready," returned the father.

" And not likely to delay us by any young-lady weaknesses—fainting, or so forth?" said Ralph.

" She may be safely trusted now," returned Bray. " I have been talking to her this morning. Here—come a little this way."

He drew Ralph Nickleby to the further end of the room, and pointed towards Gride, who sat huddled together in a corner, fumbling nervously with the buttons of his coat, and exhibiting a face of which every skulking and base expression was sharpened and aggravated to the utmost by his anxiety and trepidation.

" Look at that man," whispered Bray, emphatically. " This seems a cruel thing, after all."

" What seems a cruel thing?" inquired Ralph, with as much stolidity of face as if he really were in utter ignorance of the other's meaning.

" This marriage," answered Bray. " Don't ask me what. You know quite as well as I do."

Ralph shrugged his shoulders in silent deprecation of Bray's impatience, and elevated his eyebrows, and pursed his lips as men do when they are prepared with a sufficient answer to some remark, but wait for a more favourable opportunity of advancing it, or think it scarcely worth while to answer their adversary at all.

" Look at him. Does it not seem cruel?" said Bray.

" No!" replied Ralph boldly.

" I say it does," retorted Bray with a show of much irritation. " It is a cruel thing, by all that's bad and treacherous!"

When men are about to commit or to sanction the commission of some injustice, it is not at all uncommon for them to express pity for the object either of that or some parallel proceeding, and to feel themselves at the time quite virtuous and moral, and immensely superior to those who express no pity at all. This is a kind of upholding of faith above works, and is very comfortable. To do Ralph Nickleby justice, he seldom practised this sort of dissimulation; but he understood those who did, and therefore suffered Bray to say again and again with great vehemence that they were jointly doing a very cruel thing, before he again offered to interpose a word.

" You see what a dry, shrivelled, withered old chip it is," returned Ralph, when the other was at length silent. " If he were younger, it might be cruel, but as it is—hark'ee, Mr. Bray, he'll die soon, and leave her a rich young widow. Miss Madeline consults your taste this time; let her consult her own next."

" True, true," said Bray, biting his nails, and plainly very ill at ease. " I couldn't do anything better for her than advise her to accept these proposals, could I? Now, I ask you, Nickleby, as a man of the world—could I?"

" Surely not," answered Ralph. " I tell you what, Sir;—there are a hundred fathers within a circuit of five miles from this place, well off, good rich substantial men, who would gladly give their daughters and their own ears with them, to that very man yonder, ape and mummy as he looks."

" So there are!" exclaimed Bray, eagerly catching at anything which seemed a justification of himself. " And so I told her, both last night and to-day."

" You told her truth," said Ralph, " and did well to do so; though I must say, at the same time, that if I had a daughter, and my freedom, pleasure, nay, my very health and life, depended on her taking a husband whom I pointed out, I should hope it would not be necessary to advance any other arguments to induce her to consent to my wishes."

Bray looked at Ralph as if to see whether he spoke in earnest, and having nodded twice or thrice in unqualified assent to what had fallen from him, said,

" I must go up stairs for a few minutes to finish dressing, and when I come down, I'll bring Madeline with me. Do you know I had a very strange dream last night, which I have not remembered till this instant. I dreamt that it was this morning, and you and I had been talking, as we have been this minute ; that I went up stairs, for the very purpose for which I am going now, and that as I stretched out my hand to take Madeline's, and lead her down, the floor sunk with me, and after falling from such an indescribable and tremendous height as the imagination scarcely conceives except in dreams, I alighted in a grave."

" And you awoke, and found you were lying on your back, or with your head hanging over the bedside, or suffering some pain from indi-- gestion ?" said Ralph. " Pshaw, Mr. Bray, do as I do (you will have the opportunity now that a constant round of pleasure and enjoyment opens upon you) and occupying yourself a little more by day, have no time to think of what you dream by night."

Ralph followed him with a steady look to the door, and turning to the bridegroom, when they were again alone, said,

" Mark my words, Gride, you won't have to pay *his* annuity very long. You have the devil's luck in bargains always. If he is not booked to make the long voyage before many months are past and gone, I wear an orange for a head."

To this prophecy, so agreeable to his ears, Arthur returned no answer than a cackle of great delight, and Ralph, throwing himself into a chair, they both sat waiting in profound silence. Ralph was thinking with a sneer upon his lips on the altered manner of Bray that day, and how soon their fellowship in a bad design had lowered his pride and established a familiarity between them, when his attentive ear caught the rustling of a female dress upon the stairs, and the footstep of a man.

" Wake up," he said, stamping his foot impatiently upon the ground, " and be something like life, man, will you ? They are here. Urge those dry old bones of yours this way—quick, man, quick."

Gride shambled forward, and stood leering and bowing close by Ralph's side, when the door opened and there entered in haste—not Bray and his daughter, but Nicholas and his sister Kate.

If some tremendous apparition from the world of shadows had suddenly presented itself before him, Ralph Nickleby could not have been more thunder-stricken than he was by this surprise. His hands fell powerless by his side, he staggered back, and with open mouth, and a face of ashy paleness, stood gazing at them in speechless rage ; his eyes so prominent, and his face so convulsed and changed by the passions which raged within him, that it would have been difficult to recognise in him the same stern, composed, hard-featured man he had been not a minute ago.

" The man that came to me last night," whispered Gride, plucking at his elbow. " The man that came to me last night."

" I see," muttered Ralph, " I know. I might have guessed as much before. Across my every path, at every turn, go where I will, do what I may, he comes."

The absence of all colour from the face, the dilated nostril, the quivering of the lips which though set firmly against each other would not be still, showed what fierce emotions were struggling for the mastery with Nicholas. But he kept them down, and gently pressing Kate's arm to re-assure her, stood erect and undaunted front to front with his unworthy relative.

As the brother and sister stood side by side with a gallant bearing which became them well, a close likeness between them was apparent, which many, had they only seen them apart, might have failed to remark. The air, carriage, and very look and expression of the brother were all reflected in the sister, but softened and refined to the nicest limit of feminine delicacy and attraction. More striking still was some indefinable resemblance in the face of Ralph to both. While they had never looked more handsome nor he more ugly, while they had never held themselves more proudly, nor he shrunk half so low, there never had been a time when this resemblance was so perceptible, or when all the worst characteristics of a face rendered coarse and harsh by evil thoughts were half so manifest as now.

" Away ! " was the first word he could utter as he literally gnashed his teeth. " Away ! What brings you here—liar—scoundrel—dastard —thief."

" I come here," said Nicholas in a low deep voice, " to save your victim if I can. Liar and scoundrel you are in every action of your life, theft is your trade, and double dastard you must be or you were not here to-day. Hard words will not move me, nor would hard blows. Here I stand and will till I have done my errand."

" Girl !" said Ralph, " retire. " We can use force to him, but I would not hurt you if I could help it. Retire, you weak and silly wench, and leave this dog to be dealt with as he deserves."

" I will not retire," cried Kate, with flashing eyes and the red blood mantling in her cheeks. " You will do him no hurt that he will not repay. You may use force with me ; I think you will, for I *am* a girl, and that would well become you. But if I have a girl's weakness, I have a woman's heart, and it is not you who in a cause like this can turn that from its purpose."

" And what may your purpose be, most lofty lady ? " said Ralph.

" To offer to the unhappy subject of your treachery at this last moment," replied Nicholas, " a refuge and a home. If the near prospect of such a husband as you have provided will not prevail upon her, I hope she may be moved by the prayers and entreaties of one of her own sex. At all events they shall be tried, and I myself avowing to her father from whom I come and by whom I am commissioned, will render it an act of greater baseness, meanness, and cruelty in him if he still dares to force this marriage on. Here I wait to see him and his daughter. For this I came and brought my sister even into your vile presence. Our purpose is not to see or speak with you ; therefore to you, we stoop to say no more."

" Indeed!" said Ralph.   " You persist in remaining here, Ma'am, do you ?"

His niece's bosom heaved with the indignant excitement into which he had lashed her, but she gave him no reply.

" Now, Gride, see here," said Ralph.   " This fellow—I grieve to say my brother's son ; a reprobate and profligate, stained with every mean and selfish crime—this fellow coming here to-day to disturb a solemn ceremony, and knowing that the consequence of his presenting himself in another man's house at such a time, and persisting in remaining there, must be his being kicked into the streets and dragged through them like the vagabond he is—this fellow, mark you, brings with him his sister as a protection, thinking we would not expose a silly girl to the degradation and indignity which is no novelty to him ; and even after I have warned her of what must ensue, he still keeps her by him as you see, and clings to her apron-strings like a cowardly boy to his mother's.   Is this a pretty fellow to talk as big as you have heard him now !"

" And as I heard him last night," said Arthur Gride, " as I heard him last night when he sneaked into my house, and—he ! he! he !— very soon sneaked out again, when I nearly frightened him to death. And he wanting to marry Miss Madeline too! Oh, dear! Is there anything else he'd like—anything else we can do for him, besides giving her up? Would he like his debts paid and his house furnished, and a few bank notes for shaving paper if he shaves at all! He! he! he!"

" You will remain, girl, will you?" said Ralph, turning upon Kate again, " to be hauled down stairs like a drunken drab—as I swear you shall if you stop here ? No answer! Thank your brother for what follows. Gride, call down Bray—and not his daughter. Let them keep her above."

" If you value your head," said Nicholas, taking up a position before the door, and speaking in the same low voice in which he had spoken before, and with no more outward passion than he had before displayed ; " stay where you are."

" Mind me and not him, and call down Bray," said Ralph.

" Mind yourself rather than either of us, and stay where you are," said Nicholas.

" Will you call down Bray ?" cried Ralph passionately.

" Remember that you come near me at your peril," said Nicholas.

Gride hesitated : Ralph being by this time as furious as a baffled tiger made for the door, and attempting to pass Kate clasped her arm roughly with his hand. Nicholas with his eyes darting fire seized him by the collar. At that moment a heavy body fell with great violence on the floor above, and an instant afterwards was heard a most appalling and terrific scream.

They all stood still and gazed upon each other. Scream succeeded scream ; a heavy pattering of feet succeeded ; and many shrill voices clamouring together were heard to cry, " He is dead !"

" Stand off!" cried Nicholas, letting loose all the violent passion he

Nicholas congratulates Arthur Gride on his Wedding Morning.

had restrained till now, "if this is what I scarcely dare to hope it is, you are caught, villains, in your own toils."

He burst from the room, and darting up stairs to the quarter from whence the noise proceeded, forced his way through a crowd of persons who quite filled a small bedchamber, and found Bray lying on the floor quite dead, and his daughter clinging to the body.

"How did this happen?" he cried, looking wildly about him.

Several voices answered together that he had been observed through the half-opened door reclining in a strange and uneasy position upon a chair; that he had been spoken to several times, and not answering, was supposed to be asleep, until some person going in and shaking him by the arm, he fell heavily to the ground and was discovered to be dead.

"Who is the owner of this house?" said Nicholas, hastily.

An elderly woman was pointed out to him; and to her he said, as he knelt down and gently unwound Madeline's arms from the lifeless mass round which they were entwined: "I represent this lady's nearest friends as her servant here knows, and must remove her from this dreadful scene. This is my sister to whose charge you confide her. My name and address are upon that card, and you shall receive from me all necessary directions for the arrangements that must be made. Stand aside, every one of you, and give me room and air for God's sake."

The people fell back, scarce wondering more at what had just occurred, than at the excitement and impetuosity of him who spoke, and Nicholas, taking the insensible girl in his arms, bore her from the chamber and down stairs into the room he had just quitted, followed by his sister and the faithful servant, whom he charged to procure a coach directly, while he and Kate bent over their beautiful charge and endeavoured, but in vain, to restore her to animation. The girl performed her office with such expedition, that in a very few minutes the coach was ready.

Ralph Nickleby and Gride, stunned and paralysed by the awful event which had so suddenly overthrown their schemes (it would not otherwise, perhaps, have made much impression on them), and carried away by the extraordinary energy and precipitation of Nicholas, who bore down all before them, looked on at these proceedings like men in a dream or trance. It was not until every preparation was made for Madeline's immediate removal that Ralph broke silence by declaring she should not be taken away.

"Who says that?" cried Nicholas, starting from his knee and confronting them, but still retaining Madeline's lifeless hand in his.

"I!" answered Ralph, hoarsely.

"Hush, hush!" cried the terrified Gride, catching him by the arm again. "Hear what he says."

"Aye!" said Nicholas, extending his disengaged hand in the air, "hear what he says. That both your debts are paid in the one great debt of nature—that the bond due to-day at twelve is now waste paper—that your contemplated fraud shall be discovered yet—

that your schemes are known to man, and overthrown by Heaven —
wretches, that he defies you both to do your worst."

"This man," said Ralph, in a voice scarcely intelligible, "this man
claims his wife, and he shall have her."

"That man claims what is not his, and he should not have her
if he were fifty men, with fifty more to back him," said Nicholas.

"Who shall prevent him?"

"I will."

"By what right I should like to know," said Ralph. "By what
right I ask?"

"By this right—that, knowing what I do, you dare not tempt me
further," said Nicholas, "and by this better right, that those I serve,
and with whom you would have done me base wrong and injury,
are her nearest and her dearest friends. In their name I bear her
hence. Give way!"

"One word!" cried Ralph, foaming at the mouth.

"Not one," replied Nicholas, "I will not hear of one—save this.
Look to yourself, and heed this warning that I give you. Your day
is past, and night is coming on—"

"My curse, my bitter deadly curse, upon you, boy!"

"Whence will curses come at your command? or what avails a
curse or blessing from a man-like you? I warn you, that misfortune
and discovery are thickening about your head; that the structures
you have raised through all your ill-spent life are crumbling into
dust; that your path is beset with spies; that this very day, ten
thousand pounds of your hoarded wealth have gone in one great
crash!"

"'Tis false!" cried Ralph, shrinking back.

"'Tis true, and you shall find it so. I have no more words to
waste. Stand from the door. Kate, do you go first. Lay not a
hand on her, or on that woman, or on me, or so much as brush their
garments as they pass you by!—You let them pass and he blocks the
door again!"

Arthur Gride happened to be in the doorway, but whether inten-
tionally or from confusion was not quite apparent. Nicholas swung
him away with such violence as to cause him to spin round the room
until he was caught by a sharp angle of the wall and there knocked
down; and then taking his beautiful burden in his arms rushed
violently out. No one cared to stop him, if any were so disposed.
Making his way through a mob of people, whom a report of the
circumstances had attracted round the house, and carrying Madeline
in his great excitement as easily as if she were an infant, he reached
the coach in which Kate and the girl were already waiting, and
confiding his charge to them, jumped up beside the coachman an
bade him drive away.

TYAS'S ILLUSTRATED CLASSICS.

This day is published, to be continued Weekly, No. I., Price Threepence, of

THE LIFE AND ADVENTURES

OF

ROBINSON CRUSOE:

BY DANIEL DEFOE.

PROFUSELY ILLUSTRATED WITH ENGRAVINGS ON WOOD
FROM DESIGNS BY GRANDVILLE.

Character of the Work.

"Perhaps there exists no work, either of instruction or entertainment, in the English language, which has been more generally read, and more universally admired, than the Life and Adventures of ROBINSON CRUSOE. It is difficult to say in what the charm consists, by which persons of all classes and denominations are thus fascinated; yet the majority of readers will recollect it as among the first works that awakened and interested their youthful attention; and feel, even in advanced life, and in the maturity of their understanding, that there are still associated with ROBINSON CRUSOE, the sentiments peculiar to that period, when all is new, all glittering in prospect, and when those visions are most bright, which the experience of after life tends only to darken and destroy.

"ROBINSON CRUSOE is eagerly read by young people; and there is hardly a child so devoid of imagination as not to have supposed for himself a solitary island, in which he could act ROBINSON CRUSOE, were it but in the corner of the nursery. Neither does a re-perusal at a more advanced age, diminish early impressions. The situation is such as every man may make his own; and, being possible in itself, is, by the exquisite art of the narrator, rendered as probable as it is interesting. It has the merit, too, of that species of accurate painting which can be looked at again and again with new pleasure.

"Neither has the admiration of the work been confined to England, although ROBINSON CRUSOE himself, with his rough good sense, his prejudices, and his obstinate determination not to sink under evils which can be surmounted by exertion, forms no bad specimen of the TRUE-BORN ENGLISHMAN. It is computed that within forty years from the appearance of the original work, no less than forty-one different ROBINSONS appeared, besides fifteen imitations, in which other titles were used. Upon the whole, the work is as unlikely to lose its celebrity as it is to be equalled in its peculiar character by any other of similar excellence."—*Sir Walter Scott's Biographies of the Novelists.*

The whole Work will be completed in about Forty Numbers, Price Threepence; or Ten Monthly Parts, Price One Shilling.

LONDON: ROBERT TYAS, 50 CHEAPSIDE.
JOHN MENZIES, EDINBURGH.

Vizetelly and Co. Printers, 135 Fleet Street.

"I went my new journey, and was out five or six days."—*Page* 213.

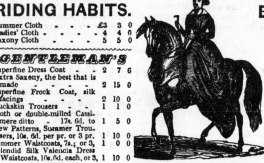

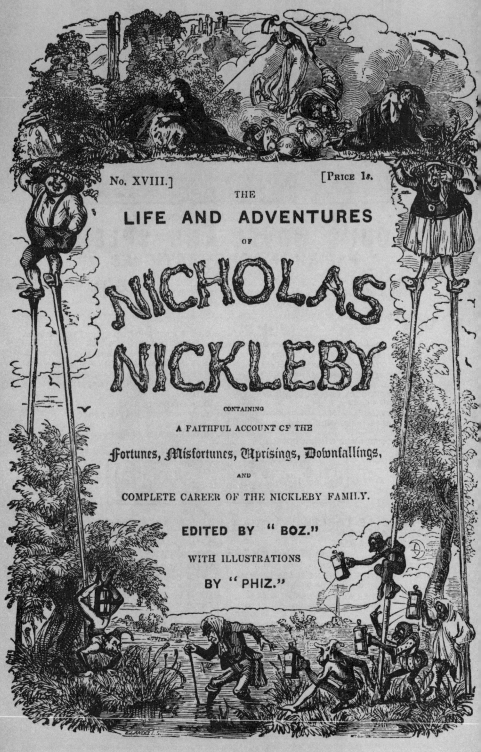

No. XVIII.] [Price 1s.

THE
LIFE AND ADVENTURES
OF
NICHOLAS
NICKLEBY

CONTAINING

A FAITHFUL ACCOUNT OF THE

Fortunes, Misfortunes, Uprisings, Downfallings,

AND

COMPLETE CAREER OF THE NICKLEBY FAMILY.

EDITED BY "BOZ."

WITH ILLUSTRATIONS

BY "PHIZ."

LONDON· CHAPMAN AND HALL 186, STRAND.

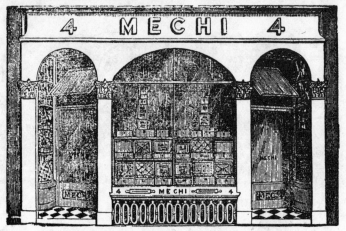

LEADENHALL STREET, LONDON.

MECHI'S NOVEL AND SPLENDID
PAPIER MACHÉ ARTICLES,

CONSISTING OF

TEA TRAYS, TEA CADDIES, LADIES' WORK, CAKE, AND NOTE BASKETS, CARD CASES, CARD POOLS, FRUIT PLATES, FRUIT BASKETS, NETTING BOXES, HAND SCREENS, CARD RACKS, CHESS BOARDS.

LADIES' COMPANIONS, or Work Cases 15s. to 2l.

LADIES' CARD CASES, in Pearl, Ivory, and Tortoiseshell . . . . . . 10s. to 5l. each.

LADIES' WORK BOXES . 25s. to 10 Guineas.

LADIES' DRESSING CASES 2l. 10s. to 50 Guineas.

LADIES' SCOTCH WORK BOXES at all prices.

LADIES' ROSEWOOD AND MAHOGANY DESKS 12s. 6d. to 10 Guineas.

LADIES' MOROCCO AND RUSSIA LEATHER WRITING CASES . . . 5s. to 5l.

LADIES' ENVELOPE CASES, various prices.

LADIES' TABLE INKSTANDS, made of British Coal (quite a novelty) . . . 7s. 6d. to 30s.

LADIES' SCOTCH TOOTH-PICK CASES.

LADIES' IVORY AND TORTOISESHELL HAIR BRUSHES . . . at 2l. to 5l. per Pair.

LADIES' SCENT AND TOILET BOTTLES in great variety.

LADIES' SCOTCH TEA CADDIES . 21s. to 40s.

LADIES' PLAYING CARD BOXES . 30s. to 5l.

LADIES' JAPAN DRESSING CASES 7s. to 15s.

LADIES' TORTOISESHELL DRESSING & SIDE COMBS.

LADIES' HAND GLASSES.

LADIES' PATENT INSTANTANEOUS PEN-MAKERS . . . 10s. 6d. and 12s. 6d.

LADIES' ELEGANT PENKNIVES AND SCISSORS 5s. to 30s.

INVENTOR OF THE PATENT CASTELLATED TOOTH BRUSHES.

TRY MECHI'S Magic STROP.

INVENTOR OF THE MECHIAN PORTABLE DRESSING CASES.

MISCELLANEOUS.

BAGATELLE TABLES	£3 10 to 5 0	POPE JOAN BOARDS	£0 13 to 1 0
BACKGAMMON TABLES	1 0 to 5 10	IVORY CHESSMEN	1 1 to 10 10
CHESS BOARDS	0 4 to 3 0	BONE & WOOD DITTO	Various Prices.

WHIST MARKERS, COUNTERS, &c.

GENT.'S DRESSING CASES, in Wood 2l. to 50l.

GENT.'S LEATHER DRESSING CASES 25s. to 24l.

GENT.'S WRITING DESKS, in Wood 30s. to 16l.

GENT.'S LEATHER WRITING DESKS 24s. 6d. to 5l.

GENT.'S WRITING & DRESSING CASE COMBINED . . . . . 5l. to 16l.

GENT.'S POCKET BOOKS WITH INSTRUMENTS 20s. to 40s.

GENT.'S ELEGANT CASES OF RAZORS 12s. to 3l.

GENT.'S SEVEN DAY RAZORS, in Fancy Woods 25s. to 5l.

GENT.'S RAZOR STROPS . 2s. to 30s.

GENT.'S SPORTING KNIVES . 12s. to 5l.

GENT.'S FANCY PENKNIVES . 8s. to 15s.

GENT.'S PEARL AND SHELL POCKET COMBS 3s. 6d. to 15s.

GENT.'S SCOTCH CIGAR BOXES 3s. 6d. to 40s.

GENT.'S COAL AND EBONY INKSTANDS 7s. 6d. to 50s.

GENT.'S IVORY AND FANCY WOOD HAIR BRUSHES . . . 20s. to 3l. 10s.

GENT.'S SETS OF BRUSHES in Russia Cases 25s. to 4l. 10s.

GENT.'S SILVER AND IVORY SHAVING BRUSHES In elegant Patterns.

GENT.'S SILVER AND SHELL TABLETS.

MECHI,  MECHI,

4. LEADENHALL ST. LONDON.

Submits, to public inspection, his Manufactures, as being of the finest quality this kingdom can produce, and at moderate prices.

A Large Stock of Table Cutlery. Plated Tea and Coffee Services, Dish Covers, Hash Covers, &c.

THE
NICKLEBY ADVERTISER.

MR. MOON, Her Majesty's Publisher and Printseller, 20, Threadneedle Street, London, has the honour to announce his intention to publish the following IMPORTANT ENGRAVINGS.

THE WATERLOO BANQUET
AT APSLEY HOUSE.

From a Picture by WILLIAM SALTER, Esq., Member of the Academies of Florence, Rome, &c

Mr. MOON has the distinguished honour to announce that Mr. Salter, who has been so long and anxiously engaged on this great and interesting National Picture, received from his Grace the Duke of Wellington the exclusive privilege of being present at the recent Banquet, with a view to its completion. Proofs before the Letters, 15l. 15s.; Proofs, 12l. 12s.; Prints, 10l. 10s.

From the TIMES.—The room in which the banquet is held, is in the picture an exact copy of the real apartment. The numerous paintings in the possession of his Grace, which decorate the walls of the apartment itself, are in the representation in Mr. Salter's picture all faithfully copied; and the details of furniture, the candelabra, the superb plateau, &c., are all elaborately set forth. The numerous portraits are good likenesses of the orginals; indeed, the eye of the spectator discovers without difficulty the face of every individual, and recognises the closeness of its resemblance to the features with which he is familiar.... The engravings will be most interesting records and excellent illustrations of the great day of victory which resulted from the talents, valour, and military skill of the illustrious Duke and his companions on the field of battle.

From the MORNING CHRONICLE.—The subject is an extremely bold and difficult one, but Mr. Salter has treated it with consummate skill, and his success may be said to be complete. A masterly style of composition has enabled him at once to preserve the order of the table, and yet to overcome the unpleasantness of straight lines in the arrangement of his figures. The dinner has been eaten, the dishes have been removed, dessert and wines have followed, the table is laden with the costly plate which grateful nations have heaped upon the invincible defender of their liberties and independence—the veteran chief himself has risen to address that remnant of his old companions in arms (upwards of sixty in number), who, surviving the shock of a hundred battles, are still left unvanquished by the hand of time. The stiffness of the party has relaxed—the chairs have somewhat receded from the table—the old warriors have grouped themselves in knots (here the mastery of the composition, aided by the fine perspective, is most conspicuously evinced), and are either attentively listening to their illustrious host, or engaged in earnest and brief conversation amongst themselves. There is a wonderful reality in the picture. The likenesses are positively startling.

Mr. MOON has felt himself compelled to address the following Circular to the various Noblemen and other Officers who have sat to the Artist for their Portraits for this great Picture.

20, Threadneedle-street.

MY LORD,—Mr. Salter's Painting of the Waterloo Banquet is now, after several years' labour, nearly completed; and as you have done the Artist the honour of sitting for your Portrait, will you allow me, as his Publisher, to solicit the favour of your Autograph, Coat of Arms, and proper Style and Titles, to prevent any mistake occurring in the due description of the distinguished individuals who are there represented? Will you, my Lord, at the same time, permit me to avail myself of the opportunity which this application affords, for laying before your Lordship the following facts?

The high honour of the valuable and exclusive privilege granted by his Grace the Duke of Wellington to Mr. Salter, has not prevented certain unscrupulous individuals from pirating the subject originally conceived by that gentleman, (the Anniversary, at Apsley House, of the Victory of Waterloo,) even while it is yet in his Study,—a proceeding hitherto held by Artists, who have any sense of justice and good faith, to be most dishonourable. No excuse can fairly be admitted, for receiving and executing a commission from any Publisher to do a thing so unusual and so unworthy. The very title, so far as these parties have dared to copy it, has been adopted, in order to deceive the Public, and in the hope of obtaining patronage, by means of misrepresentation, for a work which is without authority, and was never heard of until Mr. Salter had long been occupied upon his picture, and my advertisements had been some time before the public.

Permit me, my Lord, to state that I have entered into very heavy engagements for a Print from Mr. Salter's grand work, in the confidence that the Artist's original thought would be held sacred by his brother artists, and the belief that this most interesting and national subject was one which every Englishman would gladly see thus commemorated by the Painter. This fact, coupled with the circumstances of the very glaring attempt at piracy, which is now in the course of being carried into effect, to the serious injury of the original Painter and his Publisher, have obliged me, my Lord, in self-defence, to issue the following Advertisement:—

Mr. MOON, of 20, Threadneedle-street, who has no connexion whatever with any other Publishing House in London, begs to caution his friends and the public against any spurious publication, purporting to represent the Waterloo Heroes at Apsley House celebrating the Anniversary of the great Battle.

Mr. Salter alone has been authorised, by His Grace the Duke of Wellington, to paint the 'Waterloo Banquet' at Apsley House; and for this purpose he has been afforded every facility by His Grace, by the Commander-in-Chief, and by upwards of seventy Officers, who have expressly sat to Mr. Salter for their Portraits.

Begging leave to apologise for this intrusion upon your valuable time, I have the honour to be, my Lord, your Lordship's most obedient servant,

FRAS. GRAH. MOON.

Nearly ready for publication, the last Portrait of

HIS GRACE THE DUKE OF WELLINGTON,

In the MILITARY UNDRESS of a FIELD MARSHAL, as worn in Action.

Painted by J. SIMPSON, Esq., and Engraving in Mezzotint by B. P. GIBBON.

Price to Subscribers: Prints, 12s.; Proofs, 21s.; Proofs before Letters, 1l. 11s. 6d.

London: F. G. MOON, Her Majesty's Publisher and Printseller in Ordinary, 20, Threadneedle-street.

MOSLEY'S METALLIC PENS.

R. MOSLEY & CO. beg to call the attention of Mercantile Men, and the Public in general, to their superior Metallic Pens. They possess the highest degree of elasticity and flexibility, and are found perfectly free from all those inconveniences which have prevented so many persons making use of Metallic Pens.

Every description of writer may be suited, as these pens are manufactured of various qualities, degrees of hardness, &c. They may be had of all respectable Stationers throughout the kingdom.

Observe that every Pen is stamped, R. MOSLEY & CO., LONDON.

SPLENDID GILT FRAMES.

CHARLES M'LEAN, 181, Fleet Street, five houses east of St. Dunstan's Church, respectfully informs the Trade, Artists, and the Public, that they can be supplied with Gilt Frames, of the best manufacture, at prices never hitherto attempted.

N.B.—A SHEET OF DRAWINGS OF FRAMES, REPRESENTING THE EXACT PATTERNS, SIZES, AND PRICES, may be had gratis. (Sent in the country for single postage.)

50 by 40	6-inch moulding	70s.		21 by 17	4-inch moulding	19s.
36	28	„	36s.		18	14	„	17s.
30	25	5-inch moulding	30s.		16	12	„	15s.
24	20	4-inch ditto	22s.		14	12	„	13s.
24	18	„	21s.		12	10	„	11s.

Regilding executed for the Trade. Rosewood or Maplewood, in the length or in frames.

All Goods taken back if not approved of in Three Months.

ARTESIAN WELLS.

" The sole method of obtaining a constant and abundant supply of pure water is by the adoption of one of ROBINS'S ROYAL FILTERS, the only apparatus of real utility ; it renders the filthy liquid supplied to London houses as crystalline in brilliancy as the water from an Artesian well, and far superior to it in purity, and all the qualities that benefit health and prolong life."—*Dr. Halliday on Diet.*

Sole Depot for the sale of the above invention is No. 163, Strand, near Somerset House ; and purchasers are earnestly cautioned against spurious imitations.

CURVATURES OF THE SPINE.

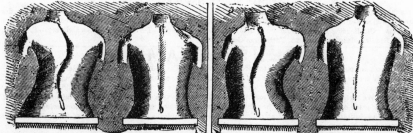

CURVATURES OF THE SPINE, with their concomitant evils, are too generally known to need any particular remarks here ; but it is a melancholy truth, and cannot be too strongly impressed, that the health and figures of an incalculable number of young persons are irremediably ruined by their having recourse to inefficacious means, or trusting to the supports of mechanists, which, instead of removing, only conceal the deformity. For some years Dr. KINGDON has given his undivided attention to these affections ; he has visited the Continental Orthopœdic Establishments, and for the last three years he has received for treatment young Ladies of the higher ranks of life into his own residence, GOTHIC HOUSE, STOCKWELL (three miles from LONDON). His success has been surprising : cases of severity, and of many years standing, have yielded to his method of treatment, where that of others had been previously tried and proved ineffectual : in fact, it has not failed in a single instance of producing the most gratifying results. He has so simplified the curative system, that it causes no embarrassment to the Patient, no confinement is required, the accomplishments may be pursued, and the ordinary occupations of life followed ; the health has in every case been either perfectly restored or considerably improved. Dr. Kingdon dislikes the medium of a public advertisement for making his system generally known ; but when he is in the daily habit of seeing persons labouring under the most distressing maladies, occasioned by long-standing deviations of the Spine, which by the seasonable aid of efficient means could have been easily redressed, he is induced to call the attention of Parents, &c. to the fact, that scarcely an instance of CURVATURE of the SPINE occurs, which may not, by timely application, be entirely cured in a very short time by his method of treatment, and even extreme cases can be greatly ameliorated. The above figures of casts, taken before and after treatment, are selected from a great many others, of Ladies who have been under his care. (Fig. 1 and 3 before treatment, Fig. 2 and 4 after ditto.)

Dr. Kingdon can be consulted on Mondays, Wednesdays, or Fridays, between the hours of 11 and 1 o'clock in the forenoon, at his town-house, 65, HARLEY STREET, CAVENDISH SQUARE, LONDON ; and at a similar time on Tuesdays, Thursdays, and Saturdays, at GOTHIC HOUSE, STOCKWELL, SURREY.

Just published, post 8vo, price 1s., with several Plates,

An ADDRESS to PARENTS, &c., on CURVATURES of the SPINE, with REMARKS on the PHYSICAL EDUCATION of YOUNG FEMALES of the Higher Ranks of Life. By RICHARD KINGDON, M.D., &c., M.R.C.S.

London: Houlston and Hughes, 154, Strand.

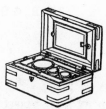
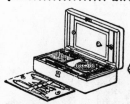
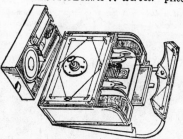

BEAUFOY AND Co., SOUTH LAMBETH, LONDON.

BEAUFOY'S INSTANT CURE

FOR THE

TOOTHACHE.

THE GENUINE PACKAGES CONTAIN

A FAC-SIMILE

OF ONE OR THE OTHER OF THESE

VIGNETTES.

SOLD BY MOST RESPECTABLE DRUGGISTS, WITH AMPLE DIRECTIONS FOR USE,
In Bottles, Price 1s. 1½d each. Stamp included.

BEAUFOY AND CO., SOUTH LAMBETH, LONDON.

[BRADBURY AND EVANS, PRINTERS, WHITEFRIARS.]

186, STRAND.
September, 1839.

NEW WORK BY BOZ.

MESSRS. CHAPMAN & HALL have the pleasure of announcing that they have completed arrangements with Mr. CHARLES DICKENS for the publication of

A NEW WORK,

ON AN ENTIRELY NEW PLAN.

The first number of this work will appear in March next.

COMPLETION OF NICHOLAS NICKLEBY.

Subscribers are informed that Nos. XIX. and XX., being the completion of NICHOLAS NICKLEBY, will be published together on the 30th of September, and will contain a PORTRAIT OF THE AUTHOR, engraved by Mr. Wm. Finden, from an original painting by D. Maclise, Esq., A.R.A.

Bradbury and Evans, Printers, Whitefriars.

CHAPTER LV.

OF FAMILY MATTERS, CARES, HOPES, DISAPPOINTMENTS, AND SORROWS.

ALTHOUGH Mrs. Nickleby had been made acquainted by her son and daughter with every circumstance of Madeline Bray's history which was known to them; although the responsible situation in which Nicholas stood had been carefully explained to her, and she had been prepared even for the possible contingency of having to receive the young lady in her own house—improbable as such a result had appeared only a few minutes before it came about—still, Mrs. Nickleby, from the moment when this confidence was first reposed in her late on the previous evening, had remained in an unsatisfactory and profoundly mystified state, from which no explanations or arguments could relieve her, and which every fresh soliloquy and reflection only aggravated more and more.

" Bless my heart, Kate," so the good lady argued, " if the Mr. Cheerybles don't want this young lady to be married, why don't they file a bill against the Lord Chancellor, make her a chancery ward, and shut her up in the Fleet prison for safety—I have read of such things in the newspapers a hundred times; or, if they are so very fond of her as Nicholas says they are, why don't they marry her themselves—one of them I mean. And even supposing they don't want her to be married, and don't want to marry her themselves, why in the name of wonder should Nicholas go about the world forbidding people's banns ?"

" I don't think you quite understand," said Kate, gently.

" Well I am sure, Kate, my dear, you're very polite," replied Mrs. Nickleby. " I have been married myself I hope, and I have seen other people married. Not understand, indeed !"

" I know you have had great experience, dear mama," said Kate ; " I mean that perhaps you don't quite understand all the circumstances in this instance. We have stated them awkwardly, I dare say."

" That I dare say you have," retorted her mother, briskly. " That's very likely. I am not to be held accountable for that ; though at the same time, as the circumstances speak for themselves, I shall take the liberty, my love, of saying that I do understand them, and perfectly well too, whatever you and Nicholas may choose to think to the contrary. Why is such a great fuss made because this Miss Magdalen is going to marry somebody who is older than herself ? Your poor papa was older than I was—four years and a half older. Jane Dibabs—the Dibabses lived in the beautiful little thatched white house one story high, covered all over with ivy and creeping plants, with an exquisite little porch with twining honeysuckles and all sorts of things, where the earwigs used to fall into one's tea on a summer evening, and always fell upon their backs and kicked dreadfully, and where the frogs used to get into the rushlight shades when one stopped all night, and sit up and look through the little holes like Christians—Jane Dibabs, *she* married a man who was a great deal older than herself, and would marry him notwithstanding all that could be said to the contrary, and she was so fond of him that nothing was ever equal to it. There was no fuss made about Jane Dibabs, and her husband was a most honourable and excellent man, and everybody spoke well of him. Then why should there be any fuss about this Magdalen?"

"Her husband is much older; he is not her own choice, his character is the very reverse of that which you have just described. Don't you see a broad distinction between the two cases?" said Kate.

To this Mrs. Nickleby only replied that she durst say she was very stupid, indeed she had no doubt she was, for her own children almost as much as told her so every day of her life; to be sure she was a little older than they, and perhaps some foolish people might think she ought reasonably to know best. However, no doubt she was wrong, of course she was—she always was—she couldn't be right, indeed—couldn't be expected to be—so she had better not expose herself any more; and to all Kate's conciliations and concessions for an hour ensuing, the good lady gave no other replies than—Oh, certainly—why did they ask *her*—*her* opinion was of no consequence—it didn't matter what *she* said—with many other rejoinders of the same class.

In this frame of mind (expressed when she had become too resigned for speech, by nods of the head, upliftings of the eyes, and little beginnings of groans, converted as they attracted attention into short coughs), Mrs. Nickleby remained until Nicholas and Kate returned with the object of their solicitude; when, having by this time asserted her own importance, and becoming besides interested in the trials of one so young and beautiful, she not only displayed the utmost zeal and solicitude, but took great credit to herself for recommending the course of procedure which her son had adopted; frequently declaring with an expressive look, that it was very fortunate things were *as* they were, and hinting, that but for great encouragement and wisdom on her own part, they never could have been brought to that pass.

Not to strain the question whether Mrs. Nickleby had or had not any great hand in bringing matters about, it is unquestionable that she had strong ground for exultation. The brothers, upon their return, bestowed such commendations upon Nicholas for the part he had taken, and evinced so much joy at the altered state of events and the recovery of their young friend from trials so great and dangers so threatening, that, as she more than once informed her daughter, she now considered the fortunes of the family "as good as" made. Mr. Charles Cheeryble, indeed, Mrs. Nickleby positively asserted had, in the first transports of his surprise and delight, "as good as" said so, and without precisely explaining what this qualification meant, she subsided, whenever she mentioned the subject, into such a mysterious and important state, and had such visions of wealth and dignity in perspective, that (vague and clouded though they were) she was at such times almost as happy as if she had really been permanently provided for on a scale of great splendour, and all her cares were over.

The sudden and terrible shock she had received, combined with the great affliction and anxiety of mind which she had for a long time endured, proved too much for Madeline's strength. Recovering from the state of stupefaction into which the sudden death of her father happily plunged her, she only exchanged that condition for one of dangerous and active illness. When the delicate physical powers which have been sustained by an unnatural strain upon the mental energies and a resolute determination not to yield, at last give way, their degree of prostration is usually proportionate to the strength of the effort which has previously upheld them. Thus it was that the illness which fell on Madeline was of no slight or temporary nature, but one which for a time threatened her reason, and—scarcely worse—her life itself.

Who, slowly recovering from a disorder so severe and dangerous, could be insensible to the unremitting attentions of such a nurse as gentle, tender, earnest Kate? On whom could the sweet soft voice, the light step, the delicate hand, the quiet, cheerful, noiseless discharge of those thousand little offices of kindness and relief which we feel so deeply when we are ill, and forget so lightly when we are well—on whom could they make so deep an impression as on a young heart stored with every pure and true affection that women cherish; almost a stranger to the endearments and devotion of its own sex, save as it learnt them from itself; and rendered by calamity and suffering keenly susceptible of the sympathy so long unknown and so long sought in vain? What wonder that days became as years in knitting them together? What wonder, if with every hour of returning health, there came some stronger and sweeter recognition of the praises which Kate, when they recalled old scenes—they seemed old now, and to have been acted years ago—would lavish on her brother; where would have been the wonder even if those praises had found a quick response in the breast of Madeline, and if, with the image of Nicholas so constantly recurring in the features of his sister that she could scarcely separate the two, she had sometimes found it equally difficult to assign to each the feelings they had first inspired, and had imperceptibly mingled with her gratitude to Nicholas, some of that warmer feeling which she had assigned to Kate?

" My dear," Mrs. Nickleby would say, coming into the room with an elaborate caution, calculated to discompose the nerves of an invalid rather more than the entry of a horse-soldier at full gallop ; " how do you find yourself to-night. I hope you are better ? "

" Almost well, mama," Kate would reply, laying down her work, and taking Madeline's hand in hers.

" Kate ! " Mrs. Nickleby would say, reprovingly, " don't talk so loud " (the worthy lady herself talking in a whisper that would have made the blood of the stoutest man run cold in his veins).

Kate would take this reproof very quietly, and Mrs. Nickleby, making every board creak, and every thread rustle as she moved stealthily about, would add—

" My son Nicholas has just come home, and I have come, according to custom, my dear, to know from your own lips exactly how you are, for he won't take my account, and never will."

" He is later than usual to-night," perhaps Madeline would reply. " Nearly half an hour."

" Well, I never saw such people in all my life as you are for time up here!" Mrs. Nickleby would exclaim in great astonishment; "I declare I never did! I had not the least idea that Nicholas was after his time—not the smallest. Mr. Nickleby used to say—your poor papa I am speaking of, Kate my dear—used to say that appetite was the best clock in the world, but you have no appetite, my dear Miss Bray, I wish you had, and upon my word I really think you ought to take something that would give you one; I am sure I don't know, but I have heard that two or three dozen native lobsters give an appetite, though that comes to the same thing after all, for I suppose you must have an appetite before you can take 'em. If I said lobsters, I meant oysters, but of course it's all the same, though really how you came to know about Nicholas——"

" We happened to be just talking about him, mama ; that was it."

" You never seem to me to be talking about anything else, Kate, and upon my word I am quite surprised at your being so very thoughtless. You can find subjects enough to talk about sometimes, and when you know how important it is to keep up Miss Bray's spirits, and interest her and all that, it really is quite extraordinary to me what can induce you to keep on prose, prose, prose, din, din, din, everlastingly upon the same theme. You are a very kind nurse, Kate, and a very good one, and I know you mean very well; but I will say this—that if it wasn't for me, I really don't know what would become of Miss Bray's spirits, and so I tell the doctor every day. He says he wonders how I sustain my own, and I am sure I very often wonder myself how I can contrive to keep up as I do. Of course it's an exertion, but still, when I know how much depends upon me in this house, I am obliged to make it. There's nothing praiseworthy in that, but it's necessary, and I do it."

With that, Mrs. Nickleby would draw up a chair, and for some three quarters of an hour run through a great variety of distracting topics in the most distracting manner possible : tearing herself away at length on the plea that she must now go and amuse Nicholas while he took his supper. After a preliminary raising of his spirits with the information that she considered the patient decidedly worse, she would further cheer him up by relating how dull, listless, and low-spirited Miss Bray was, because Kate foolishly talked about nothing else but him and family matters. When she had made Nicholas thoroughly comfortable with these and other inspiriting remarks, she would discourse at length on the arduous duties she had performed that day, and sometimes be moved to tears in wondering how, if anything were to happen to herself, the family would ever get on without her.

At other times when Nicholas came home at night, he would be accompanied by Mr. Frank Cheeryble, who was commissioned by the brothers to inquire how Madeline was that evening. On such occasions (and they were of very frequent occurrence), Mrs. Nickleby deemed it of particular importance that she should have her wits about her ; for from certain signs and tokens which had attracted her attention, she shrewdly suspected that Mr. Frank, interested as his uncles were in Madeline, came quite as much to see Kate as to inquire after her; the more especially as the brothers were in constant communication with the medical man, came backwards and forwards very frequently themselves, and received a full report from Nicholas every morning. These were proud times for Mrs. Nickleby, and never was anybody half so discreet and sage as she, or half so mysterious withal; and never was there such cunning generalship, or such unfathomable designs, as she brought to bear upon Mr. Frank, with the view of ascertaining whether her suspicions were well founded, and if so, of tantalising him into taking her into his confidence and throwing himself upon her merciful consideration. Extensive was the artillery, heavy and light, which Mrs. Nickleby brought into play for the furtherance of these great schemes, and various and opposite the means which she employed to bring about the end she had in view. At one time she was all cordiality and ease, at another, all stiffness and frigidity. Now she would seem to open her whole heart to her unhappy victim, and the next time they met receive him with the most distant and studious reserve, as if a new light had broken in upon her, and guessing his intentions, she had resolved to check them in the bud; as if she felt it her bounden duty to act with Spartan firmness, and at once and for ever to discourage hopes which never could be realised. At other times, when Nicholas was not there to overhear, and Kate was up stairs busily tending her sick friend, the worthy lady would throw out dark hints of an intention to send her to France for three or four years, or to Scotland for the improvement of her health, impaired by her late fatigues, or to America on a visit, or anywhere that threatened a long and tedious separation. Nay, she even went so far as to hint obscurely at an attachment entertained for her daughter by the son of an old neighbour of theirs, one Horatio Peltirogus (a young gentleman who might have been at that time four years old, or thereabouts), and to represent it indeed as almost a settled thing between the families—only waiting for her daughter's final decision to come off with the sanction of the church, and to the unspeakable happiness and content of all parties.

It was in the full pride and glory of having sprung this last mine one night with extraordinary success, that Mrs. Nickleby took the opportunity of being left alone with her son before retiring to rest, to sound him upon the subject which so occupied her thoughts: not doubting that they could have but one opinion respecting it. To this end, she approached the question with divers laudatory and appropriate remarks touching the general amiability of Mr. Frank Cheeryble.

" You are quite right, mother," said Nicholas, " quite right. He is a fine fellow."

" Good-looking, too," said Mrs. Nickleby.

" Decidedly good-looking," answered Nicholas.

" What may you call his nose, now, my dear?" pursued Mrs. Nickleby, wishing to interest Nicholas in the subject to the utmost.

" Call it?" repeated Nicholas.

"Ah!" returned his mother, "what style of nose—what order of architecture, if one may say so. I am not very learned in noses. Do you call it a Roman or a Grecian?"

"Upon my word, mother," said Nicholas, laughing, "as well as I remember, I should call it a kind of Composite, or mixed nose. But I have no very strong recollection upon the subject, and if it will afford you any gratification, I'll observe it more closely, and let you know."

"I wish you would, my dear," said Mrs. Nickleby, with an earnest look.

"Very well," returned Nicholas. "I will."

Nicholas returned to the perusal of the book he had been reading, when the dialogue had gone thus far. Mrs. Nickleby, after stopping a little for consideration, resumed.

"He is very much attached to you, Nicholas, my dear."

Nicholas laughingly said, as he closed his book, that he was glad to hear it, and observed that his mother seemed deep in their new friend's confidence already.

"Hem!" said Mrs. Nickleby. "I don't know about that, my dear, but I think it is very necessary that somebody should be in his confidence—highly necessary."

Elated by a look of curiosity from her son, and the consciousness of possessing a great secret all to herself, Mrs. Nickleby went on with great animation:

"I am sure, my dear Nicholas, how you can have failed to notice it is to me quite extraordinary; though I don't know why I should say that either, because of course as far as it goes, and to a certain extent, there is a great deal in this sort of thing, especially in this early stage, which however clear it may be to females, can scarcely be expected to be so evident to men. I don't say that I have any particular penetration in such matters. I may have; those about me should know best about that, and perhaps do know. Upon that point I shall express no opinion—it wouldn't become me to do so; it's quite out of the question —quite."

Nicholas snuffed the candles, put his hands in his pockets, and leaning back in his chair, assumed a look of patient suffering and melancholy resignation.

"I think it's my duty, Nicholas, my dear," resumed his mother, "to tell you what I know, not only because you have a right to know it too, and to know everything that happens in this family, but because you have it in your power to promote and assist the thing very much; and there is no doubt that the sooner one can come to a clear understanding upon such subjects, it is always better every way. There are a great many things you might do, such as taking a walk in the garden sometimes, or sitting up stairs in your own room for a little while, or making believe to fall asleep occasionally, or pretending that you recollected some business, and going out for an hour or so, and taking Mr. Smike with you. These seem very slight things, and I dare say you will be amused at my making them of so much importance; at the same time, my dear, I can assure you (and you'll find this out,

Nicholas, for yourself one of these days, if you ever fall in love with anybody, as I trust and hope you will, provided she is respectable and well conducted, and of course you'd never dream of falling in love with anybody who was not), I say, I can assure you that a great deal more depends upon these little things than you would suppose possible. If your poor papa was alive, he would tell you how much depended upon the parties being left alone. Of course you are not to go out of the room as if you meant it and did it on purpose, but as if it was quite an accident, and to come back again in the same way. If you cough in the passage before you open the door, or whistle carelessly, or hum a tune, or something of that sort, to let them know you're coming, it's always better; because of course, though it's not only natural, but perfectly correct and proper under the circumstances, still it is very confusing if you interrupt young people when they are—when they are sitting on the sofa, and—and all that sort of thing, which is very nonsensical perhaps, but still they will do it."

The profound astonishment with which her son regarded her during this long address, gradually increasing as it approached its climax, in no way discomposed Mrs. Nickleby, but rather exalted her opinion of her own cleverness; therefore, merely stopping to remark, with much complacency, that she had fully expected him to be surprised, she entered upon a vast quantity of circumstantial evidence of a particularly incoherent and perplexing kind, the upshot of which was to establish, beyond the possibility of doubt, that Mr. Frank Cheeryble had fallen desperately in love with Kate.

"With whom?" cried Nicholas.

Mrs. Nickleby repeated, with Kate.

"What! *our* Kate—my sister!"

"Lord, Nicholas!" returned Mrs. Nickleby, "whose Kate should it be, if not ours; or what should I care about it, or take any interest in it for, if it was anybody but your sister?"

"Dear mother," said Nicholas, "surely it can't be."

"Very good, my dear," replied Mrs. Nickleby, with great confidence. "Wait, and see."

Nicholas had never, until that moment, bestowed one thought upon the remote possibility of such an occurrence as that which was now communicated to him; for, besides that he had been much from home of late and closely occupied with other matters, his own jealous fears had prompted the suspicion that some secret interest in Madeline, akin to that which he felt himself, occasioned those visits of Frank Cheeryble which had recently become so frequent. Even now, although he knew that the observation of an anxious mother was much more likely to be correct in such a case than his own, and although she reminded him of many little circumstances which, taken together, were certainly susceptible of the construction she triumphantly put upon them, he was not quite convinced but that they arose from mere good-natured thoughtless gallantry, which would have dictated the same conduct towards any other girl who was young and pleasing—at all events, he hoped so, and therefore tried to believe it.

" I am very much disturbed by what you tell me," said Nicholas, after a little reflection, "though I yet hope you may be mistaken."

" I don't understand why you should hope so," said Mrs. Nickleby, " I confess ; but you may depend upon it I am not."

" What of Kate ? " inquired Nicholas.

" Why that, my dear," returned Mrs. Nickleby, " is just the. point upon which I am not yet satisfied. During this sickness, she has been constantly at Madeline's bedside—never were two people so fond of each other as they have grown—and to tell you the truth, Nicholas, I have rather kept her away now and then, because I think it's a good plan, and urges a young man on. He doesn't get too sure, you know."

She said this with such a mingling of high delight and self-congratulation, that it was inexpressibly painful to Nicholas to dash her hopes ; but he felt that there was only one honourable course before him, and that he was bound to take it.

" Dear mother," he said kindly, " don't you see that if there really were any serious inclination on the part of Mr. Frank towards Kate, and we suffered ourselves for one moment to encourage it, we should be acting a most dishonourable and ungrateful part ? I ask you if you don't see it, but I need not say that, I know you don't, or you would have been more strictly upon your guard. Let me explain my meaning to you—remember how poor we are."

Mrs. Nickleby shook her head, and said through her tears that poverty was not a crime.

" No," said Nicholas, " and for that very reason poverty should engender an honest pride, that it may not lead and tempt us to unworthy actions, and that we may preserve the self-respect which a hewer of wood and drawer of water may maintain—and does better in maintaining than a monarch his. Think what we owe to these two brothers ; remember what they have done and do every day for us with a generosity and delicacy for which the devotion of our whole lives would be a most imperfect and inadequate return. What kind of return would that be which would be comprised in our permitting their nephew, their only relative, whom they regard as a son, and for whom it would be mere childishness to suppose they have not formed plans suitably adapted to the education he has had, and the fortune he will inherit—in our permitting him to marry a portionless girl so closely connected with us, that the irresistible inference must be that he was entrapped by a plot ; that it was a deliberate scheme and a speculation amongst us three. Bring the matter clearly before yourself, mother. Now, how would you feel if they were married, and the brothers coming here on one of those kind errands which bring them here so often, you had to break out to them the truth ? Would you be at ease, and feel that you had played an honest, open, part ? "

Poor Mrs. Nickleby, crying more and more, murmured that of course Mr. Frank would ask the consent of his uncles first.

" Why, to be sure, that would place *him* in a better situation with them," said Nicholas, " but we should still be open to the same suspicions, the distance between us would still be as great, the advantages to be gained would still be as manifest as now. We may be reckoning without our host in all this," he added more cheerfully, " and I trust, and almost believe we are. If it be otherwise, I have that confidence in Kate that I know she will feel as I do, and in you, dear mother, to be assured that after a little consideration you will do the same."

After many more representations and entreaties, Nicholas obtained a promise from Mrs. Nickleby that she would try all she could to think as he did, and that if Mr. Frank persevered in his attentions she would endeavour to discourage them, or, at the least, would render him no countenance or assistance. He determined to forbear mentioning the subject to Kate until he was quite convinced there existed a real necessity for his doing so, and resolved to assure himself, as well as he could by close personal observation, of the exact position of affairs. This was a very wise resolution, but he was prevented from putting it in practice by a new source of anxiety and uneasiness.

Smike became alarmingly ill; so reduced and exhausted that he could scarcely move from room to room without assistance, and so worn and emaciated that it was painful to look upon him. Nicholas was warned by the same medical authority to whom he had at first appealed, that the last chance and hope of his life depended on his being instantly removed from London. That part of Devonshire in which Nicholas had been himself bred when a boy, was named as the most favourable spot; but this advice was cautiously coupled with the information, that whoever accompanied him thither must be prepared for the worst, for every token of rapid consumption had appeared, and he might never return alive.

The kind brothers, who were acquainted with the poor creature's sad history, despatched old Tim to be present at this consultation. That same morning, Nicholas was summoned by brother Charles into his private room, and thus addressed :

" My dear sir, no time must be lost. This lad shall not die if such human means as we can use can save his life; neither shall he die alone, and in a strange place. Remove him to-morrow morning, see that he has every comfort that his situation requires, and don't leave him— don't leave him, my dear sir, until you know that there is no longer any immediate danger. It would be hard indeed to part you now—no, no, no. Tim shall wait upon you to-night, sir; Tim shall wait upon you to-night with a parting word or two. Brother Ned, my dear fellow, Mr. Nickleby waits to shake hands and say good bye; Mr. Nickleby won't be long gone; this poor chap will soon get better—very soon get better— and then he'll find out some nice homely country people to leave him with, and go backwards and forwards sometimes—backwards and forwards you know, Ned—and there's no cause to be down-hearted, for he'll very soon get better, very soon, won't he—won't he, Ned ? "

What Tim Linkinwater said, or what he brought with him that night, needs not to be told. Next morning Nicholas and his feeble companion began their journey.

And who but one—and that one he who, but for those who crowded round him then, had never met a look of kindness, or known a word of pity—could tell what agony of mind, what blighted thoughts, what unavailing sorrow, were involved in that sad parting!

" See," cried Nicholas eagerly, as he looked from the coach window, " they are at the corner of the lane still! And now there's Kate—poor Kate, whom you said you couldn't bear to say good bye to—waving her handkerchief. Don't go without one gesture of farewell to Kate!"

" I cannot make it!" cried his trembling companion, falling back in his seat and covering his eyes. " Do you see her now? Is she there still?"

" Yes, yes!" said Nicholas earnestly. " There, she waves her hand again. I have answered it for you—and now they are out of sight. Do not give way so bitterly, dear friend, do not. You will meet them all again."

He whom he thus encouraged, raised his withered hands and clasped them fervently together.

" In heaven—I humbly pray to God—in heaven!'

It sounded like the prayer of a broken heart.

CHAPTER LVI.

RALPH NICKLEBY, BAFFLED BY HIS NEPHEW IN HIS LATE DESIGN, HATCHES A SCHEME OF RETALIATION WHICH ACCIDENT SUGGESTS TO HIM, AND TAKES INTO HIS COUNSELS A TRIED AUXILIARY.

THE course which these adventures shape out for themselves and imperatively call upon the historian to observe, now demands that they should revert to the point they attained previous to the commencement of the last chapter, when Ralph Nickleby and Arthur Gride were left together in the house where death had so suddenly reared his dark and heavy banner.

With clenched hands, and teeth ground together so firm and tight that no locking of the jaws could for the time have fixed and riveted them more securely, Ralph stood for some minutes in the same attitude in which he had last addressed his nephew: breathing heavily, but as rigid and motionless in other respects as if he had been a brazen statue. After a time, he began by slow degrees, as a man rousing himself from heavy slumber, to relax. For a moment he shook his clasped fist stealthily and savagely towards the door by which Nicholas had disappeared, and then thrusting it into his breast as if to repress by force even this show of passion, turned round and confronted the less hardy usurer, who had not yet risen from the ground.

The cowering wretch, who still shook in every limb, and whose few grey hairs trembled and quivered on his head with abject dismay, tottered to his feet as he met Ralph's eye, and shielding his face with both hands, protested while he crept towards the door that it was no fault of his.

"Who said it was, man?" returned Ralph, in a suppressed voice. "Who said it was?"

"You looked as if you thought I was to blame," said Gride, timidly.

"Pshaw!" Ralph muttered, forcing a laugh. "I blame him for not living an hour longer—one hour longer would have been long enough— I blame no one else."

"N—n—no one else?" said Gride.

"Not for this mischance," replied Ralph. "I have an old score to clear with that—that young fellow who has carried off your mistress, but that has nothing to do with his blustering just now, for we should soon have been quit of him, but for this cursed accident."

There was something so unnatural in the constrained calmness with which Ralph Nickleby spoke, when coupled with the livid face, the horrible expression of the features to which every nerve and muscle as it twitched and throbbed with a spasm whose workings no effort could conceal, gave every instant some new and frightful aspect—there was something so unnatural and ghastly in the contrast between his harsh, slow, steady voice (only altered by a certain halting of the breath which made him pause between almost every word like a drunken man bent upon speaking plainly), and these evidences of the most intense and violent passions, and the struggle he made to keep them under, that if the dead body which lay above had stood instead of him before the cowering Gride, it could scarcely have presented a spectacle which would have terrified him more.

"The coach," said Ralph after a time, during which he had struggled like some strong man against a fit. "We came in a coach. Is it —waiting?"

Gride gladly availed himself of the pretext for going to the window to see, and Ralph, keeping his face steadily the other way, tore at his shirt with the hand which he had thrust into his breast, and muttered in a hoarse whisper—

"Ten thousand pounds! He said ten thousand! The precise sum paid in but yesterday for the two mortgages, and which would have gone out again at heavy interest to-morrow. If that house has failed, and he the first to bring the news!—Is the coach there?"

"Yes, yes," said Gride, startled by the fierce tone of the inquiry. "It's here. Dear, dear, what a fiery man you are!"

"Come here," said Ralph, beckoning to him. "We mustn't make a show of being disturbed. We'll go down arm in arm."

"But you pinch me black and blue," urged Gride, writhing with pain.

Ralph threw him off impatiently, and descending the stairs with his usual firm and heavy tread, got into the coach. Arthur Gride followed. After looking doubtfully at Ralph when the man asked where he was to drive, and finding that he remained silent, and expressed no wish upon the subject, Arthur mentioned his own house, and thither they proceeded.

On their way, Ralph sat in the furthest corner with folded arms, and uttered not a word. With his chin sunk upon his breast, and his downcast eyes quite hidden by the contraction of his knotted brows, he might have been asleep for any sign of consciousness he gave, until the coach stopped, when he raised his head, and glancing through the window inquired what place that was.

" My house," answered the disconsolate Gride, affected perhaps by its loneliness. " Oh dear ! my house."

" True," said Ralph. " I have not observed the way we came. I should like a glass of water. You have that in the house, I suppose ? "

" You shall have a glass of—of anything you like," answered Gride, with a groan. " It's no use knocking, coachman. Ring the bell."

The man rang, and rang, and rang again ; then knocked until the street re-echoed with the sounds ; then listened at the keyhole of the door. Nobody came, and the house was silent as the grave.

" How's this ? " said Ralph impatiently.

" Peg is so very deaf," answered Gride with a look of anxiety and alarm. " Oh dear ! Ring again, coachman. She *sees* the bell."

Again the man rang and knocked, and knocked and rang again. Some of the neighbours threw up their windows and called across the street to each other that old Gride's housekeeper must have dropped down dead. Others collected round the coach and gave vent to various surmises ; some held that she had fallen asleep, some that she had burnt herself to death, some that she had got drunk ; and one very fat man that she had seen something to eat which had frightened her so much (not being used to it) that she had fallen into a fit. This last suggestion particularly delighted the bystanders, who cheered it rather uproariously, and were with some difficulty deterred from dropping down the area and breaking open the kitchen door to ascertain the fact. Nor was this all, for rumours having gone abroad that Arthur was to be married that morning, very particular inquiries were made after the bride, who was held by the majority to be disguised in the person of Mr. Ralph Nickleby, which gave rise to much jocose indignation at the public appearance of a bride in boots and pantaloons, and called forth a great many hoots and groans. At length the two money-lenders obtained shelter in a house next door, and being accommodated with a ladder, clambered over the wall of the back yard, which was not a high one, and descended in safety on the other side.

" I am almost afraid to go in, I declare," said Arthur, turning to Ralph when they were alone. " Suppose she should be murdered— lying with her brains knocked out by a poker—eh ? "

" Suppose she were," said Ralph, hoarsely. " I tell you I wish such things were more common than they are, and more easily done. You may stare and shiver—I do ! "

He applied himself to a pump in the yard, and having taken a deep draught of water and flung a quantity on his head and face, regained his accustomed manner and led the way into the house, Gride following close at his heels.

It was the same dark place as ever : every room dismal and silent as it was wont to be, and every ghostly article of furniture in its customary place. The iron heart of the old grim clock undisturbed by all the noise without, still beat heavily within its dusty case, the tottering presses slunk from the sight as usual in their melancholy corners, the echoes of footsteps returned the same dreary sound; the long-legged spider paused in his nimble run, and scared by the sight of men in that his dull domain, hung motionless upon the wall counterfeiting death until they should have passed him by.

From cellar to garret went the two usurers opening every creaking door and looking into every deserted room. But no Peg was there. At last they sat them down in the apartment which Arthur Gride usually inhabited, to rest after their search.

" The hag is out on some preparation for your wedding festivities, I suppose," said Ralph preparing to depart. " See here. I destroy the bond; we shall never need it now."

Gride who had been peering narrowly about the room fell at that moment upon his knees before a large chest, and uttered a terrible yell.

" How now ?" said Ralph looking sternly round.

" Robbed ! robbed !" screamed Arthur Gride.

" Robbed ! of money ?"

" No, no, no. Worse, far worse."

" Of what then ?" demanded Ralph.

" Worse than money, worse than money !" cried the old man, casting the papers out of the chest, like some beast tearing up the earth. " She had better have stolen money—all my money—I haven't much. She had better have made me a beggar, than have done this !"

" Done what ?" said Ralph. " Done what, you devil's dotard ?"

Still Gride made no answer, but tore and scratched among the papers, and yelled and screeched like a fiend in torment.

" There is something missing, you say," said Ralph, shaking him furiously by the collar. " What is it ?"

" Papers, deeds. I am a ruined man—lost—lost! I am robbed, I am ruined. She saw me reading it—reading it of late.—I did very often.—She watched me—saw me put it in the box that fitted into this —the box is gone—she has stolen it.—Damnation seize her, she has robbed me !"

" Of *what !*" cried Ralph, on whom a sudden light appeared to break, for his eyes flashed and his frame trembled with agitation as he clutched Gride by his bony arm. " Of what ?"

" She don't know what it is; she can't read !" shrieked Gride, not heeding the inquiry. " There's only one way in which money can be made of it, and that is by taking it to *her*. Somebody will read it for her and tell her what to do. She and her accomplice will get money for it and be let off besides; they'll make a merit of it—say they found it—knew it—and be evidence against me. The only person it will fall upon is me—me—me !"

" Patience !" said Ralph, clutching him still tighter and eyeing him with a sidelong look, so fixed and eager as sufficiently to denote that he had some hidden purpose in what he was about to say. " Hear reason.

She can't have been gone long. I'll call the police. Give you but information of what she has stolen, and they'll lay hands upon her, trust me.—Here—help!"

"No—no—no," screamed the old man putting his hand upon Ralph's mouth. "I can't, I daren't."

"Help! help!" cried Ralph.

"No, no, no," shrieked the other, stamping upon the ground with the energy of a madman. "I tell you no. I daren't—I daren't!"

"Daren't make this robbery public?" said Ralph eagerly.

"No!" rejoined Gride, wringing his hands. "Hush! Hush! Not a word of this; not a word must be said. I am undone. Whichever way I turn, I am undone. I am betrayed. I shall be given up. I shall die in Newgate!"

With frantic exclamations such as these, and with many others in which fear, grief, and rage, were strangely blended, the panic-stricken wretch gradually subdued his first loud outcry until it had softened down into a low despairing moan chequered now and then by a howl as, going over such papers as were left in the chest, he discovered some new loss. With very little excuse for departing so abruptly, Ralph left him, and greatly disappointing the loiterers outside the house by telling them there was nothing the matter, got into the coach and was driven to his own home.

A letter lay on his table. He let it lie there for some time as if he had not the courage to open it, but at length did so and turned deadly pale.

"The worst has happened," he said, "the house has failed. I see— the rumour was abroad in the City last night, and reached the ears of those merchants. Well—well!"

He strode violently up and down the room and stopped again.

"Ten thousand pounds! And only lying there for a day—for one day! How many anxious years, how many pinching days and sleepless nights, before I scraped together that ten thousand pounds!—Ten thousand pounds! How many proud painted dames would have fawned and smiled, and how many spendthrift blockheads done me lip-service to my face and cursed me in their hearts, while I turned that ten thousand pounds into twenty! While I ground, and pinched, and used these needy borrowers for my pleasure and profit, what smooth-tongued speeches, and courteous looks, and civil letters they would have given me! The cant of the lying world is, that men like me compass our riches by dissimulation and treachery, by fawning, cringing, and stooping. Why, how many lies, what mean and abject evasions, what humbled behaviour from upstarts who, but for my money, would spurn me aside as they do their betters every day, would that ten thousand pounds have brought me in!—Grant that I had doubled it—made cent. per cent.—for every sovereign told another—there would not be one piece of money in all that heap of coin which wouldn't represent ten thousand mean and paltry lies, told—not by the money-lender, oh no! but by the money-borrowers—your liberal, thoughtless, generous, dashing folks, who wouldn't be so mean as save a sixpence for the world."

Striving as it would seem to lose part of the bitterness of his regrets in the bitterness of these other thoughts, Ralph continued to pace the room. There was less and less of resolution in his manner as his mind gradually reverted to his loss ; and at length, dropping into his elbow-chair and grasping its sides so firmly that they creaked again, he said, between his set teeth :

" The time has been when nothing could have moved me like the loss of this great sum—nothing, for births, deaths, marriages, and every event which is of interest to most men, had (unless it is connected with gain or loss of money) no interest for me. But now I swear, I mix up with the loss, his triumph in telling it. If he had brought it about, —I almost feel as if he had—I couldn't hate him more. Let me but retaliate upon him, by degrees however slow ; let me but begin to get the better of him, let me but turn the scale, and I can bear it."

His meditations were long and deep. They terminated in his despatching a letter by Newman, addressed to Mr. Squeers at the Saracen's Head, with instructions to inquire whether he had arrived in town, and if so, to wait an answer. Newman brought back the information that Mr. Squeers had come by mail that morning, and had received the letter in bed ; but that he sent his duty, and word that he would get up and wait upon Mr. Nickleby directly.

The interval between the delivery of this message and the arrival of Mr. Squeers was very short, but before he came, Ralph had suppressed every sign of emotion, and once more regained the hard, immoveable, inflexible manner which was habitual to him, and to which, perhaps, was ascribable no small part of the influence which, over many men of no very strong prejudices on the score of morality, he could exert almost at will.

" Well, Mr. Squeers," he said, welcoming that worthy with his accustomed smile, of which a sharp look and a thoughtful frown were part and parcel.—" how do *you* do ? "

" Why, sir," said Mr. Squeers, " I'm pretty well. So's the family, and so's the boys, except for a sort of rash as is a running through the school, and rather puts 'em off their feed. But it's a ill wind as blows no good to nobody ; that's what I always say when them lads has a wisitation. A wisitation, sir, is the lot of mortality. Mortality itself, sir, is a wisitation. The world is chock full of wisitations ; and if a boy repines at a wisitation and makes you uncomfortable with his noise, he must have his head punched. That's going according to the scripter, that is."

" Mr. Squeers," said Ralph, drily.

" Sir."

" We'll avoid these precious morsels of morality if you please, and talk of business."

" With all my heart, sir," rejoined Squeers, " and first let me say——"

" First let *me* say, if you please——Noggs ! "

Newman presented himself when the summons had been twice or thrice repeated, and asked if his master called.

" I did. Go to your dinner. And go at once. Do you hear ?"

"It an't time," said Newman, doggedly.

"My time is yours, and I say it is," returned Ralph.

"You alter it every day," said Newman. "It isn't fair."

"You don't keep many cooks, and can easily apologize to them for the trouble," retorted Ralph. "Begone, sir!"

Ralph not only issued this order in his most preremptory manner, but under pretence of fetching some papers from the little office, saw it obeyed, and when Newman had left the house, chained the door to prevent the possibility of his returning secretly by means of his latch key.

"I have reason to suspect that fellow," said Ralph, when he returned to his own office. "Therefore, until I have thought of the shortest and least troublesome way of ruining him, I hold it best to keep him at a distance."

"It wouldn't take much to ruin him, I should think," said Squeers, with a grin.

"Perhaps not," answered Ralph. "Nor to ruin a great many people whom I know. You were going to say——?"

Ralph's summary and matter-of-course way of holding up this example and throwing out the hint that followed it, had evidently an effect (as doubtless it was designed to have) upon Mr. Squeers, who said, after a little hesitation and in a much more subdued tone—

"Why, what I was a going to say, sir, is, that this here business regarding of that ungrateful and hard-hearted chap Snawley senior, puts me out of my way, and occasions a inconveniency quite unparalleled, besides, as I may say, making, for whole weeks together, Mrs. Squeers a perfect widder. It's a pleasure to me to act with you, of course."

"Of course," said Ralph, drily.

"Yes, I say, of course," resumed Mr. Squeers, rubbing his knees, "but at the same time, when one comes, as I do now, better than two hundred and fifty mile to take a afferdavid, it does put a man out a good deal, letting alone the risk."

"And where may the risk be, Mr. Squeers?" said Ralph.

"I said, letting alone the risk," replied Squeers, evasively.

"And I said, where was the risk?"

"I wasn't complaining, you know, Mr. Nickleby," pleaded Squeers. "Upon my word I never see such a——"

"I ask you where is the risk?" repeated Ralph, emphatically.

"Where the risk?" returned Squeers, rubbing his knees still harder. "Why, it an't necessary to mention—certain subjects is best awoided. Oh, you know what risk I mean."

"How often have I told you," said Ralph, "and how often am I to tell you, that you run no risk? What have you sworn, or what are you asked to swear, but that at such and such a time a boy was left with you in the name of Smike; that he was at your school for a given number of years, was lost under such and such circumstances, is now found, and has been identified by you in such and such keeping. This is all true—is it not?"

" Yes," replied Squeers, " that's all true."

" Well, then," said Ralph, " what risk do you run ? Who swears to a lie but Snawley—a man whom I have paid much less than I have you ?"

" He certainly did it cheap, did Snawley," observed Squeers.

" He did it cheap !" retorted Ralph, testily, " yes, and he did it well, and carries it off with a hypocritical face and a sanctified air, but you—risk ! What do you mean by risk ? The certificates are all genuine, Snawley *had* another son, he *has* been married twice, his first wife *is* dead, none but her ghost could tell that she didn't write that letter, none but Snawley himself can tell that this is not his son and that his son is food for worms. The only perjury is Snawley's, and I fancy he is pretty well used to it. Where's your risk ?"

" Why, you know," said Squeers, fidgeting in his chair, " if you come to that, I might say where's yours ?"

" You might say where's mine !" returned Ralph ; " you may say where's mine. I don't appear in the business—neither do you. All Snawley's interest is to stick well to the story he has told, and all his risk is to depart from it in the least. Talk of *your* risk in the conspiracy !"

" I say," remonstrated Squeers, looking uneasily round ; " don't call it that—just as a favour, don't."

" Call it what you like," said Ralph, irritably, " but attend to me. This tale was originally fabricated as a means of deep annoyance against one who hurt your trade and half cudgelled you to death, and to enable you to obtain repossession of a half-dead drudge, whom you wished to regain, because while you wreaked your vengeance on him for his share in the business, you knew that the knowledge that he was again in your power would be the best punishment you could inflict upon your enemy. Is that so, Mr. Squeers ?"

" Why, sir," returned Squeers, almost overpowered by the determination which Ralph displayed to make everything tell against him, and by his stern unyielding manner, " in a measure it was."

" What does that mean ?" said Ralph, quietly.

" Why, in a measure, means," returned Squeers, " as it may be so ; that it wasn't all on my account, because you had some old grudge to satisfy, too."

" If I had not had," said Ralph, in no way abashed by the reminder, " do you think I should have helped you ?"

" Why no, I don't suppose you would," Squeers replied. " I only wanted that point to be all square and straight between us."

" How can it ever be otherwise ?" retorted Ralph. " Except that account is against me, for I spend money to gratify my hatred, and you pocket it, and gratify yours at the same time. You are at least as avaricious as you are revengeful—so am I. Which is best off ? You, who win money and revenge at the same time and by the same process, and who are at all events sure of money, if not of revenge ; or I, who am only sure of spending money in any case, and can but win bare revenge at last ?"

As Mr. Squeers could only answer this proposition by shrugs and smiles, Ralph sternly bade him be silent, and thankful that he was so well off, and then fixing his eyes steadily upon him, proceeded to say—

First, that Nicholas had thwarted him in a plan he had formed for the disposal in marriage of a certain young lady, and had, in the confusion attendant upon her father's sudden death, secured that lady himself and borne her off in triumph.

Secondly, that by some will or settlement—certainly by some instrument in writing, which must contain the young lady's name, and could be therefore easily selected from others, if access to the place where it was deposited were once secured—she was entitled to property which, if the existence of this deed ever became known to her, would make her husband (and Ralph represented that Nicholas was certain to marry her) a rich and prosperous man, and most formidable enemy.

Thirdly, that this deed had been, with others, stolen from one who had himself obtained or concealed it fraudulently, and who feared to take any steps for its recovery; and that he (Ralph) knew the thief.

To all this, Mr. Squeers listened with greedy ears that devoured every syllable, and with his one eye and his mouth wide open: marvelling for what special reason he was honoured with so much of Ralph's confidence, and to what it all tended.

" Now," said Ralph, leaning forward, and placing his hand on Squeers's arm, " hear the design which I have conceived, and which I must—I say, must, if I can ripen it—have carried into execution. No advantage can be reaped from this deed, whatever it is, save by the girl herself, or her husband, and the possession of this deed by one or other of them is indispensable to any advantage being gained. *That* I have discovered beyond the possibility of doubt. I want that deed brought here, that I may give the man who brings it fifty pounds in gold, and burn it to ashes before his face."

Mr. Squeers, after following with his eye the action of Ralph's hand towards the fire-place as if he were at that moment consuming the paper, drew a long breath, and said—

" Yes; but who's to bring it? "

" Nobody, perhaps, for much is to be done before it can be got at," said Ralph. " But if anybody—you."

Mr. Squeers's first tokens of consternation, and his flat relinquishment of the task, would have staggered most men, if they had not occasioned an utter abandonment of the proposition. On Ralph they produced not the slightest effect. Resuming when the schoolmaster had quite talked himself out of breath, as coolly as if he had never been interrupted, Ralph proceeded to expatiate on such features of the case as he deemed it most advisable to lay the greatest stress upon.

These were, the age, decrepitude, and weakness of Mrs. Sliderskew, the great improbability of her having any accomplice or even acquaintance, taking into account her secluded habits, and her long residence in such a house as Gride's; the strong reason there was to suppose that the robbery was not the result of a concerted plan, otherwise she would have watched an opportunity of carrying off a sum of money, or even of her being in want (to which the same argument applied); the difficulty she would be placed in when she began to think on what she had done, and found herself incumbered with documents of whose nature she was utterly ignorant; and the comparative ease with which somebody, with a full knowledge of her position, obtaining access to her and working upon her fears, if necessary, might worm himself into her confidence, and obtain, under one pretence or another, free possession of the deed. To these were added such considerations as the constant residence of Mr. Squeers at a long distance from London, which rendered his association with Mrs. Sliderskew a mere masquerading frolic, in which nobody was likely to recognise him either at the time or afterwards; the impossibility of Ralph's undertaking the task himself, being already known to her by sight, and various comments upon the uncommon tact and experience of Mr. Squeers, which would make his overreaching one old woman a mere matter of child's play and amusement. In addition to these influences and persuasions, Ralph drew, with his utmost skill and power, a vivid picture of the defeat which Nicholas would sustain should they succeed, in linking himself to a beggar where he expected to wed an heiress—glanced at the immeasurable importance it must be to a man situated as Squeers, to preserve such a friend as himself—dwelt on a long train of benefits conferred since their first acquaintance, when he had reported favourably of his treatment of a sickly boy who had died under his hands (and whose death was very convenient to Ralph and his clients, but this he did *not* say), and finally hinted that the fifty pounds might be increased to seventy-five, or in the event of very great success, even to a hundred.

These arguments at length concluded, Mr. Squeers crossed his legs and uncrossed them, and scratched his head, and rubbed his eye, and examined the palms of his hands, and bit his nails, and after exhibiting many other signs of restlessness and indecision, asked " whether one hundred pound was the highest that Mr. Nickleby could go." Being answered in the affirmative, he became restless again, and after some thought, and an unsuccessful inquiry " whether he couldn't go another fifty," said he supposed he must try and do the most he could for a friend, which was always his maxim, and therefore he undertook the job.

" But how are you to get at the woman?" he said; " that's what it is as puzzles me."

" I may not get at her at all," replied Ralph, " but I'll try. I have hunted down people in this city before now who have been better hid than she, and I know quarters in which a guinea or two carefully spent will often solve darker riddles than this—ay, and keep them close too, if need be. I hear my man ringing at the door. We may as well part. You had better not come to and fro, but wait till you hear from me."

" Good!" returned Squeers. " I say, if you shouldn't find her out, you'll pay expenses at the Saracen, and something for loss of time?"

" Well," said Ralph, testily; " yes. You have nothing more to say?"

Squeers, shaking his head, Ralph accompanied him to the street-door, and audibly wondering, for the edification of Newman, why it was fastened as if it were night, let him in and Squeers out, and returned to his own room.

"Now!" he muttered, doggedly. "Come what come may, for the present I am firm and unshaken. Let me but retrieve this one small portion of my loss and disgrace. Let me but defeat him in this one hope, dear to his heart as I know it must be. Let me but do this, and it shall be the first link in such a chain, which I will wind about him, as never man forged yet."

CHAPTER LVII.

HOW RALPH NICKLEBY'S AUXILIARY WENT ABOUT HIS WORK, AND
HOW HE PROSPERED WITH IT.

It was a dark, wet, gloomy night in autumn, when in an upper room of a mean house, situated in an obscure street or rather court near Lambeth, there sat all alone, a one-eyed man grotesquely habited, either for lack of better garments or for purposes of disguise, in a loose great-coat, with arms half as long again as his own, and a capacity of breadth and length which would have admitted of his winding himself in it, head and all, with the utmost ease, and without any risk of straining the old and greasy material of which it was composed.

So attired, and in a place so far removed from his usual haunts and occupations, and so very poor and wretched in its character, perhaps Mrs. Squeers herself would have had some difficulty in recognising her lord, quickened though her natural sagacity doubtless would have been by the affectionate yearnings and impulses of a tender wife. But Mrs. Squeers's lord it was; and in a tolerably disconsolate mood Mrs. Squeers's lord appeared to be, as, helping himself from a black bottle which stood on the table beside him, he cast round the chamber a look, in which very slight regard for the objects within view was plainly mingled with some regretful and impatient recollection of distant scenes and persons.

There were certainly no particular attractions, either in the room over which the glance of Mr. Squeers so discontentedly wandered, or in the narrow street into which it might have penetrated, if he had thought fit to approach the window. The attic-chamber in which he sat was bare and mean; the bedstead, and such few other articles of necessary furniture as it contained, of the commonest description, in a most crazy state, and of a most uninviting appearance. The street was muddy, dirty, and deserted. Having but one outlet, it was traversed by few but the inhabitants at any time, and the night being one of those on which most people are glad to be within doors, it now presented no other signs of life than the dull glimmering of poor candles from the dirty windows, and few sounds but the pattering of the rain, and occasionally the heavy closing of some creaking door.

Mr. Squeers continued to look disconsolately about him, and to listen to these noises in profound silence, broken only by the rustling of his large coat, as he now and then moved his arm to raise his glass to his lips—Mr. Squeers continued to do this for some time, until the increasing gloom warned him to snuff the candle. Seeming to be slightly roused by this exertion, he raised his eyes to the ceiling, and fixing them upon some uncouth and fantastic figures, traced upon it by the wet and damp which had penetrated through the roof, broke out into the following soliloquy:

"Well, this is a pretty go, is this here!—an uncommon pretty go! Here have I been a matter of how many weeks—hard upon six—a-follering up this here blessed old dowager, petty larcenerer,"—Mr. Squeers delivered himself of this epithet with great difficulty and effort —"and Dotheboys Hall a-running itself regularly to seed the while! That's the worst of ever being in with a ow-dacious chap like that old Nickleby; you never know when he's done with you, and if you're in for a penny, you're in for a pound."

This remark perhaps reminded Mr. Squeers that he was in for a hundred pound; at any rate, his countenance relaxed, and he raised his glass to his mouth with an air of greater enjoyment of its contents than he had before evinced.

"I never see," soliloquised Mr. Squeers in continuation, "I never see nor come across such a file as that old Nickleby—never. He's out of everybody's depth, he is. He's what you may a-call a rasper, is Nickleby. To see how sly and cunning he grubbed on, day after day, a-worming and plodding and tracing and turning and twining of hisself about, till he found out where this precious Mrs. Peg was hid, and cleared the ground for me to work upon—creeping and crawling and gliding, like a ugly old, bright-eyed, stagnation-blooded adder! Ah! He'd have made a good un in our line, but it would have been too limited for him; his genius would have busted all bounds, and coming over every obstacle, broke down all before it, 'till it erected itself into a monneyment of—Well, I'll think of the rest, and say it when conwenient."

Making a halt in his reflections at this place, Mr. Squeers again put his glass to his lips, and drawing a dirty letter from his pocket, proceeded to con over its contents with the air of a man who had read it very often, and now refreshed his memory rather in the absence of better amusement than for any specific information.

"The pigs is well," said Mr. Squeers, "the cows is well, and the boys is bobbish. Young Sprouter has been a-winking, has he? I'll wink him when I get back. 'Cobbey would persist in sniffing while he was a-eating his dinner, and said that the beef was so strong it made him.'—Very good, Cobbey, we'll see if we can't make you sniff a little without beef. 'Pitcher was took with another fever,'—of course he was—' and being fetched by his friends, died the day after he got home,' —of course he did, and out of aggravation; it's part of a deep-laid system.

There an't another chap in the school but that boy as would have died exactly at the end of the quarter, taking it out of me to the very last, and then carrying his spite to the utmost extremity. ' The juniorest Palmer said he wished he was in Heaven,'—I really don't know, I do not know what's to be done with that young fellow; he's always a-wishing something horrid. He said once he wished he was a donkey, because then he wouldn't have a father as didn't love him!—pretty wicious that, for a child of six !"

Mr. Squeers was so much moved by the contemplation of this hardened nature in one so young, that he angrily put up the letter, and sought, in a new train of ideas, a subject of consolation.

"It's a long time to have been a-lingering in London," he said, " and this is a precious hole to come and live in, even if it has been only for a week or so. Still, one hundred pound is five boys, and five boys takes a whole year to pay one hundred pound, and there's their keep to be substracted, besides. There's nothing lost, neither, by one's being here; because the boys' money comes in just the same as if I was at home, and Mrs. Squeers she keeps them in order. There'll be some lost time to make up, of course—there'll be an arrear of flogging as'll have to be gone through; still, a couple of days makes that all right, and one don't mind a little extra work for one hundred pound. It's pretty nigh the time to wait upon the old woman. From what she said last night, I suspect that if I'm to succeed at all, I shall succeed to-night, so I'll have half a glass more to wish myself success, and put myself in spirits. Mrs. Squeers, my dear, your health."

Leering with his one eye as if the lady to whom he drank had been actually present, Mr. Squeers—in his enthusiasm, no doubt—poured out a full glass, and emptied it; and as the liquor was raw spirits, and he had applied himself to the same bottle more than once already, it is not surprising that he found himself by this time in an extremely cheerful state, and quite enough excited for his purpose.

What his purpose was, soon appeared; for, after a few turns about the room to steady himself, he took the bottle under his arm and the glass in his hand, and blowing out the candle as if he purposed being gone some time, stole out upon the staircase, and creeping softly to a door opposite his own, tapped gently at it.

" But what's the use of tapping?" he said, " she'll never hear. I suppose she isn't doing anything very particular, and if she is, it don't much matter that I see."

With this brief preface, Mr. Squeers applied his hand to the latch of the door, and thrusting his head into a garret far more deplorable than that he had just left, and seeing that there was nobody there but an old woman, who was bending over a wretched fire (for although the weather was still warm, the evening was chilly), walked in, and tapped her on the shoulder.

" Well, my Slider," said Mr. Squeers, jocularly.

" Is that you ?" inquired Peg.

" Ah ! it's me, and me's the first person singular, nominative case, agreeing with the verb ' it's,' and governed by Squeers understood, as a acorn, a hour ; but when the h is sounded, the a only is to be used, as a hand, a heart, a highway," replied Mr. Squeers, quoting at random from the grammar, " at least if it isn't, you don't know any better, and if it is, I've done it accidentally."

Delivering this reply in his accustomed tone of voice, in which of course it was inaudible to Peg, Mr. Squeers drew a stool up to the fire, and placing himself over against her, and the bottle and glass on the floor between them, roared out again very loud,

" Well, my Slider."

" I hear you," said Peg, receiving him very graciously.

" I've come according to promise," roared Squeers.

" So they used to say in that part of the country I come from," observed Peg, complacently, " but I think oil's better."

" Better than what ?" shouted Squeers, adding some rather strong language in an under-tone.

" No," said Peg, " of course not."

" I never saw such a monster as you are ! " muttered Squeers, looking as amiable as he possibly could the while ; for Peg's eye was upon him, and she was chuckling fearfully, as though in delight at having made a choice repartee. " Do you see this ? this is a bottle."

" I see it," answered Peg.

" Well, and do you see *this* ?" bawled Squeers. " This is a glass ?" Peg saw that too.

" See here, then," said Squeers, accompanying his remarks with appropriate action, " I fill the glass from the bottle, and I say, ' your health, Slider,' and empty it ; then I rinse it genteelly with a little drop, which I'm forced to throw into the fire—Hallo ! we shall have the chimbley alight next—fill it again, and hand it over to you."

" *Your* health," said Peg.

" She understands that, anyways," muttered Squeers, watching Mrs. Sliderskew as she despatched her portion, and choked and gasped in a most awful manner after so doing ; " now then, let's have a talk. How's the rheumatics ?"

Mrs. Sliderskew, with much blinking and chuckling, and with looks expressive of her strong admiration of Mr. Squeers, his person, manners, and conversation, replied that the rheumatics were better.

" What's the reason," said Mr. Squeers, deriving fresh facetiousness from the bottle ; " what's the reason of rheumatics, what do they mean, what do people have 'em for—eh ? "

Mrs. Sliderskew didn't know, but suggested that it was possibly because they couldn't help it.

" Measles, rheumatics, hooping-cough, fevers, agues, and lumbagers," said Mr. Squeers, " is all philosophy together, that's what it is. The heavenly bodies is philosophy, and the earthly bodies is philosophy. If there's a screw loose in a heavenly body, that's philosophy, and if there's a screw loose in a earthly body that's philosophy too ; or it may be that sometimes there's a little metaphysics in it, but that's not often. Philosophy's the chap for me. If a parent asks a question in the classical, commercial, or mathematical line, says I, gravely, ' Why, sir, in the first place, are you a philosopher?'—'No, Mr. Squeers,' he says, 'I an't.' 'Then, sir,' says I, 'I am sorry for you, for I shan't be able to explain it.' Naturally the parent goes away and wishes he was a philosopher, and equally naturally, thinks I'm one."

Saying this and a great deal more with tipsy profundity and a serio-comic air, and keeping his eye all the time on Mrs. Sliderskew, who was unable to hear one word, Mr. Squeers concluded by helping himself and passing the bottle, to which Peg did becoming reverence.

"That's the time of day!" said Mr. Squeers. "You look twenty pound ten better than you did."

Again Mrs. Sliderskew chuckled, but modesty forbade her assenting verbally to the compliment.

"Twenty pound ten better," repeated Mr. Squeers, "than you did that day when I first introduced myself—don't you know?"

"Ah!" said Peg, shaking her head, "but you frightened me that day."

"Did I?" said Squeers, "well, it was rather a startling thing for a stranger to come and recommend himself by saying that he knew all about you, and what your name was, and why you were living so quiet here, and what you had boned, and who you boned it from, wasn't it?"

Peg nodded her head in strong assent.

"But I know everything that happens in that way, you see," continued Squeers. "Nothing takes place of that kind that I an't up to entirely. I'm a sort of a lawyer, Slider, of first-rate standing, and understanding too; I'm the intimate friend and confidental adwiser of pretty nigh every man, woman, and child that gets themselves into difficulties by being too nimble with their fingers, I'm——"

Mr. Squeers's catalogue of his own merits and accomplishments, which was partly the result of a concerted plan between himself and Ralph Nickleby, and flowed, in part, from the black bottle, was here interrupted by Mrs. Sliderskew.

"Ha, ha, ha!" she cried, folding her arms and wagging her head; "and so he wasn't married after all, wasn't he—not married after all?"

"No," replied Squeers, "that he wasn't!"

"And a young lover come and carried off the bride, eh?" said Peg.

"From under his very nose," replied Squeers; "and I'm told the young chap cut up rough besides, and broke the winders, and forced him to swaller his wedding favor, which nearly choked him."

"Tell me all about it again," cried Peg, with a malicious relish of her old master's defeat, which made her natural hideousness something quite fearful; "let's hear it all again, beginning at the beginning now, as if you'd never told me. Let's have it every word—now—now—beginning at the very first, you know, when he went to the house that morning."

Mr. Squeers, plying Mrs. Sliderskew freely with the liquor, and sustaining himself under the exertion of speaking so loud by frequent applications to it himself, complied with this request by describing the discomfiture of Arthur Gride, with such improvements on the truth as happened to occur to him, and the ingenious invention and application of which had been very instrumental in recommending him to her notice in the beginning of their acquaintance. Mrs. Sliderskew was in an ecstacy of delight, rolling her head about, drawing up her skinny shoulders, and wrinkling her cadaverous face into so many and such complicated forms of ugliness, as awakened the unbounded astonishment and disgust even of Mr. Squeers.

"He's a treacherous old goat," said Peg, "and cozened me with cunning tricks and lying promises, but never mind—I'm even with him —I'm even with him."

"More than even, Slider," returned Squeers; "you'd have been even with him if he'd got married, but with the disappointment besides, you're a long way a-head—out of sight, Slider, quite out of sight. And that reminds me," he added, handing her the glass, "if you want me to give you my opinion of them deeds, and tell you what you'd better keep and what you'd better burn, why, now's your time, Slider."

"There an't no hurry for that," said Peg, with several knowing looks and winks.

"Oh! very well!" observed Squeers, "it don't matter to me; you asked me, you know. I shouldn't charge you nothing, being a friend. You're the best judge of course, but you're a bold woman, Slider— that's all."

"How do you mean—bold?" said Peg.

"Why, I only mean that if it was me, I wouldn't keep papers as might hang me, littering about when they might be turned into money; them as wasn't useful made away with, and them as was, laid by somewheres safe, that's all," returned Squeers; "but everybody's the best judge of their own affairs. All as I say is, Slider, *I* wouldn't do it."

"Come," said Peg, "then you shall see 'em."

"*I* don't want to see 'em," replied Squeers, affecting to be out of humour, "don't talk as if it was a treat. Show 'em to somebody else and take their advice."

Mr. Squeers would very likely have carried on the farce of being offended a little longer, if Mrs. Sliderskew, in her anxiety to restore herself to her former high position in his good graces, had not become so extremely affectionate that he stood at some risk of being smothered by her caresses. Repressing, with as good a grace as possible, these little familiarities—for which there is reason to believe that the black bottle was at least as much to blame as any constitutional infirmity on the part of Mrs. Sliderskew—he protested that he had only been joking, and, in proof of his unimpaired good humour, that he was ready to examine the deeds at once, if, by so doing, he could afford any satisfaction or relief of mind to his fair friend.

"And now you're up, my Slider," bawled Squeers, as she rose to fetch them, "bolt the door."

Peg trotted to the door, and after fumbling at the bolt, crept to the other end of the room, and from beneath the coals which filled the bottom of the cupboard, drew forth a small deal box. Having placed this on the floor at Squeers's feet, she brought from under the pillow of her bed, a small key, with which she signed to that gentleman to open it. Mr. Squeers, who had eagerly followed her every motion, lost no time in obeying this hint, and throwing back the lid, gazed with rapture on the documents which lay within.

"Now you see," said Peg, kneeling down on the floor beside him, and staying his impatient hand; "what's of no use we'll burn, what we can get any money by we'll keep, and if there's any we could get him into trouble by, and fret and waste away his heart to shreds, those we'll take particular care of, for that's what I want to do, and hoped to do when I left him."

"I thought," said Squeers, "that you didn't bear him any particular good-will. But I say, why didn't you take some money besides?"

"Some what?" asked Peg.

"Some money," roared Squeers. "I do believe the woman hears me, and wants to make me break a wessel, so that she may have the pleasure of nursing me. Some money, Slider—money."

"Why, what a man you are to ask!" cried Peg, with some contempt. "If I had taken money from Arthur Gride, he'd have scoured the whole earth to find me—aye, and he'd have smelt it out, and raked it up somehow if I had buried it at the bottom of the deepest well in England. No, no! I knew better than that. I took what I thought his secrets were hid in, and them he couldn't afford to make public, let 'em be worth ever so much money. He's an old dog, a sly, old, cunning, thankless dog. He first starved and then tricked me, and if I could, I'd kill him."

"All right, and very laudable," said Squeers. "But first and foremost, Slider, burn the box. You should never keep things as may lead to discovery—always mind that. So while you pull it to pieces (which you can easily do, for it's very old and rickety) and burn it in little bits, I'll look over the papers and tell you what they are."

Peg, expressing her acquiescence in this arrangement, Mr. Squeers turned the box bottom upwards, and tumbling the contents upon the floor, handed it to her; the destruction of the box being an extemporary device for engaging her attention, in case it should prove desirable to distract it from his own proceedings.

"There," said Squeers, "you poke the pieces between the bars, and make up a good fire, and I'll read the while—let me see—let me see." And taking! the candle down beside him, Mr. Squeers, with great eagerness and a cunning grin overspreading his face, entered upon his task of examination.

If the old woman had not been very deaf, she must have heard, when she last went to the door, the breathing of two persons close behind it, and if those two persons had been unacquainted with her infirmity they must probably have chosen that moment either for presenting themselves or taking to flight. But, knowing with whom they had to deal, they remained quite still, and now, not only appeared unobserved at the door—which was not bolted, for the bolt had no hasp —but warily, and with noiseless footsteps, advanced into the room.

As they stole further and further in by slight and scarcely perceptible

Mr Squeers and Mrs Sliderskew unconscious of Visitors.

degrees, and with such caution that they scarcely seemed to breathe, the old hag and Squeers little dreaming of any such invasion, and utterly unconscious of there being any soul near but themselves, were busily occupied with their tasks. The old woman with her wrinkled face close to the bars of the stove, puffing at the dull embers which had not yet caught the wood—Squeers stooping down to the candle, which brought out the full ugliness of his face, as the light of the fire did that of his companion—both intently engaged, and wearing faces of exultation which contrasted strongly with the anxious looks of those behind, who took advantage of the slightest sound to cover their advance, and almost before they had moved an inch, and all was silent, stopped again —this, with the large bare room, damp walls, and flickering doubtful light, combined to form a scene which the most careless and indifferent spectator—could any have been present—could scarcely have failed to derive some interest from, and would not readily have forgotten.

Of the stealthy comers Frank Cheeryble was one, and Newman Noggs the other. Newman had caught up by the rusty nozzle an old pair of bellows, which were just undergoing a flourish in the air preparatory to a descent upon the head of Mr. Squeers, when Frank, with an earnest gesture, stayed his arm, and taking another step in advance, came so close behind the schoolmaster that, by leaning slightly forward, he could plainly distinguish the writing which he held up to his eye.

Mr. Squeers not being remarkably erudite, appeared to be considerably puzzled by this first prize, which was in an engrossing hand, and not very legible except to a practised eye. Having tried it by reading from left to right and from right to left, and finding it equally clear both ways, he turned it upside down with no better success.

"Ha, ha, ha!" chuckled Peg, who, on her knees before the fire, was feeding it with fragments of the box, and grinning in most devilish exultation. "What's that writing about, eh?"

"Nothing particular," replied Squeers, tossing it towards her. "It's only an old lease, as well as I can make out. Throw it in the fire."

Mrs. Sliderskew complied, and inquired what the next one was.

"This," said Squeers, "is a bundle of over-due acceptances and renewed bills of six or eight young gentlemen, but they're all M.P.'s., so it's of no use to anybody. Throw it in the fire."

Peg did as she was bidden, and waited for the next.

"This," said Squeers, "seems to be some deed of sale of the right of presentation to the rectory of Purechurch, in the valley of Cashup. Take care of that, Slider—literally for God's sake. It'll fetch its price at the Auction Mart."

"What's the next?" inquired Peg.

"Why, this," said Squeers, "seems, from the two letters that's with it, to be a bond from a curate down in the country to pay half-a-year's wages of forty pound for borrowing twenty. Take care of that, for if he don't pay it, his bishop will very soon be down upon him. We know what the camel and the needle's eye means—no man as can't live upon his income, whatever it is, must expect to go to heaven at any price—it's very odd. I don't see anything like it yet."

"What's the matter?" said Peg.

"Nothing," replied Squeers, "only I'm looking for——"

Newman raised the bellows again, and once more Frank, by a rapid motion of his arm, unaccompanied by any noise, checked him in his purpose.

"Here you are," said Squeers, "bonds—take care of them. Warrant of attorney—take care of that. Two cognovits—take care of them. Lease and release—burn that. Ah! 'Madeline Bray—come of age or marry—the said Madeline'—Here, burn *that*."

Eagerly throwing towards the old woman a parchment that he caught up for the purpose, Squeers, as she turned her head, thrust into the breast of his large coat, the deed in which these words had caught his eye, and burst into a shout of triumph.

"I've got it!" said Squeers. "I've got it. Hurrah! The plan was a good one though the chance was desperate, and the day's our own at last!"

Peg demanded what he laughed at, but no answer was returned, for Newman's arm could no longer be restrained; the bellows descending heavily and with unerring aim on the very centre of Mr. Squeers's head, felled him to the floor, and stretched him on it flat and senseless.

CHAPTER LVIII.

IN WHICH ONE SCENE OF THIS HISTORY IS CLOSED.

Dividing the distance into two days' journey, in order that his charge might sustain the less exhaustion and fatigue from travelling so far, Nicholas, at the end of the second day from their leaving home, found himself within a very few miles of the spot where the happiest years of his life had been passed, and which, while it filled his mind with pleasant and peaceful thoughts, brought back many painful and vivid recollections of the circumstances in which he and his had wandered forth from their old home, cast upon the rough world and the mercy of strangers.

It needed no such reflections as those which the memory of old days, and wanderings among scenes where our childhood has been passed, usually awaken in the most insensible minds, to soften the heart of Nicholas, and render him more than usually mindful of his drooping friend. By night and day, at all times and seasons, always watchful, attentive, and solicitous, and never varying in the discharge of his self-imposed duty to one so friendless and helpless as he whose sands of life were now fast running out and dwindling rapidly away, he was ever at his side. He never left him; to encourage and animate him, administer to his wants, support and cheer him to the utmost of his power, was now his constant and unceasing occupation.

They procured a humble lodging in a small farm-house, surrounded by meadows, where Nicholas had often revelled when a child with a troop of merry schoolfellows ; and here they took up their rest.

At first, Smike was strong enough to walk about for short distances at a time, with no other support or aid than that which Nicholas could afford him. At this time, nothing appeared to interest him so much as visiting those places which had been most familiar to his friend in bygone days. Yielding to this fancy, and pleased to find that its indulgence beguiled the sick boy of many tedious hours, and never failed to afford him matter for thought and conversation afterwards, Nicholas made such spots the scenes of their daily rambles : driving him from place to place in a little pony-chair, and supporting him on his arm while they walked slowly among these old haunts, or lingered in the sunlight to take long parting looks of those which were most quiet and beautiful.

It was on such occasions as these, that Nicholas, yielding almost unconsciously to the interest of old associations, would point out some tree that he had climbed a hundred times to peep at the young birds in their nest, and the branch from which he used to shout to little Kate, who stood below terrified at the height he had gained, and yet urging him higher still by the intensity of her admiration. There was the old house too, which they would pass every day, looking up at the tiny window through which the sun used to stream in and wake him on the summer mornings—they were all summer mornings then— and climbing up the garden-wall and looking over, Nicholas could see the very rose-bush which had come a present to Kate from some little lover and she had planted with her own hands. There were the hedge-rows where the brother and sister had so often gathered wild flowers together, and the green fields and shady paths where they had so often strayed. There was not a lane, or brook, or copse, or cottage near, with which some childish event was not entwined, and back it came upon the mind as events of childhood do—nothing in itself : perhaps a word, a laugh, a look, some slight distress, a passing thought or fear— and yet more strongly and distinctly marked, and better far remembered, than the hardest trials or severest sorrows of but a year ago.

One of these expeditions led them through the churchyard where was his father's grave. " Even here," said Nicholas, softly, " we used to loiter before we knew what death was, and when we little thought whose ashes would rest beneath, and wondering at the silence, sit down to rest and speak below our breath. Once Kate was lost, and after an hour of fruitless search, they found her fast asleep under that tree which shades my father's grave. He was very fond of her, and said when he took her up in his arms, still sleeping, that whenever he died he would wish to be buried where his dear little child had laid her head. You see his wish was not forgotten."

Nothing more passed at the time, but that night, as Nicholas sat beside his bed, Smike started up from what had seemed to be a slumber, and laying his hand in his, prayed, as the tears coursed down his face, that he would make him one solemn promise.

"What is that?" said Nicholas, kindly. "If I can redeem it, or hope to do so, you know I will."

"I am sure you will," was the reply. "Promise me that when I die, I shall be buried near—as near as they can make my grave—to the tree we saw to-day."

Nicholas gave the promise; he had few words to give it in, but they were solemn and earnest. His poor friend kept his hand in his, and turned as if to sleep. But there were stifled sobs; and the hand was pressed more than once, or twice, or thrice, before he sank to rest, and slowly loosed his hold.

In a fortnight's time, he became too ill to move about. Once or twice Nicholas drove him out, propped up with pillows, but the motion of the chaise was painful to him, and brought on fits of fainting, which, in his weakened state, were dangerous. There was an old couch in the house which was his favourite resting-place by day; when the sun shone, and the weather was warm, Nicholas had this wheeled into a little orchard which was close at hand, and his charge being well wrapt up and carried out to it, they used to sit there sometimes for hours together.

It was on one of these occasions that a circumstance took place, which Nicholas at the time thoroughly believed to be the mere delusion of an imagination affected by disease, but which he had afterwards too good reason to know was of real and actual occurrence.

He had brought Smike out in his arms—poor fellow! a child might have carried him then—to see the sunset, and, having arranged his couch, had taken his seat beside it. He had been watching the whole of the night before, and being greatly fatigued both in mind and body, gradually fell asleep.

He could not have closed his eyes five minutes, when he was awakened by a scream, and starting up in that kind of terror which affects a person suddenly roused, saw to his great astonishment that his charge had struggled into a sitting posture, and with eyes almost starting from their sockets, the cold dew standing on his forehead, and in a fit of trembling which quite convulsed his frame, was shrieking to him for help.

"Good Heaven, what is this!" cried Nicholas, bending over him. "Be calm; you have been dreaming."

"No, no, no!" cried Smike, clinging to him. "Hold me tight. Don't let me go. There—there—behind the tree!"

Nicholas followed his eyes, which were directed to some distance behind the chair from which he himself had just risen. But there was nothing there.

"This is nothing but your fancy," he said, as he strove to compose him; "nothing else indeed."

"I know better. I saw as plain as I see now," was the answer. "Oh! say you'll keep me with you—swear you won't leave me for an instant!"

"Do I ever leave you?" returned Nicholas. "Lie down again now—there. You see I'm here. Now tell me—what was it?"

"Do you remember," said Smike, in a low voice, and glancing fear-

The recognition.

fully round, " do you remember my telling you of the man who first took me to the school ? "

" Yes, surely."

" I raised my eyes just now towards that tree—that one with the thick trunk—and there, with his eyes fixed on me, he stood."

" Only reflect for one moment," said Nicholas; " granting for an instant that it's likely he is alive and wandering about a lonely place like this, so far removed from the public road, do you think that at this distance of time you could possibly know that man again ? "

" Anywhere—in any dress," returned Smike ; " but just now, he stood leaning upon his stick and looking at me, exactly as I told you I remembered him. He was dusty with walking, and poorly dressed —I think his clothes were ragged—but directly I saw him, the wet night, his face when he left me, the parlour I was left in, and the people that were there, all seemed to come back together. When he knew I saw him, he looked frightened, for he started and shrunk away. I have thought of him by day, and dreamt of him by night. He looked in my sleep when I was quite a little child, and has looked in my sleep ever since, as he did just now."

Nicholas endeavoured, by every persuasion and argument he could think of, to convince the terrified creature that his imagination had deceived him, and that this close resemblance between the creation of his dreams and the man he supposed he had seen was but a proof of it ; but all in vain. When he could persuade him to remain for a few moments in the care of the people to whom the house belonged, he instituted a strict inquiry whether any stranger had been seen, and searched himself behind the tree, and through the orchard, and upon the land immediately adjoining, and in every place near, where it was possible for a man to lie concealed, but all in vain. Satisfied that he was right in his original conjecture, he ultimately applied himself to calming the fears of Smike, which after some time he partially succeeded in doing, though not in removing the impression upon his mind, for he still declared again and again in the most solemn and fervid manner, that he had positively seen what he described, and that nothing could ever remove his firm conviction of its reality.

And now Nicholas began to see that hope was gone, and that upon the partner of his poverty, and the sharer of his better fortune, the world was closing fast. There was little pain, little uneasiness, but there was no rallying, no effort, no struggle for life. He was worn and wasted to the last degree ; his voice had sunk so low, that he could scarce be heard to speak. Nature was thoroughly exhausted, and he had lain him down to die.

On a fine, mild autumn day, when all was tranquil and at peace, when the soft sweet air crept in at the open window of the quiet room, and not a sound was heard but the gentle rustling of the leaves, Nicholas sat in his old place by the bedside, and knew that the, time was nearly come. So very still it was, that every now and then he bent down his ear to listen for the breathing of him who lay asleep, as if to assure himself that life was still there, and that he had not fallen into that deep slumber from which on earth there is no waking.

While he was thus employed, the closed eyes opened, and on the pale face there came a placid smile.

" That's well," said Nicholas. " The sleep has done you good."

" I have had such pleasant dreams," was the answer. " Such pleasant, happy dreams!"

" Of what?" said Nicholas.

The dying boy turned towards him, and putting his arm about his neck, made answer, " I shall soon be there!"

After a short silence, he spoke again.

" I am not afraid to die," he said, " I am quite contented. I almost think that if I could rise from this bed quite well, I would not wish to do so now. You have so often told me we shall meet again— so very often lately, and now I feel the truth of that so strongly—that I can even bear to part from you."

The trembling voice and tearful eye, and the closer grasp of the arm which accompanied these latter words, showed how they filled the speaker's heart; nor were there wanting indications of how deeply they had touched the heart of him to whom they were addressed.

" You say well," returned Nicholas at length, " and comfort me very much, dear fellow. Let me hear you say you are happy, if you can."

" I must tell you something first. I should not have a secret from you. You would not blame me at a time like this, I know."

" *I* blame you!" exclaimed Nicholas.

" I am sure you would not. You asked me why I was so changed, and—and sat so much alone. Shall I tell you why?"

" Not if it pains you," said Nicholas. " I only asked that I might make you happier if I could."

" I know—I felt that at the time." He drew his friend closer to him. " You will forgive me; I could not help it, but though I would have died to make her happy, it broke my heart to see—I know he loves her dearly—Oh! who could find that out so soon as I!"

The words which followed were feebly and faintly uttered, and broken by long pauses; but from them Nicholas learnt, for the first time, that the dying boy, with all the ardour of a nature concentrated on one absorbing, hopeless, secret passion, loved his sister Kate.

He had procured a lock of her hair, which hung at his breast, folded in one or two slight ribands she had worn. He prayed that when he was dead, Nicholas would take it off, so that no eyes but his might see it, and that when he was laid in his coffin and about to be placed in the earth, he would hang it round his neck again, that it might rest with him in the grave.

Upon his knees Nicholas gave him this pledge, and promised again that he should rest in the spot he had pointed out. They embraced, and kissed each other on the cheek.

" Now," he murmured, " I am happy."

He fell into a slight slumber, and waking, smiled as before; then spoke of beautiful gardens, which he said stretched out before him, and were filled with figures of men, women, and many children, all with light upon their faces; then whispered that it was Eden—and so died.

Shower Baths, Japanned Bamboo, with Brass Force-pump attached, to throw the water into the cistern, the very best made, with copper conducting tubes, and curtains complete, £5.

Hip Baths, Japanned Bamboo, £1. 2s.

Spunging Baths, Round, 30 inches diameter, 7 inches deep, 20s.

Open Baths, 3 ft. 6 in. long, 30s.; 4 ft. long, 35s.; 4 ft. 6in. long, 50s.; 5 ft. long, 60s.; 5 ft. 6 in. long, 70s.

Feet Baths, Japanned Bamboo, small size, 6s. 6d.; large, 7s 6d.; tub shape, with hoops, 11s.

Table Lamps, Bronze or Gilt, with ground glass globe shades.

Hall Lamps or Lanterns, with glass shade over top, complete with burner, Bronzed or Gilt.

Bottle Jacks, Japanned, 7s. 6d.; Brass, 9s. 6d. each.

Brass Stair Rods, per doz. 21 inches long, 3s. 0d.; 24 in. 3s. 9d.; 27 in. 4s. 6d.; 30 in. 5s. 6d.

Brass Curtain Poles, warranted solid, 1½ inch diameter, 1s. 3d. per foot; 2 in. 1s. 8d. per foot.

Brass Poles, complete with end ornaments, rings, hooks and brackets, 3ft. long, 14s.; 3ft. 6 in. 16s.; 4ft. 18s. 6d.

Brass Curtain Bands, 1¼ in. wide, 2s. per pair, 1½ in. 2s. 6d.; 2 in. 3s. 6d. Richer patterns, 1¼ in. 4s.; 2 in. 5s.

Finger Plates for Doors, newest and richest patterns, long, 1s. 2d.; short, 10d. each.

Copper Coal Scoops, small, 10s. 6d.; middle, 13s. large, 14s. 6d. Helmet Shape, 15s. 0d., 16s. 6d., 18s. 6d.; Square Shape, with Hand Scoop, 28s.

Copper Tea Kettles, Oval Shape, very strong, with barrel handle, 2 quarts, 5s. 6d.; 3 quarts, 6s.; 4 quarts, 7s. The strongest quality made, 2 quarts 9s. 6d.; 3 quarts, 10s. 6d.; 4 quarts, 11s. 6d.

Copper Stewpans; Soup or Stock Pots, and Fish Kettles, with Brazing Pan; Saucepans & Preserving Pans; Cutlet Pans, Frying Pans, and Omelette Pans, at prices proportionate with the above.

Copper Warming Pans, with handles, for fire, 6s. 6d. to 9s. 6d.; Ditto, for water, 9s. 6d.

Fire Irons.

Large strong Wrought Iron, for Kitchens, 5s.6d. to 12s. 0
Wrought Iron, suitable for Servants' Bed Rooms   2 0
Small Polished Steel, for better Bed Rooms   .   4 6
Large ditto, for Libraries   :   .   7 0
Ditto ditto, for Dining Rooms   .   .   8 6
Ditto ditto, with Cut Heads, for ditto .   .   11 6
Ditto very highly polished Steel, plain good pattern 20 0
Ditto ditto, richly cut   .   25s. to 50 0

Cruet Frames, Black Japanned, with 3 Glasses, 3s. 8d.; 4 Glasses, 4s. 9d.; 5 Glasses, 6s.; 6 Glasses, 7s.

Corkscrews, Patent, 3s. 6d. each; Common ditto, 6d., 9d., 1s., 1s. 6d., and 2s.

Smoke Jack, with Chains and Spit, £6. Superior Self-acting do. with Dangle and Horizontal Spit, £10. N. B. Experienced Workmen employed to clean, repair, and oil Smoke Jacks, which are so constantly put out of order by the treatment they meet with from chimney sweepers.

Captains' Cabin Lamps, with 1 quart kettles, 6s.

Britannia Metal Goods.

To hold . -	1½ Pts.	1 Qt.	2½ Pts.
Teapots, with Black Handles and Black Knobs .	1s. 6d.	2s. 0d.	2s. 9d.
Ditto, very strong .	3 0	3 6	4 0
Ditto, with Pearl Knobs	4 6	5 6	6 6
Ditto with Pearl Knobs and Metal Handles .	6 6	8 0	9 6

Coffee Biggins, 1s. 6d. each size extra.
Table Candlesticks, 8 in. 3s. per pair; 9in. 4s. 6d.; 10in. 7s. 6d.
Chamber Candlesticks with Extinguishers, 2s. each.
Ditto with Gadroon Edges, complete with Snuffers and Extinguisher, 4s. each.
Mustards, with Blue Earthen Lining, 1s. each.
Salt Cellars with ditto, 1s. 4d. per pair.
Pepper Boxes, 1s. each.

Britannia Metal Hot Water Dishes, with wells for gravy, and gadroon edges, 16 inches long, 30s.; 18 in., 36s.; 20 in., 43s.; 22 in., 51s.; 24 in., 57s. Hot Water Plates, 6s. 6d. each. Block Tin ditto, with loose earthen tops, 2s. 3d. each.

Reading Candlesticks, with Shade and Light to slide, one light, 5s. 6d.; two lights, 7s. 6d.

Coffee Filterers, for making Coffee without boiling.

To hold .	1 Pint.	1½ Pts.	1 Qt.	3 Pts.
Best Block Tin .	4s. 0d.	4s. 6d.	5s. 6d.	7s. 0d.
Bronzed . .	5 6	6 6	7 6	9 6

Beart's Patent Pneumatic Filterer, which will make Coffee with boiling water in five minutes, as clear as crystal, without waste, and superior in flavour to that made by any other mode. 8s., 10s., & 12s.

Etnas, for boiling a Pint of Water in three minutes, 3s. each; larger size, 4s. each.

Coffee and **Pepper Mills,** small, 3s.; middle, 4s.; large, 4s. 6d.
Ditto, to fix, small, 4s. 6d.; middle, 5s. 6d.; large, 6s. 6d.

Iron Digesters, for making Soup, to hold 2 galls. 7s.; 3 galls. 9s. 6d.; 4 galls. 13s.

Tea Urns, Globe shape. to hold four quarts, 27s. each. Modern Shapes, 45s. to 60s. each.

Improved Wove Wire Gauze Window Blinds, in mahogany frames, made to any size, and painted to any shade of colour, 2s. 3d. per square foot.
Ornamenting with shaded lines, 1s. 6d. each blind.
Ditto, with lines and corner ornaments, 3s. each blind.
Blinds, ornamented with landscape, in mahogany frames, 4s. per square foot.
Old Blind Frames filled with new wire, and painted any colour, at 1s. 4d. per square foot.

Servants' Wire Lanterns, Open Tops, with Doors, 1s. 6d. each. Closed Tops, with Doors, 2s.

Rush Safes, Open Tops, 2s. 3d. each. Closed Tops, with Doors, 2s. 9d. each.

Fire Guards, painted Green, with Dome Tops, 14 inch, 1s. 6d.; 16 in. 1s. 9d.; 18 in. 2s. 3d. Brass Wire, 6s., 6s. 6d.. and 7s. 6d.

Egg Whisks, Tinned Wire, 10d. each.

Wire Work.—All kinds of useful and ornamental Wire Work made to order.

Family Weighing Machines, or Balances, complete, with weights from ¼ oz. to 14lbs., 26s.

Ditto Patent Spring Weighing Machines, which do not require weights, 6s. 6d. to 22s.

DISH COVERS.

Inches long	9	10	11	12	14	16	18	Set of 6.	Set of 7.
The commonest are in sets of the six first sizes, which cannot be separated	...	...	...	...	...	...		£0 6s. 6d	
Block Tin . . .	1s. 6d	1s. 9d	2s. 0d	2s. 6d	3s. 3d	3s. 6d	5s. 6d	0 11 6	£0 17s. 0d
Ditto, Anti-Patent shape . .	1 9	2 0	2 6	3 0	4 0	4 6	8 0	0 16 0	1 4 0
Ditto, O. G. shape . .	2 0	2 6	3 0	3 6	4 6	6 0	8 6	1 1 0	1 9 6
Ditto, Patent Imperial Silver shape. The Tops raised in one piece, the very best made, except Plated or Silver . .	3 6	4 0	4 9	6 0	7 6	9 6	11 6	1 15 0	2 5 0
Wove Wire Fly-proof, tin rims, apanned .	...	2 0	...	2 6	3 0	3 6	4 6		

FENDERS.

The immense variety which the Show Rooms contain, and the constant change of patterns of Fenders, render it impossible to give the prices of but a small portion of them. The following Scale, however, may be taken as a guide, and the prices generally will be found about 25 per cent. below any other house whatever.

	3 Feet.	3 Feet 3.	3 Feet 6.	3 Feet 9.	4 Feet.
	s. d.	s. d.	s. d.		
Green, with Brass Top, suitable for Bed Rooms	9 6	10 0	11 0	13s. 0d.	14s. 0d.
All Brass	8 0	9 0	10 0	11 0	11 6
Black Iron for Dining Rooms or Libraries	11 0	12 0	13 0	14 0	15 0
Bronzed for ditto	13 6	15 0	16 6	17 0	18 0
Fenders, with bright Steel Tops	16 6	17 6	20 0	22 0	24 0
Ditto, very handsome, with Steel Tops and Steel Bottom Moulding					
Very rich Pattern, with Scroll Centre, Steel Rod and Steel Ends, for Drawing Rooms [all sizes]	...	...	...	from	50 0
Green painted Wire Nursery Guard Fenders, Brass Tops, 18 in. high	15 0	16 3	17 6	18 9	20 0
Ditto, 24 inches high	18 0	19 6	21 0	22 6	24 0
Iron Kitchen Fenders, with Sliding Bars	6 0	6 6	7 0	7 6	

STOVES.

Inches wide	18	20	22	24	26	28	30	32	34	36
Elliptic or Rumford Stoves, for Bed Rooms	4s. 6d.	5s. 0d.	5s. 6d.	6s. 0d.	6s. 6d.	7s. 0d.	7s. 6d.	-	-	-
Register Stoves of superior patterns	-	-	-	14 0	15 2	16 4	17 6	18s. 8d.	19s. 10	21s. 0d

Register Stoves, fine Cast, 3 feet wide, 2*l*. 5*s*., 2*l*. 10*s*., and 3*l*.—Ground Bright Front Register Stoves with Bronzed and Steel Ornaments, and with bright and black bars, 3 feet wide, 4*l*. 10*s*., 5*l*. and 5*l*. 10*s*.
Ironing Stoves for Laundries, complete, with Frame and Ash Pan, 1*l*. 5*s*.

KITCHEN RANGES.

To fit an opening of	3 Ft. 2.	3 Ft. 4.	3 Ft. 6.	4 Ft.	4 Ft. 4.	5 Ft.
With Oven and Boiler	50s.	54s.	58s.			
Self-acting ditto, with Oven and Boiler, Sliding Cheek, and Wrought Iron Bars (recommended)	90	95	100	110s.	126s.	140s.

Iron Saucepans and Tea Kettles.

	1 pint.	1½ pint.	1 Quart.	3 pint.	2 Quart.	3 Quart.	4 Quart.	6 Quart.	8 Quart.
Iron Saucepan and Cover	0s. 11d.	1s. 1d.	1s. 3d.	1s. 6d.	1s. 9d.	2s. 2d.	2s. 8d.	3s. 6d.	4s. 0d.
Iron Stewpan and Cover	...	...	1 4	1 10	2 3	3 3	4 0	5 6	6 6
Round Iron Tea Kettles	...	...	...	...	2 9	4 3	5 0	7 0	9 0
Oval ditto	...	...	...	...	3 3	4 9	5 6	7 6	9 6

Iron Boiling Pots.

	2½ Gall.	3 Gall.	3½ Gall.	4 Gall.	5 Gall.	6 Gall.
Oval Iron Boiling Pot and Cover	5s. 6d.	6s. 0d.	7s. 0d.	8s. 0d.	10s. 0d.	11s. 6d.
Tea Kitchens, or Water Fountains, with Brass Pipe & Cock	13 0	14 0	14 6	16 0	18 6

Iron Coal Scoops and Boxes.

	14 in. long.	16 in. long.	18 in. long.
Coal Boxes, Japanned with Covers, ornamented with Gold Lines	10s. 6d.	12s. 6d.	16s. 6d.
Coal Scoops, Iron, for Kitchen Use	1 6	2 6	3 6
Ditto, lined with Zinc, the most serviceable article of the kind ever made	5 0	6 6	7 6
Upright Hods	1 6	2 6	3 6

Japanned Goods.

Inches long	18	20	22	24	26	28	30
TEA TRAYS, good common quality	1s. 3d.	1s. 6d.	1s. 9d.	2s. 3d.	2s. 9d.	3s. 3d.	3s. 9d.
Ditto, best common quality	2 6	3 0	3 6	4 6	5 6	6 0	7 0
Ditto, paper shape, black	5 6	7 0	8 0	9 6	11 0	12 6	14 0
Ditto, Gothic paper shape, black	9 6	11 0	12 6	14 0	15 6	17 0	19 0

Bread and Knife Trays, each 9d., 1s., 1s. 6d., 2s. and 2s. 6d.
Middle quality ditto, at 2s. and 2s. 6d.
Best quality ditto, Gothic shape, 3s. 6d., 4s. 6d. and 5s. 6d. each.
Tea Trays, paper, Gothic shape, in sets of one each of 18, 24, and 30 inches, £5.
Ditto, richest patterns, the set, £6. and £7.
Toast Racks, plain black, 1s. 6d. Ornamented, 2s.
Ditto, marone or green, ornamented all over, 2s. 9d.
Cheese Trays, 2s., 2s. 6d., 3s., and 3s. 6d.
Snuffer Trays, 6d., 9d., 1s., 1s. 3d., and 1s. 6d.
Paper ditto, 2s., 2s. 6d., 3s., 3s. 6d., and 4s.
Paper Decanter Stands, plain black, 3s. 6d. per pair.
Ditto, ditto, red, 4s. per pair.

Plate Warmers, upright shape, with gilt lines, 21s.
Ditto, long shape, £1. 10s.
Toilet Cans and Toilet Pails, 7s. 6d. each.
Chamber Slop Pails, japanned green outside and red inside, small, 3s.; middle, 4s.; large, 5s. 6d.
Chamber Candlesticks, complete, with Snuffers and Extinguisher, 6d. Ditto, better, 9d. to 3s.
Cash Boxes, with Tumbler Locks, small size, 5s. 6d.
Ditto, ditto, middle size, 6s. 6d.; large size, 7s. 6d.
Ditto, ditto, with Patent Locks, 10s. 6d.
Deed Boxes, Japanned Brown, with Locks, 12 inches long, 11s.; 14 in. 15s.; 16 in. 18s.; 18 in. 21s.
Candle Boxes, 1s. 4d. each.
Candle or Rush Safes, 2s. 6d. each.
Cinder Pails or Sifters, Japanned, Brown, 9s. 6d. each.

TIN GOODS.

To hold	1 Pt.	1 Qt.	3 Pt.	2 Qt.	3 Qt.	4 Qt.	6 Qt.	8 Qt.	9 Qt.	10 Qt.
SAUCEPANS, strong common. with Covers	0s. 3d	0s. 4d	0s. 6d	0s. 8d	0s. 10	1s. 1d	1s. 2d	1s. 4d	1s. 8d	2s. 0d
Strongest Tin, with Iron Handles	0 9	1 0	1 4	1 10	2 2	2 9	3. 6	4 0	4 6	5 0
Block Tin	1 4	2 0	2 6	3 0	3 9	4 6	6 0			
Saucepans and Steamers	—	—	—	2 9	3 6	4 0	4 6			

Coffee and Chocolate Pots, Block Tin, to hold 1 quart, 1s. 4d.; 3 pints, 1s. 10d.; 2 quarts, 2s. 3d
Colanders, small, 10d.; large, 1s. 4d.
Ditto, Block Tin, small, 3s. 6d.; large, 4s. 6d.
Dripping Pans, with wells, small, 3s.; mid., 6s.; large, 7s.
Fish Kettles, small, 4s. 6d.; middle, 5s. 6d.; large, 6s.6d.

Turbot Pans, or Kettles, Turbot shape, 21s.
Meat Screens for Bottle Jacks, 15s. each.
Ditto, Wood, Elliptic Shape, lined with Tin, upon Rollers, with Shelf and Door, 3 feet wide, £1. 10s.
Larger sizes in proportion.
Stomach Warmers, each 2s. 6d.

To hold	3 Pts.	2 Qts.	3 Qts.	4 Qts.
TEA KETTLES, Oval shape, strong Common Tin	1s. 0d.	1s. 2d.	1s. 4d.	1s. 6d.
Ditto, strongest Tin	2 0	2 6	3 0	3 6
Block Tin, with Iron Handles and Iron Spouts	4 0	4 3	5 3	6 3
Oblong shape, with round Barrel Handles and Iron Spout	4 9	5 6	6 6	7 6

RIPPON & BURTON'S Prices of STRONG SETS of IRON and TIN
KITCHEN FURNITURE.

Small Set.

1 Bread Grater	0s.	6
1 Pair Brass Candlesticks	2	6
1 Bottle Jack	7	6
1 Tin Candlestick	1	3
1 Candle Box	0	10
1 Meat Chopper	1	6
1 Cinder Sifter	1	0
1 Coffee Pot	1	0
1 Colander	1	0
1 Dripping Pan & Stand	5	0
1 Dust Pan	0	6
1 Slice	0	6
1 Fish Kettle	4	0
1 Flour Box	0	8
2 Flat Irons	1	8
1 Fryingpan	1	2
1 Gridiron	1	0
1 Mustard Pot	1	0
1 Salt Cellar	0	8
1 Pepper Box	0	6
1 Block Tin Butter Sauce-pan	1	6
2 Iron Saucepans	6	0
2 Iron Stewpans	3	6
1 Boiling Pot, Iron	7	0
1 Set of Skewers	0	6
6 Knives and Forks	4	6
3 Spoons	0	9
1 Tea Pot and 1 Tea Tray	6	0
1 Toasting Fork	0	6
1 Tea Kettle	4	6

£3 10 0

Middle Set.

1 Bread Grater	1s.	0
1 Pair Brass Candlesticks	3	0
1 Bottle Jack	7	6
1 Pair of Bellows	1	4
2 Tin Candlesticks	2	6
1 Candle Box	1	4
1 Cheese Toaster	1	4
1 Chopper	1	9
1 Cinder Sifter	1	3
1 Coffee Pot	1	3
1 Colander	1	3
1 Dripping Pan & Stand	5	6
1 Dust Pan	0	8
1 Fish Slice	1	0
1 Fish Kettle	5	6
Pepper and Flour Boxes	1	2
3 Flat Irons	3	0
1 Fryingpan	1	9
1 Gridiron	1	3
2 Jelly Moulds	5	6
1 Mustard Pot	1	0
1 Salt Cellar	0	8
1 Plate Basket	5	6
2 Block Tin Saucepans	3	6
3 Iron Saucepans	7	6
1 Saucepan and Steamer	3	6
1 Large Boiling Pot	9	6
3 Stewpans	7	0
1 Set of Skewers	0	6
6 Knives and Forks	5	6
6 Iron Spoons	1	6
1 Tea Pot & 1 Tea Tray	6	0
1 Toasting Fork	0	6
1 Tea Kettle	6	6

£5 7 6

Large Set.

1 Bread Grater	1s.	0
1 Pair Brass Candlesticks	3	6
1 Bottle Jack	9	6
1 Pair of Bellows	2	0
2 Deep Tin Candlesticks	2	8
1 Candle Box	1	4
1 Cheese Toaster	1	10
1 Chopper, for Meat	2	0
1 Cinder Sifter	1	6
1 Coffee Pot	2	3
1 Coal Shovel	2	6
1 Colander	1	6
1 Dripping Pan and Stand	7	0
1 Dust Pan	1	0
1 Egg Slice	0	6
1 Fish Slice	1	3
2 Fish Kettles	10	6
1 Flour Box	0	6
3 Flat Irons	4	0
2 Fryingpans	4	6
1 Gridiron, with fluted Bars	3	6
1 Wood Meat Screen	30	0
3 Jelly Moulds	8	3
1 Mustard Pot	1	0
1 Salt Cellar	0	8
1 Pepper Box	0	6
1 Wicker Plate Basket, lined with Tin	7	6
3 Block Tin Saucepans	6	0
4 Iron Saucepans	12	3
1 Saucepan and Steamer	4	6
1 Large Boiling Pot, Iron	10	6
4 Stewpans, Iron	9	0
2 Sets of Skewers	1	0
6 Knives and Forks	5	6
6 Iron Spoons	1	6
1 Tea Pot	3	0
1 Tea Tray	4	0
1 Toasting Fork	1	0
1 Egg Whisk	0	9
1 Tea Kettle	7	6

£8 19 3

In submitting to the Public the foregoing Catalogue, RIPPON & BURTON beg to state, that they will continue to offer Articles of the VERY BEST MANUFACTURE only, as they have hitherto done, at prices which, when compared with others of the same quality, will be found much lower than any that have ever yet been quoted. The knowledge which RIPPON & BURTON have obtained by their long connexion with the largest Manufacturers, and the principle upon which they conduct their business, afford great advantages to the purchaser; all Articles being bought in very large quantities for Cash, and marked for sale at Cash prices, which are not subject to discount or abatement of any kind; thus giving the ready money purchaser all the advantages that can be obtained over the plan usually adopted by others, of marking their goods at prices which will enable them to give credit, and pay for that credit which they take; allowing those, who pay cash, 5 per cent. discount from prices 25 per cent. higher than they should fairly be charged. The many years RIPPON & BURTON's business has been established, and the very extensive patronage they have met with, will be some proof that the public have not been deceived by them; but, as a further security against the impositions practised by many, RIPPON & BURTON will continue to exchange, or return the money for every article that is not approved of, if returned in good condition and free of expense within one month of the time it was purchased.

J. Bradley, Printer, 76, Great Titchfield-street, London.

The Saint Ann's Society Schools,

BRIXTON HILL AND ALDERSGATE,

INSTITUTED 1709,

Supported by Voluntary Contributions,

For Educating, Clothing and wholly Maintaining the Legitimate Children of Necessitous Parents, and of those more especially who have seen Better Days,

FROM ALL PARTS, WHETHER ORPHANS OR NOT.

Under the Patronage of

HER MOST GRACIOUS MAJESTY.
HER MAJESTY THE QUEEN DOWAGER.
H. R. H. THE DUCHESS OF KENT.
H. R. H. THE LANDGRAVINE OF HESSE HOMBERG.
H. R. H. THE DUKE OF SUSSEX, K. G.

President.
HIS GRACE THE ARCHBISHOP OF CANTERBURY.

Ladies President.
HER GRACE THE DUCHESS OF NORTHUMBERLAND.
MRS. PARTIS.

THIS Institution, which affords relief to the fallen parent and helps him in the maintenance of his child, is the *only Charity*, supported by voluntary contributions and unchecked by local boundaries, which feels for the agonized father or mother in times of sudden misfortune, and aids *at once*, without waiting till their offspring becomes an orphan.

The SAINT ANN'S SOCIETY SCHOOLS were founded by the union of a few individuals in 1709, to form a Day School, each member presenting a child in turn. That School still exists, where 30 Boys and 30 Girls are clothed and educated, and 2 Girls also wholly maintained; but the nobler Charity has been grafted on it.

The Asylum at Brixton contains at present 160 Children, who are *wholly maintained Clothed* and *Educated* by the Society, which waits but the extension of its Funds to extend its benefits.

Children from all parts of the world are eligible for admission.

A *Building Fund* has recently been established for the purpose of enlarging the Country Asylum, to afford greater accommodation to the inmates, and to meet the increasing claims of Candidates.

So laudable an Institution surely cannot fail to obtain the warm approbation and the best wishes of every reflecting and benevolent member of the community. *On what portion of our fellow creatures can the bounty of the respectable and wealthy classes of society be more appropriately and beneficially conferred, than on the helpless and unoffending offspring of the numerous individuals who have been visited by adversity, and crushed by poverty?* How often, in this age of competition and enterprise, has the Merchant, the Manufacturer, the Trader, the Agriculturist, notwithstanding the utmost exertion of talent and industry, been reduced to the privations and the hardships attendant on the failure of his reasonable calculations! And what greater solace can be offered to the mind of a father or a mother, under such melancholy circumstances, than the cheering reflection that their destitute Children may find an Asylum in an Institution, where, protected from pauperism, and from constant exposure to vicious example, they may in some degree obtain those advantages which their unfortunate parents have no longer the means of bestowing.

For such an Institution,

the continued liberality of the Public is most respectfully and earnestly solicited.

A Yearly Subscription of One Guinea or more constitutes an *Annual* Governor.

A Subscription of Ten Guineas or upwards at one payment constitutes a Governor for *Life.*

Governors are entitled to Votes, at the *half-yearly* Ballot for the admission of Children into the *Brixton Asylum*, according to the amount of their Subscription: they are likewise, in rotation, from the date of their Subscription, entitled to present a Child into the *Day School* in Town.

Every Governor has the right to nominate a Candidate, Boy or Girl, at each Election, either from the Children in the *Day* School, or not; but all Children are required to be between the ages of *Seven* and *Eleven* years.

Every Governor has as many Votes at each Election as there are Children to be admitted, and may give the *whole* of them to any one Candidate, or divide them, instead of being restricted to the giving a *single vote* to any one child.

Governors become entitled to vote, and to all other privileges, *immediately* on the payment of their Subscriptions.

Proprietors of Pulpits, who may lend them for a Sermon in aid of the Charity, become Honorary Life Governors.

Clergymen preaching for the Charity receive the privileges of Life Governors; or, should they prefer it from being interested in any case at the Ballot, may receive the privilege of a Governor at the next Election for each Guinea collected after their Sermon.

The Executors of Benefactors by will become entitled to the privileges of Life Governors according to the amount of the Bequest.

A Contribution of One Hundred Guineas, *in one payment*, entitles the Donor to the privilege of immediately placing a Child, either Boy or Girl, on the Foundation at *Brixton*.

A Contribution of Two Hundred and Fifty Guineas, in one payment, entitles the Donor to the privilege, *for life*, of always keeping one Child, either Boy or Girl, on the Foundation at Brixton. And a Contribution of Seven Hundred and Fifty Pounds, gives that privelege in perpetuity.

The Elections are half-yearly; on the second Thursday in February and August.

Lists of the Governors and of the Contributions to this Charity are published yearly, at the charge of One Shilling each, (which is applied in reduction of the Printing Expenses), and may be had on application to the Secretary, who will at all times be most happy to give any information relative to the Institution.

Subscriptions and Donations will be most thankfully received by

MATTHIAS ATTWOOD, Esq. M.P. V.P. (Treasurer), 27, Gracechurch-street.
Messrs. WILLIS, PERCIVAL & Co. 76, Lombard-street.
Messrs. WILLIAMS, DEACON & Co. Birchin-lane.
Messrs. HODGSON, British and Foreign Library, Great Marylebone-street.
Mr. NISBET, Library, Berners-street.
Mr. SAMS, Royal Subscription Library, St. James's-street.
The Rev. D. LAING, (Chaplain), 67, Great Portland-street.
Each of the HOUSE STEWARDS.———Each MEMBER of the COMMITTEE.
EDWARD FRED. LEEKS (Secretary), 2, Charlotte-row, Mansion-house, and 12, James-street, Buckingham Palace.
Mr. GEORGE BLEADEN, (Collector), 47, Lothbury.
At the Brixton Asylum, and at the Town School.

And in the Country, by the following Bankers and others, who remit the same to the Secretary Six Weeks prior to every Election.

Bath—Messrs. Tuffnell & Co. Bladud Bank.	*Liverpool*—Manchester & Liverpool District Bank.
Brighton—Mr. W. H. Parsons, Royal Marine Library.	*Maidstone*—Mr. Smith, Library.
Brixton Hill—Mr. J. Arnold; Mr. Houghton.	*Manchester*—Manchester & Liverpool District Bank.
Chelmsford—Messrs. Sparrow & Co. Bankers; Messrs. Chalk, Meggy & Chalk; Mr. H. Guy, Bookseller.	*Midhurst*—J. W. Wood, Esq.
Chesterfield—Mr. John Roberts, Post-office.	*Newbury*—Mr. Job Wells.
Chipping Sodbury—John Pater, Esq.	*Oxford*—Mr. Hobdell. [Hotel.
Croydon—Mrs. Markby, Library.	*Portsea*—Mr. R. Totterdell, Commercial
Gloucester—Mr. Lea, Library.	*Ramsgate*—Messrs. Phipps & Bleaden.
Hull—Messrs. Harrison, Watson & Locke, Bankers; Messrs. Samuel Smith, Brothers & Co. Bankers.	*Ryde*—Messrs. Hale & Co. Pier Hotel.
	Southampton—Mr. Gye, Dolphin Hotel.
	Stroud—Mr. Brisley.
	Weymouth—Messrs. Elliot, Old Bank.

FORM OF BEQUEST.

" I give and bequeath unto the Treasurer, for the time being, of an Institution called or known by the name of ' THE SAINT ANN'S SOCIETY SCHOOLS,' established in the year 1709, the sum of   to be raised and paid by and out of my ready money, plate, goods and personal effects, which by law I may or can charge with the payment of the same, (and not out of any part of my lands, tenements or hereditaments), to be applied towards carrying on the laudable designs of the said Institution."

N.B. Devises of land, or bequests of money charged on land, are void by the Statute of Mortmain; but money or stock may be given by will, the same not being directed to be laid out.

Society's Office,   EDW. FRED. LEEKS,
2, Charlotte-row, Mansion-house.   Secretary.

Recently published,

The SCRIPTURE EXERCISES, written for the Children by the Honorary Chaplain, and dedicated, by permission, to Her Majesty the Queen Dowager.

The HOLY BIBLE, written at various periods during 4000 years, THE ONE DESIGN OF ONE ETERNAL MIND; a series of Texts, illustrating the connection between the Old and New Testaments. By the Rev. D. LAING, M.A., Honorary Chaplain to the St. Ann's Society Schools, and Chaplain to the Middlesex Hospital.

Smith, Elder & Co., 65, Cornhill; and J. Nisbet & Co., 21, Berners-street.

Powell & Brewster, Printers, Hand Court, Upper Thames Street.

ILLUSTRATED
BEAUTIES OF THE BALLET.

Under this title, Jefferys & Co. publish all the pleasing **Musical** novelties of the Ballet—with Portraits of the principal performers and correct representations of the respective Costumes in which the various dances are introduced :—the illustrated edition *and the only genuine Copy of the Cachucha and Valse Sentimentale* can be published alone by them :— these two popular dances form

No. 1, of the Series, WITH LIKENESS OF DUVERNAY,
price   ..   ..   **2s. 0d.**

No. 2, THE SHAWL DANCE (with Taglioni's
Portrait,)   ..   ..   **2s. 0d.**

No. 3, PAS DE DEUX (Portrait of Madame
Taglioni and Paul Taglioni)   **2s. 6d.**

No. 4, THE PAS STYRIEN (with two National
Costumes)   ..   ..   **2s. 0d.**

No. 5, THE BOHEMIAN   Do.   **2s. 0d.**

No. 6, THE GREEK ROMAIKA, (Portrait of
Celeste)   ..   ..   **2s. 0d.**

No. 7, THE POLSKI MAZOURKA (with like-
nesses of Herminie Elsler & Mad. Guibilei) **2s. 0d.**

No. 8, CVERTURE, (Spirit of Air,) ELIASON **2s. 6d.**

No 9, PAS DE SABOTS   ..   ditto   **2s. 0d.**

No. 10, CHARACTERISTIC DANCE do.   **2s. 0d.**

No. 11, VALSE NORMANDE   do.   **2s. 0d.**

No. 12, GRAND PAS DEUX   do.   **2s. 0d.**

No. 13, MAZURKA in La Gitana, with fine
Portrait of MAD. TAGLIONI   **2s. 0d.**

NOTE.—The Public is cautioned against several imitations of the above works calculated to mislead those persons only under whose notice the genuine copies have not yet fallen :—the publishers issuing these spurious things have several times acknowledged the vast superiority of J. & Co.'s editions, by their endeavours to obtain the services of the Artists and Musicians engaged on the original publications ;— these attempts have, however, hitherto proved as abortive as the desire to supplant the excellent productions in question.

JEFFERYS & Co., LONDON,
and to be had of
All Music Sellers in Great Britain & Ireland.

PIANOFORTE MUSIC
FOR THE BALL-ROOM.

QUADRILLES.
(Pianoforte Solos).

•FLÉCHE'S 6th set, "THE MAIDS OF HONOUR," .. 3s.
(dedicated to the Honorable Matilda Paget).

•FLÉCHE'S 5th set, "THE COURT BEAUTIES," .. 3s.
(dedicated to the Honorable Harriett Pitt.)

•FLÉCHE'S 4th set "THE CORONATION QUADRILLES," 3s.
(dedicated to H. R. H. The Duchess of Kent).

FLÉCHE'S 3rd set, " THE BIRTH-DAY," .. 3s.
(dedicated, by command, to Her Majesty).

FLÉCHE'S 2nd set, " LA FOLIE," 3s,
(dedicated to Miss Hutchinson).

•MONTGOMERY'S "COURT QUADRILLES " with Waltz containing Rule Britannia and God save the Queen. .. 4s.

•MONTGOMERY'S *ALLBLACKS* QUADRILLES, 1st set 2s. 6d.
Ditto   Ditto   2nd set, 2s. 6d.
(These two sets contain all the Popular American Negro Melodies).

MONTANO'S Promenade Quadrilles "LE PÉRUQUIER DU REGENT," played with extraordinary éclat at all the London Promenade Concerts. .. .. 3s.

•"MY GRANDMOTHER'S QUADRILLES," containing five genuine old National Airs, arranged by Joan Strauss. .. 2s.

•"THE GIPSY QUADRILLES," containing the "GIPSY KING," the "GIPSY QUEEN," "GOING A GIPSYING," "GIPSY'S INVITATION," and "THE GREENWOOD TREE." .. .. 2s. 6d.

QUADRILLE-DUETS,
(for four hands on the Pianoforte).

"THE MAIDS OF HONOUR," by G. Fléche. .. 4s.
"THE COURT BEAUTIES," arranged by G. Fléche. 4s.
"THE BIRTH-DAY QUADRILLES," Hunten. 4s.
"LES DEUX AMIES," composed by Montgomery. 4s.
"THE FESTIVAL QUADRILLES," Ditto .. 4s.
"THE BAYADERE'S QUADRILLES," Ditto .. 4s.
"THE CORONATION QUADRILLES," arranged by Clarke. 4s.

Note.—The above Quadrilles have been selected from the Publications of the last two Seasons as the most worthy of commendation: — the Compositions by Fléche abound in sprightly and agreeable melody, richly harmonized, and well adapted for the Pianoforte, for which instrument they are expressly written, an advantage *not possessed* by the Compositions of MUSARD, TOLBECQUE, STRAUSS, and many other eminent Writers for the Dance, whose music is written for a full Band, and generally arranged by persons altogether ignorant of the capabilities of the Pianoforte.

THE QUEEN'S COUNTRY DANCES.

Her Majesty's predilection for the "good old Country Dance," has restored this species of entertainment to the ranks of Fashion, and has caused an immense demand for appropriate Music—Guinness, Weippert's principal Leader of the Court Balls, has arranged nearly fifty of the best old national airs, for the Pianoforte, precisely as they are played at the Royal Palaces, and they are now published under the title of "The QUEEN'S COUNTRY DANCES," in two sets with all the figures, by

JEFFERYS & Co., 31, Frith Street, Soho,
and may be had of every Music Seller in the Kingdom.

DR. PERRENGTON'S
TONIC APERIENT LIQUEUR.

THE mischief which is continually entailed on the Public by the use of harsh, drastic, debilitating medicines for the cure of INDIGESTION, has long been a subject of deep regret to the most distinguished members of the MEDICAL PROFESSION.

For when we consider that Indigestion mainly depends on want of VITAL TONE in the stomach ;—and that it is owing to this want of vital tone that the intestines become loaded—their secretions vitiated—the liver torpid—and that it is from the same cause that the food ferments, producing ACIDITY, FLATULENCE, HEARTBURN, and SPASM,—REASON will lead us to expect what EXPERIENCE actually proves, namely, that the use of mere purgatives for the cure of indigestion, invariably (at the expense perhaps of a transient relief) aggravates the symptoms they were intended to remove. In fact, to use the words of the em'nent ANTHONY TODD THOMPSON, M.D., F.R.S., PROFESSOR IN UNIVERSITY COLLEGE, " The secretions instead of being improved are deteriorated, owing to the constant irritation communicated through the excretory ducts, hurrying the natural functions of the liver, and thereby rendering the secretion imperfect, if not vitiated."

To put an effectual check to these evils, DR. PERRENGTON has determined to bring into popular use his

TONIC APERIENT LIQUEUR;

a Preparation, the utility of which may be estimated from the following passage in a work recently published by DR. HOLLAND, Physician Extraordinary to the QUEEN. " I wish to suggest the value of a direct combination of Tonics with Aperients ; *a form of prescription which might well be brought into more general use.* In the greater number of instances, weakness in the proper action of the bowels is the cause of costiveness, and in seeking to remove the effect by means which act through irritation merely, we do but add to the mischief. The Tonic conjoined with the Aperient enforces its action without weakening the organs."—" This practice is of more especial use in those languid and strumous habits in which strength and good digestion are so carefully to be maintained."

The name of the TONIC APERIENT LIQUEUR is a compendium of its properties. It is a TONIC containing the concentrated essence of the most valuable INDIGENOUS and EXOTIC INVIGORANTS ; strengthening the stomach, sharpening the appetite, exhilarating the spirits, promoting nutrition, and bracing the nerves. As an APERIENT, it acts with the most insurpassable gentleness and cordiality, without nausea, griping, or flatulence, whilst, to crown the whole, its taste is a combination of the slightest but finest bitterness, with the most EXQUISITE AROMA and DELICATE FLAVOUR that ever met the approbation of the most refined palate.

The following letter, the original of which may be seen at 44, Gerrard Street, was recently sent in the most handsome manner to Dr. Perrengton, and will explain the nature of some of the symptoms which this medicine is capable of removing.

TO DR. PERRENGTON.

" Sir,--Having long suffered from indigestion, with great pain after eating (whatever it might have been that I had taken), attended with constant flatulence, restless nights, and a running of clear water from the stomach, I was persuaded to try your Tonic Aperient Liqueur, and am most happy to say that after having taken a few bottles, I am so far recovered as to be able to take my meals without experiencing those pains afterwards, and I sleep soundly. It also removed bilious feelings, from which I was a great sufferer, and kept my bowels regular.

" I am, Sir, your obliged and obedient servant,
(Signed)   " W. B. ROBARTSON.
" No. 1, Ladbrooke Terrace, Notting Hill, Kensington, July 1st, 1839."

For further particulars respecting the composition and properties of this medicine, we must refer to

A POPULAR TREATISE ON THE STOMACH;
WITH CERTAIN NEW AND IMPORTANT PRINCIPLES IN THE TREATMENT OF INDIGESTION.
BY DE S. PERRENGTON, M.D.P.

A work, containing a concise but complete account of the anatomy of the digestive organs, of the causes which disorder them, and of the treatment of the most important varieties of Indigestion—especially of *Acidity, Biliousness,* and *Flatulence.* There is many an elderly gentleman who will be grateful for the observations which it offers on the Nature, Cause, and Prevention of Corpulence ; and many a young and studious dyspeptic, whose fears of mortal disease will be dispelled by the comments on Hypochondriasis ; whilst (to quote from a popular Magazine). " it is written in a style so lively and perspicuous, that no one can help reading it through when once they have taken it in hand."

This interesting work is enclosed with every bottle of the Tonic Aperient Liqueur, which is sold in bottles, at 2s. 9d., 4s. 6d., and 11s., at the

CENTRAL DEPOT, 44, GERRARD STREET, SOHO ;
At 6, Bruton Street, Bond Street ; by Powel and Co., Boston ; and by every Medicine Vendor of repute in the British Empire and the United States of America.

REFORM YOUR TAILORS' BILLS!

LADIES' ELEGANT
RIDING HABITS.

Summer Cloth	£3	3 0
Ladies' Cloth	4	4 0
Saxony Cloth	5	5 0

GENTLEMAN'S

Superfine Dress Coat	2	7 6
Extra Saxony, the best that is made	2	15 0
Superfine Frock Coat, silk facings	2	10 0
Buckskin Trousers	1	1 0
Cloth or double-milled Cassimere ditto - 17s. 6d. to	1	5 0
New Patterns, Summer Trousers, 10s. 6d. per pr. or 3 pr.	1	10 0
Summer Waistcoats, 7s.; or 3,	1	0 0
Splendid Silk Valencia Dress Waistcoats, 10s. 6d. each, or 3,	1	10 0

FIRST-RATE
BOYS' CLOTHING.

Skeleton Dresses	£0	15 0
Tunic and Hussar Suits,	1	10 0
Camlet Cloaks	0	8 6
Cloth Cloaks	0	15 6

GENTLEMAN'S

Morning Coats and Dressing Gowns	0	18 0
Petersham Great Coats and Pilot P Jackets, bound, and Velvet Collar	1	10 0
Camlet Cloak, lined all through	1	1 0
Cloth Opera Cloak	1	10 0
Army Cloth Blue Spanish Cloak, 9½ yards round	2	10 0
Super Cloth ditto	3	3 0
Cloth or Tweed Fishing or Travelling Trousers	0	13 6

THE CELEBRITY THE
CITY CLOTHING ESTABLISHMENT

Has so many years maintained, being the

BEST AS WELL AS THE CHEAPEST HOUSE,

Renders any Assurance as to STYLE and QUALITY unnecessary. The NOBILITY and GENTRY are invited to the
SHOW-ROOMS, TO VIEW THE IMMENSE & SPLENDID STOCK.

The numerous Applications for
REGIMENTALS & NAVAL UNIFORMS,

Have induced E. P. D. & SON to make ample Arrangements for an extensive Business in this particular Branch: a perusal of their List of Prices (which can be had gratis) will show the EXORBITANT CHARGES to which OFFICERS OF THE ARMY AND NAVY HAVE SO LONG BEEN SUBJECTED.

CONTRACTS BY THE YEAR,

Originated by E. P. D. & SON, are universally adopted by CLERGYMEN and PROFESSIONAL GENTLEMEN, as being MORE REGULAR and ECONOMICAL. THE PRICES ARE THE LOWEST EVER OFFERED:—

Two Suits per Year, Superfine,	7 7	—Extra Saxony, the best that is made,	8 5
Three Suits per Year, ditto	10 17	—Extra Saxony, ditto	12 6
Four Suits per Year, ditto	14 6	—Extra Saxony, ditto	15 18

(THE OLD SUITS TO BE RETURNED.)

Capital Shooting Jackets, 21s. The new Waterproof Cloak, 21s.

COUNTRY GENTLEMEN,

Preferring their Clothes Fashionably made, at a FIRST-RATE LONDON HOUSE, are respectfully informed, that by a Post-paid Application, they will receive a Prospectus explanatory of the System of Business, Directions for Measurement, and a Statement of Prices. Or if Three or Four Gentlemen unite, one of the Travellers will be dispatched immediately to wait on them.

STATE LIVERIES SPLENDIDLY MADE.
Footman's Suit of Liveries, £3 3. Scarlet Hunting Coat, £3 3

E. P. DOUDNEY AND SON,
49, LOMBARD-STREET. 1784.
Established

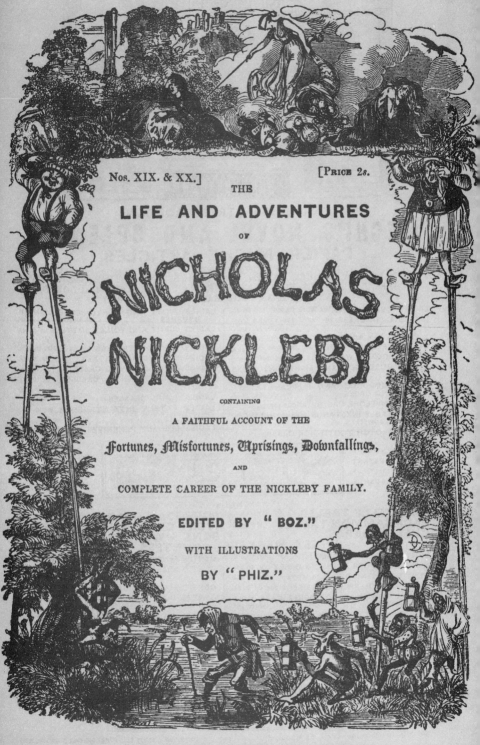

Nos. XIX. & XX.]
[Price 2s.

THE
LIFE AND ADVENTURES

of

NICHOLAS
NICKLEBY

CONTAINING

A FAITHFUL ACCOUNT OF THE

Fortunes, Misfortunes, Uprisings, Downfallings,

AND

COMPLETE CAREER OF THE NICKLEBY FAMILY.

EDITED BY "BOZ."

WITH ILLUSTRATIONS

BY "PHIZ."

LONDON: CHAPMAN AND HALL, 186, STRAND.

LEADENHALL STREET, LONDON.

MECHI'S NOVEL AND SPLENDID
PAPIER MACHÉ ARTICLES,

CONSISTING OF

TEA TRAYS, TEA CADDIES, LADIES' WORK, CAKE, AND NOTE BASKETS, CARD CASES, CARD POOLS, FRUIT PLATES, FRUIT BASKETS, NETTING BOXES, HAND SCREENS, CARD RACKS, CHESS BOARDS.

LADIES' COMPANIONS, or Work Cases 15s. to 2l.	LADIES' IVORY AND TORTOISESHELL HAIR BRUSHES . . . at 2l. to 5l. per Pair.
LADIES' CARD CASES, in Pearl, Ivory, and Tortoiseshell . . . . 10s. to 5l. each.	LADIES' SCENT AND TOILET BOTTLES in great variety.
LADIES' WORK BOXES . 25s. to 10 Guineas.	LADIES' SCOTCH TEA CADDIES . 21s. to 40s.
LADIES' DRESSING CASES 2l. 10s. to 90 Guineas.	LADIES' PLAYING CARD BOXES . 30s. to 5l.
LADIES' SCOTCH WORK BOXES at all prices.	LADIES' JAPAN DRESSING CASES 7s. to 15s.
LADIES' ROSEWOOD AND MAHOGANY DESKS 12s. 6d. to 10 Guineas.	LADIES' TORTOISESHELL DRESSING & SIDE COMBS.
LADIES' MOROCCO AND RUSSIA LEATHER WRITING CASES . . . . 5s. to 5l.	LADIES' HAND GLASSES.
LADIES' ENVELOPE CASES, various prices.	LADIES' PATENT INSTANTANEOUS PEN-MAKERS . . . . 10s. 6d. and 12s. 6d.
LADIES' TABLE INKSTANDS, made of British Coal (quite a novelty) . . . 7s. 6d. to 30s.	LADIES' ELEGANT PENKNIVES AND SCISSORS 5s. to 30s.
LADIES' SCOTCH TOOTH-PICK CASES.	

INVENTOR OF THE PATENT CASTELLATED TOOTH BRUSHES.

INVENTOR OF THE MECHIAN PORTABLE DRESSING CASES.

MISCELLANEOUS.

BAGATELLE TABLES	£3 10 to 5 0	POPE JOAN BOARDS	£0 13 to 1 0
BACKGAMMON TABLES	1 0 to 5 10	IVORY CHESSMEN	1 1 to 10 10
CHESS BOARDS	0 4 to 3 0	BONE & WOOD DITTO	Various Prices.

WHIST MARKERS, COUNTERS, &c.

GENT.'S DRESSING CASES, in Wood	2l. to 50l.	GENT.'S FANCY PENKNIVES 5s. to 15s.
GENT.'S LEATHER DRESSING CASES 25s. to 24l.		GENT.'S PEARL AND SHELL POCKET COMBS 3s. 6d. to 15s.
GENT.'S WRITING DESKS, in Wood	30s. to 16l.	
GENT.'S LEATHER WRITING DESKS 24s. 6d. to 5l.		GENT.'S SCOTCH CIGAR BOXES 3s. 6d. to 40s.
GENT.'S WRITING & DRESSING CASE COMBINED . . . . 5l. to 16l.		GENT.'S COAL AND EBONY INKSTANDS 7s. 6d. to 50s.
GENT.'S POCKET BOOKS WITH INSTRUMENTS 20s. to 46s.		GENT.'S IVORY AND FANCY WOOD HAIR BRUSHES . . . . 20s. to 2l. 10s.
GENT.'S ELEGANT CASES OF RAZORS 12s. to 8l.		GENT.'S SETS OF BRUSHES in Russia Cases 25s. to 4l. 10s.
GENT.'S SEVEN DAY RAZORS, in Fancy Woods 25s. to 5l.		GENT.'S SILVER AND IVORY SHAVING BRUSHES In elegant Patterns.
GENT.'S RAZOR STROPS . 2s. to 30s.		
GENT.'S SPORTING KNIVES . 19s. to 5l.		GENT.'S SILVER AND SHELL TABLETS.

MECHI,

MECHI,

ON MONDAY, DECEMBER 2, WILL BE PUBLISHED,

No. I.,

TO BE COMPLETED IN NOT EXCEEDING TWENTY MONTHLY NUMBERS,

PRICE ONE SHILLING EACH,

OF

POOR JACK.

BY CAPTAIN MARRYAT,

AUTHOR OF "PETER SIMPLE," ETC. ETC.

ILLUSTRATED WITH NUMEROUS WOOD ENGRAVINGS,

FROM DRAWINGS

BY CLARKSON STANFIELD, R.A.

LONDON:
LONGMAN, ORME, BROWN, GREEN, AND LONGMANS.

*** The Conclusion of " CAPTAIN MARRYAT's DIARY IN AMERICA" will
be published early in January.

POPULAR JUVENILE BOOKS,

ELEGANTLY EMBELLISHED.

AN EXTRAORDINARY CASE OF CURE

OF THE FOLLOWING LONG-STANDING COMPLAINTS.

To Mr. Thomas Gardner, General Hygeian Agent for India.

Sir,—I am induced by a sense of gratitude to Mr. Morison, and of interest in the welfare of my fellow-creatures, to inform you of the cure performed on me by Morison's Universal Medicines.

I came to India a Private in the Artillery in 1816, and during the first few years of my residence in the country I suffered very much from illness. In 1818, at Dum Dum, I was seriously ill during six or seven successive months; and have been informed, that a funeral party was warned for my burial more than once.

In 1825, I was appointed Quarter-Master Serjeant to the 19th Regiment, and the officers of the corps can testify, that I have suffered more from bad health than is usually the fate of man. 1st. When at Agra in 1822, the Surgeon considered me a fit subject for the invalids; but being anxious to remain in the service, I was kindly permitted to do so at that period. In 1835, at Barrackpore, I was dangerously ill with pain in the lower intestines, and after a consultation of Surgeons on my case, the most active measures were resorted to for my recovery, but without avail. At this time, when in a hopeless state, a friend advised me to try Morison's Pills, which I did, taking 5 of No. 1, and most grateful was I to the Almighty for his blessing the means resorted to for my recovery. I then increased the dose gradually up to 25 and 30, taking No. 1 and 2 alternately; and here I must remark, that after a fortnight I was extremely ill, and thought it was all over with me. I formed a thousand different opinions of the Pills; and often asked myself, How can the Pills hurt me now, after having done me so much good? However, I was alarmed, for so weak was I as to be unable to rise from my bed without help; and I did not take any pills on that night or the following morning. But during the next day I was as well and as cheerful as in my childhood, which encouraged me to persevere with the Universal Medicine; and in the course of a month I was restored to perfect health.

The following is a list of the diseases with which I had been afflicted, and having been cured by Morison's Pills alone, under Divine Providence, I have reason to consider them a Universal remedy:

1st. Severe pain in the lower intestines.
2nd. Liver complaint during fifteen years.
3rd. Palpitation of the heart seven years.
4th. Extreme costiveness fifteen years.
5th. Weakness of sight, and giddiness, often falling helpless to the ground, ten years.
6th. Teeth loose from taking calomel.

I acknowledge with gratitude that Morison's Pills have cured me of all the above diseases. In January 1836, at my present station, Cuttack, I lifted a heavy box, and immediately felt a pain across the small of the back, and five minutes afterwards was unable to move; at night I took 15 Pills of No. 2, the next morning 20 of the same, and at night 20 of No. 1, and the following morning 25 of No. 2, continuing to take large doses. The morning after my injury, the Surgeon of the regiment kindly came to see me, at the request of the Adjutant, but I declined taking any medicine but Morison's Pills, and the Surgeon allowed me to have my own way. He sent me some ointment to apply externally, but I did not use it. On the third day I was entirely free from pain.

When afflicted with the illness above mentioned, I was constantly impelled to drink spirits and water as a stimulant; but now I am so strong and cheerful that I do not feel the necessity of anything of the kind, nor do I ever take it.

Temperance Societies have done and are still doing good; but sometimes when people are weak and melancholy they will drink spirits in spite of these societies; and it is my firm belief that the object of Temperance Societies would be much promoted by persuading people to attend more to their health, and to take the Universal Vegetable Medicines, they would then be cheerful and vigorous from good health, and would no longer have to

> " Keep their spirits up
> By pouring spirits down,"

as is now too common a practice. Notwithstanding my complicated and long-continued illness, and that I have been upwards of 21 years in India, I am now quite hearty and strong, considering my sufferings, and the officers of the regiment tell me they never before saw me in such good health.

To you who have been the means of introducing Morison's Universal Medicines in India, I beg leave to offer my best thanks, while I am ready and willing to take oath to its truth, if required.

I remain,
Your most obedient Servant,
MICHAEL CONDON,
Late Sergeant-Major, 19th Regiment, N.I.,
Now retired on Full Pay.

CAUTION.

Whereas spurious imitations of my Medicines are now in circulation, I, JAMES MORISON, the Hygeist, hereby give notice, that none can be genuine without the words " MORISON'S UNIVERSAL MEDICINES " are engraved on the Government Stamp, affixed to each box, IN WHITE LETTERS UPON A RED GROUND. Sold only by the General Agents to the British College of Health and their Sub-Agents. No Chemist or Druggist is authorised by me to dispose of the same. In witness whereof I have hereunto set my hand, JAMES MORISON, the Hygeist.

BRITISH COLLEGE OF HEALTH, 2, Hamilton Place, New Road, London, 1839.

Sold in Boxes, at 1s. 1½d., 2s. 9d., 4s. 6d., and Family Packets, containing three 4s. 6d. Boxes, 11s. each. Also the Vegetable Cleansing Powders, 1s. 1½d. per Box.

J. & E. ATKINSON,
PERFUMERS,
24, OLD BOND STREET, LONDON,

Beg to inform the Nobility and Gentry that the Perfumery manufactured or imported by them, is sold by appointment by most Perfumers and Hair Dressers in Town and Country; but as there are numerous counterfeits, particularly in small Country Towns, sold under the fictitious names of " William Atkinson," &c., they respectfully request that purchasers will observe the name and address distinct on the Label; and also a small Address Stamp, printed in colours similar to a patent medicine stamp. The opposite is a fac-simile, excepting the colours.

ATKINSON'S OLD BROWN WINDSOR SOAP

Is principally composed of fine vegetable oils, and is very highly perfumed. It is peculiarly mild in quality, very softening to the skin, and economical in use, going nearly twice as far as new Soaps. Price 2s. 6d. a packet.

N.B. The numerous articles sold under the above name, are only the common alkaline Soaps, coloured, and slightly perfumed; and the effect on a delicate skin is very destructive.

ATKINSON'S ALMOND SOAP,

Made from the purest Oil of Almonds; combining all the softening and beautifying qualities of the Almond, with the detersive properties of the common alkaline Soaps. It far surpasses all others for softening the skin, and making it beautifully white, however injured or discoloured by neglect, change of climate, or any other cause.

ATKINSON'S BEAR'S GREASE,
FOR THE GROWTH OF HAIR.

This article is procured from the animal in its native climate, it being known to possess more vivifying properties when so procured, than when the animal is in a domesticated state. It is of the finest quality, and is sent out without any admixture, except a little perfume to keep it sweet; and for the growth of Hair it is no doubt far superior to anything hitherto known: for dressing the Hair it is very pleasant and useful, cleaning the head from dandriff, and making the Hair beautifully soft and glossy.

* As many articles are sold as Bear's Grease which are mere deceptions, being only strong rancid fats mixed with pungent essential oils, and are extremely deleterious, some of the counterfeits so closely imitate the genuine in their outward appearance, that it requires a near inspection to perceive the difference; several of them are a fac-simile of his pot, with the word ' Genuine,' instead of the name ' Atkinson,' and some say ' William ' instead of ' James.' J. and E. Atkinson's are enclosed in a wrapper, with the signature and address distinct, and the pots have a Bear on the top surrounded with a circle, and the words ' ATKINSON'S BEAR'S GREASE FOR THE GROWTH OF THE HAIR,' and underneath ' PRICE 2s. 6d. or 4s.'

ATKINSON'S COLD CREAM OF ROSES.

This article is of the very best quality, and is always fresh, their consumption requiring them to make it twice a week; but it will keep good for six months. Nothing surpasses it for cooling and softening the Skin, and curing and preventing its chapping.

EAU DE COLOGNE,
FROM JEAN MARIA FARINA.

There are few articles that the Public are more imposed upon than Eau de Cologne; at least 99 in 100 bottles sold under that name, are made in this country from strong alcohol, mixed with hot, essential oils, and, used internally, are highly pernicious. The real Eau from Cologne owes its superiority to the grape-spirit which composes it, distilled with balsamic herbs indigenous to the borders of the Rhine, and can no more be made in this country than brandy; and as the duty and expense is about 14s. per dozen, the genuine only gives a reasonable profit to the vender at One Guinea the Case.

BOUQUET DE LA REINE VICTORIA.

This fashionable Perfume combines the fragrance of the choicest vernal flowers, and is equally permanent as odoriferous. Also, the COURT BOUQUET, BOUQUET MILITAIRE, EXTRACT OF SPRING FLOWERS, &c., and various others from France and Italy, selected from the best Perfumers in the respective countries.

ATKINSON'S DEPILATORY

For removing superfluous Hair from the face, neck, and arms, with equal certainty and safety, leaving the Skin softer and whiter than before the application.

MAHOMED'S DYE

For changing the Hair on the head, eyebrows, or whiskers, to a permanent brown or black by one application, without staining the skin or the finest linen.

NAPLES SOAP,

Imported from the first manufacturer in Naples. J. & E. A. can with confidence recommend their present stock as of a very choice character; some is perfumed with the Rose, which is never to be obtained to a great extent.

PROPRIETARY ARTICLES.

ROWLAND'S MACASSAR OIL, ARNOLD'S IMPERIAL CREAM, WILLIS'S MIRIFIC BALSAM, OLDRIDGE'S BALM OF COLOMBIA, SMYTH'S LAVENDER WATER, RIGGE'S SOAP, and all other Perfumery of established character.

HAIR BRUSHES,

With Ivory backs, and in various fancy Wood, in great variety, warranted.

NAIL, TOOTH, AND SHAVING BRUSHES.

COMBS,

In Tortoiseshell, Bone, and Ivory, of every description.

Perfumery of all kinds of the best quality, nothing inferior being kept, wholesale and retail.

N.B. An allowance on taking six or more of one kind of article.

24, OLD BOND STREET, SEPTEMBER 1839.

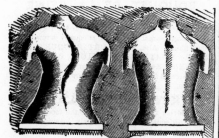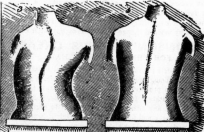

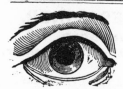

IMPORTANT TO INVALIDS AND OTHERS.
BY THE KING'S ROYAL LETTERS PATENT.

Wholesale Upholstery, Cabinet and Chair Manufactory,
33, GERRARD STREET, SOHO.

G. MINTER's PATENT SELF-ACTING RECLINING AND ELEVATING CHAIRS are manufactured with every attention to the comforts of a Sick Chamber, as well as for the use of the Dining-room, Drawing-room, or Library, as useful and indulgent Articles of Furniture; the merits of the Chair only require inspecting to be convinced of its superiority over all others. Prices, from Six to Twelve Guineas.

Every description of Bath and Brighton Garden Wheel Chairs made with G. M.'s Patent Self-Acting Seats and Backs, so as to form an inclined plane for an Invalid to lie at full length. Merlin Chairs, Portable Carriage Chairs, Exercising Chamber Horses, Water Beds, and every Article for the comfort of the Invalid and Infirm.

G. M. having obtained a Verdict in his favour in the Court of King's Bench, and also in the Court of Exchequer, against two Individuals who infringed his Patent, a handsome Reward will be given to any Person giving information leading to the Conviction of any Offender.

LADIES' & GENTLEMENS' DRESSING CASES.

Ladies' Dressing Case,
Neatly finished in Rosewood, price .... £1. 8s.

Superior Rosewood
Ladies' Dressing Case,
With Jewel Drawer .. £4. 15s.

In Mahogany, brass-finished,
Gentlemens' Neatly-finished Dressing Case,
price .... 18s. 6d.

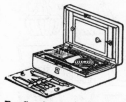 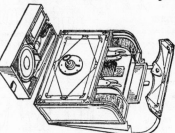 

For Gentlemen, in Spanish Mahogany, the
One Guinea Dressing Case,
With Looking Glass, and completely fitted with Brushes, Cutlery, &c.

In Real Russia Leather,
Gentlemens' Dressing Case,
Approved upright pattern, fitted with superior Cutlery and Brushes, ... 50s.

In Rosewood, brass-finished,
Gentlemens' Multum in Parvo Dressing Case,
Completely fitted, £2.

Show Room for Desks, Dressing Cases, &c. at
THE BRITISH PAPER WAREHOUSE,
No. 46 CORNHILL, LONDON.

APSLEY PELLATT'S

ABRIDGED LIST OF
Net Cash Prices for the best Flint Glass Ware.

DECANTERS.

25 Strong quart Nelson shape decanters, cut all over, bold flutes and cut brim & stopper, P.M. each 10s6d. to 12 0

26 Do. three-ringed royal shape, cut on and between rings, turned out stop, P.M. each 10 0

Do. do. not cut on or between rings, nor turned out stopper, P.M. ea. 8s to 9 0

27 Fancy shapes, cut all over, eight flutes, spire stopper, &c. each, P.M. 16s. to 18 0

Do. six flutes only, each, P.M. 24s. to 27 0

DISHES.

31 Dishes, oblong, pillar moulded, scolloped edges, cut star.

| 5-in. | 7-in. | 9-in. | 10-in. |
| 3s. 6d. | 6s. 6d. | 11s. | 13s. each. |

32 Oval cup sprig, shell pattern,

| 5-in. | 7-in. | 9-in. | 11-in. |
| 7s. 6d. | 9s. 6d. | 16s. | 19s. each. |

33 Square shape pillar, moulded star,

| 5-in. | 7-in | 9-in. | 10-in. |
| 4s. | 8s. | 12s. 6d. | 15s. each. |

FINGER CUPS.

37 Fluted finger-cups, strong, about 14 oz. each 2 6

Do. plain flint, punted, per doz..... 18 0

Do. coloured, per doz.......18s. to 21 0

38 Ten-fluted round, very strong, each. 5 0

Eight-fluted do., each 8 0

39 Medicean shape, moulded pillar, pearl upper part, cut flat flutes, each .. 5 0

PICKLES

46 Pickles, half fluted for 3 in. holes, RM ea. 4 6

47 Strong, moulded bottom, 3-in. hole, cut all over, flat flutes, R.M. each. 5 0

Best cut star do. for 3½-in. hole, PM ea. 7 6

Very strong and best cut, P.M. each 14 6

WATER JUGS

59 Quarts, neatly fluted and cut rings, each...................14s. to 18 0

60 Ewer shape, best cut handles, &c... 21 0

61 Silver do. scolloped edges, ex. lar. flutes 25 0

WATER BOTTLES

70 Moulded pillar body, cut neck, each. 3 0

71 Cut neck and star................. 3 0

72 Double fluted cut rings 3 6

73 Very strong pillar, moulded body, cut neck and rings 5 6

74 Grecian shape, fluted all over 7 0

TUMBLERS

	78 79	80 81 82 83 84 85 86 87	
Tale 5s.			
Flint,	7s. 10s. 12s. 12s. 10s. 12s. 14s. 18s. 18s.		Doz.
	to to to to to to to to to		
	8s. 12s. 14s. 15s. 12s.	18s. 21s. 21s. 30s. do.	

WINES

88	89	90	91	92	93	94	95	96	97	98	99
7s.	7s.	7s.	7s.	8s.	14s.	12s.	13s.	15s.	18s.	21s.	20s.
to		to	to	to							
8s.		9s.	9s.	9s.	10s.						

Glass Blowing, Cutting, and Engraving, may be inspected by Purchasers, at Mr. Pellatt's Extensive Flint Glass and Steam Cutting Works, in Holland Street, near Blackfriars' Bridge, any Tuesday, Wednesday, or Thursday.

Merchants and the Trade supplied on equitable Terms.

No Abatement from the above specified Ready Money Prices.

No Connexion with any other Establishment.

M. & W. Collis, Printers, 104, Bishopsgate Street Within.

BEAUFOY AND Co., SOUTH LAMBETH, LONDON.

BEAUFOY'S INSTANT CURE

FOR THE

TOOTHACHE.

THE GENUINE PACKAGES CONTAIN

A FAC-SIMILE

OF ONE OR THE OTHER OF THESE

VIGNETTES.

SOLD BY MOST RESPECTABLE DRUGGISTS, WITH AMPLE DIRECTIONS FOR USE,
In Bottles, Price 1s. 1½d each. Stamp included.

BEAUFOY AND CO., SOUTH LAMBETH, LONDON.

[BRADBURY AND EVANS, PRINTERS, WHITEFRIARS.]

Faithfully Yours

Charles Dickens

Painted by D. Maclise A.R.A.

Engraved by Finden.

Printed by J. Yates

London, Published Oct.ʳ 1, 1839 by Chapman & Hall, 186 Strand.

PORTRAIT OF MR. DICKENS.

PROOF IMPRESSIONS will be ready on the 21st October.

PRICE.—In quarto, plain paper . . . . . One Shilling.
,,   folio, India paper . . . . Two Shillings.

NEW WORK BY "BOZ."

MESSRS. CHAPMAN & HALL have the pleasure
of announcing that they have completed arrangements with Mr. CHARLES DICKENS for the
publication of

A NEW WORK,

ON AN ENTIRELY NEW PLAN.

The first number of this work will appear in
March next.

186, STRAND,
  September 30, 1839.

NICHOLAS NICKLEBY.

THE Public and the Trade are respectfully informed that NICHOLAS NICKLEBY, complete in One Volume, will be ready for delivery on the 21st October.

Price, neatly bound in cloth	£1	1	0
„ „ „ Half morocco, marble edges	1	4	6
„ „ Whole bound morocco, gilt edges	1	6	6

SUBSCRIBERS desirous of having their copies bound in a similar style can have them done by the Publishers, or through their Booksellers, at the following prices—

Whole bound, morocco, gilt edges . . . . 6*s.* 6*d.*
Half bound, „ marble leaves 4 6
In cloth, lettered 1 6

CHAPMAN AND HALL, 186, 'STRAND.

CHAPTER LIX.

THE PLOTS BEGIN TO FAIL, AND DOUBTS AND DANGERS TO DISTURB THE PLOTTER.

RALPH sat alone in the solitary room where he was accustomed to take his meals, and to sit of nights when no profitable occupation called him abroad; before him was an untasted breakfast, and near to where his fingers beat restlessly upon the table, lay his watch. It was long past the time at which, for many years, he had put it in his pocket and gone with measured steps down stairs to the business of the day, but he took as little heed of its monotonous warning, as of the meat and drink before him, and remained with his head resting on one hand, and his eyes fixed moodily on the ground.

This departure from his regular and constant habit in one so regular and unvarying in all that appertained to the daily pursuit of riches, would almost of itself have told that the usurer was not well. That he laboured under some mental or bodily indisposition, and that it was one of no slight kind so to affect a man like him, was sufficiently shown by his haggard face, jaded air, and hollow languid eyes, which he raised at last with a start and a hasty glance around him, as one who suddenly awakes from sleep, and cannot immediately recognise the place in which he finds himself.

"What is this," he said, "that hangs over me, and I cannot shake off? I have never pampered myself, and should not be ill. I have never moped, and pined, and yielded to fancies; but what *can* a man do without rest?"

He pressed his hand upon his forehead.

"Night after night comes and goes, and I have no rest. If I sleep, what rest is that which is disturbed by constant dreams of the same detested faces crowding round me—of the same detested people in every variety of action, mingling with all I say and do, and always to my defeat? Waking, what rest have I, constantly haunted by this heavy shadow of—I know not what, which is its worst character I must have rest. One night's unbroken rest, and I should be a man again."

Pushing the table from him while he spoke, as though he loathed the sight of food, he encountered the watch; the hands of which were almost upon noon.

"This is strange!" he said, "noon, and Noggs not here! what drunken brawl keeps him away? I would give something now, something in money even after that dreadful loss, if he had stabbed a man in a tavern scuffle, or broken into a house, or picked a pocket, or done anything that would send him abroad with an iron ring upon his leg, and rid me of him. Better still if I could throw temptation in his way, and lure him on to rob me. He should be welcome to what he took, so I brought the law upon him, for he is a traitor, I swear; how or when or where I don't know, though I suspect."

After waiting for another half-hour, he despatched the woman who kept his house to Newman's lodging, to inquire if he were ill, and why he had not come or sent. She brought back answer that he had not been home all night, and that no one could tell her anything about him.

" But there is a gentleman, Sir," she said, " below, who was standing at the door when I came in, and he says——"

" What says he ?" demanded Ralph, turning angrily upon her. "I told you I would see nobody."

" He says," replied the woman, abashed by his harshness, " that he comes on very particular business which admits of no excuse, and I thought perhaps it might be about——"

" About what, in the devil's name ?" said Ralph hastily. " You spy and speculate on people's business with me, do you, woman ?"

" Dear, no, Sir! I saw you were anxious, and thought it might be about Mr. Noggs, that's all."

" Saw I was anxious !" muttered Ralph ; " they all watch me now. Where is this person? You did not say I was not down yet, I hope?"

The woman replied that he was in the little office, and that she had said her master was engaged, but she would take the message.

" Well," said Ralph, " I'll see him. Go you to your kitchen, and keep there,—do you mind me ? "

Glad to be released, the woman quickly disappeared. Collecting himself, and assuming as much of his accustomed manner as his utmost resolution could summon, Ralph descended the stairs, and after pausing for a few moments with his hand upon the lock, entered Newman's room, and confronted Mr. Charles Cheeryble.

Of all men alive, this was one of the last he would have wished to meet at any time ; but now that he recognised in him only the patron and protector of Nicholas, he would rather have seen a spectre. One beneficial effect, however, the encounter had upon him. It instantly roused all his dormant energies, rekindled in his breast the passions that for many years had found an improving home there, called up all his wrath, hatred, and malice ; restored the sneer to his lip, and the scowl to his brow, and made him again in all outward appearance the same Ralph Nickleby that so many had bitter cause to remember.

" Humph," said Ralph, pausing at the door. " This is an unexpected favour, Sir."

" And an unwelcome one," said brother Charles ; " an unwelcome one, I know."

" Men say you are truth itself, Sir," sneered Ralph. " You speak truth now at all events, and I'll not contradict you. The favour is at least as unwelcome as it is unexpected. I can scarcely say more ! "

" Plainly, Sir——" began brother Charles.

" Plainly, Sir," interrupted Ralph, " I wish this conference to be a short one, and to end where it begins. I guess the subject upon which you are about to speak, and I'll not hear you. You like plainness, I believe,—there it is. Here is the door as you see. Our way lies in very different directions. Take yours I beg of you, and leave me to pursue mine in quiet."

" In quiet ! " repeated brother Charles mildly, and looking at him with more of pity than reproach. " To pursue his way in quiet ! "

" You will scarcely remain in my house, I presume, Sir, against my will," said Ralph; " or you can scarcely hope to make an impression upon a man who closes his ears to all that you can say, and is firmly and resolutely determined not to hear you."

" Mr. Nickleby, Sir," returned brother Charles, no less mildly than before, but firmly too, " I come here against my will—sorely and grievously against my will. I have never been in this house before; and to speak my mind, Sir, I don't feel at home or easy in it, and have no wish ever to be here again. You do not guess the subject on which I come to speak to you, you do not indeed. I am sure of that, or your manner would be a very different one."

Ralph glanced keenly at him, but the clear eye and open countenance of the honest old merchant underwent no change of expression, and met his look without reserve.

" Shall I go on?" said Mr. Cheeryble.

" Oh, by all means, if you please," returned Ralph drily. " Here are walls to speak to, Sir, a desk, and two stools—most attentive auditors, and certain not to interrupt you. Go on, I beg; make my house yours, and perhaps by the time I return from my walk, you will have finished what you have to say, and will yield me up possession again."

So saying, he buttoned his coat, and turning into the passage, took down his hat. The old gentleman followed, and was about to speak, when Ralph waved him off impatiently, and said :

" Not a word. I tell you, Sir, not a word. Virtuous as you are, you are not an angel yet, to appear in men's houses whether they will or no, and pour your speech into unwilling ears. Preach to the walls I tell you—not to me."

" I am no angel, Heaven knows," returned brother Charles, shaking his head, " but an erring and imperfect man; nevertheless, there is one quality which all men have in common with the angels blessed opportunities of exercising if they will—mercy. It is an errand of mercy that brings me here. Pray, let me discharge it."

" I show no mercy," retorted Ralph with a triumphant smile, " and I ask none. Seek no mercy from me, Sir, in behalf of the fellow who has imposed upon your childish credulity, but let him expect the worst that I can do."

" He ask mercy at your hands ! " exclaimed the old merchant warmly, " ask it at his, Sir, ask it at his. If you will not hear me now when you may, hear me when you must, or anticipate what I would say, and take measures to prevent our ever meeting again. Your nephew is a noble lad, Sir, an honest, noble lad. What you are, Mr. Nickleby, I will not say; but what you have done, I know. Now, Sir, when you go about the business in which you have been recently engaged, and find it difficult of pursuing, come to me and my brother Ned, and Tim Linkinwater, Sir, and we'll explain it for you—and come soon, or it may be too late, and you may have it explained with a little more roughness, and a little less delicacy—and never forget, Sir, that I came here this morning in mercy to you, and am still ready to talk to you in the same spirit."

With these words, uttered with great emphasis and emotion, brother Charles put on his broad-brimmed hat, and passing Ralph Nickleby

without any further remark, trotted nimbly into the street. Ralph
looked after him, but neither moved nor spoke for some time, when he
broke what almost seemed the silence of stupefaction, by a scornful laugh.

"This," he said, "from its wildness, should be another of those
dreams that have so broken my rest of late. In mercy to me!—Pho!
The old simpleton has gone mad."

Although he expressed himself in this derisive and contemptuous
manner, it was plain that the more Ralph pondered, the more ill at
ease he became, and the more he laboured under some vague anxiety
and alarm, which increased as the time passed on and no tidings of
Newman Noggs appeared. After waiting until late in the afternoon
tortured by various apprehensions and misgivings, and the recollection
of the warning which his nephew had given him when they last met,
the further confirmation of which now presented itself in one shape of
probability now in another, and haunted him perpetually, he left home,
and scarcely knowing why, save that he was in a suspicious and agitated
mood, betook himself to Snawley's house. His wife presented herself,
and of her Ralph inquired whether her husband was at home.

"No," she said sharply, "he is not indeed, and I don't think he will
be at home for a very long time, that's more."

"Do you know who I am?" asked Ralph.

"Oh yes, I know you very well—too well, perhaps, and perhaps he
does too, and sorry am I that I should have to say it."

"Tell him that I saw him through the window-blind above, as I
crossed the road just now, and that I would speak to him on business,"
said Ralph sarcastically. "Do you hear?"

"I hear," rejoined Mrs. Snawley, taking no further notice of the
request.

"I knew this woman was a hypocrite in the way of psalms and
Scripture phrases," said Ralph, passing quietly by, "but I never knew
she drank before."

"Stop! You don't come in here," said Mr. Snawley's better-half,
interposing her person, which was a robust one, in the doorway. "You
have said more than enough to him on business before now. I always
told him what dealing with you and working out your schemes would
come to. It was either you or the schoolmaster—one of you, or the
two between you—that got the forged letter done, remember that.
That wasn't his doing, so don't lay it at his door."

"Hold your tongue, you Jezebel," said Ralph, looking fearfully round.

"Ah, I know when to hold my tongue, and when to speak, Mr.
Nickleby," retorted the dame. "Take care that other people know
when to hold theirs."

"You jade," said Ralph, grinning with rage; "if your husband
has been idiot enough to trust you with his secrets, keep them—keep
them, she-devil that you are."

"Not so much his secrets as other people's secrets perhaps," retorted
the woman; "not so much his secrets as yours. None of your black
looks at me. You'll want 'em all perhaps for another time. You had
better keep 'em."

"Will you," said Ralph, suppressing his passion as well as he could, and clutching her tightly by the wrist: " will you go to your husband and tell him that I know he is at home, and that I must see him ? And will you tell me what it is that you and he mean by this new style of behaviour ?"

" No," replied the woman, violently disengaging herself, " I'll do neither."

" You set me at defiance, do you ?" said Ralph.

" Yes," was the answer. " I do."

For an instant Ralph had his hand raised as though he were about to strike her, but checking himself, and nodding his head, and muttering as though to assure her he would not forget this, walked away.

Thence, he went straight to the inn which Mr. Squeers frequented and inquired when he had been there last ; in the vague hope that whether successful or unsuccessful, he might by this time have returned from his mission and be able to assure him that all was safe. But Mr. Squeers had not been there for ten days, and all that the people could tell about him was, that he had left his luggage and his bill.

Disturbed by a thousand fears and surmises, and bent upon ascertaining whether Squeers had any suspicion of Snawley, or was in any way a party to this altered behaviour, Ralph determined to hazard the extreme step of inquiring for him at the Lambeth lodging, and having an interview with him even there. Bent upon this purpose, and in that mood in which delay is insupportable, he repaired at once to the place, and being by description perfectly acquainted with the situation of his room, crept up stairs and knocked gently at the door.

Not one, nor two, nor three, nor yet a dozen knocks served to convince Ralph against his wish that there was nobody inside. He reasoned that he might be asleep ; and, listening, almost persuaded himself that he could hear him breathe. Even when he was satisfied that he could not be there, he sat patiently down upon a broken stair and waited ; arguing that he had gone out upon some slight errand and must soon return.

Many feet came up the creaking stairs, and the step of some seemed to his listening ear so like that of the man for whom he waited, that Ralph often stood up to be ready to address him when he reached the top ; but one by one each person turned off into some room short of the place where he was stationed, and at every such disappointment he felt quite chilled and lonely.

At length he felt it was hopeless to remain, and going down stairs again, inquired of one of the lodgers if he knew anything of Mr. Squeers's movements—mentioning that worthy by an assumed name which had been agreed upon between them. By this lodger he was referred to another, and by him to some one else, from whom he learnt that late on the previous night he had gone out hastily with two men, who had shortly afterwards returned for the old woman who lived on the same floor ; and that although the circumstance had attracted the attention of the informant, he had not spoken to them at the time, nor made any inquiry afterwards.

This possessed him with the idea that perhaps Peg Sliderskew had been apprehended for the robbery, and that Mr. Squeers being with her at the time, had been apprehended also on suspicion of being a confederate. If this were so, the fact must be known to Gride ; and to Gride's house he directed his steps ; now thoroughly alarmed, and fearful that there were indeed plots afoot tending to his discomfiture and ruin.

Arrived at the usurer's house, he found the windows close shut, the dingy blinds drawn down : all silent, melancholy, and deserted. But this was its usual aspect. He knocked—gently at first, then loud and vigorously, but nobody came. He wrote a few words in pencil on a card, and having thrust it under the door was going away, when a noise above as though a window-sash were stealthily raised caught his ear, and looking up he could just discern the face of Gride himself cautiously peering over the house parapet from the window of the garret. Seeing who was below, he drew it in again ; not so quickly however but that Ralph let him know he was observed, and called to him to come down.

The call being repeated, Gride looked out again so cautiously that no part of the old man's body was visible, and the sharp features and white hair appearing alone above the parapet looked like a severed head garnishing the wall.

"Hush !" he cried. " Go away—go away !"

" Come down," said Ralph, beckoning him.

" Go a—way !" squeaked Gride, shaking his head in a sort of ecstacy of impatience. " Don't speak to me, don't knock, don't call attention to the house, but go away."

" I'll knock I swear till I have your neighbours up in arms," said Ralph, " if you don't tell me what you mean by lurking there, you whining cur."

" I can't hear what you say—don't talk to me, it isn't safe—go away —go away," returned Gride.

" Come down, I say. Will you come down !" said Ralph fiercely.

" No—o—o—o," snarled Gride. He drew in his head ; and Ralph, left standing in the street, could hear the sash closed as gently and carefully as it had been opened.

" How is this," said he, " that they all fall from me and shun me like the plague—these men who have licked the dust from my feet ! *Is* my day past, and is this indeed the coming on of night ? I'll know what it means, I will, at any cost. I am firmer and more myself just now than I have been these many days."

Turning from the door, which in the first transport of his rage he had meditated battering upon until Gride's very fears impelled him to open it, he turned his face towards the city, and working his way steadily through the crowd which was pouring from it (it was by this time between five and six o'clock in the afternoon) went straight to the house of business of the Brothers Cheeryble, and putting his head into the glass case, found Tim Linkinwater alone.

" My name's Nickleby," said Ralph.

" I know it," replied Tim, surveying him through his spectacles.

" Which of your firm was it who called on me this morning ?" demanded Ralph.

" Mr. Charles."

"Then tell Mr. Charles I want to see him."

"You shall see," said Tim, getting off his stool with great agility. "You shall see not only Mr. Charles, but Mr. Ned likewise."

Tim stopped, looked steadily and severely at Ralph, nodded his head once in a curt manner which seemed to say there was a little more behind, and vanished. After a short interval he returned, and ushering Ralph into the presence of the two brothers, remained in the room himself.

"I want to speak to you, who spoke to me this morning," said Ralph, pointing out with his finger the man whom he addressed.

"I have no secrets from my brother Ned, or from Tim Linkinwater," observed Brother Charles quietly.

"I have," said Ralph.

"Mr. Nickleby, Sir," said brother Ned, "the matter upon which my brother Charles called upon you this morning is one which is already perfectly well known to us three and to others besides, and must unhappily soon become known to a great many more. He waited upon you, Sir, this morning alone, as a matter of delicacy and consideration. We feel now that further delicacy and consideration would be misplaced, and if we confer together it must be as we are or not at all."

"Well, gentlemen," said Ralph with a curl of the lip, "talking in riddles would seem to be the peculiar forte of you two, and I suppose your clerk, like a prudent man, has studied the art also with a view to your good graces. Talk in company, gentlemen, in God's name. I'll humour you."

"Humour!" cried Tim Linkinwater, suddenly growing very red in the face, "He'll humour us! He'll humour Cheeryble Brothers! Do you hear that? Do you hear him? Do you hear him say he'll humour Cheeryble Brothers?"

"Tim," said Charles and Ned together, "pray Tim, pray now don't."

Tim, taking the hint, stifled his indignation as well as he could and suffered it to escape through his spectacles, with the additional safety-valve of a short hysterical laugh now and then, which seemed to relieve him mightily.

"As nobody bids me to a seat," said Ralph looking round, "I'll take one, for I am fatigued with walking. And now if you please, gentlemen, I wish to know—I demand to know; I have the right—what you have to say to me which justifies such a tone as you have assumed, and that underhand interference in my affairs which I have reason to suppose you have been practising. I tell you plainly, gentlemen, that little as I care for the opinion of the world (as the slang goes) I don't choose to submit quietly to slander and malice. Whether you suffer yourselves to be imposed upon too easily, or wilfully make yourselves parties to it, the result to me is the same, and in either case you can't expect from a plain man like myself much consideration or forbearance."

So coolly and deliberately was this said, that nine men out of ten, ignorant of the circumstances, would have supposed Ralph to be really an injured man. There he sat with folded arms; paler than usual certainly and sufficiently ill-favoured, but quite collected—far more so than the brothers or the exasperated Tim, and ready to face out the very worst.

" Very well, Sir," said brother Charles. " Very well. Brother Ned, will you ring the bell ?"

" Charles, my dear fellow ! stop one instant," returned the other. " It will be better for Mr. Nickleby and for our object that he should remain silent if he can, till we have said what we have to say. I wish him to understand that."

" Quite right, quite right," said brother Charles.

Ralph smiled but made no reply. The bell was rung, the room-door opened ; a man came in with a halting walk ; and, looking round, Ralph's eyes met those of Newman Noggs. From that moment his heart began to fail him.

" This is a good beginning," he said bitterly. " Oh ! this is a good beginning. You are candid, honest, open-hearted, fair-dealing men ! I always knew the real worth of such characters as yours ! To tamper with a fellow like this, who would sell his soul (if he had one) for drink, and whose every word is a lie,—what men are safe if this is done ? Oh it's a good beginning !"

" I *will* speak," cried Newman, standing on tiptoe to look over Tim's head, who had interposed to prevent him. " Hallo, you Sir—old Nickleby—what do you mean when you talk of ' a fellow like this ?' Who made me ' a fellow like this ?' If I would sell my soul for drink, why wasn't I a thief, swindler, housebreaker, area sneak, robber of pence out of the trays of blind men's dogs, rather than your drudge and packhorse ? If my every word was a lie, why wasn't I a pet and favourite of yours ? Lie ! When did I ever cringe and fawn to you— eh ? Tell me that. I served you faithfully. I did more work because I was poor, and took more hard words from you because I despised you and them, than any man you could have got from the parish workhouse. I did. I served you because I was proud ; because I was a lonely man with you, and there were no other drudges to see my degradation, and because nobody knew better than you that I was a ruined man, that I hadn't always been what I am, and that I might have been better off if I hadn't been a fool and fallen into the hands of you and others who were knaves. Do you deny that—eh ?"

" Gently," reasoned Tim, " you said you wouldn't."

" I said I wouldn't !" cried Newman, thrusting him aside, and moving his hand as Tim moved, so as to keep him at arm's-length, " don't tell me. Here, you Nickleby, don't pretend not to mind me ; it won't do, I know better. You were talking of tampering just now. Who tampered with Yorkshire schoolmasters, and, while they sent the drudge out that he shouldn't overhear, forgot that such great caution might render him suspicious, and that he might watch his master out at nights, and might set other eyes to watch the schoolmaster besides ? Who tampered with a selfish father, urging him to sell his daughter to old Arthur Gride, and tampered with Gride too, and did so in the little office *with a closet in the room ?*"

Ralph had put a great command upon himself, but he could not have suppressed a slight start, if he had been certain to be beheaded for it next moment.

" Aha !" cried Newman, "you mind me now, do you ? What first set this fag to be jealous of his master's actions, and to feel that if he hadn't crossed him when he might, he would have been as bad as he, or worse? That master's cruel treatment of his own flesh and blood, and vile designs upon a young girl who interested even his broken-down, drunken, miserable hack, and made him linger in his service, in the hope of doing her some good (as, thank God, he had done others once or twice before), when he would otherwise have relieved his feelings by pummelling his master soundly, and then going to the Devil. He would—mark that; and mark this—that I'm here now because these gentlemen thought it best. When I sought them out (as I did—there was no tampering with me) I told them I wanted help to find you out, to trace you down, to go through with what I had begun, to help the right; and that when I had done it, I'd burst into your room and tell you all, face to face, man to man, and like a man. Now I've said my say, and let anybody else say theirs, and fire away."

With this concluding sentiment, Newman Noggs, who had been perpetually sitting down and getting up again all through his speech which he had delivered in a series of jerks, and who was, from the violent exercise and the excitement combined, in a state of most intense and fiery heat, became, without passing through any intermediate stage, stiff, upright, and motionless, and so remained, staring at Ralph Nickleby with all his might and main.

Ralph looked at him for an instant, and for an instant only; then waved his hand, and, beating the ground with his foot, said in a choking voice,

"Go on, gentlemen, go on. I'm patient, you see. There's law to be had, there's law. I shall call you to an account for this. Take care what you say; I shall make you prove it."

"The proof is ready," returned Brother Charles, "quite ready to our hands. The man Snawley last night made a confession."

"Who may 'the man Snawley' be," returned Ralph, "and what may his 'confession' have to do with my affairs?"

To this inquiry, put with a dogged inflexibility of manner which language cannot express, the old gentleman returned no answer, but went on to say that to show him how much they were in earnest, it would be necessary to tell him not only what accusations were made against him, but what proof of them they had, and how that proof had been acquired. This laying open the whole question, brought up Brother Ned, Tim Linkinwater, and Newman Noggs, all three at once, who, after a vast deal of talking together, and a scene of great confusion, laid before Ralph in distinct terms the following statement.

That Newman, having been solemnly assured by one not then producible that Smike was not the son of Snawley, and this person having offered to make oath to that effect if necessary, they had by this communication been first led to doubt the claim set up, which they would otherwise have seen no reason to dispute, supported as it was by evidence which they had no power of disproving. That once suspecting the existence of a conspiracy, they had no difficulty in tracing back its origin to the malice of Ralph and the vindictiveness and avarice of Squeers. That suspicion and proof being two very different things, they

had been advised by a lawyer, eminent for his sagacity and acuteness
in such practice, to resist the proceedings taken on the other side for
the recovery of the youth as slowly and artfully as possible, and meanwhile to beset Snawley (with whom it was clear the main falsehood
must rest), to lead him, if possible, into contradictory and conflicting
statements, to harass him by all available means, and so to practise on
his fears and regard for his own safety as to induce him to divulge the
whole scheme, and to give up his employer and whomsoever else he
could implicate. That all this had been skilfully done; but that
Snawley, who was well practised in the arts of low cunning and
intrigue, had successfully baffled all their attempts, until an unexpected
circumstance had brought him last night upon his knees.

It thus arose. When Newman Noggs reported that Squeers was
again in town, and that an interview of such secrecy had taken place
between him and Ralph that he had been sent out of the house, plainly
lest he should overhear a word, a watch was set upon the schoolmaster,
in the hope that something might be discovered which would throw
some light upon the suspected plot. It being found, however, that
he held no further communication with Ralph nor any with Snawley,
and lived quite alone, they were completely at fault; the watch was
withdrawn, and they would have observed his motions no longer, if it
had not happened that one night Newman stumbled unobserved upon
him and Ralph in the street together. Following them, he discovered,
to his great suprise, that they repaired to various low lodging-houses,
and taverns kept by broken gamblers, to more than one of whom Ralph
was known, and were in pursuit—so he found by inquiries when they
had left—of an old woman, whose description exactly tallied with that
of deaf Mrs. Sliderskew. Affairs now appearing to assume a more
serious complexion, the watch was renewed with increased vigilance;
an officer was procured who took up his abode in the same tavern with
Squeers; and by him and Frank Cheeryble the footsteps of the unconscious
schoolmaster were dogged, until he was safely housed in the lodging
at Lambeth. Mr. Squeers having shifted his lodging, the officer
shifted his, and, lying concealed in the same street, and, indeed, in the
opposite house, soon found that Mr. Squeers and Mrs. Sliderskew were
in constant communication.

In this state of things Arthur Gride was appealed to. The robbery,
partly owing to the inquisitiveness of the neighbours, and partly to his
own grief and rage, had long ago become known; but he positively
refused to give his sanction or yield any assistance to the old woman's
capture, and was seized with such a panic at the idea of being called
upon to give evidence against her, that he shut himself up close in
his house, and refused to hold communication with anybody. Upon
this, the pursuers took counsel together, and, coming so near the truth
as to arrive at the conclusion that Gride and Ralph, with Squeers for
their instrument, were negotiating for the recovery of some of the
stolen papers which would not bear the light, and might possibly
explain the hints relative to Madeline which Newman had overheard,
resolved that Mrs. Sliderskew should be taken into custody before she
had parted with them, and Squeers too, if anything suspicious could be

attached to him. Accordingly, a search-warrant being procured, and all prepared, Mr. Squeers's window was watched, until his light was put out, and the time arrived when, as had been previously ascertained, he usually visited Mrs. Sliderskew. This done, Frank Cheeryble and Newman stole up stairs to listen to their discourse, and to give the signal to the officer at the most favourable time. At what an opportune moment they arrived, how they listened, and what they heard, is already known to the reader. Mr. Squeers, still half stunned, was hurried off with a stolen deed in his possession, and Mrs. Sliderskew was apprehended likewise. The information being promptly carried to Snawley that Squeers was in custody—he was not told for what—that worthy, first extorting a promise that he should be kept harmless, declared the whole tale concerning Smike to be a fiction and forgery, and implicated Ralph Nickleby to the fullest extent. As to Mr. Squeers, he had that morning undergone a private examination before a magistrate, and being unable to account satisfactorily for his possession of the deed or his companionship with Mrs. Sliderskew, had been, with her, remanded for a week.

All these discoveries were now related to Ralph circumstantially and in detail. Whatever impression they secretly produced, he suffered no sign of emotion to escape him, but sat perfectly still, not raising his frowning eyes from the ground, and covering his mouth with his hand. When the narrative was concluded, he raised his head hastily, as if about to speak, but on brother Charles resuming, fell into his old attitude again.

"I told you this morning," said the old gentleman, laying his hand upon his brother's shoulder, "that I came to you in mercy. How far you may be implicated in this last transaction, or how far the person who is now in custody may criminate you, you best know. But justice must take its course against the parties implicated in the plot against this poor, unoffending, injured lad. It is not in my power, or in the power of my brother Ned, to save you from the consequences. The utmost we can do is to warn you in time, and to give you an opportunity of escaping them. We would not have an old man like you disgraced and punished by your near relation, nor would we have him forget, like you, all ties of blood and nature. We entreat you—brother Ned, you join me, I know, in this entreaty, and so Tim Linkinwater do you, although you pretend to be an obstinate dog, Sir, and sit there frowning as if you didn't—we entreat you to retire from London, to take shelter in some place where you will be safe from the consequences of these wicked designs, and where you may have time, Sir, to atone for them, and to become a better man."

"And do you think," returned Ralph, rising, with the sneer of a devil, "and do you think you will so easily crush me? Do you think that a hundred well-arranged plans, or a hundred suborned witnesses, or a hundred false curs at my heels, or a hundred canting speeches full of oily words, will move me? I thank you for disclosing your schemes, which I am now prepared for. You have not the man to deal with that you think; try me, and remember that I spit upon your fair words and false dealings, and dare you—provoke you—taunt you—to do to me the very worst you can."

Thus they parted for that time; but the worst had not come yet.

CHAPTER LX.

THE DANGERS THICKEN, AND THE WORST IS TOLD.

INSTEAD of going home, Ralph threw himself into the first street cabriolet he could find, and directing the driver towards the police-office of the district in which Mr. Squeers's misfortunes had occurred, alighted at a short distance from it, and, discharging the man, went the rest of his way thither on foot. Inquiring for the object of his solicitude, he learnt that he had timed his visit well, for Mr. Squeers was in fact at that moment waiting for a hackney-coach he had ordered, and in which he purposed proceeding to his week's retirement, like a gentleman.

Demanding speech with the prisoner, he was ushered into a kind of waiting-room in which, by reason of his scholastic profession and superior respectability, Mr..Squeers had been permitted to pass the day. Here, by the light of a guttering and blackened candle, he could barely discern the schoolmaster fast asleep on a bench in a remote corner. An empty glass stood on a table before him, and this, with his somnolent condition and a very strong smell of brandy and water, forewarned the visitor that Mr. Squeers had been seeking in creature comforts a temporary forgetfulness of his unpleasant situation.

It was not a very easy matter to rouse him : so lethargic and heavy were his slumbers. Regaining his faculties by slow and faint glimmerings, he at length sat upright, and displaying a very yellow face, a very red nose, and a very bristly beard, the joint effect of which was considerably heightened by a dirty white handkerchief, spotted with blood, drawn over the crown of his head and tied under his chin, stared ruefully at Ralph in silence, until his feelings found a vent in this pithy sentence :

" I say, young fellow, you've been and done it now, you have ! "

" What's the matter with your head ? " asked Ralph.

" Why, your man, your informing kidnapping man, has been and broke it," rejoined Squeers sulkily, " that's what's the matter with it. You've come at last, have you ? "

" Why have you not sent to me ? " said Ralph. " How could I come till I knew what had befallen you ? "

" My family ! " hiccupped Mr. Squeers, raising his eye to the ceiling ; " my daughter as is at that age when all the sensibilities is a coming out strong in blow—my son as is the young Norval of private life, and the pride and ornament of a doting willage—here's a shock for the family ! The coat of arms of the Squeerses is tore, and their sun is gone down into the ocean wave ! "

" You have been drinking," said Ralph, " and have not yet slept yourself sober."

" I haven't been drinking your health, my codger," replied Mr. Squeers, " so you have nothing to do with that."

Ralph suppressed the indignation which the schoolmaster's altered and insolent manner awakened, and asked again why he had not sent to him.

" What should I get by sending to you ? " returned Squeers. " To be known to be in with you, wouldn't do me a great deal of good, and they won't take bail till they know something more of the case, so here am I hard and fast, and there are you loose and comfortable."

" And so must you be in a few days," retorted Ralph, with affected good-humour. " They can't hurt you, man."

" Why, I suppose they can't do much to me if I explain how it was that I got into the good company of that there ca-daverous old Slider," replied Squeers viciously, " who I wish was dead and buried, and resurrected and dissected, and hung upon wires in a anatomical museum, before ever I'd had anything to do with her. This is what him with the powdered head says this morning, in so many words—' Prisoner, as you have been found in company with this woman ; as you were detected in possession of this document ; and as you were engaged with her in fraudulently destroying others, and can give no satisfactory account of yourself, I shall remand you for a week, in order that inquiries may be made, and evidence got—and meanwhile I can't take any bail for your appearance.' Well then, what I say now is, that I *can* give a satisfactory account of myself ; I can hand in the card of my establishment and say, ' *I* am the Wackford Squeers as is therein named, Sir. I am the man as is guaranteed by unimpeachable references to be a out-and-outer in morals and uprightness of principle. Whatever is wrong in this business is no fault of mine. I had no evil design in it, Sir. I was not aware that anything was wrong. I was merely employed by a friend —my friend Mr. Ralph Nickleby, of Golden Square—send for him, Sir, and ask him what he has to say—he's the man ; not me.' "

" What document was it that you had ? " asked Ralph, evading for the moment the point just raised.

" What document ? Why, *the* document," replied Squeers. " The Madeline what's-her-name one. It was a will, that's what it was."

" Of what nature, whose will, when dated, how benefiting her, to what extent ? " asked Ralph hurriedly.

" A will in her favour, that's all I know," rejoined Squeers ; " and that's more than you'd have known, if you'd had them bellows on your head. It's all owing to your precious caution that they got hold of it. If you had let me burn it, and taken my word that it was gone, it would have been a heap of ashes behind the fire, instead of being whole and sound inside of my great-coat."

" Beaten at every point ! " muttered Ralph, gnawing his fingers.

" Ah ! " sighed Squeers, who, between the brandy and water and his broken head, wandered strangely, " at the delightful village of Dotheboys near Greta Bridge in Yorkshire, youth are boarded, clothed, booked, washed, furnished with pocket money, provided with all necessaries, instructed in all languages living and dead, mathematics, orthography, geometry, astronomy, trigonometry—this is a altered state of trigonomics, this is—a double l—all, everything—a cobbler's weapon. U-p-up, adjective, not down. S-q-u-double e-r-s-Squeers, noun substantive, a educator of youth. Total, all up with Squeers ! "

His running on in this way had afforded Ralph an opportunity of recovering his presence of mind, which at once suggested to him the necessity of removing as far as possible the schoolmaster's misgivings, and leading him to believe that his safety and best policy lay in the preservation of a rigid silence.

"I tell you once again," he said, "they can't hurt you. You shall have an action for false imprisonment, and make a profit of this yet. We will devise a story for you that should carry you through twenty times such a trivial scrape as this; and if they want security in a thousand pounds for your reappearance in case you should be called upon, you shall have it. All you have to do is to keep back the truth. You're a little fuddled to-night, and may not be able to see this as clearly as you would at another time, but this is what you must do, and you'll need all your senses about you, for a slip might be awkward."

"Oh!" said Squeers, who had looked cunningly at him, with his head stuck on one side like an old raven. "That's what I'm to do, is it? Now then, just you hear a word or two from me. I an't a going to have any stories made for me, and I an't a going to stick to any. If I find matters going against me, I shall expect you to take your share, and I'll take care you do. You never said anything about danger. I never bargained for being brought into such a plight as this, and I don't mean to take it as quiet as you think. I let you lead me on from one thing to another, because we had been mixed up together in a certain sort of a way, and if you had liked to be ill-natured you might perhaps have hurt the business, and if you liked to be good-natured you might throw a good deal in my way. Well; if all goes right now, that's quite correct, and I don't mind it; but if anything goes wrong, then times are altered, and I shall just say and do whatever I think may serve me most; and take advice from nobody. My moral influence with them lads," added Mr. Squeers, with deeper gravity, "is a tottering to its basis. The images of Mrs. Squeers, my daughter, and my son Wackford, all short of vittles, is perpetually before me; every other consideration melts away and vanishes in front of these, and the only number in all arithmetic that I know of as a husband and a father is number one, under this here most fatal go!"

How long Mr. Squeers might have declaimed, or how stormy a discussion his declamation might have led to, nobody knows. Being interrupted at this point by the arrival of the coach and an attendant who was to bear him company, he perched his hat with great dignity on the top of the handkerchief that bound his head, and thrusting one hand in his pocket, and taking the attendant's arm with the other, suffered himself to be led forth.

"As I supposed, from his not sending!" thought Ralph. "This fellow, I plainly see through all his tipsy fooling, has made up his mind to turn upon me. I am so beset and hemmed in that they are not only all struck with fear, but, like the beasts in the fable have their fling at me now, though time was, and no longer ago than yesterday too, when they were all civility and compliance. But they shall not move me. I'll not give way. I will not budge one inch!"

He went home, and was glad to find the housekeeper complaining of illness that he might have an excuse for being alone and sending her away to where she lived, which was hard by. Then he sat down by the light of a single candle, and began to think, for the first time, on all that had taken place that day.

He had neither eaten nor drunk since last night, and in addition to the anxiety of mind he had undergone, had been travelling about from place to place almost incessantly for many hours. He felt sick and exhausted, but could taste nothing save a glass of water, and continued to sit with his head upon his hand—not resting or thinking, but laboriously trying to do both, and feeling that every sense, but one of weariness and desolation, was for the time benumbed.

It was nearly ten o'clock when he heard a knocking at the door, and still sat quiet as before, as if he could not even bring his thoughts to bear upon that. It had been often repeated, and he had several times heard a voice outside, saying there was a light in the window (meaning, as he knew, his own candle), before he could rouse himself and go down stairs.

" Mr. Nickleby, there is terrible news for you, and I am sent to beg you will come with me directly," said a voice he seemed to recognise. He held his hand above his eyes, and looking out, saw Tim Linkinwater on the steps.

" Come where ? " demanded Ralph.

" To our house—where you came this morning. I have a coach here."

" Why should I go there?" said Ralph.

" Don't ask me why, but pray come with me."

" Another edition of to-day ! " returned Ralph, making as though he would shut the door.

" No, no ! " cried Tim, catching him by the arm and speaking most earnestly ; " it is only that you may hear something that has occurred —something very dreadful, Mr. Nickleby, which concerns you nearly. Do you think I would tell you so, or come to you like this, if it were not the case ? "

Ralph looked at him more closely, and seeing that he was indeed greatly excited, faltered, and could not tell what to say or think.

" You had better hear this now than at any other time," said Tim, " it may have some influence with you. For Heaven's sake come ! "

Perhaps at another time Ralph's obstinacy and dislike would have been proof against any appeal from such a quarter, however emphatically urged, but now, after a moment's hesitation, he went into the hall for his hat, and returning got into the coach without speaking a word.

Tim well remembered afterwards, and often said, that as Ralph Nickleby went into the house for this purpose, he saw him by the light of the candle which he had set down upon a chair, reel and stagger like a drunken man. He well remembered too that when he had placed his foot upon the coach steps, he turned round and looked upon him with a face so ashy pale and so very wild and vacant that it made him shudder, and for the moment almost afraid to follow. People were fond of saying that he had some dark presentiment upon him then, but his emotion might perhaps, with greater show of reason, be referred to what he had undergone that day.

A profound silence was observed during the ride. Arrived at their place of destination, Ralph followed his conductor into the house, and into a room where the two brothers were.   He was so astounded, not to say awed, by something of a mute compassion for himself which was visible in their manner and in that of the old clerk, that he could scarcely speak.

Having taken a seat, however, he contrived to say, though in broken words, " What—what have you to say to me—more than has been said already ? "

The room was old and large, very imperfectly lighted, and terminated in a bay window, about which hung some heavy drapery.   Casting his eyes in this direction as he spoke, he thought he made out the dusky figure of a man, and was confirmed in this impression by seeing that the object moved as if uneasy under his scrutiny.

" Who's that yonder ? " he said.

" One who has conveyed to us within these two hours the intelligence which caused our sending to you," replied brother Charles.   " Let him be, Sir, let him be for the present."

" More riddles ! " said Ralph, faintly.   " Well, Sir ? "

In turning his face towards the brothers he was obliged to avert it from the window, but before either of them could speak, he had looked round again.   It was evident that he was rendered restless and uncomfortable by the presence of the unseen person, for he repeated this action several times, and at length, as if in a nervous state which rendered him positively unable to turn away from the place, sat so as to have it opposite him, and muttered as an excuse that he could not bear the light.

The brothers conferred apart for a short time: their manner showing that they were agitated.   Ralph glanced at them twice or thrice, and ultimately said, with a great effort to recover his self-possession, " Now, what is this ?   If I am brought from home at this time of night, let it be for something.   What have you got to tell me ? "   After a short pause, he added, " Is my niece dead ? "

He had struck upon a key which rendered the task of commencement an easier one.   Brother Charles turned, and said that it was a death of which they had to tell him, but that his niece was well.

" You don't mean to tell me," said Ralph, as his eyes brightened, " that her brother's dead.   No, that's too good.   I'd not believe it if you told me so.   It would be too welcome news to be true."

" Shame on you, you hardened and unnatural man," cried the other brother, warmly ; " prepare yourself for intelligence, which if you have any human feeling in your breast, will make even you shrink and tremble.   What if we tell you that a poor unfortunate boy, a child in everything but never having known one of those tender endearments, or one of those lightsome hours which make our childhood a time to be remembered like a happy dream through all our after life—a warm-hearted, harmless, affectionate creature, who never offended you or did you wrong, but on whom you have vented the malice and hatred you have conceived for your nephew, and whom you have made an instrument for wreaking your bad passions upon him—what if we tell you that, sinking under your persecution, Sir, and the misery and ill-usage of a life short in years but long in suffering, this poor creature has gone to tell his sad tale where, for your part in it, you must surely answer ? "

"If you tell me," said Ralph, eagerly; "if you tell me that he is dead, I forgive you all else. If you tell me that he is dead, I am in your debt and bound to you for life. He is! I see it in your faces. Who triumphs now? Is this your dreadful news, this your terrible intelligence? You see how it moves me. You did well to send. I would have travelled a hundred miles a-foot, through mud, mire, and darkness, to hear this news just at this time."

Even then, moved as he was by this savage joy, Ralph could see in the faces of the two brothers, mingling with their look of disgust and horror, something of that indefinable compassion for himself which he had noticed before.

"And *he* brought you the intelligence, did he?" said Ralph, pointing with his finger towards the recess already mentioned; "and sat there, no doubt, to see me prostrated and overwhelmed by it! Ha, ha, ha! But I tell him that I'll be a sharp thorn in his side for many a long day to come, and I tell you two again that you don't know him yet, and that you'll rue the day you took compassion on the vagabond."

"You take me for your nephew," said a hollow, dejected voice; "it would be better for you and for me too if I were he indeed."

The figure that he had seen so dimly, rose, and came slowly down. He started back, for he found that he confronted—not Nicholas, as he had supposed, but Brooker.

Ralph had no reason that he knew, to fear this man; he had never feared him before; but the pallor which had been observed in his face when he issued forth that night, came upon him again; he was seen to tremble, and his voice changed as he said, keeping his eyes upon him,

"What does this fellow here? Do you know he is a convict—a felon —a common thief!"

"Hear what he has to tell you—oh, Mr. Nickleby, hear what he has to tell you, be he what he may," cried the brothers, with such emphatic earnestness, that Ralph turned to them in wonder. They pointed to Brooker, and Ralph again gazed at him: as it seemed mechanically.

"That boy," said the man, "that these gentlemen have been talking of—"

"That boy," repeated Ralph, looking vacantly at him.

"Whom I saw stretched dead and cold upon his bed, and who is now in his grave——"

"Who is now in his grave," echoed Ralph, like one who talks in his sleep.

The man raised his eyes, and clasped his hands solemnly together:

"——Was your only son, so help me God in heaven!"

In the midst of a dead silence, Ralph sat down, pressing his two hands upon his temples. He removed them after a minute, and never was there seen part of a living man, undisfigured by any wound, such a ghastly face as he then disclosed. He looked fixedly at Brooker, who was by this time standing at a short distance from him, but did not say one word or make the slightest sound or gesture.

"Gentlemen," said the man, "I offer no excuses for myself. I am long past that. If in telling you how this has happened, I tell you that I was harshly used and perhaps driven out of my real nature, I do it only as a necessary part of my story, and not to shield myself; I am a guilty man."

He stopped as if to recollect, and looking away from Ralph and addressing himself to the brothers, proceeded in a subdued and humble tone :

"Among those who once had dealings with this man, gentlemen—that's from twenty to five-and-twenty years ago—there was one, a rough fox-hunting, hard-drinking gentleman, who had run through his own fortune, and wanted to squander away that of his sister; they were both orphans, and she lived with him and managed his house. I don't know whether it was originally to back his influence and try to over-persuade the young woman or not, but he," pointing to Ralph, "used to go down to the house in Leicestershire pretty often, and stop there many days at a time. They had had a great many dealings together, and he may have gone on some of those, or to patch up his client's affairs, which were in a ruinous state—of course he went for profit. The gentlewoman was not a girl, but she was, I have heard say, handsome, and entitled to a pretty large property. In course of time he married her. The same love of gain which led him to contract this marriage, led to its being kept strictly private, for a clause in her father's will declared that if she married without her brother's consent, the property, in which she had only some life interest while she remained single, should pass away altogether to another branch of the family. The brother would give no consent that the sister didn't buy and pay for handsomely; Mr. Nickleby would consent to no such sacrifice, and so they went on keeping their marriage secret, and waiting for him to break his neck or die of a fever. He did neither, and meanwhile the result of this private marriage was a son. The child was put out to nurse a long way off, his mother never saw him but once or twice and then by stealth, and his father—so eagerly did he thirst after the money which seemed to come almost within his grasp now, for his brother-in-law was very ill, and breaking more and more every day—never went near him, to avoid raising any suspicion. The brother lingered on, Mr. Nickleby's wife constantly urged him to avow their marriage, he peremptorily refused. She remained alone in a dull country house, seeing little or no company but riotous, drunken sportsmen. He lived in London and clung to his business. Angry quarrels and recriminations took place, and when they had been married nearly seven years, and were within a few weeks of the time when the brother's death would have adjusted all, she eloped with a younger man and left him."

Here he paused, but Ralph did not stir, and the brothers signed to him to proceed.

"It was then that I became acquainted with these circumstances from his own lips. They were no secrets then, for the brother and others knew them, but they were communicated to me not on this account, but because I was wanted. He followed the fugitives—some said to make money of his wife's shame, but I believe to take some violent revenge, for that was as much his character as the other—perhaps more. He didn't find them, and she died not long after. I don't know whether he began to think he might like the child, or whether he wished to make sure that it should never fall into its mother's hands, but before he went, he entrusted me with the charge of bringing it home. And I did so."

He went on from this point in a still more humble tone, and spoke in a very low voice, pointing to Ralph as he resumed.

" He had used me ill—cruelly—I reminded him in what, not long ago when I met him in the street—and I hated him. I brought the child home to his own house and lodged him in the front garret. Neglect had made him very sickly, and I was obliged to call in a doctor, who said he must be removed for change of air or he would die. I think that first put it in my head. I did it then. He was gone six weeks, and when he came back, I told him—with every circumstance well planned and proved ; nobody could have suspected me—that the child was dead and buried. He might have been disappointed in some intention he had formed, or he might have had some natural affection, but he *was* grieved at *that*, and I was confirmed in my design of opening up the secret one day, and making it a means of getting money from him. I had heard, like most other men, of Yorkshire schools. I took the child to one kept by a man named Squeers, and left it there. I gave him the name of Smike. I paid twenty pounds a-year for him for six years, never breathing the secret all the time, for I had left his father's service after more hard usage, and quarrelled with him again. I was sent away from this country. I have been away nearly eight years. Directly I came home again I travelled down into Yorkshire, and skulking in the village of an evening time, made inquiries about the boys at the school, and found that this one, whom I had placed there, had run away with a young man bearing the name of his own father. I sought his father out in London, and hinting at what I could tell him, tried for a little money to support life, but he repulsed me with threats. I then found out his clerk, and going on from little to little, and showing him that there were good reasons for communicating with me, learnt what was going on ; and it was I who told him that the boy was no son of the man who claimed to be his father. All this time I had never seen the boy. At length I heard from this same source that he was very ill, and where he was. I travelled down there that I might reveal myself, if possible, to his recollection and confirm my story. I came upon him unexpectedly ; but before I could speak he knew me—he had good cause to remember me, poor lad—and I would have sworn to him if I had met him in the Indies ; I knew the piteous face I had seen in the little child. After a few days' indecision, I applied to the young gentleman in whose care he was, and I found that he was dead. He knows how quickly he recognised me again, how often he had described me and my leaving him at the school, and how he told him of a garret he recollected, which is the one I have spoken of, and in his father's house to this day. This is my story ; I demand to be brought face to face with the schoolmaster, and put to any possible proof of any part of it, and I will show that it's too true, and that I have this guilt upon my soul."

" Unhappy man ! " said the brothers. " What reparation can you make for this ? "

" None, gentlemen, none ! I have none to make, and nothing to hope now. I am old in years, and older still in misery and care. This confession can bring nothing upon me but new suffering and punishment ; but I make it, and will abide by it whatever comes. I have been made the instrument of working out this dreadful retribution upon the head of a man who, in the hot pursuit of his bad ends, has persecuted and hunted down his own child to death. It must descend upon me too—I know it must fall—my reparation comes too late, and neither in this world nor in the next can I have hope again!"

He had hardly spoken, when the lamp, which stood upon the table close to where Ralph was seated, and which was the only one in the room, was thrown to the ground and left them in utter darkness. There was some trifling confusion in obtaining another light; the interval was a mere nothing; but when it appeared, Ralph Nickleby was gone.

The good brothers and Tim Linkinwater occupied some time in discussing the probability of his return, and when it became apparent that he would not come back, they hesitated whether or no to send after him. At length, remembering how strangely and silently he had sat in one immoveable position during the interview, and thinking he might possibly be ill, they determined, although it was now very late, to send to his house on some pretence, and finding an excuse in the presence of Brooker, whom they knew not how to dispose of without consulting his wishes, they concluded to act upon this resolution before going to bed.

CHAPTER LXI.

WHEREIN NICHOLAS AND HIS SISTER FORFEIT THE GOOD OPINION OF ALL WORLDLY AND PRUDENT PEOPLE.

On the next morning after Brooker's disclosure had been made, Nicholas returned home. The meeting between him and those whom he had left there, was not without strong emotion on both sides, for they had been informed by his letters of what had occurred; and besides that, his griefs were theirs, they mourned with him the death of one whose forlorn and helpless state had first established a claim upon their compassion, and whose truth of heart and grateful earnest nature had every day endeared him to them more and more.

"I am sure," said Mrs. Nickleby, wiping her eyes, and sobbing bitterly, " I have lost the best, the most zealous, and most attentive creature that has ever been a companion to me in my life—putting you, my dear Nicholas, and Kate, and your poor papa, and that well-behaved nurse who ran away with the linen and the twelve small forks, out of the question of course. Of all the tractable, equal-tempered, attached, and faithful beings that ever lived, I believe he was the most so. To look round upon the garden now, that he took so much pride in, or to go into his room and see it filled with so many of those little contrivances for our comfort that he was so fond of making, and made so well, and so little thought he would leave unfinished—I can't bear it, I cannot really. Ah! This is a great trial to me, a great trial. It will be a comfort to you, my dear Nicholas, to the end of your life to recollect how kind and good you always were to him—so it will be to me to think what excellent terms we were always upon, and how fond he always was of me, poor fellow! It was very natural you should have been attached to him, my dear—very—and of course you were, and are very much cut up by this; I am sure it's only necessary to look at you and see how changed you are, to see that; but nobody knows what my feelings are—nobody can—it's quite impossible!"

While Mrs. Nickleby, with the utmost sincerity, gave vent to her sorrows after her own peculiar fashion of considering herself foremost, she was not the only one who indulged such feelings. Kate, although well accustomed to forget herself when others were to be considered, could not repress her grief; Madeline was scarcely less moved than she; and poor, hearty, honest, little Miss La Creevy, who had come upon one of her visits while Nicholas was away, and had done nothing since the sad news arrived but console and cheer them all, no sooner beheld him coming in at the door, than she sat herself down upon the stairs, and bursting into a flood of tears, refused for a long time to be comforted.

"It hurts me so," cried the poor body, "to see him come back alone. I can't help thinking what he must have suffered himself. I wouldn't mind so much if he gave way a little more, but he bears it so manfully."

"Why, so I should," said Nicholas, "should I not?"

"Yes, yes," replied the little woman, "and bless you for a good creature; but this does seem at first to a simple soul like me—I know it's wrong to say so, and I shall be sorry for it presently—this does seem such a poor reward for all you have done."

"Nay," said Nicholas gently, "what better reward could I have than the knowledge that his last days were peaceful and happy, and the recollection that I was his constant companion, and was not prevented, as I might have been by a hundred circumstances, from being beside him?"

"To be sure," sobbed Miss La Creevy, "it's very true, and I'm an ungrateful, impious, wicked little fool, I know."

With that, the good soul fell to crying afresh, and, endeavouring to recover herself, tried to laugh. The laugh and the cry meeting each other thus abruptly had a struggle for the mastery, and the result was that it was a drawn battle, and Miss La Creevy went into hysterics.

Waiting until they were all tolerably quiet and composed again, Nicholas, who stood in need of some rest after his long journey, retired to his own room, and throwing himself, dressed as he was, upon the bed, fell into a sound sleep. When he awoke he found Kate sitting by his bedside, who, seeing that he had opened his eyes, stooped down to kiss him.

"I came to tell you how glad I am to see you home again."

"But I can't tell you how glad I am to see you, Kate."

"We have been wearying so for your return," said Kate, "mama and I, and—and Madeline."

"You said in your last letter that she was quite well," said Nicholas, rather hastily, and colouring as he spoke. "Has nothing been said since I have been away about any future arrangements that the brothers have in contemplation for her?"

"Oh, not a word," replied Kate, "I can't think of parting from her without sorrow; and surely, Nicholas, you don't wish it."

Nicholas coloured again, and, sitting down beside his sister on a little couch near the window, said,

"No, Kate, no, I do not. I might strive to disguise my real

feelings from anybody but you; but I will tell you that—briefly and plainly, Kate—that I love her."

Kate's eyes brightened, and she was going to make some reply, when Nicholas laid his hand upon her arm, and went on :

" Nobody must know this but you. She last of all."

" Dear Nicholas!"

" Last of all—never, though never is a long day. Sometimes I try to think that the time may come when I may honestly tell her this; but it is so far off, in such distant perspective, so many years must elapse before it comes, and when it does come (if ever), I shall be so unlike what I am now, and shall have so outlived my days of youth and romance—though not, I am sure, of love for her—that even I feel how visionary all such hopes must be, and try to crush them rudely my-self and have the pain over, rather than suffer time to wither them, and keep the disappointment in store. No, Kate; since I have been absent, I have had, in that poor fellow who is gone, perpetually before my eyes another instance of the munificent liberality of these noble brothers. As far as in me lies I will deserve it, and if I have wavered in my bounden duty to them before, I am now determined to discharge it rigidly, and to put further delays and temptations beyond my reach."

" Before you say another word, dear Nicholas," said Kate, turning pale, "you must hear what I have to tell you. I came on purpose, but I had not the courage. What you say now gives me new heart." She faltered, and burst into tears.

There was that in her manner which prepared Nicholas for what was coming. Kate tried to speak, but her tears prevented her.

" Come, you foolish girl," said Nicholas; " why Kate, Kate, be a woman. I think I know what you would tell me. It concerns Mr. Frank, does it not ?"

Kate sunk her head upon his shoulder, and sobbed out " Yes."

" And he has offered you his hand, perhaps, since I have been away," said Nicholas; " is that it ? Yes. Well, well; it's not so difficult, you see, to tell me, after all. He offered you his hand ?"

" Which I refused," said Kate.

" Yes; and why ?"

" I told him," she said, in a trembling voice, " all that I have since found you told mama, and while I could not conceal from him, and cannot from you that—that it was a pang and a great trial, I did so firmly, and begged him not to see me any more."

" That's my own brave Kate!" said Nicholas, pressing her to his breast. " I knew you would."

" He tried to alter my resolution," said Kate, " and declared that be my decision what it might, he would not only inform his uncles of the step he had taken, but would communicate it to you also, directly you returned. I am afraid," she added, her momentary composure for-saking her, " I am afraid I may not have said strongly enough how highly I felt such disinterested love should be regarded, and how earnestly I prayed for his future happiness. If you do talk together, I should—I should like him to know that."

" And did you suppose, Kate, when you had made this sacrifice to what you knew was right and honourable, that I should shrink from mine?" said Nicholas tenderly.

"Oh, no! not if your position had been the same, but—"

"But it is the same," interrupted Nicholas; "Madeline is not the near relation of our benefactors, but she is closely bound to them by ties as dear, and I was first entrusted with her history, specially because they reposed unbounded confidence in me, and believed that I was true as steel. How base would it be of me to take advantage of the circumstances which placed her here, or of the slight service I was happily able to render her, and to seek to engage her affections when the result must be, if I succeeded, that the brothers would be disappointed in their darling wish of establishing her as their own child, and that I must seem to hope to build my fortunes on their compassion for the young creature whom I had so meanly and unworthily entrapped, turning her very gratitude and warmth of heart to my own purpose and account, and trading in her misfortunes! I, too, whose duty and pride and pleasure, Kate, it is, to have other claims upon me which I will never forget, and who have the means of a comfortable and happy life already, and have no right to look beyond it! I have determined to remove this weight from my mind; I doubt whether I have not done wrong even now; and to-day I will without reserve or equivocation disclose my real reasons to Mr. Cheeryble, and implore him to take immediate measures for removing this young lady to the shelter of some other roof."

"To-day? so very soon!"

"I have thought of this for weeks, and why should I postpone it? If the scene through which I have just passed has taught me to reflect and awakened me to a more anxious and careful sense of duty, why should I wait until the impression has cooled? You would not dissuade me, Kate; now would you?"

"You may grow rich you know," said Kate.

"I may grow rich!" repeated Nicholas, with a mournful smile, "ay, and I may grow old. But rich or poor, or old or young, we shall ever be the same to each other, and in that our comfort lies. What if we have but one home? It can never be a solitary one to you and me. What if we were to remain so true to these first impressions as to form no others? It is but one more link to the strong chain that binds us together. It seems but yesterday that we were playfellows, Kate, and it will seem but to-morrow that we are staid old people, looking back then to these cares as we look back now to those of our childish days, and recollecting with a melancholy pleasure that the time was when they could move us. Perhaps then, when we are quaint old folks and talk of the times when our step was lighter and our hair not grey, we may be even thankful for the trials that so endeared us to each other, and turned our lives into that current down which we shall have glided so peacefully and calmly. And having caught some inkling of our story, the young people about us—as young as you and I are now, Kate—shall come to us for sympathy, and pour distresses which hope and inexperience could scarcely feel enough for, into the compassionate ears of the old bachelor brother and his maiden sister."

Kate smiled through her tears as Nicholas drew this picture, but they were not tears of sorrow, although they continued to fall when he had ceased to speak.

"Am I not right, Kate?" he said, after a short silence.

"Quite, quite, dear brother; and I cannot tell you how happy I am that I have acted as you would have had me."

"You don't regret?"

"N--n--no," said Kate timidly, tracing some pattern upon the ground with her little foot. "I don't regret having done what was honourable and right, of course, but I do regret that this should have ever happened—at least sometimes I regret it, and sometimes I—I don't know what I say; I am but a weak girl Nicholas, and it has agitated me very much."

It is no vaunt to affirm that if Nicholas had had ten thousand pounds at the minute, he would, in his generous affection for the owner of that blushing cheek and downcast eye, have bestowed its utmost farthing, in perfect forgetfulness of himself, to secure her happiness. But all he could do was to comfort and console her by kind words; and words they were of such love and kindness and cheerful encouragement, that poor Kate threw her arms about his neck and declared she would weep no more.

"What man," thought Nicholas proudly, while on his way soon afterwards to the Brothers' house, "would not be sufficiently rewarded for any sacrifice of fortune, by the possession of such a heart as that, which, but that hearts weigh light and gold and silver heavy, is beyond all praise. Frank has money and wants no more. Where would it buy him such a treasure as Kate! And yet in unequal marriages, the rich party is always supposed to make a great sacrifice, and the other to get a good bargain! But I am thinking like a lover, or like an ass, which I suppose is pretty nearly the same."

Checking thoughts so little adapted to the business on which he was bound by such self-reproofs as this and many others no less sturdy, he proceeded on his way and presented himself before Tim Linkinwater.

"Ah! Mr. Nickleby," cried Tim, "God bless you! how d'ye do! Well? Say you're quite well and never better—do now."

"Quite," said Nicholas, shaking him by both hands.

"Ah!" said Tim, "you look tired though, now I come to look at you. Hark! there he is, d'ye hear him? That was Dick the blackbird. He hasn't been himself since you've been gone. He'd never get on without you now; he takes as naturally to you, as he does to me."

"Dick is a far less sagacious fellow than I supposed him, if he thinks I am half so well worthy of his notice as you," replied Nicholas.

"Why I'll tell you what, Sir," said Tim, standing in his favourite attitude and pointing up to the cage with the feather of his pen, "it's a very extraordinary thing about that bird, that the only people he ever takes the smallest notice of are Mr. Charles and Mr. Ned and you and me."

Here Tim stopped and glanced anxiously at Nicholas; then unexpectedly catching his eye repeated, "and you and me, Sir, and you and me." And then he glanced at Nicholas again, and, squeezing his hand, said, "I am a bad one at putting off anything I am interested in. I didn't mean to ask you, but I should like to hear a few particulars about that poor boy. Did he mention Cheeryble Brothers at all?"

"Yes," said Nicholas, "many and many a time."

" That was right of him," returned Tim, wiping his eyes, " that was very right of him."

" And he mentioned your name a score of times," said Nicholas, " and often bade me carry back his love to Mr. Linkinwater."

" No, no, did he though ?" rejoined Tim, sobbing outright. " Poor fellow ! I wish we could have had him buried in town. There isn't such a burying-ground in all London as that little one on the other side of the square—there are counting-houses all round it, and if you go in there on a fine day you can see the books and safes through the open windows. And he sent his love to me, did he ? I didn't expect he would have thought of me. Poor fellow, poor fellow ! His love too !"

Tim was so completely overcome by this little mark of recollection, that he was quite unequal to any further conversation at the moment. Nicholas therefore slipped quietly out, and went to Brother Charles's room.

If he had previously sustained his firmness and fortitude, it had been by an effort which had cost him no little pain; but the warm welcome, the hearty manner, the homely unaffected commiseration of the good old man went to his heart, and no inward struggle could prevent his showing it.

" Come, come, my dear Sir," said the benevolent merchant ; " we must not be cast down, no, no. We must learn to bear misfortune, and we must remember that there are many sources of consolation even in death. Every day that this poor lad had lived, he must have been less and less qualified for the world, and more unhappy in his own deficiencies. It is better as it is, my dear Sir. Yes, yes, yes, it's better as it is."

" I have thought of all that, Sir," replied Nicholas, clearing his throat. " I feel it, I assure you."

" Yes, that's well," replied Mr. Cheeryble, who, in the midst of all his comforting, was quite as much taken aback as honest old Tim ; " that's well. Where is my brother Ned ? Tim Linkinwater, Sir, where is my brother Ned ?"

" Gone out with Mr. Trimmers, about getting that unfortunate man into the hospital, and sending a nurse to his children," said Tim.

" My brother Ned is a fine fellow—a great fellow !" exclaimed brother Charles as he shut the door and returned to Nicholas. " He will be over-joyed to see you, my dear Sir: we have been speaking of you every day."

" To tell you the truth, Sir, I am glad to find you alone," said Nicholas, with some natural hesitation, " for I am anxious to say something to you. Can you spare me a very few minutes ?"

" Surely, surely," returned brother Charles, looking at him with an anxious countenance. " Say on, my dear Sir, say on."

" I scarcely know how or where to begin," said Nicholas. " If ever one mortal had reason to be penetrated with love and reverence for another, with such attachment as would make the hardest service in his behalf a pleasure and delight, with such grateful recollections as must rouse the utmost zeal and fidelity of his nature, those are the feelings which I should entertain for you, and do, from my heart and soul, believe me."

" I do believe you," replied the old gentleman, " and I am happy in the belief. I have never doubted it; I never shall. I am sure I never shall."

" Your telling me that so kindly," said Nicholas, "emboldens me to proceed. When you first took me into your confidence and despatched me on those missions to Miss Bray, I should have told you that I had seen her long before, that her beauty had made an impression upon me which I could not efface, and that I had fruitlessly endeavoured to trace her and become acquainted with her history. I did not tell you so, because I vainly thought I could conquer my weaker feelings, and render every consideration subservient to my duty to you."

" Mr. Nickleby," said brother Charles, "you did not violate the confidence I placed in you, or take an unworthy advantage of it. I am sure you did not."

" I did not," said Nicholas, firmly. "Although I found that the necessity for self-command and restraint became every day more imperious and the difficulty greater, I never for one instant spoke or looked but as I would have done had you been by. I never for one moment deserted my trust, nor have I to this instant. But I find that constant association and companionship with this sweet girl is fatal to my peace of mind, and may prove destructive to the resolutions I made in the beginning and up to this time have faithfully kept. In short, Sir, I cannot trust myself, and I implore and beseech you to remove this young lady from under the charge of my mother and sister without delay. I know that to any one but myself—to you who consider the immeasurable distance between me and this young lady, who is now your ward and the object of your peculiar care—my loving her even in thought must appear the height of rashness and presumption. I know it is so. But who can see her as I have seen,—who can know what her life has been, and not love her ? I have no excuse but that, and as I cannot fly from this temptation, and cannot repress this passion with its object constantly before me, what can I do but pray and beseech you to remove it, and to leave me to forget her !"

" Mr. Nickleby," said the old man, after a short silence, " you can do no more. I was wrong to expose a young man like you to this trial. I might have foreseen what would happen. Thank you, Sir, thank you. Madeline shall be removed."

" If you would grant me one favour, dear Sir, and suffer her to remember me with esteem by never revealing to her this confession—"

" I will take care,"—said Mr. Cheeryble. " And now, is this all you have to tell me ? "

" No ! " returned Nicholas, meeting his eye, " it is not."

" I know the rest," said Mr. Cheeryble, apparently very much relieved by this prompt reply. " When did it come to your knowledge ? "

" When I reached home this morning."

" You felt it your duty immediately to come to me, and tell me what your sister no doubt acquainted you with ? "

" I did," said Nicholas, " though I could have wished to have spoken to Mr. Frank first."

" Frank was with me last night," replied the old gentleman. " You have done well, Mr. Nickleby—very well, Sir—and I thank you again."

Upon this head Nicholas requested permission to add a few words. He ventured to hope that nothing he had said would lead to the estrangement of Kate and Madeline, who had formed an attachment for each other, any interruption of which would, he knew, be attended with great pain to them, and, most of all, with remorse and pain to him, as its unhappy cause. When these things were all forgotten he hoped that Frank and he might still be warm friends, and that no word or thought of his humble home, or of her who was well contented to remain there and share his quiet fortunes, would ever again disturb the harmony between them. He recounted, as nearly as he could, what had passed between him and Kate that morning; speaking of her with such warmth of pride and affection, and dwelling so cheerfully upon the confidence they had of overcoming any selfish regrets and living contented and happy in each other's love, that few could have heard him unmoved. More moved himself than he had been yet, he expressed in a few hurried words—as expressive perhaps as the most eloquent phrases—his devotion to the brothers, and his hope that he might live and die in their service.

To all this, brother Charles listened in profound silence, and with his chair so turned from Nicholas that his face could not be seen. He had not spoken either in his accustomed manner, but with a certain stiffness and embarrassment very foreign to it. Nicholas feared he had offended him. He said, "No—no—he had done quite right," but that was all.

"Frank is a heedless, foolish fellow," he said, after Nicholas had paused for some time, "a very heedless, foolish fellow. I will take care that this is brought to a close without delay. Let us say no more upon the subject; it's a very painful one to me. Come to me in half an hour, I have strange things to tell you, my dear Sir, and your uncle has appointed this afternoon for your waiting upon him with me."

"Waiting upon him! With you, Sir!" cried Nicholas.

"Ay, with me," replied the old gentleman. "Return to me in half an hour, and I'll tell you more."

Nicholas waited upon him at the time mentioned, and then learnt all that had taken place on the previous day, and all that was known of the appointment Ralph had made with the brothers which was for that night, and for the better understanding of which it will be requisite to return and follow his own footsteps from the house of the twin brothers. Therefore we leave Nicholas somewhat reassured by the restored kindness of their manner towards him, and yet sensible that it was different from what it had been (though he scarcely knew in what respect), and full of uneasiness, uncertainty, and disquiet.

CHAPTER LXII.

RALPH MAKES ONE LAST APPOINTMENT—AND KEEPS IT.

CREEPING from the house and slinking off like a thief: groping with his hands when first he got into the street as if he were a blind man, and looking often over his shoulder while he hurried away, as though he were followed in imagination or reality by some one anxious to question or detain him, Ralph Nickleby left the city behind him and took the road to his own home.

The night was dark, and a cold wind blew, driving the clouds furiously and fast before it.   There was one black, gloomy mass that seemed to follow him ; not hurrying in the wild chase with the others, but lingering sullenly behind, and gliding darkly and stealthily on. He often looked back at this, and more than once stopped to let it pass over, but somehow, when he went forward again it was still behind him, coming mournfully and slowly up like a shadowy funeral train.

He had to pass a poor, mean burial-ground—a dismal place raised a few feet above the level of the street, and parted from it by a low parapet wall and an iron railing ; a rank, unwholesome, rotten spot, where the very grass and weeds seemed, in their frowsy growth, to tell that they had sprung from paupers' bodies, and struck their roots in the graves of men, sodden in steaming courts and drunken hungry dens. And here in truth they lay, parted from the living by a little earth and a board or two—lay thick and close—corrupting in body as they had in mind; a dense and squalid crowd.   Here they lay cheek by jowl with life: no deeper down than the feet of the throng that passed there every day, and piled high as their throats.   Here they lay, a grisly family, all those dear departed brothers and sisters of the ruddy clergy-man who did his task so speedily when they were hidden in the ground !

As he passed here, Ralph called to mind that he had been one of a jury long before, on the body of a man who had cut his throat ; and that he was buried in this place.   He could not tell how he came to recollect it now, when he had so often passed and never thought about him, or how it was that he felt an interest in the circumstance, but he did both, and stopping, and clasping the iron railings with his hands, looked eagerly in, wondering which might be his grave.

While he was thus engaged, there came towards him, with noise of shouts and singing, some fellows full of drink, followed by others, who were remonstrating with them and urging them to go home in quiet.   They were in high good-humour, and one of them, a little, weazen, hump-backed man, began to dance.   He was a grotesque, fan-tastic figure, and the few by-standers laughed.   Ralph himself was moved to mirth, and echoed the laugh of one who stood near and who looked round in his face.   When they had passed on and he was left alone again, he resumed his speculation with a new kind of interest, for he recollected that the last person who had seen the suicide alive had left him very merry, and he remembered how strange he and the other jurors had thought that at the time.

He could not fix upon the spot among such a heap of graves, but he conjured up a strong and vivid idea of the man himself, and how he looked, and what had led him to do it, all of which he recalled with ease.   By dint of dwelling upon this theme, he carried the impression with him when he went away, as he remembered when a child to have had frequently before him the figure of some goblin he had once seen chalked upon a door.   But as he drew nearer and nearer home he forgot it again, and began to think how very dull and solitary the house would be inside.

This feeling became so strong at last, that when he reached his own door, he could hardly make up his mind to turn the key and open it— when he had done that and gone into the passage, he felt as though to shut it again would be to shut out the world. But he let it go, and it closed with a loud noise. There was no light. How very dreary, cold, and still it was!

Shivering from head to foot he made his way up stairs into the room where he had been last disturbed. He had made a kind of compact with himself that he would not think of what had happened until he got home. He was at home now, and suffered himself for the first time to consider it.

His own child—his own child! He never doubted the tale; he felt it was true, knew it as well now as if he had been privy to it all along. His own child! And dead too. Dying beside Nicholas—loving him, and looking upon him as something like an angel! That was the worst.

They had all turned from him and deserted him in his very first need, even money could not buy them now; everything must come out, and everybody must know all. Here was the young lord dead, his companion abroad and beyond his reach, ten thousand pounds gone at one blow, his plot with Gride overset at the very moment of triumph, his after schemes discovered, himself in danger, the object of his persecution and Nicholas's love, his own wretched boy; everything crumbled and fallen upon him, and he beaten down beneath the ruins and grovelling in the dust.

If he had known his child to be alive, if no deceit had been ever practised and he had grown up beneath his eye, he might have been a careless, indifferent, rough, harsh father—like enough—he felt that; but the thought would come that he might have been otherwise, and that his son might have been a comfort to him and they two happy together. He began to think now, that his supposed death and his wife's flight had had some share in making him the morose, hard man he was. He seemed to remember a time when he was not quite so rough and obdurate, and almost thought that he had first hated Nicholas because he was young and gallant, and perhaps like the stripling who had brought dishonour and loss of fortune on his head.

But one tender thought, or one of natural regret in that whirlwind of passion and remorse, was as a drop of calm water in a stormy maddened sea. His hatred of Nicholas had been fed upon his own defeat, nourished on his interference with his schemes, fattened upon his old defiance and success. There were reasons for its increase; it had grown and strengthened gradually. Now it attained a height which was sheer wild lunacy. That his of all others should have been the hands to rescue his miserable child, that he should have been his protector and faithful friend, that he should have shown him that love and tenderness which from the wretched moment of his birth he had never known, that he should have taught him to hate his own parent and execrate his very name, that he should now know and feel all this and triumph in the recollection, was gall and madness to the usurer's heart. The dead boy's love for Nicholas, and the attachment of Nicholas to him, was insupportable agony. The picture of his death-bed, with Nicholas at his side tending and supporting him, and he breathing out his thanks, and expiring in his arms, when he would have had them mortal enemies and hating each other to the last, drove him frantic. He gnashed his teeth and smote the air, and looking wildly round, with eyes which gleamed through the darkness, cried aloud :

" I am trampled down and ruined. The wretch told me true. The night has come. Is there no way to rob them of further triumph, and spurn their mercy and compassion ? Is there no devil to help me ? "

Swiftly there glided again into his brain the figure he had raised that night. It seemed to lie before him. The head was covered now. So it was when he first saw it. The rigid, upturned, marble feet too, he remembered well. Then came before him the pale and trembling relatives who had told their tale upon the inquest—the shrieks of women—the silent dread of men—the consternation and disquiet—the victory achieved by that heap of clay which with one motion of its hand had let out the life and made this stir among them——

He spoke no more, but after a pause softly groped his way out of the room, and up the echoing stairs—up to the top—to the front garret —where he closed the door behind him, and remained——

It was a mere lumber-room now, but it yet contained an old dismantled bedstead : the one on which his son had slept, for no other had ever been there. He avoided it hastily, and sat down as far from it as he could.

The weakened glare of the lights in the street below, shining through the window which had no blind or curtain to intercept it, was enough to show the character of the room, though not sufficient fully to reveal the various articles of lumber, old corded trunks and broken furniture, which were scattered about. It had a shelving roof ; high in one part, and at another descending almost to the floor. It was towards the highest part that Ralph directed his eyes, and upon it he kept them fixed steadily for some minutes, when he rose, and dragging thither an old chest upon which he had been seated, mounted upon it, and felt along the wall above his head with both hands. At length they touched a large iron hook firmly driven into one of the beams.

At that moment he was interrupted by a loud knocking at the door below. After a little hesitation he opened the window, and demanded who it was.

" I want Mr. Nickleby," replied a voice.

" What with him ? "

" That's not Mr. Nickleby's voice surely," was the rejoinder.

It was not like it ; but it was Ralph who spoke, and so he said.

The voice made answer that the twin brothers wished to know whether the man whom he had seen that night was to be detained, and that although it was now midnight they had sent in their anxiety to do right.

" Yes," cried Ralph, " detain him till to-morrow ; then let them bring him here—him and my nephew—and come themselves, and be sure that I will be ready to receive them."

" At what hour ? " asked the voice.

" At any hour," replied Ralph fiercely. " In the afternoon, tell them. At any hour—at any minute—all times will be alike to me."

He listened to the man's retreating footsteps until the sound had passed, and then gazing up into the sky saw, or thought he saw, the same black cloud that had seemed to follow him home, and which now appeared to hover directly above the house.

" I know its meaning now," he muttered, " and the restless nights, the dreams, and why I have quailed of late ;—all pointed to this. Oh ! if men by selling their own souls could ride rampant for a term, for how short a term would I barter mine to-night !"

The sound of a deep bell came along the wind. One.

" Lie on !" cried the usurer, " with your iron tongue; ring merrily for births that make expectants writhe, and marriages that are made in hell, and toll ruefully for the dead whose shoes are worn already. Call men to prayers who are godly because not found out, and ring chimes for the coming in of every year that brings this cursed world nearer to its end. No bell or book for me ; throw me on a dunghill, and let me rot there to infect the air !"

With a wild look around, in which frenzy, hatred, and despair, were horribly mingled, he shook his clenched hand at the sky above him, which was still dark and threatening, and closed the window.

The rain and hail pattered against the glass, the chimneys quaked and rocked ; the crazy casement rattled with the wind as though an impatient hand inside were striving to burst it open. But no hand was there, and it opened no more.

*   *   *   *   *   *   *

" How's this ?" cried one, " the gentlemen say they can't make anybody hear, and have been trying these two hours ?"

" And yet he came home last night," said another, " for he spoke to somebody out of that window up stairs."

They were a little knot of men, and, the window being mentioned, went out in the road to look up at it. This occasioned their observing that the house was still close shut, as the housekeeper had said she had left it on the previous night, and led to a great many suggestions, which terminated in two or three of the boldest getting round to the back and so entering by a window, while the others remained outside in impatient expectation.

They looked into all the rooms below, opening the shutters as they went to admit the fading light ; and still finding nobody, and everything quiet and in its place, doubted whether they should go farther. One man, however, remarking that they had not yet been into the garret, and that it was there he had been last seen, they agreed to look there too, and went up softly, for the mystery and silence made them timid.

After they had stood for an instant on the landing eyeing each other, he who had proposed their carrying the search so far turned the handle of the door, and pushing it open looked through the chink, and fell back directly.

" It's very odd," he whispered, " he's hiding behind the door ! Look !"

They pressed forward to see, but one among them thrusting the others aside with a loud exclamation, drew a clasp knife from his pocket and dashing into the room cut down the body.

He had torn a rope from one of the old trunks and hung himself on an iron hook immediately below the trap-door in the ceiling—in the very place to which the eyes of his son, a lonely, desolate, little creature, had so often been directed in childish terror fourteen years before.

CHAPTER LXIII.

THE BROTHERS CHEERYBLE MAKE VARIOUS DECLARATIONS FOR THEM-
SELVES AND OTHERS; AND TIM LINKINWATER MAKES A DECLARATION
FOR HIMSELF.

SOME weeks had passed, and the first shock of these events had subsided. Madeline had been removed; Frank had been absent; and
Nicholas and Kate had begun to try in good earnest to stifle their own
regrets, and to live for each other and for their mother, who, poor lady,
could in no wise be reconciled to this dull and altered state of affairs,
when there came one evening, per favour of Mr. Linkinwater, an invitation from the Brothers to dinner on the next day but one, comprehending not only Mrs. Nickleby, Kate, and Nicholas, but little Miss
La Creevy, who was most particularly mentioned.

"Now, my dears," said Mrs. Nickleby, when they had done becoming honour to the bidding, and Tim had taken his departure, "what
does *this* mean?"

"What do *you* mean, mother?" asked Nicholas, smiling.

"I say, my dear," rejoined that lady, with a face of unfathomable
mystery, "what does this invitation to dinner mean,—what is its
intention and object?"

"I conclude it means, that on such a day we are to eat and drink in
their house, and that its intent and object is to confer pleasure upon us,"
said Nicholas.

"And that's all you conclude it is, my dear?"

"I have not yet arrived at anything deeper, mother."

"Then I'll just tell you one thing," said Mrs. Nickleby, "you'll find
yourself a little surprised, that's all. You may depend upon it that
this means something besides dinner."

"Tea and supper, perhaps," suggested Nicholas.

"I wouldn't be absurd, my dear, if I were you," replied Mrs.
Nickleby, in a lofty manner, "because it's not by any means becoming,
and doesn't suit you at all. What I mean to say is, that the Mr.
Cheerybles don't ask us to dinner with all this ceremony for nothing.
Never mind, wait and see. You won't believe anything I say, of
course. It's much better to wait, a great deal better, it's satisfactory
to all parties, and there can be no disputing. All I say is, remember
what I say now, and when I say I said so, don't say I didn't."

With this stipulation, Mrs. Nickleby, who was troubled night and
day with a vision of a hot messenger tearing up to the door to announce
that Nicholas had been taken into partnership, quitted that branch of
the subject, and entered upon a new one.

"It's a very extraordinary thing," she said, "a most extraordinary
thing, that they should have invited Miss La Creevy. It quite asto-
nishes me, upon my word it does. Of course it's very pleasant that
she should be invited, very pleasant, and I have no doubt that she'll
conduct herself extremely well; she always does. It's very gratifying
to think that we should have been the means of introducing her into

such society, and I'm quite glad of it, quite rejoiced, for she certainly is an exceedingly well-behaved and good-natured little person. I could wish that some friend would mention to her how very badly she has her cap trimmed, and what very preposterous bows those are, but of course that's impossible; and if she likes to make a fright of herself, no doubt she has a perfect right to do so. We never see ourselves— never do and never did—and I suppose we never shall."

This moral reflection reminding her of the necessity of being peculiarly smart upon the occasion, so as to counterbalance Miss La Creevy, and be herself an effectual set-off and atonement, led Mrs. Nickleby into a consultation with her daughter relative to certain ribands, gloves, and trimmings, which, being a complicated question, and one of paramount importance, soon routed the previous one, and put it to flight.

The great day arriving, the good lady put herself under Kate's hands an hour or so after breakfast, and, dressing by easy stages, completed her toilet in sufficient time to allow of her daughter's making hers, which was very simple and not very long, though so satisfactory that she had never appeared more charming or looked more lovely. Miss La Creevy, too, arrived with two bandboxes (whereof the bottoms fell out as they were handed from the coach) and something in a newspaper, which a gentleman had sat upon, coming down, and which was obliged to be ironed again before it was fit for service. At last everybody was dressed, including Nicholas, who had come home to fetch them, and they went away in a coach sent by the Brothers for the purpose : Mrs. Nickleby wondering very much what they would have for dinner, and cross-examining Nicholas as to the extent of his discoveries in the morning, whether he had smelt anything cooking at all like turtle, and if not, what he had smelt ; and diversifying the conversation with reminiscences of dinners to which she had gone some twenty years ago, concerning which she particularized not only the dishes but the guests, in whom her hearers did not feel a very absorbing interest, as not one of them had ever chanced to hear their names before.

The old butler received them with profound respect and many smiles, and ushered them into the drawing-room, where they were received by the Brothers with so much cordiality and kindness that Mrs. Nickleby was quite in a flutter, and had scarcely presence of mind enough even to patronise Miss La Creevy. Kate was still more affected by the reception, for knowing that the Brothers were acquainted with all that had passed between her and Frank, she felt her position a most delicate and trying one, and was trembling upon the arm of Nicholas when Mr. Charles took her in his, and led her to another part of the room.

"Have you seen Madeline, my dear," he said, "since she left your house?"

" No, Sir?" replied Kate. " Not once."

" And not heard from her, eh ? Not heard from her ?"

" I have only had one letter," rejoined Kate, gently. " I thought she would not have forgotten me quite so soon."

" Ah !" said the old man, patting her on the head and speaking as affectionately as if she had been his favourite child. " Poor dear ! what do you think of this, brother Ned ? Madeline has only written to her once—only once, Ned, and she didn't think she would have forgotten her quite so soon, Ned."

" Oh ! sad, sad—very sad !" said Ned.

The brothers interchanged a glance, and looking at Kate for a little time without speaking, shook hands, and nodded as if they were congratulating each other upon something very delightful.

"Well, well," said brother Charles, "go into that room, my dear, that door yonder, and see if there's not a letter for you from her. I think there's one upon the table. You needn't hurry back, my love, if there is, for we don't dine just yet, and there's plenty of time—plenty of time."

Kate retired as she was directed, and brother Charles having followed her graceful figure with his eyes, turned to Mrs. Nickleby and said—

" We took the liberty of naming one hour before the real dinner-time, ma'am, because we had a little business to speak about, which would occupy the interval. Ned, my dear fellow, will you mention what we agreed upon ? Mr. Nickleby, Sir, have the goodness to follow me."

Without any further explanation, Mrs. Nickleby, Miss La Creevy, and brother Ned, were left alone together, and Nicholas followed brother Charles into his private room, where to his great astonishment he encountered Frank whom he supposed to be abroad.

" Young men," said Mr. Cheeryble, " shake hands."

" I need no bidding to do that," said Nicholas, extending his.

" Nor I," rejoined Frank, as he clasped it heartily.

The old gentleman thought that two handsomer or finer young fellows could scarcely stand side by side than those on whom he looked with so much pleasure. Suffering his eyes to rest upon them for a short time in silence, he said, while he seated himself at his desk,

" I wish to see you friends—close and firm friends—and if I thought you otherwise, I should hesitate in what I am about to say. Frank, look here. Mr. Nickleby, will you come on the other side ?"

The young men stepped up on either hand of brother Charles, who produced a paper from his desk and unfolded it.

" This," he said, " is a copy of the will of Madeline's maternal grandfather, bequeathing her the sum of twelve thousand pounds, payable either upon her coming of age or marrying. It would appear that this gentleman, angry with her (his only relation) because she would not put herself under his protection, and detach herself from the society of her father, in compliance with his repeated overtures, made a will leaving this property, which was all he possessed, to a charitable institution. He would seem to have repented this determination, however, for three weeks afterwards, and in the same month, he executed this. By some fraud it was abstracted immediately after his decease, and the other—the only will found—was proved and administered. Friendly negotiations, which have only just now terminated, have been proceeding since this instrument came into our hands, and as there is no doubt of its authenticity, and the witnesses have been discovered (after some trouble), the money has been refunded. Madeline has therefore obtained her right, and is, or will be, when either of the contingencies which I have mentioned has arisen, mistress of this fortune. You understand me ?"

Frank replied in the affirmative. Nicholas, who could not trust himself to speak lest his voice should be heard to falter, bowed his head.

" Now, Frank," said the old gentleman, " you were the immediate means of recovering this deed. The fortune is but a small one, but we love Madeline, and such as it is, we would rather see you allied to her with that, than to any other girl we know who has three times the money. Will you become a suitor to her for her hand ?"

" No, Sir : I interested myself in the recovery of that instrument, believing that her hand was already pledged to one who has a thousand times the claims upon her gratitude, and, if I mistake not, upon her heart, than I or any other man can ever urge. In this it seems I judged hastily."

" As you always do, Sir," cried brother Charles, utterly forgetting his assumed dignity, " as you always do. How dare you think, Frank, that we would have you marry for money, when youth, beauty, and every amiable virtue and excellence, were to be had for love? How dared you, Frank, go and make love to Mr. Nickleby's sister without telling us first what you meant to do, and letting us speak for you ?"

" I hardly dared to hope."

" You hardly dared to hope ! Then, so much the greater reason for having our assistance. Mr. Nickleby, Sir, Frank, although he judged hastily, judged for once correctly. Madeline's heart *is* occupied— give me your hand, Sir ; it is occupied by you, and worthily and naturally. This fortune is destined to be yours, but you have a greater fortune in her, Sir, than you would have in money were it forty times told. She chooses you, Mr. Nickleby. She chooses as we, her dearest friends, would have her choose. Frank chooses as we would have *him* choose. He should have your sister's little hand, Sir, if she had refused it a score of times—ay, he should, and he shall ! You acted nobly not knowing our sentiments, but now you know them, Sir, and must do as you are bid. What ! You are the children of a worthy gentleman ! The time was, Sir, when my dear brother Ned and I were two poor simple-hearted boys, wandering almost barefoot to seek our fortunes ; are we changed in anything but years and worldly circumstances since that time ? No, God forbid ! Oh, Ned, Ned, Ned, what a happy day this is for you and me ; if our poor mother had only lived to see us now, Ned, how proud it would have made her dear heart at last !"

Thus apostrophised, brother Ned, who had entered with Mrs. Nickleby, and who had been before unobserved by the young men, darted forward, and fairly hugged brother Charles in his arms.

" Bring in my little Kate," said the latter, after a short silence. " Bring her in, Ned. Let me see Kate, let me kiss her. I have a right to do so now ; I was very near it when she first came ; I have often been very near it. Ah ! Did you find the letter, my bird ? Did you find Madeline herself, waiting for you and expecting you ? Did you find that she had not quite forgotten her friend and nurse and sweet companion ? Why, this is almost the best of all !"

" Come, come," said Ned, " Frank will be jealous, and we shall have some cutting of throats before dinner."

" Then let him take her away, Ned, let him take her away.
Madeline's in the next room. Let all the lovers get out of the way,
and talk among themselves, if they've anything to say. Turn 'em out,
Ned, every one."

Brother Charles began the clearance by leading the blushing girl
himself to the door, and dismissing her with a kiss. Frank was not
very slow to follow, and Nicholas had disappeared first of all. So there
only remained Mrs. Nickleby and Miss La Creevy, who were both
sobbing heartily; the two brothers, and Tim Linkinwater, who now
came in to shake hands with everybody, his round face all radiant
and beaming with smiles.

" Well, Tim Linkinwater, Sir," said brother Charles, who was
always spokesman, " now the young folks are happy, Sir."

" You didn't keep 'em in suspense as long as you said you would,
though," returned Tim, archly. " Why, Mr. Nickleby and Mr. Frank
were to have been in your room for I don't know how long ; and I
don't know what you weren't to have told them before you came out
with the truth."

" Now, did you ever know such a villain as this, Ned ?" said the
old gentleman, " did you ever know such a villain as Tim Linkinwater? He accusing me of being impatient, and he the very man who
has been wearying us morning, noon, and night, and torturing us for
leave to go and tell 'em what was in store, before our plans were half
complete, or we had arranged a single thing—a treacherous dog !"

" So he is, brother Charles," returned Ned, " Tim is a treacherous
dog. Tim is not to be trusted. Tim is a wild young fellow—he wants
gravity and steadiness; he must sow his wild oats, and then perhaps
he'll become in time a respectable member of society."

This being one of the standing jokes between the old fellows and
Tim, they all three laughed very heartily, and might have laughed
much longer, but that the brothers seeing that Mrs. Nickleby was
labouring to express her feelings, and was really overwhelmed by the
happiness of the time, took her between them, and led her from the
room under pretence of having to consult her on some most important
arrangements.

Now Tim and Miss La Creevy had met very often, and had always
been very chatty and pleasant together—had always been great friends
—and consequently it was the most natural thing in the world that Tim,
finding that she still sobbed, should endeavour to console her. As Miss
La Creevy sat on a large old-fashioned window-seat, where there was
ample room for two, it was also natural that Tim should sit down
beside her ; and as to Tim's being unusually spruce and particular in
his attire that day, why it was a high festival and a great occasion, and
that was the most natural thing of all.

Tim sat down beside Miss La Creevy, and crossing one leg over the
other so that his foot—he had very comely feet, and happened to be
wearing the neatest shoes and black silk stockings possible—should
come easily within the range of her eye, said in a soothing way :

" Don't cry."

" I must," rejoined Miss La Creevy.

"No don't," said Tim. "Please don't; pray don't."

"I am so happy!" sobbed the little woman.

"Then laugh," said Tim, "do laugh."

What in the world Tim was doing with his arm it is impossible to conjecture, but he knocked his elbow against that part of the window which was quite on the other side of Miss La Creevy; and it is clear that it could have no business there.

"Do laugh," said Tim, "or I'll cry."

"Why should you cry?" asked Miss La Creevy, smiling.

"Because I'm happy too," said Tim. "We are both happy, and I should like to do as you do."

Surely there never was a man who fidgetted as Tim must have done then, for he knocked the window again—almost in the same place—and Miss La Creevy said she was sure he'd break it.

"I knew," said Tim, "that you would be pleased with this scene."

"It was very thoughtful and kind to remember me," returned Miss La Creevy. "Nothing could have delighted me half so much."

Why on earth should Miss La Creevy and Tim Linkinwater have said all this in a whisper? It was no secret. And why should Tim Linkinwater have looked so hard at Miss La Creevy, and why should Miss La Creevy have looked so hard at the ground?

"It's a pleasant thing," said Tim, "to people like us, who have passed all our lives in the world alone, to see young folks that we are fond of brought together with so many years of happiness before them."

"Ah!" cried the little woman with all her heart, "that it is!"

"Although," pursued Tim—"although it makes one feel quite solitary and cast away—now don't it?"

Miss La Creevy said she didn't know. And why should she say she didn't know? Because she must have known whether it did or not.

"It's almost enough to make us get married after all, isn't it?" said Tim.

"Oh nonsense!" replied Miss La Creevy, laughing, "we are too old."

"Not a bit," said Tim, "we are too old to be single—why shouldn't we both be married instead of sitting through the long winter evenings by our solitary firesides? Why shouldn't we make one fireside of it, and marry each other?"

"Oh Mr. Linkinwater, you're joking!"

"No, no, I'm not. I'm not indeed," said Tim. "I will if you will. Do, my dear."

"It would make people laugh so."

"Let 'em laugh," cried Tim, stoutly, "we have good tempers I know, and we'll laugh too. Why what hearty laughs we have had since we've known each other."

"So we have," cried Miss La Creevy—giving way a little, as Tim thought.

"It has been the happiest time in all my life—at least, away from the counting-house and Cheeryble Brothers," said Tim. "Do, my dear. Now say you will."

"No, no, we mustn't think of it," returned Miss La Creevy. "What would the Brothers say?"

"Why, God bless your soul!" cried Tim, innocently, "you don't suppose I should think of such a thing without their knowing it! Why they left us here on purpose."

"I can never look 'em in the face again!" exclaimed Miss La Creevy, faintly.

"Come," said Tim, "let's be a comfortable couple. We shall live in the old house here, where I have been for four-and-forty year; we shall go to the old church, where I've been every Sunday morning all through that time; we shall have all my old friends about us—Dick, the archway, the pump, the flower-pots, and Mr. Frank's children, and Mr. Nickleby's children, that we shall seem like grandfather and grandmother to. Let's be a comfortable couple, and take care of each other, and if we should get deaf, or lame, or blind, or bed-ridden, how glad we shall be that we have somebody we are fond of always to talk to and sit with! Let's be a comfortable couple. Now do, my dear."

Five minutes after this honest and straight-forward speech, little Miss La Creevy and Tim were talking as pleasantly as if they had been married for a score of years, and had never once quarrelled all the time; and five minutes after that, when Miss La Creevy had bustled out to see if her eyes were red and put her hair to rights, Tim moved with a stately step towards the drawing-room exclaiming as he went, "There an't such another woman in all London—I *know* there an't."

By this time the apoplectic butler was nearly in fits, in consequence of the unheard-of postponement of dinner. Nicholas, who had been engaged in a manner which every reader may imagine for himself or herself, was hurrying down stairs in obedience to his angry summons when he encountered a new surprise.

Upon his way down, he overtook in one of the passages a stranger genteelly dressed in black who was also moving towards the dining-room. As he was rather lame and walked slowly Nicholas lingered behind, and was following him step by step, wondering who he was, when he suddenly turned round and caught him by both hands.

"Newman Noggs!" cried Nicholas joyfully.

"Ah! Newman, your own Newman, your own old faithful Newman. My dear boy, my dear Nick, I give you joy—health, happiness, every blessing. I can't bear it, it's too much, my dear boy—it makes a child of me!"

"Where have you been?" said Nicholas, "what have you been doing! How often have I inquired for you, and been told that I should hear before long!"

"I know, I know," returned Newman, "they wanted all the happiness to come together. I've been helping 'em. I—I—look at me, Nick, look at me."

"You would never let *me* do that," said Nicholas in a tone of gentle reproach.

"I didn't mind what I was then. I shouldn't have had the heart to put on gentleman's clothes. They would have reminded me of old times and made me miserable; I am another man now, Nick. My dear boy, I can't speak—don't say anything to me—don't think the worse of me for these tears—you don't know what I feel to-day; you can't and never will!"

They walked in to dinner arm-in-arm, and sat down side by side. Never was such a dinner as that since the world began. There was the superannuated bank clerk Tim Linkinwater's friend, and there was the chubby old lady Tim Linkinwater's sister, and there was so much attention from Tim Linkinwater's sister to Miss La Creevy, and there were so many jokes from the superannuated bank clerk, and Tim Linkinwater himself was in such tiptop spirits, and little Miss La Creevy was in such a comical state, that of themselves they would have composed the pleasantest party conceivable. Then there was Mrs. Nickleby so grand and complacent, Madeline and Kate so blushing and beautiful, Nicholas and Frank so devoted and proud, and all four so silently and tremblingly happy—there was Newman so subdued yet so overjoyed, and there were the twin Brothers so delighted and interchanging such looks, that the old servant stood transfixed behind his master's chair and felt his eyes grow dim as they wandered round the table.

When the first novelty of the meeting had worn off, and they began truly to feel how happy they were, the conversation became more general and the harmony and pleasure if possible increased. The Brothers were in a perfect ecstacy, and their insisting on saluting the ladies all round before they would permit them to retire, gave occasion to the superannuated bank clerk to say so many good things that he quite outshone himself, and was looked upon as a prodigy of humour.

"Kate, my dear," said Mrs. Nickleby, taking her daughter aside directly they got up stairs, "you don't really mean to tell me that this is actually true about Miss La Creevy and Mr. Linkinwater?"

"Indeed it is, mama."

"Why I never heard such a thing in my life!" exclaimed Mrs. Nickleby.

"Mr. Linkinwater is a most excellent creature," reasoned Kate, "and for his age, quite young still."

"For *his* age, my dear!" returned Mrs. Nickleby, "yes; nobody says anything against him, except that I think he is the weakest and most foolish man I ever knew. It's *her* age I speak of. That he should have gone and offered himself to a woman who must be—ah, half as old again as I am, and that she should have dared to accept him! It don't signify, Kate;—I'm disgusted with her!"

Shaking her head very emphatically indeed, Mrs. Nickleby swept away; and all the evening, in the midst of the merriment and enjoyment that ensued, and in which with that exception she freely participated, conducted herself towards Miss La Creevy in a stately and distant manner, designed to mark her sense of the impropriety of her conduct, and to signify her extreme and cutting disapprobation of the misdemeanour she had so flagrantly committed.

CHAPTER LXIV.

AN OLD ACQUAINTANCE IS RECOGNISED UNDER MELANCHOLY CIRCUMSTANCES, AND DOTHEBOYS HALL BREAKS UP FOR EVER.

NICHOLAS was one of those whose joy is incomplete unless it is shared by the friends of adverse and less fortunate days. Surrounded by every fascination of love and hope, his warm heart yearned towards plain

John Browdie. He remembered their first meeting with a smile, and their second with a tear; saw poor Smike once again with the bundle on his shoulder trudging patiently by his side, and heard the honest Yorkshireman's rough words of encouragement as he left them on their road to London.

Madeline and he sat down very many times, jointly to produce a letter which should acquaint John at full length with his altered fortunes, and assure him of his friendship and gratitude. It so happened, however, that the letter could never be written. Although they applied themselves to it with the best intentions in the world, it chanced that they always fell to talking about something else, and when Nicholas tried it by himself, he found it impossible to write one half of what he wished to say, or to pen anything, indeed, which on re-perusal did not appear cold and unsatisfactory compared with what he had in his mind. At last, after going on thus from day to day, and reproaching himself more and more, he resolved (the more readily as Madeline strongly urged him) to make a hasty trip into Yorkshire, and present himself before Mr. and Mrs. Browdie without a word of notice.

Thus it was that between seven and eight o'clock one evening, he and Kate found themselves in the Saracen's Head booking-office, securing a place to Greta Bridge by the next morning's coach. They had to go westward to procure some little necessaries for his journey, and as it was a fine night, they agreed to walk there and ride home.

The place they had just been in called up so many recollections, and Kate had so many anecdotes of Madeline, and Nicholas so many anecdotes of Frank, and each was so interested in what the other said, and both were so happy and confiding, and had so much to talk about, that it was not until they had plunged for a full half hour into that labyrinth of streets which lies between Seven Dials and Soho without emerging into any large thoroughfare, that Nicholas began to think it just possible they might have lost their way.

The possibility was soon converted into a certainty, for on looking about, and walking first to one end of the street and then to the other, he could find no land-mark he could recognise, and was fain to turn back again in quest of some place at which he could seek a direction.

It was a by-street, and there was nobody about, or in the few wretched shops they passed. Making towards a faint gleam of light, which streamed across the pavement from a cellar, Nicholas was about to descend two or three steps so as to render himself visible to those below and make his inquiry, when he was arrested by a loud noise of scolding in a woman's voice.

"Oh come away!" said Kate, "they are quarrelling. You'll be hurt."

"Wait one instant, Kate. Let us hear if there's anything the matter," returned her brother. "Hush!"

"You nasty, idle, vicious, good-for-nothing brute," cried the woman, stamping on the ground, "why don't you turn the mangle?"

"So I am, my life and soul!" replied a man's voice. "I am always turning, I am perpetually turning, like a demd old horse in a demnition mill. My life is one demd horrid grind!"

"Then why don't you go and list for a soldier?" retorted the woman, "you're welcome to."

Reduced circumstances of Mr Mantalini.

"For a soldier!" cried the man. "For a soldier! Would his joy and gladness see him in a coarse red coat with a little tail? Would she hear of his being slapped and beat by drummers demnebly? Would she have him fire off real guns, and have his hair cut and his whiskers shaved, and his eyes turned right and left, and his trousers pipe-clayed?"

"Dear Nicholas," whispered Kate, "you don't know who that is. It's Mr. Mantalini I am confident."

"Do make sure; peep at him while I ask the way," said Nicholas. "Come down a step or two—come."

Drawing her after him, Nicholas crept down the steps and looked into a small boarded cellar. There, amidst clothes-baskets and clothes, stripped to his shirt-sleeves, but wearing still an old patched pair of pantaloons of superlative make, a once brilliant waistcoat, and moustache and whiskers as of yore, but lacking their lustrous dye—there, endeavouring to mollify the wrath of a buxom female, the proprietress of the concern, and grinding meanwhile as if for very life at the mangle, whose creaking noise, mingled with her shrill tones, appeared almost to deafen him—there was the graceful, elegant, fascinating, and once dashing Mantalini.

"Oh you false traitor!" cried the lady, threatening personal violence on Mr. Mantalini's face.

"False! Oh dem! Now my soul, my gentle, captivating, bewitching, and most demnebly enslaving chick-a-biddy, be calm," said Mr. Mantalini, humbly.

"I won't!" screamed the woman. "I'll tear your eyes out!"

"Oh! What a demd savage lamb!" cried Mr. Mantalini.

"You're never to be trusted," screamed the woman, "you were out all day yesterday, and gallivanting somewhere I know—you know you were. Isn't it enough that I paid two pound fourteen for you, and took you out of prison and let you live here like a gentleman, but must you go on like this: breaking my heart besides?"

"I will never break its heart, I will be a good boy, and never do so any more; I will never be naughty again; I beg its little pardon," said Mr. Mantalini, dropping the handle of the mangle, and folding his palms together, "it is all up with its handsome friend, he has gone to the demnition bow-wows. It will have pity? it will not scratch and claw, but pet and comfort? Oh, demmit."

Very little affected, to judge from her action, by this tender appeal, the lady was on the point of returning some angry reply, when Nicholas, raising his voice, asked his way to Piccadilly.

Mr. Mantalini turned round, caught sight of Kate, and, without another word, leapt at one bound into a bed which stood behind the door, and drew the counterpane over his face, kicking meanwhile convulsively.

"Demmit," he cried, in a suffocating voice, "it's little Nickleby! Shut the door, put out the candle, turn me up in the bedstead; oh, dem, dem, dem!"

The woman looked first at Nicholas, and then at Mr. Mantalini, as if uncertain on whom to visit this extraordinary behaviour, but Mr. Mantalini happening by ill luck to thrust his nose from under the bed-clothes, in his anxiety to ascertain whether the visitors were gone, she suddenly, and with a dexterity which could only have been acquired by long practice, flung a pretty heavy clothes-basket at him, with so good an aim that he kicked more violently than before, though without venturing to make any effort to disengage his head, which was quite extinguished. Thinking this a favourable opportunity for departing before any of the torrent of her wrath discharged itself upon him, Nicholas hurried Kate off, and left the unfortunate subject of this unexpected recognition to explain his conduct as he best could.

The next morning he began his journey. It was now cold, winter weather, forcibly recalling to his mind under what circumstances he had first travelled that road, and how many vicissitudes and changes he had since undergone. He was alone inside the greater part of the way, and sometimes, when he had fallen into a doze, and, rousing himself, looked out of the window, and recognised some place which he well remembered as having passed either on his journey down, or in the long walk back with poor Smike, he could hardly believe but that all which had since happened had been a dream, and that they were still plodding wearily on towards London, with the world before them.

To render these recollections the more vivid, it came on to snow as night set in, and passing though Stamford and Grantham, and by the little alehouse where he had heard the story of the bold Baron of Grogswig, everything looked as if he had seen it but yesterday, and not even a flake of the white crust upon the roofs had melted away. Encouraging the train of ideas which flocked upon him, he could almost persuade himself that he sat again outside the coach, with Squeers and the boys, that he heard their voices in the air, and that he felt again, but with a mingled sensation of pain and pleasure now, that old sinking of the heart and longing after home. While he was yet yielding himself up to these fancies he fell asleep, and, dreaming of Madeline, forgot them.

He slept at the inn at Greta Bridge on the night of his arrival, and, rising at a very early hour next morning, walked to the market town, and inquired for John Browdie's house. John lived in the outskirts now he was a family man, and, as everybody knew him, Nicholas had no difficulty in finding a boy who undertook to guide him to his residence.

Dismissing his guide at the gate, and in his impatience not even stopping to admire the thriving look of cottage or garden either, Nicholas made his way to the kitchen door, and knocked lustily with his stick.

"Halloa!" cried a voice inside, "waat be the matther noo? Be the toon a-fire? Ding, but thou mak'est noise eneaf!"

With these words John Browdie opened the door himself, and opening his eyes too to their utmost width, cried, as he clapped his hands together and burst into a hearty roar,

"Ecod, it be the godfeyther, it be the godfeyther! Tilly, here be Misther Nickleby. Gi' us thee hond, mun. Coom awa', coom awa'. In wi' un, doon beside the fire; tak' a soop o' thot. Dinnot say a word till thou'st droonk it a', oop wi' it, mun. Ding! but I'm reeght glod to see thee."

Adapting his action to his text, John dragged Nicholas into the kitchen, forced him down upon a huge settle beside a blazing fire, poured out from an enormous bottle about a quarter of a pint of spirits, thrust it into his hand, opened his mouth and threw back his head as a sign to him to drink it instantly, and stood with a broad grin of welcome overspreading his great red face, like a jolly giant.

" I might ha' knowa'd," said John, " that nobody but thou would ha' coom wi' sike a knock as yon. Thot was the wa' thou knocked at schoolmeasther's door eh? Ha, ha, ha! But I say—waa't be a' this aboot schoolmeasther?"

" You know it then?" said Nicholas.

" They were talking aboot it doon toon last neeght," replied John, " but neane on 'em seemed quite to un'erstan' it loike."

" After various shiftings and delays," said Nicholas, " he has been sentenced to be transported for seven years, for being in the unlawful possession of a stolen will; and after that, he has to suffer the consequence of a conspiracy."

" Whew!" cried John, " a conspiracy! Soomat in the pooder plot wa'—eh? Sooma't in the Guy Faurx line?"

" No, no, no, a conspiracy connected with his school; I'll explain it presently."

" Thot's reeght!" said John, " explain it arter breakfast, not noo, for thou bees't hoongry, and so am I; and Tilly she mun' be at the bottom o' a' explanations, for she says thot's the mutual confidence. Ha, ha, ha! Ecod it's a room start is the mutual confidence!"

The entrance of Mrs. Browdie with a smart cap on and very many apologies for their having been detected in the act of breakfasting in the kitchen, stopped John in his discussion of this grave subject, and hastened the breakfast, which being composed of vast mounds of toast, new-laid eggs, boiled ham, Yorkshire pie, and other cold substantials (of which heavy relays were constantly appearing from another kitchen under the direction of a very plump servant), was admirably adapted to the cold bleak morning, and received the utmost justice from all parties. At last it came to a close, and the fire which had been lighted in the best parlour having by this time burnt up, they adjourned thither to hear what Nicholas had to tell.

Nicholas told them all, and never was there a story which awakened so many emotions in the breasts of two eager listeners. At one time honest John groaned in sympathy, and at another roared with joy; at one time he vowed to go up to London on purpose to get a sight of the Brothers Cheeryble, and at another swore that Tim Linkinwater should receive such a ham by coach, and carriage free, as mortal knife had never carved. When Nicholas began to describe Madeline, he sat with his mouth wide open nudging Mrs. Browdie from time to time, and exclaiming under his breath that she must be " raa'ther a tidy sort," and when he heard at last that his young friend had come down purposely to communicate his good fortune, and to convey to him all those assurances of friendship which he could not state with sufficient warmth in writing—that the only object of his journey was to share his happiness with them, and to tell them that when he was married they must come up to see him, and that Madeline insisted on it as well as he— John could hold out no longer, but after looking indignantly at his wife

and demanding to know what she was whimpering for, drew his coat-
sleeve over his eyes and blubbered outright.

"Telle'e waa't though," said John seriously, when a great deal had
been said on both sides, "to return to schoolmeasther: if this news
aboot 'un has reached school to-day, the old 'ooman wean't have a whole
boan in her boddy, nor Fanny neither."

"Oh John!" cried Mrs. Browdie.

"Ah! and Oh John agean," replied the Yorkshireman. "I dinnot
know what they lads mightn't do. When it first got aboot that
schoolmeasther was in trouble, soom feythers and moothers sent and
took their young chaps awa'. If them as is left should know waa'ts
coom tiv'un, there'll be sike a revolution and rebel!—Ding! But I
think they'll a' gang daft, and spill bluid like wather!"

In fact John Browdie's apprehensions were so strong that he determined to ride over to the school without delay, and invited Nicholas to
accompany him, which however he declined, pleading that his presence
might perhaps aggravate the bitterness of their adversity.

"Thot's true!" said John, "I should ne'er ha' thought o' thot."

"I must return to-morrow," said Nicholas, "but I mean to dine
with you to-day, and if Mrs. Browdie can give me a bed—"

"Bed!" cried John, "I wish thou could'st sleep in fower beds at
once. Ecod thou should'st have 'em a'. Bide till I coom back, on'y
bide till I coom back, and ecod we'll mak' a day of it."

Giving his wife a hearty kiss, and Nicholas a no less hearty shake
of the hand, John mounted his horse and rode off: leaving Mrs.
Browdie to apply herself to hospitable preparations, and his young
friend to stroll about the neighbourhood, and revisit spots which were
rendered familiar to him by many a miserable association.

John cantered away, and arriving at Dotheboys Hall tied his horse to
a gate and made his way to the schoolroom door, which he found locked
on the inside. A tremendous noise and riot arose from within, and
applying his eye to a convenient crevice in the wall, he did not remain
long in ignorance of its meaning.

The news of Mr. Squeers's downfall had reached Dotheboys; that
was quite clear. To all appearance it had very recently become known
to the young gentlemen, for the rebellion had just broken out.

It was one of the brimstone-and-treacle mornings, and Mrs. Squeers
had entered school according to custom with the large bowl and spoon,
followed by Miss Squeers and the amiable Wackford, who during his
father's absence had taken upon him such minor branches of the executive as kicking the pupils with his nailed boots, pulling the hair of
some of the smaller boys, pinching the others in aggravating places, and rendering himself in various similar ways a great comfort and happiness to
his mother. Their entrance, whether by premeditation or a simultane-
ous impulse, was the signal of revolt. While one detachment rushed
to the door and locked it, and another mounted upon the desks and
forms, the stoutest (and consequently the newest) boy seized the cane,
and confronting Mrs. Squeers with a stern countenance, snatched off
her cap and beaver-bonnet, put it on his own head, armed himself with the wooden spoon, and bade her, on pain of death, go

The "breaking up" at Dotheboys Hall.

down upon her knees, and take a dose directly. Before that estimable lady could recover herself or offer the slightest retaliation, she was forced into a kneeling posture by a crowd of shouting tormentors, and compelled to swallow a spoonful of the odious mixture, rendered more than usually savoury by the immersion in the bowl of Master Wackford's head, whose ducking was entrusted to another rebel. The success of this first achievement prompted the malicious crowd, whose faces were clustered together in every variety of lank and half-starved ugliness, to further acts of outrage. The leader was insisting upon Mrs. Squeers repeating her dose, Master Squeers was undergoing another dip in the treacle, and a violent assault had been commenced on Miss Squeers, when John Browdie, bursting open the door with one vigorous kick, rushed to the rescue. The shouts, screams, groans, hoots, and clapping of hands, suddenly ceased, and a dead silence ensued.

" Ye be noice chaps," said John, looking steadily round. " What's to do here, thou yoong dogs !"

" Squeers is in prison, and we are going to run away !" cried a score of shrill voices. " We won't stop, we won't stop !"

" Weel then, dinnot stop," replied John, " who waants thee to stop ? Roon awa' loike men, but dinnot hurt the women."

" Hurrah !" cried the shrill voices, more shrilly still.

" Hurrah !" repeated John. " Weel, hurrah loike men too. Noo then, look out. Hip—hip—hip—hurrah !"

" Hurrah !" cried the voices.

" Hurrah agean," said John. " Looder still."

The boys obeyed.

" Anoother !" said John. " Dinnot be afeard on it. Let's have a good 'un."

" Hurrah !"

" Noo then," said John, " let's have yan more to end wi', and then coot off as quick as you loike. Tak' a good breath noo—Squeers be in jail—the school's brokken oop—it's a' ower—past and gane—think o' thot, and let it be a hearty 'un. Hurrah !"

Such a cheer arose as the walls of Dotheboys Hall had never echoed before, and were destined never to respond to again. When the sound had died away the school was empty, and of the busy noisy crowd which had peopled it but five minutes before, not one remained.

" Very well, Mr. Browdie !" said Miss Squeers, hot and flushed from the recent encounter, but vixenish to the last ; " you've been and excited our boys to run away. Now see if we don't pay you out for that, Sir ! If my pa is unfortunate and trod down by henemies, we're not going to be basely crowed and conquered over by you and Tilda."

" Noa !" replied John bluntly, " thou bean't. Tak' thy oath o' thot. Think betther o' us, Fanny. I tell'ee both that I'm glod the auld man has been caught out at last—dom'd glod—but ye'll sooffer eneaf wi'out any crowin' fra' me, and I be not the mun to crow nor be Tilly the lass, so I tell'ee flat. More than thot, I tell'ee noo, that if thou need'st friends to help thee awa' from this place—dinnot turn up thy nose, Fanny, thou may'st—thou'lt foind Tilly and I wi' a thout o' old times aboot us, ready to lend thee a hond. And when I say thot, dinnot think I be asheamed of waa't I've deane, for I say agean, Hurrah! and dom the schoolmeasther—there!"

His parting words concluded, John Browdie strode heavily out, remounted his nag, put him once more into a smart canter, and, carolling lustily forth some fragments of an old song, to which the horse's hoofs rang a merry accompaniment, sped back to his pretty wife and to Nicholas.

For some days afterwards the neighbouring country was overrun with boys, who, the report went, had been secretly furnished by Mr. and Mrs. Browdie, not only with a hearty meal of bread and meat, but with sundry shillings and sixpences to help them on their way. To this rumour John always returned a stout denial, which he accompanied, however, with a lurking grin, that rendered the suspicious doubtful, and fully confirmed all previous believers in their opinion.

There were a few timid young children, who, miserable as they had been, and many as were the tears they had shed in the wretched school, still knew no other home, and had formed for it a sort of attachment, which made them weep when the bolder spirits fled, and cling to it as a refuge. Of these, some were found crying under hedges and in such places, frightened at the solitude. One had a dead bird in a little cage; he had wandered nearly twenty miles, and when his poor favourite died, lost courage, and lay down beside him. Another was discovered in a yard hard by the school, sleeping with a dog, who bit at those who came to remove him, and licked the sleeping child's pale face.

They were taken back, and some other stragglers were recovered, but by degrees they were claimed, or lost again; and in course of time Dotheboys Hall and its last breaking up began to be forgotten by the neighbours, or to be only spoken of as among the things that had been.

CHAPTER LXV.

CONCLUSION.

When her term of mourning had expired, Madeline gave her hand and fortune to Nicholas, and on the same day and at the same time Kate became Mrs. Frank Cheeryble. It was expected that Tim Linkinwater and Miss La Creevy would have made a third couple on the occasion, but they declined, and two or three weeks afterwards went out together one morning before breakfast, and coming back with merry faces, were found to have been quietly married that day.

The money which Nicholas acquired in right of his wife he invested in the firm of Cheeryble Brothers, in which Frank had become a partner. Before many years elapsed, the business began to be carried on in the names of "Cheeryble and Nickleby," so that Mrs. Nickleby's prophetic anticipations were realised at last.

The twin brothers retired. Who needs to be told that *they* were happy? They were surrounded by happiness of their own creation, and lived but to increase it.

Tim Linkinwater condescended, after much entreaty and browbeating, to accept a share in the house, but he could never be prevailed upon to suffer the publication of his name as a partner, and always persisted in the punctual and regular discharge of his clerkly duties.

He and his wife lived in the old house, and occupied the very bed-chamber in which he had slept for four-and-forty years. As his wife grew older, she became even a more cheerful and light-hearted little creature; and it was a common saying among their friends, that it was impossible to say which looked the happier—Tim as he sat calmly smiling in his elbow-chair on one side of the fire, or his brisk little wife chatting and laughing, and constantly bustling in and out of hers, on the other.

Dick, the blackbird, was removed from the counting-house and pro-moted to a warm corner in the common sitting-room. Beneath his cage hung two miniatures, of Mrs. Linkinwater's execution: one representing herself and the other Tim, and both smiling very hard at all beholders. Tim's head being powdered like a twelfth cake, and his spectacles copied with great nicety, strangers detected a close resemblance to him at the first glance, and this leading them to suspect that the other must be his wife, and emboldening them to say so without scruple, Mrs. Linkin-water grew very proud of these achievements in time, and considered them among the most successful likenesses she had ever painted. Tim had the profoundest faith in them likewise, for upon this, as upon all other subjects, they held but one opinion, and if ever there were a " comfortable couple" in the world, it was Mr. and Mrs. Linkinwater.

Ralph having died intestate, and having no relations but those with whom he had lived in such enmity, they would have become in legal course his heirs. But they could not bear the thought of grow-ing rich on money so acquired, and felt as though they could never hope to prosper with it. They made no claim to his wealth; and the riches for which he had toiled all his days, and burdened his soul with so many evil deeds, were swept at last into the coffers of the state, and no man was the better or the happier for them.

Arthur Gride was tried for the unlawful possession of the will, which he had either procured to be stolen, or dishonestly acquired and retained by other means as bad. By dint of an ingenious counsel, and a legal flaw, he escaped, but only to undergo a worse punishment; for some years afterwards his house was broken open in the night by robbers, tempted by the rumours of his great wealth, and he was found horribly murdered in his bed.

Mrs. Sliderskew went beyond the seas at nearly the same time as Squeers, and in the course of nature never returned. Brooker died penitent. Sir Mulberry Hawk lived abroad for some years, courted and caressed, and in high repute as a fine dashing fellow; and ulti-mately, returning to this country, was thrown into jail for debt, and there perished miserably, as such high, noble spirits generally do.

The first act of Nicholas, when he became a rich and prosperous merchant, was to buy his father's old house. As time crept on, and there came gradually about him a group of lovely children, it was altered and enlarged, but none of the old rooms were ever pulled down, no old tree was rooted up, nothing with which there was any associa-tion of bygone times was ever removed or changed.

Within a stone's-throw was another retreat, enlivened by children's pleasant voices too, and here was Kate, with many new cares and occupations, and many new faces courting her sweet smile (and one so like her own, that to her mother she seemed a child again), the same true gentle creature, the same fond sister, the same in the love of all about her, as in her girlish days.

Mrs. Nickleby lived sometimes with her daughter, and sometimes with her son, accompanying one or other of them to London at those periods when the cares of business obliged both families to reside there, and always preserving a great appearance of dignity, and relating her experiences (especially on points connected with the management and bringing-up of children) with much solemnity and importance. It was a very long time before she could be induced to receive Mrs. Linkinwater into favour, and it is even doubtful whether she ever thoroughly forgave her.

There was one grey-haired, quiet, harmless gentleman, who, winter and summer, lived in a little cottage hard by Nicholas's house, and when he was not there, assumed the superintendence of affairs. His chief pleasure and delight was in the children, with whom he was a child himself, and master of the revels. The little people could do nothing without dear Newman Noggs.

The grass was green above the dead boy's grave, and trodden by feet so small and light, that not a daisy drooped its head beneath their pressure. Through all the spring and summer-time, garlands of fresh flowers wreathed by infant hands rested upon the stone, and when the children came to change them lest they should wither and be pleasant to him no longer, their eyes filled with tears, and they spoke low and softly of their poor dead cousin.

THE END.

LONDON:
BRADBURY AND EVANS, PRINTERS, WHITEFRIARS.

The children at their cousin's grave.

LIFE AND ADVENTURES

OF

NICHOLAS NICKLEBY.

THE

LIFE AND ADVENTURES

OF

NICHOLAS NICKLEBY.

BY CHARLES DICKENS.

WITH ILLUSTRATIONS BY PHIZ.

LONDON:

CHAPMAN AND HALL, 186, STRAND.

MDCCCXXXIX.

LONDON:
BRADBURY AND EVANS, PRINTERS, WHITEFRIARS.

TO

W. C. MACREADY, ESQ.,

THE FOLLOWING PAGES

ARE INSCRIBED,

AS A SLIGHT TOKEN OF ADMIRATION AND REGARD,

BY HIS FRIEND,

THE AUTHOR.

PREFACE.

It has afforded the Author great amusement and satisfaction, during the progress of this work, to learn from country friends and from a variety of ludicrous statements concerning himself in provincial newspapers, that more than one Yorkshire schoolmaster lays claim to being the original of Mr. Squeers. One worthy, he has reason to believe, has actually consulted authorities learned in the law, as to his having good grounds on which to rest an action for libel; another has meditated a journey to London, for the express purpose of committing an assault and battery upon his traducer; a third perfectly remembers being waited on last January twelvemonth by two gentlemen, one of whom held him in conversation while the other took his likeness; and, although Mr. Squeers has but one eye, and he has two, and the published sketch does not resemble him (whoever he may be) in any other respect, still he and all his friends and neighbours know at once for whom it is meant, because—the character is *so* like him.

While the Author cannot but feel the full force of the compliment thus conveyed to him, he ventures to suggest that these contentions may arise from the fact, that Mr. Squeers is the representative of a class, and not of an individual. Where

imposture, ignorance, and brutal cupidity, are the stock in
trade of a small body of men, and one is described by these
characteristics, all his fellows will recognise something belonging
to themselves, and each will have a misgiving that the portrait
is his own.

To this general description, as to most others, there may be
some exceptions; and although the Author neither saw nor
heard of any in the course of an excursion which he made into
Yorkshire, before he commenced these adventures, or before
or since, it affords him much more pleasure to assume their
existence than to doubt it. He has dwelt thus long upon this
point, because his object in calling public attention to the
system would be very imperfectly fulfilled, if he did not state
now in his own person, emphatically and earnestly, that Mr.
Squeers and his school are faint and feeble pictures of an existing reality, purposely subdued and kept down lest they should
be deemed impossible—that there are upon record trials at law
in which damages have been sought as a poor recompense for
lasting agonies and disfigurements inflicted upon children by
the treatment of the master in these places, involving such
offensive and foul details of neglect, cruelty, and disease, as no
writer of fiction would have the boldness to imagine—and that,
since he has been engaged upon these Adventures, he has
received from private quarters far beyond the reach of suspicion
or distrust, accounts of atrocities, in the perpetration of which
upon neglected or repudiated children these schools have been
the main instruments, very far exceeding any that appear in
these pages.

To turn to a more pleasant subject, it may be right to say,
that there *are* two characters in this book which are drawn
from life. It is remarkable that what we call the world, which

is so very credulous in what professes to be true, is most incredulous in what professes to be imaginary; and that while every day in real life it will allow in one man no blemishes, and in another no virtues, it will seldom admit a very strongly-marked character, either good or bad, in a fictitious narrative, to be within the limits of probability. For this reason, they have been very slightly and imperfectly sketched. Those who take an interest in this tale will be glad to learn that the BROTHERS CHEERYBLE live; that their liberal charity, their singleness of heart, their noble nature, and their unbounded benevolence, are no creations of the Author's brain; but are prompting every day (and oftenest by stealth) some munificent and generous deed in that town of which they are the pride and honour.

It only now remains for the writer of these passages, with that feeling of regret with which we leave almost any pursuit that has for a long time occupied us and engaged our thoughts, and which is naturally augmented in such a case as this, when that pursuit has been surrounded by all that could animate and cheer him on,—it only now remains for him, before abandoning his task, to bid his readers farewell.

" The author of a periodical performance," says Mackenzie, " has indeed a claim to the attention and regard of his readers, more interesting than that of any other writer. Other writers submit their sentiments to their readers, with the reserve and circumspection of him who has had time to prepare for a public appearance. He who has followed Horace's rule, of keeping his book nine years in his study, must have withdrawn many an idea which in the warmth of composition he had conceived, and altered many an expression which in the hurry of writing he had set down. But the periodical essayist commits to his readers the feelings of the day, in the language which those feelings have prompted. As he has delivered himself with the freedom of intimacy and the cordiality of friendship, he will naturally look for the indulgence which those relations may claim; and when he bids his readers adieu, will hope, as well as feel, the regrets of an acquaintance, and the tenderness of a friend."

With such feelings and such hopes the periodical essayist, the Author of these pages, now lays them before his readers in a completed form, flattering himself, like the writer just quoted, that on the first of next month they may miss his company at the accustomed time as something which used to be expected with pleasure; and think of the papers which on that day of so many past months they have read, as the correspondence of one who wished their happiness, and contributed to their amusement.

CONTENTS.

———•———

LIST OF PLATES.

———•———

SPECIMEN PAGE.

THE INVISIBLE BURGLARS.

" Here, Jerry," continued the host, " run out for the policeman; " and Jerry, of course, ran with all possible speed.

" You'd better come down there, you wagabonds," cried the landlord.

" Hexcuse us," said Jim, " you are werry perlite."

" If you don't, I'll blow you bang through the pot ! " cried the land-lord.

" You haven't enough powder," said the invisible Joe.

The policeman here entered, and bustling up to the grate, shouted " now, young fellows, come along, I wants you."

" *Do* you," said one of the young fellows.

" It's o' no use, you know," cried the policeman, who held his authority to be contemned, and his dignity insulted, by that tranquil remark. " You'd better come at once, you know, my rum uns."

" That's werry good advice, I des-say," said one of the rum uns. " ony *we* doesn't think so."

" Why, it taint o' no use," urged the policeman, " you an't got a ha'porth o' chance. Here, give us hold of a stick or a broom," said he to the waiter; and the chambermaid ran to fetch one; when another policeman entered, to whom the first said, " Smith, go and stand by them ere chimley pots, will yer," and accordingly up Smith went with the boots.

" Now then," said the policeman, having got a long broom, " if you don't come down, my crickets, in course I shall make you, and that's all about it."

In reply to this acute observation, one of the " crickets " indulged in a contemptuous laugh, which so enraged the policeman, that he on the instant introduced the long broom up the chimney, and brought down of course a sufficient quantity of soot to fill an imperial bushel measure. This remarkable descension, being on his part wholly unexpected, caused him to spit and sneeze with considerable vehemence, while his face was sufficiently black to win the sympathies of any regular philan-thropist going.

" Now then, you sirs ! " shouted Smith from the top; " Do you mean to come up or go down ? *Ony* say !"

As soon as the first fit of sneezing had subsided, the policeman below was just about to give vent to the indignation which swelled his official breast, when he was seized with another, which in its effects proved far more violent than the first.

" Good luck to you," said he on regaining the power to speak, " give us something to wash it down, or I shall choke. It 'll be all the worse for you, my kids, when I gets you. Do you mean to come down now ? *that's* all about it. It's o' no use, you know, for in course we don't leave you. Once for all, do you mean to come down."

" You are *werry* perlite," replied one of the kids, " but we'd much rayther not."

" Why then," said the constable in disguise, who, as far as the making up of his face was concerned, appeared perfectly ready to mur-der *Othello* —" in course we must make you."

SPECIMEN

OF THE

ILLUSTRATIONS

OF

Printed by J.R. Jobbins, litho.

T. Onwhyn delt.

Uncle John in extacies.

VALENTINE VOX,

THE

VENTRILOQUIST.

This day, handsomely bound in cloth, price 14s,

HEADS OF THE PEOPLE;

CONTAINING FIFTY PORTRAITS OF THE ENGLISH.

DRAWN BY KENNY MEADOWS,

ENGRAVED BY ORRIN SMITH,

WITH ORIGINAL ARTICLES BY DISTINGUISHED WRITERS.

" THIS work will in every respect be a National Work ! "

Such was the promise of the projectors on the commencement of the " HEADS OF THE PEOPLE ; " and such has been the public feeling as regards its comprehensiveness of design, and the striking fidelity with which its characters (characters of the present day, who " live' and move, and have their being," about us) have been portrayed, that the Proprietors have the proudest satisfaction in alluding to the sentiments of the most influential portion of the Press, that, in its many notices of the work, in its daily quotations from its pages, have, in the most emphatic manner, distinguished it from the numerous ephemera put forth only to be forgotten. The " HEADS OF THE PEOPLE " has been welcomed by public writers as a work which, marked by the greatest originality in its design, is destined to become a part of the country's literature, containing, as it is its purpose to do, PICTURES OF HUMAN LIFE ; not life as dreamt of by the fashionable novelmonger ; not human nature as daubed and distorted by the caricaturist ; but LIFE AS IT IS ; the writers delineating it showing that, in fact, there is nothing apparently so commonplace, nothing so familiar, from which new and striking associations may not be gathered ; in which sympathies long dormant may not be awakened. To the philosophic observer there is nothing barren.

The originality and success of the " HEADS OF THE PEOPLE " (for ten thousand subscribers do monthly honour to it) are made manifest by the many imitations of its design. Not only is the work translated into French, and published weekly in Paris, but Frenchmen, copying its purpose as applicable to themselves, have put forth " Les François, ou Mœurs Contemporaines," in precisely the same vein as the English original ; a compliment at once declaratory of the usefulness and peculiarity of its purpose. More : at home its brief essays have been the subject matter of long and elaborate discussions in reviews of the first character ; whilst books in " 3 vols. 8vo," have been christened after its subjects, and the essence of eight pages has served to leaven a thousand of the manufacturing novelist.

The " HEADS OF THE PEOPLE " is, in fact, a Picture Gallery of the English Nation in all its profound, affecting, and humorous varieties of character. The volume contains

The Dress-Maker	D. JERROLD	The Teetotaler	L. BLANCHARD	The Street Conjuror	A. CROWQUILL
The Diner-out	D. JERROLD	The Factory Child	D. JERROLD	The Ballad Singer	D. JERROLD
The Stock-broker	C. WHITEHEAD	Omnibus Conductor	LEIGH HUNT	The Irish Peasant	S. LOVER
The Lawyer's Clerk	LEMAN REDE	Common Informer	D. JERROLD	Captain Rook	W. THACKERAY
" Lion " of a Party	D. JERROLD	Family Governess	MISS WINTER	The Pigeon	W. THACKERAY
Medical Student	P. LEIGH	The Midshipman	E. HOWARD	The Cockney	D. JERROLD
Maid of All-Work	C. WEBBE	The Pew-Opener	D. JERROLD	The Theatrical Manager	R. B. PEAKE
Fashionable Physician	R. H. HORNE	The Last Go	C. WHITEHEAD		
The Spoilt Child	R. H. HORNE	Man of Many Goes	C. WHITEHEAD	The Retired Tradesman	J. OGDEN
The Old Lord	E. CHATFIELD	The Chimney-Sweep	J. OGDEN	The English Pauper	J. L. HUNT
The Parish Beadle	C. WEBBE	The Undertaker	D. JERROLD	The Hangman	D. JERROLD
Draper's Assistant	D. JERROLD	Sentimental Singer	C. WHITEHEAD	Prime Minister	L. BLANCHARD
The Monthly Nurse	LEIGH HUNT	The President	C. WHITEHEAD	The Exciseman	
The Auctioneer	D. JERROLD	Old Housekeeper	ALICE	The Apothecary	
The Landlady	C. WHITEHEAD	The Postman	D. JERROLD	The Farmer's Daughter	W. HOWITT
The Parlour Orator	C. WHITEHEAD	The Young Lord	D. JERROLD		
The Barmaid :	C. WHITEHEAD	The English Peasant	WM. HOWITT	The Printer's Devil	D. JERROLD
		CommercialTraveller	L. BLANCHARD		

☞ No. I of a new series of this popular work will be issued on the first of December, and be continued monthly.

TYAS'S
LEGAL HAND-BOOKS.

"IGNORANTIA JURIS NON EXCUSAT."

ADVERTISEMENT.

It has been a cause of general complaint with reference to the means of acquiring a useful knowledge of the Outlines of Law, or such branches of it as might suit the taste of some or affect the interests of others, that the expensive nature of Law Books renders them attainable but by few; and that, when within the reach of that few, they are so replete with technical terms as to be, in part, unintelligible to non-professional readers, without great pains and trouble of reference, to arrive at the meaning of those terms.

To remedy in part these evils, and with the view of laying open in a simple and concise form, divested of technicalities, and made plain to every capacity, and within the reach of all, general outlines of such Branches of Law as it has been thought might be useful to non-professional readers, it is purposed to lay before the public

A SERIES OF LEGAL HAND-BOOKS;

and in order to ensure a correct and faithful statement of the Law, as it now stands, on each subject, so as to render the series truly worthy of the patronage of the public, the publisher has great confidence in announcing that they will be prepared for publication

BY A BARRISTER OF THE MIDDLE TEMPLE.

The series will be published at the lowest remunerating price, and as nearly as possible in the following order, one every alternate month, commencing as soon as the manuscripts are so far prepared as to ensure their regular appearance.

1. DEBTOR AND CREDITOR.
2. REAL PROPERTY.
3. PERSONAL PROPERTY.
4. WILLS.
5. EXECUTORS AND ADMINISTRATORS.—TRUSTEES.
6. HUSBAND AND WIFE.
7. LANDLORD AND TENANT.
8. BILLS OF EXCHANGE AND PROMISSORY NOTES.
9. COMMERCIAL LAW.
10. PRINCIPAL AND AGENT.—PRINCIPAL AND SURETY.
11. MASTER AND SERVANT.
12. LEGACIES.
13. BAILMENTS.
14. ELECTION LAW.
15. LAW OF NATIONS.
16. PARTNERSHIP.

" Ignorance of the Law excuseth no man."

ROBERT TYAS, 50, CHEAPSIDE.

HAND-BOOKS FOR THE MILLION!

PRICE ONE SHILLING EACH.

ANGLING.—The Angler's Hand-Book is a complete Guide to the Art, with descriptions and coloured figures of Artificial Flies.

ARCHERY.—The Hand-Book of Archery contains descriptions of the various implements used therein, with directions for their use; and interesting anecdotes of the art. Illustrated by a View of a Bow Meeting.

ARCHITECTURE.—The Hand-Book of Architecture is a Guide to the most important terms used in Grecian, Roman, Gothic, and Church Architecture; indispensable to all who are desirous of being able to describe, or converse upon, the various parts of a building, &c., &c. With Pictorial Illustrations.

ASTRONOMY.—The Hand-Book of Astronomy comprises all the elements of that noble science, illustrated by numerous wood cuts.

BANKING.—Ten Minutes Advice about Keeping a Banker, addressed to the middle class of people, by a practical Banker.

CARVING.—The Hand-Book of Carving. With Hints on the Etiquette of the Dinner Table, and many Figures.

CHEMISTRY.—The Hand-book of Chemistry is a popular treatise on the principles of the science, adapted to those who are unacquainted with its elements.

CHEMICAL EXPERIMENTS.—The Hand-Book of Chemical Amusements contains a series of experiments, illustrating the Hand-Book of Chemistry, with full directions for manufacturing the implements required, at the least possible cost.

CHESS.—The Chess-Player's Hand-Book contains directions for the most speedy acquisition of a competent knowledge of this interesting and scientific game; the moves of the pieces, their value, and the Laws of the Game. With illustrative Engravings.

CONCHOLOGY.—The Hand-Book of Conchology contains a comprehensive introduction to the science, illustrated by engraved specimens of these beautiful productions of the Animal Kingdom.

COOKERY.—The Hand-Book of Domestic Cookery; containing an immense mass of useful information, with directions for preparing and cooking the best and most economical dishes for domestic use.

CRIBBAGE.—Dee's Hand-Book of the Game of Cribbage.
" This treatise is the only one extant worthy of commendation."—*English Gentleman.*

CRICKET.—The Cricketer's Hand-Book. All the Laws of the Game, with an Engraved Frontispiece, being a view of Lord's Cricket Ground.

ELECTRICITY.—The Hand-Book of Electricity comprises all the elements of this interesting science, with many experiments illustrative of its principles.

FRENCH LANGUAGE.—The French Scholar's Hand-Book; containing a compendious Grammar of the French Language, a copious and well-arranged Vocabulary, and a quantity of Phrases in common use.

FRENCH AS IT MUST BE SPOKEN.—Hand-Book of the Intonations and Elisions of the French Language; or French as it must be Spoken. By J. Tourrier.

GEOLOGY.—The Hand-Book of Geology gives a general view of this attractive science. With a Coloured Frontispiece.

GERMAN.—" The German Scholar's Hand-Book is an unassuming little work, which fully carries out its title. It contains a clear and concise Synopsis of the German Grammar, and also a very useful Vocabulary, and list of phrases; and will no doubt be found invaluable as an introduction to the more voluminous and complicated works on the subject. It ought to be the companion of every one who wishes to obtain a knowledge of the German Language,"—*Sherwood's Miscellany.*

HELIOGRAPHY.—The Hand-Book of Heliography; or, the Art of obtaining Drawings from Nature by the Action of Light, as discovered and perfected by M. Daguerre, with Engravings and Descriptions of the Apparatus, and a History of the Invention; with the Art of Dioramic Painting. For M. Daguerre's secret the French Government has just granted a pension of 10,000 francs.

HERALDRY.—The Hand-Book of Heraldry; or, complete Accidence of Armorie, in the simplest terms and the shortest possible space. With numerous Engravings.

LANGUAGE OF FLOWERS.—The Hand-Book of the Language and Sentiment of Flowers, containing the name of every Flower to which an Emblem has been assigned (arranged alphabetically), with its power in language annexed. Preceded by an Essay on the Sentimental Language of Flowers, by the author of " The Sentiments of Flowers," and illustrated by a coloured Frontispiece.

MAGIC.—" The Hand-book of Magic is a pretty little brochure for the waistcoat pocket, detailing the mysteries of a series of philosophical amusements, simple deceptions, tricks with cards and money, sleight of hand, &c., for the benefit of intelligent little boys and girls. All the more difficult portions of the text are illustrated by neatly-executed wood engravings; and most of the directions are studiously simple and intelligible."—*United Service Gazette.*

MINERALOGY.—The Hand-Book of Mineralogy contains the Elements of the science illustrated by Engravings.

MORALS.—The Hand-Book of Morals is a collection of Common Sayings, with Annotations, &c.

NATURAL PHENOMENA.—The Hand-book of Natural Phenomena contains a full account of Natural Appearances, stating their causes and effects as far as has been satisfactorily ascertained. One of the most interesting and instructive little books ever published. Illustrated by elegant Engravings on wood.

SINGING BIRDS.—The Hand-Book of Singing Birds; with directions for Breeding and Rearing the finest Songsters, and the best general mode of treatment. With many Engravings.

SHORT-HAND.—Short Hints on Short-Hand. By which the Student may speedily acquire a competent knowledge of this polite and useful accomplishment. With four plates.

STEAM ENGINE.—The Hand-Book of the Steam Engine is explanatory of the principle on which steam is made to act upon machinery, and contains an account of the various modes by which it is made subservient to the use of man.

SWIMMING.—The Swimmer's Hand-Book; wherein are many valuable precepts, which if the Reader strictly follow, he will soon become an expert swimmer. With eight Illustrations.

WHIST.—The Whist-player's Hand-Book; containing Rules and Directions for playing the universally popular Game of Whist; Laws of the Game, &c. &c.

" Elegant and useful publications."—*Doncaster Chronicle.*

⁎⁎⁎ Several others on Popular Subjects are in course of preparation

THE CHRISTIAN LIBRARY.

IN an age when the press teems with cheap publications, it is to be deplored that by far the greater portion are light and trifling in their nature.

In general literature, all the productions of the most celebrated authors of the last century have been presented in every varied form, for the use of all classes of Society, while Standard Religious Works have received but little attention. To supply the desideratum which this neglect has occasioned is the intention of the Publisher of the CHRISTIAN LIBRARY. The plan and conditions of publication may be stated in few words.

The work will be printed on the very best paper, in medium 8vo, double columns, from a beautiful type cast expressly for the purpose.

All the Books appearing in this series will be carefully revised by a competent Editor; and, when deemed necessary, illustrative notes will be annexed.

WORKS ALREADY PUBLISHED.

1. ELISHA, UNABRIDGED, by the Author of " Elijah the Tishbite." *Price* 1s. 9d.

2. CECIL'S LIFE OF NEWTON. *Price 9d.*

3. *HANNAH MORE'S PRACTICAL PIETY. 1s. 4d.

4. SCOTT'S FORCE OF TRUTH. *Price 6d.*

5. MELMOTH'S GREAT IMPORTANCE OF A RELIGIOUS LIFE. *Price 6d.*

6. PALEY'S EVIDENCES OF CHRISTIANITY. 2s.

7. DODDRIDGE'S RISE AND PROGRESS OF RELIGION IN THE SOUL OF MAN. 2s.

Which will be followed by

8. ELIJAH THE TISHBITE.

NOTICES OF THE WORK.

The *Christian Library* is a series of cheap reprints of standard religious Works which have lately fallen under our observation. Three parts lie before us, consisting severally of "Cecil's Life of Newton," "Hannah More's Practical Piety," and "Krummacher's Elisha." All these, of whose excellence it is unnecessary to speak, may now be had for less money than any one of them could previously be purchased for. The paper and type are really beautiful.—*Christian Advocate,* April 29.

The *Christian Library* promises to become a valuable addition to our cheaper works upon theological subjects. It is printed on excellent paper, in double columns, and does great credit to the publisher. The works announced as part of the series are of most sterling and recognised value, and we cordially wish success to the enterprise.—*Christian Remembrancer,* May, 1839.

A selection of popular religious Works are in course of being reprinted in an edition under the title of *Christian Library Edition,* neatly and cheaply. Before us is "Cecil's Memoirs of Newton," published for Ninepence, and in good form; and "Krummacher's Elisha," also very cheap, considering that it is given unabridged.—*Tait's Magazine,* April, 1839.

* An Edition of this excellent work is also printed in a pocket size, neatly done up in cloth, **2s. 6d.** or morocco, price 4s. 6d.

NEW AND SPLENDID EDITION OF GULLIVER'S TRAVELS.

TO BE COMPLETED IN EIGHT MONTHLY PARTS.

On the 1st of October will be published, beautifully printed in large Octavo,
Price 2s. 6d.

PART I.

OF THE NEW STANDARD EDITION

OF

GULLIVER'S TRAVELS:

ILLUSTRATED WITH UPWARDS OF
FOUR HUNDRED WOOD-CUTS AFTER DESIGNS BY GRANDVILLE:

WITH NOTES AND ELUCIDATIONS
FROM VARIOUS ORIGINAL AND MANUSCRIPT SOURCES;
AN ESSAY ON PHILOSOPHIC AND SATIRICAL FICTIONS;

AND

A NEW LIFE OF SWIFT.

BY W. C. TAYLOR, LL.D. M.R.A.S. ETC.

OF TRINITY COLLEGE, DUBLIN.

GRANDVILLE's extraordinary skill in humorous and characteristic Delineations
is celebrated throughout Europe; but perhaps there never was a work so
admirably calculated to bring out his peculiar powers as Gulliver's Travels,

for there is none in which all the weak points of humanity are so admirably developed. The artist manifestly felt that he was illustrating the work of a cognate mind; he has therefore, as in a labour of love, put forth all his strength, with a success which has astonished even his oldest and warmest admirers. In bringing out these Illustrations for the English Public, the Proprietors felt that something more was wanting than a mere republication of the text; the striking similarity between the present state of Political Parties and that which prevailed during the reigns of the first two Georges, the absolute identity of the Watch-words used by rival Politicians, and the repetition of nearly the same Projects and Speculations, render Gulliver's Travels more interesting now than at any period since their first publication. At the same time, the lapse of a century has cleared away much of the darkness that veiled the countless political intrigues which followed the Accession of the House of Brunswick; the publication of State Papers, Memoirs, and collections of Letters, and the gradual decline of that jealousy which watched over an ancestor's MSS. not less rigorously than a Sultan over his harem, have enabled the Editor to point out most of the objects against which Swift's "satiric touches" were directed, and to elucidate the scope and purport of his fiction. Under these circumstances it may without presumption be said, that the forthcoming edition of Gulliver will deserve to rank as a Standard, and will recommend itself not only to general readers, but to the lover of Fine Arts, the Philosopher, the Statesman, and the Politician.

LONDON: HAYWARD & MOORE, 53, PATERNOSTER-ROW.
1839.

[Printed by Manning and Mason, 12, Ivy lane, St. Paul's.]

HILL'S
SEAL WAFERS.

These Wafers are adapted to all uses to which Sealing Wax and common Wafers have been hitherto applied. They are made of every variety of form, size, and colour; and with any inscription or device, from a simple Initial to a Coat of Arms. These Wafers will be found superior in neatness and simplicity of application to any thing previously introduced for the purpose, and they are sold at a price which may ensure their universal adoption.

TO THE NOBILITY AND FAMILIES OF DISTINCTION they are recommended as a substitute for wax, not only for their brilliancy of colour and beauty of appearance, but for their presenting the most perfect impressions of Armorial Bearings and Crests, without giving the least trouble in producing them. They will also be found admirably adapted for a possessive mark on Library Books, &c.

TO PRIVATE FAMILIES the neatness and facility with which their Initials can be affixed to their Notes and Letters will induce the adoption of the Seal Wafer.

PUBLIC COMPANIES will see the advantage of using a seal bearing their peculiar designation, and which can be applied with so little trouble.

TO MERCANTILE AND COMMERCIAL FIRMS, the use of a Wafer, which never obliterates any portion of their correspondence, will be obvious.

MANUFACTURERS AND RETAIL DEALERS will find these Wafers of the most essential service, as they may have neat Labels in the most novel style, producing a medallion effect, which at the time they are circulating their address, will afford the greatest security against fraud.

MANUFACTURED AND SOLD BY

EDWIN HILL, Coventry Road, BIRMINGHAM.

LONDON AGENTS,

J. & F. HARWOOD, 26, FENCHURCH STREET

DE FOE'S NOVELS AND MISCELLANEOUS WORKS,

IN MONTHLY VOLUMES.

On NOVEMBER 1st will appear Vol. I. of

THE NOVELS

AND

MISCELLANEOUS WORKS

OF

DANIEL DE FOE.

WITH A BIOGRAPHICAL MEMOIR OF THE AUTHOR,

LITERARY PREFACES TO THE VARIOUS PIECES, ILLUSTRATIVE NOTES, ETC.,

BY THE LATE

SIR WALTER SCOTT AND OTHERS.

THE magic name of ROBINSON CRUSOE carries us back at once to the green freshness of boyhood, and awakens up a thousand delightful sensations, which we remember to have felt while we hung, fascinated, over that beautiful romance. Nor are the charms of this wonderful fiction confined to us or to any nation : it belongs to the world. Yet universal as is the celebrity of Robinson Crusoe, how few, comparatively, are aware that the great magician who conjured up the desert island and its solitary occupant, did not thereupon break his wand and "bury his book"—how few are aware that he left behind other volumes teeming with the same spirit of adventure, the same hair-breadth 'scapes by land and flood; others again, full of the life and manners of De Foe's own age and city ; and that in all these he so faithfully and minutely portrayed the various scenes and characters—the outward word and gesture, and inward thought and feeling —as to bring them immediately and vividly before the reader.

The influence of De Foe's works upon our national character has been correspondingly great: the young of successive generations, while hanging with delight over his imperishable fictions, imbibed that love of adventure, and trust upon Divine Providence, which have contributed so largely to our commercial and maritime greatness.

Notwithstanding this, the only attempt that has hitherto been made to bring these fictions together, is the edition of De Foe's Novels, edited by Sir Walter Scott, in twelve volumes ; yet, even this, (admirable so far as it goes, but always unsatisfactory, from its incompleteness,) is become rare, and difficult to procure. We cannot, therefore, feel a doubt but we shall be well encouraged by the Public, in our endeavour to carry nearer to perfection the work so well begun by the great Modern Novelist.

What we propose to do is :—

First : To reprint the Novels edited by Sir Walter Scott, with the addition of all those omitted by him, known to be De Foe's.

Secondly : To reprint, uniformly with these, a selection of the most interesting and standard treatises of De Foe, in Theology, Morals, Politics, Magic and Witchcraft, Poetry, &c.

Thirdly : To prefix the Biographical Memoir of Sir Walter Scott; and to retain his Literary Prefaces, Notes, &c. to the pieces contained in his edition, and to supply them, as nearly uniform as possible, to the remainder.

It only remains to be said that the work will be correctly and elegantly printed by Mr. Talboys, of Oxford, with a new type expressly cast for the purpose; that by a discreet economy, without any sacrifice of elegance, each volume will contain nearly two of Sir Walter Scott's edition; that the entire collection will form eighteen volumes in small octavo; and that, for the convenience of all parties, it will be published in monthly volumes at 5s. each, neatly bound in cloth.

The following is the order of publication :—

VOL.

1 & 2. LIFE OF THE AUTHOR. ADVENTURES OF ROBINSON CRUSOE.

3. LIFE, ADVENTURES, AND PIRACIES OF CAPTAIN SINGLETON.

4. THE FORTUNES AND MISFORTUNES OF MOLL FLANDERS

5. LIFE AND ADVENTURES OF COLONEL JACK.

6. MEMOIRS OF A CAVALIER.

7. THE FORTUNATE MISTRESS; OR, LIFE OF ROXANA.

8. VOYAGE ROUND THE WORLD, BY A COURSE NEVER SAILED BEFORE.

9. CARLETON'S MEMOIRS. LIFE OF MRS. DAVIES, COMMONLY CALLED "MOTHER ROSS."

10. HISTORY OF THE PLAGUE. THE CONSOLIDATOR.

11. HISTORY OF THE DEVIL. APPARITION OF MRS. VEAL.

12. SYSTEM OF MAGIC, AND HISTORY OF THE BLACK ART.

13. SECRETS OF THE INVISIBLE WORLD, AND HISTORY OF APPARITIONS.

14. RELIGIOUS COURTSHIP.

15 & 16. THE FAMILY INSTRUCTOR.

17 & 18. MISCELLANEOUS PIECES IN PROSE AND VERSE, not of a temporary or local character.

A FEW TESTIMONIALS, OUT OF THOUSANDS, IN FAVOUR OF DANIEL DE FOE AND HIS WRITINGS.

" There cannot be a more national writer than De Foe,—every thought of his, every word, every image, is entirely English : there is not a page of his that does not remind us the author was born in London, and lived in the days of King William and Queen Anne. It is one of the chief reproaches of our press that no uniform collected edition of his works has ever appeared in England."—*Chalmers*.

" But whatever way he acquired his knowledge of low life, De Foe certainly possessed it in the most extensive sense, and applied it in the composition of several works of fiction in the style termed by the Spaniards *gusto picaresco*, of which no man was ever a greater master. This class of the fictitious narrative may be termed the Romance of Roguery, the subjects being the adventures of thieves, rogues, vagabonds, and swindlers, including viragos and courtezans. The improved taste of the present age has justly rejected this coarse species of amusement; nevertheless, the strange and blackguard scenes which De Foe describes, are fit to be compared to the gipsy-boys of the Spanish painter Murillo, which are so justly admired, as being, in truth of conception, and spirit of execution, the very *chefs-d'œuvre* of art."—*Sir Walter Scott*.

" De Foe visited Scotland about the time of the Union, and it is evident that the anecdotes concerning this unhappy period must have been peculiarly interesting to a man of his liveliness of imagination, who excelled all others in dramatising a story, and presenting it in actual speech and action before the reader."—*Quarterly Review*, vol. xvi. p. 454.

" His (Caleb Williams') disguises and escapes in London, though detailed at too great length, have a frightful reality, perhaps nowhere paralleled in our language, except it be in some paintings of Daniel De Foe, with whom it is distinction to bear comparison. There are several somewhat similar scenes in ' Colonel Jack' of that admirable writer, which, among his novels, is indeed only the second ; but which could be second to none but Robinson Crusoe, one of those very few books which are equally popular in every country of Europe, and which delight every reader, from the philosopher to the child. Caleb Williams resembles the novels of De Foe, in the austerity with which it rejects the agency of women and the power of love."—*Edin. Rev.* xxv. 488.

" We come now to the merits of De Foe as a writer of fiction, in respect to which he was a mighty magician indeed. No writer upon earth ever exceeded him in a mastery over those thoughts which come home to the business and bosoms of the general run of mankind: and of course when he represents such, he is the very genius of verisimilitude."—*Westminster Review*, vol. xiii.

" Few men have been more accurate observers of life and manners, and of the mechanism of society, than De Foe."—*Quarterly Review*, vol. xxiv. 361.

" Most of our readers are probably familiar with De Foe's history of that great calamity (the Plague)—a work in which fabulous incidents and circumstances are combined with authentic narratives, with an art and verisimilitude which no other writer has ever been able to communicate to fiction."—*Edin. Rev.* xxvi. 461.

OXFORD: PRINTED BY D. A. TALBOYS, FOR THOMAS TEGG, LONDON.